Archie®

MODERN

CLASSICS

· VOL ___ O ·

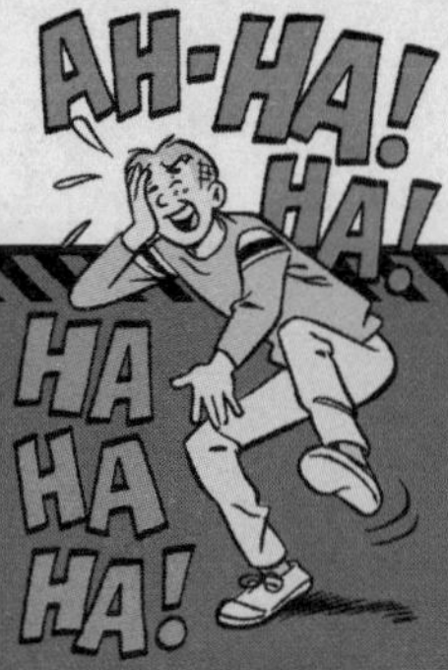
AH-HA!
HA!
HA
HA
HA!

Publisher / Co-CEO: Jon Goldwater

Co-President / Editor-In-Chief: Victor Gorelick

Co-President: Mike Pellerito

Co-President: Alex Segura

Chief Creative Officer: Roberto Aguirre-Sacasa

Chief Operating Officer: William Mooar

Chief Financial Officer: Robert Wintle

Director: Jonathan Betancourt

Art Director: Vincent Lovallo

Production Manager: Stephen Oswald

Lead Designer: Kari McLachlan

Associate Editor: Carlos Antunes

Editor: Jamie Lee Rotante

Co-CEO: Nancy Silberkleit

Published by Archie Comic Publications, Inc. 629 Fifth Avenue, Suite 100, Pelham, NY 10803-1242

ISBN: 978-1-64576-967-5

STORIES

BILL GOLLIHER, FRANCIS BONNET, ANGELO DᴇCESARE,
JACK MORELLI, VICTOR GORELICK, BILL BETTWY,
DAN PARENT & RON ROBBINS

ART

JEFF SHULTZ, PAT KENNEDY, TIM KENNEDY,
DAN PARENT, BILL GOLLIHER, BILL GALVAN, JIM AMASH,
BOB SMITH, RICH KOSLOWSKI, BEN GALVAN,
GLENN WHITMORE & JACK MORELLI

CONTENTS

VERONICA
BETTY
SHULTZ

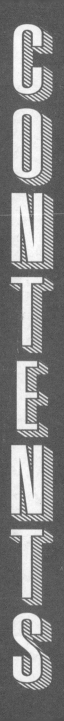

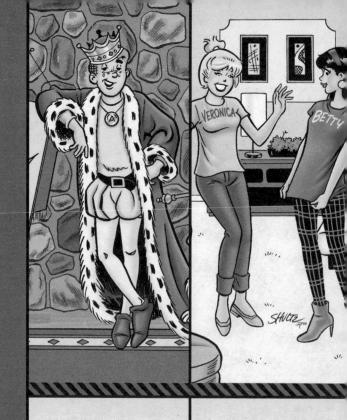

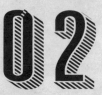

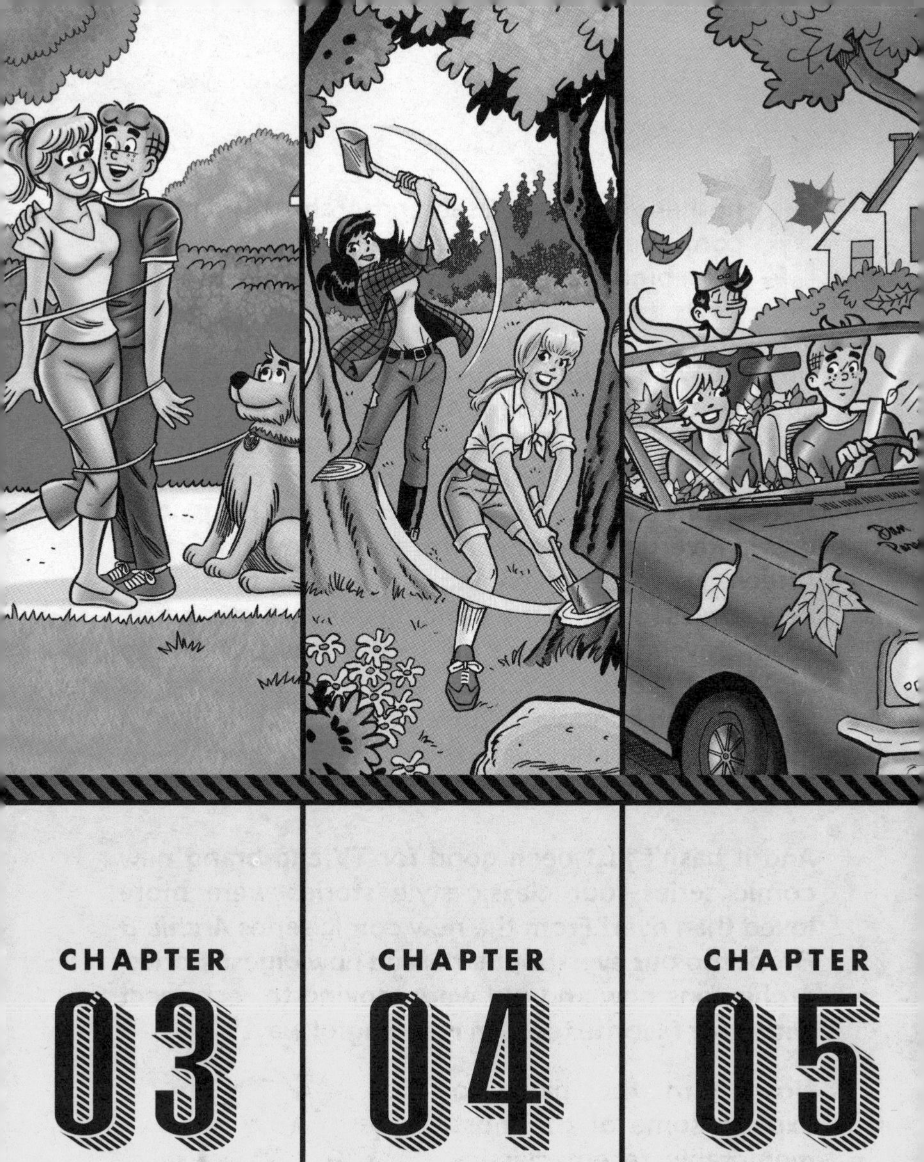

Another year has passed and Archie Comics has continued to deliver fresh takes, fun stories and even bigger and better events than ever before!

While *Riverdale* continues to heat up the airwaves on the CW and *Chilling Adventures of Sabrina* casts a spell on its Netflix viewers, Archie Comics announced another television show to add to its growing roster: *Katy Keene*, which is slated to premiere on the CW network in early 2020. While Archie and his pals 'n' gals in Riverdale and beyond are taking over the small screen, we've been keeping up with the times with new stories for our long-standing comics fans as well. From traveling back in time to the '40s and '50s to looking ahead to the future, namely the teens' senior year of high school, to time traveling all over with Jughead, Archie has been showcasing what makes it just so timeless in the standard comic series.

And it hasn't just been good for TV and brand new comic series—our classic-style stories were more loved than ever! From the new comic series *Archie & Friends* to our ever-popular brand new digest stories, Archie fans new and old were looking to reconnect with their favorite teens in meaningful ways!

Now, turn the page to explore some of the most memorable recent classic-style Archie stories!

01 ARCHIE COMICS

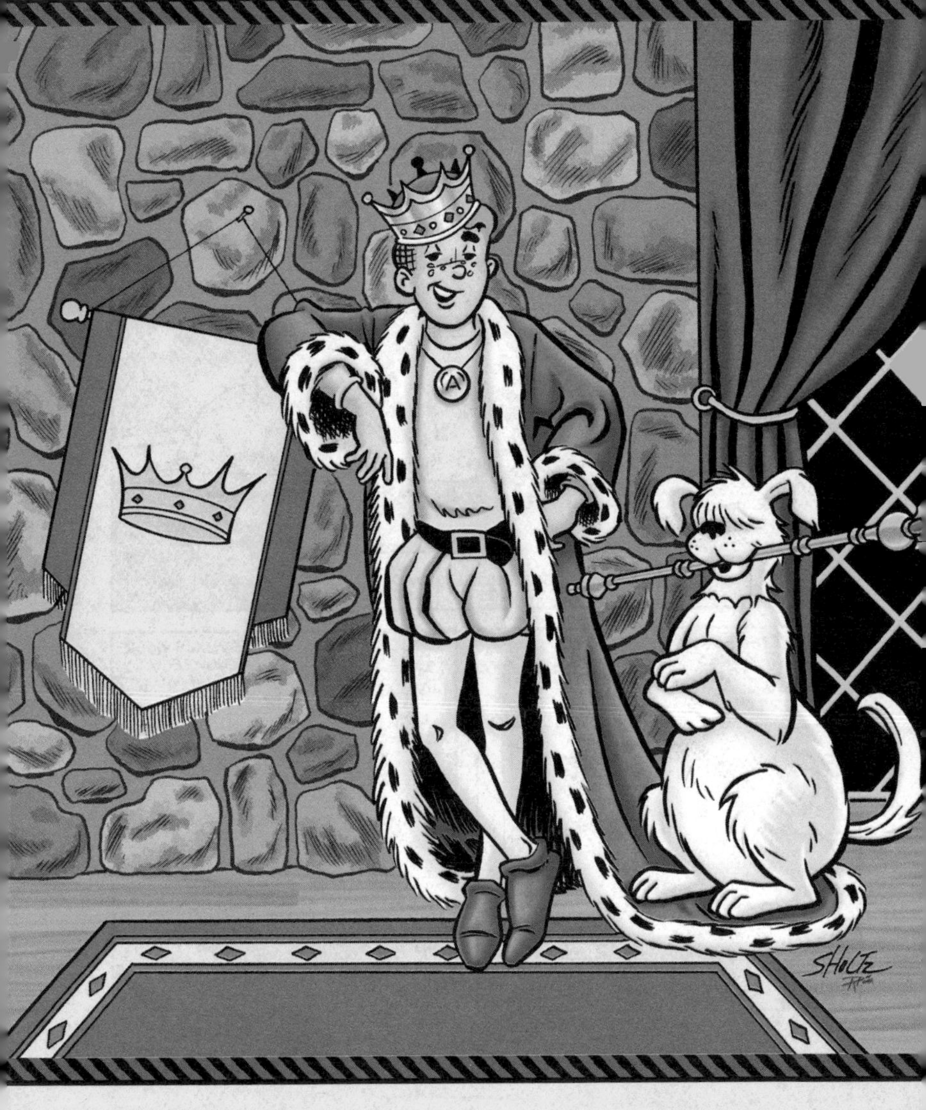

Archie in Love Those L.I.P.S.!

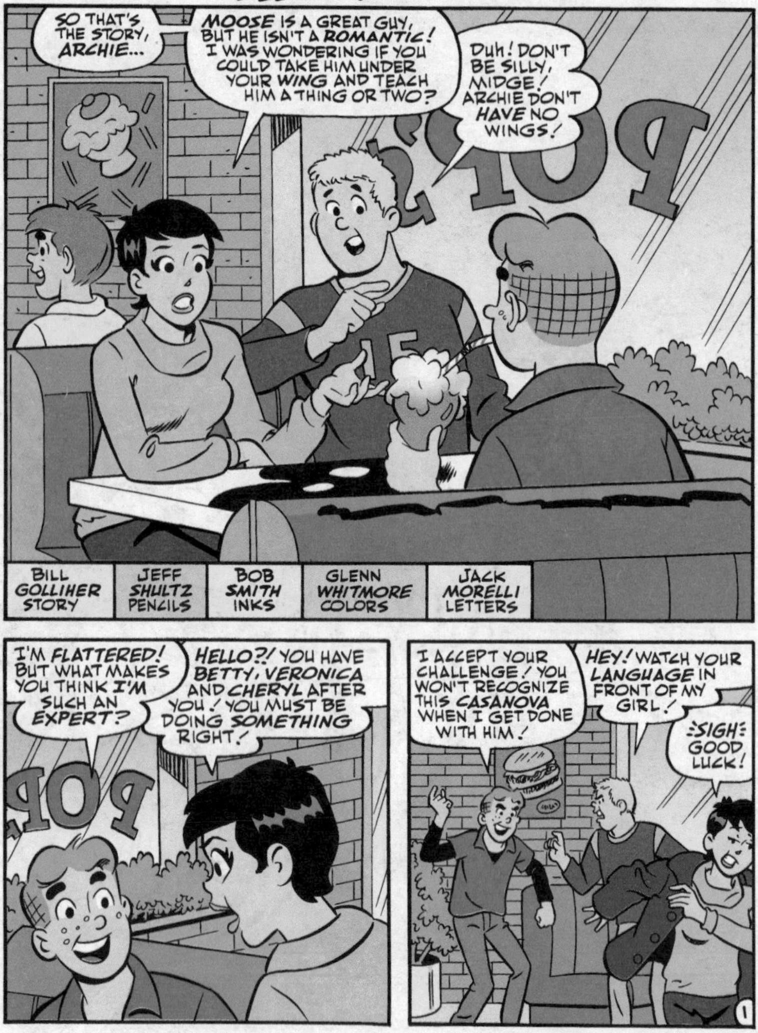
SO THAT'S THE STORY, ARCHIE...
MOOSE IS A GREAT GUY, BUT HE ISN'T A ROMANTIC! I WAS WONDERING IF YOU COULD TAKE HIM UNDER YOUR WING AND TEACH HIM A THING OR TWO?
Duh! DON'T BE SILLY, MIDGE! ARCHIE DON'T HAVE NO WINGS!
POP'S
BILL GOLLIHER STORY
JEFF SHULTZ PENCILS
BOB SMITH INKS
GLENN WHITMORE COLORS
JACK MORELLI LETTERS
I'M FLATTERED! BUT WHAT MAKES YOU THINK I'M SUCH AN EXPERT?
HELLO?! YOU HAVE BETTY, VERONICA AND CHERYL AFTER YOU! YOU MUST BE DOING SOMETHING RIGHT!
I ACCEPT YOUR CHALLENGE! YOU WON'T RECOGNIZE THIS CASANOVA WHEN I GET DONE WITH HIM!
HEY! WATCH YOUR LANGUAGE IN FRONT OF MY GIRL!
SIGH GOOD LUCK!
1

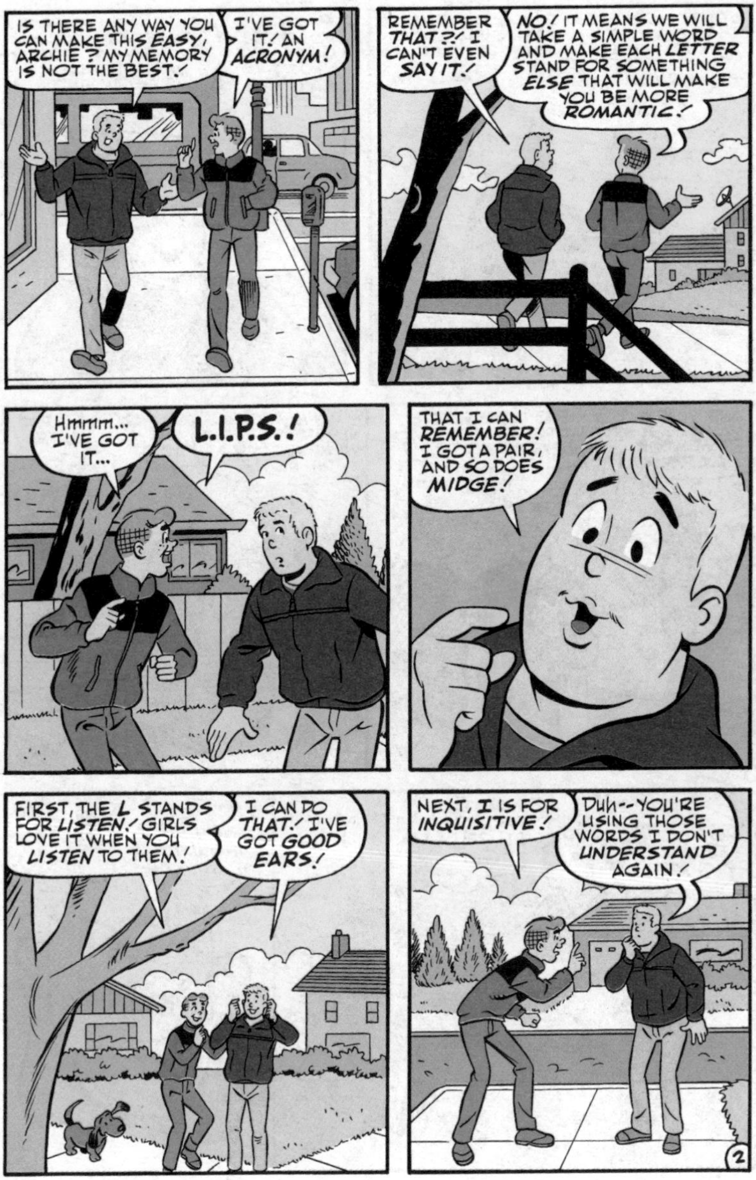
IS THERE ANY WAY YOU CAN MAKE THIS EASY, ARCHIE ? MY MEMORY IS NOT THE BEST.!
I'VE GOT IT! AN ACRONYM!
REMEMBER THAT?! I CAN'T EVEN SAY IT!
NO! IT MEANS WE WILL TAKE A SIMPLE WORD AND MAKE EACH LETTER STAND FOR SOMETHING ELSE THAT WILL MAKE YOU BE MORE ROMANTIC!
Hmmm... I'VE GOT IT...
L.I.P.S.!
THAT I CAN REMEMBER! I GOT A PAIR, AND SO DOES MIDGE!
FIRST, THE L STANDS FOR LISTEN! GIRLS LOVE IT WHEN YOU LISTEN TO THEM!
I CAN DO THAT! I'VE GOT GOOD EARS!
NEXT, I IS FOR INQUISITIVE!
Duh--YOU'RE USING THOSE WORDS I DON'T UNDERSTAND AGAIN!
2

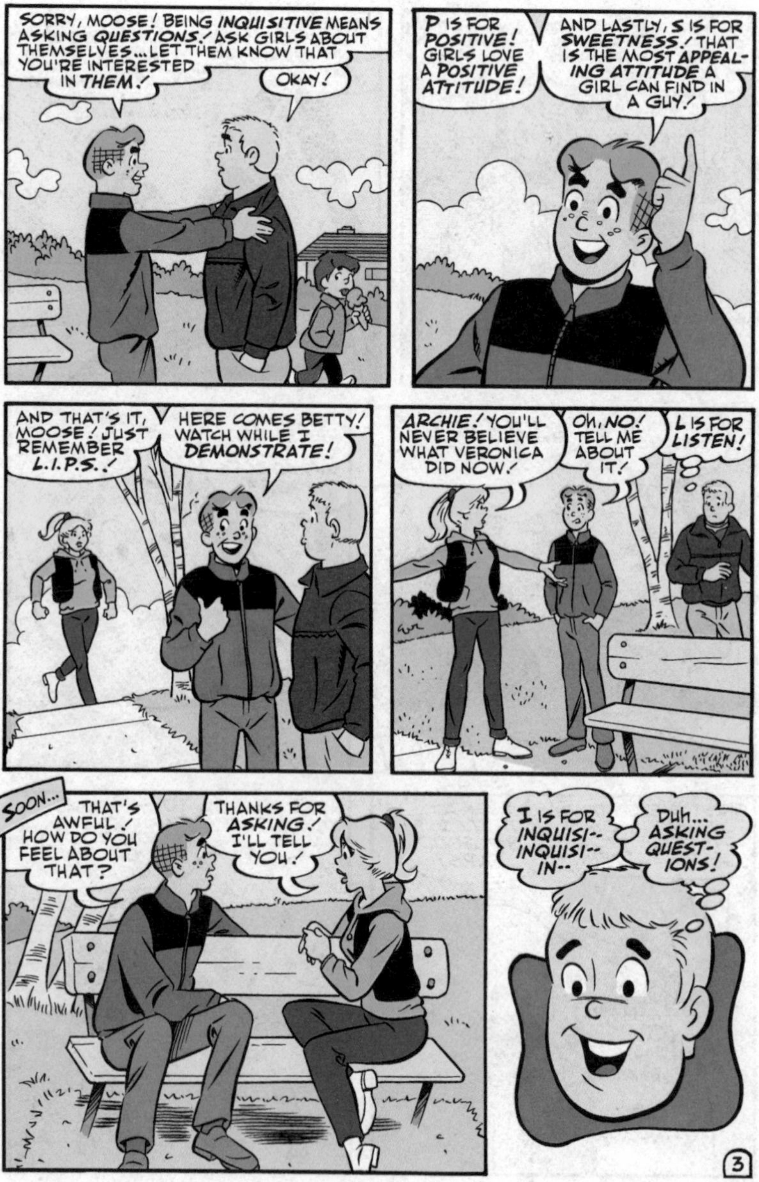
SORRY, MOOSE! BEING INQUISITIVE MEANS ASKING QUESTIONS! ASK GIRLS ABOUT THEMSELVES... LET THEM KNOW THAT YOU'RE INTERESTED IN THEM!
OKAY!
P IS FOR POSITIVE! GIRLS LOVE A POSITIVE ATTITUDE!
AND LASTLY, S IS FOR SWEETNESS! THAT IS THE MOST APPEALING ATTITUDE A GIRL CAN FIND IN A GUY!
AND THAT'S IT, MOOSE! JUST REMEMBER L.I.P.S.!
HERE COMES BETTY! WATCH WHILE I DEMONSTRATE!
ARCHIE! YOU'LL NEVER BELIEVE WHAT VERONICA DID NOW!
OH, NO! TELL ME ABOUT IT!
L IS FOR LISTEN!
SOON...
THAT'S AWFUL! HOW DO YOU FEEL ABOUT THAT?
THANKS FOR ASKING! I'LL TELL YOU!
I IS FOR INQUISI-- INQUISI-- IN--
DUH... ASKING QUEST-IONS!
3

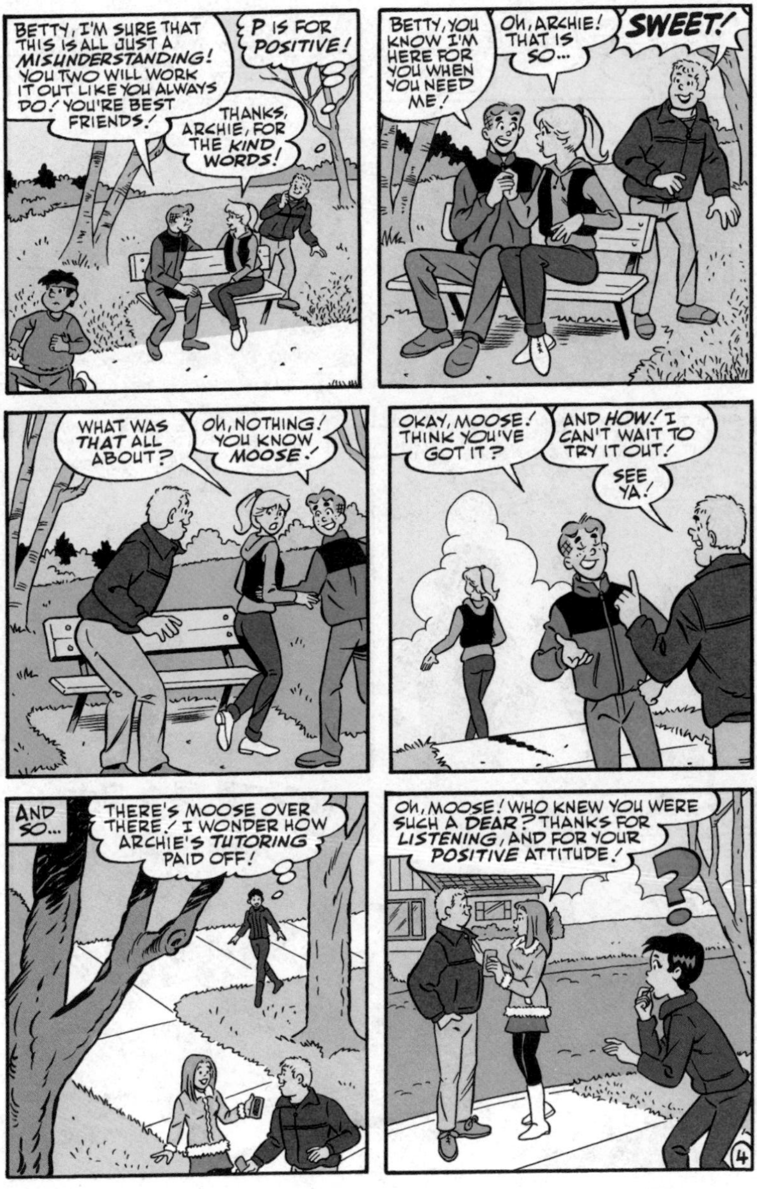
BETTY, I'M SURE THAT THIS IS ALL JUST A MISUNDERSTANDING! YOU TWO WILL WORK IT OUT LIKE YOU ALWAYS DO! YOU'RE BEST FRIENDS!
P IS FOR POSITIVE!
THANKS, ARCHIE, FOR THE KIND WORDS!
BETTY, YOU KNOW I'M HERE FOR YOU WHEN YOU NEED ME!
OH, ARCHIE! THAT IS SO...
SWEET!
WHAT WAS THAT ALL ABOUT?
OH, NOTHING! YOU KNOW MOOSE!
OKAY, MOOSE! THINK YOU'VE GOT IT?
AND HOW! I CAN'T WAIT TO TRY IT OUT!
SEE YA!
AND SO...
THERE'S MOOSE OVER THERE! I WONDER HOW ARCHIE'S TUTORING PAID OFF!
OH, MOOSE! WHO KNEW YOU WERE SUCH A DEAR? THANKS FOR LISTENING, AND FOR YOUR POSITIVE ATTITUDE!
?
4

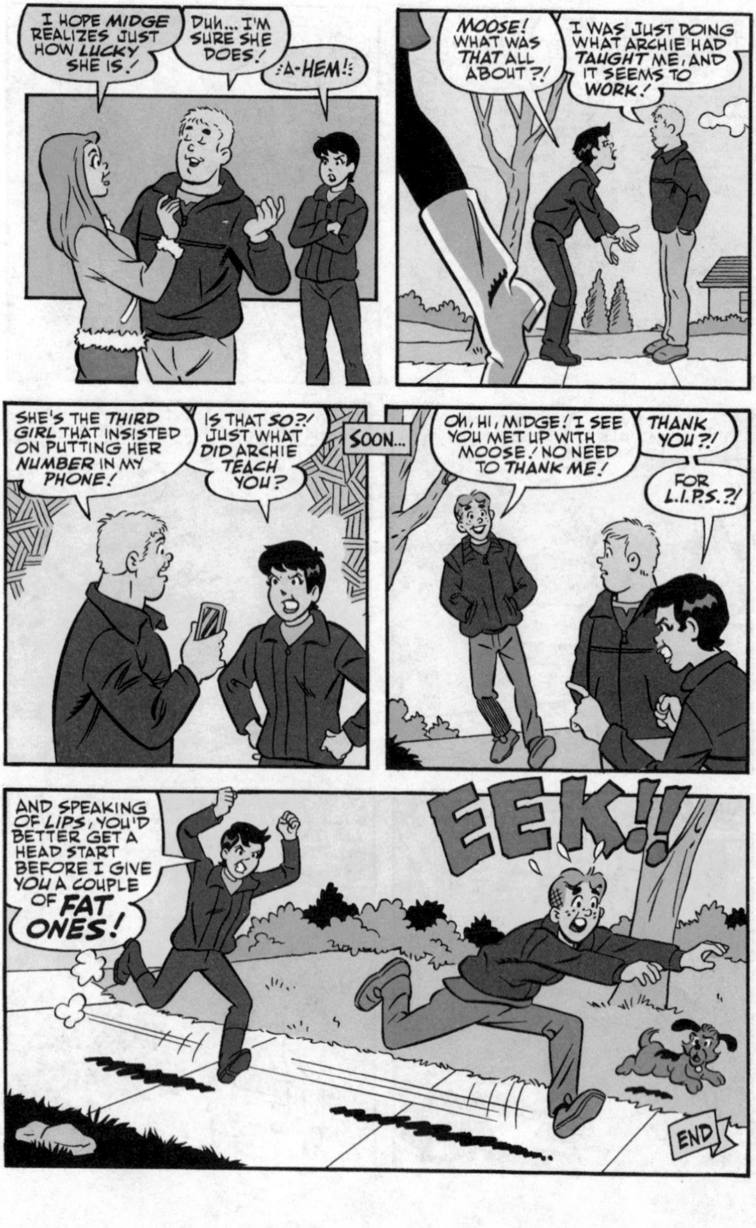
I HOPE MIDGE REALIZES JUST HOW LUCKY SHE IS!
DUH... I'M SURE SHE DOES!
A-HEM!
MOOSE! WHAT WAS THAT ALL ABOUT?!
I WAS JUST DOING WHAT ARCHIE HAD TAUGHT ME, AND IT SEEMS TO WORK!
SHE'S THE THIRD GIRL THAT INSISTED ON PUTTING HER NUMBER IN MY PHONE!
IS THAT SO?! JUST WHAT DID ARCHIE TEACH YOU?
SOON...
OH, HI, MIDGE! I SEE YOU MET UP WITH MOOSE! NO NEED TO THANK ME!
THANK YOU?!
FOR L.I.P.S.?!
AND SPEAKING OF LIPS, YOU'D BETTER GET A HEAD START BEFORE I GIVE YOU A COUPLE OF FAT ONES!
EEK!!
END

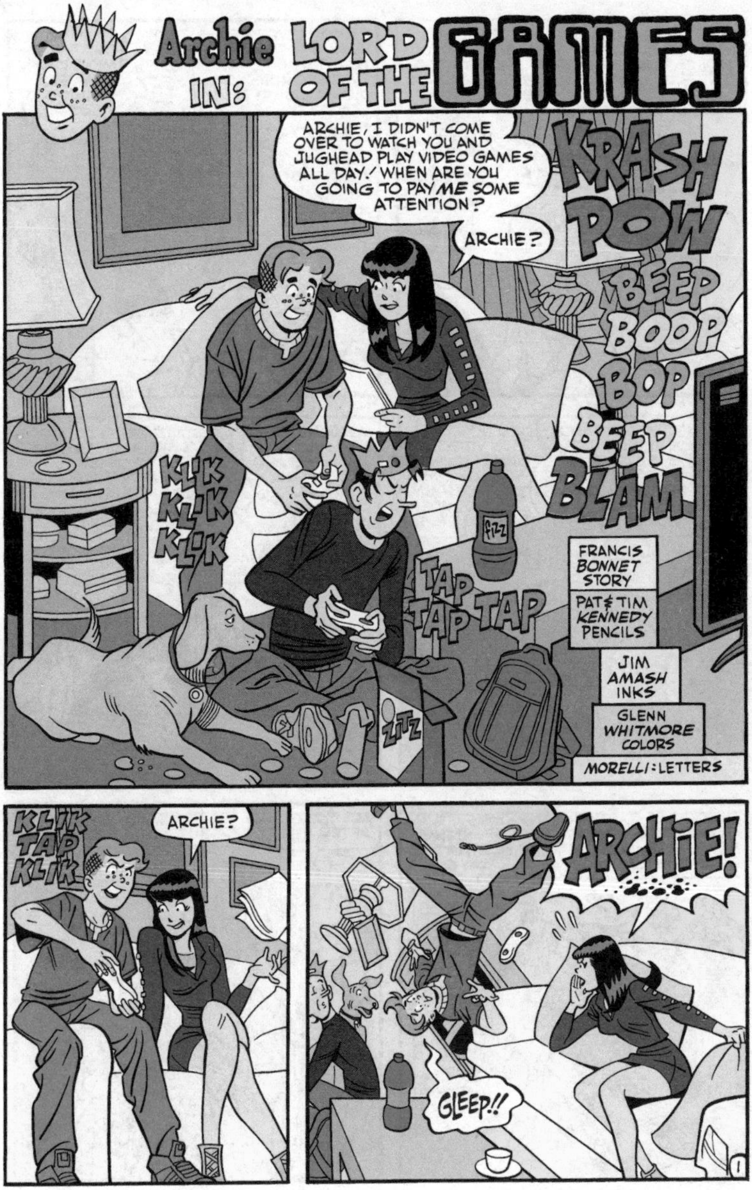
Archie IN: LORD OF THE GAMES
ARCHIE, I DIDN'T COME OVER TO WATCH YOU AND JUGHEAD PLAY VIDEO GAMES ALL DAY! WHEN ARE YOU GOING TO PAY ME SOME ATTENTION?
ARCHIE?
KRASH
POW
BEEP
BOOP
BOP
BEEP
BLAM
KLIK KLIK KLIK
TAP TAP TAP TAP
FIZZ
ZITZ
FRANCIS BONNET STORY
PAT & TIM KENNEDY PENCILS
JIM AMASH INKS
GLENN WHITMORE COLORS
MORELLI: LETTERS
KLIK TAP KLIK
ARCHIE?
ARCHIE!
GLEEP!!
1

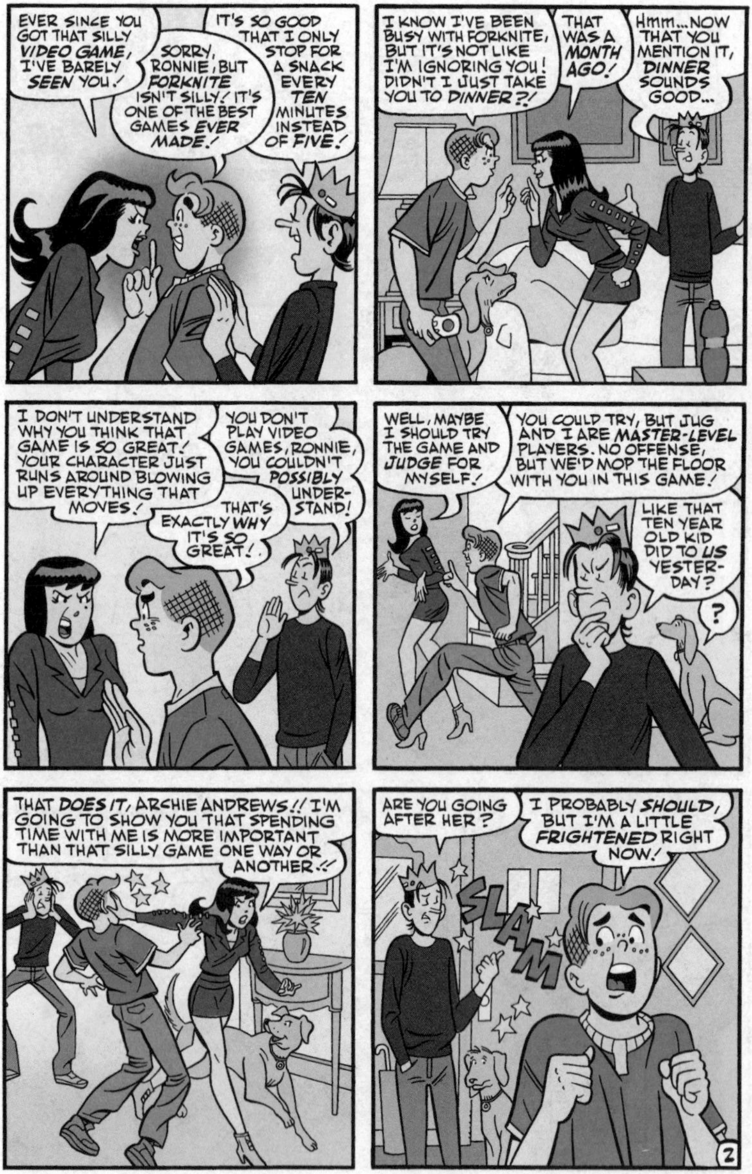
EVER SINCE YOU GOT THAT SILLY VIDEO GAME, I'VE BARELY SEEN YOU!
SORRY, RONNIE, BUT FORKNITE ISN'T SILLY! IT'S ONE OF THE BEST GAMES EVER MADE!
IT'S SO GOOD THAT I ONLY STOP FOR A SNACK EVERY TEN MINUTES INSTEAD OF FIVE!
I KNOW I'VE BEEN BUSY WITH FORKNITE, BUT IT'S NOT LIKE I'M IGNORING YOU! DIDN'T I JUST TAKE YOU TO DINNER?!
THAT WAS A MONTH AGO!
Hmm... NOW THAT YOU MENTION IT, DINNER SOUNDS GOOD...
I DON'T UNDERSTAND WHY YOU THINK THAT GAME IS SO GREAT! YOUR CHARACTER JUST RUNS AROUND BLOWING UP EVERYTHING THAT MOVES!
YOU DON'T PLAY VIDEO GAMES, RONNIE, YOU COULDN'T POSSIBLY UNDERSTAND!
THAT'S EXACTLY WHY IT'S SO GREAT!
WELL, MAYBE I SHOULD TRY THE GAME AND JUDGE FOR MYSELF!
YOU COULD TRY, BUT JUG AND I ARE MASTER-LEVEL PLAYERS. NO OFFENSE, BUT WE'D MOP THE FLOOR WITH YOU IN THIS GAME!
LIKE THAT TEN YEAR OLD KID DID TO US YESTERDAY?
?
THAT DOES IT, ARCHIE ANDREWS!! I'M GOING TO SHOW YOU THAT SPENDING TIME WITH ME IS MORE IMPORTANT THAN THAT SILLY GAME ONE WAY OR ANOTHER!!
ARE YOU GOING AFTER HER?
I PROBABLY SHOULD, BUT I'M A LITTLE FRIGHTENED RIGHT NOW!
SLAM
2

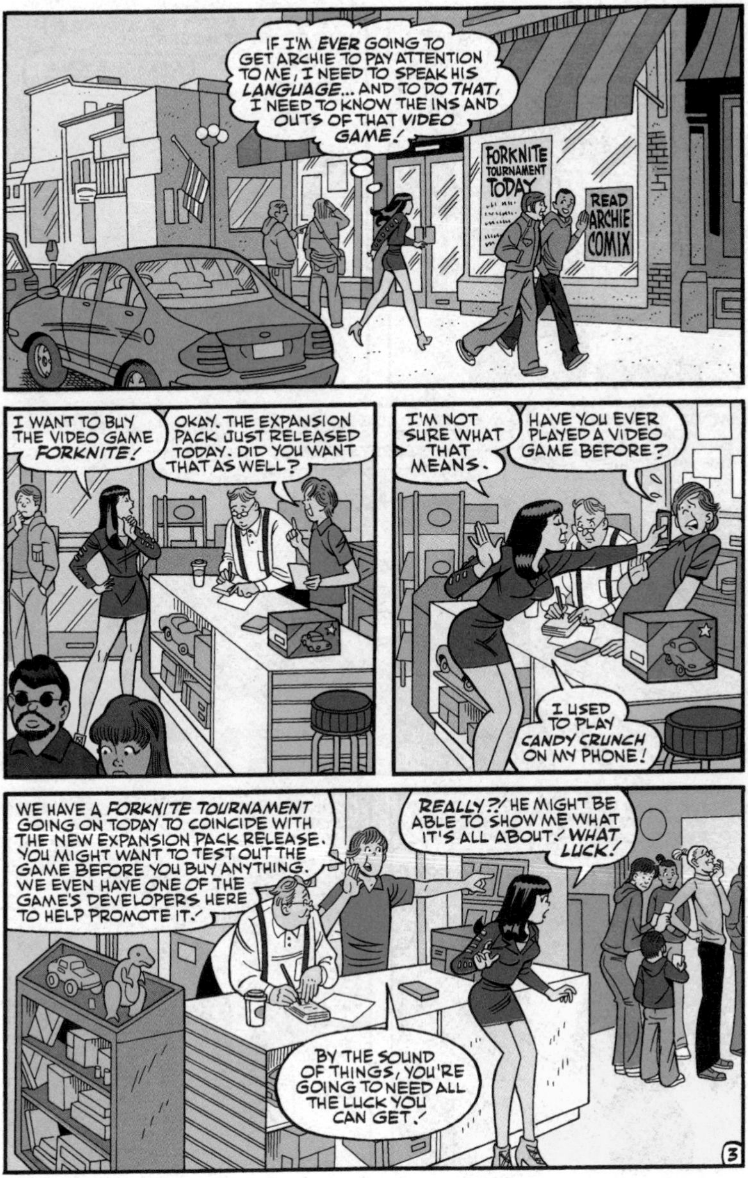
IF I'M EVER GOING TO GET ARCHIE TO PAY ATTENTION TO ME, I NEED TO SPEAK HIS LANGUAGE... AND TO DO THAT, I NEED TO KNOW THE INS AND OUTS OF THAT VIDEO GAME!
FORKNITE TOURNAMENT TODAY
READ ARCHIE COMIX
I WANT TO BUY THE VIDEO GAME FORKNITE!
OKAY. THE EXPANSION PACK JUST RELEASED TODAY. DID YOU WANT THAT AS WELL?
I'M NOT SURE WHAT THAT MEANS.
HAVE YOU EVER PLAYED A VIDEO GAME BEFORE?
I USED TO PLAY CANDY CRUNCH ON MY PHONE!
WE HAVE A FORKNITE TOURNAMENT GOING ON TODAY TO COINCIDE WITH THE NEW EXPANSION PACK RELEASE. YOU MIGHT WANT TO TEST OUT THE GAME BEFORE YOU BUY ANYTHING. WE EVEN HAVE ONE OF THE GAME'S DEVELOPERS HERE TO HELP PROMOTE IT!
REALLY?! HE MIGHT BE ABLE TO SHOW ME WHAT IT'S ALL ABOUT! WHAT LUCK!
BY THE SOUND OF THINGS, YOU'RE GOING TO NEED ALL THE LUCK YOU CAN GET!
3

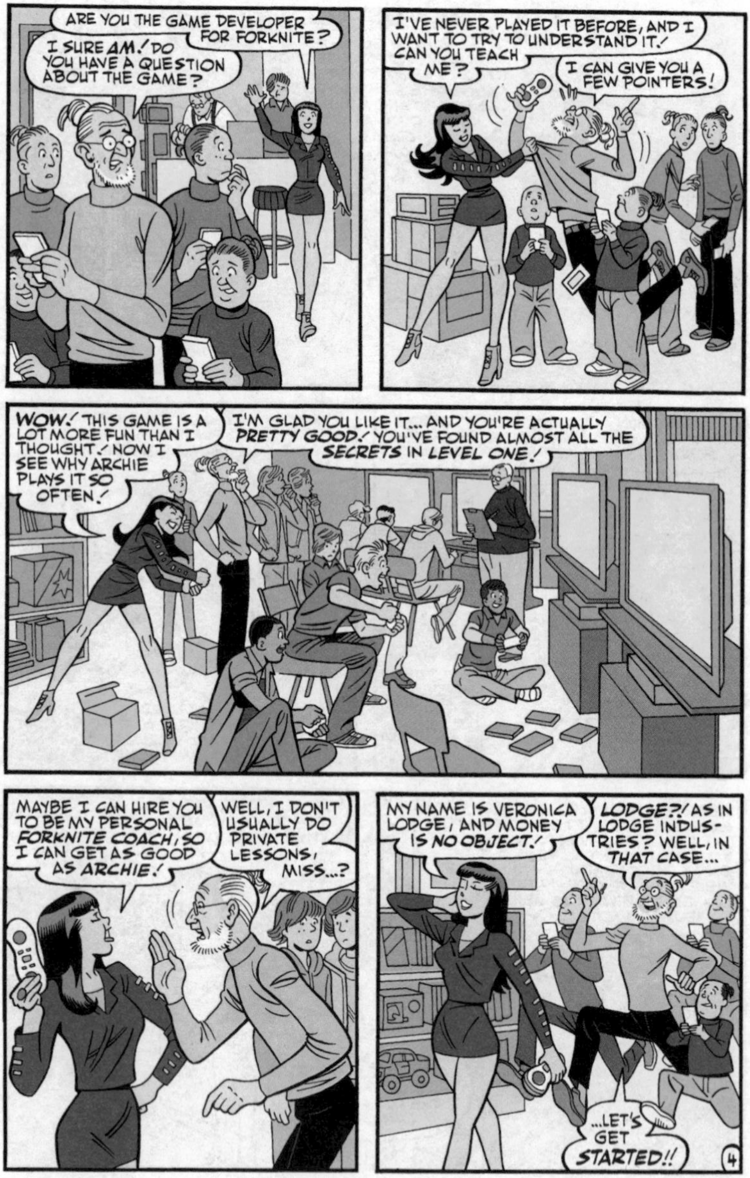
ARE YOU THE GAME DEVELOPER FOR FORKNITE?
I SURE AM! DO YOU HAVE A QUESTION ABOUT THE GAME?
I'VE NEVER PLAYED IT BEFORE, AND I WANT TO TRY TO UNDERSTAND IT! CAN YOU TEACH ME?
I CAN GIVE YOU A FEW POINTERS!
WOW! THIS GAME IS A LOT MORE FUN THAN I THOUGHT! NOW I SEE WHY ARCHIE PLAYS IT SO OFTEN!
I'M GLAD YOU LIKE IT... AND YOU'RE ACTUALLY PRETTY GOOD! YOU'VE FOUND ALMOST ALL THE SECRETS IN LEVEL ONE!
MAYBE I CAN HIRE YOU TO BE MY PERSONAL FORKNITE COACH, SO I CAN GET AS GOOD AS ARCHIE!
WELL, I DON'T USUALLY DO PRIVATE LESSONS, MISS...?
MY NAME IS VERONICA LODGE, AND MONEY IS NO OBJECT!
LODGE?! AS IN LODGE INDUSTRIES? WELL, IN THAT CASE...
...LET'S GET STARTED!!
4

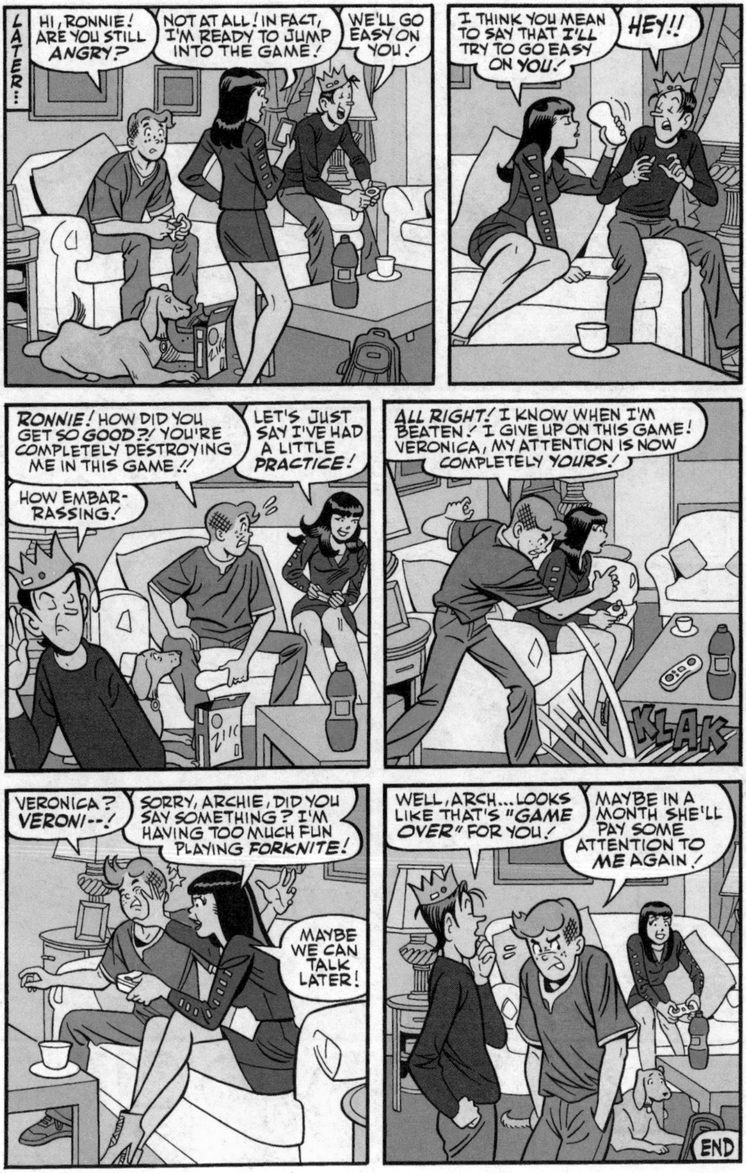
LATER...
HI, RONNIE! ARE YOU STILL ANGRY?
NOT AT ALL! IN FACT, I'M READY TO JUMP INTO THE GAME!
WE'LL GO EASY ON YOU!
I THINK YOU MEAN TO SAY THAT I'LL TRY TO GO EASY ON YOU!
HEY!!
RONNIE! HOW DID YOU GET SO GOOD?! YOU'RE COMPLETELY DESTROYING ME IN THIS GAME!!
LET'S JUST SAY I'VE HAD A LITTLE PRACTICE!
HOW EMBARRASSING!
ALL RIGHT! I KNOW WHEN I'M BEATEN! I GIVE UP ON THIS GAME! VERONICA, MY ATTENTION IS NOW COMPLETELY YOURS!
KLAK
VERONICA? VERONI--!
SORRY, ARCHIE, DID YOU SAY SOMETHING? I'M HAVING TOO MUCH FUN PLAYING FORKNITE!
MAYBE WE CAN TALK LATER!
WELL, ARCH... LOOKS LIKE THAT'S "GAME OVER" FOR YOU!
MAYBE IN A MONTH SHE'LL PAY SOME ATTENTION TO ME AGAIN!
END

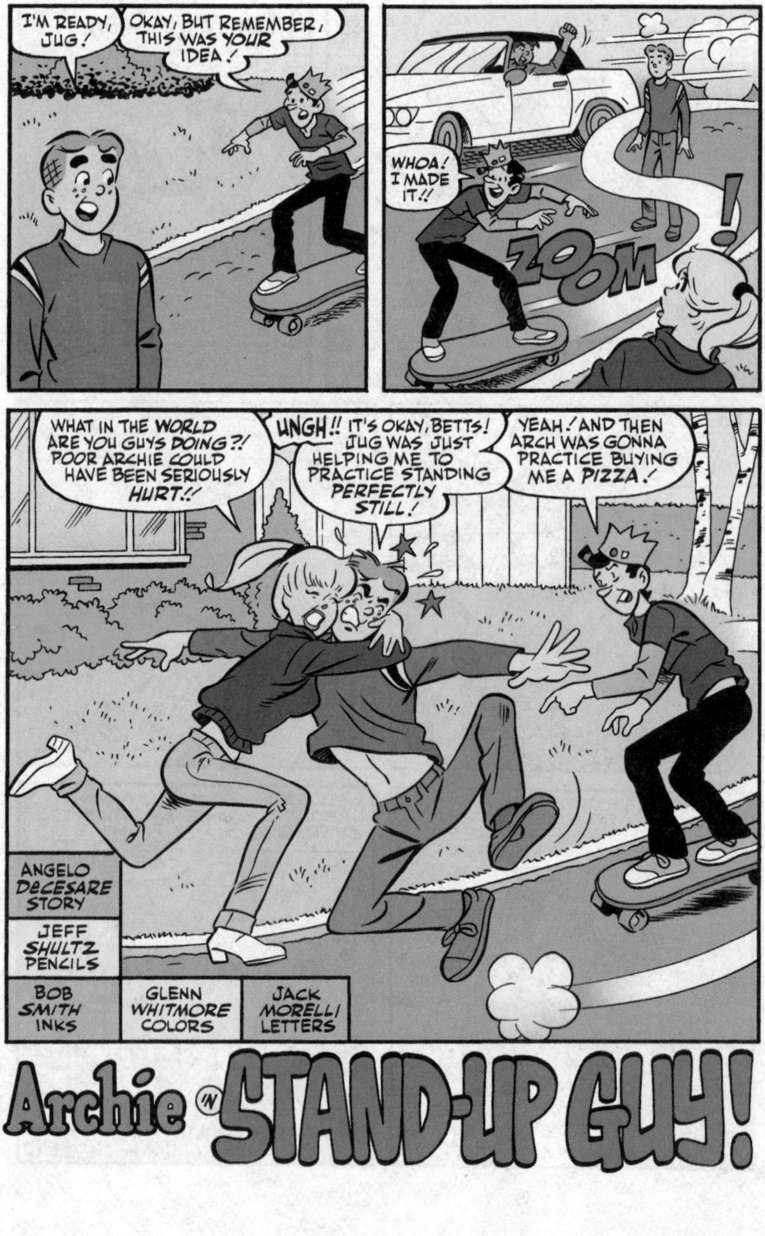

I'M READY, JUG!
OKAY, BUT REMEMBER, THIS WAS YOUR IDEA!
WHOA! I MADE IT!!
ZOOM
!
WHAT IN THE WORLD ARE YOU GUYS DOING?! POOR ARCHIE COULD HAVE BEEN SERIOUSLY HURT!!
UNGH!! IT'S OKAY, BETTS! JUG WAS JUST HELPING ME TO PRACTICE STANDING PERFECTLY STILL!
YEAH! AND THEN ARCH WAS GONNA PRACTICE BUYING ME A PIZZA!
ANGELO DeCESARE STORY
JEFF SHULTZ PENCILS
BOB SMITH INKS
GLENN WHITMORE COLORS
JACK MORELLI LETTERS
Archie IN STAND-UP GUY!

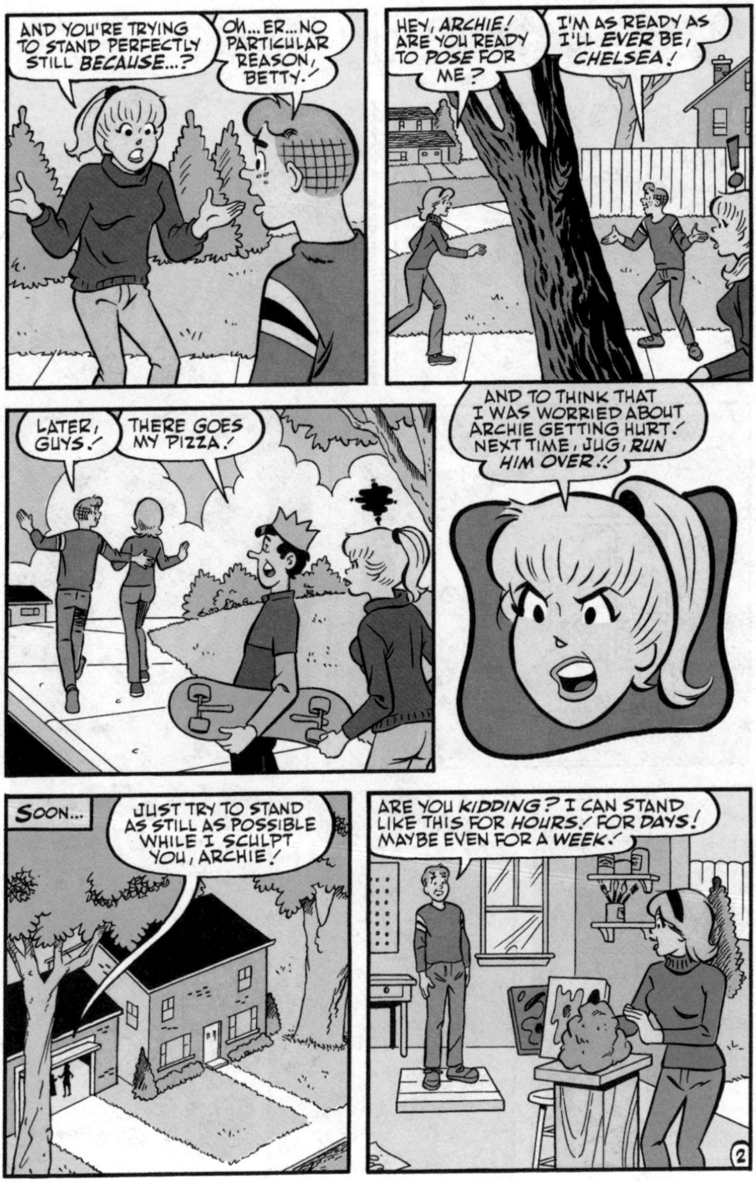
AND YOU'RE TRYING TO STAND PERFECTLY STILL BECAUSE...?
OH... ER... NO PARTICULAR REASON, BETTY!
HEY, ARCHIE! ARE YOU READY TO POSE FOR ME?
I'M AS READY AS I'LL EVER BE, CHELSEA!
LATER, GUYS!
THERE GOES MY PIZZA!
AND TO THINK THAT I WAS WORRIED ABOUT ARCHIE GETTING HURT! NEXT TIME, JUG, RUN HIM OVER!!
SOON...
JUST TRY TO STAND AS STILL AS POSSIBLE WHILE I SCULPT YOU, ARCHIE!
ARE YOU KIDDING? I CAN STAND LIKE THIS FOR HOURS! FOR DAYS! MAYBE EVEN FOR A WEEK!
2

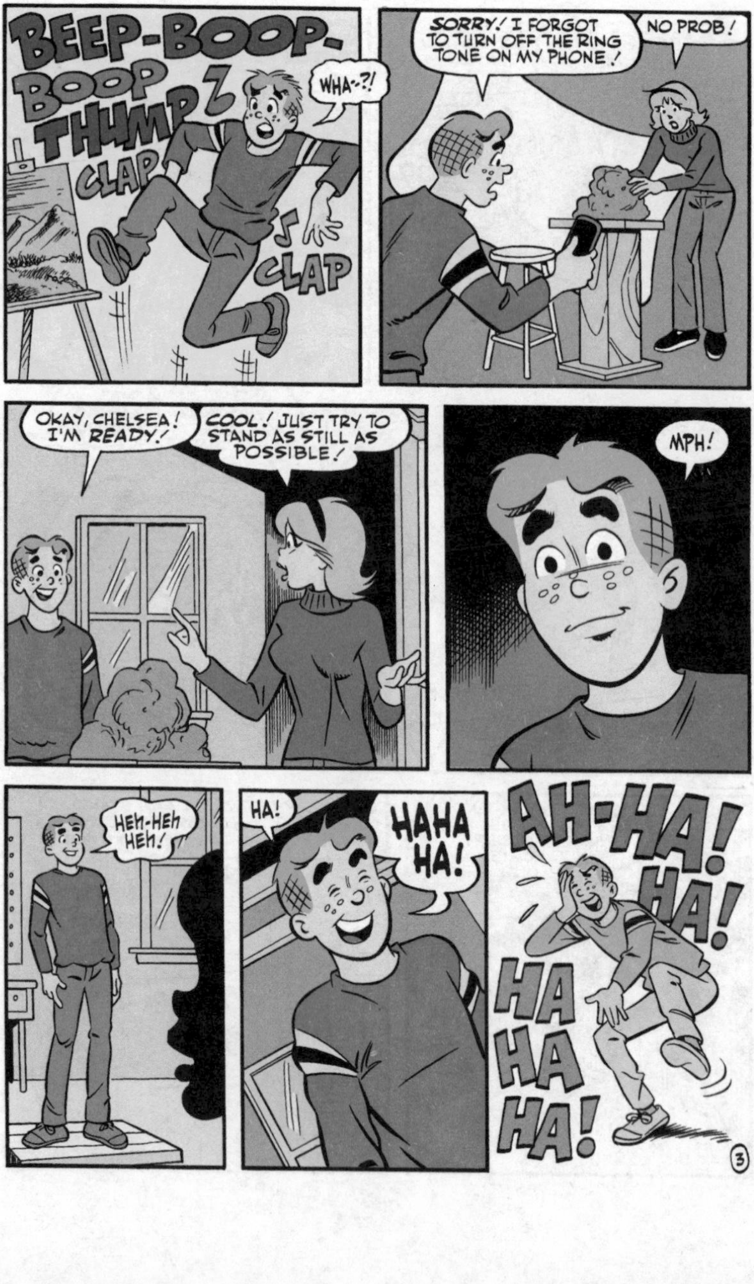
BEEP-BOOP-BOOP
THUMP
CLAP
CLAP
WHA-?!
SORRY! I FORGOT TO TURN OFF THE RING TONE ON MY PHONE!
NO PROB!
OKAY, CHELSEA! I'M READY!
COOL! JUST TRY TO STAND AS STILL AS POSSIBLE!
MPH!
HEH-HEH HEH!
HA!
HAHA HA!
AH-HA! HA! HA HA HA HA HA!
3

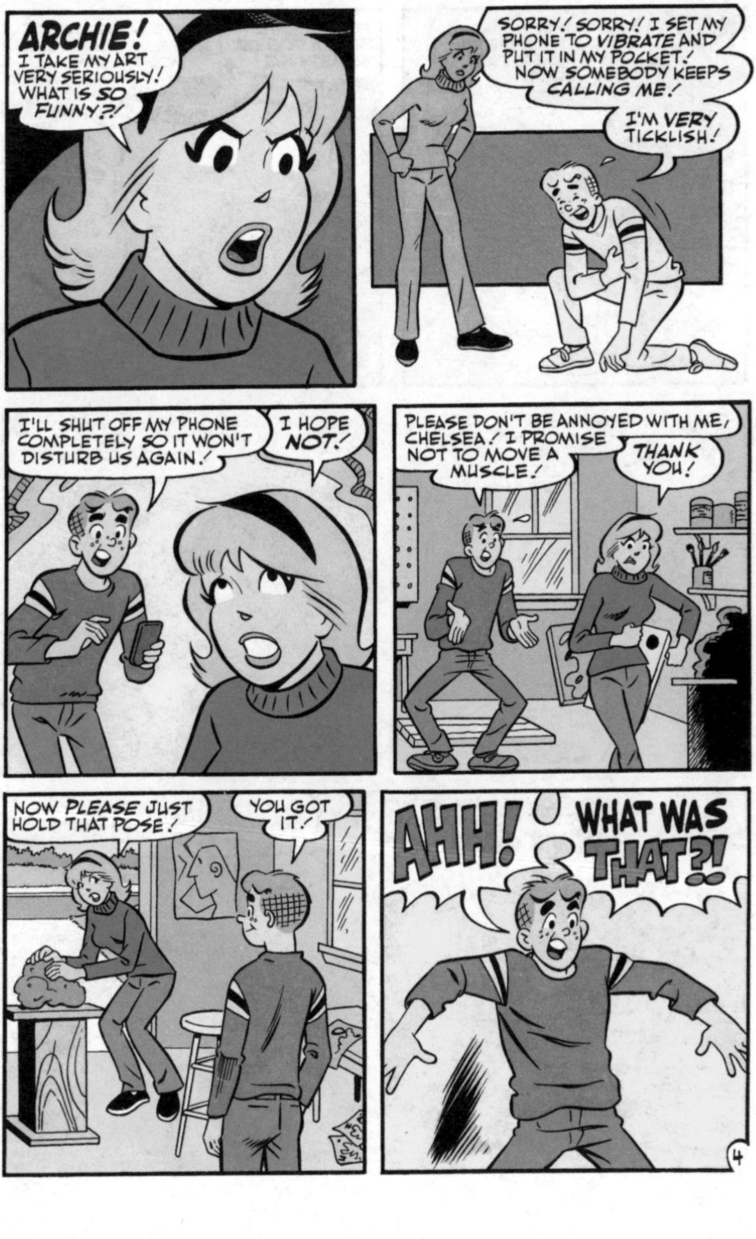
ARCHIE! I TAKE MY ART VERY SERIOUSLY! WHAT IS SO FUNNY?!
SORRY! SORRY! I SET MY PHONE TO VIBRATE AND PUT IT IN MY POCKET! NOW SOMEBODY KEEPS CALLING ME!
I'M VERY TICKLISH!
I'LL SHUT OFF MY PHONE COMPLETELY SO IT WON'T DISTURB US AGAIN!
I HOPE NOT!
PLEASE DON'T BE ANNOYED WITH ME, CHELSEA! I PROMISE NOT TO MOVE A MUSCLE!
THANK YOU!
NOW PLEASE JUST HOLD THAT POSE!
YOU GOT IT!
AHH!
WHAT WAS THAT?!
4

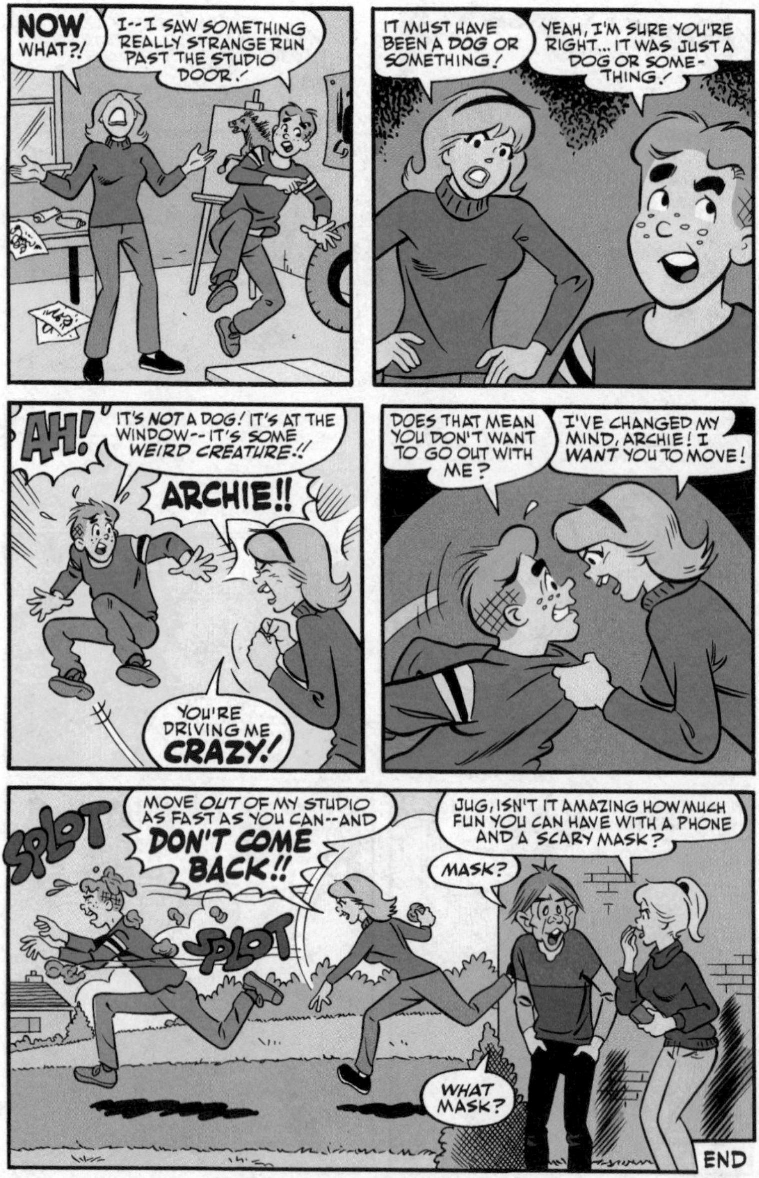
NOW WHAT?!
I--I SAW SOMETHING REALLY STRANGE RUN PAST THE STUDIO DOOR!
IT MUST HAVE BEEN A DOG OR SOMETHING!
YEAH, I'M SURE YOU'RE RIGHT... IT WAS JUST A DOG OR SOMETHING!
AH!
IT'S NOT A DOG! IT'S AT THE WINDOW-- IT'S SOME WEIRD CREATURE!!
ARCHIE!!
YOU'RE DRIVING ME CRAZY!
DOES THAT MEAN YOU DON'T WANT TO GO OUT WITH ME?
I'VE CHANGED MY MIND, ARCHIE! I WANT YOU TO MOVE!
SPLOT
MOVE OUT OF MY STUDIO AS FAST AS YOU CAN--AND DON'T COME BACK!!
SPLOT
JUG, ISN'T IT AMAZING HOW MUCH FUN YOU CAN HAVE WITH A PHONE AND A SCARY MASK?
MASK?
WHAT MASK?
END

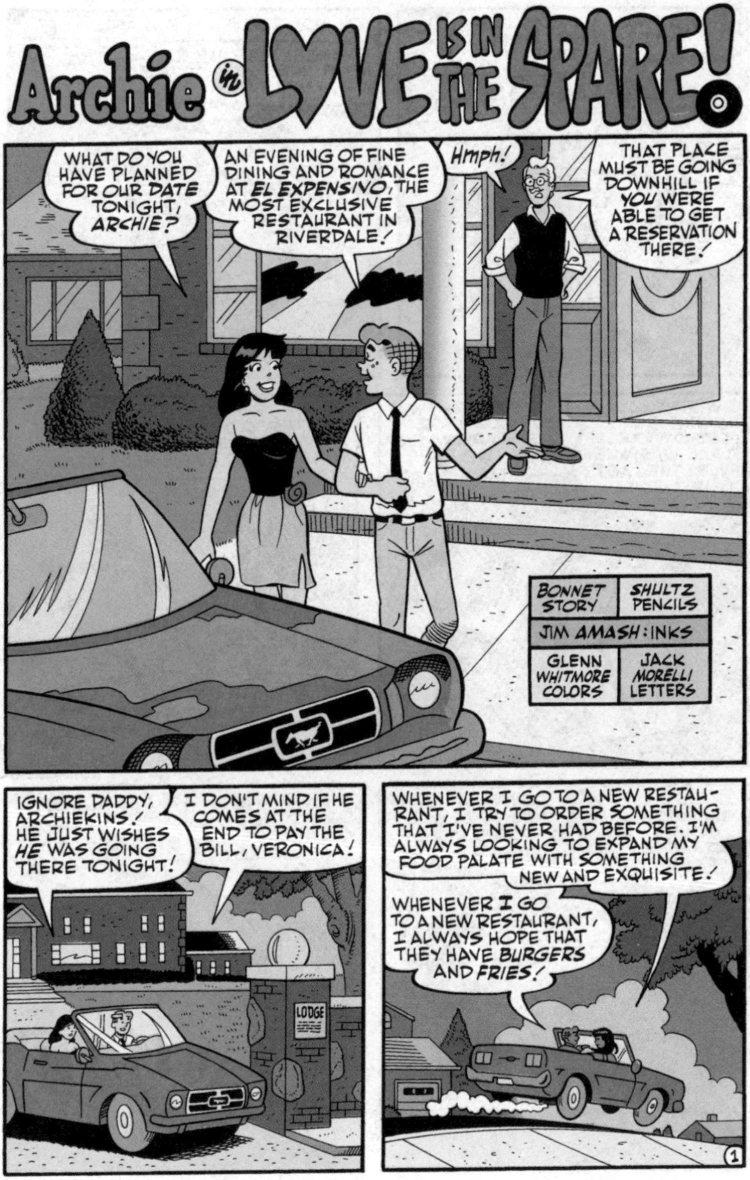
Archie in LOVE IS IN THE SPARE!
WHAT DO YOU HAVE PLANNED FOR OUR DATE TONIGHT, ARCHIE?
AN EVENING OF FINE DINING AND ROMANCE AT EL EXPENSIVO, THE MOST EXCLUSIVE RESTAURANT IN RIVERDALE!
Hmph!
THAT PLACE MUST BE GOING DOWNHILL IF YOU WERE ABLE TO GET A RESERVATION THERE!
BONNET STORY
SHULTZ PENCILS
JIM AMASH: INKS
GLENN WHITMORE COLORS
JACK MORELLI LETTERS
IGNORE DADDY, ARCHIEKINS! HE JUST WISHES HE WAS GOING THERE TONIGHT!
I DON'T MIND IF HE COMES AT THE END TO PAY THE BILL, VERONICA!
LODGE
WHENEVER I GO TO A NEW RESTAU-RANT, I TRY TO ORDER SOMETHING THAT I'VE NEVER HAD BEFORE. I'M ALWAYS LOOKING TO EXPAND MY FOOD PALATE WITH SOMETHING NEW AND EXQUISITE!
WHENEVER I GO TO A NEW RESTAURANT, I ALWAYS HOPE THAT THEY HAVE BURGERS AND FRIES!
1

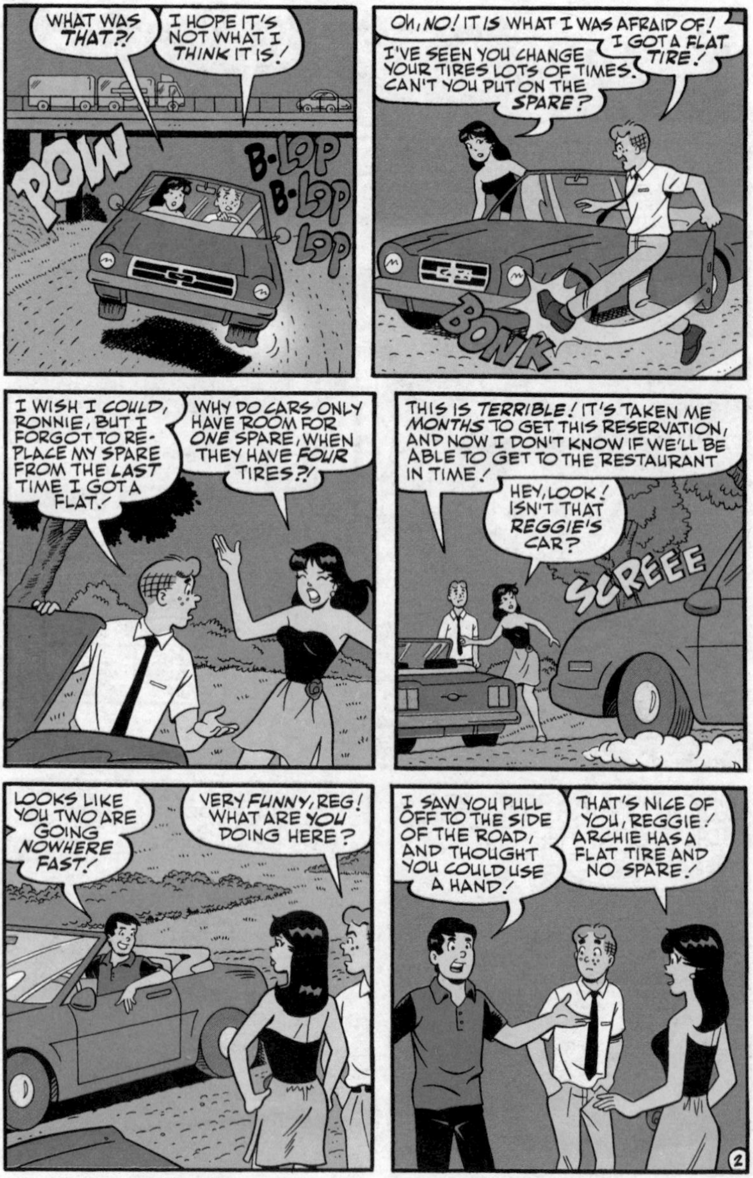
WHAT WAS THAT?!
I HOPE IT'S NOT WHAT I THINK IT IS!
POW
B-LOP B-LOP LOP
OH, NO! IT IS WHAT I WAS AFRAID OF! I GOT A FLAT TIRE!
I'VE SEEN YOU CHANGE YOUR TIRES LOTS OF TIMES. CAN'T YOU PUT ON THE SPARE?
BONK
I WISH I COULD, RONNIE, BUT I FORGOT TO RE-PLACE MY SPARE FROM THE LAST TIME I GOT A FLAT!
WHY DO CARS ONLY HAVE ROOM FOR ONE SPARE, WHEN THEY HAVE FOUR TIRES?!
THIS IS TERRIBLE! IT'S TAKEN ME MONTHS TO GET THIS RESERVATION, AND NOW I DON'T KNOW IF WE'LL BE ABLE TO GET TO THE RESTAURANT IN TIME!
HEY, LOOK! ISN'T THAT REGGIE'S CAR?
SCREEE
LOOKS LIKE YOU TWO ARE GOING NOWHERE FAST!
VERY FUNNY, REG! WHAT ARE YOU DOING HERE?
I SAW YOU PULL OFF TO THE SIDE OF THE ROAD, AND THOUGHT YOU COULD USE A HAND!
THAT'S NICE OF YOU, REGGIE! ARCHIE HAS A FLAT TIRE AND NO SPARE!
2

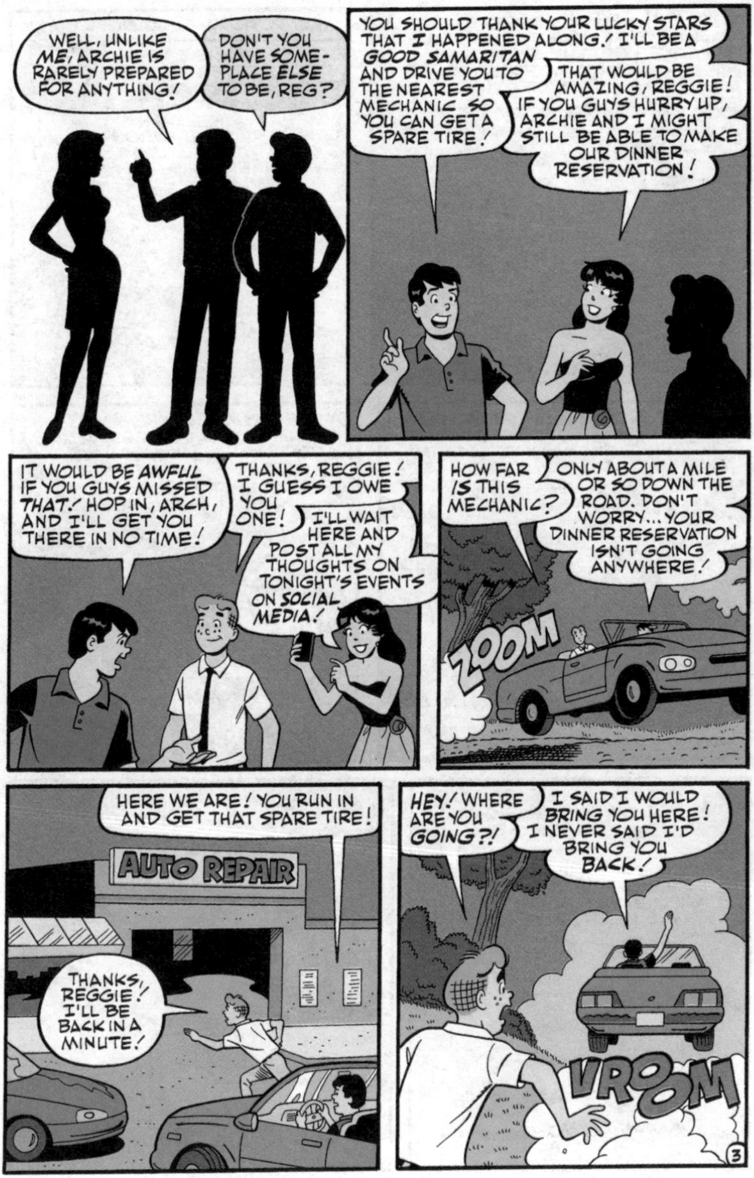
WELL, UNLIKE ME, ARCHIE IS RARELY PREPARED FOR ANYTHING!
DON'T YOU HAVE SOME-PLACE ELSE TO BE, REG?
YOU SHOULD THANK YOUR LUCKY STARS THAT I HAPPENED ALONG! I'LL BE A GOOD SAMARITAN AND DRIVE YOU TO THE NEAREST MECHANIC SO YOU CAN GET A SPARE TIRE!
THAT WOULD BE AMAZING, REGGIE! IF YOU GUYS HURRY UP, ARCHIE AND I MIGHT STILL BE ABLE TO MAKE OUR DINNER RESERVATION!
IT WOULD BE AWFUL IF YOU GUYS MISSED THAT! HOP IN, ARCH, AND I'LL GET YOU THERE IN NO TIME!
THANKS, REGGIE! I GUESS I OWE YOU ONE!
I'LL WAIT HERE AND POST ALL MY THOUGHTS ON TONIGHT'S EVENTS ON SOCIAL MEDIA!
HOW FAR IS THIS MECHANIC?
ONLY ABOUT A MILE OR SO DOWN THE ROAD. DON'T WORRY... YOUR DINNER RESERVATION ISN'T GOING ANYWHERE!
ZOOM
HERE WE ARE! YOU RUN IN AND GET THAT SPARE TIRE!
AUTO REPAIR
THANKS, REGGIE! I'LL BE BACK IN A MINUTE!
HEY! WHERE ARE YOU GOING?!
I SAID I WOULD BRING YOU HERE! I NEVER SAID I'D BRING YOU BACK!
VROOM
3

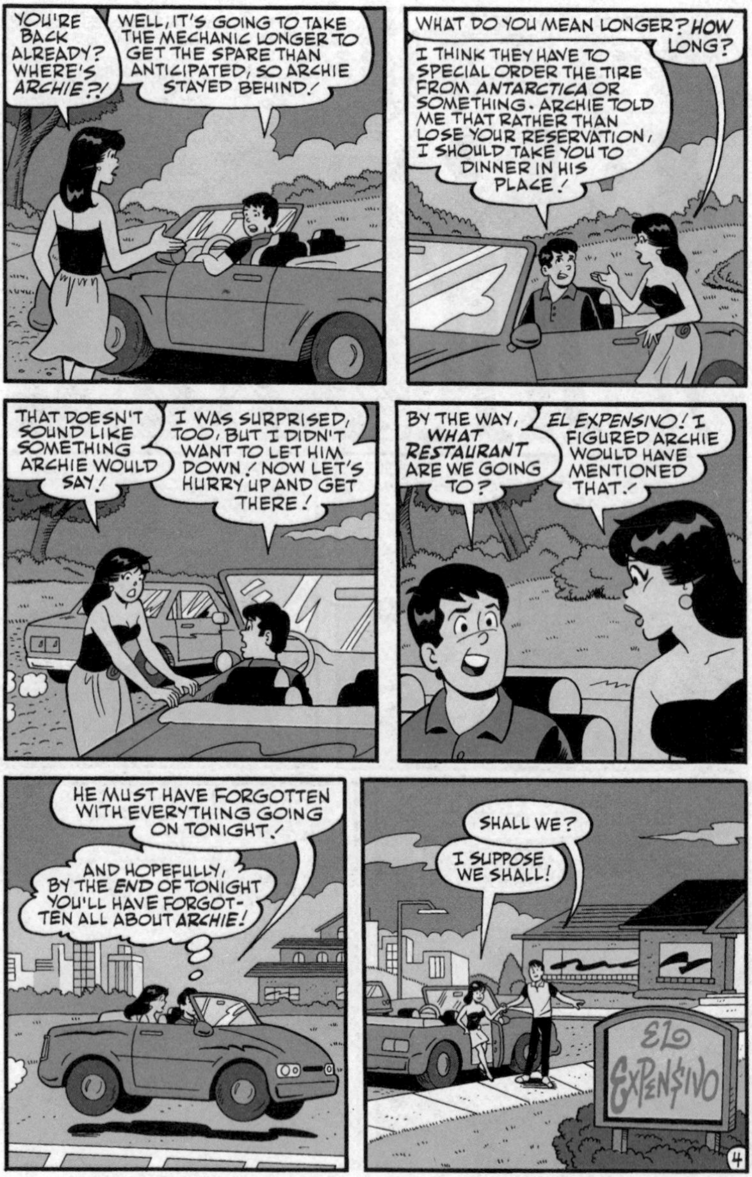
YOU'RE BACK ALREADY? WHERE'S ARCHIE?!
WELL, IT'S GOING TO TAKE THE MECHANIC LONGER TO GET THE SPARE THAN ANTICIPATED, SO ARCHIE STAYED BEHIND!
WHAT DO YOU MEAN LONGER? HOW LONG?
I THINK THEY HAVE TO SPECIAL ORDER THE TIRE FROM ANTARCTICA OR SOMETHING. ARCHIE TOLD ME THAT RATHER THAN LOSE YOUR RESERVATION, I SHOULD TAKE YOU TO DINNER IN HIS PLACE!
THAT DOESN'T SOUND LIKE SOMETHING ARCHIE WOULD SAY!
I WAS SURPRISED, TOO, BUT I DIDN'T WANT TO LET HIM DOWN! NOW LET'S HURRY UP AND GET THERE!
BY THE WAY, WHAT RESTAURANT ARE WE GOING TO?
EL EXPENSIVO! I FIGURED ARCHIE WOULD HAVE MENTIONED THAT!
HE MUST HAVE FORGOTTEN WITH EVERYTHING GOING ON TONIGHT!
AND HOPEFULLY, BY THE END OF TONIGHT YOU'LL HAVE FORGOTTEN ALL ABOUT ARCHIE!
SHALL WE?
I SUPPOSE WE SHALL!
EL EXPENSIVO
4

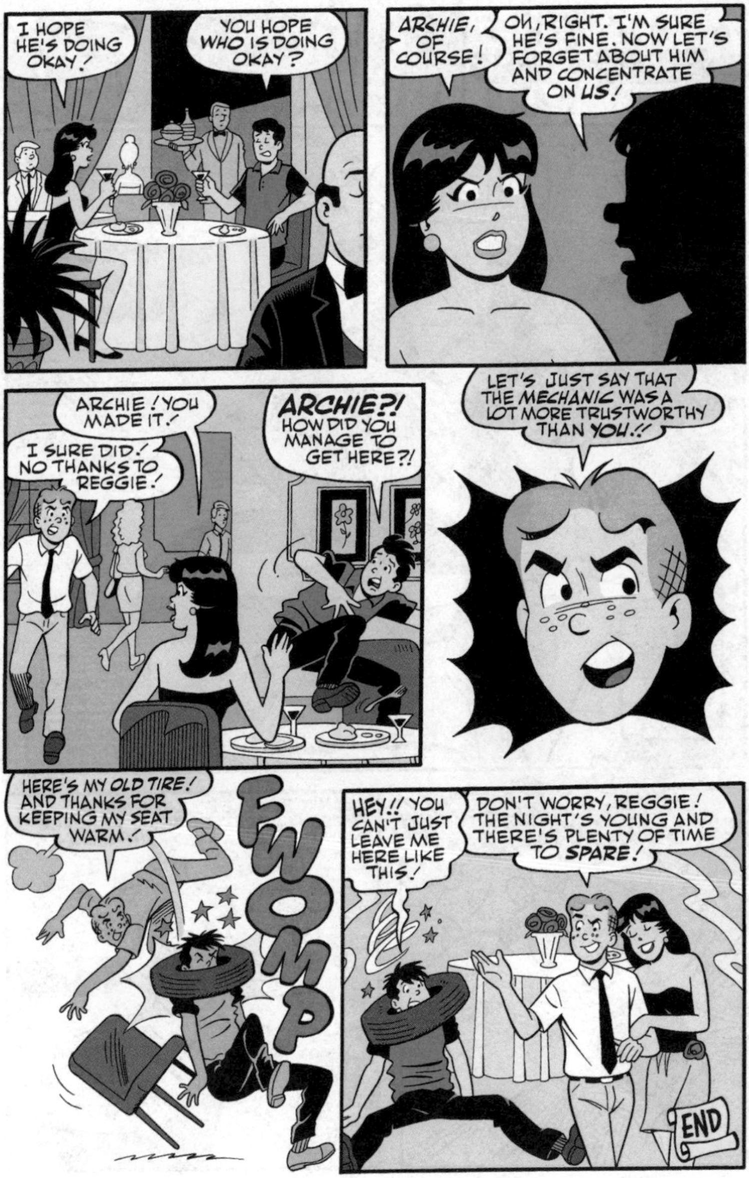

I HOPE HE'S DOING OKAY!
YOU HOPE WHO IS DOING OKAY?
ARCHIE, OF COURSE!
OH, RIGHT. I'M SURE HE'S FINE. NOW LET'S FORGET ABOUT HIM AND CONCENTRATE ON US!
ARCHIE! YOU MADE IT!
I SURE DID! NO THANKS TO REGGIE!
ARCHIE?! HOW DID YOU MANAGE TO GET HERE?!
LET'S JUST SAY THAT THE MECHANIC WAS A LOT MORE TRUSTWORTHY THAN YOU!!
HERE'S MY OLD TIRE! AND THANKS FOR KEEPING MY SEAT WARM!
FWOMP
HEY!! YOU CAN'T JUST LEAVE ME HERE LIKE THIS!
DON'T WORRY, REGGIE! THE NIGHT'S YOUNG AND THERE'S PLENTY OF TIME TO SPARE!
END

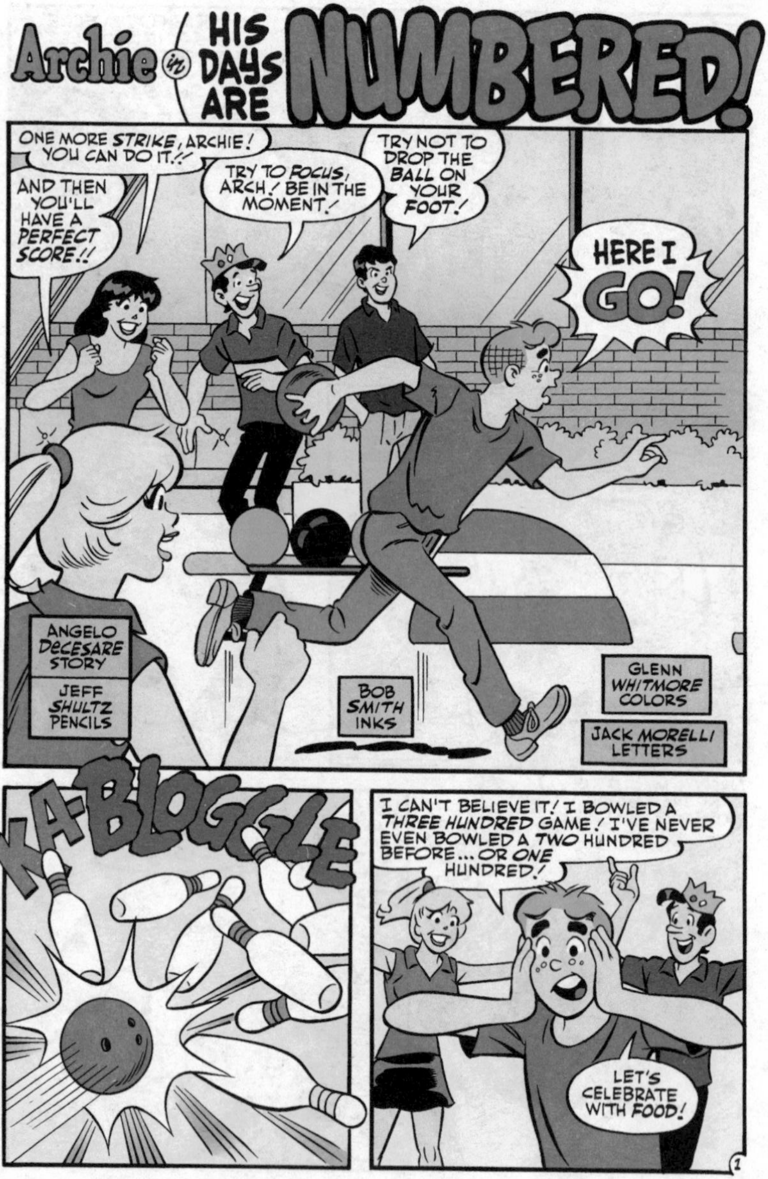
Archie in
HIS DAYS ARE NUMBERED!
ONE MORE STRIKE, ARCHIE! YOU CAN DO IT.!!
AND THEN YOU'LL HAVE A PERFECT SCORE!!
TRY TO FOCUS, ARCH! BE IN THE MOMENT!
TRY NOT TO DROP THE BALL ON YOUR FOOT!
HERE I GO!
ANGELO DECESARE STORY
JEFF SHULTZ PENCILS
BOB SMITH INKS
GLENN WHITMORE COLORS
JACK MORELLI LETTERS
KA-BLOGGLE
I CAN'T BELIEVE IT! I BOWLED A THREE HUNDRED GAME! I'VE NEVER EVEN BOWLED A TWO HUNDRED BEFORE... OR ONE HUNDRED!
LET'S CELEBRATE WITH FOOD!
1

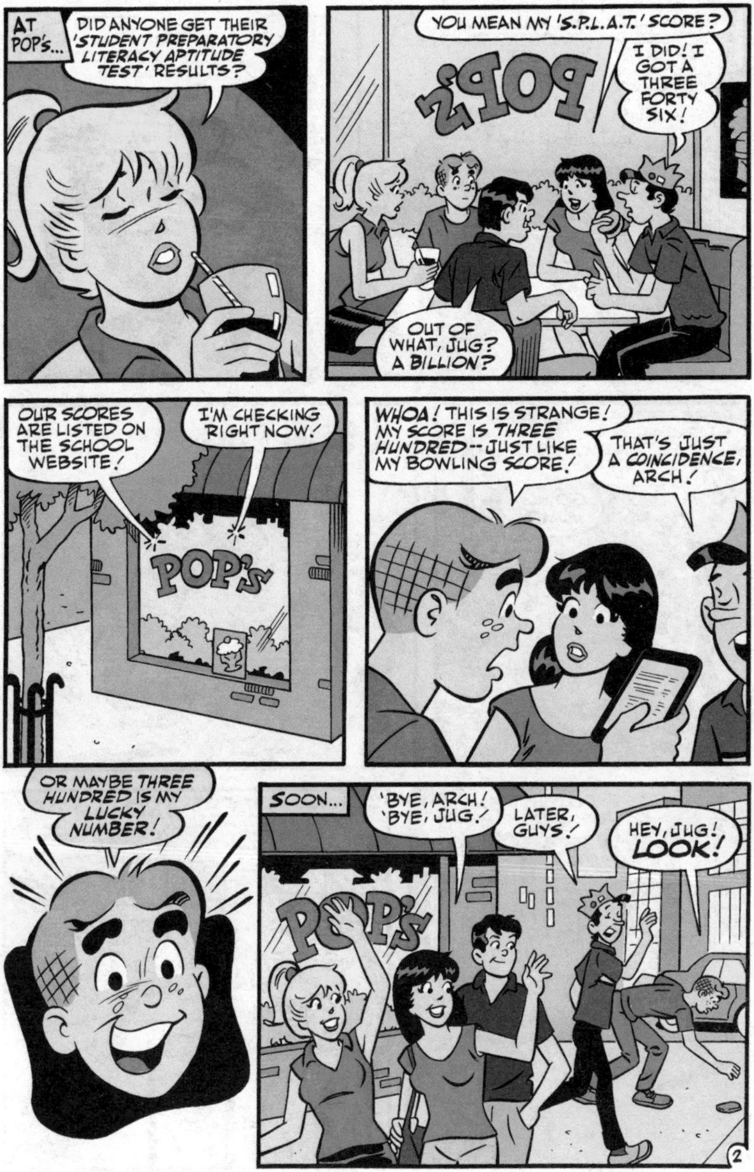
AT POP'S...
DID ANYONE GET THEIR 'STUDENT PREPARATORY LITERACY APTITUDE TEST' RESULTS?
YOU MEAN MY 'S.P.L.A.T.' SCORE?
I DID! I GOT A THREE FORTY SIX!
POP'S
OUT OF WHAT, JUG? A BILLION?
OUR SCORES ARE LISTED ON THE SCHOOL WEBSITE!
I'M CHECKING RIGHT NOW!
POP'S
WHOA! THIS IS STRANGE! MY SCORE IS THREE HUNDRED -- JUST LIKE MY BOWLING SCORE!
THAT'S JUST A COINCIDENCE, ARCH!
OR MAYBE THREE HUNDRED IS MY LUCKY NUMBER!
SOON...
'BYE, ARCH! 'BYE, JUG!
LATER, GUYS!
HEY, JUG! LOOK!
2

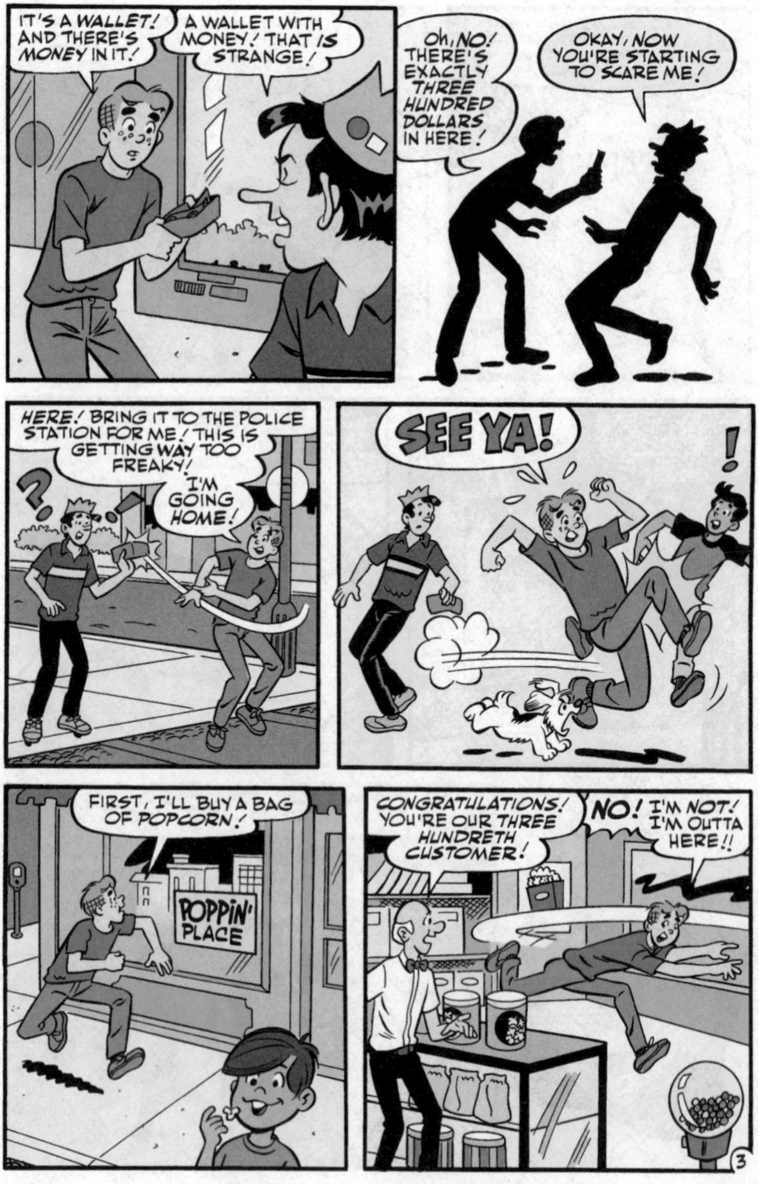
IT'S A WALLET! AND THERE'S MONEY IN IT!
A WALLET WITH MONEY! THAT IS STRANGE!
OH, NO! THERE'S EXACTLY THREE HUNDRED DOLLARS IN HERE!
OKAY, NOW YOU'RE STARTING TO SCARE ME!
HERE! BRING IT TO THE POLICE STATION FOR ME! THIS IS GETTING WAY TOO FREAKY!
I'M GOING HOME!
?
!
SEE YA!
!
FIRST, I'LL BUY A BAG OF POPCORN!
POPPIN' PLACE
CONGRATULATIONS! YOU'RE OUR THREE HUNDRETH CUSTOMER!
NO! I'M NOT! I'M OUTTA HERE!!
3

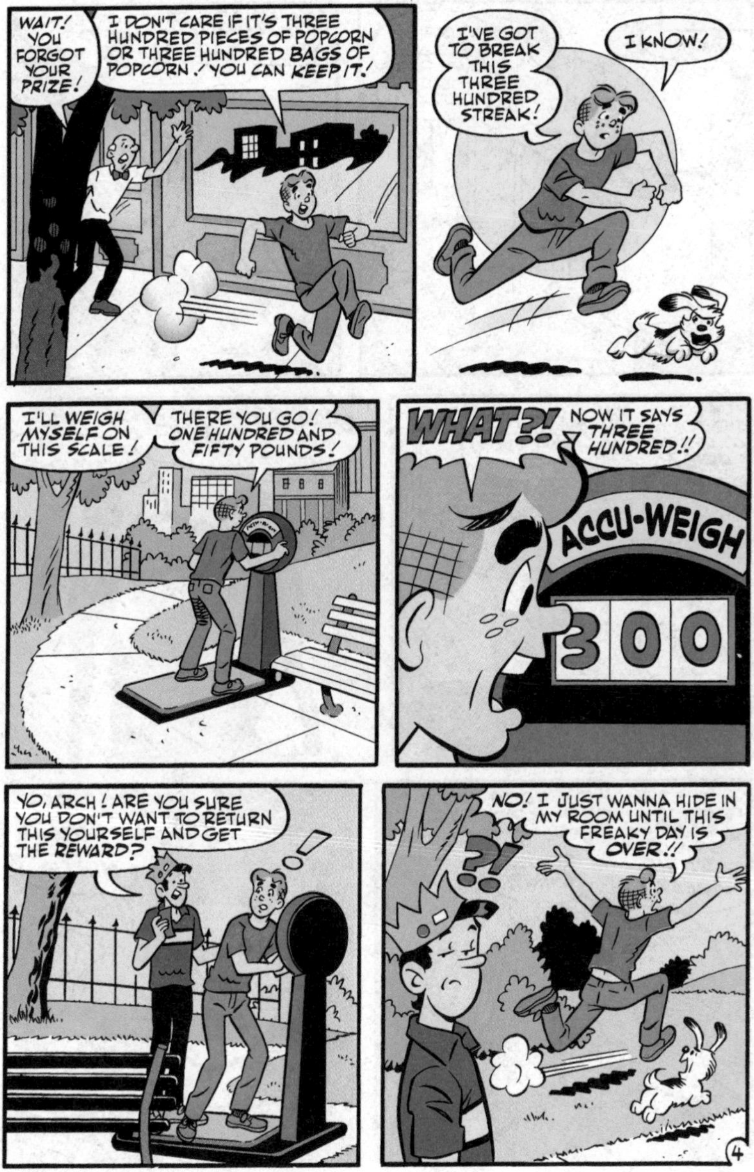
WAIT! YOU FORGOT YOUR PRIZE!
I DON'T CARE IF IT'S THREE HUNDRED PIECES OF POPCORN OR THREE HUNDRED BAGS OF POPCORN! YOU CAN KEEP IT!
I'VE GOT TO BREAK THIS THREE HUNDRED STREAK!
I KNOW!
I'LL WEIGH MYSELF ON THIS SCALE!
THERE YOU GO! ONE HUNDRED AND FIFTY POUNDS!
WHAT?!
NOW IT SAYS THREE HUNDRED!!
ACCU-WEIGH
300
YO, ARCH! ARE YOU SURE YOU DON'T WANT TO RETURN THIS YOURSELF AND GET THE REWARD?
!
?!
NO! I JUST WANNA HIDE IN MY ROOM UNTIL THIS FREAKY DAY IS OVER!!
4

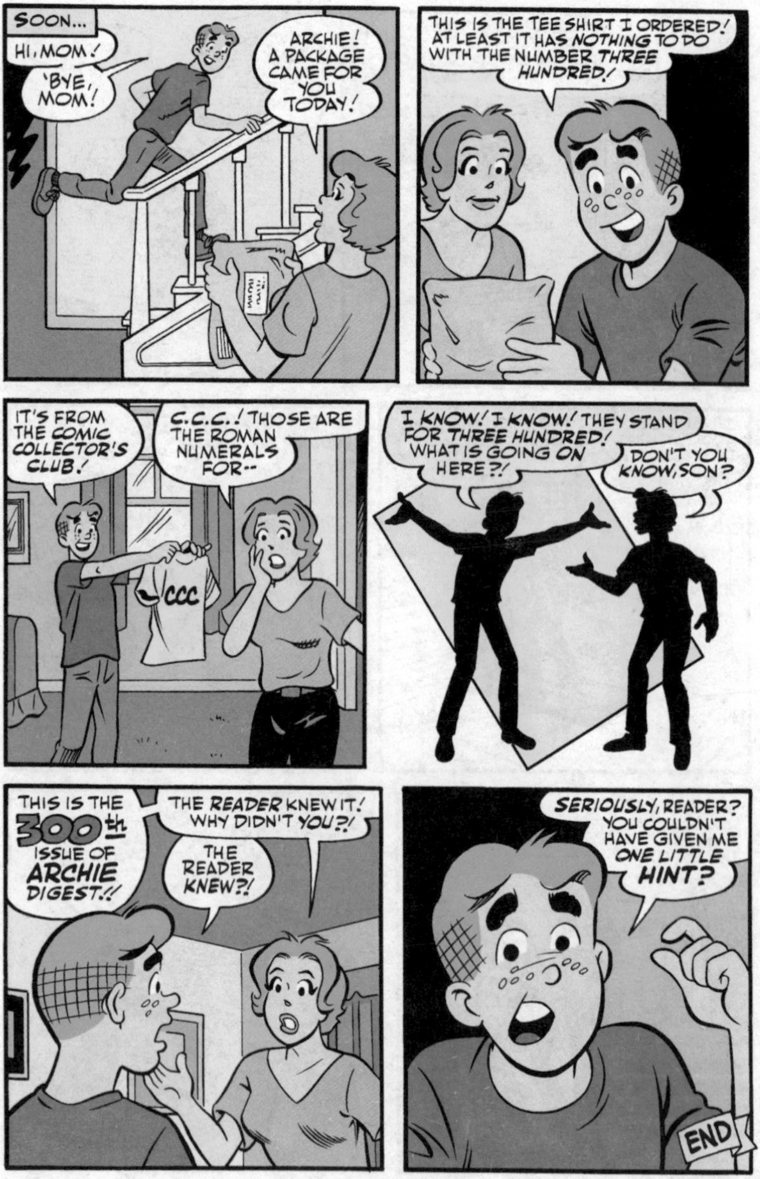
SOON...
HI, MOM!
'BYE, MOM!
ARCHIE! A PACKAGE CAME FOR YOU TODAY!
THIS IS THE TEE SHIRT I ORDERED! AT LEAST IT HAS NOTHING TO DO WITH THE NUMBER THREE HUNDRED!
IT'S FROM THE COMIC COLLECTOR'S CLUB!
C.C.C.! THOSE ARE THE ROMAN NUMERALS FOR--
CCC
I KNOW! I KNOW! THEY STAND FOR THREE HUNDRED! WHAT IS GOING ON HERE?!
DON'T YOU KNOW, SON?
THIS IS THE 300th ISSUE OF ARCHIE DIGEST!!
THE READER KNEW IT! WHY DIDN'T YOU?!
THE READER KNEW?!
SERIOUSLY, READER? YOU COULDN'T HAVE GIVEN ME ONE LITTLE HINT?
END

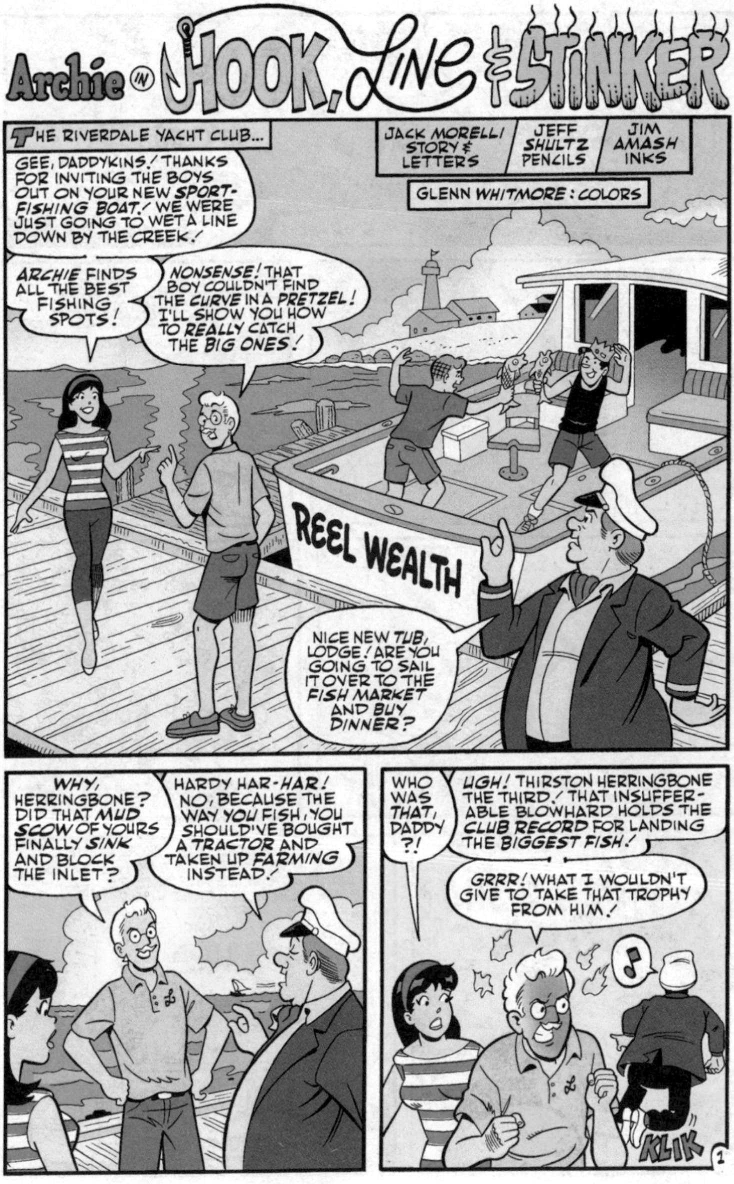
Archie in HOOK, LINE & STINKER
THE RIVERDALE YACHT CLUB...
JACK MORELLI STORY & LETTERS
JEFF SHULTZ PENCILS
JIM AMASH INKS
GLENN WHITMORE : COLORS
GEE, DADDYKINS! THANKS FOR INVITING THE BOYS OUT ON YOUR NEW SPORT-FISHING BOAT! WE WERE JUST GOING TO WET A LINE DOWN BY THE CREEK!
ARCHIE FINDS ALL THE BEST FISHING SPOTS!
NONSENSE! THAT BOY COULDN'T FIND THE CURVE IN A PRETZEL! I'LL SHOW YOU HOW TO REALLY CATCH THE BIG ONES!
REEL WEALTH
NICE NEW TUB, LODGE! ARE YOU GOING TO SAIL IT OVER TO THE FISH MARKET AND BUY DINNER?
WHY, HERRINGBONE? DID THAT MUD SCOW OF YOURS FINALLY SINK AND BLOCK THE INLET?
HARDY HAR-HAR! NO, BECAUSE THE WAY YOU FISH, YOU SHOULD'VE BOUGHT A TRACTOR AND TAKEN UP FARMING INSTEAD!
WHO WAS THAT, DADDY?!
UGH! THIRSTON HERRINGBONE THE THIRD! THAT INSUFFER-ABLE BLOWHARD HOLDS THE CLUB RECORD FOR LANDING THE BIGGEST FISH!
GRRR! WHAT I WOULDN'T GIVE TO TAKE THAT TROPHY FROM HIM!
KLIK
1

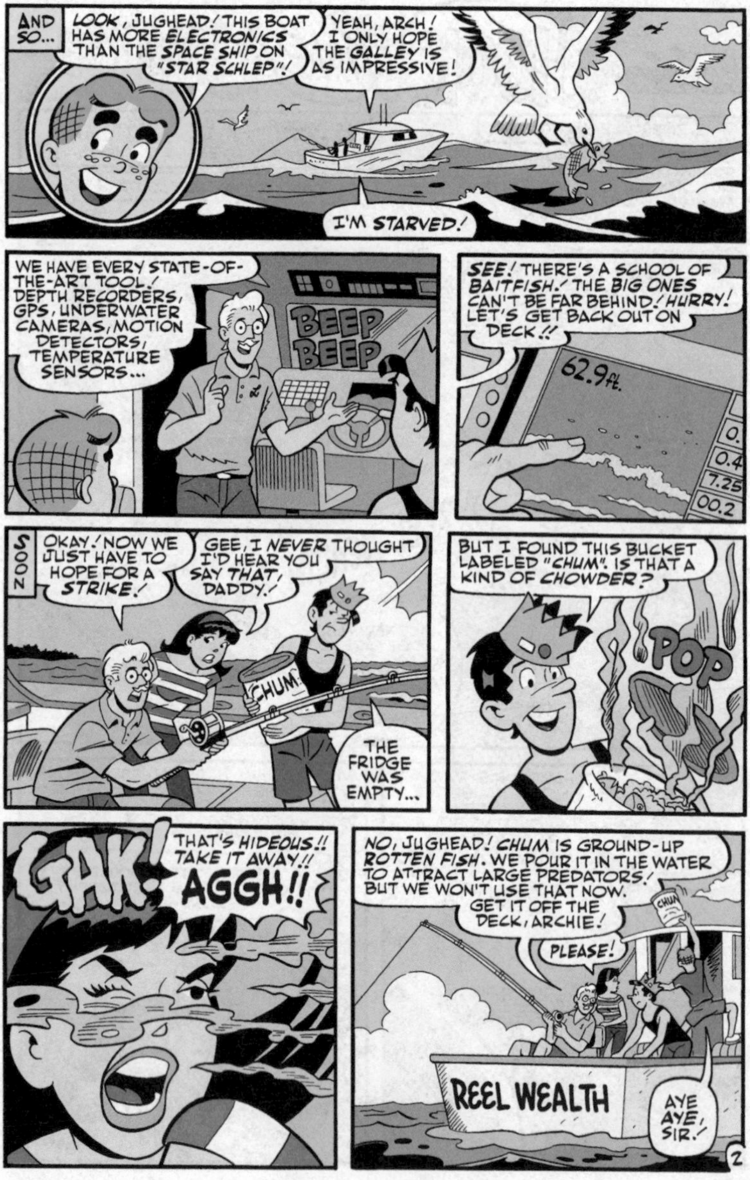
AND SO...
LOOK, JUGHEAD! THIS BOAT HAS MORE ELECTRONICS THAN THE SPACE SHIP ON "STAR SCHLEP"!
YEAH, ARCH! I ONLY HOPE THE GALLEY IS AS IMPRESSIVE!
I'M STARVED!
WE HAVE EVERY STATE-OF-THE-ART TOOL! DEPTH RECORDERS, GPS, UNDERWATER CAMERAS, MOTION DETECTORS, TEMPERATURE SENSORS...
BEEP BEEP
SEE! THERE'S A SCHOOL OF BAITFISH! THE BIG ONES CAN'T BE FAR BEHIND! HURRY! LET'S GET BACK OUT ON DECK!!
62.9ft.
0.4
7.25
00.2
SOON
OKAY! NOW WE JUST HAVE TO HOPE FOR A STRIKE!
GEE, I NEVER THOUGHT I'D HEAR YOU SAY THAT, DADDY!
CHUM
THE FRIDGE WAS EMPTY...
BUT I FOUND THIS BUCKET LABELED "CHUM". IS THAT A KIND OF CHOWDER?
POP
GAK!
THAT'S HIDEOUS!! TAKE IT AWAY!!
AGGH!!
NO, JUGHEAD! CHUM IS GROUND-UP ROTTEN FISH. WE POUR IT IN THE WATER TO ATTRACT LARGE PREDATORS! BUT WE WON'T USE THAT NOW.
GET IT OFF THE DECK, ARCHIE!
PLEASE!
CHUM
REEL WEALTH
AYE AYE, SIR!
2

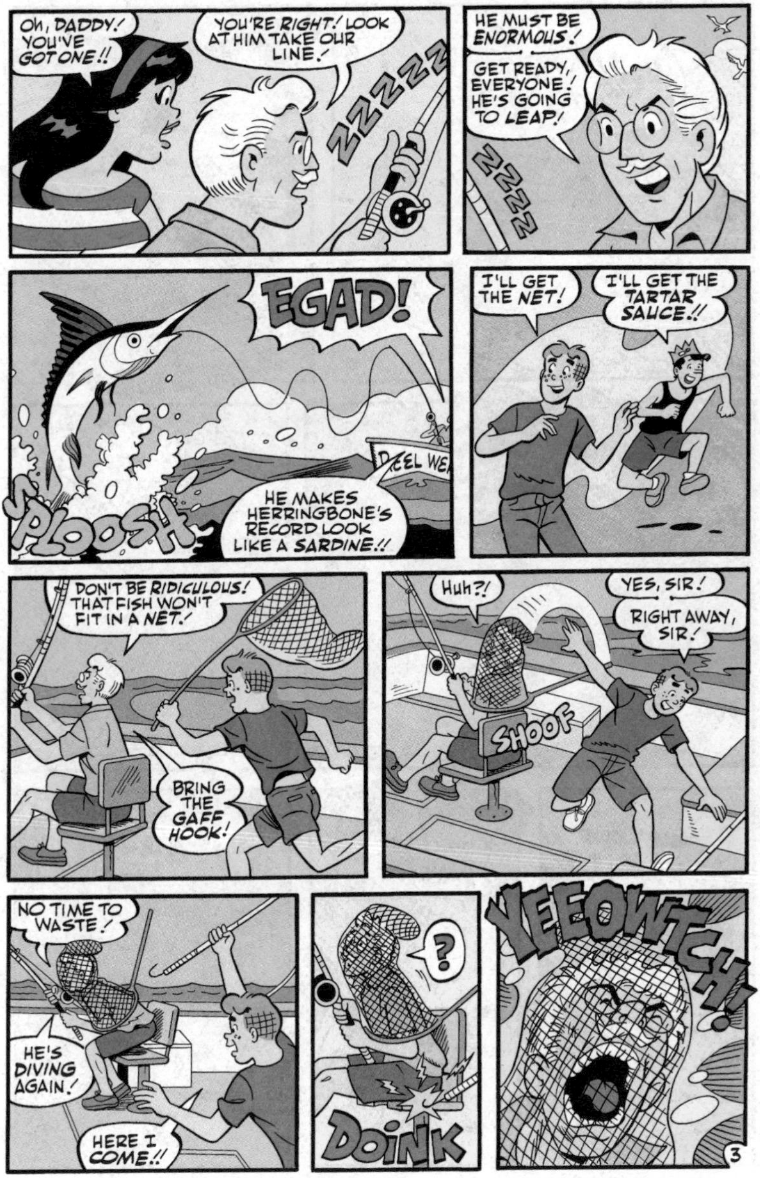

OH, DADDY! YOU'VE GOT ONE!!
YOU'RE RIGHT! LOOK AT HIM TAKE OUR LINE!
ZZZZZ
HE MUST BE ENORMOUS!
GET READY, EVERYONE! HE'S GOING TO LEAP!
ZZZZ
EGAD!
SPLOOSH
REEL WE
HE MAKES HERRINGBONE'S RECORD LOOK LIKE A SARDINE!!
I'LL GET THE NET!
I'LL GET THE TARTAR SAUCE!!
DON'T BE RIDICULOUS! THAT FISH WON'T FIT IN A NET!
BRING THE GAFF HOOK!
HUH?!
YES, SIR!
RIGHT AWAY, SIR!
SHOOF
NO TIME TO WASTE!
HE'S DIVING AGAIN!
HERE I COME!!
?
DOINK
YEEOWTCH!
3

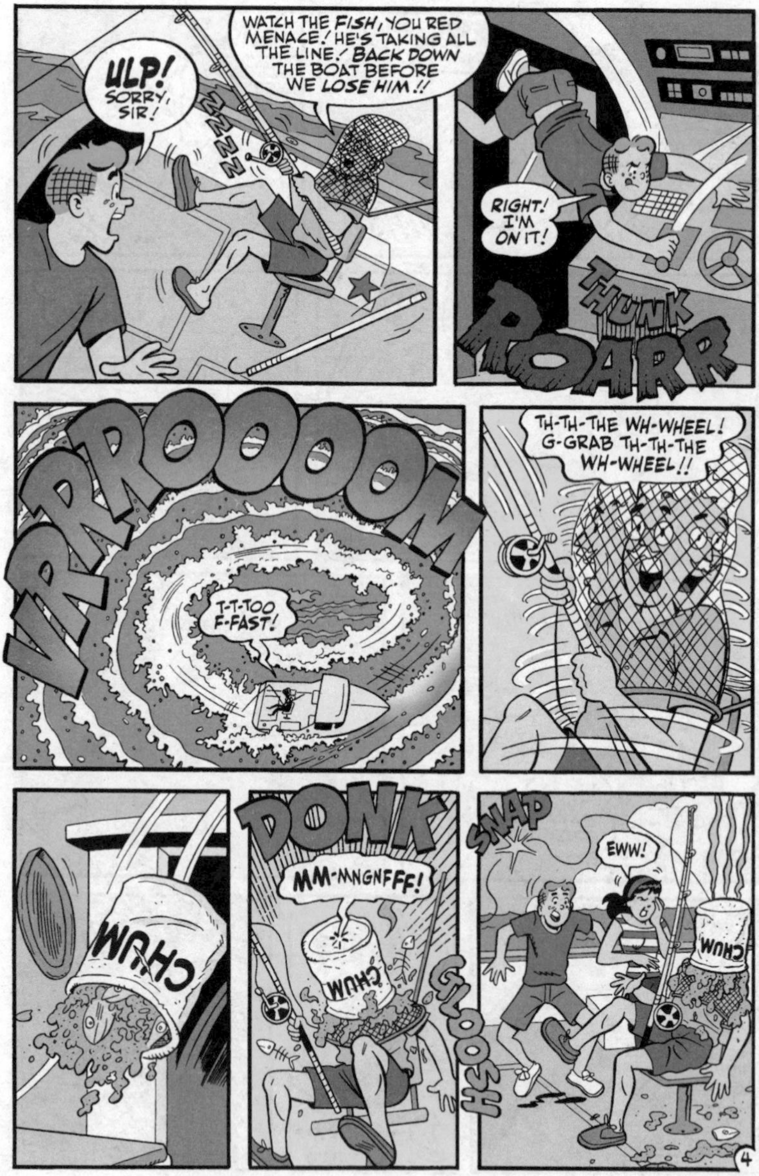
WATCH THE FISH, YOU RED MENACE! HE'S TAKING ALL THE LINE! BACK DOWN THE BOAT BEFORE WE LOSE HIM!!
ULP! SORRY, SIR!
ZZZZ
RIGHT! I'M ON IT!
THUNK
ROARR
VRROOOOOM
T-T-TOO F-FAST!
TH-TH-THE WH-WHEEL! G-GRAB TH-TH-THE WH-WHEEL!!
CHUM
DONK
MM-MNGNFFF!
CHUM
GLOOSH
SNAP
EWW!
CHUM
4

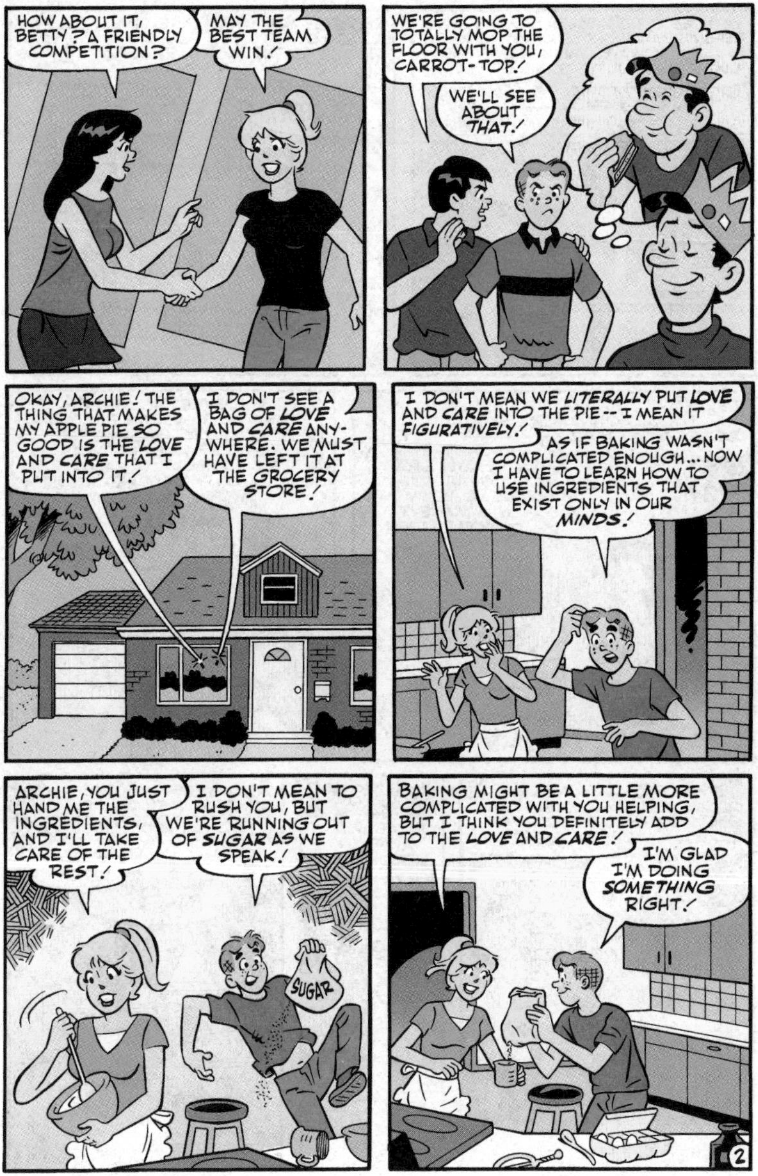
HOW ABOUT IT, BETTY? A FRIENDLY COMPETITION?
MAY THE BEST TEAM WIN!
WE'RE GOING TO TOTALLY MOP THE FLOOR WITH YOU, CARROT-TOP!
WE'LL SEE ABOUT THAT!
OKAY, ARCHIE! THE THING THAT MAKES MY APPLE PIE SO GOOD IS THE LOVE AND CARE THAT I PUT INTO IT!
I DON'T SEE A BAG OF LOVE AND CARE ANYWHERE. WE MUST HAVE LEFT IT AT THE GROCERY STORE!
I DON'T MEAN WE LITERALLY PUT LOVE AND CARE INTO THE PIE -- I MEAN IT FIGURATIVELY!
AS IF BAKING WASN'T COMPLICATED ENOUGH... NOW I HAVE TO LEARN HOW TO USE INGREDIENTS THAT EXIST ONLY IN OUR MINDS!
ARCHIE, YOU JUST HAND ME THE INGREDIENTS, AND I'LL TAKE CARE OF THE REST!
I DON'T MEAN TO RUSH YOU, BUT WE'RE RUNNING OUT OF SUGAR AS WE SPEAK!
SUGAR
BAKING MIGHT BE A LITTLE MORE COMPLICATED WITH YOU HELPING, BUT I THINK YOU DEFINITELY ADD TO THE LOVE AND CARE!
I'M GLAD I'M DOING SOMETHING RIGHT!
2

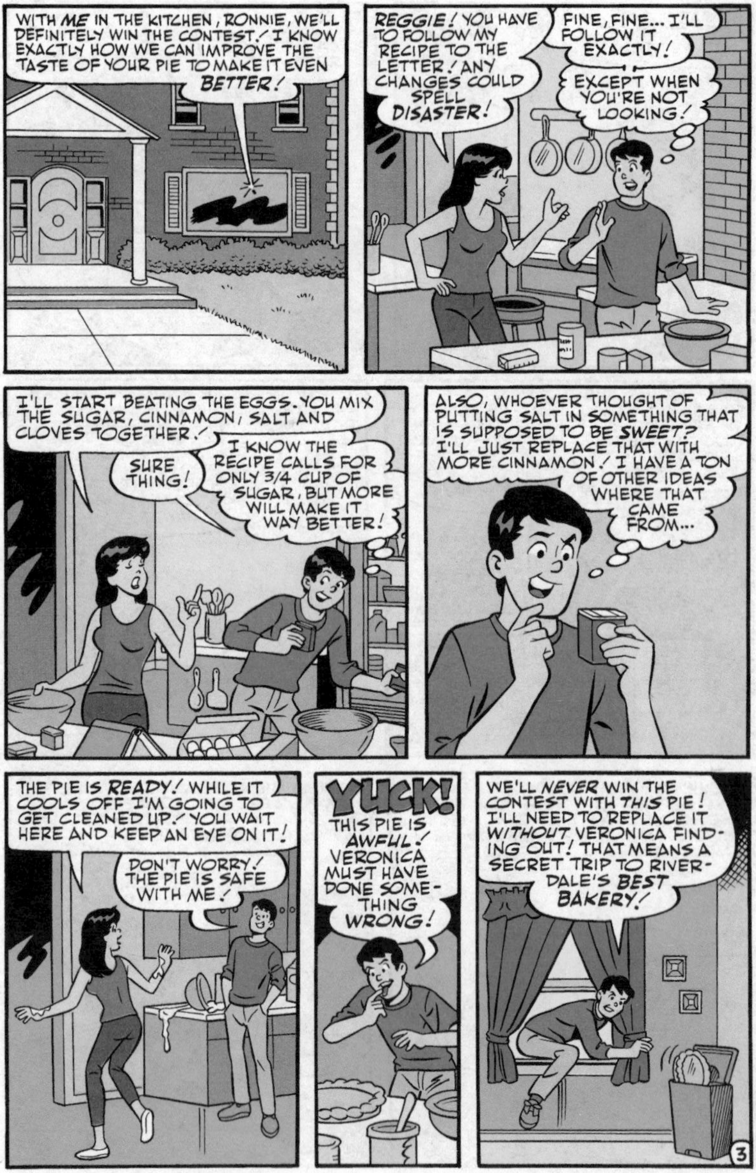
WITH ME IN THE KITCHEN, RONNIE, WE'LL DEFINITELY WIN THE CONTEST! I KNOW EXACTLY HOW WE CAN IMPROVE THE TASTE OF YOUR PIE TO MAKE IT EVEN BETTER!
REGGIE! YOU HAVE TO FOLLOW MY RECIPE TO THE LETTER! ANY CHANGES COULD SPELL DISASTER!
FINE, FINE... I'LL FOLLOW IT EXACTLY!
EXCEPT WHEN YOU'RE NOT LOOKING!
I'LL START BEATING THE EGGS. YOU MIX THE SUGAR, CINNAMON, SALT AND CLOVES TOGETHER!
SURE THING!
I KNOW THE RECIPE CALLS FOR ONLY 3/4 CUP OF SUGAR, BUT MORE WILL MAKE IT WAY BETTER!
ALSO, WHOEVER THOUGHT OF PUTTING SALT IN SOMETHING THAT IS SUPPOSED TO BE SWEET? I'LL JUST REPLACE THAT WITH MORE CINNAMON! I HAVE A TON OF OTHER IDEAS WHERE THAT CAME FROM...
THE PIE IS READY! WHILE IT COOLS OFF I'M GOING TO GET CLEANED UP! YOU WAIT HERE AND KEEP AN EYE ON IT!
DON'T WORRY! THE PIE IS SAFE WITH ME!
YUCK!
THIS PIE IS AWFUL! VERONICA MUST HAVE DONE SOME-THING WRONG!
WE'LL NEVER WIN THE CONTEST WITH THIS PIE! I'LL NEED TO REPLACE IT WITHOUT VERONICA FIND-ING OUT! THAT MEANS A SECRET TRIP TO RIVER-DALE'S BEST BAKERY!
3

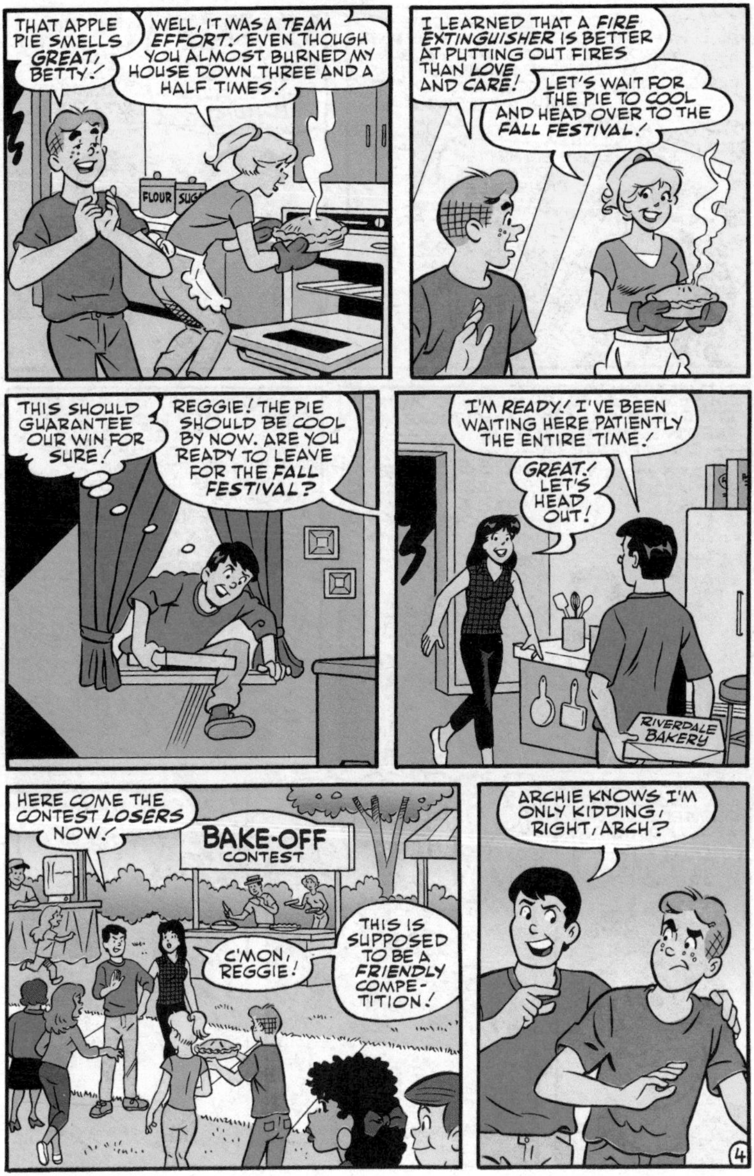
THAT APPLE PIE SMELLS GREAT, BETTY!
WELL, IT WAS A TEAM EFFORT! EVEN THOUGH YOU ALMOST BURNED MY HOUSE DOWN THREE AND A HALF TIMES!
FLOUR
I LEARNED THAT A FIRE EXTINGUISHER IS BETTER AT PUTTING OUT FIRES THAN LOVE AND CARE!
LET'S WAIT FOR THE PIE TO COOL AND HEAD OVER TO THE FALL FESTIVAL!
THIS SHOULD GUARANTEE OUR WIN FOR SURE!
REGGIE! THE PIE SHOULD BE COOL BY NOW. ARE YOU READY TO LEAVE FOR THE FALL FESTIVAL?
I'M READY! I'VE BEEN WAITING HERE PATIENTLY THE ENTIRE TIME!
GREAT! LET'S HEAD OUT!
RIVERDALE BAKERY
HERE COME THE CONTEST LOSERS NOW!
BAKE-OFF CONTEST
C'MON, REGGIE!
THIS IS SUPPOSED TO BE A FRIENDLY COMPETITION!
ARCHIE KNOWS I'M ONLY KIDDING, RIGHT, ARCH?
4

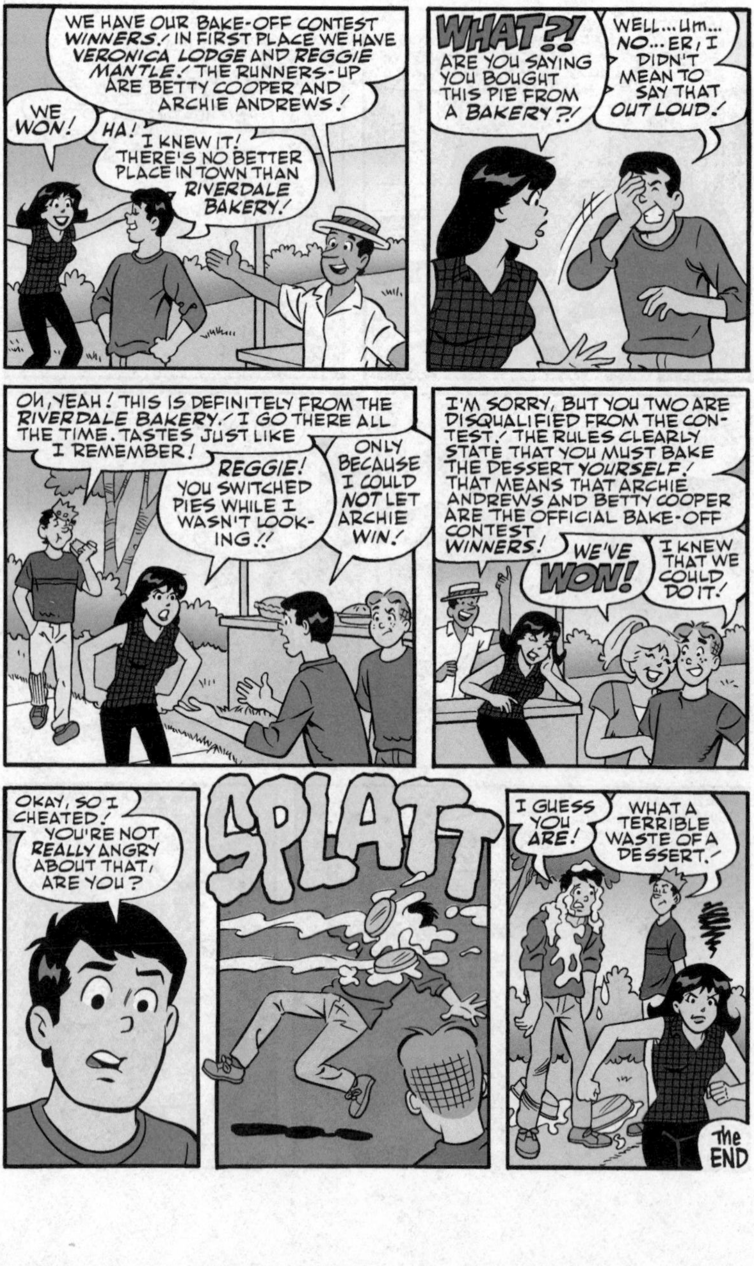
WE HAVE OUR BAKE-OFF CONTEST WINNERS! IN FIRST PLACE WE HAVE VERONICA LODGE AND REGGIE MANTLE! THE RUNNERS-UP ARE BETTY COOPER AND ARCHIE ANDREWS!
WE WON!
HA! I KNEW IT! THERE'S NO BETTER PLACE IN TOWN THAN RIVERDALE BAKERY!
WHAT?! ARE YOU SAYING YOU BOUGHT THIS PIE FROM A BAKERY?!
WELL...UM... NO...ER, I DIDN'T MEAN TO SAY THAT OUT LOUD!
OH, YEAH! THIS IS DEFINITELY FROM THE RIVERDALE BAKERY! I GO THERE ALL THE TIME. TASTES JUST LIKE I REMEMBER!
REGGIE! YOU SWITCHED PIES WHILE I WASN'T LOOKING!!
ONLY BECAUSE I COULD NOT LET ARCHIE WIN!
I'M SORRY, BUT YOU TWO ARE DISQUALIFIED FROM THE CONTEST! THE RULES CLEARLY STATE THAT YOU MUST BAKE THE DESSERT YOURSELF! THAT MEANS THAT ARCHIE ANDREWS AND BETTY COOPER ARE THE OFFICIAL BAKE-OFF CONTEST WINNERS!
WE'VE WON!
I KNEW THAT WE COULD DO IT!
OKAY, SO I CHEATED! YOU'RE NOT REALLY ANGRY ABOUT THAT, ARE YOU?
SPLATT
I GUESS YOU ARE!
WHAT A TERRIBLE WASTE OF A DESSERT!
THE END

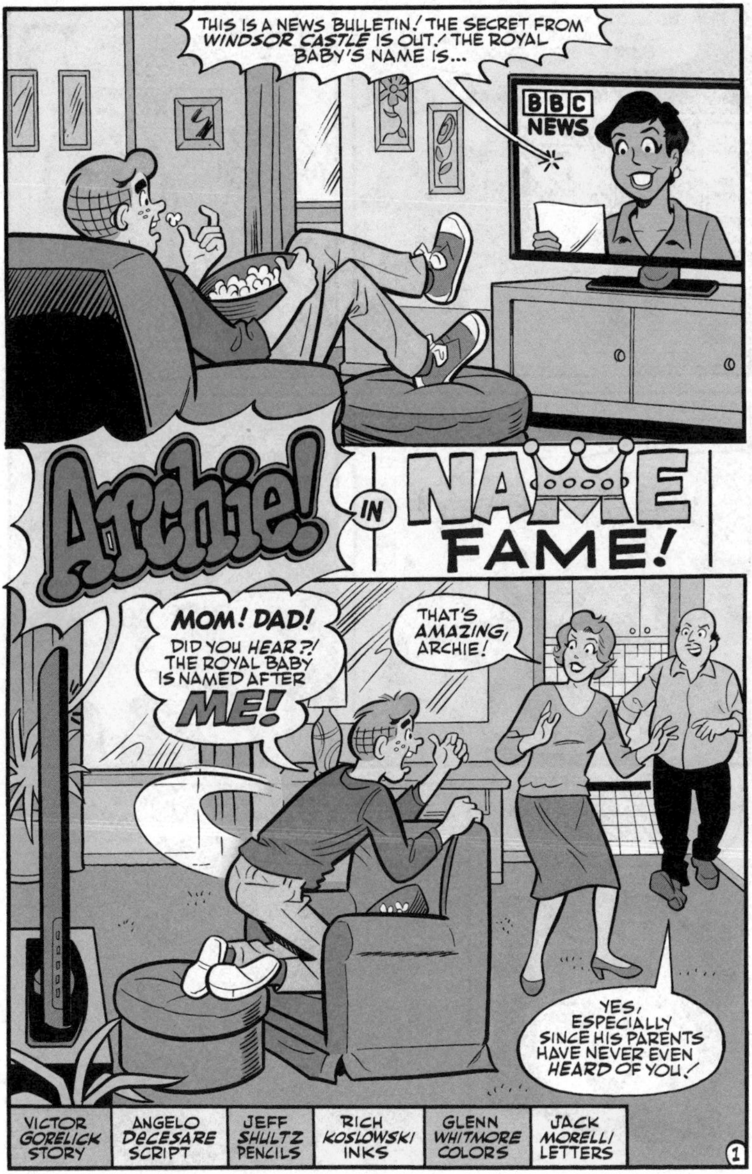
THIS IS A NEWS BULLETIN! THE SECRET FROM WINDSOR CASTLE IS OUT! THE ROYAL BABY'S NAME IS...
BBC NEWS
ARCHIE! IN NAME FAME!
MOM! DAD! DID YOU HEAR?! THE ROYAL BABY IS NAMED AFTER ME!
THAT'S AMAZING, ARCHIE!
YES, ESPECIALLY SINCE HIS PARENTS HAVE NEVER EVEN HEARD OF YOU!
VICTOR GORELICK STORY
ANGELO DECESARE SCRIPT
JEFF SHULTZ PENCILS
RICH KOSLOWSKI INKS
GLENN WHITMORE COLORS
JACK MORELLI LETTERS
1

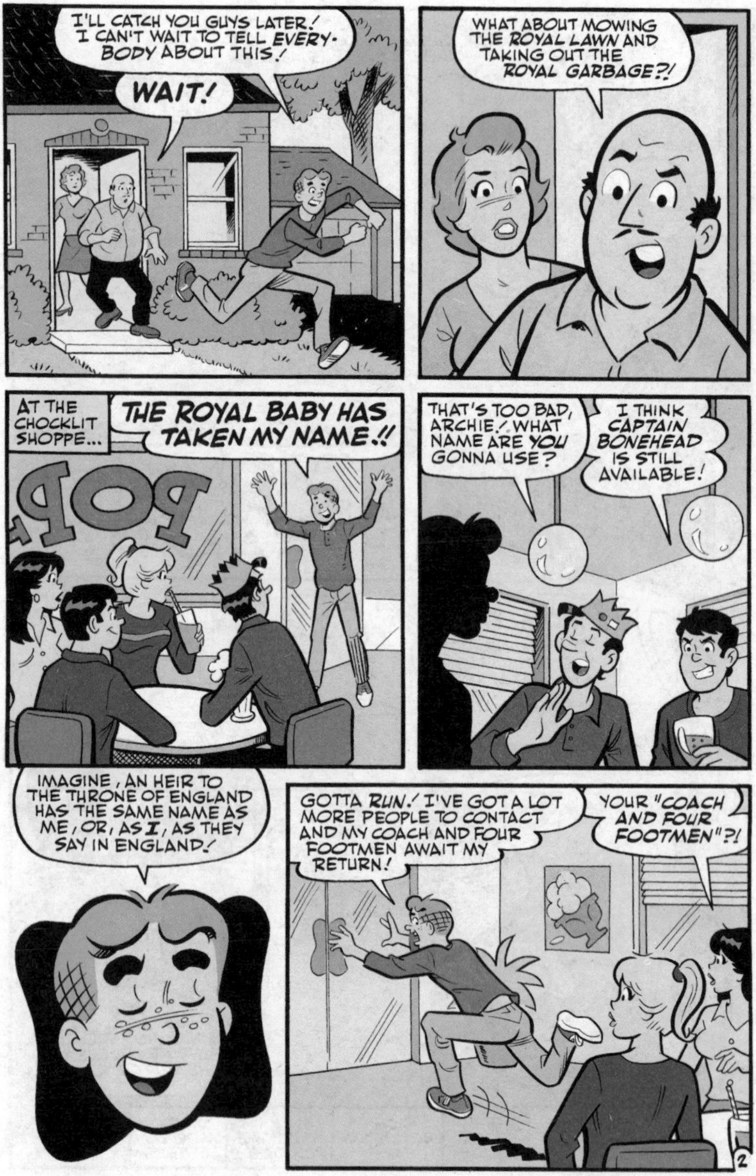
I'LL CATCH YOU GUYS LATER! I CAN'T WAIT TO TELL EVERY-BODY ABOUT THIS!
WAIT!
WHAT ABOUT MOWING THE ROYAL LAWN AND TAKING OUT THE ROYAL GARBAGE?!
AT THE CHOCKLIT SHOPPE...
THE ROYAL BABY HAS TAKEN MY NAME!!
POP
THAT'S TOO BAD, ARCHIE! WHAT NAME ARE YOU GONNA USE?
I THINK CAPTAIN BONEHEAD IS STILL AVAILABLE!
IMAGINE, AN HEIR TO THE THRONE OF ENGLAND HAS THE SAME NAME AS ME, OR, AS I, AS THEY SAY IN ENGLAND!
GOTTA RUN! I'VE GOT A LOT MORE PEOPLE TO CONTACT AND MY COACH AND FOUR FOOTMEN AWAIT MY RETURN!
YOUR "COACH AND FOUR FOOTMEN"?!
2

MY CAR AND FOUR TIRES!
LATER...
THAT'S RIGHT, GRANDMA ANDREWS! SOMEDAY THERE MAY BE A KING ARCHIE!
YOU'LL ALWAYS BE MY LITTLE PRINCE!
IT'S GETTING LATE, ARCHIE! AND YOU HAVE SCHOOL TOMORROW.
I'M GOING TO SLEEP RIGHT NOW, MOM!
I CAN'T WAIT FOR SCHOOL SO I CAN SEE THE FACES OF ALL THE STUDENTS, NOT TO MENTION THE CHEERLEADERS! HAVING A ROYAL CONNECTION IS GONNA BE AWESOME!
SOON...
THANKS FOR HELPING ME PICK A PRINCESS, GRANDMA!
ANYTHING FOR MY LITTLE PRINCE!
Z!
YOUR ROYAL BREAKFAST IS SERVED, YOUR HIGHNESS! ROYAL COLD PIZZA FROM YESTERDAY'S ROYAL BOWLING PARTY!
BARUM!
3

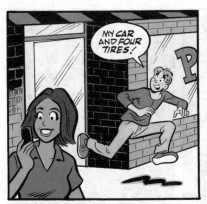

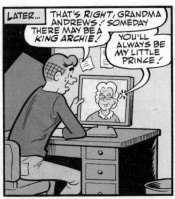

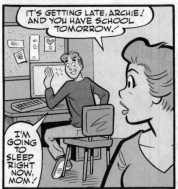

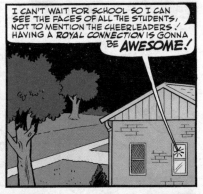

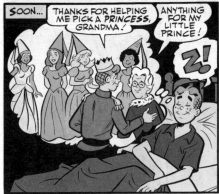

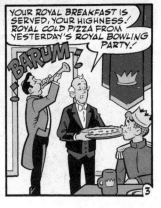

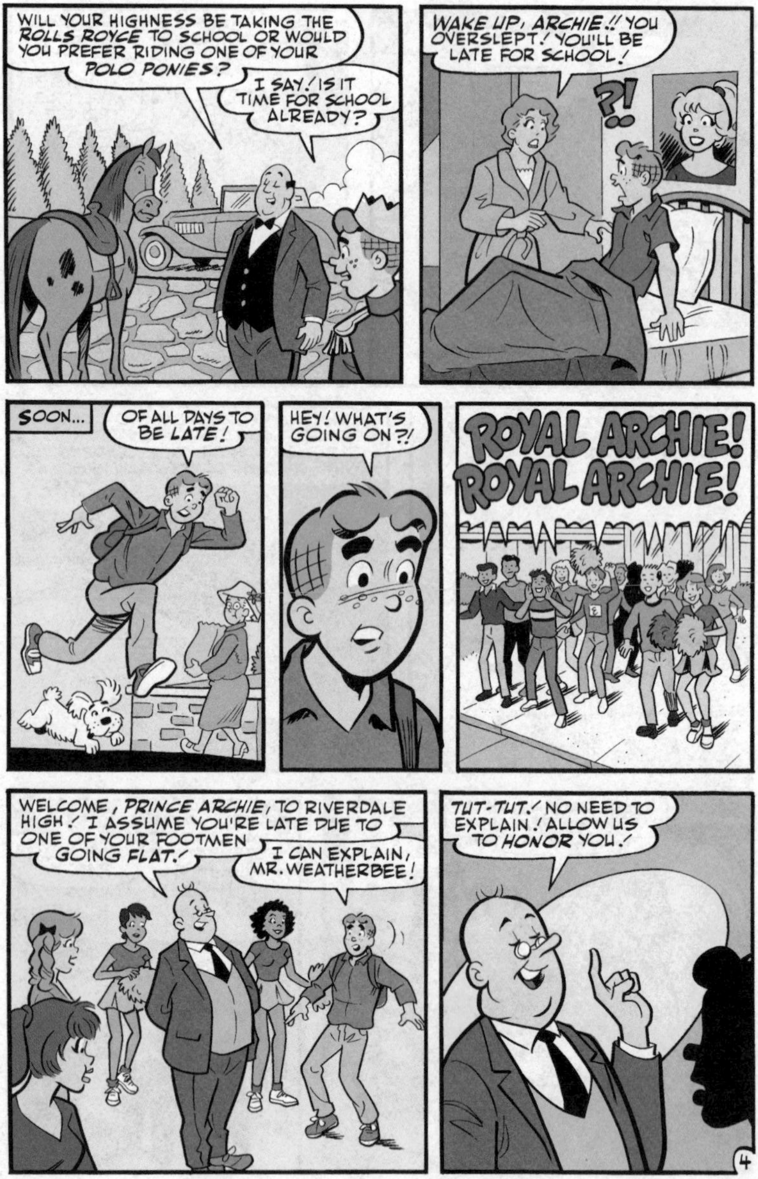
WILL YOUR HIGHNESS BE TAKING THE ROLLS ROYCE TO SCHOOL OR WOULD YOU PREFER RIDING ONE OF YOUR POLO PONIES?
I SAY! IS IT TIME FOR SCHOOL ALREADY?
WAKE UP, ARCHIE!! YOU OVERSLEPT! YOU'LL BE LATE FOR SCHOOL!
?!
SOON...
OF ALL DAYS TO BE LATE!
HEY! WHAT'S GOING ON?!
ROYAL ARCHIE! ROYAL ARCHIE!
WELCOME, PRINCE ARCHIE, TO RIVERDALE HIGH! I ASSUME YOU'RE LATE DUE TO ONE OF YOUR FOOTMEN GOING FLAT!
I CAN EXPLAIN, MR. WEATHERBEE!
TUT-TUT! NO NEED TO EXPLAIN! ALLOW US TO HONOR YOU!
4

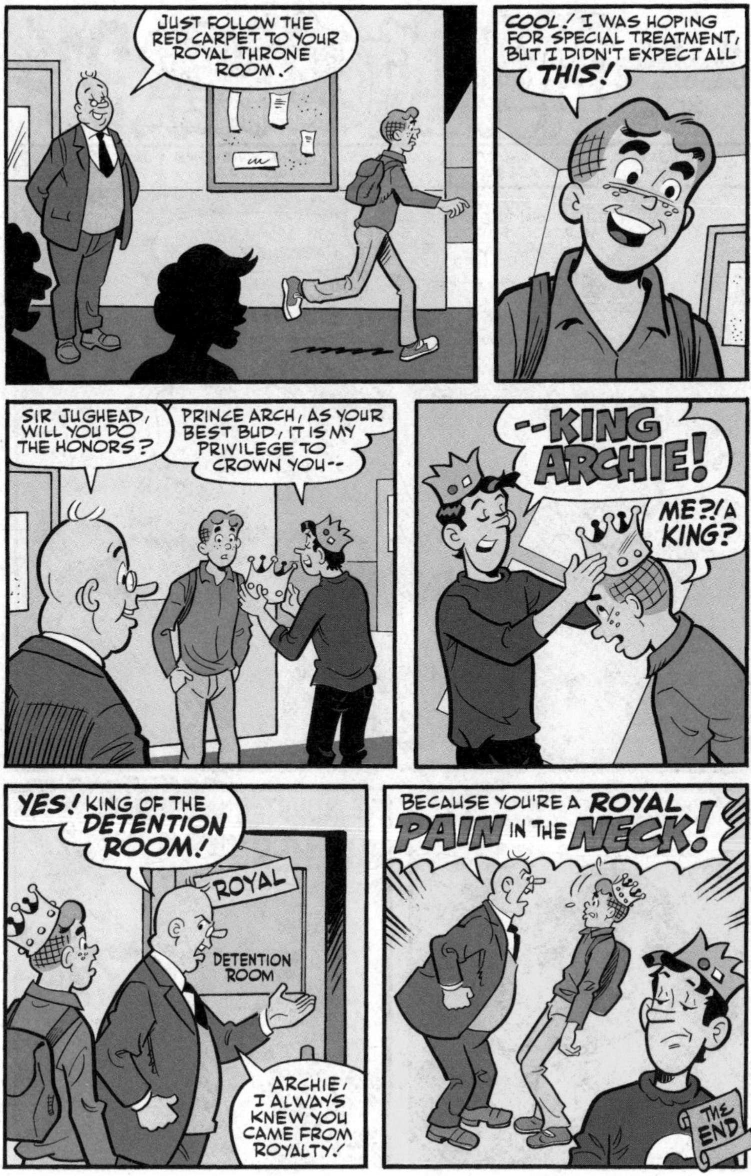
JUST FOLLOW THE RED CARPET TO YOUR ROYAL THRONE ROOM!
COOL! I WAS HOPING FOR SPECIAL TREATMENT, BUT I DIDN'T EXPECT ALL THIS!
SIR JUGHEAD, WILL YOU DO THE HONORS?
PRINCE ARCH, AS YOUR BEST BUD, IT IS MY PRIVILEGE TO CROWN YOU--
--KING ARCHIE!
ME?! A KING?
YES! KING OF THE DETENTION ROOM!
ROYAL
DETENTION ROOM
ARCHIE, I ALWAYS KNEW YOU CAME FROM ROYALTY!
BECAUSE YOU'RE A ROYAL PAIN IN THE NECK!
THE END

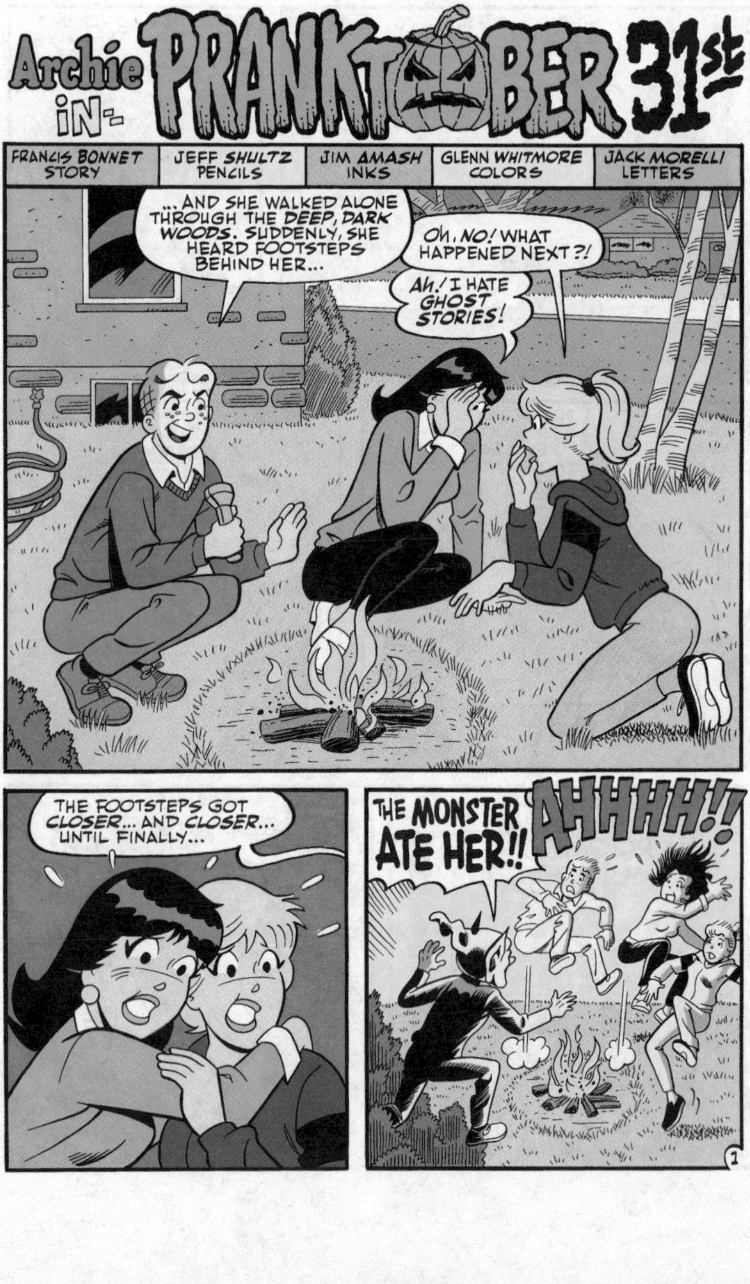
Archie in-
PRANKTOBER 31st
FRANCIS BONNET STORY
JEFF SHULTZ PENCILS
JIM AMASH INKS
GLENN WHITMORE COLORS
JACK MORELLI LETTERS
...AND SHE WALKED ALONE THROUGH THE DEEP, DARK WOODS. SUDDENLY, SHE HEARD FOOTSTEPS BEHIND HER...
Oh, NO! WHAT HAPPENED NEXT?!
Ah! I HATE GHOST STORIES!
THE FOOTSTEPS GOT CLOSER... AND CLOSER... UNTIL FINALLY...
THE MONSTER ATE HER!!
AHHHH!!
1

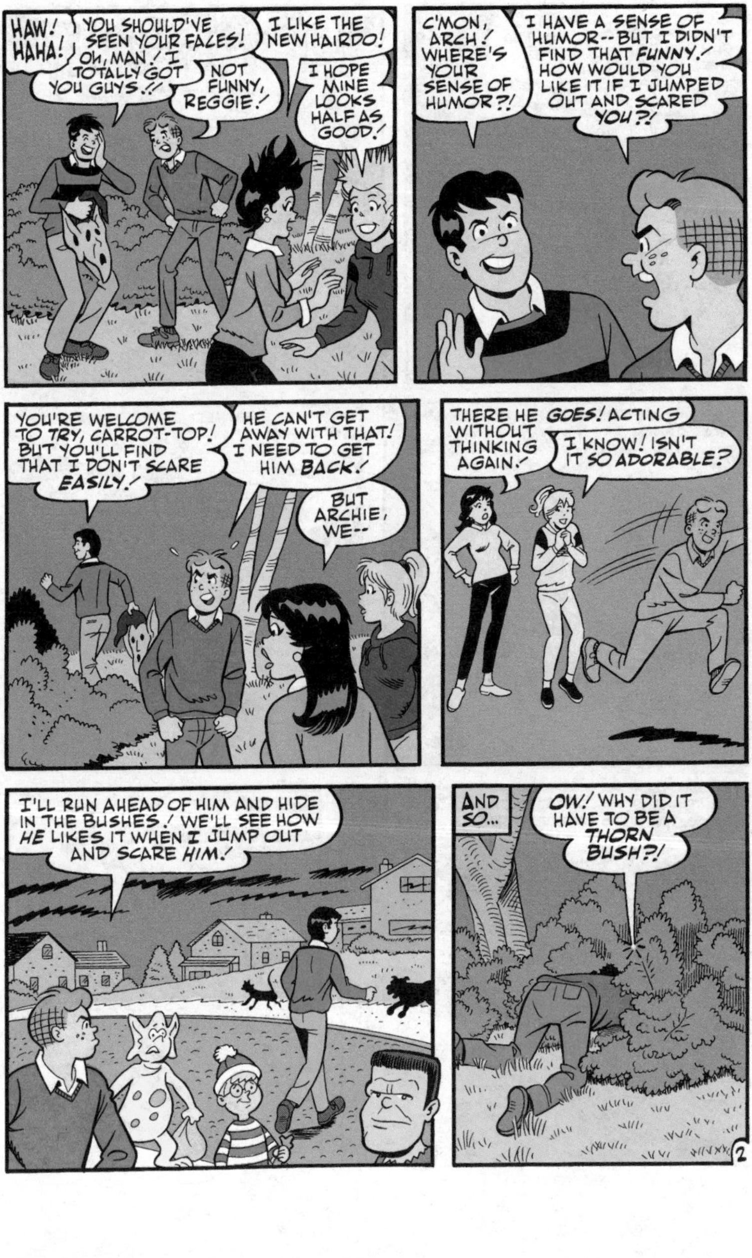
HAW! HAHA!
YOU SHOULD'VE SEEN YOUR FACES! OH, MAN! I TOTALLY GOT YOU GUYS.!!
NOT FUNNY, REGGIE!
I LIKE THE NEW HAIRDO!
I HOPE MINE LOOKS HALF AS GOOD!
C'MON, ARCH! WHERE'S YOUR SENSE OF HUMOR?!
I HAVE A SENSE OF HUMOR--BUT I DIDN'T FIND THAT FUNNY! HOW WOULD YOU LIKE IT IF I JUMPED OUT AND SCARED YOU?!
YOU'RE WELCOME TO TRY, CARROT-TOP! BUT YOU'LL FIND THAT I DON'T SCARE EASILY!
HE CAN'T GET AWAY WITH THAT! I NEED TO GET HIM BACK!
BUT ARCHIE, WE--
THERE HE GOES! ACTING WITHOUT THINKING AGAIN!
I KNOW! ISN'T IT SO ADORABLE?
I'LL RUN AHEAD OF HIM AND HIDE IN THE BUSHES! WE'LL SEE HOW HE LIKES IT WHEN I JUMP OUT AND SCARE HIM!
AND SO...
OW! WHY DID IT HAVE TO BE A THORN BUSH?!
2

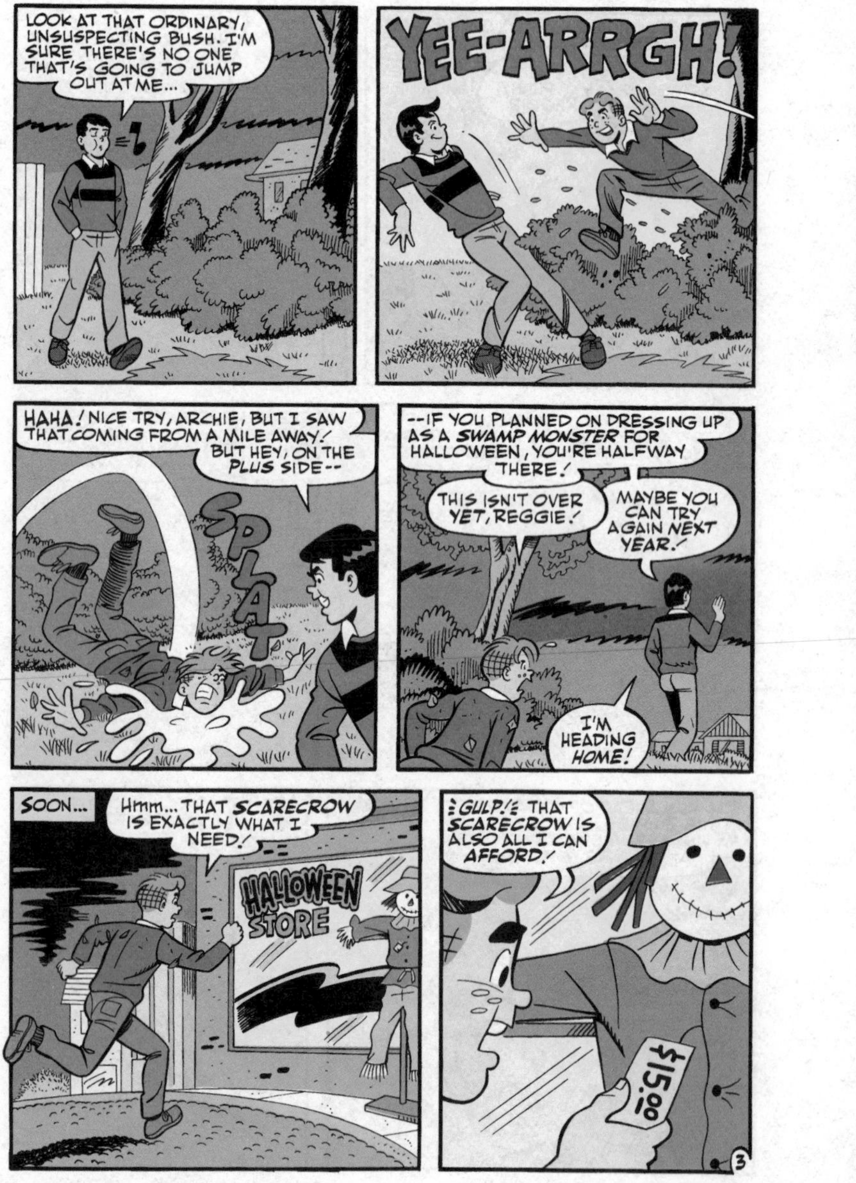
LOOK AT THAT ORDINARY, UNSUSPECTING BUSH. I'M SURE THERE'S NO ONE THAT'S GOING TO JUMP OUT AT ME...
YEE-ARRGH!
HAHA! NICE TRY, ARCHIE, BUT I SAW THAT COMING FROM A MILE AWAY!
BUT HEY, ON THE PLUS SIDE--
SPLAT
--IF YOU PLANNED ON DRESSING UP AS A SWAMP MONSTER FOR HALLOWEEN, YOU'RE HALFWAY THERE!
THIS ISN'T OVER YET, REGGIE!
MAYBE YOU CAN TRY AGAIN NEXT YEAR!
I'M HEADING HOME!
SOON...
Hmm... THAT SCARECROW IS EXACTLY WHAT I NEED!
HALLOWEEN STORE
GULP! THAT SCARECROW IS ALSO ALL I CAN AFFORD!
$15.00
3

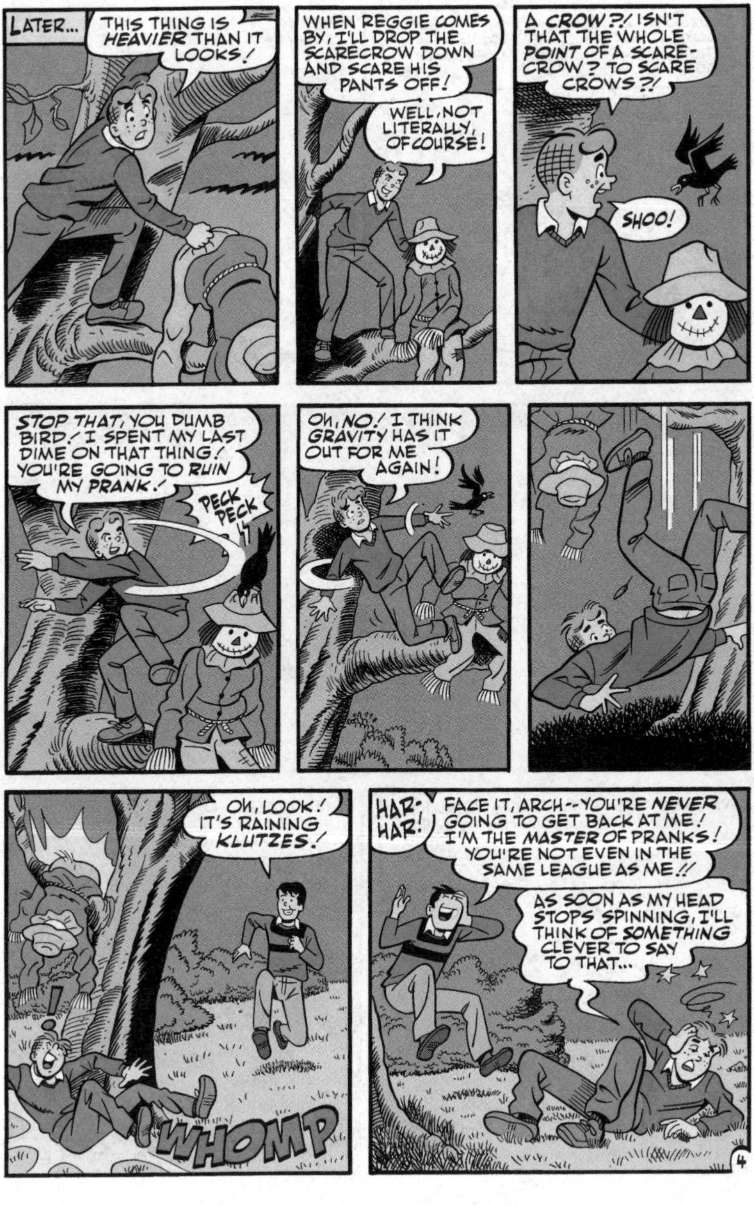
LATER...
THIS THING IS HEAVIER THAN IT LOOKS!
WHEN REGGIE COMES BY, I'LL DROP THE SCARECROW DOWN AND SCARE HIS PANTS OFF!
WELL, NOT LITERALLY, OF COURSE!
A CROW?! ISN'T THAT THE WHOLE POINT OF A SCARE-CROW? TO SCARE CROWS?!
SHOO!
STOP THAT, YOU DUMB BIRD! I SPENT MY LAST DIME ON THAT THING! YOU'RE GOING TO RUIN MY PRANK!
PECK PECK
OH, NO! I THINK GRAVITY HAS IT OUT FOR ME AGAIN!
OH, LOOK! IT'S RAINING KLUTZES!
!
WHOMP
HAR-HAR!
FACE IT, ARCH-- YOU'RE NEVER GOING TO GET BACK AT ME! I'M THE MASTER OF PRANKS! YOU'RE NOT EVEN IN THE SAME LEAGUE AS ME!!
AS SOON AS MY HEAD STOPS SPINNING, I'LL THINK OF SOMETHING CLEVER TO SAY TO THAT...
4

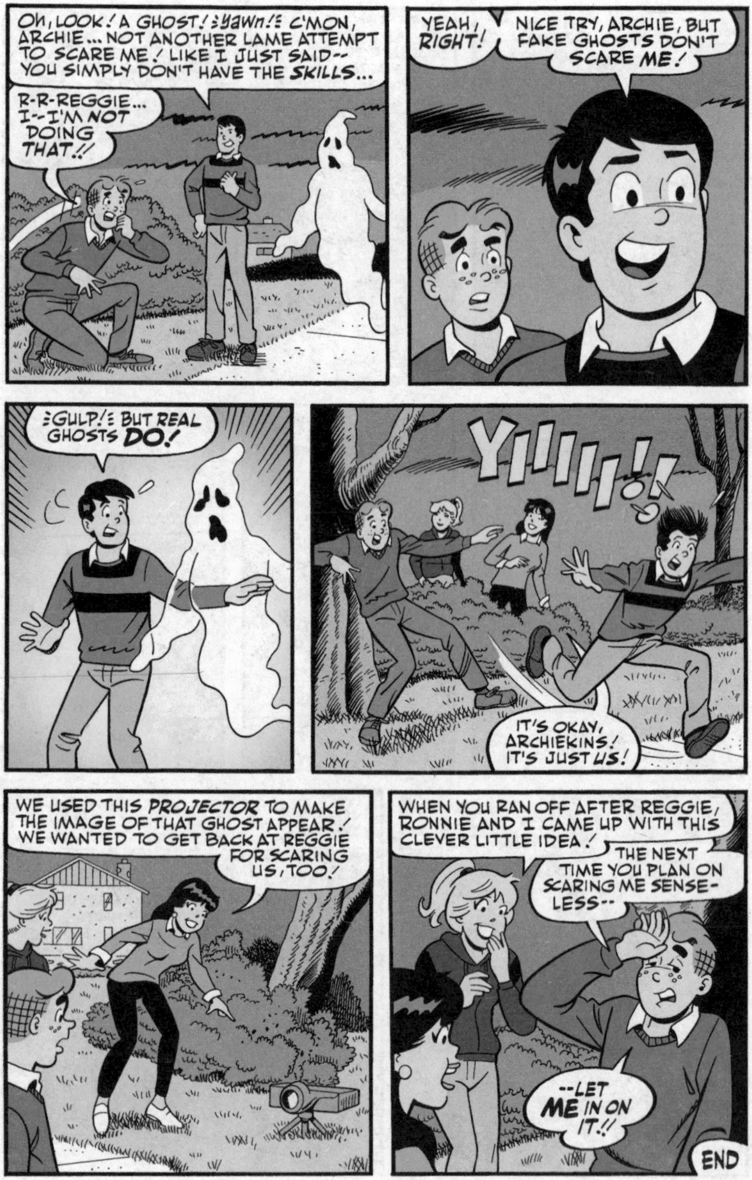
OH, LOOK! A GHOST! ⁝YAWN!⁝ C'MON, ARCHIE... NOT ANOTHER LAME ATTEMPT TO SCARE ME! LIKE I JUST SAID-- YOU SIMPLY DON'T HAVE THE SKILLS...
R-R-REGGIE... I--I'M NOT DOING THAT!!
YEAH, RIGHT!
NICE TRY, ARCHIE, BUT FAKE GHOSTS DON'T SCARE ME!
⁝GULP!⁝ BUT REAL GHOSTS DO!
YIIIII!!
IT'S OKAY, ARCHIEKINS! IT'S JUST US!
WE USED THIS PROJECTOR TO MAKE THE IMAGE OF THAT GHOST APPEAR! WE WANTED TO GET BACK AT REGGIE FOR SCARING US, TOO!
WHEN YOU RAN OFF AFTER REGGIE, RONNIE AND I CAME UP WITH THIS CLEVER LITTLE IDEA!
THE NEXT TIME YOU PLAN ON SCARING ME SENSE-LESS--
--LET ME IN ON IT!!
END

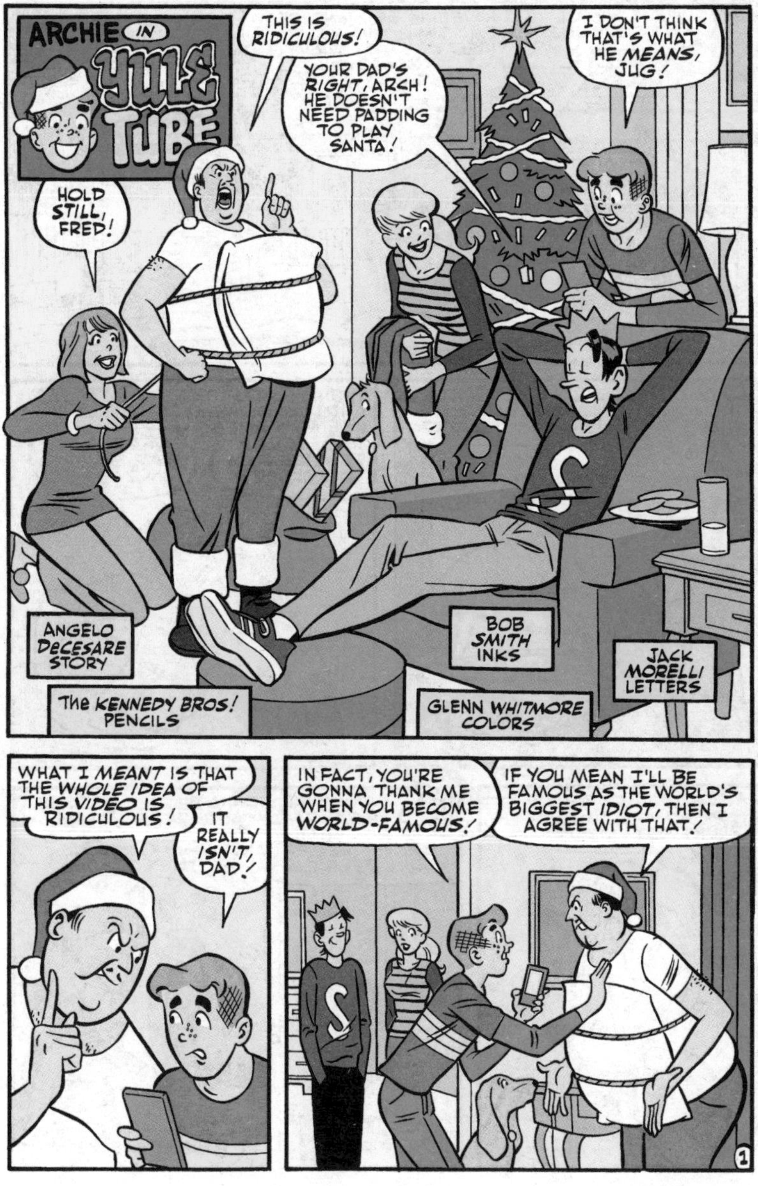
ARCHIE IN YULE TUBE
THIS IS RIDICULOUS!
HOLD STILL, FRED!
YOUR DAD'S RIGHT, ARCH! HE DOESN'T NEED PADDING TO PLAY SANTA!
I DON'T THINK THAT'S WHAT HE MEANS, JUG!
ANGELO DECESARE STORY
The KENNEDY BROS! PENCILS
BOB SMITH INKS
GLENN WHITMORE COLORS
JACK MORELLI LETTERS
WHAT I MEANT IS THAT THE WHOLE IDEA OF THIS VIDEO IS RIDICULOUS!
IT REALLY ISN'T, DAD!
IN FACT, YOU'RE GONNA THANK ME WHEN YOU BECOME WORLD-FAMOUS!
IF YOU MEAN I'LL BE FAMOUS AS THE WORLD'S BIGGEST IDIOT, THEN I AGREE WITH THAT!
1

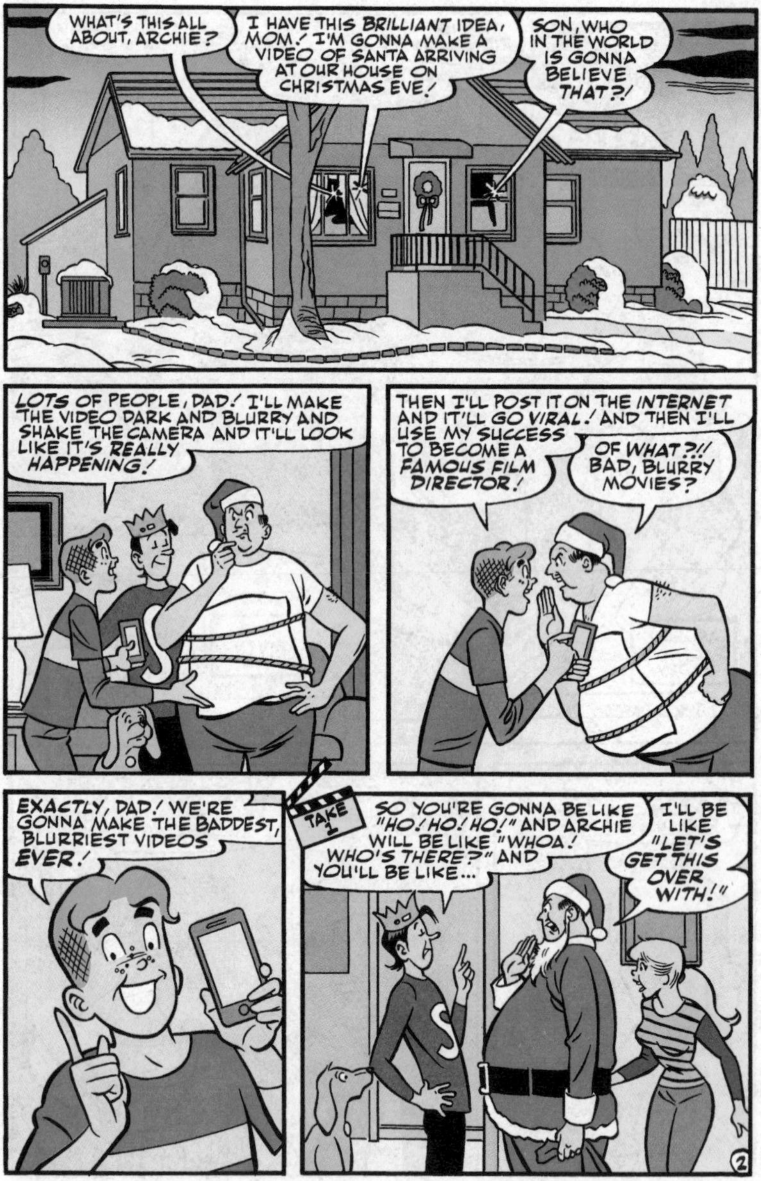
WHAT'S THIS ALL ABOUT, ARCHIE?
I HAVE THIS BRILLIANT IDEA, MOM! I'M GONNA MAKE A VIDEO OF SANTA ARRIVING AT OUR HOUSE ON CHRISTMAS EVE!
SON, WHO IN THE WORLD IS GONNA BELIEVE THAT?!
LOTS OF PEOPLE, DAD! I'LL MAKE THE VIDEO DARK AND BLURRY AND SHAKE THE CAMERA AND IT'LL LOOK LIKE IT'S REALLY HAPPENING!
THEN I'LL POST IT ON THE INTERNET AND IT'LL GO VIRAL! AND THEN I'LL USE MY SUCCESS TO BECOME A FAMOUS FILM DIRECTOR!
OF WHAT?!! BAD, BLURRY MOVIES?
EXACTLY, DAD! WE'RE GONNA MAKE THE BADDEST, BLURRIEST VIDEOS EVER!
TAKE 1
SO YOU'RE GONNA BE LIKE "HO! HO! HO!" AND ARCHIE WILL BE LIKE "WHOA! WHO'S THERE?" AND YOU'LL BE LIKE...
I'LL BE LIKE "LET'S GET THIS OVER WITH!"
2

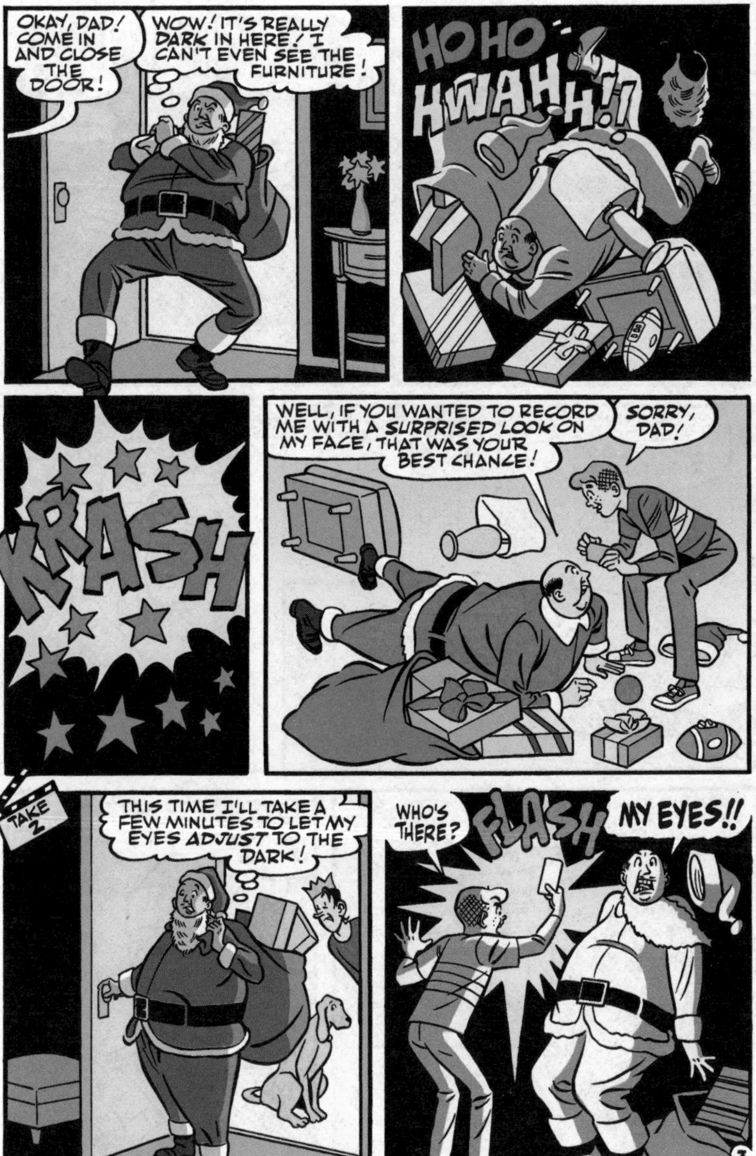
OKAY, DAD! COME IN AND CLOSE THE DOOR!
WOW! IT'S REALLY DARK IN HERE! I CAN'T EVEN SEE THE FURNITURE!
HO HO HWAHH!!
KRASH
WELL, IF YOU WANTED TO RECORD ME WITH A SURPRISED LOOK ON MY FACE, THAT WAS YOUR BEST CHANCE!
SORRY, DAD!
TAKE 2
THIS TIME I'LL TAKE A FEW MINUTES TO LET MY EYES ADJUST TO THE DARK!
WHO'S THERE?
FLASH
MY EYES!!
3

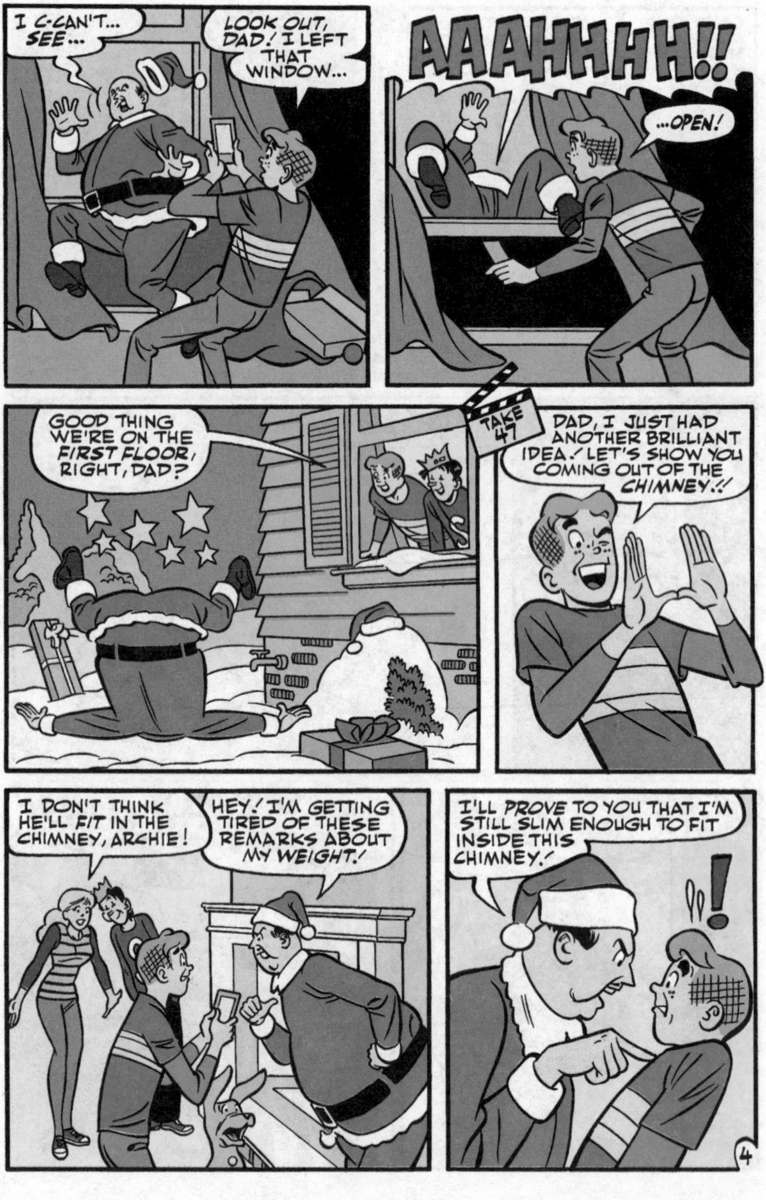
I C-CAN'T... SEE...
LOOK OUT, DAD! I LEFT THAT WINDOW...
AAAHHHH!!
...OPEN!
TAKE 47
GOOD THING WE'RE ON THE FIRST FLOOR, RIGHT, DAD?
DAD, I JUST HAD ANOTHER BRILLIANT IDEA! LET'S SHOW YOU COMING OUT OF THE CHIMNEY!!
I DON'T THINK HE'LL FIT IN THE CHIMNEY, ARCHIE!
HEY! I'M GETTING TIRED OF THESE REMARKS ABOUT MY WEIGHT!
I'LL PROVE TO YOU THAT I'M STILL SLIM ENOUGH TO FIT INSIDE THIS CHIMNEY!
!
4

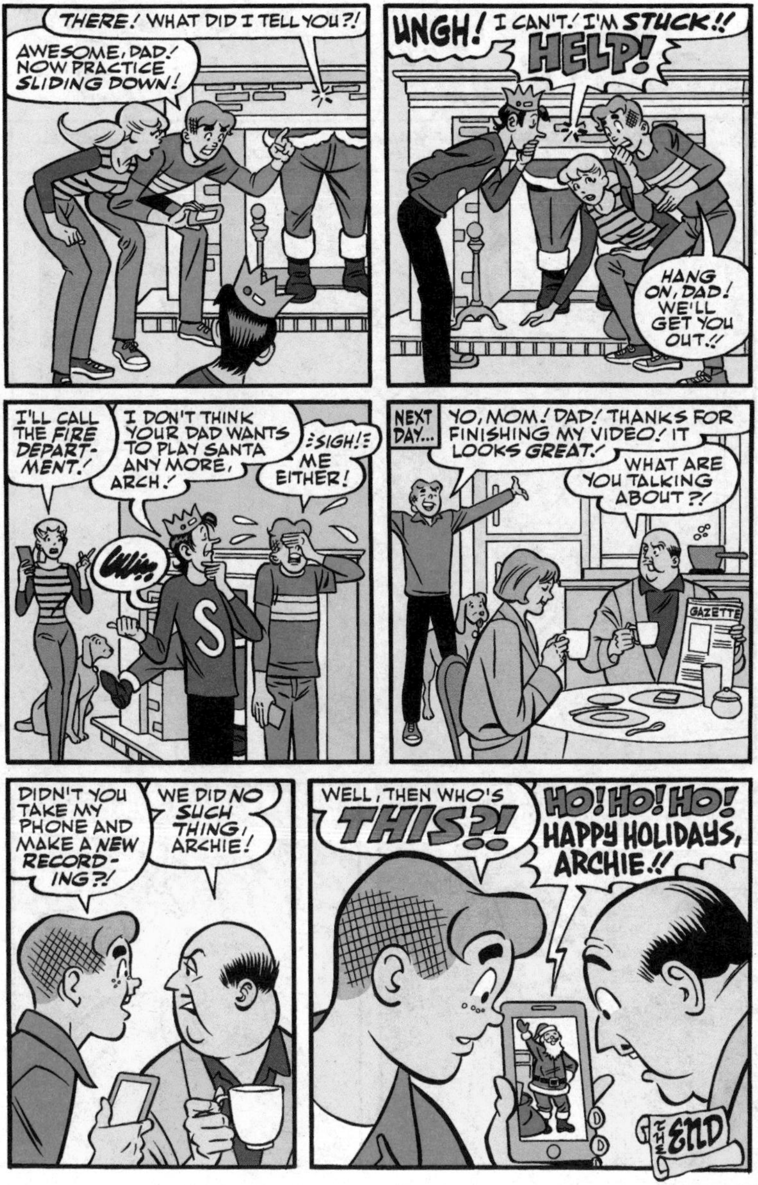
THERE! WHAT DID I TELL YOU?!
AWESOME, DAD! NOW PRACTICE SLIDING DOWN!
UNGH! I CAN'T! I'M STUCK!!
HELP!
HANG ON, DAD! WE'LL GET YOU OUT!!
I'LL CALL THE FIRE DEPARTMENT!
I DON'T THINK YOUR DAD WANTS TO PLAY SANTA ANY MORE, ARCH!
SIGH!
ME EITHER!
NEXT DAY...
YO, MOM! DAD! THANKS FOR FINISHING MY VIDEO! IT LOOKS GREAT!
WHAT ARE YOU TALKING ABOUT?!
GAZETTE
DIDN'T YOU TAKE MY PHONE AND MAKE A NEW RECORDING?!
WE DID NO SUCH THING, ARCHIE!
WELL, THEN WHO'S THIS?!
HO! HO! HO! HAPPY HOLIDAYS, ARCHIE!!
THE END

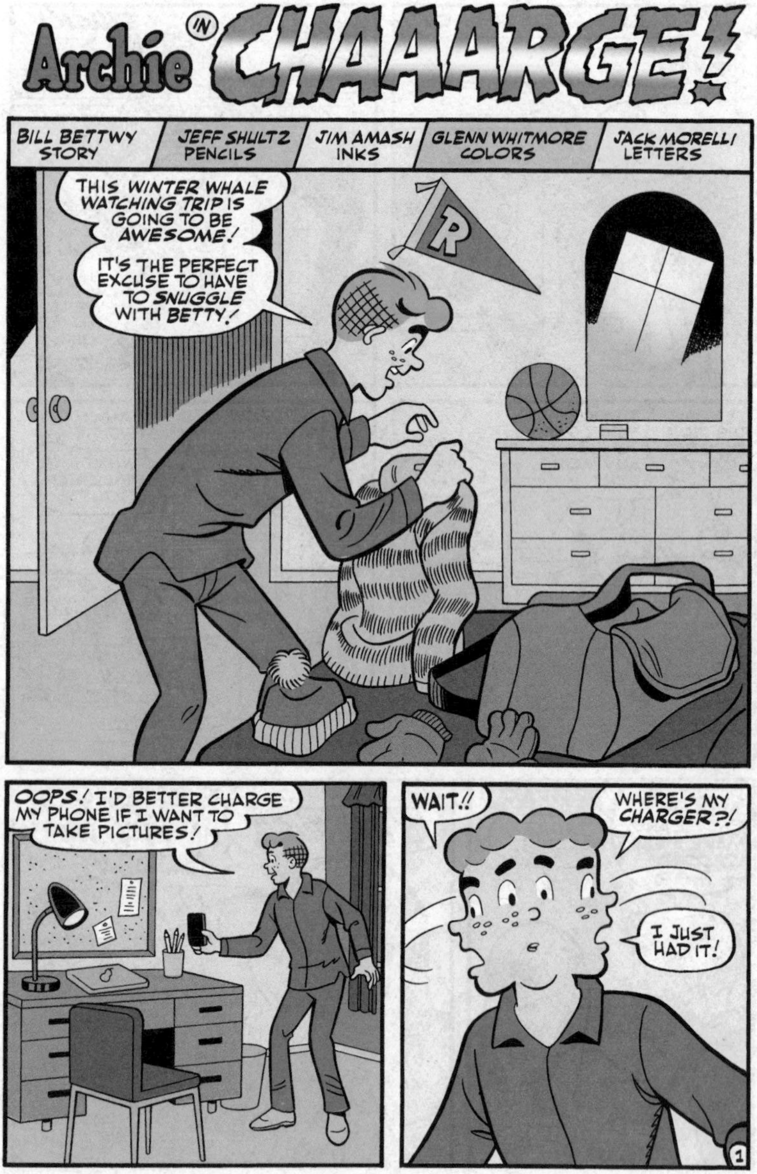
Archie in CHAAARGE!
BILL BETTWY STORY
JEFF SHULTZ PENCILS
JIM AMASH INKS
GLENN WHITMORE COLORS
JACK MORELLI LETTERS
THIS WINTER WHALE WATCHING TRIP IS GOING TO BE AWESOME!
IT'S THE PERFECT EXCUSE TO HAVE TO SNUGGLE WITH BETTY!
R
OOPS! I'D BETTER CHARGE MY PHONE IF I WANT TO TAKE PICTURES!
WAIT!!
WHERE'S MY CHARGER?!
I JUST HAD IT!
1

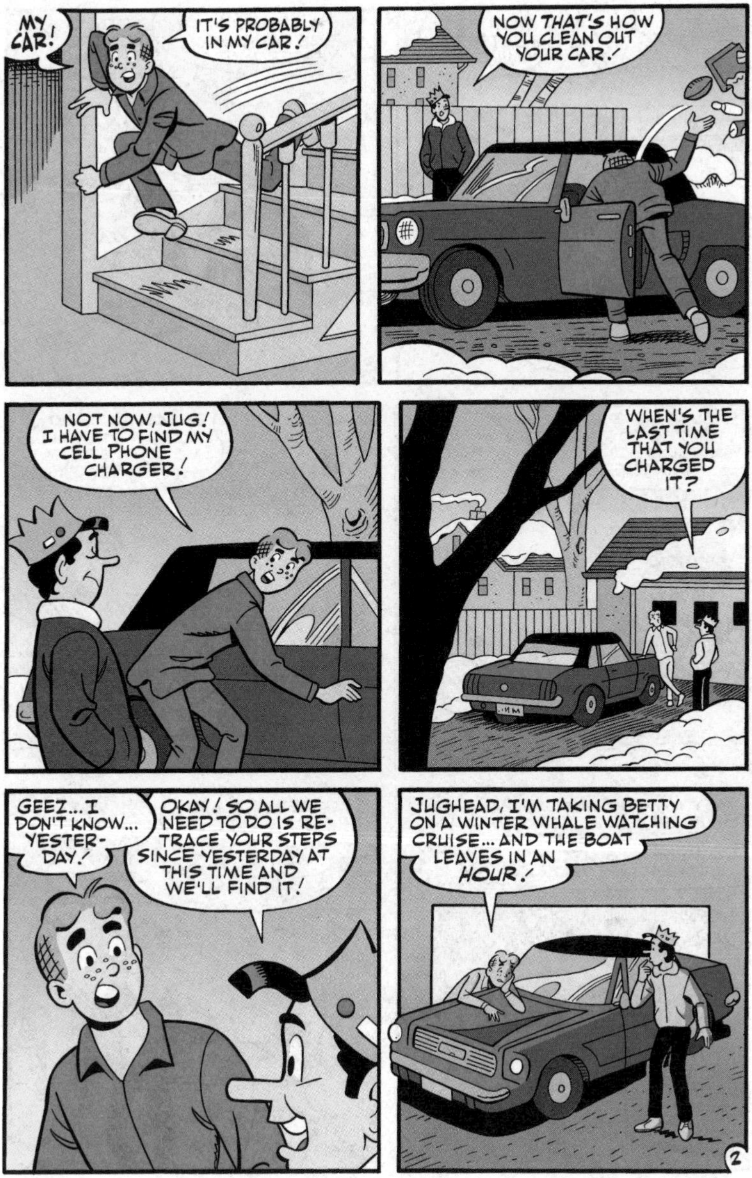
MY CAR!
IT'S PROBABLY IN MY CAR!
NOW THAT'S HOW YOU CLEAN OUT YOUR CAR!
NOT NOW, JUG! I HAVE TO FIND MY CELL PHONE CHARGER!
WHEN'S THE LAST TIME THAT YOU CHARGED IT?
GEEZ... I DON'T KNOW... YESTER-DAY!
OKAY! SO ALL WE NEED TO DO IS RE-TRACE YOUR STEPS SINCE YESTERDAY AT THIS TIME AND WE'LL FIND IT!
JUGHEAD, I'M TAKING BETTY ON A WINTER WHALE WATCHING CRUISE... AND THE BOAT LEAVES IN AN HOUR!
2

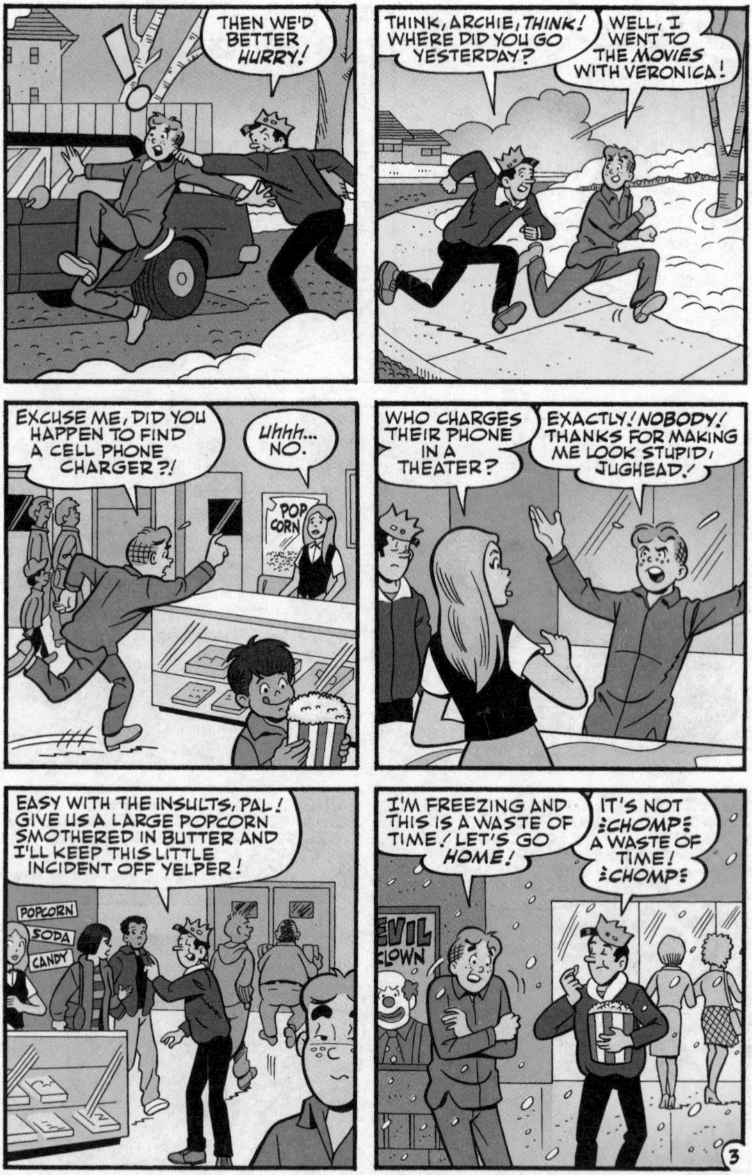
THEN WE'D BETTER HURRY!
THINK, ARCHIE, THINK! WHERE DID YOU GO YESTERDAY?
WELL, I WENT TO THE MOVIES WITH VERONICA!
EXCUSE ME, DID YOU HAPPEN TO FIND A CELL PHONE CHARGER?!
uhhh... NO.
POP CORN
WHO CHARGES THEIR PHONE IN A THEATER?
EXACTLY! NOBODY! THANKS FOR MAKING ME LOOK STUPID, JUGHEAD!
EASY WITH THE INSULTS, PAL! GIVE US A LARGE POPCORN SMOTHERED IN BUTTER AND I'LL KEEP THIS LITTLE INCIDENT OFF YELPER!
POPCORN
SODA
CANDY
I'M FREEZING AND THIS IS A WASTE OF TIME! LET'S GO HOME!
IT'S NOT CHOMP A WASTE OF TIME! CHOMP
EVIL CLOWN
3

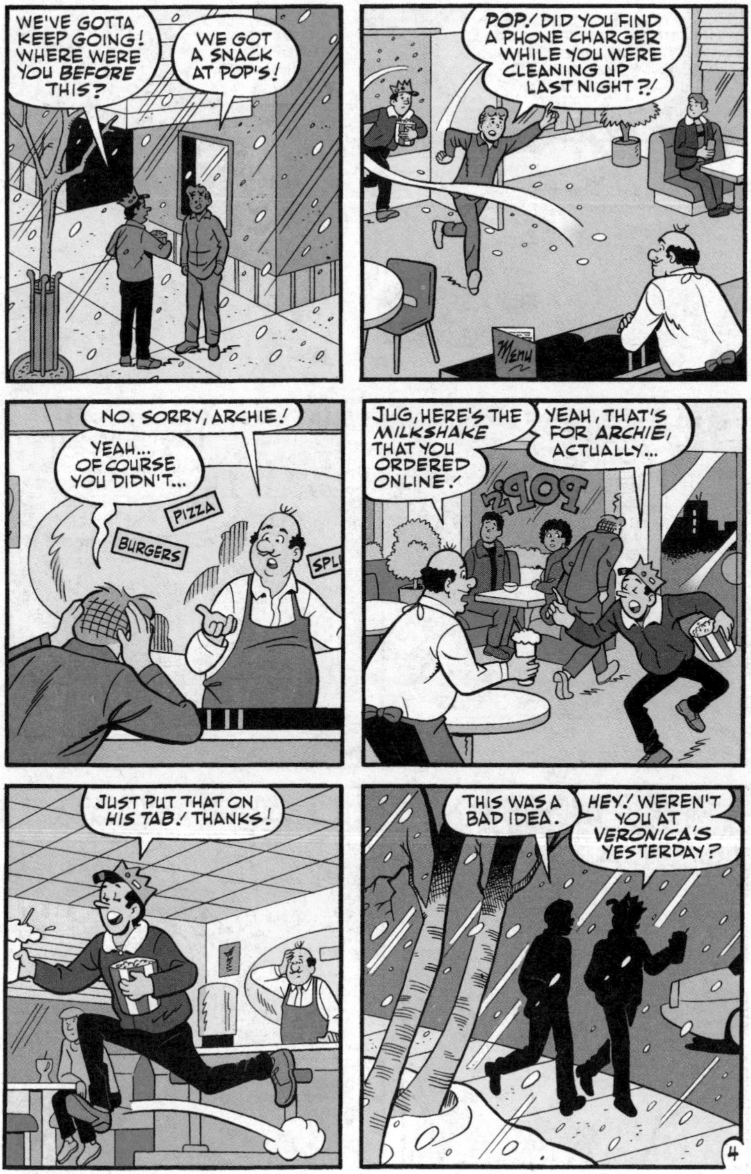
WE'VE GOTTA KEEP GOING! WHERE WERE YOU BEFORE THIS?
WE GOT A SNACK AT POP'S!
POP! DID YOU FIND A PHONE CHARGER WHILE YOU WERE CLEANING UP LAST NIGHT?!
MENU
NO. SORRY, ARCHIE!
YEAH... OF COURSE YOU DIDN'T...
PIZZA
BURGERS
JUG, HERE'S THE MILKSHAKE THAT YOU ORDERED ONLINE!
YEAH, THAT'S FOR ARCHIE, ACTUALLY...
POP'S
JUST PUT THAT ON HIS TAB! THANKS!
THIS WAS A BAD IDEA.
HEY! WEREN'T YOU AT VERONICA'S YESTERDAY?

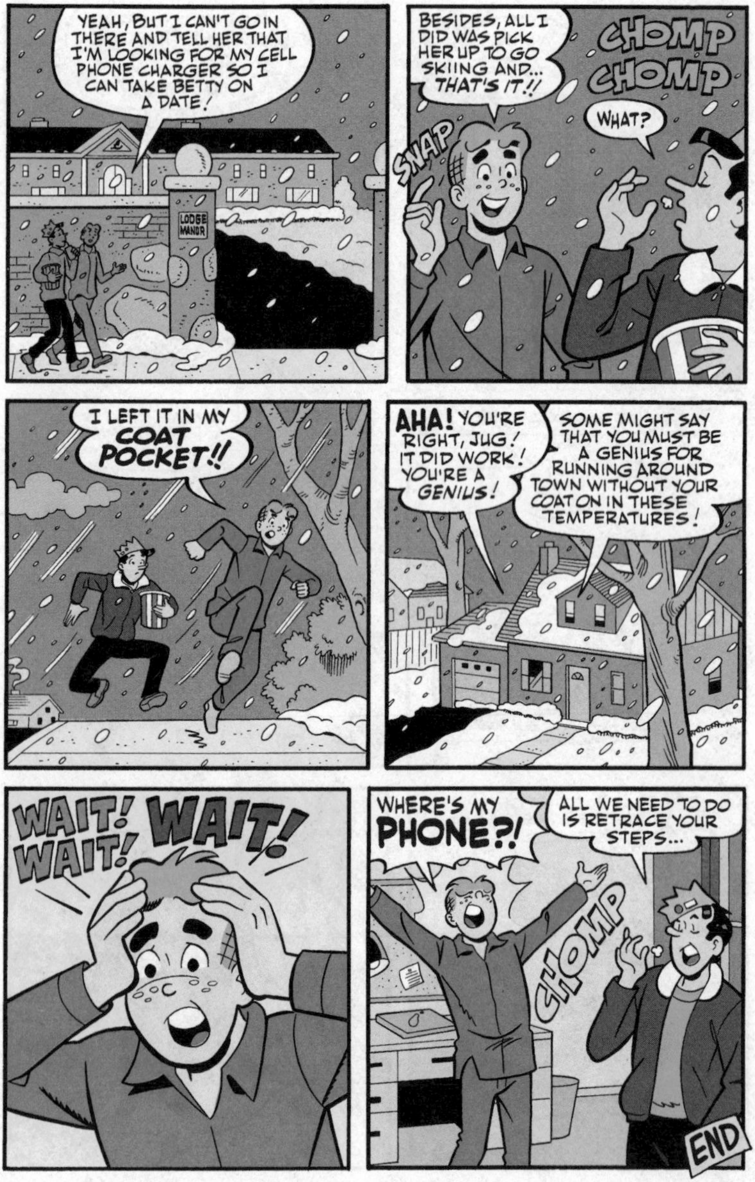

YEAH, BUT I CAN'T GO IN THERE AND TELL HER THAT I'M LOOKING FOR MY CELL PHONE CHARGER SO I CAN TAKE BETTY ON A DATE!
LODGE MANOR
BESIDES, ALL I DID WAS PICK HER UP TO GO SKIING AND... THAT'S IT!!
SNAP
CHOMP CHOMP
WHAT?
I LEFT IT IN MY COAT POCKET!!
AHA! YOU'RE RIGHT, JUG! IT DID WORK! YOU'RE A GENIUS!
SOME MIGHT SAY THAT YOU MUST BE A GENIUS FOR RUNNING AROUND TOWN WITHOUT YOUR COAT ON IN THESE TEMPERATURES!
WAIT! WAIT! WAIT!
WHERE'S MY PHONE?!
ALL WE NEED TO DO IS RETRACE YOUR STEPS...
CHOMP
END

02 BETTY & VERONICA

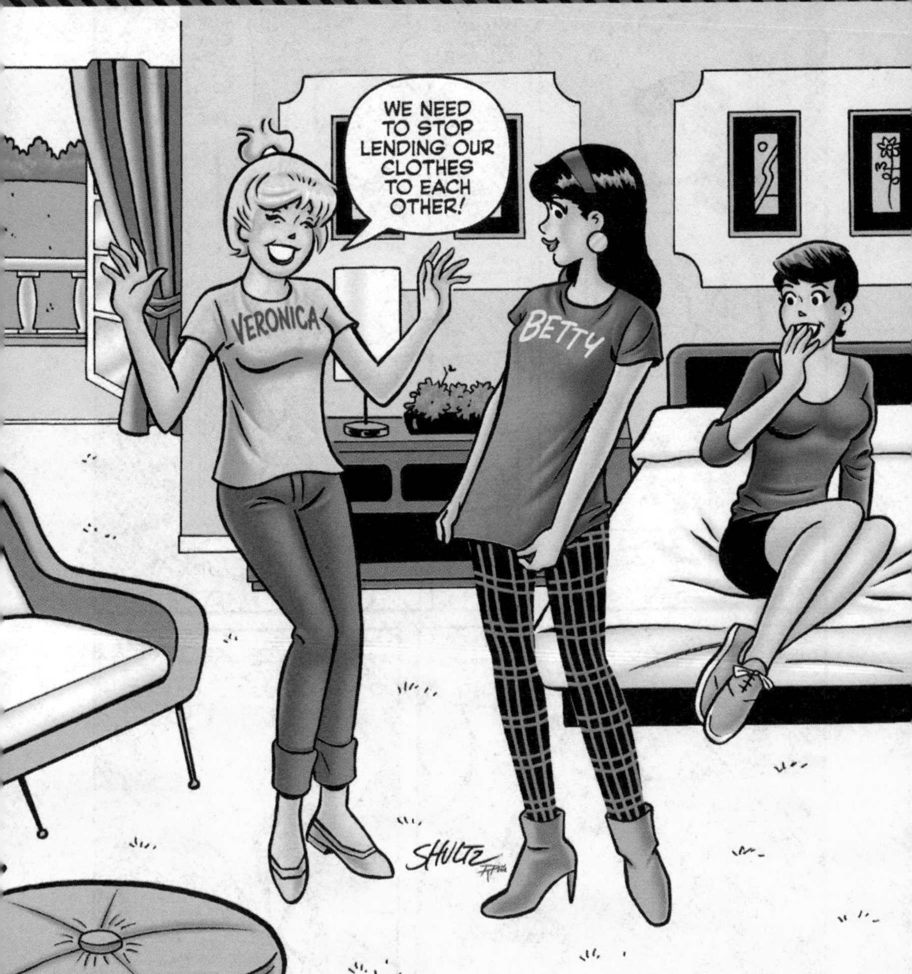
WE NEED TO STOP LENDING OUR CLOTHES TO EACH OTHER!
VERONICA
BETTY
SHULTZ

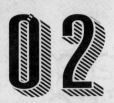

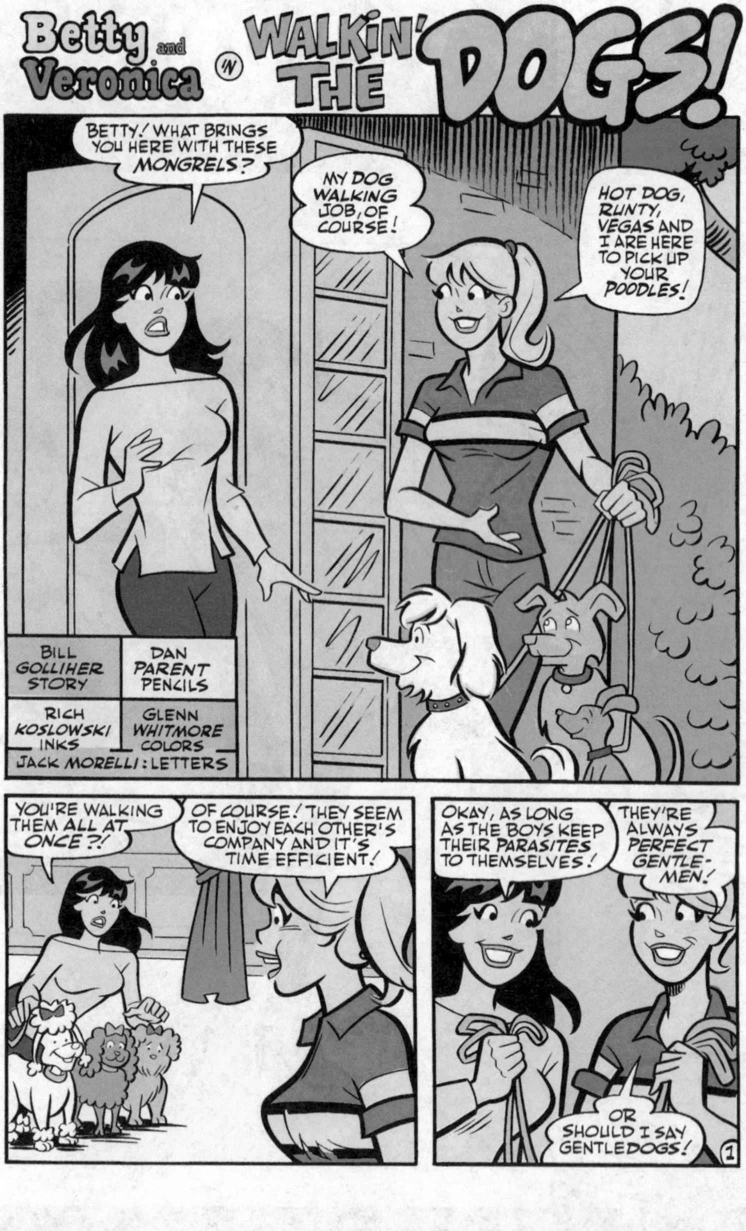
Betty and Veronica in WALKIN' THE DOGS!
BETTY! WHAT BRINGS YOU HERE WITH THESE MONGRELS?
MY DOG WALKING JOB, OF COURSE!
HOT DOG, RUNTY, VEGAS AND I ARE HERE TO PICK UP YOUR POODLES!
BILL GOLLIHER STORY
DAN PARENT PENCILS
RICH KOSLOWSKI INKS
GLENN WHITMORE COLORS
JACK MORELLI : LETTERS
YOU'RE WALKING THEM ALL AT ONCE?!
OF COURSE! THEY SEEM TO ENJOY EACH OTHER'S COMPANY AND IT'S TIME EFFICIENT!
OKAY, AS LONG AS THE BOYS KEEP THEIR PARASITES TO THEMSELVES!
THEY'RE ALWAYS PERFECT GENTLE-MEN!
OR SHOULD I SAY GENTLEDOGS!
1

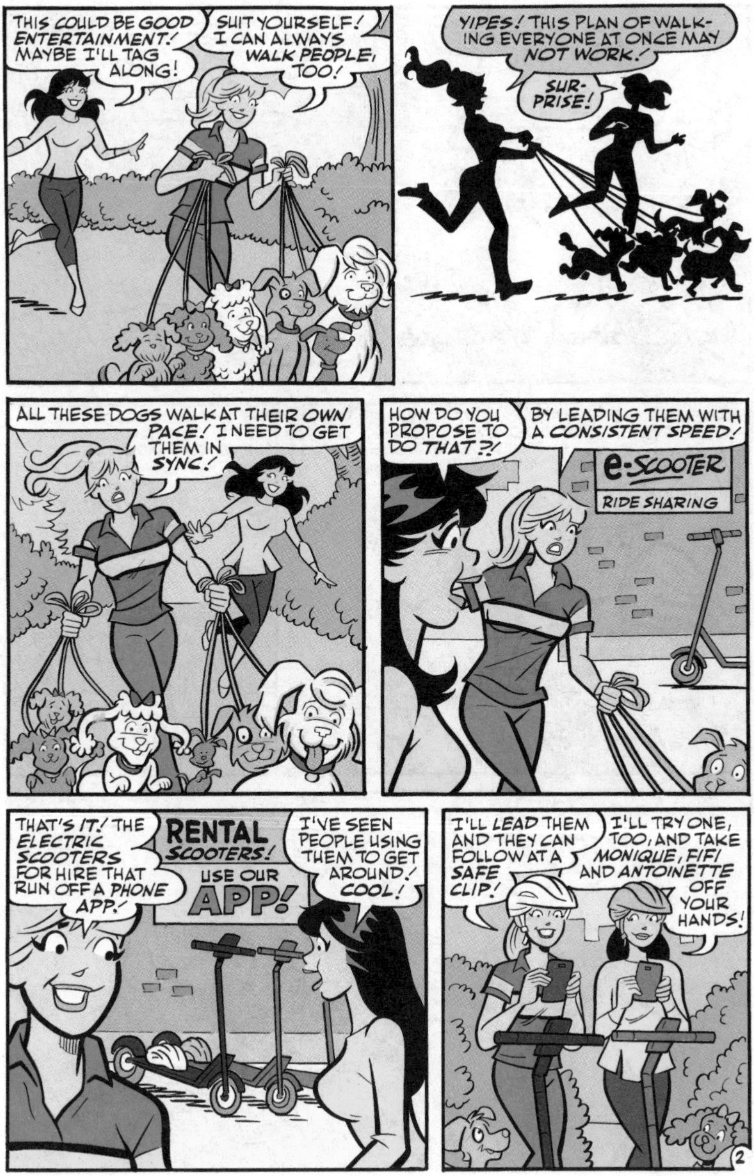
THIS COULD BE GOOD ENTERTAINMENT! MAYBE I'LL TAG ALONG!
SUIT YOURSELF! I CAN ALWAYS WALK PEOPLE, TOO!
YIPES! THIS PLAN OF WALKING EVERYONE AT ONCE MAY NOT WORK!
SURPRISE!
ALL THESE DOGS WALK AT THEIR OWN PACE! I NEED TO GET THEM IN SYNC!
HOW DO YOU PROPOSE TO DO THAT?!
BY LEADING THEM WITH A CONSISTENT SPEED!
e-SCOOTER
RIDE SHARING
THAT'S IT! THE ELECTRIC SCOOTERS FOR HIRE THAT RUN OFF A PHONE APP!
RENTAL SCOOTERS!
USE OUR APP!
I'VE SEEN PEOPLE USING THEM TO GET AROUND! COOL!
I'LL LEAD THEM AND THEY CAN FOLLOW AT A SAFE CLIP!
I'LL TRY ONE, TOO, AND TAKE MONIQUE, FIFI AND ANTOINETTE OFF YOUR HANDS!
2

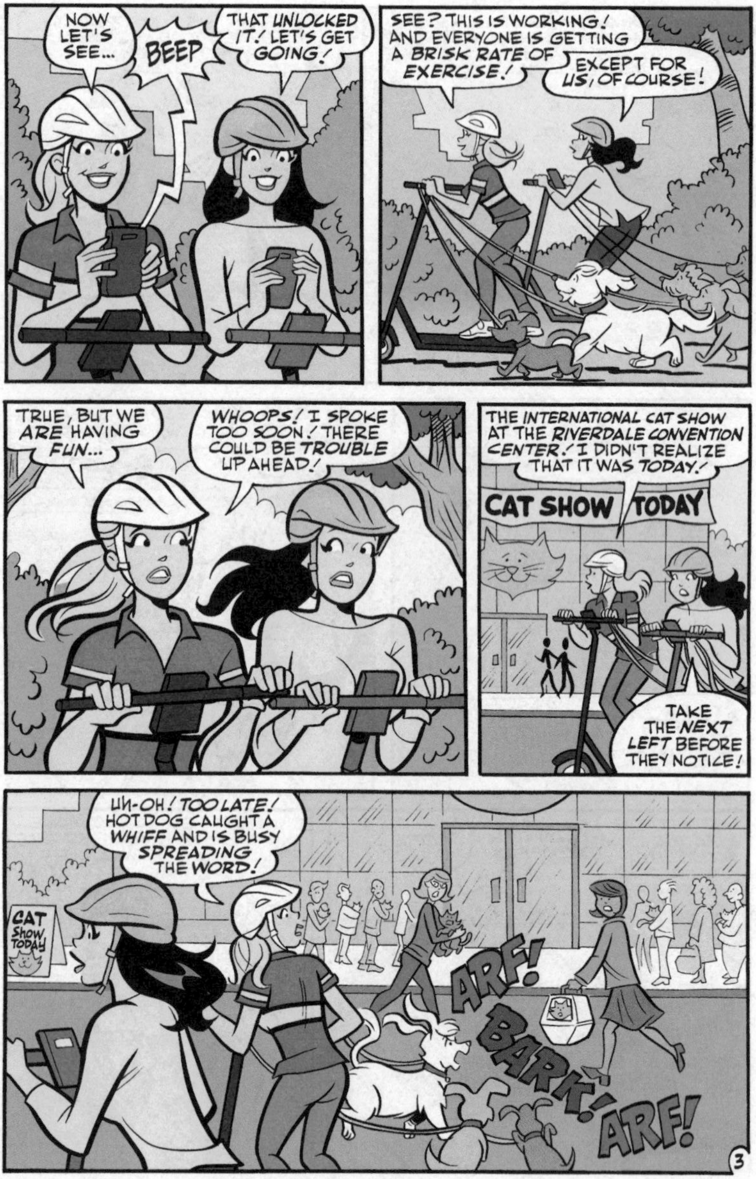
NOW LET'S SEE...
BEEP
THAT UNLOCKED IT! LET'S GET GOING!
SEE? THIS IS WORKING! AND EVERYONE IS GETTING A BRISK RATE OF EXERCISE!
EXCEPT FOR US, OF COURSE!
TRUE, BUT WE ARE HAVING FUN...
WHOOPS! I SPOKE TOO SOON! THERE COULD BE TROUBLE UP AHEAD!
THE INTERNATIONAL CAT SHOW AT THE RIVERDALE CONVENTION CENTER! I DIDN'T REALIZE THAT IT WAS TODAY!
CAT SHOW TODAY
TAKE THE NEXT LEFT BEFORE THEY NOTICE!
UH-OH! TOO LATE! HOT DOG CAUGHT A WHIFF AND IS BUSY SPREADING THE WORD!
CAT SHOW TODAY
ARF!
BARK!
ARF!
3

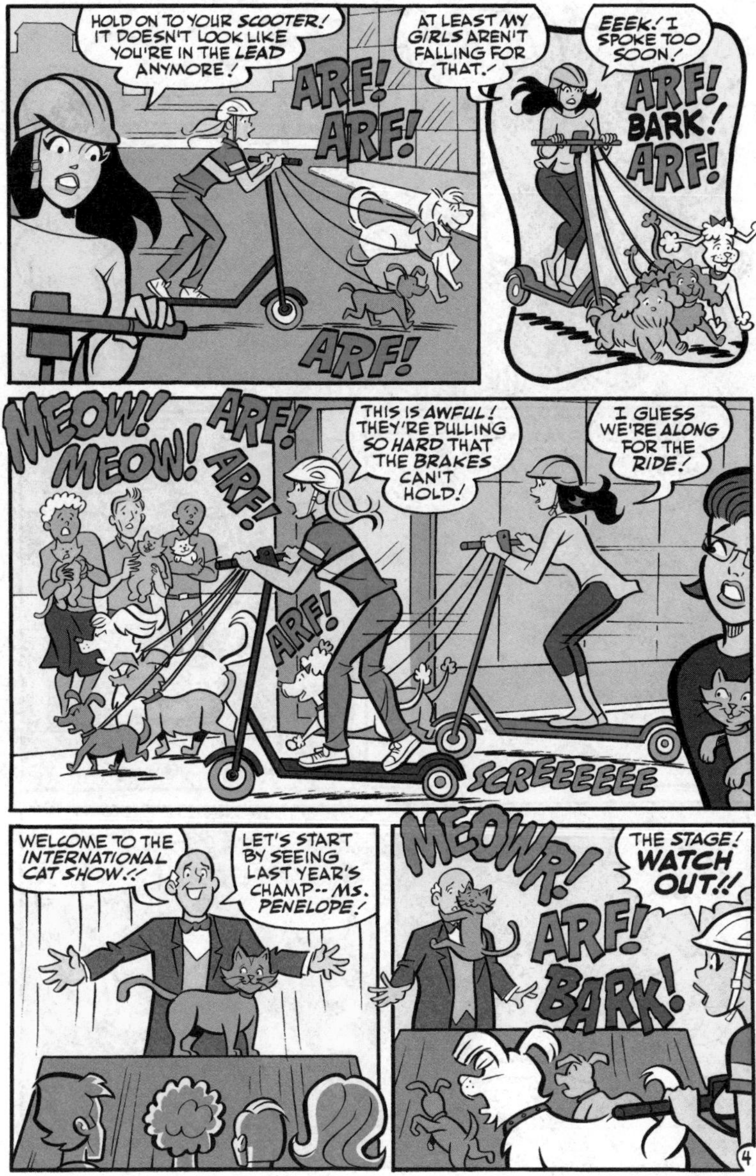
HOLD ON TO YOUR SCOOTER! IT DOESN'T LOOK LIKE YOU'RE IN THE LEAD ANYMORE!
ARF! ARF!
ARF!
AT LEAST MY GIRLS AREN'T FALLING FOR THAT.
EEEK! I SPOKE TOO SOON!
ARF! BARK! ARF!
MEOW! MEOW!
ARF! ARF!
THIS IS AWFUL! THEY'RE PULLING SO HARD THAT THE BRAKES CAN'T HOLD!
I GUESS WE'RE ALONG FOR THE RIDE!
ARF!
SCREEEEEEE
WELCOME TO THE INTERNATIONAL CAT SHOW!!
LET'S START BY SEEING LAST YEAR'S CHAMP-- MS. PENELOPE!
MEOWR!
THE STAGE! WATCH OUT!!
ARF! BARK!
4

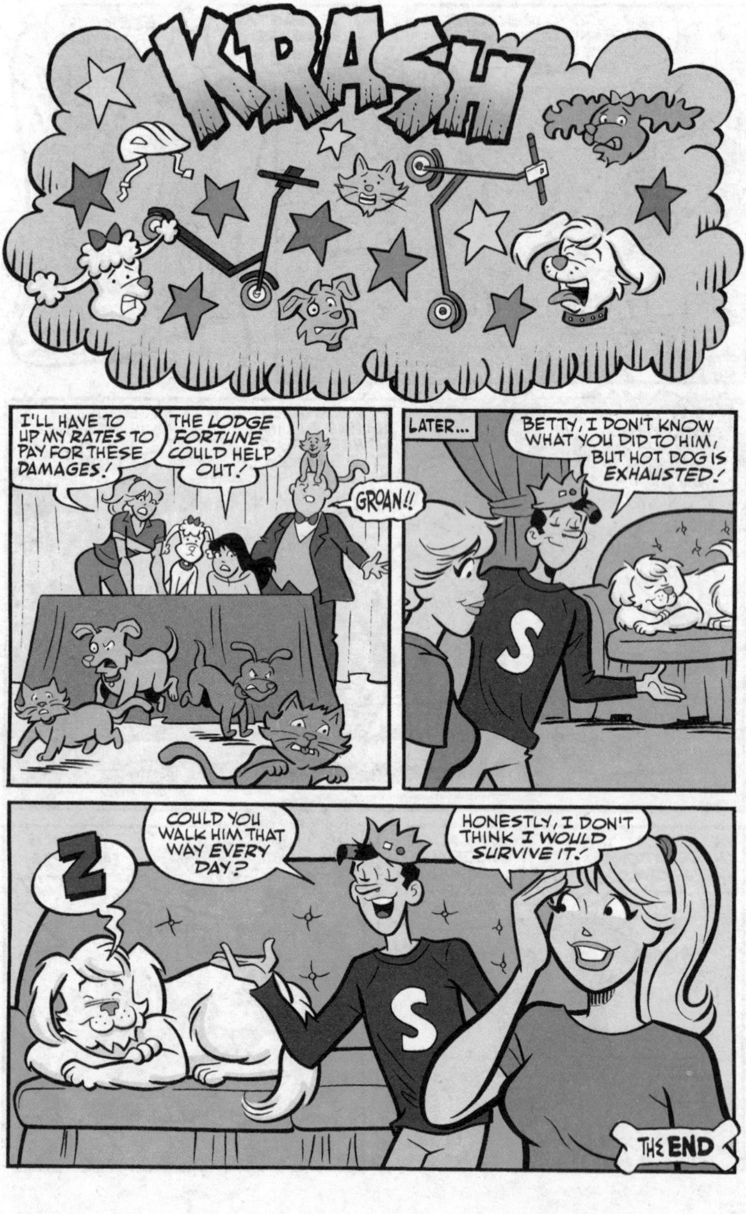
KRASH
I'LL HAVE TO UP MY RATES TO PAY FOR THESE DAMAGES!
THE LODGE FORTUNE COULD HELP OUT!
GROAN!!
LATER...
BETTY, I DON'T KNOW WHAT YOU DID TO HIM, BUT HOT DOG IS EXHAUSTED!
Z
COULD YOU WALK HIM THAT WAY EVERY DAY?
HONESTLY, I DON'T THINK I WOULD SURVIVE IT.!
THE END

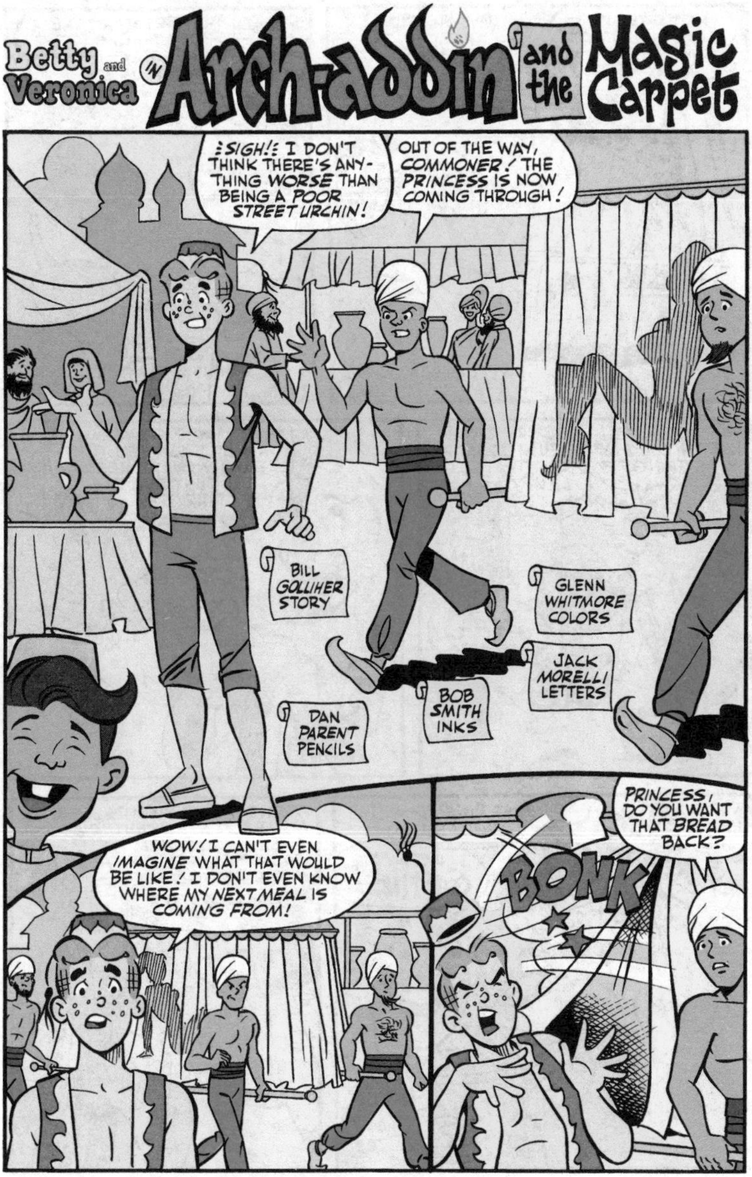

Betty and Veronica in
Arch-addin and the Magic Carpet
:SIGH!: I DON'T THINK THERE'S ANY-THING WORSE THAN BEING A POOR STREET URCHIN!
OUT OF THE WAY, COMMONER! THE PRINCESS IS NOW COMING THROUGH!
BILL GOLLIHER STORY
DAN PARENT PENCILS
BOB SMITH INKS
GLENN WHITMORE COLORS
JACK MORELLI LETTERS
WOW! I CAN'T EVEN IMAGINE WHAT THAT WOULD BE LIKE! I DON'T EVEN KNOW WHERE MY NEXT MEAL IS COMING FROM!
BONK
PRINCESS, DO YOU WANT THAT BREAD BACK?

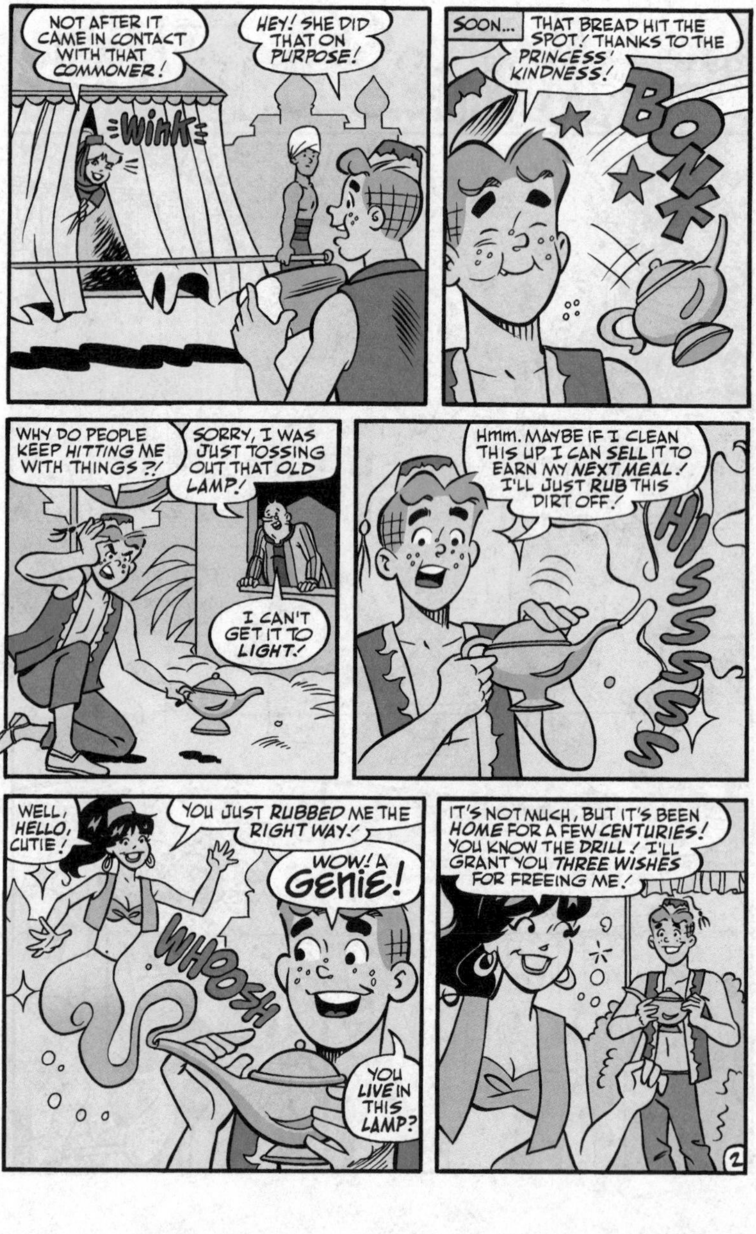
NOT AFTER IT CAME IN CONTACT WITH THAT COMMONER!
HEY! SHE DID THAT ON PURPOSE!
WINK
SOON...
THAT BREAD HIT THE SPOT! THANKS TO THE PRINCESS' KINDNESS!
BONK
WHY DO PEOPLE KEEP HITTING ME WITH THINGS?!
SORRY, I WAS JUST TOSSING OUT THAT OLD LAMP!
I CAN'T GET IT TO LIGHT!
Hmm. MAYBE IF I CLEAN THIS UP I CAN SELL IT TO EARN MY NEXT MEAL! I'LL JUST RUB THIS DIRT OFF!
HISSSSSS
WELL, HELLO, CUTIE!
YOU JUST RUBBED ME THE RIGHT WAY!
WOW! A GENIE!
WHOOSH
YOU LIVE IN THIS LAMP?
IT'S NOT MUCH, BUT IT'S BEEN HOME FOR A FEW CENTURIES! YOU KNOW THE DRILL! I'LL GRANT YOU THREE WISHES FOR FREEING ME!
2

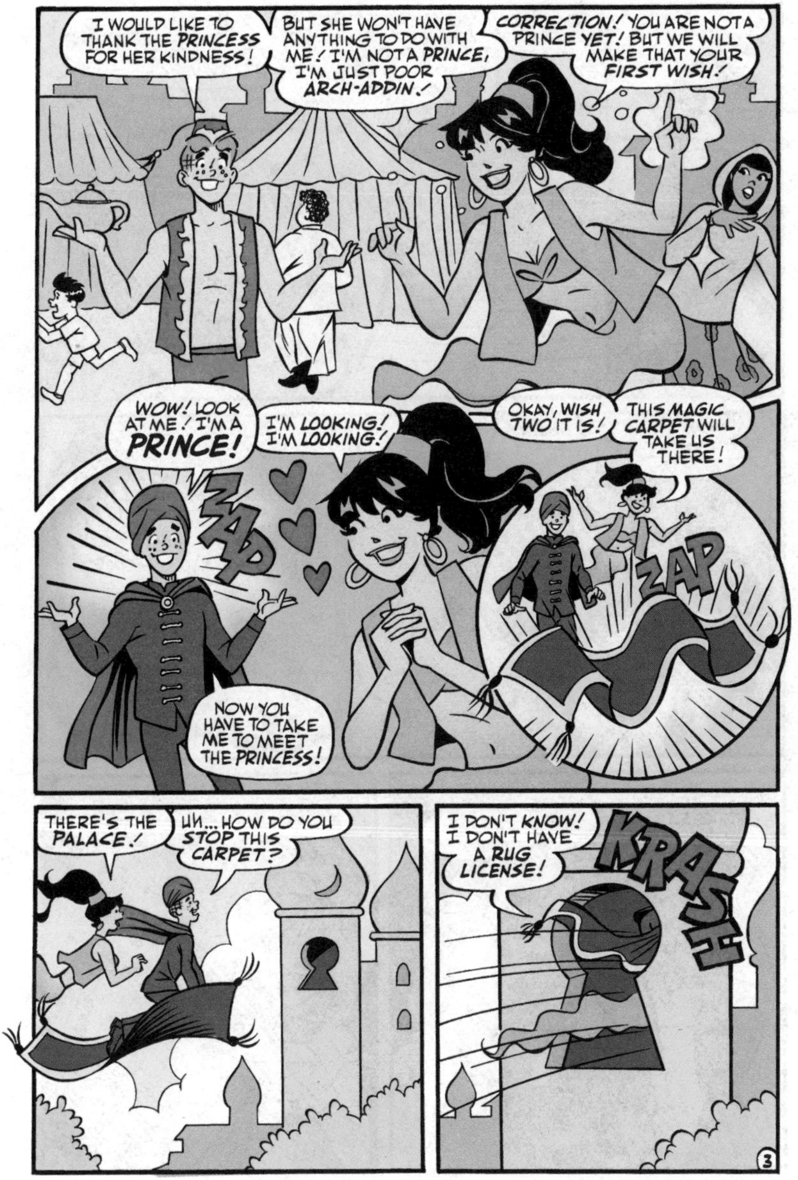
I WOULD LIKE TO THANK THE PRINCESS FOR HER KINDNESS!
BUT SHE WON'T HAVE ANYTHING TO DO WITH ME! I'M NOT A PRINCE, I'M JUST POOR ARCH-ADDIN!
CORRECTION! YOU ARE NOT A PRINCE YET! BUT WE WILL MAKE THAT YOUR FIRST WISH!
WOW! LOOK AT ME! I'M A PRINCE!
I'M LOOKING! I'M LOOKING!
ZAP
NOW YOU HAVE TO TAKE ME TO MEET THE PRINCESS!
OKAY, WISH TWO IT IS!
THIS MAGIC CARPET WILL TAKE US THERE!
ZAP
THERE'S THE PALACE!
UH... HOW DO YOU STOP THIS CARPET?
I DON'T KNOW! I DON'T HAVE A RUG LICENSE!
KRASH
3

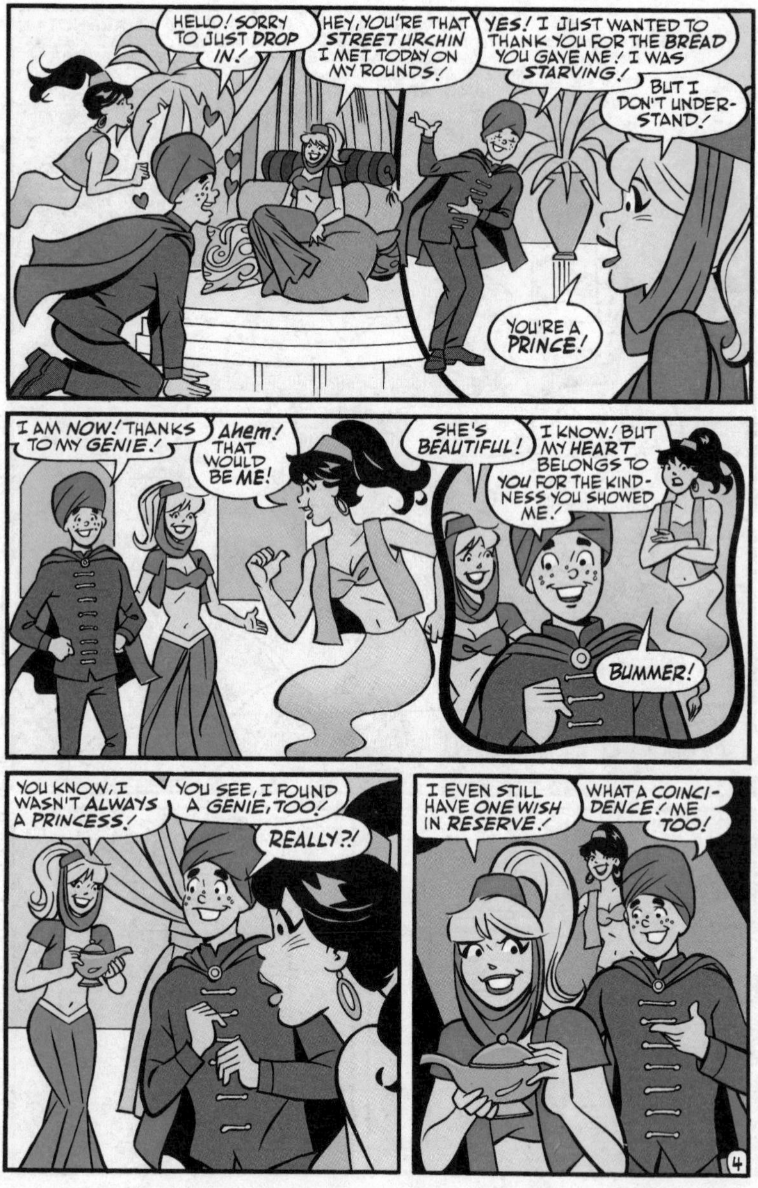
HELLO! SORRY TO JUST DROP IN!
HEY, YOU'RE THAT STREET URCHIN I MET TODAY ON MY ROUNDS!
YES! I JUST WANTED TO THANK YOU FOR THE BREAD YOU GAVE ME! I WAS STARVING!
BUT I DON'T UNDER-STAND!
YOU'RE A PRINCE!
I AM NOW! THANKS TO MY GENIE!
Ahem! THAT WOULD BE ME!
SHE'S BEAUTIFUL!
I KNOW! BUT MY HEART BELONGS TO YOU FOR THE KIND-NESS YOU SHOWED ME!
BUMMER!
YOU KNOW, I WASN'T ALWAYS A PRINCESS!
YOU SEE, I FOUND A GENIE, TOO!
REALLY?!
I EVEN STILL HAVE ONE WISH IN RESERVE!
WHAT A COINCI-DENCE! ME TOO!
4

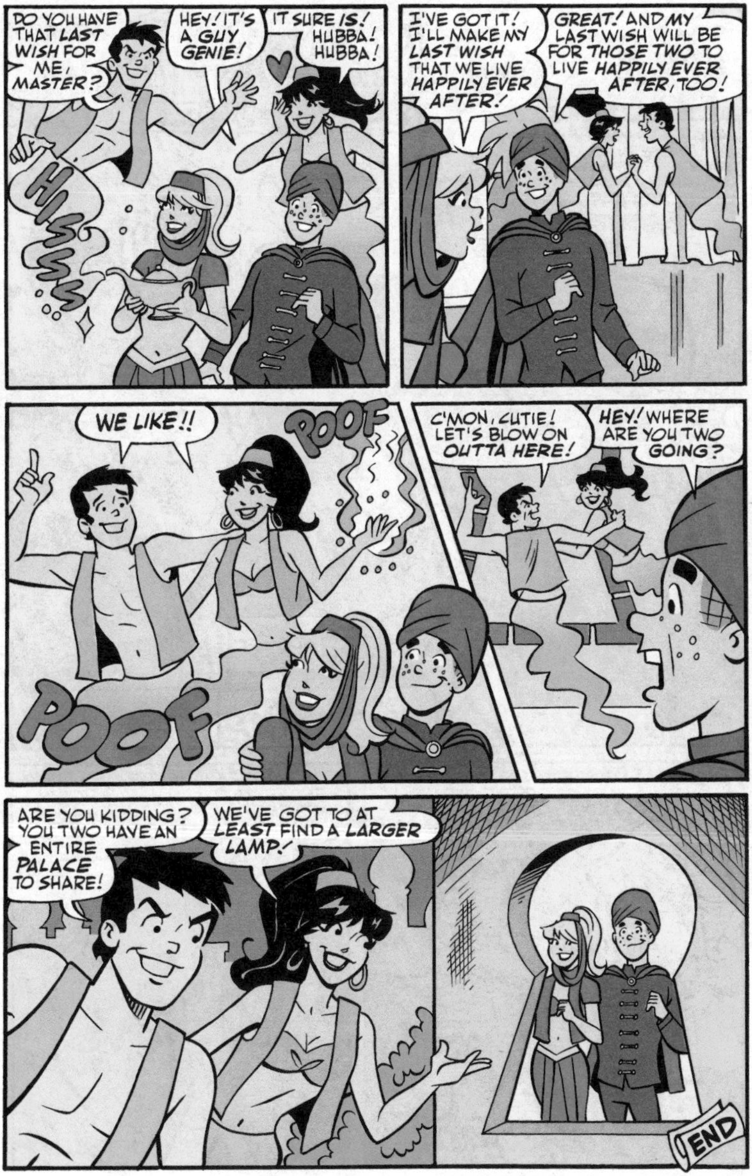
DO YOU HAVE THAT LAST WISH FOR ME, MASTER?
HEY! IT'S A GUY GENIE!
IT SURE IS! HUBBA! HUBBA!
HISSSS
I'VE GOT IT! I'LL MAKE MY LAST WISH THAT WE LIVE HAPPILY EVER AFTER!
GREAT! AND MY LAST WISH WILL BE FOR THOSE TWO TO LIVE HAPPILY EVER AFTER, TOO!
WE LIKE!!
POOF
POOF
C'MON, CUTIE! LET'S BLOW ON OUTTA HERE!
HEY! WHERE ARE YOU TWO GOING?
ARE YOU KIDDING? YOU TWO HAVE AN ENTIRE PALACE TO SHARE!
WE'VE GOT TO AT LEAST FIND A LARGER LAMP!
END

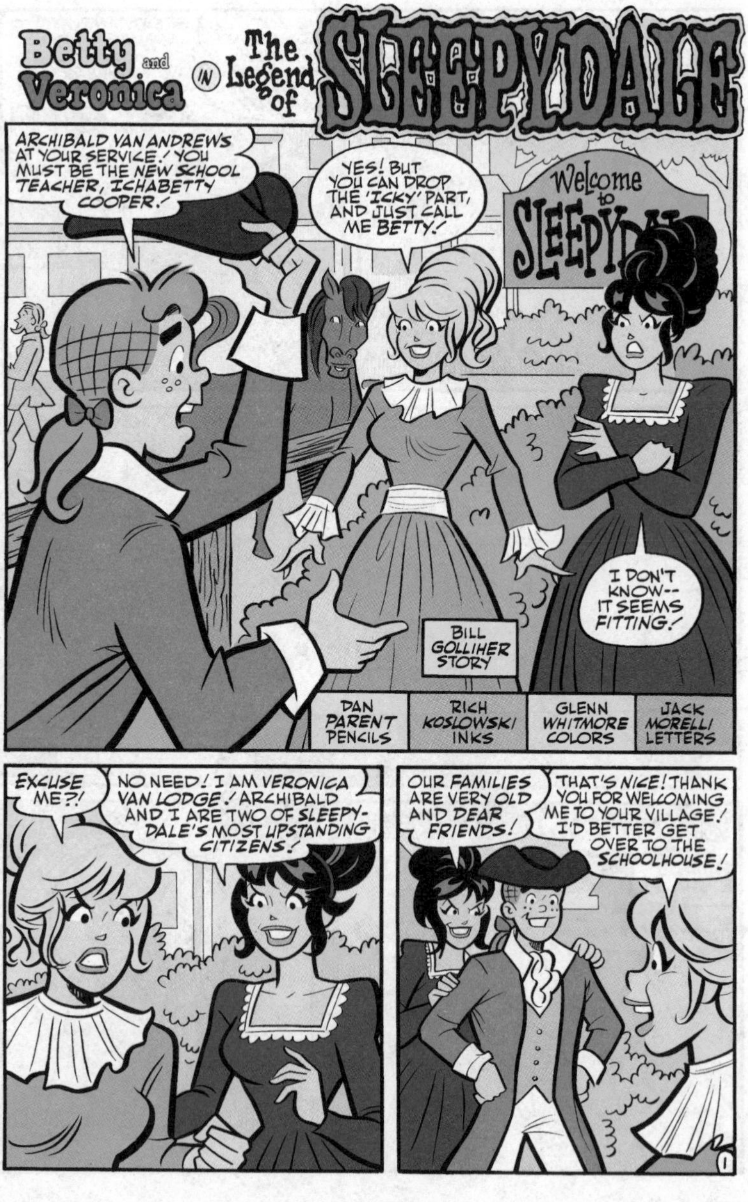
Betty and Veronica IN The Legend of SLEEPYDALE
ARCHIBALD VAN ANDREWS AT YOUR SERVICE! YOU MUST BE THE NEW SCHOOL TEACHER, ICHABETTY COOPER!
YES! BUT YOU CAN DROP THE 'ICKY' PART, AND JUST CALL ME BETTY!
Welcome to SLEEPYD
I DON'T KNOW-- IT SEEMS FITTING!
BILL GOLLIHER STORY
DAN PARENT PENCILS
RICH KOSLOWSKI INKS
GLENN WHITMORE COLORS
JACK MORELLI LETTERS
EXCUSE ME?!
NO NEED! I AM VERONICA VAN LODGE! ARCHIBALD AND I ARE TWO OF SLEEPY-DALE'S MOST UPSTANDING CITIZENS!
OUR FAMILIES ARE VERY OLD AND DEAR FRIENDS!
THAT'S NICE! THANK YOU FOR WELCOMING ME TO YOUR VILLAGE! I'D BETTER GET OVER TO THE SCHOOLHOUSE!
1

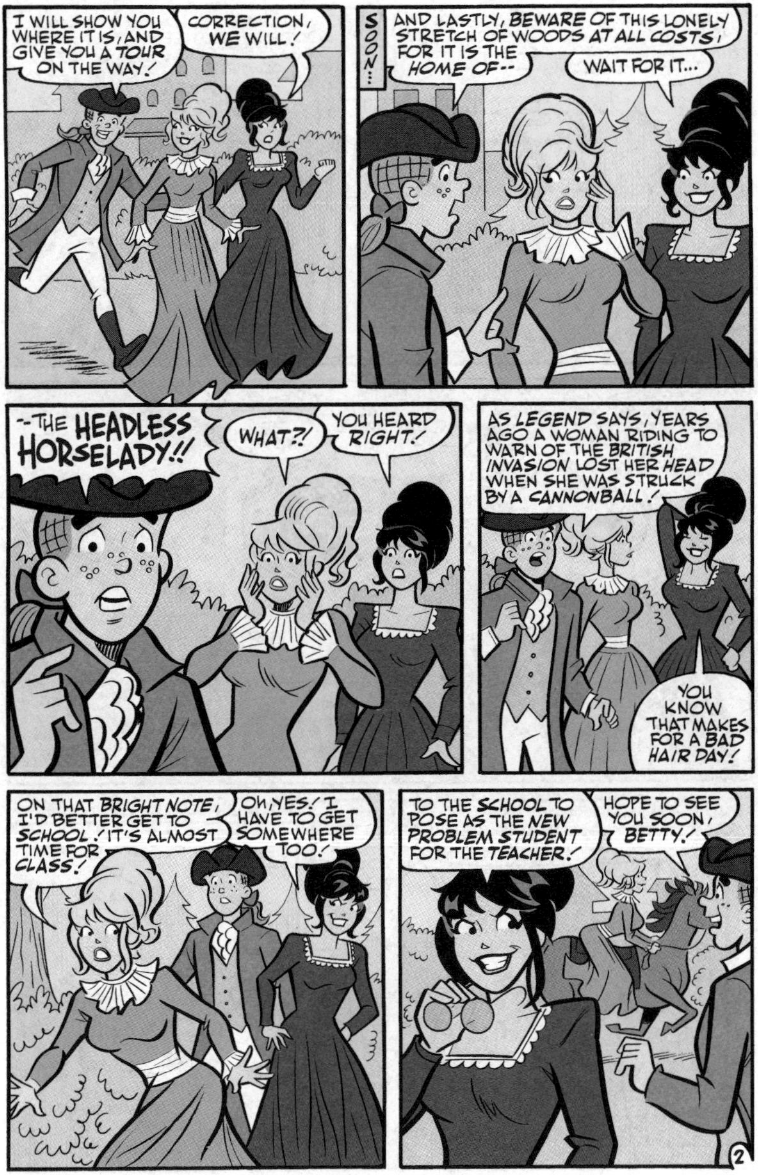
I WILL SHOW YOU WHERE IT IS, AND GIVE YOU A TOUR ON THE WAY!
CORRECTION, WE WILL!
SOON...
AND LASTLY, BEWARE OF THIS LONELY STRETCH OF WOODS AT ALL COSTS, FOR IT IS THE HOME OF--
WAIT FOR IT...
--THE HEADLESS HORSELADY!!
WHAT?!
YOU HEARD RIGHT!
AS LEGEND SAYS, YEARS AGO A WOMAN RIDING TO WARN OF THE BRITISH INVASION LOST HER HEAD WHEN SHE WAS STRUCK BY A CANNONBALL!
YOU KNOW THAT MAKES FOR A BAD HAIR DAY!
ON THAT BRIGHT NOTE, I'D BETTER GET TO SCHOOL! IT'S ALMOST TIME FOR CLASS!
OH, YES! I HAVE TO GET SOMEWHERE TOO!
TO THE SCHOOL TO POSE AS THE NEW PROBLEM STUDENT FOR THE TEACHER!
HOPE TO SEE YOU SOON, BETTY!
2

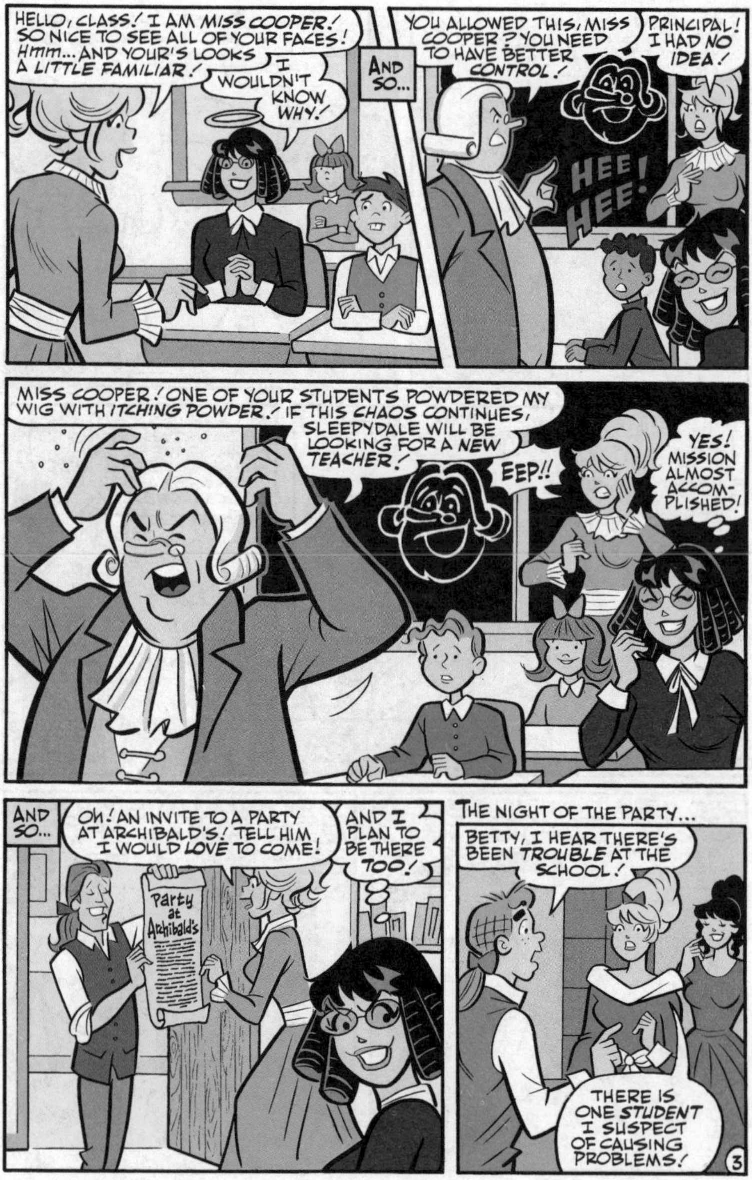
HELLO, CLASS! I AM MISS COOPER! SO NICE TO SEE ALL OF YOUR FACES! Hmm... AND YOUR'S LOOKS A LITTLE FAMILIAR!
I WOULDN'T KNOW WHY!
AND SO...
YOU ALLOWED THIS, MISS COOPER? YOU NEED TO HAVE BETTER CONTROL!
PRINCIPAL! I HAD NO IDEA!
HEE! HEE!
MISS COOPER! ONE OF YOUR STUDENTS POWDERED MY WIG WITH ITCHING POWDER! IF THIS CHAOS CONTINUES, SLEEPYDALE WILL BE LOOKING FOR A NEW TEACHER!
EEP!!
YES! MISSION ALMOST ACCOMPLISHED!
AND SO...
Oh! AN INVITE TO A PARTY AT ARCHIBALD'S! TELL HIM I WOULD LOVE TO COME!
AND I PLAN TO BE THERE TOO!
Party at Archibald's
THE NIGHT OF THE PARTY...
BETTY, I HEAR THERE'S BEEN TROUBLE AT THE SCHOOL!
THERE IS ONE STUDENT I SUSPECT OF CAUSING PROBLEMS!
3

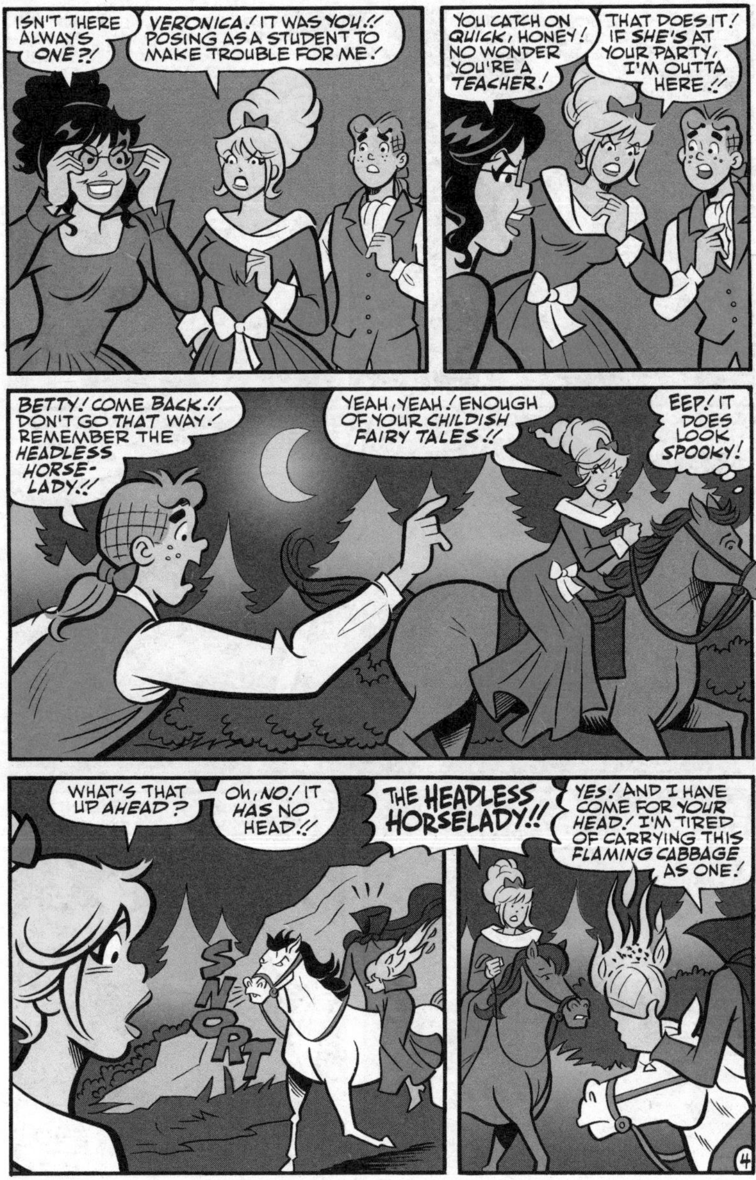

ISN'T THERE ALWAYS ONE ?!
VERONICA! IT WAS YOU!! POSING AS A STUDENT TO MAKE TROUBLE FOR ME!
YOU CATCH ON QUICK, HONEY! NO WONDER YOU'RE A TEACHER!
THAT DOES IT! IF SHE'S AT YOUR PARTY, I'M OUTTA HERE!!
BETTY! COME BACK!! DON'T GO THAT WAY! REMEMBER THE HEADLESS HORSE-LADY!!
YEAH, YEAH! ENOUGH OF YOUR CHILDISH FAIRY TALES!!
EEP! IT DOES LOOK SPOOKY!
WHAT'S THAT UP AHEAD?
OH, NO! IT HAS NO HEAD!!
SNORT
THE HEADLESS HORSELADY!!
YES! AND I HAVE COME FOR YOUR HEAD! I'M TIRED OF CARRYING THIS FLAMING CABBAGE AS ONE!
4

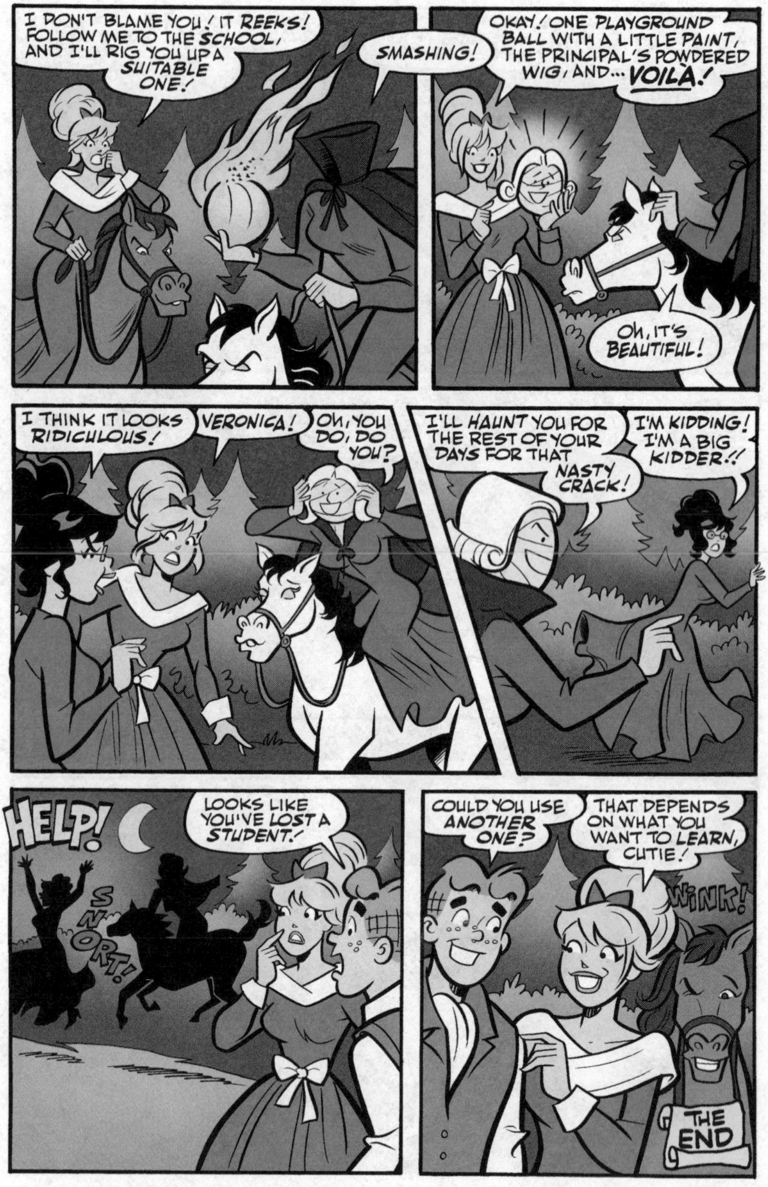
I DON'T BLAME YOU! IT REEKS! FOLLOW ME TO THE SCHOOL, AND I'LL RIG YOU UP A SUITABLE ONE!
SMASHING!
OKAY! ONE PLAYGROUND BALL WITH A LITTLE PAINT, THE PRINCIPAL'S POWDERED WIG, AND... VOILÀ!
OH, IT'S BEAUTIFUL!
I THINK IT LOOKS RIDICULOUS!
VERONICA!
OH, YOU DO, DO YOU?
I'LL HAUNT YOU FOR THE REST OF YOUR DAYS FOR THAT NASTY CRACK!
I'M KIDDING! I'M A BIG KIDDER!!
HELP!
SNORT!
LOOKS LIKE YOU'VE LOST A STUDENT!
COULD YOU USE ANOTHER ONE?
THAT DEPENDS ON WHAT YOU WANT TO LEARN, CUTIE!
WINK!
THE END

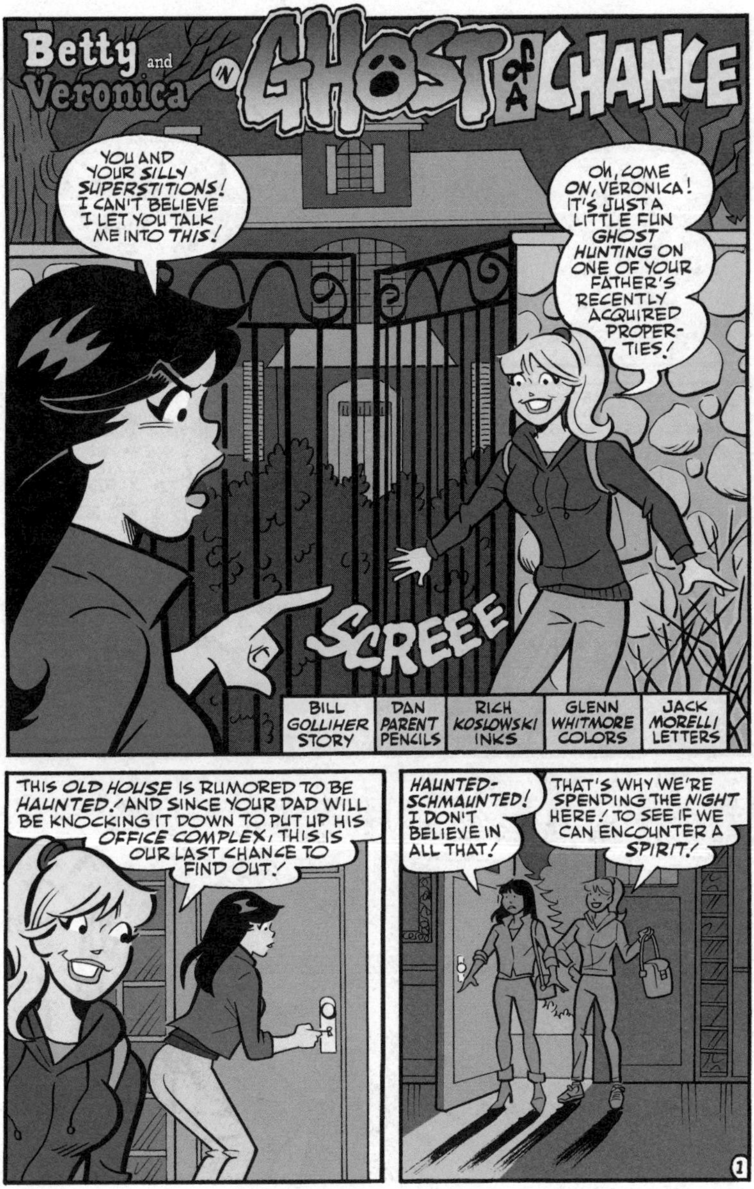
Betty and Veronica
IN
GHOST of A CHANCE
YOU AND YOUR SILLY SUPERSTITIONS! I CAN'T BELIEVE I LET YOU TALK ME INTO THIS!
OH, COME ON, VERONICA! IT'S JUST A LITTLE FUN GHOST HUNTING ON ONE OF YOUR FATHER'S RECENTLY ACQUIRED PROPER-TIES!
SCREEE
BILL GOLLIHER STORY
DAN PARENT PENCILS
RICH KOSLOWSKI INKS
GLENN WHITMORE COLORS
JACK MORELLI LETTERS
THIS OLD HOUSE IS RUMORED TO BE HAUNTED! AND SINCE YOUR DAD WILL BE KNOCKING IT DOWN TO PUT UP HIS OFFICE COMPLEX, THIS IS OUR LAST CHANCE TO FIND OUT!
HAUNTED-SCHMAUNTED! I DON'T BELIEVE IN ALL THAT!
THAT'S WHY WE'RE SPENDING THE NIGHT HERE! TO SEE IF WE CAN ENCOUNTER A SPIRIT!
1

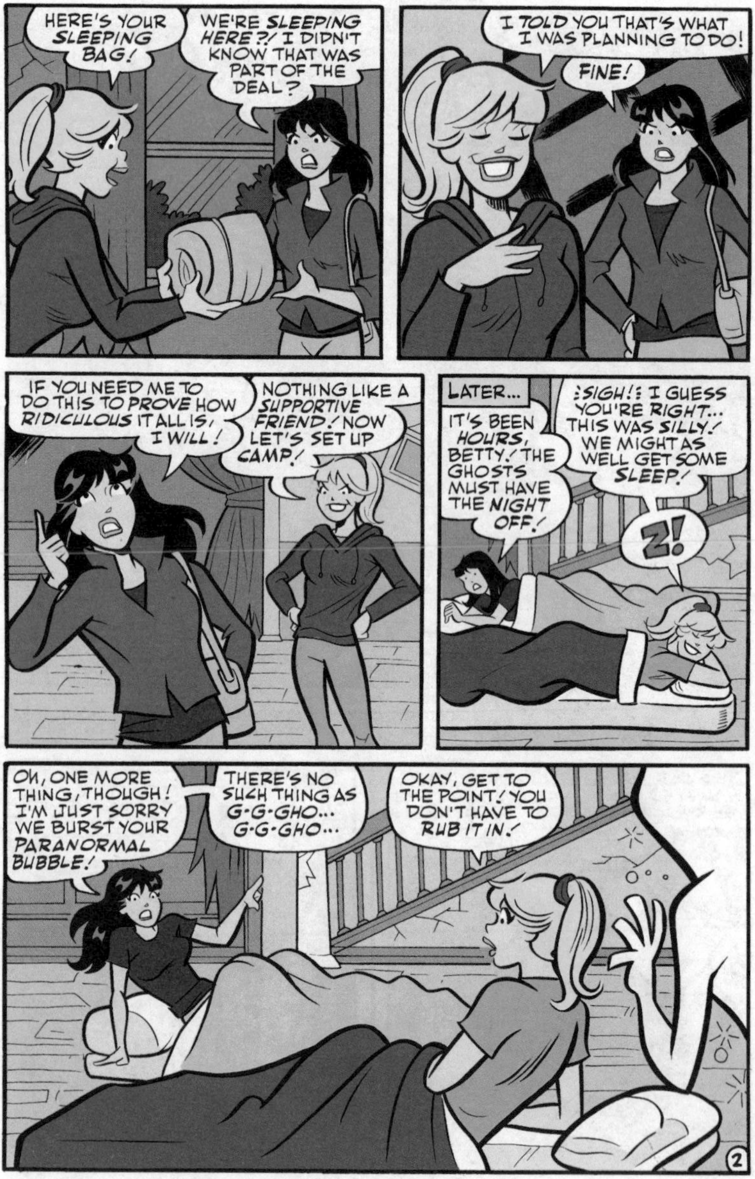
HERE'S YOUR SLEEPING BAG!
WE'RE SLEEPING HERE?! I DIDN'T KNOW THAT WAS PART OF THE DEAL?
I TOLD YOU THAT'S WHAT I WAS PLANNING TO DO!
FINE!
IF YOU NEED ME TO DO THIS TO PROVE HOW RIDICULOUS IT ALL IS, I WILL!
NOTHING LIKE A SUPPORTIVE FRIEND! NOW LET'S SET UP CAMP!
LATER...
IT'S BEEN HOURS, BETTY! THE GHOSTS MUST HAVE THE NIGHT OFF!
:SIGH!: I GUESS YOU'RE RIGHT... THIS WAS SILLY! WE MIGHT AS WELL GET SOME SLEEP!
Z!
OH, ONE MORE THING, THOUGH! I'M JUST SORRY WE BURST YOUR PARANORMAL BUBBLE!
THERE'S NO SUCH THING AS G-G-GHO... G-G-GHO...
OKAY, GET TO THE POINT! YOU DON'T HAVE TO RUB IT IN!
2

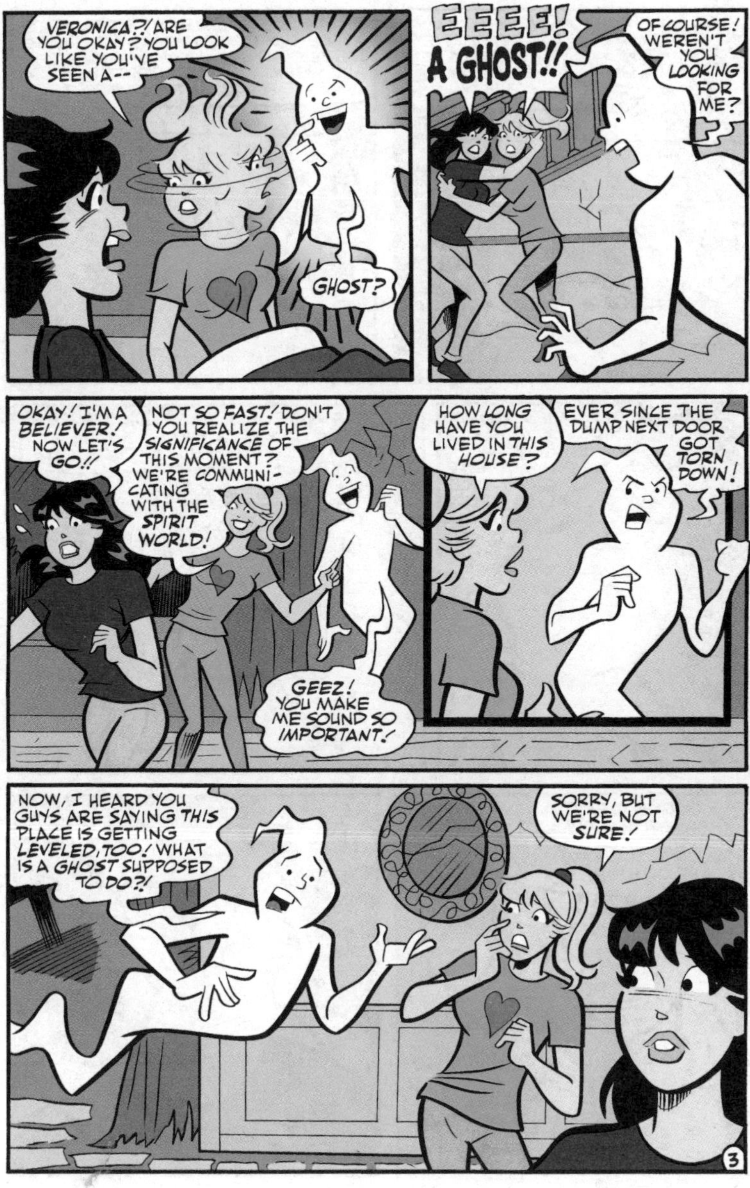
VERONICA?! ARE YOU OKAY? YOU LOOK LIKE YOU'VE SEEN A--
GHOST?
EEEE! A GHOST!!
OF COURSE! WEREN'T YOU LOOKING FOR ME?
OKAY! I'M A BELIEVER! NOW LET'S GO!!
NOT SO FAST! DON'T YOU REALIZE THE SIGNIFICANCE OF THIS MOMENT? WE'RE COMMUNICATING WITH THE SPIRIT WORLD!
GEEZ! YOU MAKE ME SOUND SO IMPORTANT!
HOW LONG HAVE YOU LIVED IN THIS HOUSE?
EVER SINCE THE DUMP NEXT DOOR GOT TORN DOWN!
NOW, I HEARD YOU GUYS ARE SAYING THIS PLACE IS GETTING LEVELED, TOO! WHAT IS A GHOST SUPPOSED TO DO?!
SORRY, BUT WE'RE NOT SURE!
3

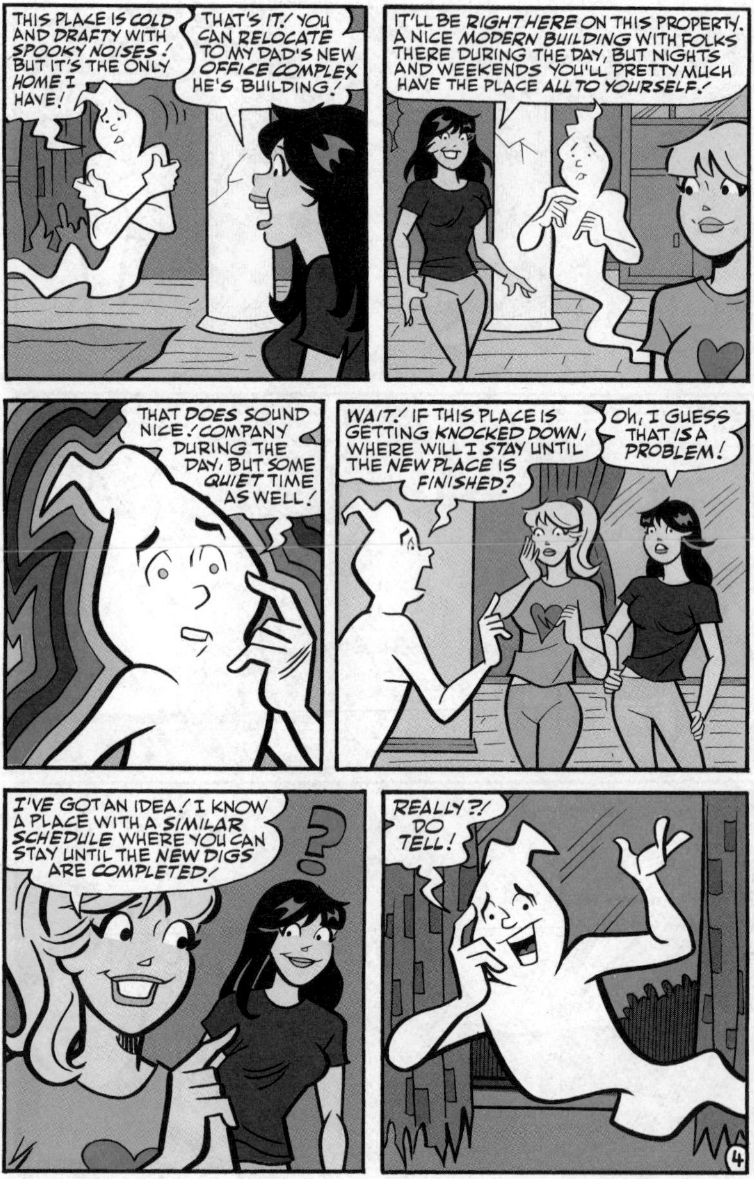
THIS PLACE IS COLD AND DRAFTY WITH SPOOKY NOISES! BUT IT'S THE ONLY HOME I HAVE!
THAT'S IT! YOU CAN RELOCATE TO MY DAD'S NEW OFFICE COMPLEX HE'S BUILDING!
IT'LL BE RIGHT HERE ON THIS PROPERTY. A NICE MODERN BUILDING WITH FOLKS THERE DURING THE DAY, BUT NIGHTS AND WEEKENDS YOU'LL PRETTY MUCH HAVE THE PLACE ALL TO YOURSELF!
THAT DOES SOUND NICE! COMPANY DURING THE DAY, BUT SOME QUIET TIME AS WELL!
WAIT! IF THIS PLACE IS GETTING KNOCKED DOWN, WHERE WILL I STAY UNTIL THE NEW PLACE IS FINISHED?
Oh, I GUESS THAT IS A PROBLEM!
I'VE GOT AN IDEA! I KNOW A PLACE WITH A SIMILAR SCHEDULE WHERE YOU CAN STAY UNTIL THE NEW DIGS ARE COMPLETED!
?
REALLY?! DO TELL!
4

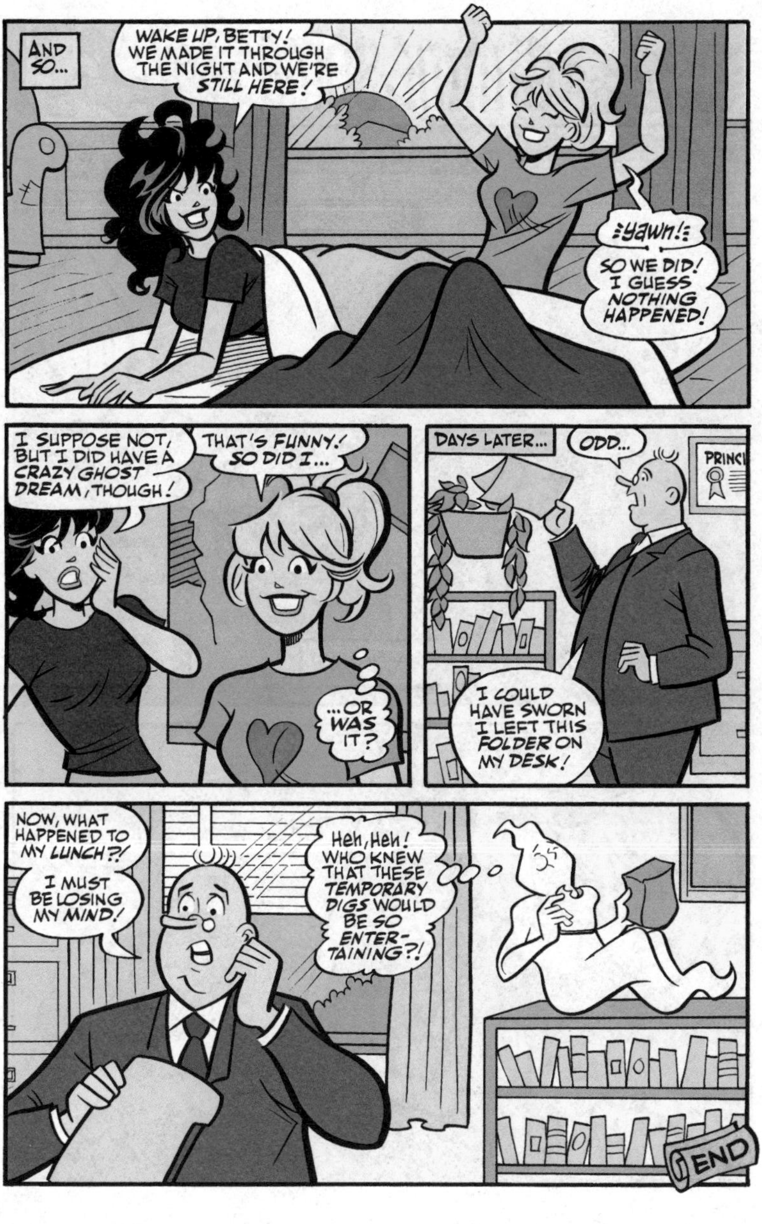
AND SO...
WAKE UP, BETTY! WE MADE IT THROUGH THE NIGHT AND WE'RE STILL HERE!
yawn!
SO WE DID! I GUESS NOTHING HAPPENED!
I SUPPOSE NOT, BUT I DID HAVE A CRAZY GHOST DREAM, THOUGH!
THAT'S FUNNY! SO DID I...
...OR WAS IT?
DAYS LATER...
ODD...
PRINCI
I COULD HAVE SWORN I LEFT THIS FOLDER ON MY DESK!
NOW, WHAT HAPPENED TO MY LUNCH?!
I MUST BE LOSING MY MIND!
Heh, Heh! WHO KNEW THAT THESE TEMPORARY DIGS WOULD BE SO ENTERTAINING?!
END

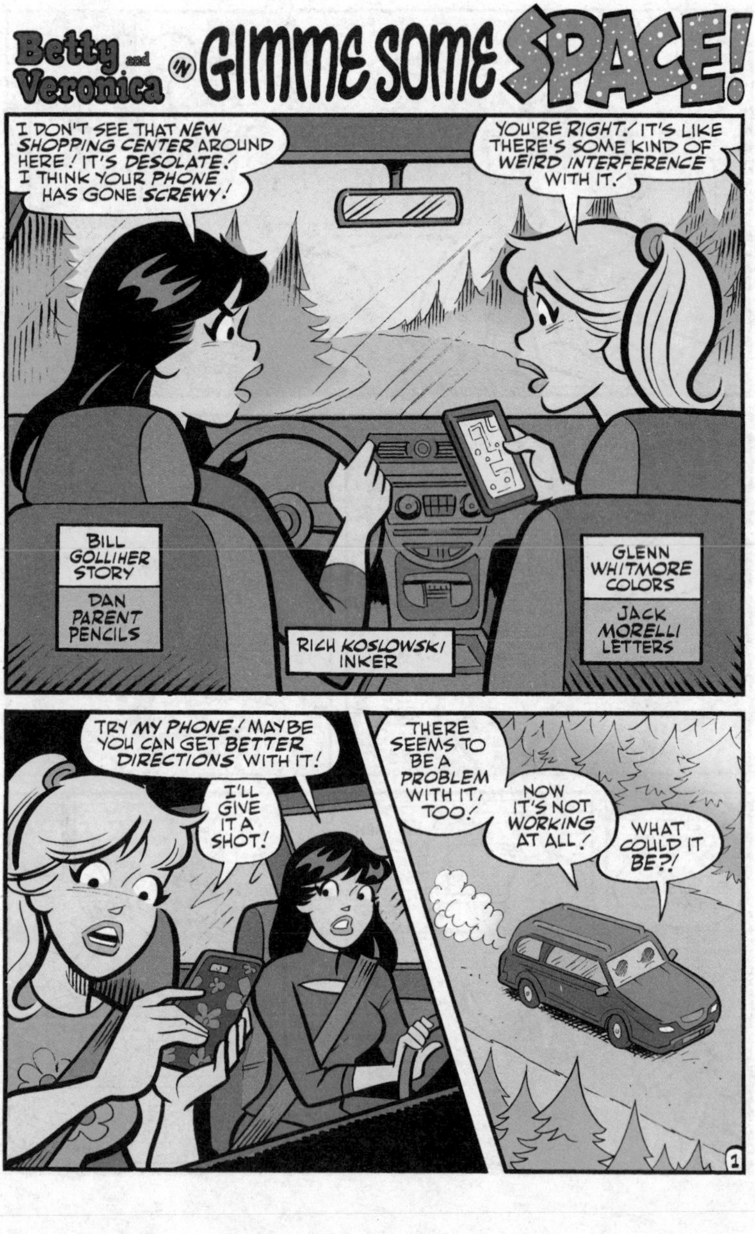
Betty and Veronica in GIMME SOME SPACE!
I DON'T SEE THAT NEW SHOPPING CENTER AROUND HERE! IT'S DESOLATE! I THINK YOUR PHONE HAS GONE SCREWY!
YOU'RE RIGHT! IT'S LIKE THERE'S SOME KIND OF WEIRD INTERFERENCE WITH IT!
BILL GOLLIHER STORY
DAN PARENT PENCILS
RICH KOSLOWSKI INKER
GLENN WHITMORE COLORS
JACK MORELLI LETTERS
TRY MY PHONE! MAYBE YOU CAN GET BETTER DIRECTIONS WITH IT!
I'LL GIVE IT A SHOT!
THERE SEEMS TO BE A PROBLEM WITH IT, TOO!
NOW IT'S NOT WORKING AT ALL!
WHAT COULD IT BE?!
1

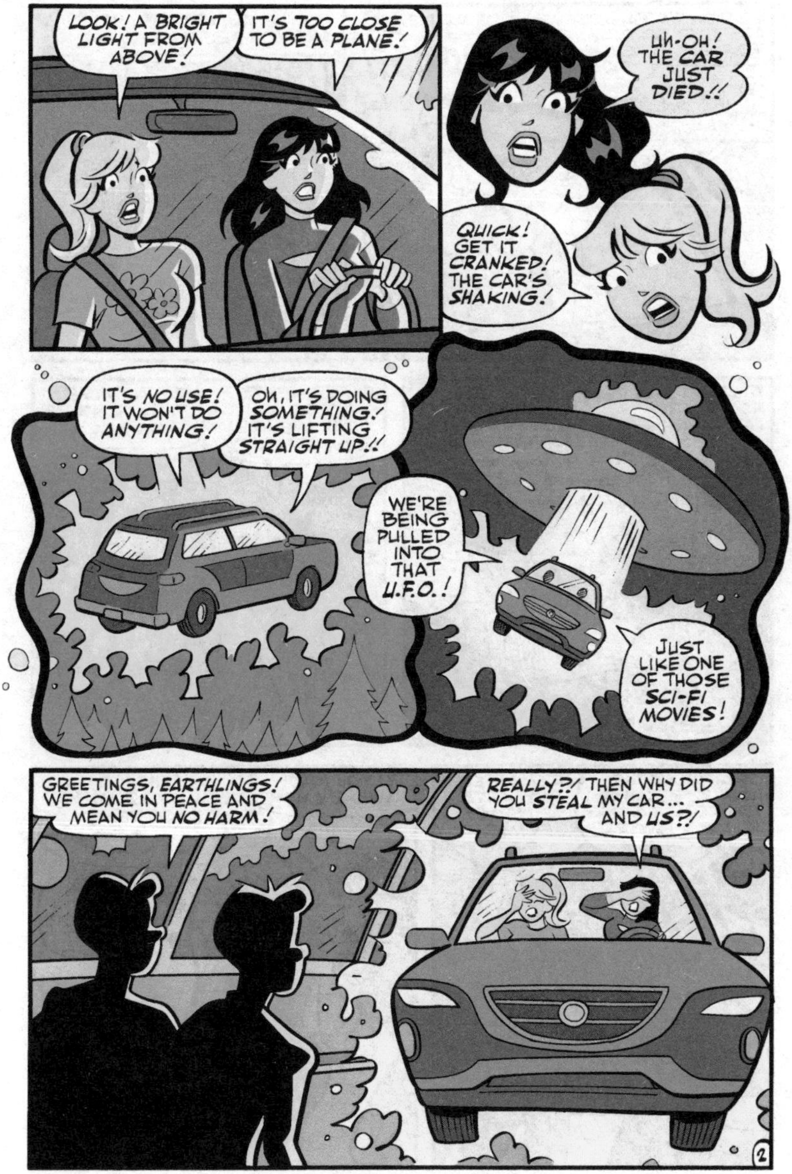
LOOK! A BRIGHT LIGHT FROM ABOVE!
IT'S TOO CLOSE TO BE A PLANE!
UH-OH! THE CAR JUST DIED!!
QUICK! GET IT CRANKED! THE CAR'S SHAKING!
IT'S NO USE! IT WON'T DO ANYTHING!
OH, IT'S DOING SOMETHING! IT'S LIFTING STRAIGHT UP!!
WE'RE BEING PULLED INTO THAT U.F.O.!
JUST LIKE ONE OF THOSE SCI-FI MOVIES!
GREETINGS, EARTHLINGS! WE COME IN PEACE AND MEAN YOU NO HARM!
REALLY?! THEN WHY DID YOU STEAL MY CAR... AND US?!
2

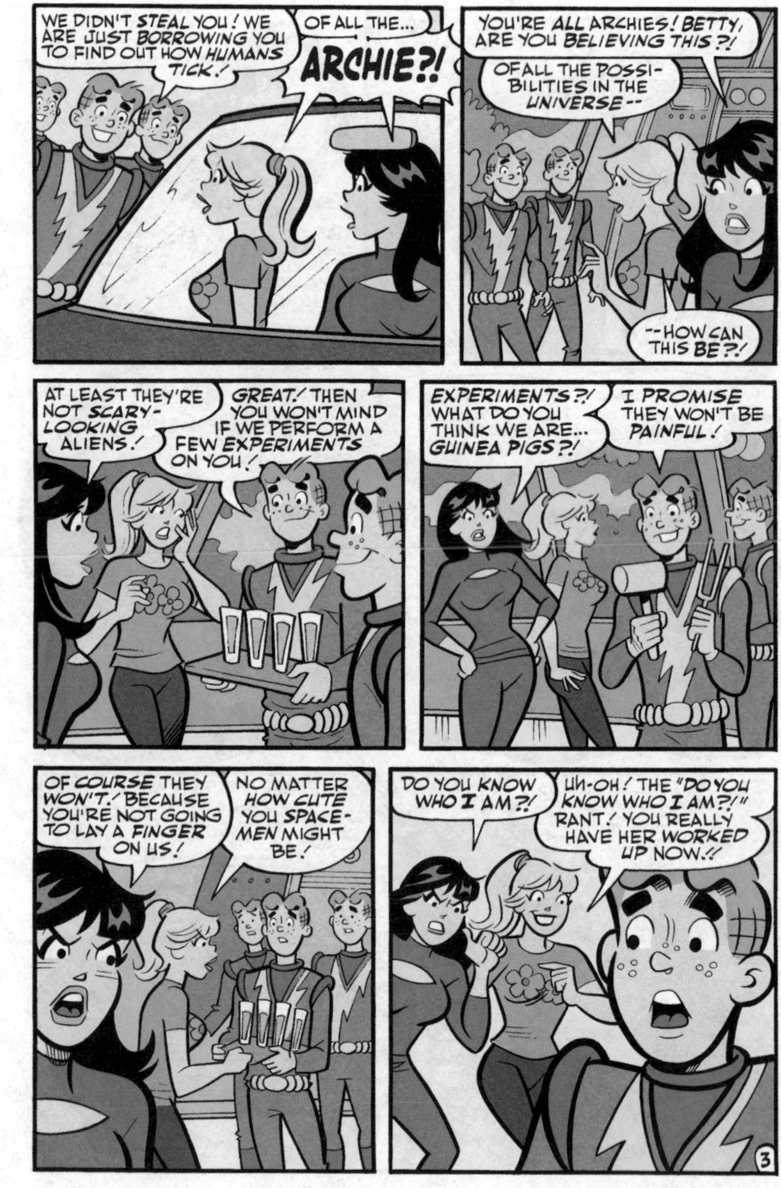
WE DIDN'T STEAL YOU! WE ARE JUST BORROWING YOU TO FIND OUT HOW HUMANS TICK!
OF ALL THE...
ARCHIE?!
YOU'RE ALL ARCHIES! BETTY, ARE YOU BELIEVING THIS?!
OF ALL THE POSSIBILITIES IN THE UNIVERSE --
-- HOW CAN THIS BE?!
AT LEAST THEY'RE NOT SCARY-LOOKING ALIENS!
GREAT! THEN YOU WON'T MIND IF WE PERFORM A FEW EXPERIMENTS ON YOU!
EXPERIMENTS?! WHAT DO YOU THINK WE ARE... GUINEA PIGS?!
I PROMISE THEY WON'T BE PAINFUL!
OF COURSE THEY WON'T! BECAUSE YOU'RE NOT GOING TO LAY A FINGER ON US!
NO MATTER HOW CUTE YOU SPACE-MEN MIGHT BE!
DO YOU KNOW WHO I AM?!
UH-OH! THE "DO YOU KNOW WHO I AM?!" RANT! YOU REALLY HAVE HER WORKED UP NOW!!
3

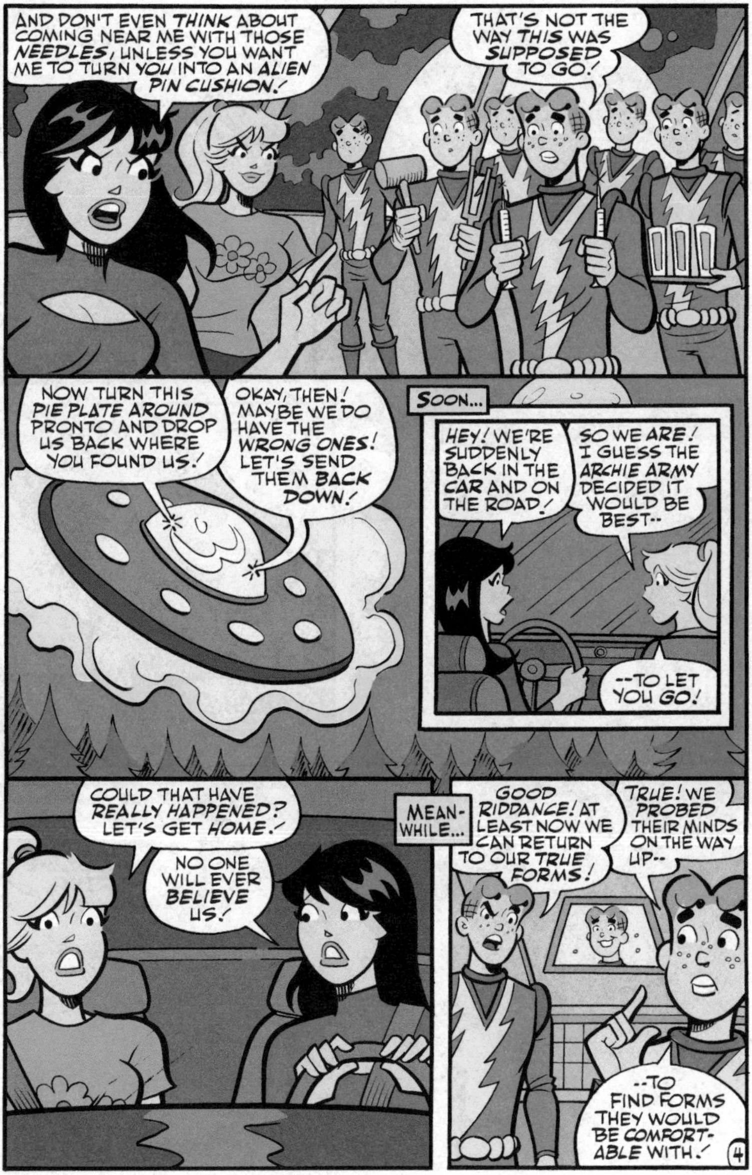
AND DON'T EVEN THINK ABOUT COMING NEAR ME WITH THOSE NEEDLES, UNLESS YOU WANT ME TO TURN YOU INTO AN ALIEN PIN CUSHION!
THAT'S NOT THE WAY THIS WAS SUPPOSED TO GO!
NOW TURN THIS PIE PLATE AROUND PRONTO AND DROP US BACK WHERE YOU FOUND US!
OKAY, THEN! MAYBE WE DO HAVE THE WRONG ONES! LET'S SEND THEM BACK DOWN!
SOON...
HEY! WE'RE SUDDENLY BACK IN THE CAR AND ON THE ROAD!
SO WE ARE! I GUESS THE ARCHIE ARMY DECIDED IT WOULD BE BEST--
--TO LET YOU GO!
COULD THAT HAVE REALLY HAPPENED? LET'S GET HOME!
NO ONE WILL EVER BELIEVE US!
MEAN-WHILE...
GOOD RIDDANCE! AT LEAST NOW WE CAN RETURN TO OUR TRUE FORMS!
TRUE! WE PROBED THEIR MINDS ON THE WAY UP--
--TO FIND FORMS THEY WOULD BE COMFORT-ABLE WITH!
4

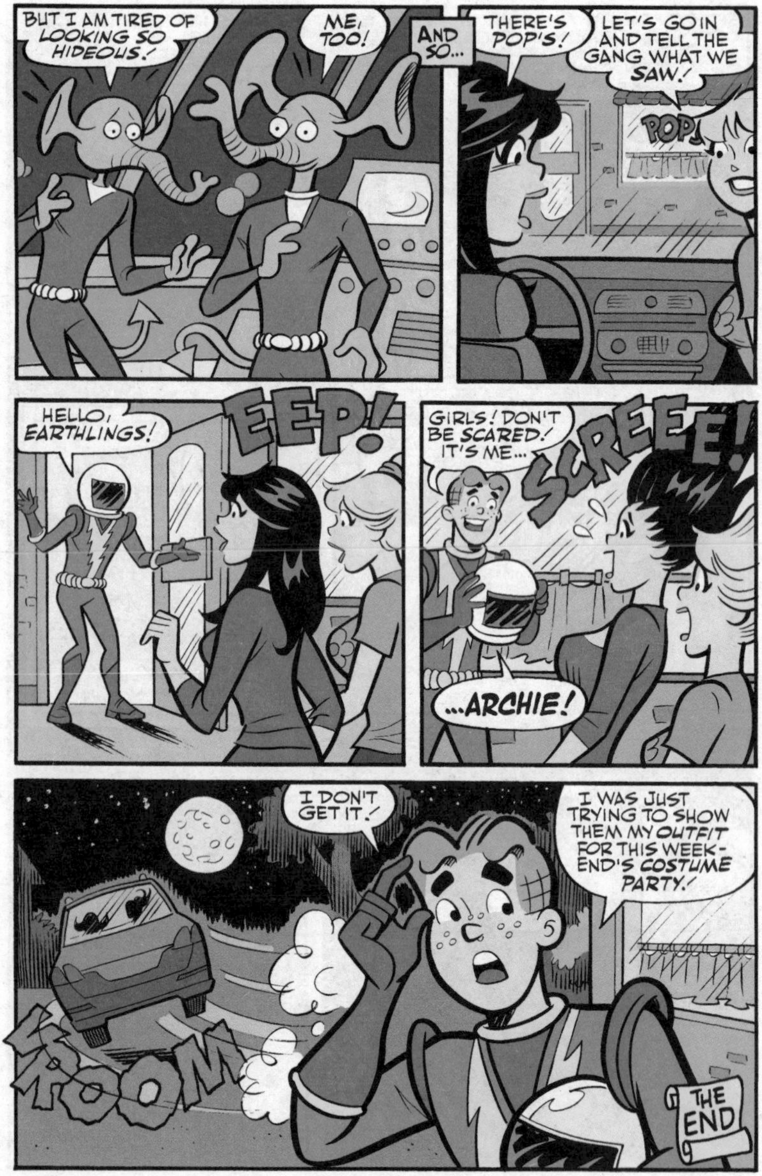
BUT I AM TIRED OF LOOKING SO HIDEOUS!
ME, TOO!
AND SO...
THERE'S POP'S!
LET'S GO IN AND TELL THE GANG WHAT WE SAW!
POP'S
HELLO, EARTHLINGS!
EEP!
GIRLS! DON'T BE SCARED! IT'S ME...
SCREEEE!
...ARCHIE!
I DON'T GET IT!
I WAS JUST TRYING TO SHOW THEM MY OUTFIT FOR THIS WEEK-END'S COSTUME PARTY!
VROOM
THE END

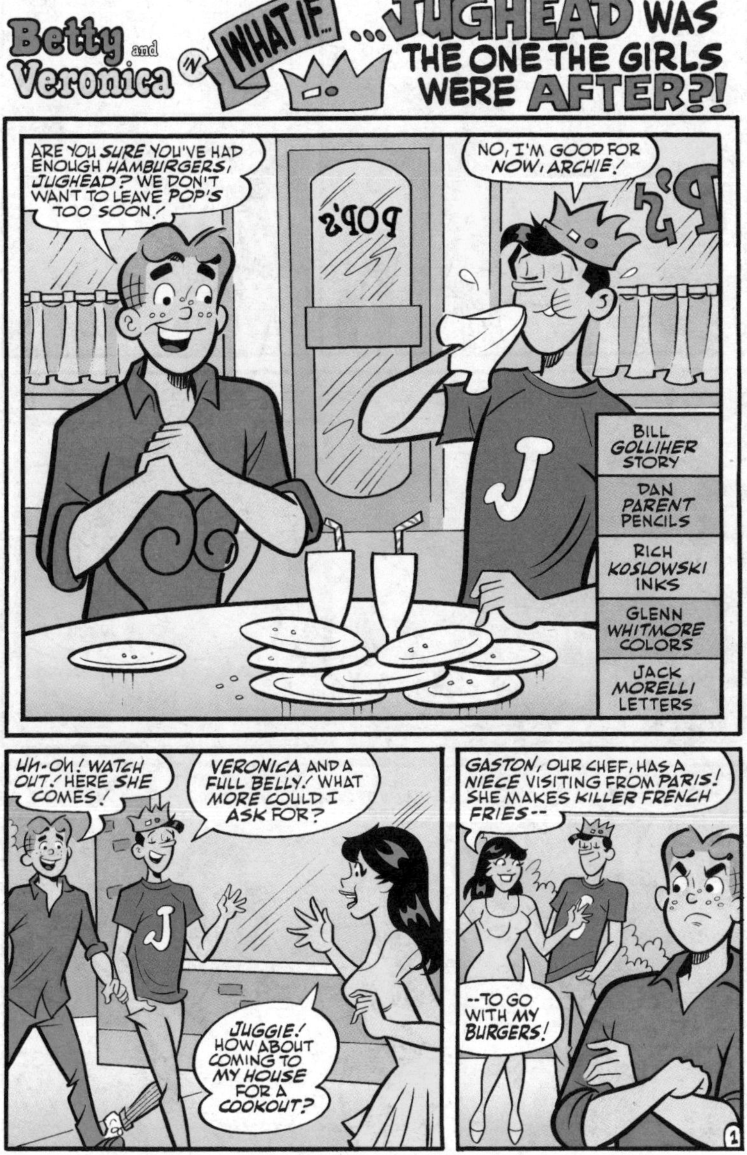
Betty and Veronica
IN
WHAT IF...
...JUGHEAD WAS THE ONE THE GIRLS WERE AFTER?!
ARE YOU SURE YOU'VE HAD ENOUGH HAMBURGERS, JUGHEAD? WE DON'T WANT TO LEAVE POP'S TOO SOON!
NO, I'M GOOD FOR NOW, ARCHIE!
POP'S
BILL GOLLIHER STORY
DAN PARENT PENCILS
RICH KOSLOWSKI INKS
GLENN WHITMORE COLORS
JACK MORELLI LETTERS
UH-OH! WATCH OUT! HERE SHE COMES!
VERONICA AND A FULL BELLY! WHAT MORE COULD I ASK FOR?
JUGGIE! HOW ABOUT COMING TO MY HOUSE FOR A COOKOUT?
GASTON, OUR CHEF, HAS A NIECE VISITING FROM PARIS! SHE MAKES KILLER FRENCH FRIES--
--TO GO WITH MY BURGERS!
1

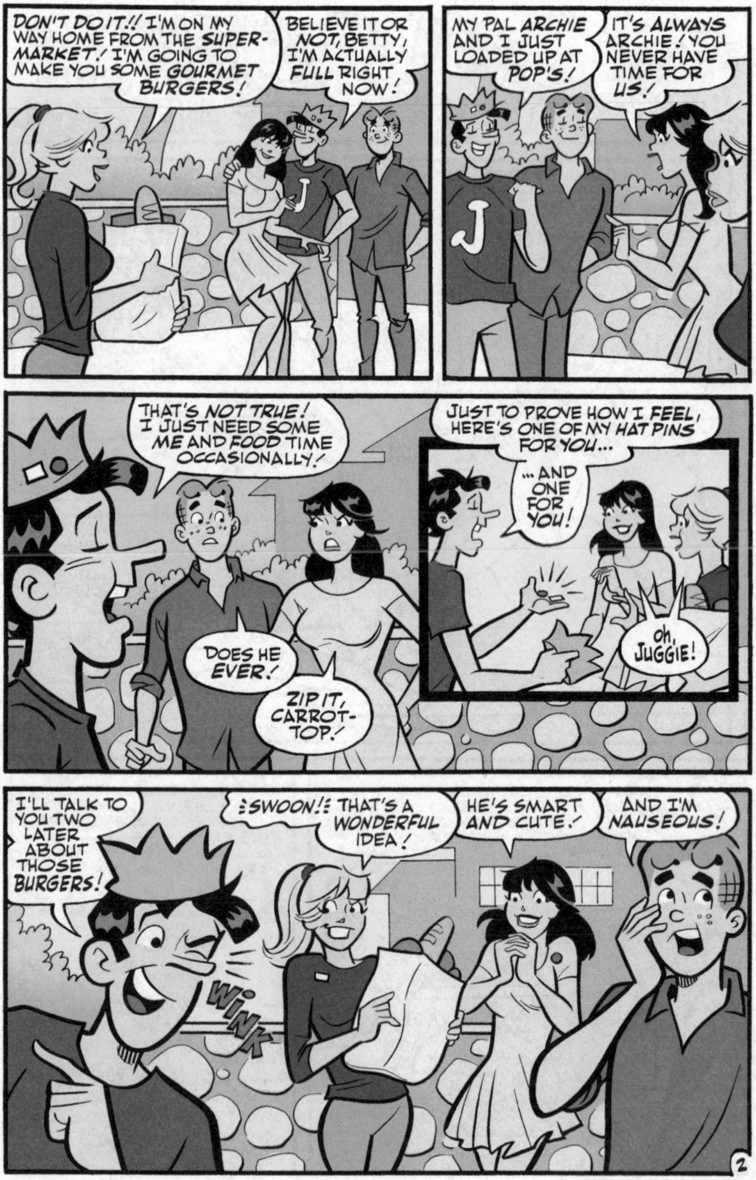
DON'T DO IT!! I'M ON MY WAY HOME FROM THE SUPER-MARKET! I'M GOING TO MAKE YOU SOME GOURMET BURGERS!
BELIEVE IT OR NOT, BETTY, I'M ACTUALLY FULL RIGHT NOW!
MY PAL ARCHIE AND I JUST LOADED UP AT POP'S!
IT'S ALWAYS ARCHIE! YOU NEVER HAVE TIME FOR US!
THAT'S NOT TRUE! I JUST NEED SOME ME AND FOOD TIME OCCASIONALLY!
DOES HE EVER!
ZIP IT, CARROT-TOP!
JUST TO PROVE HOW I FEEL, HERE'S ONE OF MY HAT PINS FOR YOU...
...AND ONE FOR YOU!
oh, JUGGIE!
I'LL TALK TO YOU TWO LATER ABOUT THOSE BURGERS!
WINK
SWOON! THAT'S A WONDERFUL IDEA!
HE'S SMART AND CUTE!
AND I'M NAUSEOUS!
2

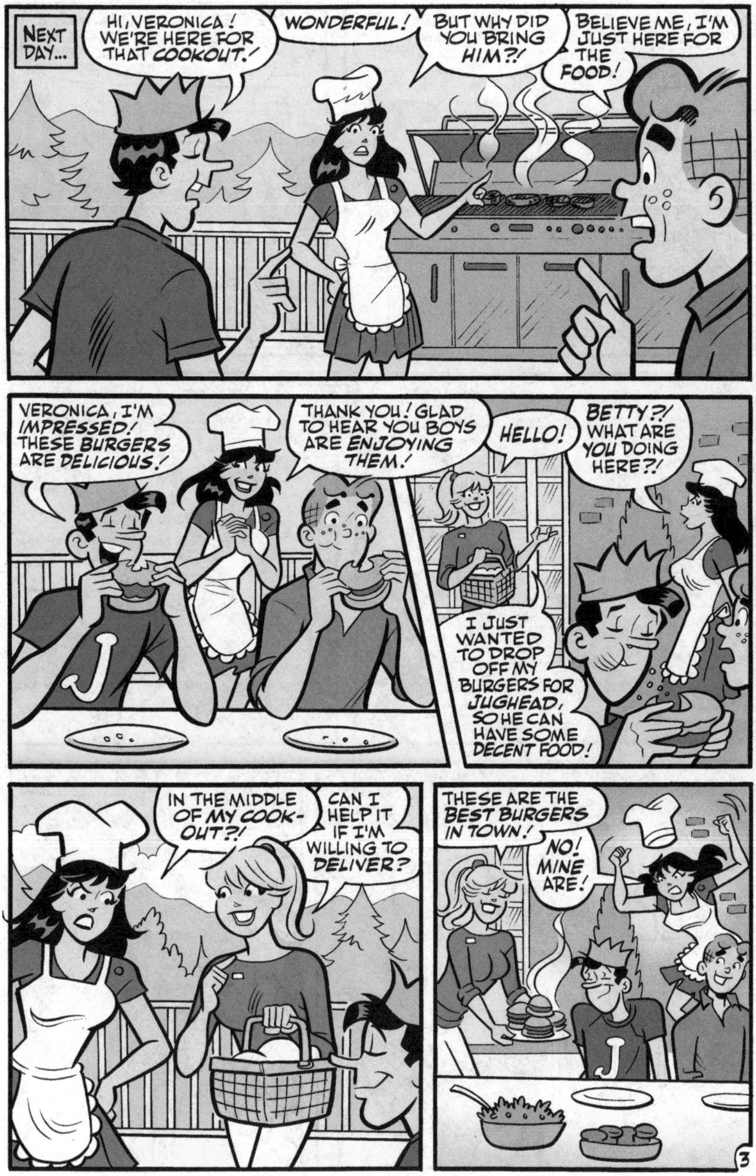
NEXT DAY...
HI, VERONICA! WE'RE HERE FOR THAT COOKOUT.!
WONDERFUL!
BUT WHY DID YOU BRING HIM?!
BELIEVE ME, I'M JUST HERE FOR THE FOOD!
VERONICA, I'M IMPRESSED! THESE BURGERS ARE DELICIOUS!
THANK YOU! GLAD TO HEAR YOU BOYS ARE ENJOYING THEM!
HELLO!
BETTY?! WHAT ARE YOU DOING HERE?!
I JUST WANTED TO DROP OFF MY BURGERS FOR JUGHEAD, SO HE CAN HAVE SOME DECENT FOOD!
IN THE MIDDLE OF MY COOK-OUT?!
CAN I HELP IT IF I'M WILLING TO DELIVER?
THESE ARE THE BEST BURGERS IN TOWN!
NO! MINE ARE!
3

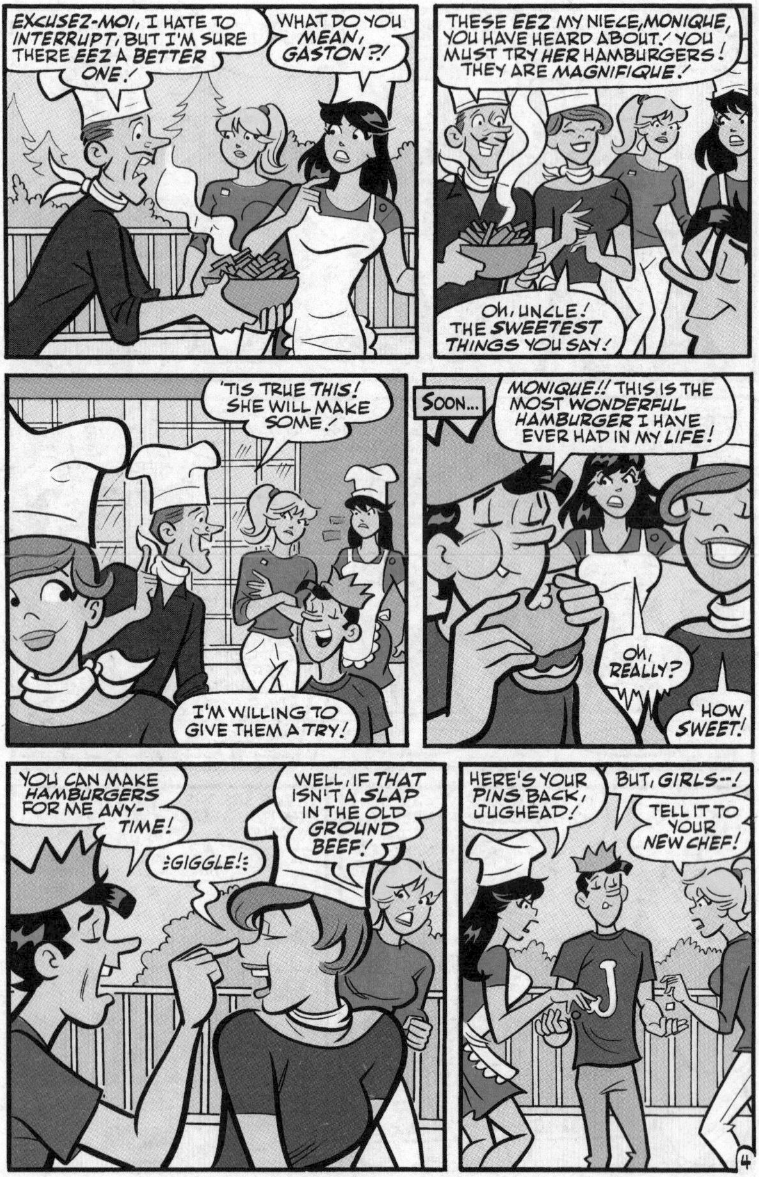
EXCUSEZ-MOI, I HATE TO INTERRUPT, BUT I'M SURE THERE EEZ A BETTER ONE!
WHAT DO YOU MEAN, GASTON?!
THESE EEZ MY NIECE, MONIQUE, YOU HAVE HEARD ABOUT! YOU MUST TRY HER HAMBURGERS! THEY ARE MAGNIFIQUE!
OH, UNCLE! THE SWEETEST THINGS YOU SAY!
'TIS TRUE THIS! SHE WILL MAKE SOME!
I'M WILLING TO GIVE THEM A TRY!
SOON...
MONIQUE!! THIS IS THE MOST WONDERFUL HAMBURGER I HAVE EVER HAD IN MY LIFE!
OH, REALLY?
HOW SWEET!
YOU CAN MAKE HAMBURGERS FOR ME ANY-TIME!
GIGGLE!
WELL, IF THAT ISN'T A SLAP IN THE OLD GROUND BEEF!
HERE'S YOUR PINS BACK, JUGHEAD!
BUT, GIRLS--!
TELL IT TO YOUR NEW CHEF!
4

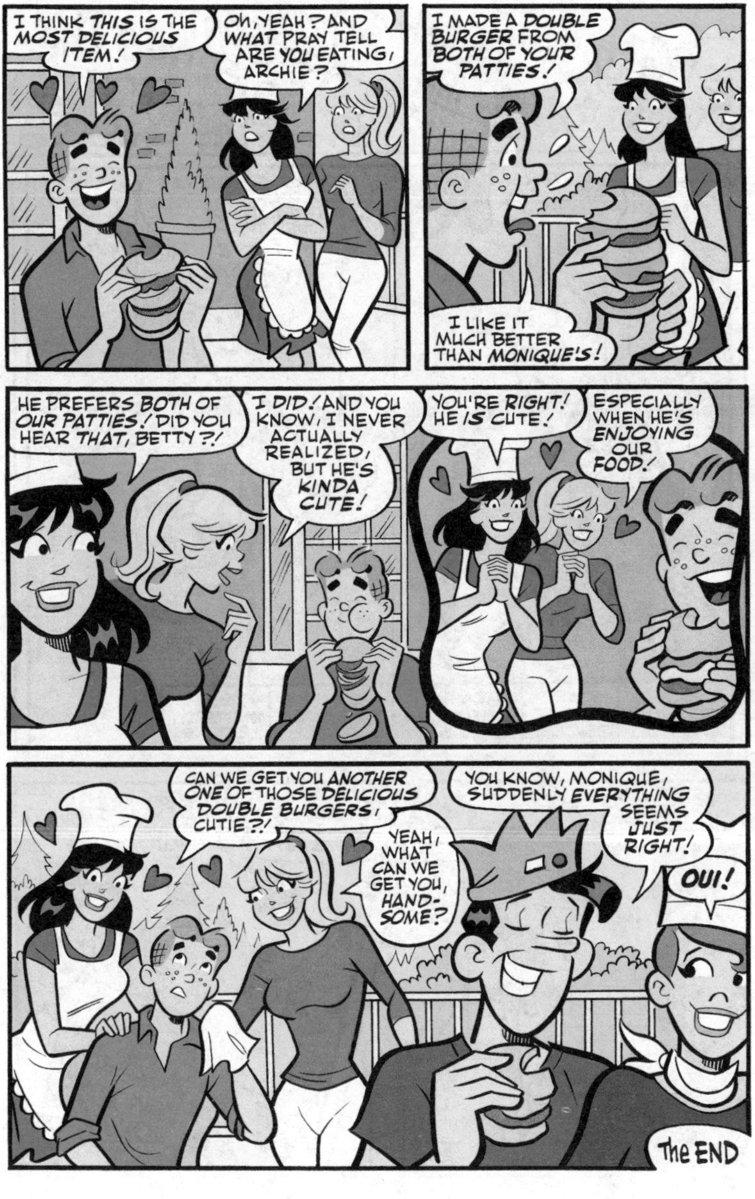
I THINK THIS IS THE MOST DELICIOUS ITEM!
OH, YEAH? AND WHAT PRAY TELL ARE YOU EATING, ARCHIE?
I MADE A DOUBLE BURGER FROM BOTH OF YOUR PATTIES!
I LIKE IT MUCH BETTER THAN MONIQUE'S!
HE PREFERS BOTH OF OUR PATTIES! DID YOU HEAR THAT, BETTY?!
I DID! AND YOU KNOW, I NEVER ACTUALLY REALIZED, BUT HE'S KINDA CUTE!
YOU'RE RIGHT! HE IS CUTE!
ESPECIALLY WHEN HE'S ENJOYING OUR FOOD!
CAN WE GET YOU ANOTHER ONE OF THOSE DELICIOUS DOUBLE BURGERS, CUTIE?!
YEAH, WHAT CAN WE GET YOU, HANDSOME?
YOU KNOW, MONIQUE, SUDDENLY EVERYTHING SEEMS JUST RIGHT!
OUI!
The END

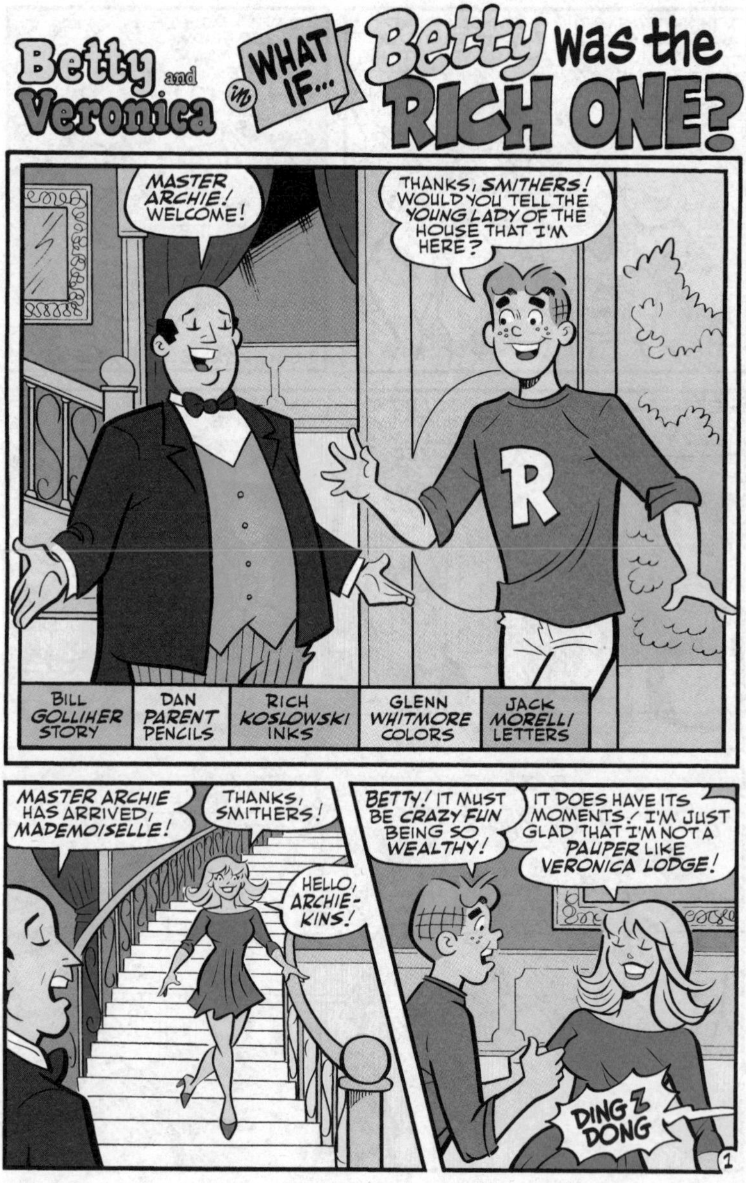
Betty and Veronica in WHAT IF... Betty was the RICH ONE?
MASTER ARCHIE! WELCOME!
THANKS, SMITHERS! WOULD YOU TELL THE YOUNG LADY OF THE HOUSE THAT I'M HERE?
BILL GOLLIHER STORY
DAN PARENT PENCILS
RICH KOSLOWSKI INKS
GLENN WHITMORE COLORS
JACK MORELLI LETTERS
MASTER ARCHIE HAS ARRIVED, MADEMOISELLE!
THANKS, SMITHERS!
HELLO, ARCHIE-KINS!
BETTY! IT MUST BE CRAZY FUN BEING SO WEALTHY!
IT DOES HAVE ITS MOMENTS! I'M JUST GLAD THAT I'M NOT A PAUPER LIKE VERONICA LODGE!
DING DONG
1

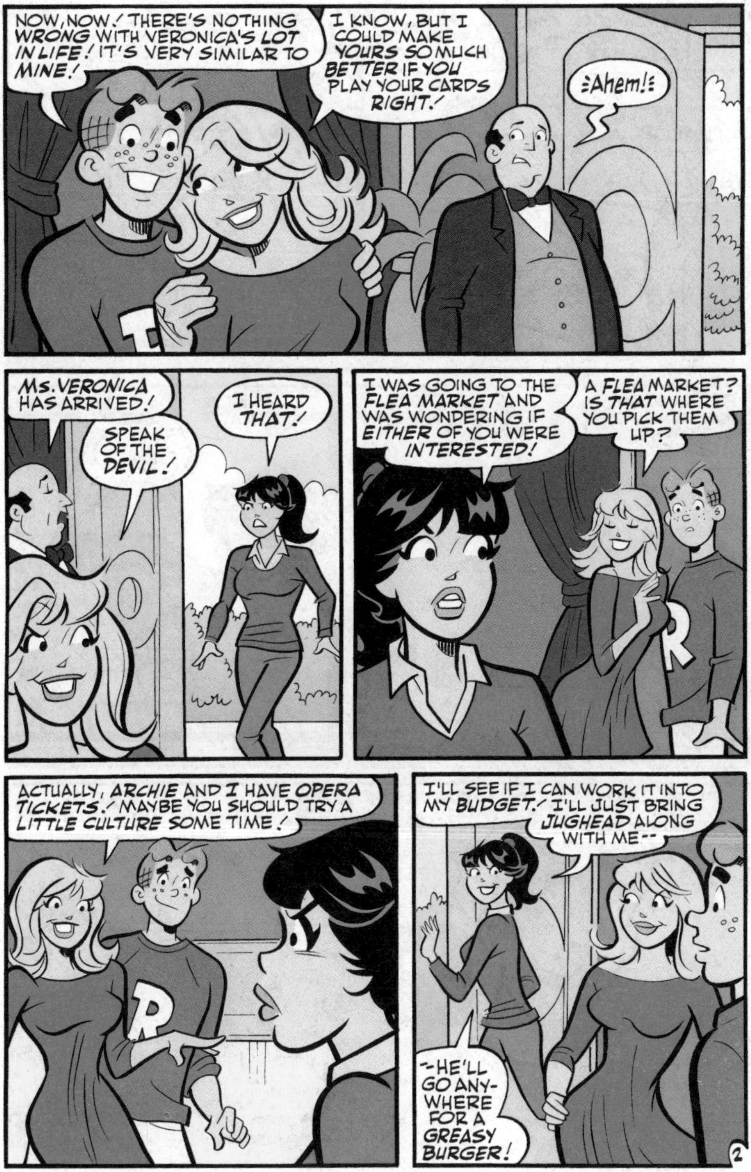
NOW, NOW! THERE'S NOTHING WRONG WITH VERONICA'S LOT IN LIFE! IT'S VERY SIMILAR TO MINE!
I KNOW, BUT I COULD MAKE YOURS SO MUCH BETTER IF YOU PLAY YOUR CARDS RIGHT!
Ahem!
MS. VERONICA HAS ARRIVED!
SPEAK OF THE DEVIL!
I HEARD THAT!
I WAS GOING TO THE FLEA MARKET AND WAS WONDERING IF EITHER OF YOU WERE INTERESTED!
A FLEA MARKET? IS THAT WHERE YOU PICK THEM UP?
ACTUALLY, ARCHIE AND I HAVE OPERA TICKETS! MAYBE YOU SHOULD TRY A LITTLE CULTURE SOME TIME!
I'LL SEE IF I CAN WORK IT INTO MY BUDGET! I'LL JUST BRING JUGHEAD ALONG WITH ME--
--HE'LL GO ANYWHERE FOR A GREASY BURGER!
2

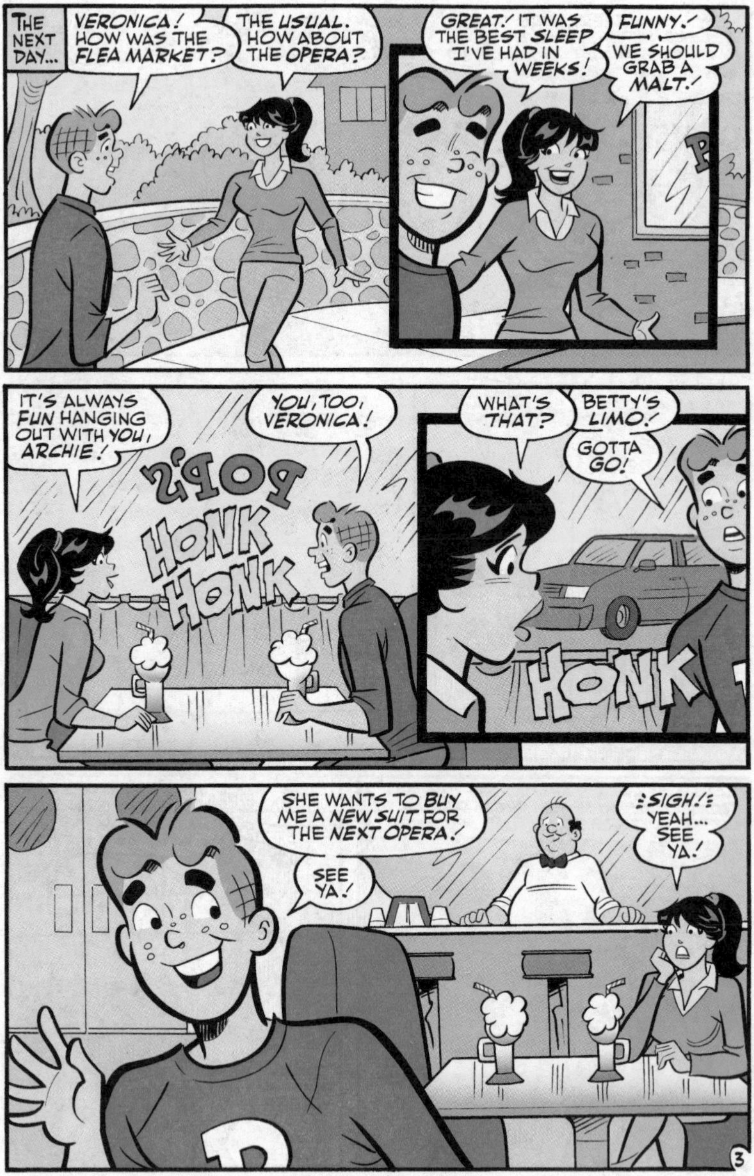
THE NEXT DAY...
VERONICA! HOW WAS THE FLEA MARKET?
THE USUAL. HOW ABOUT THE OPERA?
GREAT! IT WAS THE BEST SLEEP I'VE HAD IN WEEKS!
FUNNY!
WE SHOULD GRAB A MALT!
IT'S ALWAYS FUN HANGING OUT WITH YOU, ARCHIE!
YOU, TOO, VERONICA!
POP'S
HONK HONK
WHAT'S THAT?
BETTY'S LIMO!
GOTTA GO!
HONK
SHE WANTS TO BUY ME A NEW SUIT FOR THE NEXT OPERA!
SEE YA!
SIGH! YEAH... SEE YA!
3

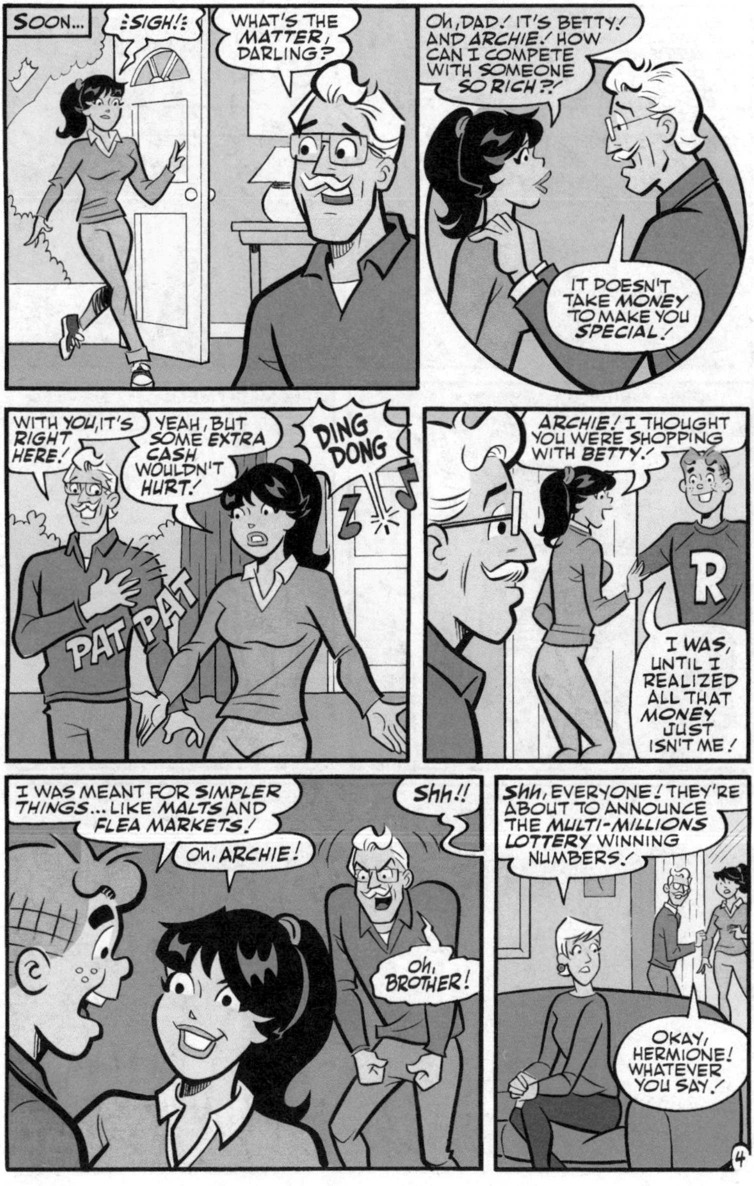
SOON...
:SIGH!:
WHAT'S THE MATTER, DARLING?
Oh, DAD! IT'S BETTY! AND ARCHIE! HOW CAN I COMPETE WITH SOMEONE SO RICH?!
IT DOESN'T TAKE MONEY TO MAKE YOU SPECIAL!
WITH YOU, IT'S RIGHT HERE!
PAT PAT
YEAH, BUT SOME EXTRA CASH WOULDN'T HURT!
DING DONG
ARCHIE! I THOUGHT YOU WERE SHOPPING WITH BETTY!
I WAS, UNTIL I REALIZED ALL THAT MONEY JUST ISN'T ME!
I WAS MEANT FOR SIMPLER THINGS... LIKE MALTS AND FLEA MARKETS!
Oh, ARCHIE!
Shh!!
Oh, BROTHER!
Shh, EVERYONE! THEY'RE ABOUT TO ANNOUNCE THE MULTI-MILLIONS LOTTERY WINNING NUMBERS!
OKAY, HERMIONE! WHATEVER YOU SAY!
4

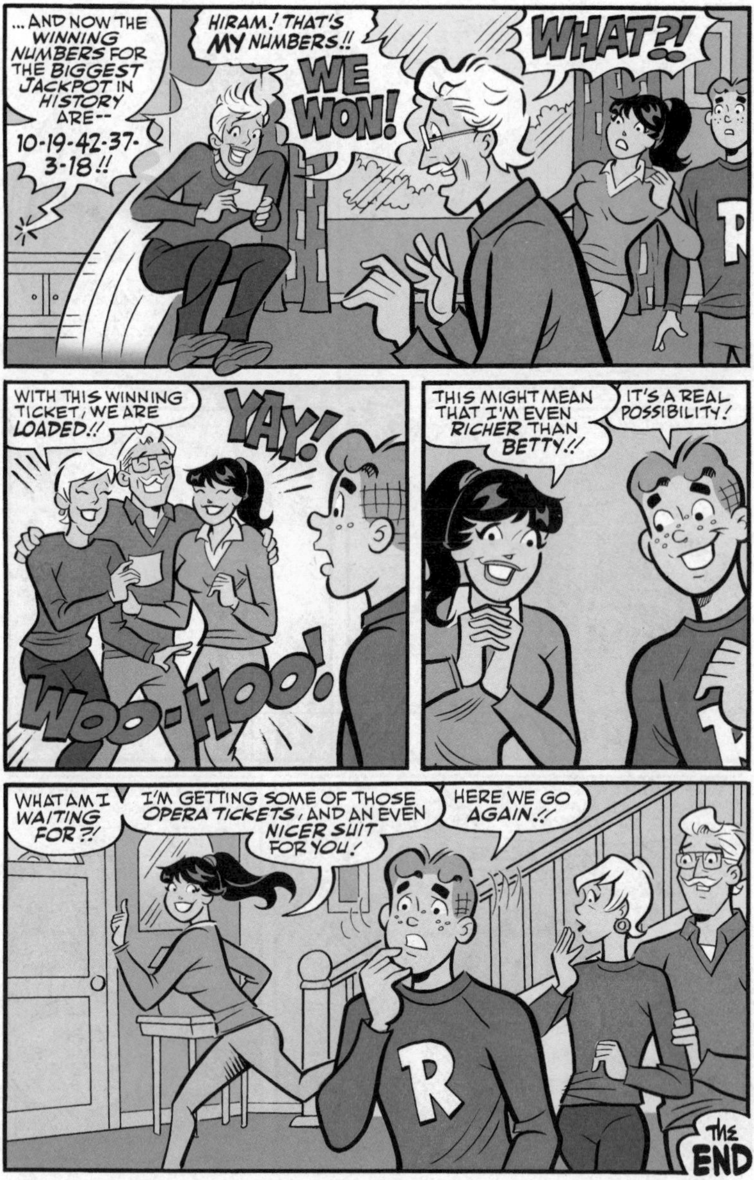
...AND NOW THE WINNING NUMBERS FOR THE BIGGEST JACKPOT IN HISTORY ARE-- 10-19-42-37-3-18!!
HIRAM! THAT'S MY NUMBERS!!
WE WON!
WHAT?!
WITH THIS WINNING TICKET, WE ARE LOADED!!
YAY!
WOO-HOO!
THIS MIGHT MEAN THAT I'M EVEN RICHER THAN BETTY!!
IT'S A REAL POSSIBILITY!
WHAT AM I WAITING FOR?!
I'M GETTING SOME OF THOSE OPERA TICKETS, AND AN EVEN NICER SUIT FOR YOU!
HERE WE GO AGAIN!!
THE END

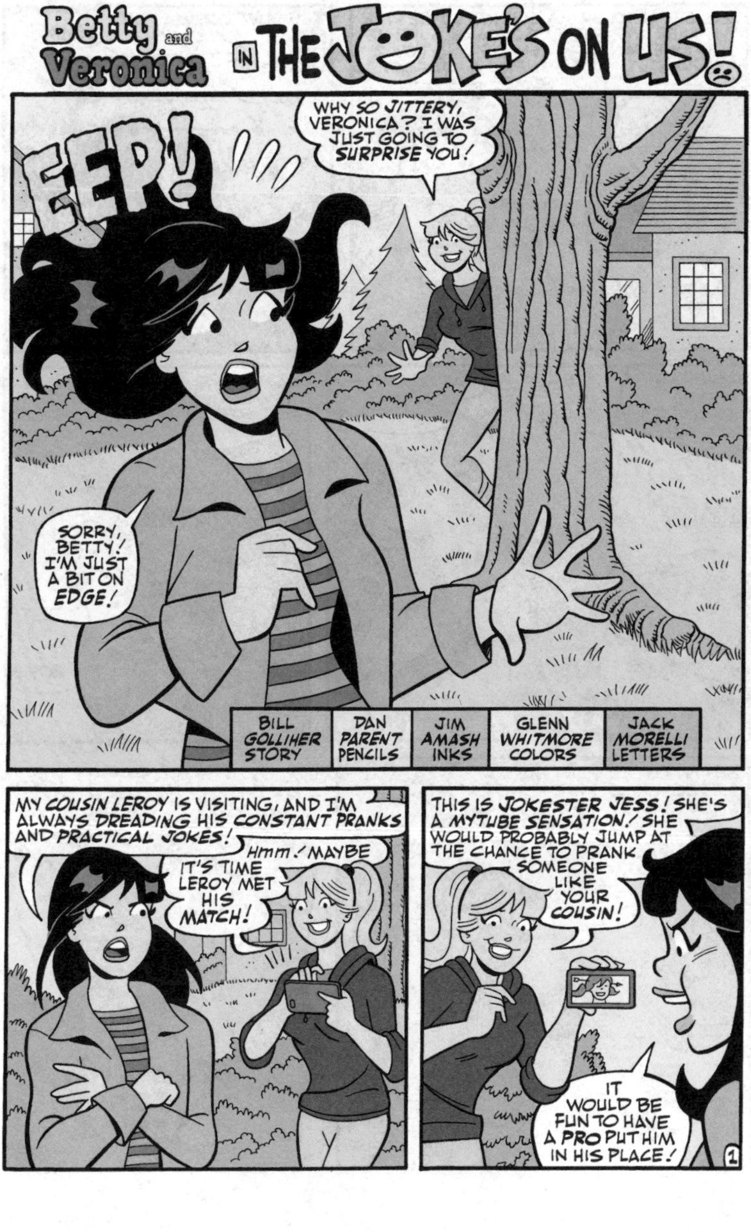
Betty and Veronica
IN THE JOKE'S ON US!
EEP!
WHY SO JITTERY, VERONICA? I WAS JUST GOING TO SURPRISE YOU!
SORRY, BETTY! I'M JUST A BIT ON EDGE!
BILL GOLLIHER STORY
DAN PARENT PENCILS
JIM AMASH INKS
GLENN WHITMORE COLORS
JACK MORELLI LETTERS
MY COUSIN LEROY IS VISITING, AND I'M ALWAYS DREADING HIS CONSTANT PRANKS AND PRACTICAL JOKES!
Hmm! MAYBE IT'S TIME LEROY MET HIS MATCH!
THIS IS JOKESTER JESS! SHE'S A MYTUBE SENSATION! SHE WOULD PROBABLY JUMP AT THE CHANCE TO PRANK SOMEONE LIKE YOUR COUSIN!
IT WOULD BE FUN TO HAVE A PRO PUT HIM IN HIS PLACE!
1

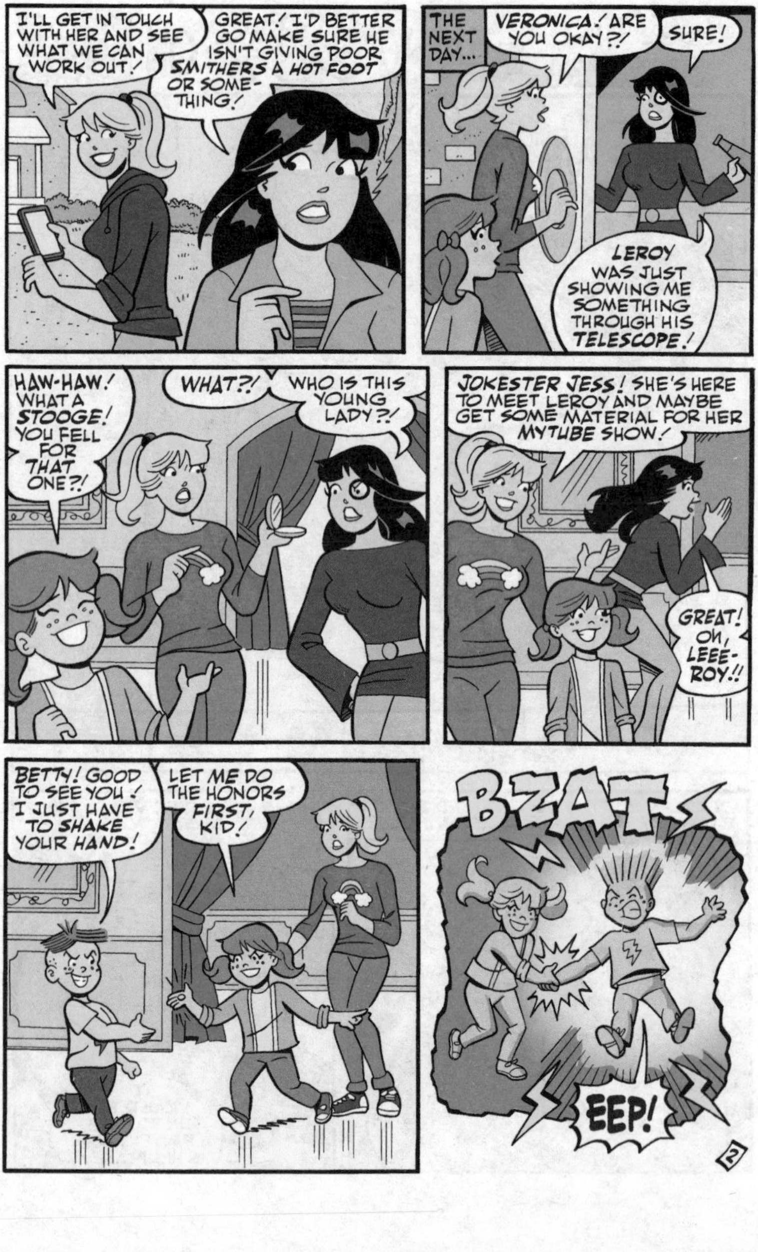
I'LL GET IN TOUCH WITH HER AND SEE WHAT WE CAN WORK OUT!
GREAT! I'D BETTER GO MAKE SURE HE ISN'T GIVING POOR SMITHERS A HOT FOOT OR SOME-THING!
THE NEXT DAY...
VERONICA! ARE YOU OKAY?!
SURE!
LEROY WAS JUST SHOWING ME SOMETHING THROUGH HIS TELESCOPE!
HAW-HAW! WHAT A STOOGE! YOU FELL FOR THAT ONE?!
WHAT?!
WHO IS THIS YOUNG LADY?!
JOKESTER JESS! SHE'S HERE TO MEET LEROY AND MAYBE GET SOME MATERIAL FOR HER MYTUBE SHOW!
GREAT! OH, LEEE-ROY!!
BETTY! GOOD TO SEE YOU! I JUST HAVE TO SHAKE YOUR HAND!
LET ME DO THE HONORS FIRST, KID!
BZAT
EEP!
2

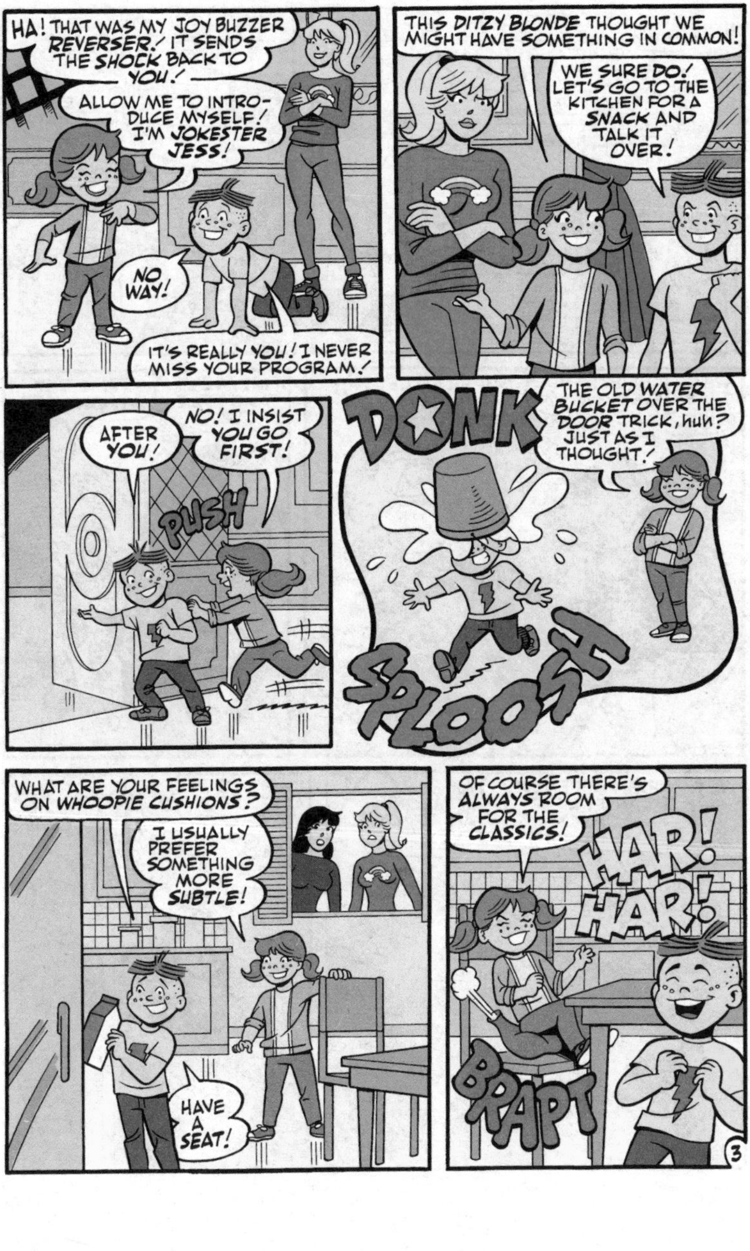
HA! THAT WAS MY JOY BUZZER REVERSER! IT SENDS THE SHOCK BACK TO YOU!
ALLOW ME TO INTRODUCE MYSELF! I'M JOKESTER JESS!
NO WAY!
IT'S REALLY YOU! I NEVER MISS YOUR PROGRAM!
THIS DITZY BLONDE THOUGHT WE MIGHT HAVE SOMETHING IN COMMON!
WE SURE DO! LET'S GO TO THE KITCHEN FOR A SNACK AND TALK IT OVER!
AFTER YOU!
NO! I INSIST YOU GO FIRST!
PUSH
DONK
THE OLD WATER BUCKET OVER THE DOOR TRICK, huh? JUST AS I THOUGHT!
SPLOOSH
WHAT ARE YOUR FEELINGS ON WHOOPIE CUSHIONS?
I USUALLY PREFER SOMETHING MORE SUBTLE!
HAVE A SEAT!
OF COURSE THERE'S ALWAYS ROOM FOR THE CLASSICS!
HAR! HAR!
BRAPT
3

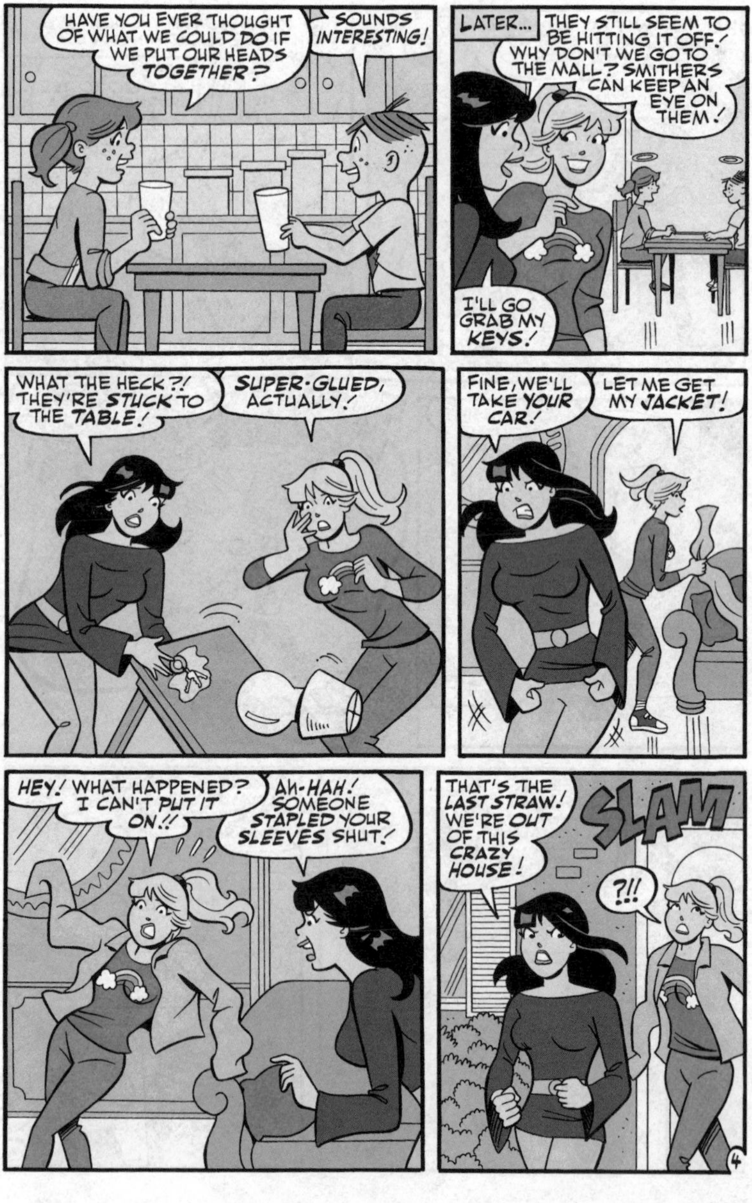
HAVE YOU EVER THOUGHT OF WHAT WE COULD DO IF WE PUT OUR HEADS TOGETHER?
SOUNDS INTERESTING!
LATER...
THEY STILL SEEM TO BE HITTING IT OFF! WHY DON'T WE GO TO THE MALL? SMITHERS CAN KEEP AN EYE ON THEM!
I'LL GO GRAB MY KEYS!
WHAT THE HECK?! THEY'RE STUCK TO THE TABLE!
SUPER-GLUED, ACTUALLY!
FINE, WE'LL TAKE YOUR CAR!
LET ME GET MY JACKET!
HEY! WHAT HAPPENED? I CAN'T PUT IT ON!!
AH-HAH! SOMEONE STAPLED YOUR SLEEVES SHUT!
THAT'S THE LAST STRAW! WE'RE OUT OF THIS CRAZY HOUSE!
SLAM
?!!
4

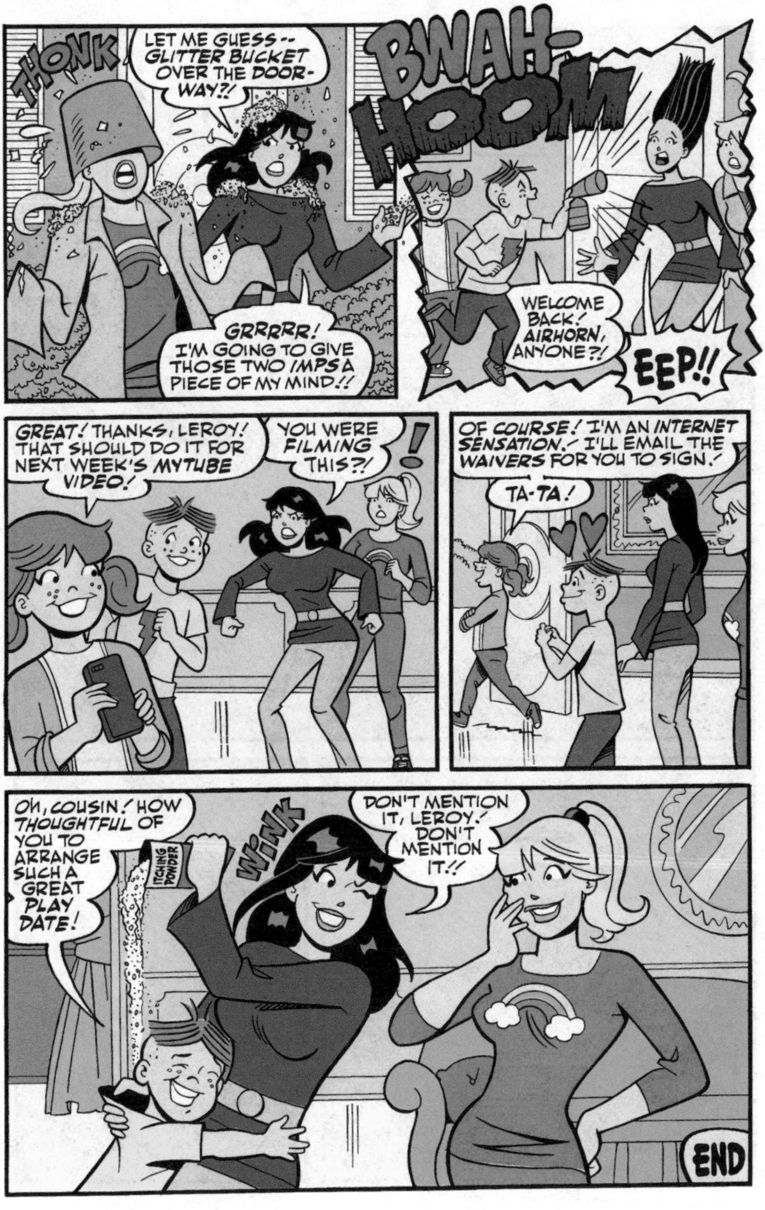
THONK
LET ME GUESS -- GLITTER BUCKET OVER THE DOORWAY?!
GRRRRR! I'M GOING TO GIVE THOSE TWO IMPS A PIECE OF MY MIND!!
BWAH-HOOM
WELCOME BACK! AIRHORN, ANYONE?!
EEP!!
GREAT! THANKS, LEROY! THAT SHOULD DO IT FOR NEXT WEEK'S MYTUBE VIDEO!
YOU WERE FILMING THIS?!
!
OF COURSE! I'M AN INTERNET SENSATION. I'LL EMAIL THE WAIVERS FOR YOU TO SIGN.
TA-TA!
OH, COUSIN! HOW THOUGHTFUL OF YOU TO ARRANGE SUCH A GREAT PLAY DATE!
WINK
ITCHING POWDER
DON'T MENTION IT, LEROY. DON'T MENTION IT!!
END

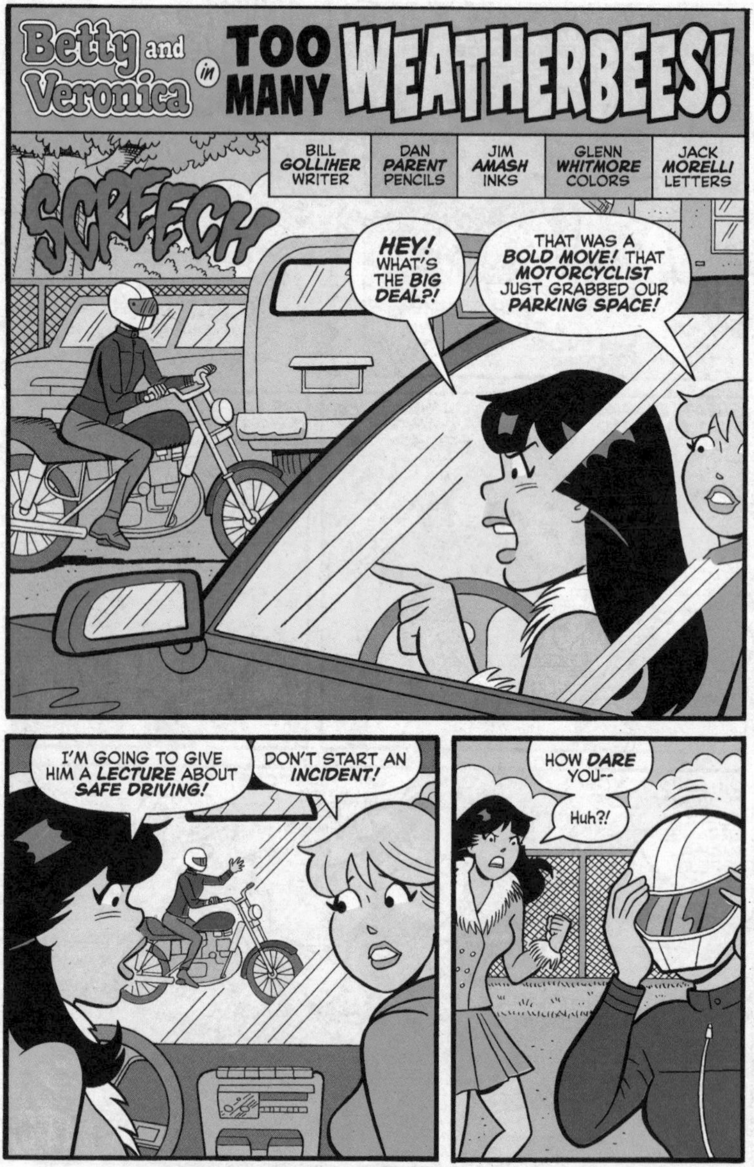
Betty and Veronica in TOO MANY WEATHERBEES!
BILL GOLLIHER WRITER
DAN PARENT PENCILS
JIM AMASH INKS
GLENN WHITMORE COLORS
JACK MORELLI LETTERS
SCREECH
HEY! WHAT'S THE BIG DEAL?!
THAT WAS A BOLD MOVE! THAT MOTORCYCLIST JUST GRABBED OUR PARKING SPACE!
I'M GOING TO GIVE HIM A LECTURE ABOUT SAFE DRIVING!
DON'T START AN INCIDENT!
HOW DARE YOU--
Huh?!

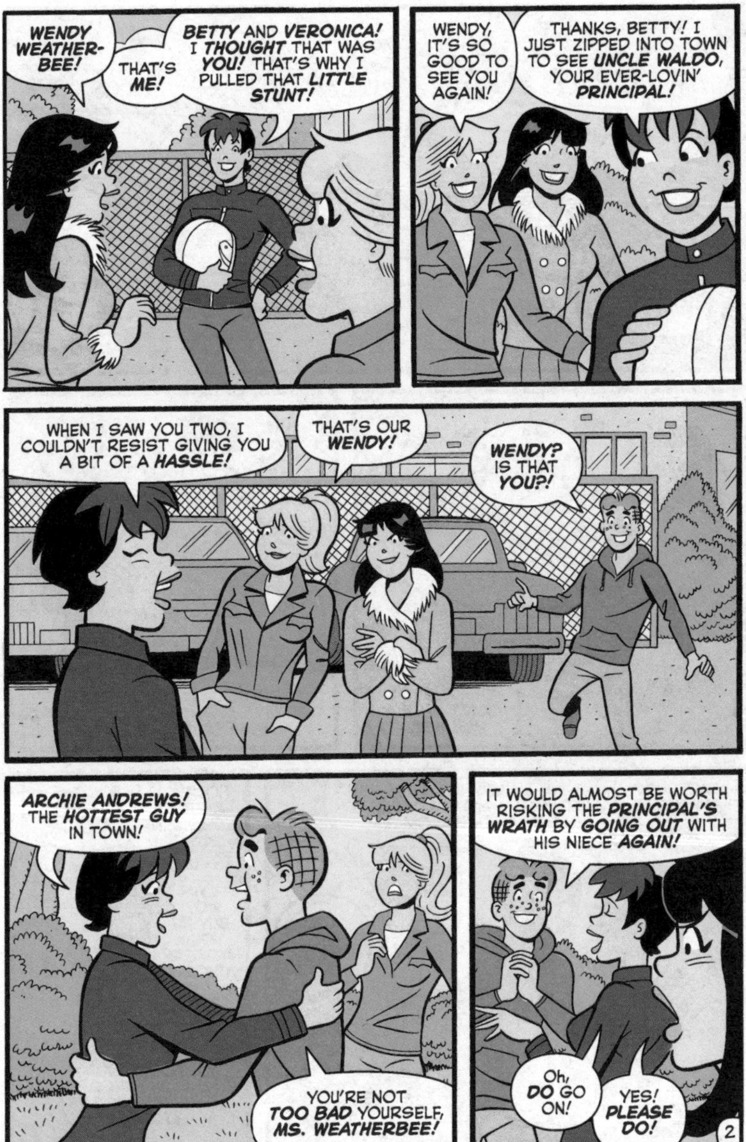
WENDY WEATHER-BEE!
THAT'S ME!
BETTY AND VERONICA! I THOUGHT THAT WAS YOU! THAT'S WHY I PULLED THAT LITTLE STUNT!
WENDY, IT'S SO GOOD TO SEE YOU AGAIN!
THANKS, BETTY! I JUST ZIPPED INTO TOWN TO SEE UNCLE WALDO, YOUR EVER-LOVIN' PRINCIPAL!
WHEN I SAW YOU TWO, I COULDN'T RESIST GIVING YOU A BIT OF A HASSLE!
THAT'S OUR WENDY!
WENDY? IS THAT YOU?!
ARCHIE ANDREWS! THE HOTTEST GUY IN TOWN!
YOU'RE NOT TOO BAD YOURSELF, MS. WEATHERBEE!
IT WOULD ALMOST BE WORTH RISKING THE PRINCIPAL'S WRATH BY GOING OUT WITH HIS NIECE AGAIN!
Oh, DO GO ON!
YES! PLEASE DO!
2

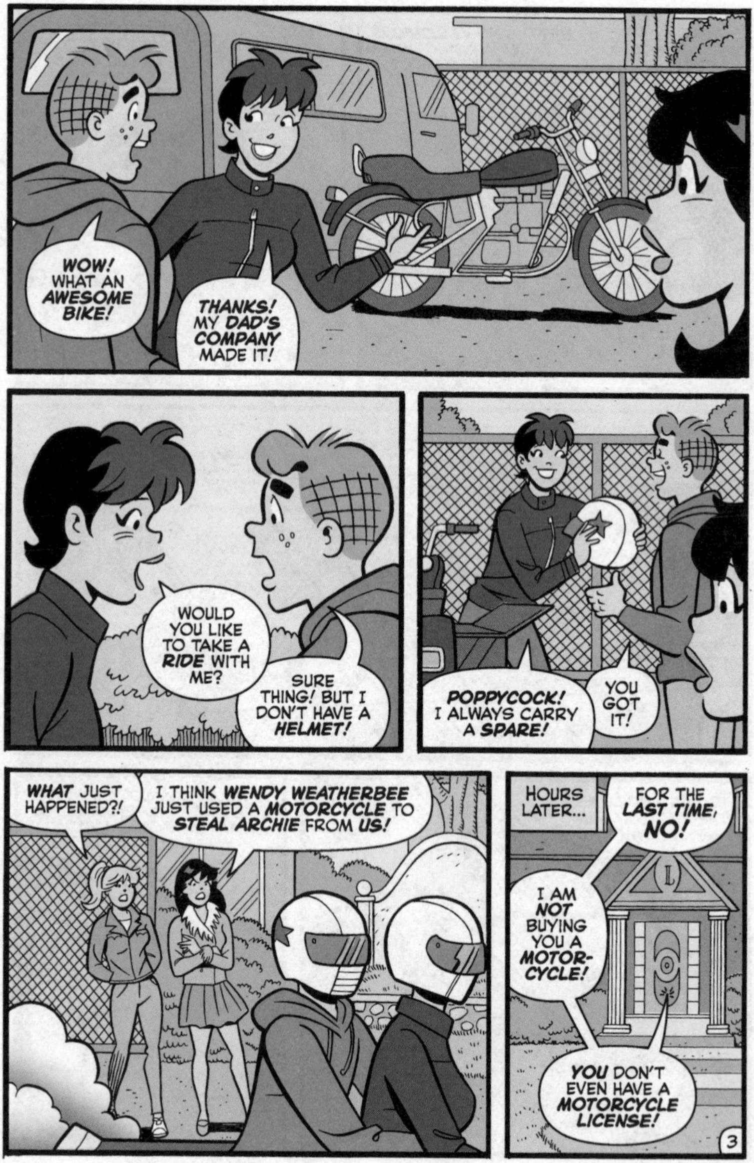
WOW! WHAT AN AWESOME BIKE!
THANKS! MY DAD'S COMPANY MADE IT!
WOULD YOU LIKE TO TAKE A RIDE WITH ME?
SURE THING! BUT I DON'T HAVE A HELMET!
POPPYCOCK! I ALWAYS CARRY A SPARE!
YOU GOT IT!
WHAT JUST HAPPENED?!
I THINK WENDY WEATHERBEE JUST USED A MOTORCYCLE TO STEAL ARCHIE FROM US!
HOURS LATER...
FOR THE LAST TIME, NO!
I AM NOT BUYING YOU A MOTOR-CYCLE!
YOU DON'T EVEN HAVE A MOTORCYCLE LICENSE!
3

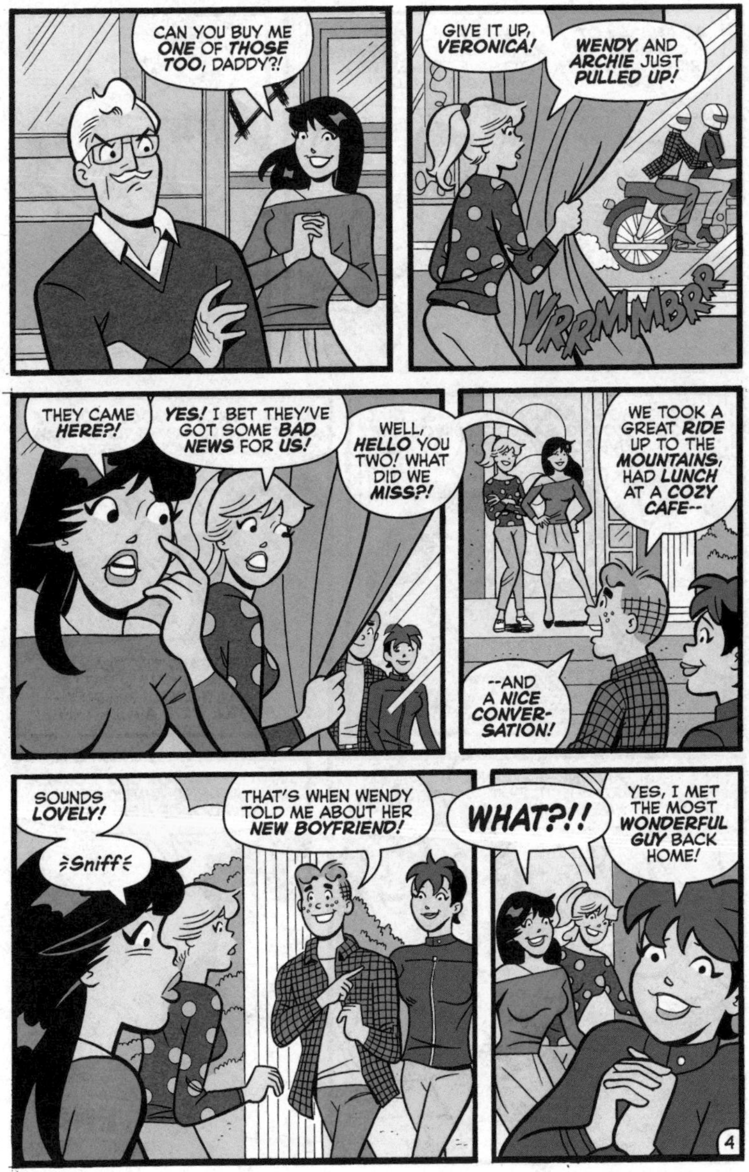
CAN YOU BUY ME ONE OF THOSE TOO, DADDY?!
GIVE IT UP, VERONICA!
WENDY AND ARCHIE JUST PULLED UP!
VRRMMBRR
THEY CAME HERE?!
YES! I BET THEY'VE GOT SOME BAD NEWS FOR US!
WELL, HELLO YOU TWO! WHAT DID WE MISS?!
WE TOOK A GREAT RIDE UP TO THE MOUNTAINS, HAD LUNCH AT A COZY CAFE--
--AND A NICE CONVER-SATION!
SOUNDS LOVELY!
Sniff
THAT'S WHEN WENDY TOLD ME ABOUT HER NEW BOYFRIEND!
WHAT?!!
YES, I MET THE MOST WONDERFUL GUY BACK HOME!
4

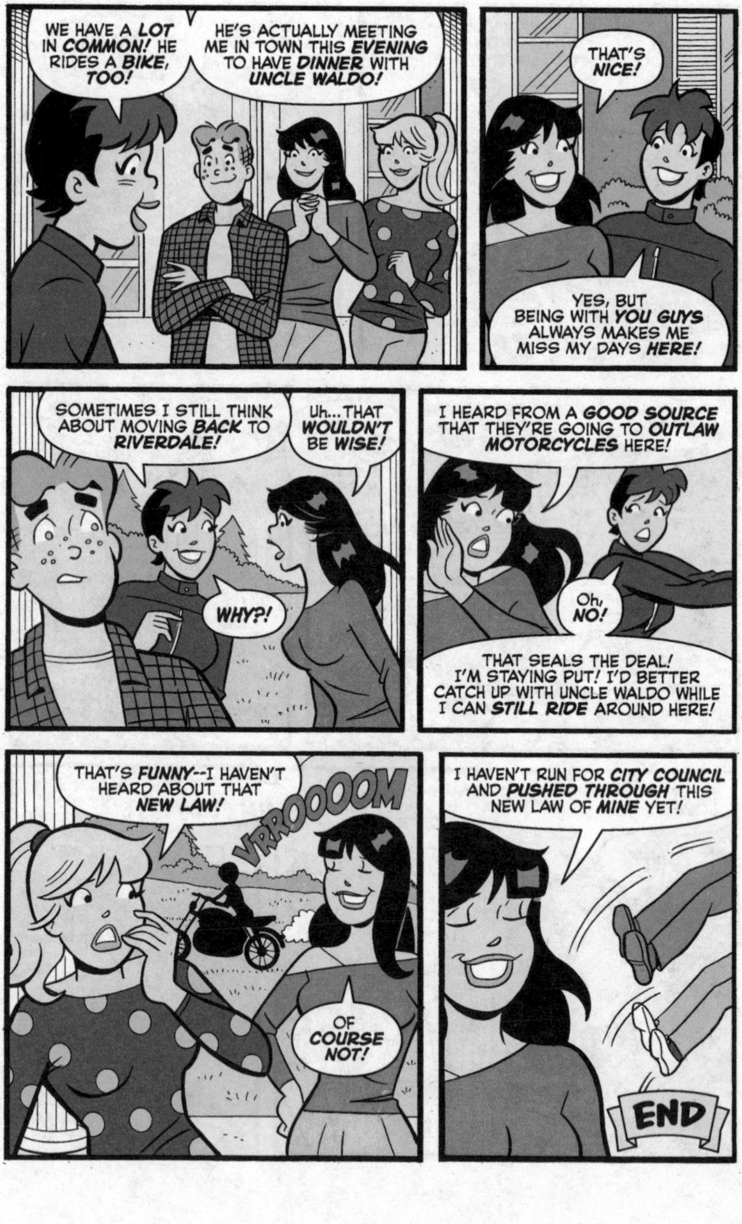
WE HAVE A LOT IN COMMON! HE RIDES A BIKE, TOO!
HE'S ACTUALLY MEETING ME IN TOWN THIS EVENING TO HAVE DINNER WITH UNCLE WALDO!
THAT'S NICE!
YES, BUT BEING WITH YOU GUYS ALWAYS MAKES ME MISS MY DAYS HERE!
SOMETIMES I STILL THINK ABOUT MOVING BACK TO RIVERDALE!
Uh...THAT WOULDN'T BE WISE!
WHY?!
I HEARD FROM A GOOD SOURCE THAT THEY'RE GOING TO OUTLAW MOTORCYCLES HERE!
Oh, NO!
THAT SEALS THE DEAL! I'M STAYING PUT! I'D BETTER CATCH UP WITH UNCLE WALDO WHILE I CAN STILL RIDE AROUND HERE!
THAT'S FUNNY--I HAVEN'T HEARD ABOUT THAT NEW LAW!
VRROOOOOM
OF COURSE NOT!
I HAVEN'T RUN FOR CITY COUNCIL AND PUSHED THROUGH THIS NEW LAW OF MINE YET!
END

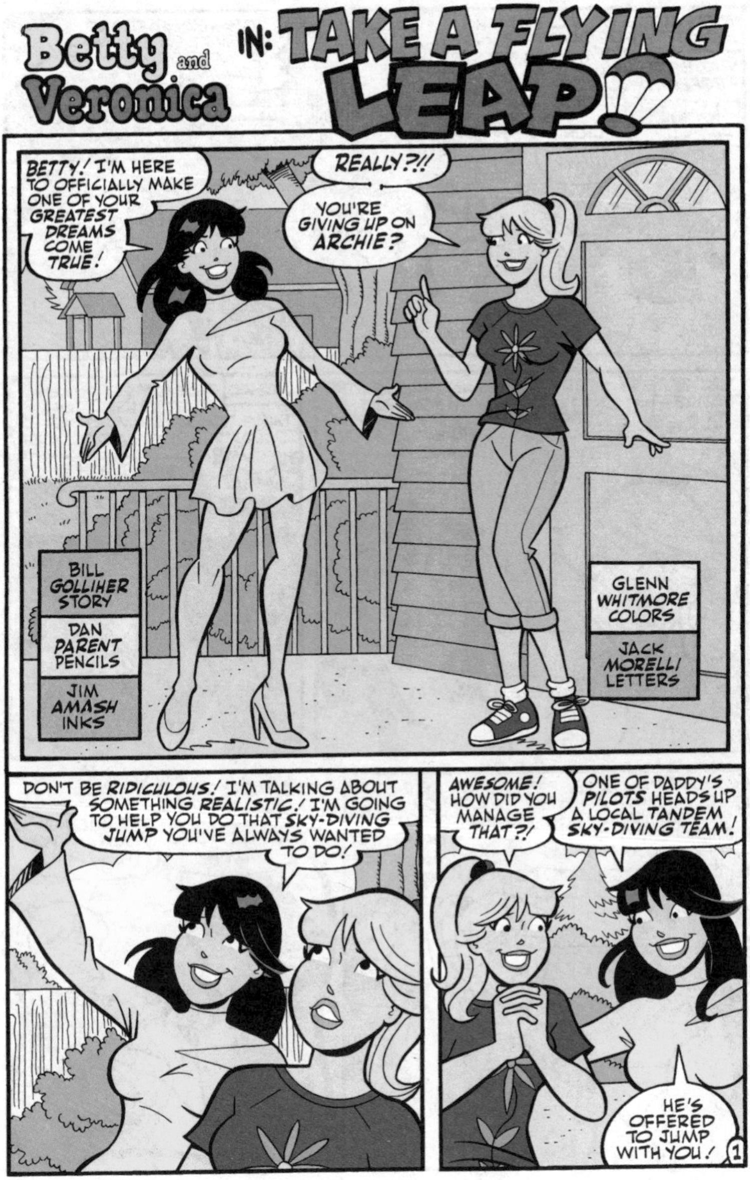
Betty and Veronica
IN: TAKE A FLYING LEAP!
BETTY! I'M HERE TO OFFICIALLY MAKE ONE OF YOUR GREATEST DREAMS COME TRUE!
REALLY?!!
YOU'RE GIVING UP ON ARCHIE?
BILL GOLLIHER STORY
DAN PARENT PENCILS
JIM AMASH INKS
GLENN WHITMORE COLORS
JACK MORELLI LETTERS
DON'T BE RIDICULOUS! I'M TALKING ABOUT SOMETHING REALISTIC! I'M GOING TO HELP YOU DO THAT SKY-DIVING JUMP YOU'VE ALWAYS WANTED TO DO!
AWESOME! HOW DID YOU MANAGE THAT?!
ONE OF DADDY'S PILOTS HEADS UP A LOCAL TANDEM SKY-DIVING TEAM!
HE'S OFFERED TO JUMP WITH YOU!
1

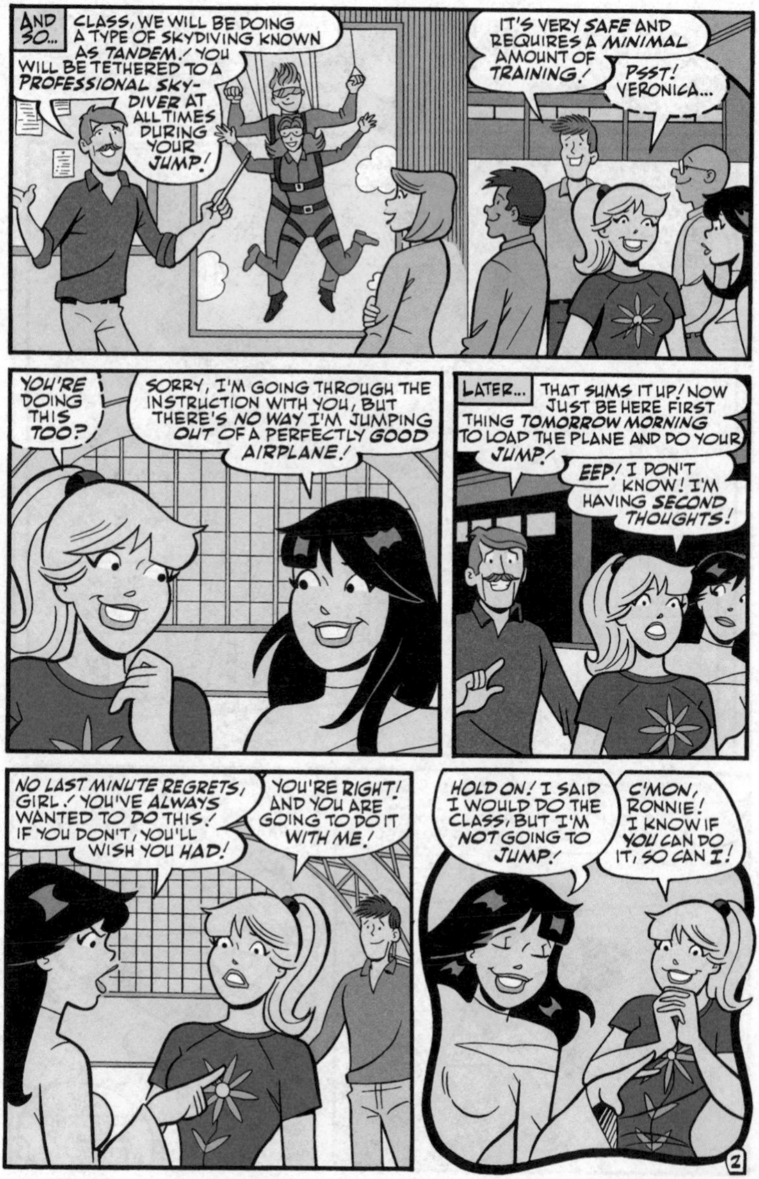
AND SO...
CLASS, WE WILL BE DOING A TYPE OF SKYDIVING KNOWN AS TANDEM! YOU WILL BE TETHERED TO A PROFESSIONAL SKY-DIVER AT ALL TIMES DURING YOUR JUMP!
IT'S VERY SAFE AND REQUIRES A MINIMAL AMOUNT OF TRAINING!
PSST! VERONICA...
YOU'RE DOING THIS TOO?
SORRY, I'M GOING THROUGH THE INSTRUCTION WITH YOU, BUT THERE'S NO WAY I'M JUMPING OUT OF A PERFECTLY GOOD AIRPLANE!
LATER...
THAT SUMS IT UP! NOW JUST BE HERE FIRST THING TOMORROW MORNING TO LOAD THE PLANE AND DO YOUR JUMP!
EEP! I DON'T KNOW! I'M HAVING SECOND THOUGHTS!
NO LAST MINUTE REGRETS, GIRL! YOU'VE ALWAYS WANTED TO DO THIS! IF YOU DON'T, YOU'LL WISH YOU HAD!
YOU'RE RIGHT! AND YOU ARE GOING TO DO IT WITH ME!
HOLD ON! I SAID I WOULD DO THE CLASS, BUT I'M NOT GOING TO JUMP!
C'MON, RONNIE! I KNOW IF YOU CAN DO IT, SO CAN I!
2

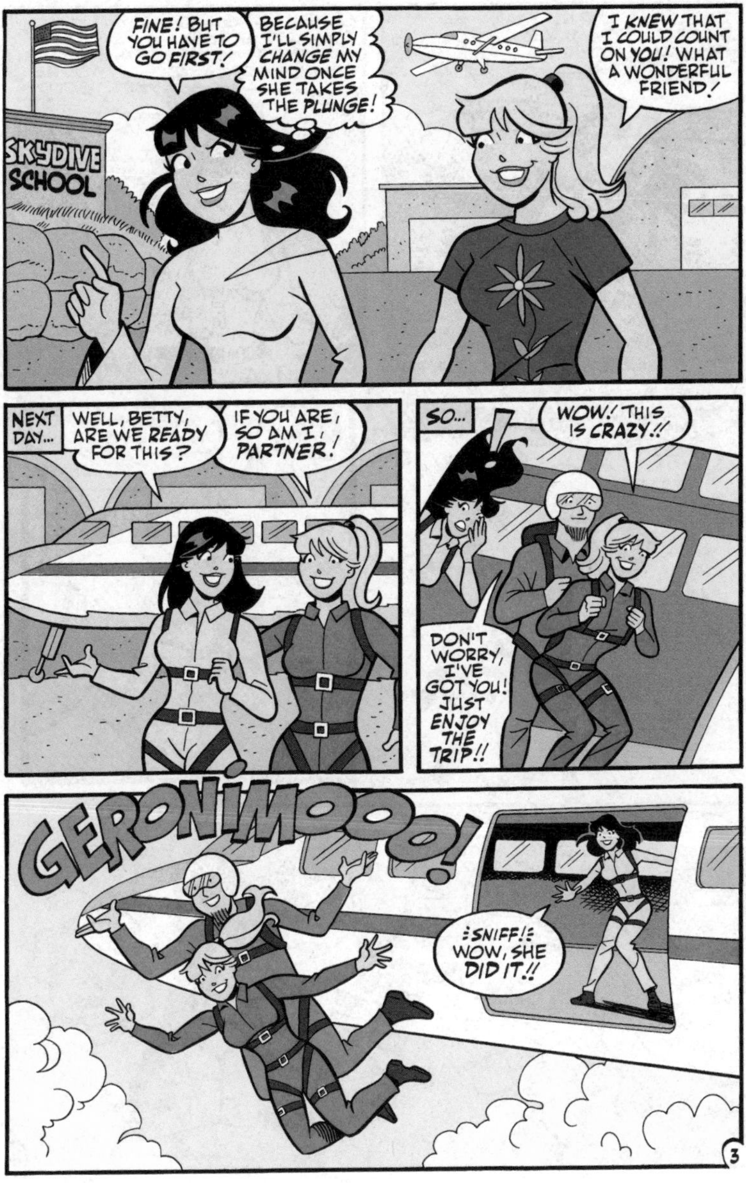
FINE! BUT YOU HAVE TO GO FIRST!
BECAUSE I'LL SIMPLY CHANGE MY MIND ONCE SHE TAKES THE PLUNGE!
I KNEW THAT I COULD COUNT ON YOU! WHAT A WONDERFUL FRIEND!
SKYDIVE SCHOOL
NEXT DAY...
WELL, BETTY, ARE WE READY FOR THIS?
IF YOU ARE, SO AM I, PARTNER!
SO...
WOW! THIS IS CRAZY!!
!
DON'T WORRY, I'VE GOT YOU! JUST ENJOY THE TRIP!!
GERONIMOOOO!
:SNIFF!: WOW, SHE DID IT!!
3

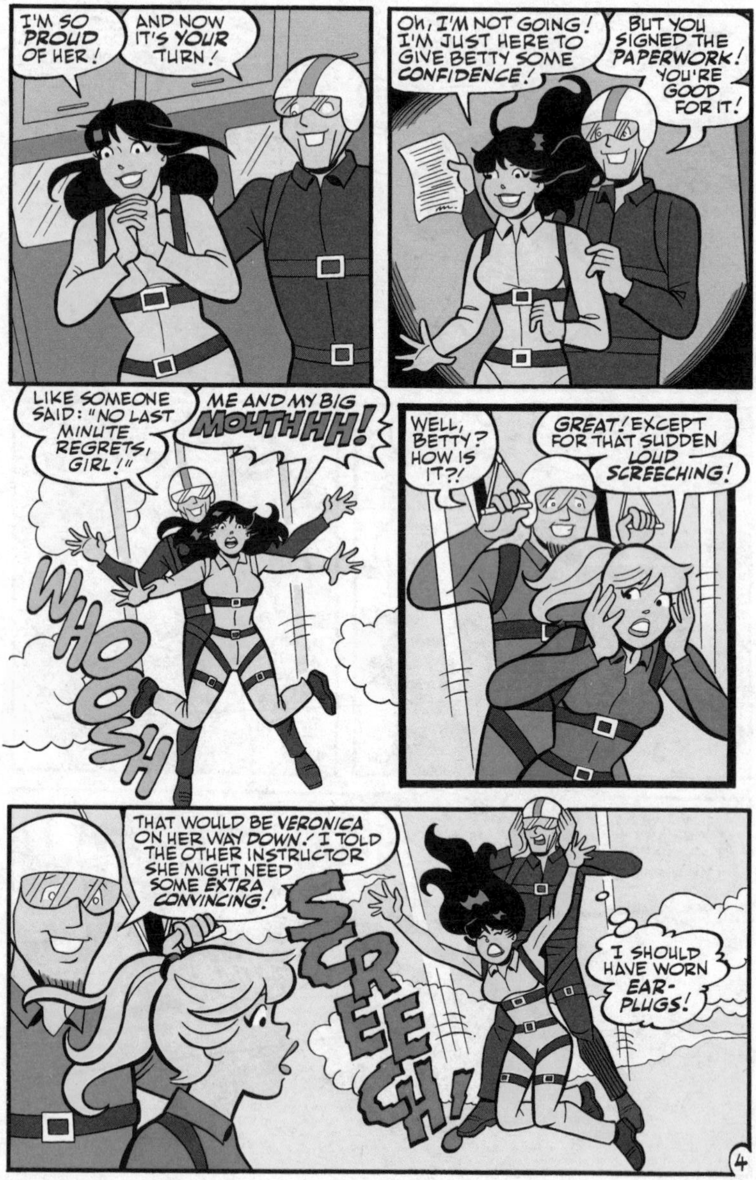

I'M SO PROUD OF HER!
AND NOW IT'S YOUR TURN!
OH, I'M NOT GOING! I'M JUST HERE TO GIVE BETTY SOME CONFIDENCE!
BUT YOU SIGNED THE PAPERWORK! YOU'RE GOOD FOR IT!
LIKE SOMEONE SAID: "NO LAST MINUTE REGRETS, GIRL!"
ME AND MY BIG MOUTHHH!
WHOOOSH
WELL, BETTY? HOW IS IT?!
GREAT! EXCEPT FOR THAT SUDDEN LOUD SCREECHING!
THAT WOULD BE VERONICA ON HER WAY DOWN! I TOLD THE OTHER INSTRUCTOR SHE MIGHT NEED SOME EXTRA CONVINCING!
SCREEECH!
I SHOULD HAVE WORN EAR-PLUGS!
4

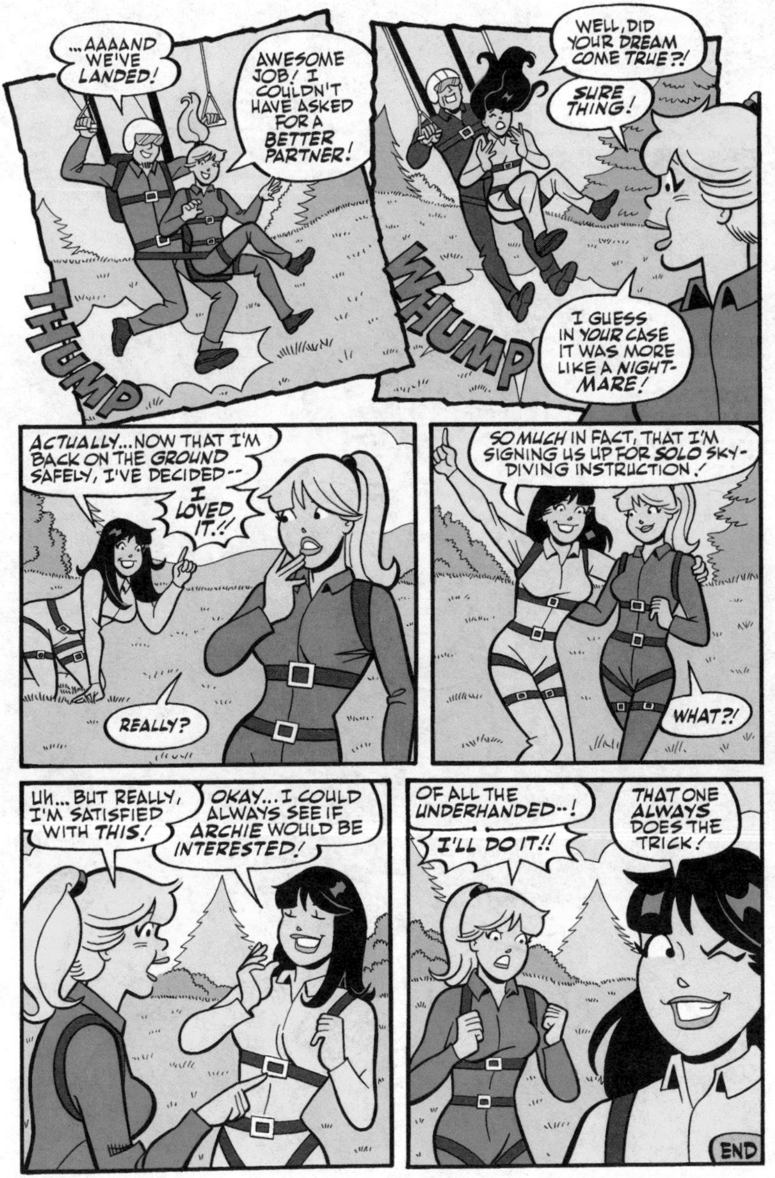
...AAAAND WE'VE LANDED!
AWESOME JOB! I COULDN'T HAVE ASKED FOR A BETTER PARTNER!
THUMP
WELL, DID YOUR DREAM COME TRUE?!
SURE THING!
WHUMP
I GUESS IN YOUR CASE IT WAS MORE LIKE A NIGHT-MARE!
ACTUALLY... NOW THAT I'M BACK ON THE GROUND SAFELY, I'VE DECIDED--
I LOVED IT!!
REALLY?
SO MUCH IN FACT, THAT I'M SIGNING US UP FOR SOLO SKY-DIVING INSTRUCTION!
WHAT?!
UH... BUT REALLY, I'M SATISFIED WITH THIS!
OKAY... I COULD ALWAYS SEE IF ARCHIE WOULD BE INTERESTED!
OF ALL THE UNDERHANDED--!
I'LL DO IT!!
THAT ONE ALWAYS DOES THE TRICK!
END

03 ARCHIE & ME

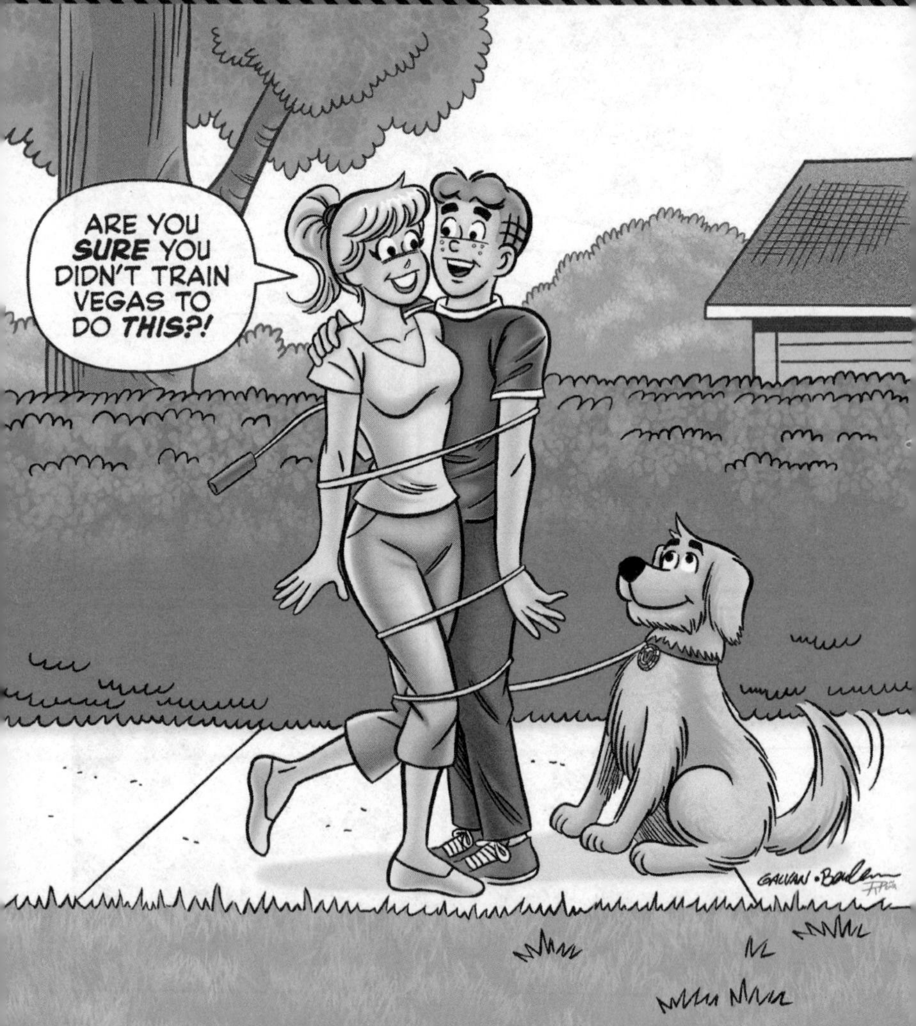
ARE YOU SURE YOU DIDN'T TRAIN VEGAS TO DO THIS?!
GALVAN • BOLLING

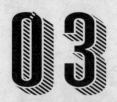

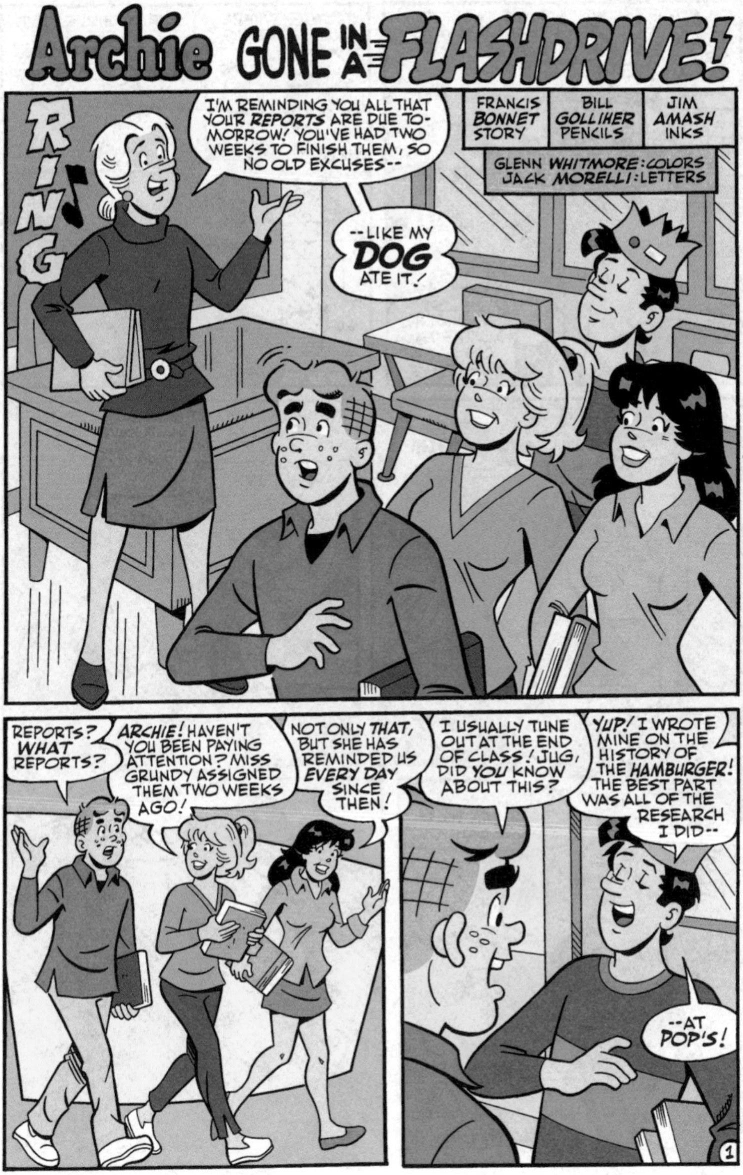
Archie GONE IN A FLASHDRIVE!
FRANCIS BONNET STORY
BILL GOLLIHER PENCILS
JIM AMASH INKS
GLENN WHITMORE: COLORS
JACK MORELLI: LETTERS
RING
I'M REMINDING YOU ALL THAT YOUR REPORTS ARE DUE TOMORROW! YOU'VE HAD TWO WEEKS TO FINISH THEM, SO NO OLD EXCUSES--
--LIKE MY DOG ATE IT!
REPORTS? WHAT REPORTS?
ARCHIE! HAVEN'T YOU BEEN PAYING ATTENTION? MISS GRUNDY ASSIGNED THEM TWO WEEKS AGO!
NOT ONLY THAT, BUT SHE HAS REMINDED US EVERY DAY SINCE THEN!
I USUALLY TUNE OUT AT THE END OF CLASS! JUG, DID YOU KNOW ABOUT THIS?
YUP! I WROTE MINE ON THE HISTORY OF THE HAMBURGER! THE BEST PART WAS ALL OF THE RESEARCH I DID--
--AT POP'S!
1

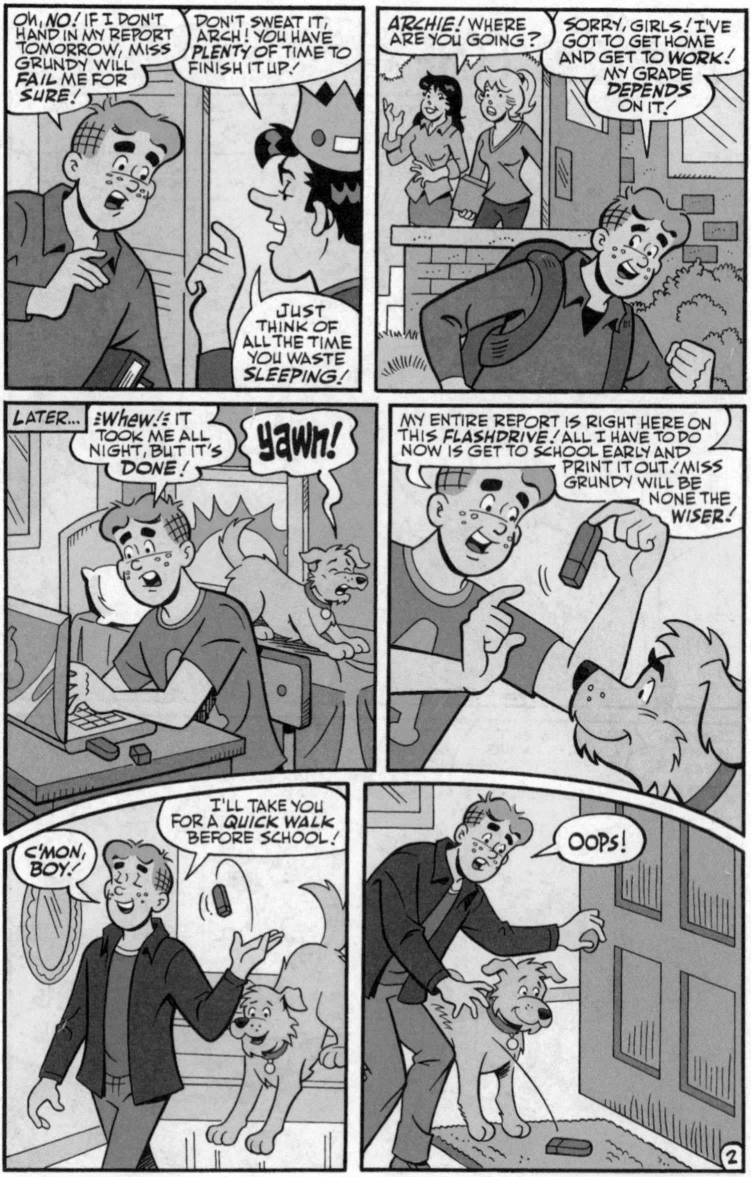
OH, NO! IF I DON'T HAND IN MY REPORT TOMORROW, MISS GRUNDY WILL FAIL ME FOR SURE!
DON'T SWEAT IT, ARCH! YOU HAVE PLENTY OF TIME TO FINISH IT UP!
JUST THINK OF ALL THE TIME YOU WASTE SLEEPING!
ARCHIE! WHERE ARE YOU GOING?
SORRY, GIRLS! I'VE GOT TO GET HOME AND GET TO WORK! MY GRADE DEPENDS ON IT!
LATER...
WHEW! IT TOOK ME ALL NIGHT, BUT IT'S DONE!
YAWN!
MY ENTIRE REPORT IS RIGHT HERE ON THIS FLASHDRIVE! ALL I HAVE TO DO NOW IS GET TO SCHOOL EARLY AND PRINT IT OUT! MISS GRUNDY WILL BE NONE THE WISER!
C'MON, BOY!
I'LL TAKE YOU FOR A QUICK WALK BEFORE SCHOOL!
OOPS!
2

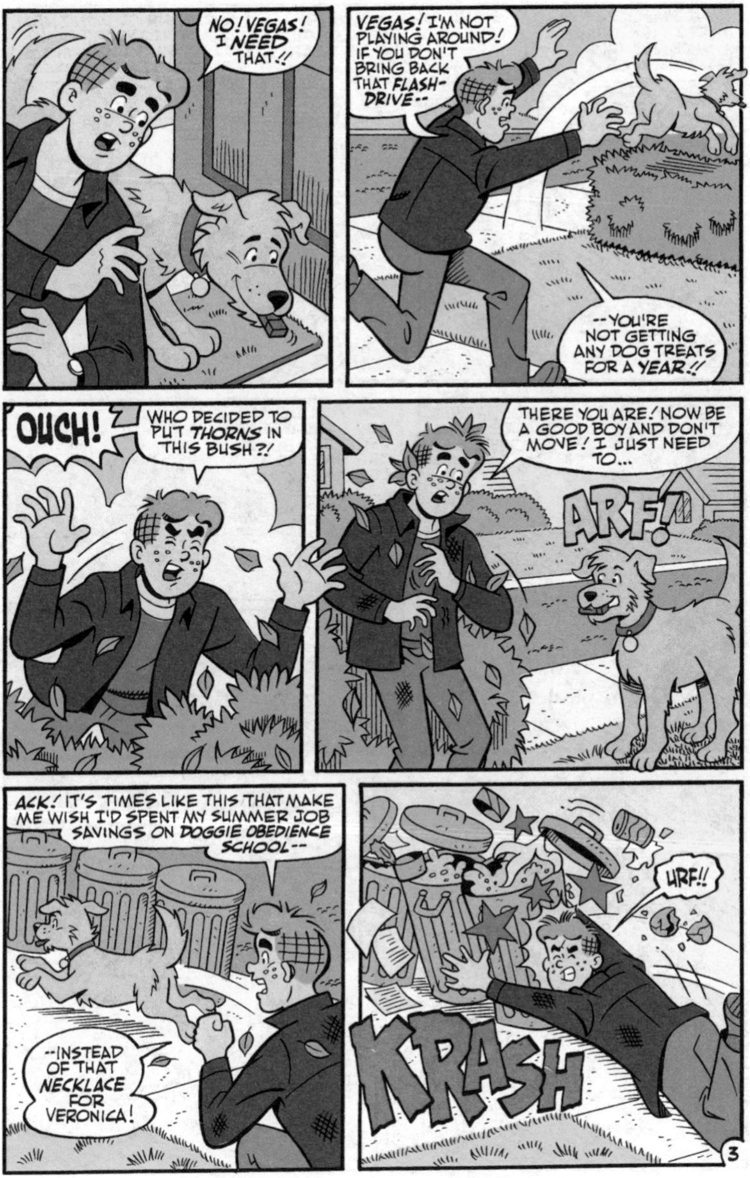
NO! VEGAS! I NEED THAT!!
VEGAS! I'M NOT PLAYING AROUND! IF YOU DON'T BRING BACK THAT FLASH-DRIVE--
--YOU'RE NOT GETTING ANY DOG TREATS FOR A YEAR!!
OUCH!
WHO DECIDED TO PUT THORNS IN THIS BUSH?!
THERE YOU ARE! NOW BE A GOOD BOY AND DON'T MOVE! I JUST NEED TO...
ARF!
ACK! IT'S TIMES LIKE THIS THAT MAKE ME WISH I'D SPENT MY SUMMER JOB SAVINGS ON DOGGIE OBEDIENCE SCHOOL--
--INSTEAD OF THAT NECKLACE FOR VERONICA!
URF!!
KRASH
3

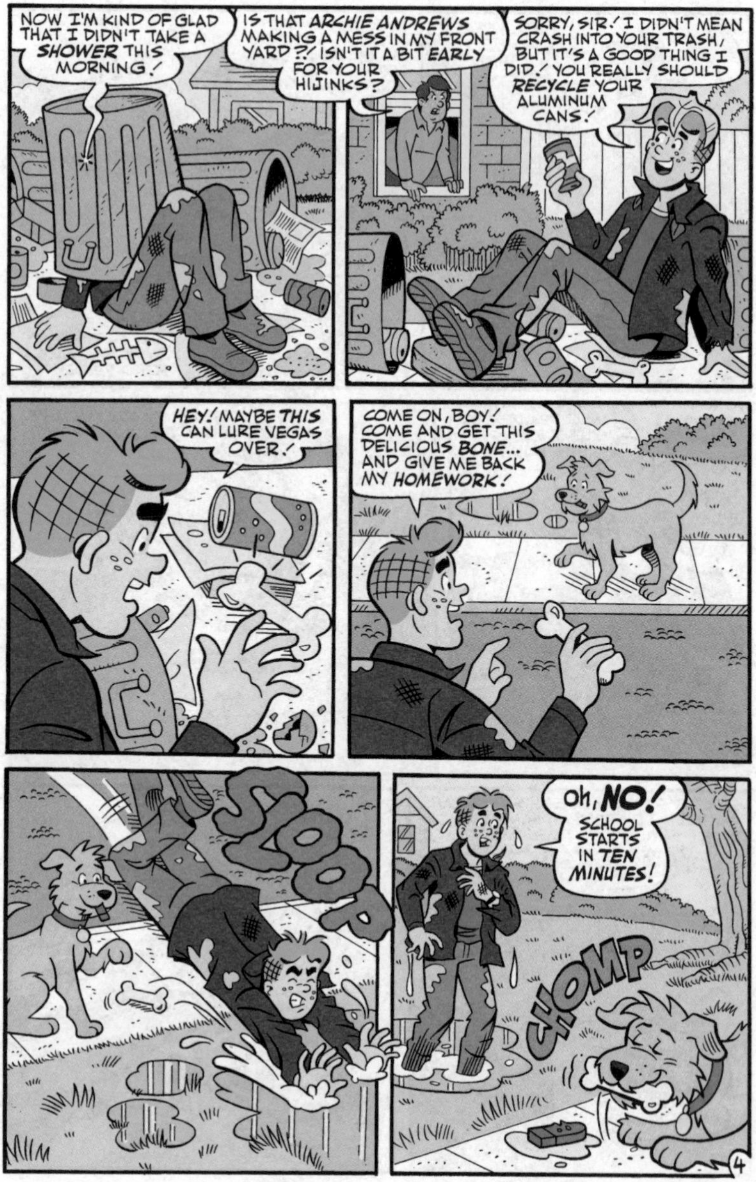
NOW I'M KIND OF GLAD THAT I DIDN'T TAKE A SHOWER THIS MORNING!
IS THAT ARCHIE ANDREWS MAKING A MESS IN MY FRONT YARD?! ISN'T IT A BIT EARLY FOR YOUR HIJINKS?
SORRY, SIR! I DIDN'T MEAN CRASH INTO YOUR TRASH, BUT IT'S A GOOD THING I DID! YOU REALLY SHOULD RECYCLE YOUR ALUMINUM CANS!
HEY! MAYBE THIS CAN LURE VEGAS OVER!
COME ON, BOY! COME AND GET THIS DELICIOUS BONE... AND GIVE ME BACK MY HOMEWORK!
SLOOP
Oh, NO! SCHOOL STARTS IN TEN MINUTES!
CHOMP
4

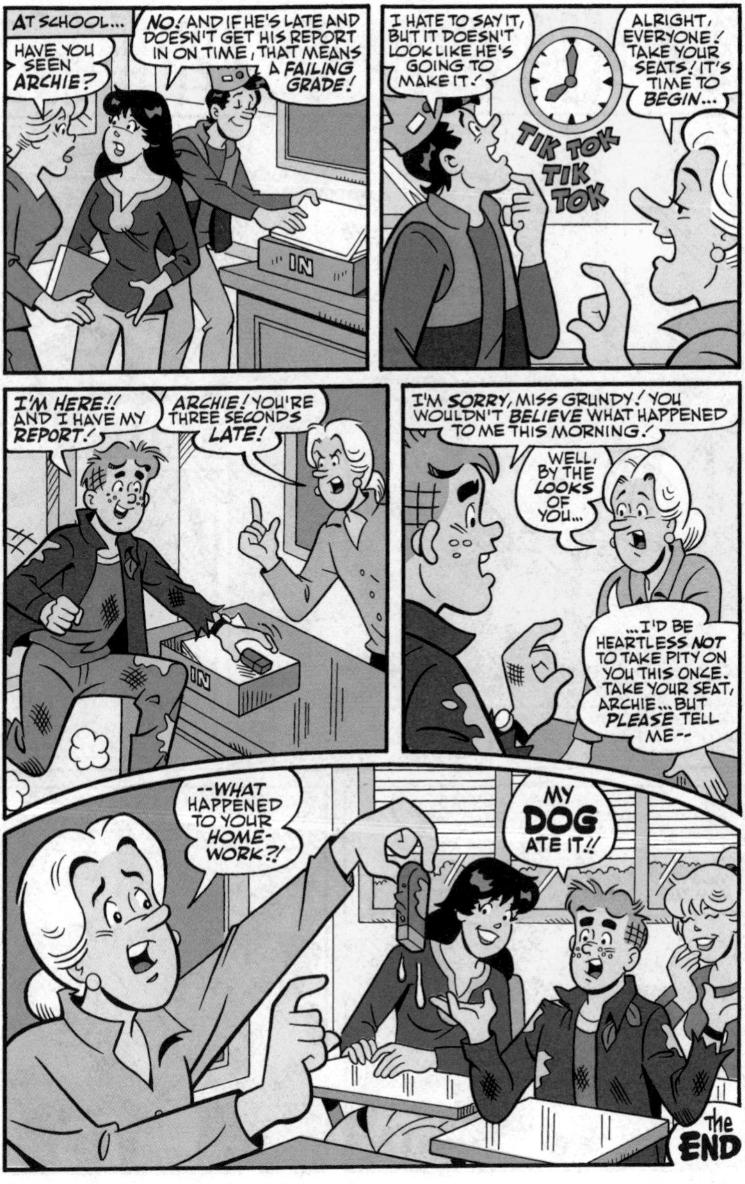
AT SCHOOL...
HAVE YOU SEEN ARCHIE?
NO! AND IF HE'S LATE AND DOESN'T GET HIS REPORT IN ON TIME, THAT MEANS A FAILING GRADE!
IN
I HATE TO SAY IT, BUT IT DOESN'T LOOK LIKE HE'S GOING TO MAKE IT!
ALRIGHT, EVERYONE! TAKE YOUR SEATS! IT'S TIME TO BEGIN...
TIK TOK TIK TOK
I'M HERE!! AND I HAVE MY REPORT!
ARCHIE! YOU'RE THREE SECONDS LATE!
IN
I'M SORRY, MISS GRUNDY! YOU WOULDN'T BELIEVE WHAT HAPPENED TO ME THIS MORNING!
WELL, BY THE LOOKS OF YOU...
...I'D BE HEARTLESS NOT TO TAKE PITY ON YOU THIS ONCE. TAKE YOUR SEAT, ARCHIE... BUT PLEASE TELL ME--
--WHAT HAPPENED TO YOUR HOME-WORK?!
MY DOG ATE IT!!
THE END

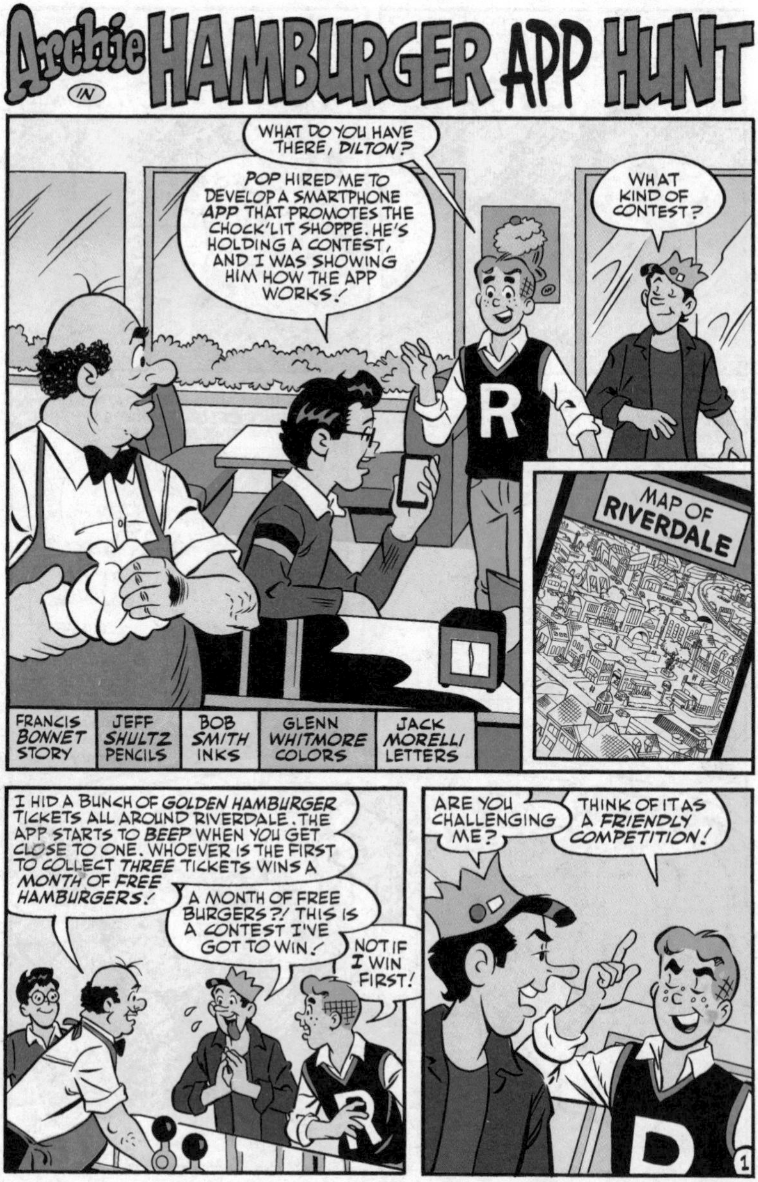
Archie
IN
HAMBURGER APP HUNT
WHAT DO YOU HAVE THERE, DILTON?
POP HIRED ME TO DEVELOP A SMARTPHONE APP THAT PROMOTES THE CHOCK'LIT SHOPPE. HE'S HOLDING A CONTEST, AND I WAS SHOWING HIM HOW THE APP WORKS!
WHAT KIND OF CONTEST?
MAP OF RIVERDALE
FRANCIS BONNET STORY
JEFF SHULTZ PENCILS
BOB SMITH INKS
GLENN WHITMORE COLORS
JACK MORELLI LETTERS
I HID A BUNCH OF GOLDEN HAMBURGER TICKETS ALL AROUND RIVERDALE. THE APP STARTS TO BEEP WHEN YOU GET CLOSE TO ONE. WHOEVER IS THE FIRST TO COLLECT THREE TICKETS WINS A MONTH OF FREE HAMBURGERS!
A MONTH OF FREE BURGERS?! THIS IS A CONTEST I'VE GOT TO WIN!
NOT IF I WIN FIRST!
ARE YOU CHALLENGING ME?
THINK OF IT AS A FRIENDLY COMPETITION!
1

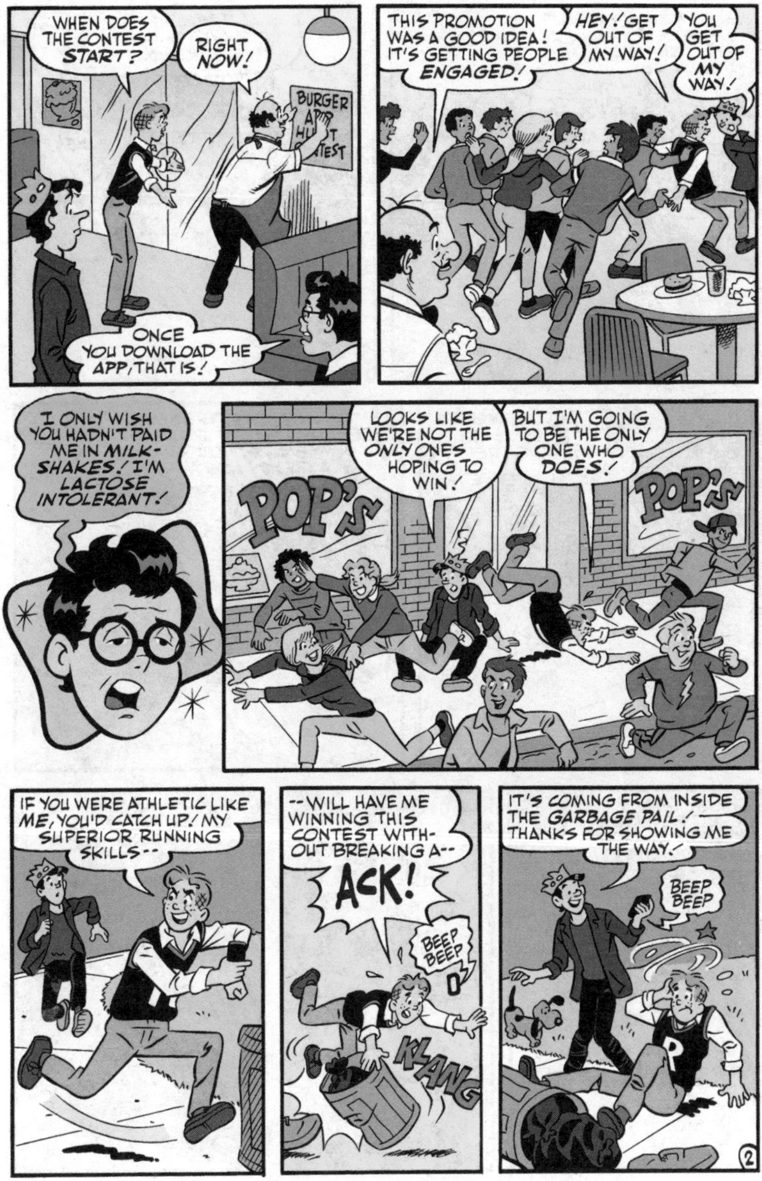
WHEN DOES THE CONTEST START?
RIGHT NOW!
BURGER APP HUNT CONTEST
ONCE YOU DOWNLOAD THE APP, THAT IS!
THIS PROMOTION WAS A GOOD IDEA! IT'S GETTING PEOPLE ENGAGED!
HEY! GET OUT OF MY WAY!
YOU GET OUT OF MY WAY!
I ONLY WISH YOU HADN'T PAID ME IN MILK-SHAKES! I'M LACTOSE INTOLERANT!
LOOKS LIKE WE'RE NOT THE ONLY ONES HOPING TO WIN!
BUT I'M GOING TO BE THE ONLY ONE WHO DOES!
POP'S
POP'S
IF YOU WERE ATHLETIC LIKE ME, YOU'D CATCH UP! MY SUPERIOR RUNNING SKILLS--
--WILL HAVE ME WINNING THIS CONTEST WITH-OUT BREAKING A--
ACK!
BEEP BEEP
KLANG
IT'S COMING FROM INSIDE THE GARBAGE PAIL! THANKS FOR SHOWING ME THE WAY!
BEEP BEEP
2

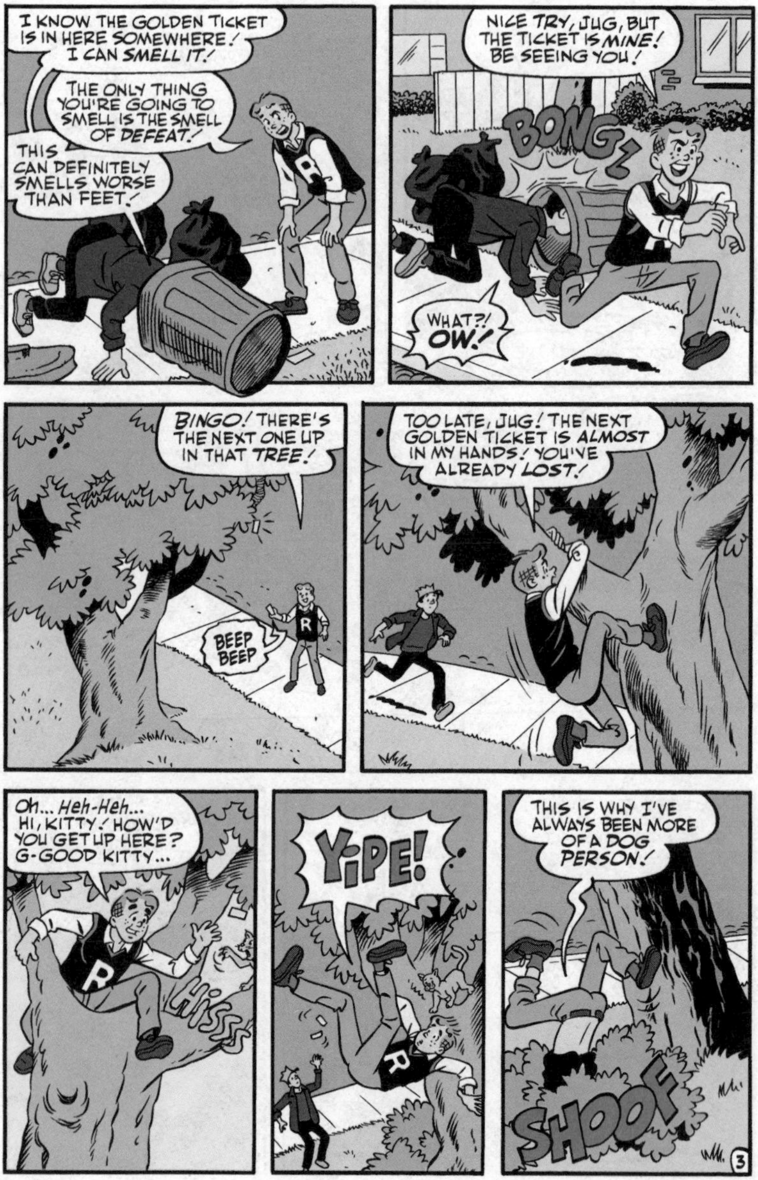
I KNOW THE GOLDEN TICKET IS IN HERE SOMEWHERE! I CAN SMELL IT!
THE ONLY THING YOU'RE GOING TO SMELL IS THE SMELL OF DEFEAT!
THIS CAN DEFINITELY SMELLS WORSE THAN FEET!
NICE TRY, JUG, BUT THE TICKET IS MINE! BE SEEING YOU!
BONG!
WHAT?! OW!
BINGO! THERE'S THE NEXT ONE UP IN THAT TREE!
BEEP BEEP
TOO LATE, JUG! THE NEXT GOLDEN TICKET IS ALMOST IN MY HANDS! YOU'VE ALREADY LOST!
Oh... Heh-Heh... HI, KITTY! HOW'D YOU GET UP HERE? G-GOOD KITTY...
HISSS
YIPE!
THIS IS WHY I'VE ALWAYS BEEN MORE OF A DOG PERSON!
SHOOF
3

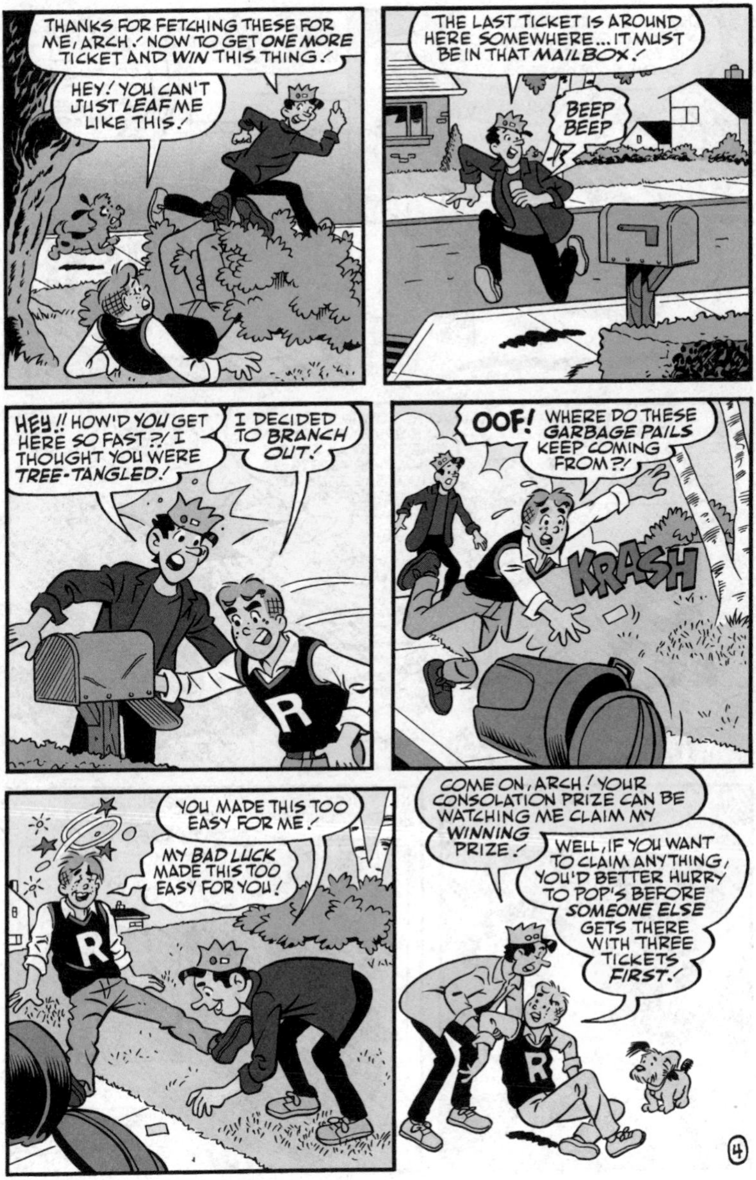
THANKS FOR FETCHING THESE FOR ME, ARCH.! NOW TO GET ONE MORE TICKET AND WIN THIS THING.!
HEY! YOU CAN'T JUST LEAF ME LIKE THIS!
THE LAST TICKET IS AROUND HERE SOMEWHERE... IT MUST BE IN THAT MAILBOX!
BEEP BEEP
HEY!! HOW'D YOU GET HERE SO FAST?! I THOUGHT YOU WERE TREE-TANGLED!
I DECIDED TO BRANCH OUT!
OOF!
WHERE DO THESE GARBAGE PAILS KEEP COMING FROM?!
KRASH
YOU MADE THIS TOO EASY FOR ME!
MY BAD LUCK MADE THIS TOO EASY FOR YOU!
COME ON, ARCH! YOUR CONSOLATION PRIZE CAN BE WATCHING ME CLAIM MY WINNING PRIZE!
WELL, IF YOU WANT TO CLAIM ANYTHING, YOU'D BETTER HURRY TO POP'S BEFORE SOMEONE ELSE GETS THERE WITH THREE TICKETS FIRST!
4

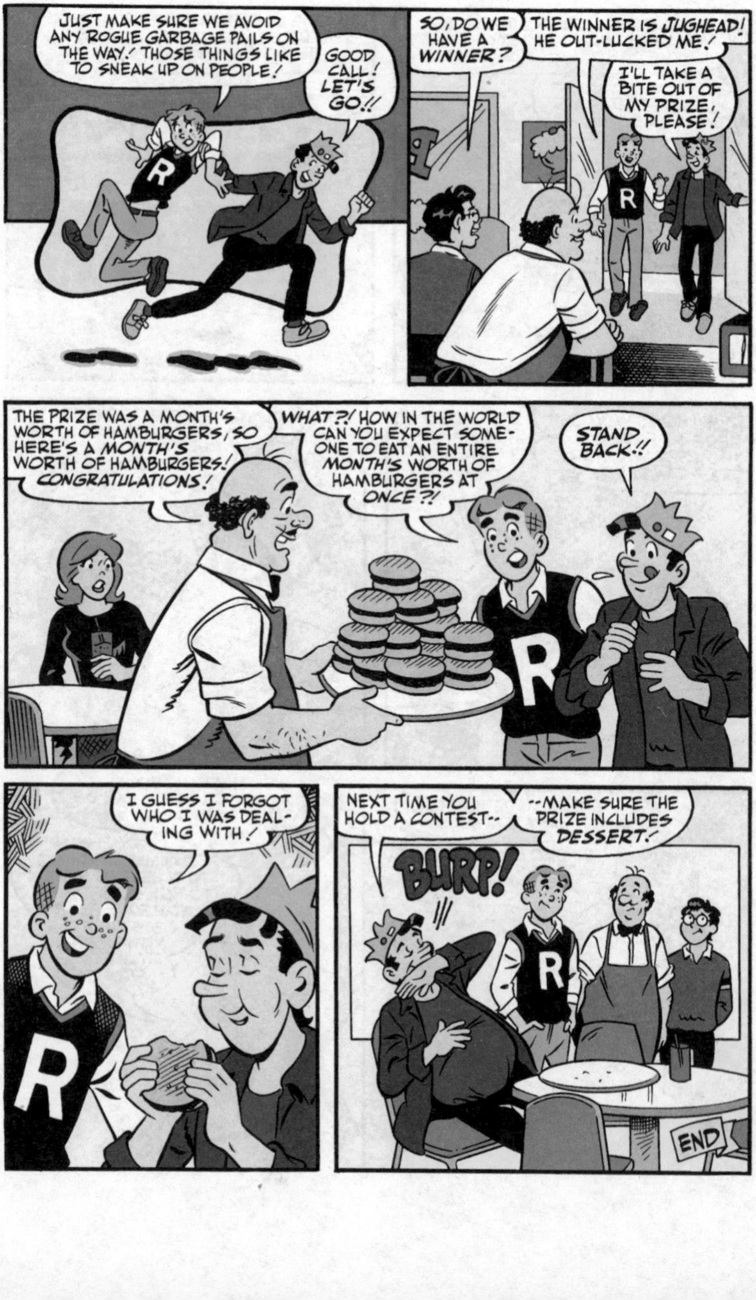
JUST MAKE SURE WE AVOID ANY ROGUE GARBAGE PAILS ON THE WAY! THOSE THINGS LIKE TO SNEAK UP ON PEOPLE!
GOOD CALL! LET'S GO!!
SO, DO WE HAVE A WINNER?
THE WINNER IS JUGHEAD! HE OUT-LUCKED ME!
I'LL TAKE A BITE OUT OF MY PRIZE, PLEASE!
THE PRIZE WAS A MONTH'S WORTH OF HAMBURGERS, SO HERE'S A MONTH'S WORTH OF HAMBURGERS! CONGRATULATIONS!
WHAT?! HOW IN THE WORLD CAN YOU EXPECT SOME-ONE TO EAT AN ENTIRE MONTH'S WORTH OF HAMBURGERS AT ONCE?!
STAND BACK!!
I GUESS I FORGOT WHO I WAS DEAL-ING WITH!
NEXT TIME YOU HOLD A CONTEST--
--MAKE SURE THE PRIZE INCLUDES DESSERT!
BURP!
END

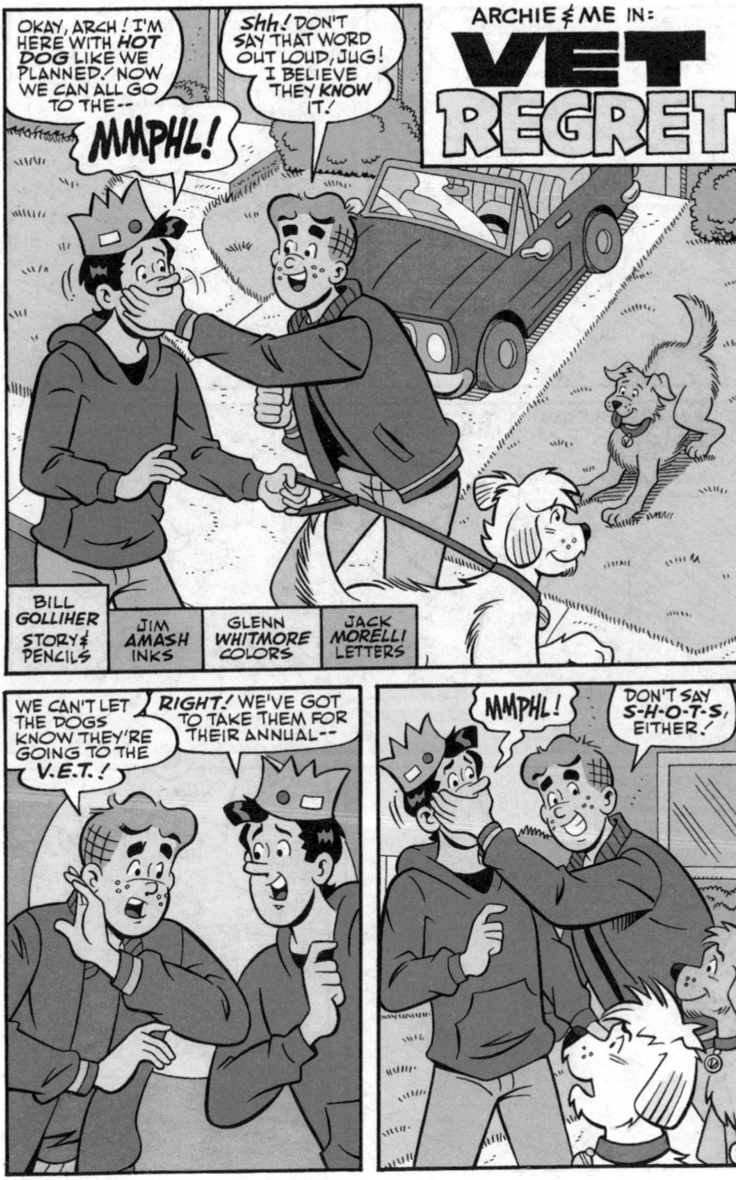
OKAY, ARCH! I'M HERE WITH HOT DOG LIKE WE PLANNED! NOW WE CAN ALL GO TO THE--
MMPHL!
Shh! DON'T SAY THAT WORD OUT LOUD, JUG! I BELIEVE THEY KNOW IT!
ARCHIE & ME IN:
VET REGRET
BILL GOLLIHER STORY & PENCILS
JIM AMASH INKS
GLENN WHITMORE COLORS
JACK MORELLI LETTERS
WE CAN'T LET THE DOGS KNOW THEY'RE GOING TO THE V.E.T.!
RIGHT! WE'VE GOT TO TAKE THEM FOR THEIR ANNUAL--
MMPHL!
DON'T SAY S-H-O-T-S, EITHER!
1

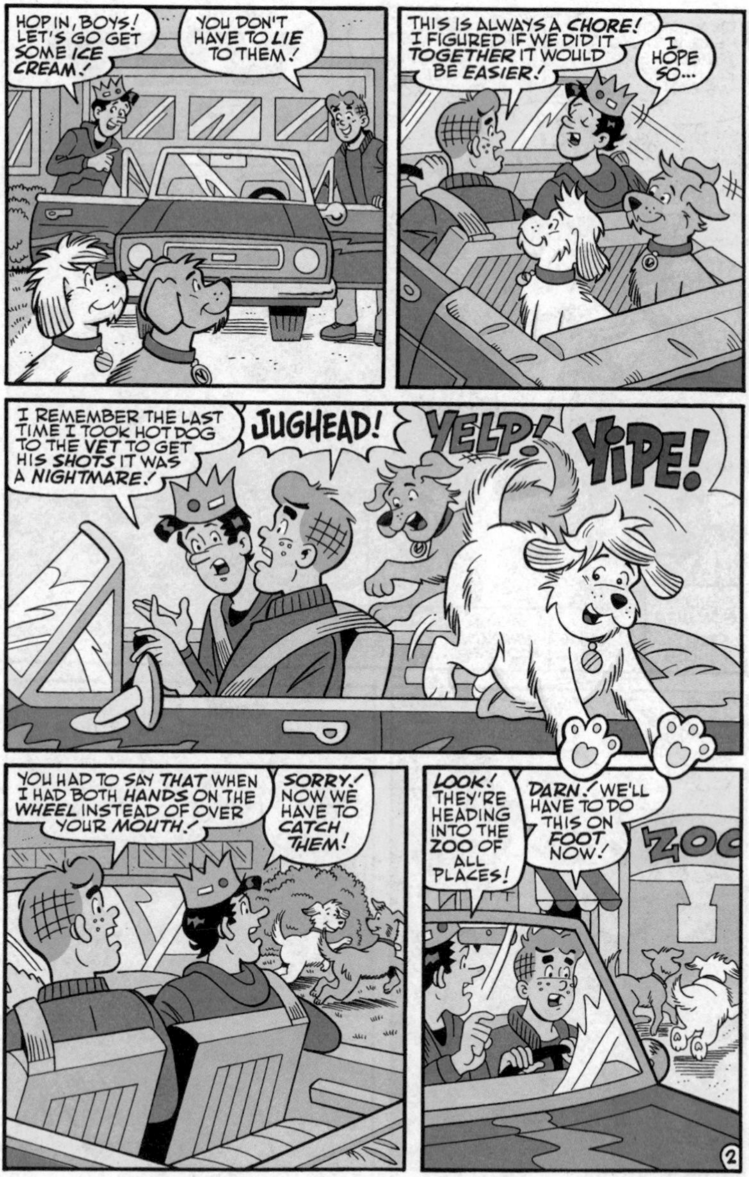
HOP IN, BOYS! LET'S GO GET SOME ICE CREAM!
YOU DON'T HAVE TO LIE TO THEM!
THIS IS ALWAYS A CHORE! I FIGURED IF WE DID IT TOGETHER IT WOULD BE EASIER!
I HOPE SO...
I REMEMBER THE LAST TIME I TOOK HOT DOG TO THE VET TO GET HIS SHOTS IT WAS A NIGHTMARE!
JUGHEAD!
YELP!
YIPE!
YOU HAD TO SAY THAT WHEN I HAD BOTH HANDS ON THE WHEEL INSTEAD OF OVER YOUR MOUTH!
SORRY! NOW WE HAVE TO CATCH THEM!
LOOK! THEY'RE HEADING INTO THE ZOO OF ALL PLACES!
DARN! WE'LL HAVE TO DO THIS ON FOOT NOW!
2

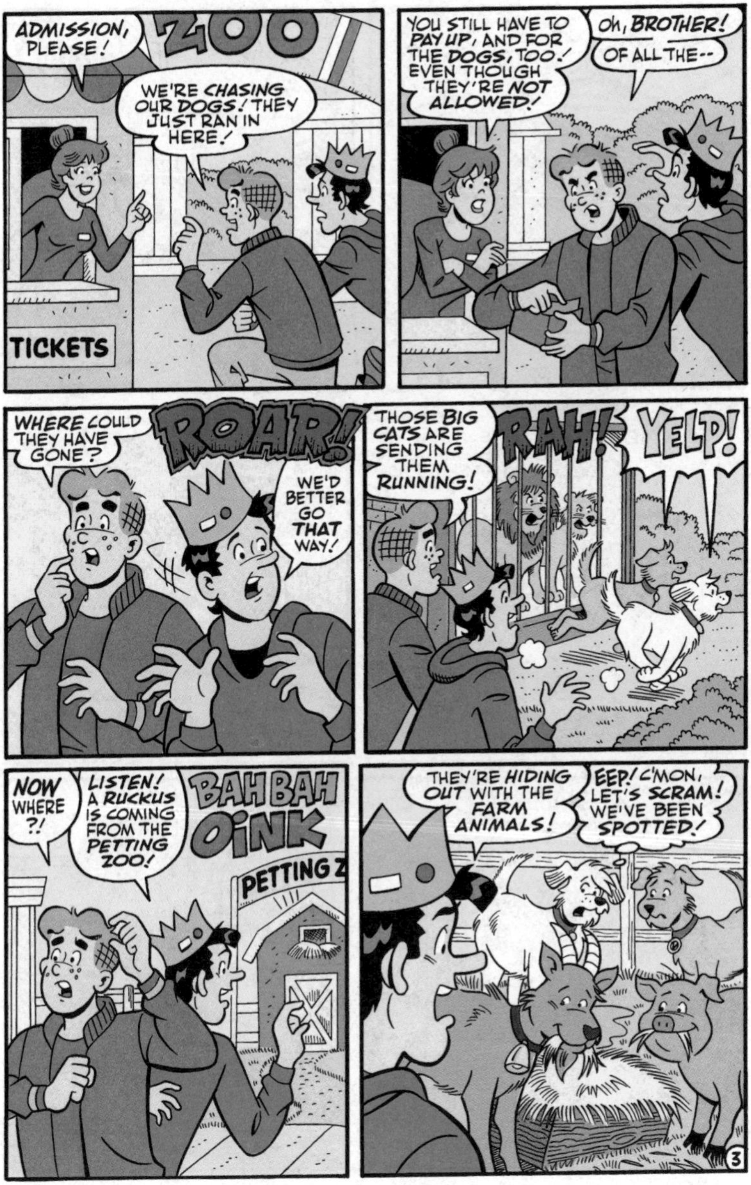
ADMISSION, PLEASE!
ZOO
WE'RE CHASING OUR DOGS! THEY JUST RAN IN HERE!
TICKETS
YOU STILL HAVE TO PAY UP, AND FOR THE DOGS, TOO! EVEN THOUGH THEY'RE NOT ALLOWED!
Oh, BROTHER!
OF ALL THE--
WHERE COULD THEY HAVE GONE?
ROAR!
WE'D BETTER GO THAT WAY!
THOSE BIG CATS ARE SENDING THEM RUNNING!
RAH!
YELP!
NOW WHERE ?!
LISTEN! A RUCKUS IS COMING FROM THE PETTING ZOO!
BAH BAH
OINK
PETTING Z
THEY'RE HIDING OUT WITH THE FARM ANIMALS!
EEP! C'MON, LET'S SCRAM! WE'VE BEEN SPOTTED!
3

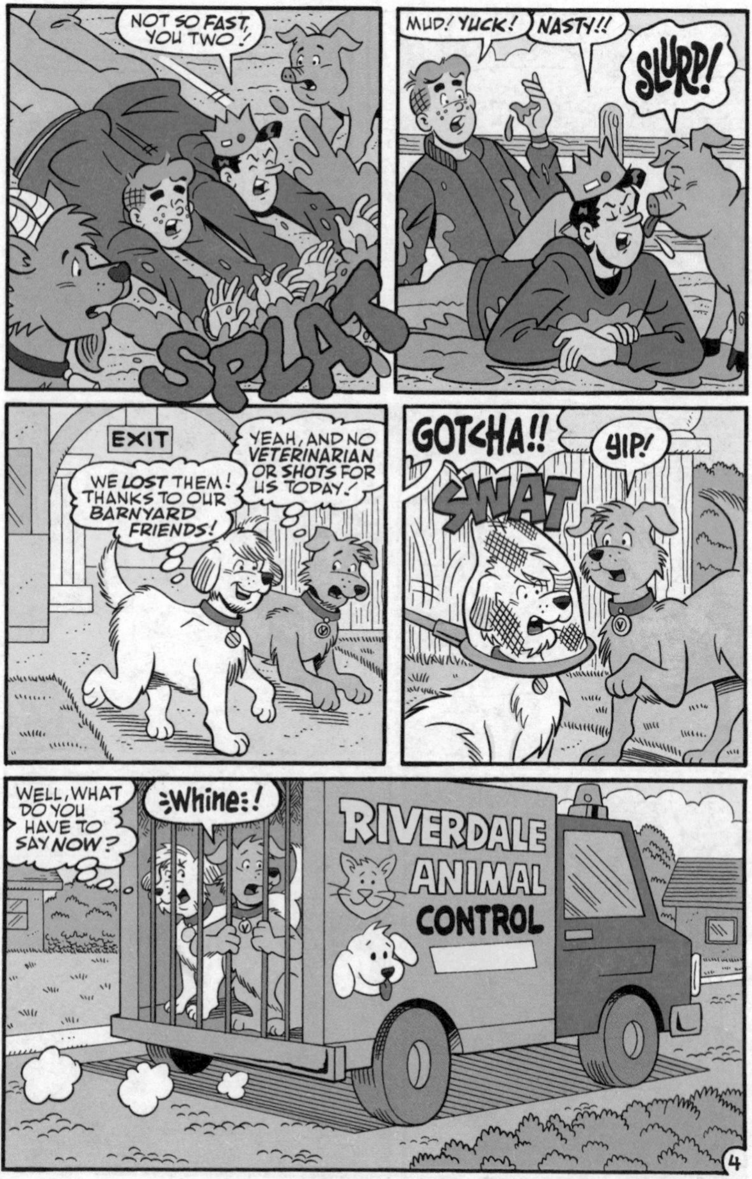
NOT SO FAST, YOU TWO!
SPLAT
MUD! YUCK!
NASTY!!
SLURP!
EXIT
WE LOST THEM! THANKS TO OUR BARNYARD FRIENDS!
YEAH, AND NO VETERINARIAN OR SHOTS FOR US TODAY!
GOTCHA!!
SWAT
YIP!
WELL, WHAT DO YOU HAVE TO SAY NOW?
Whine!
RIVERDALE ANIMAL CONTROL
4

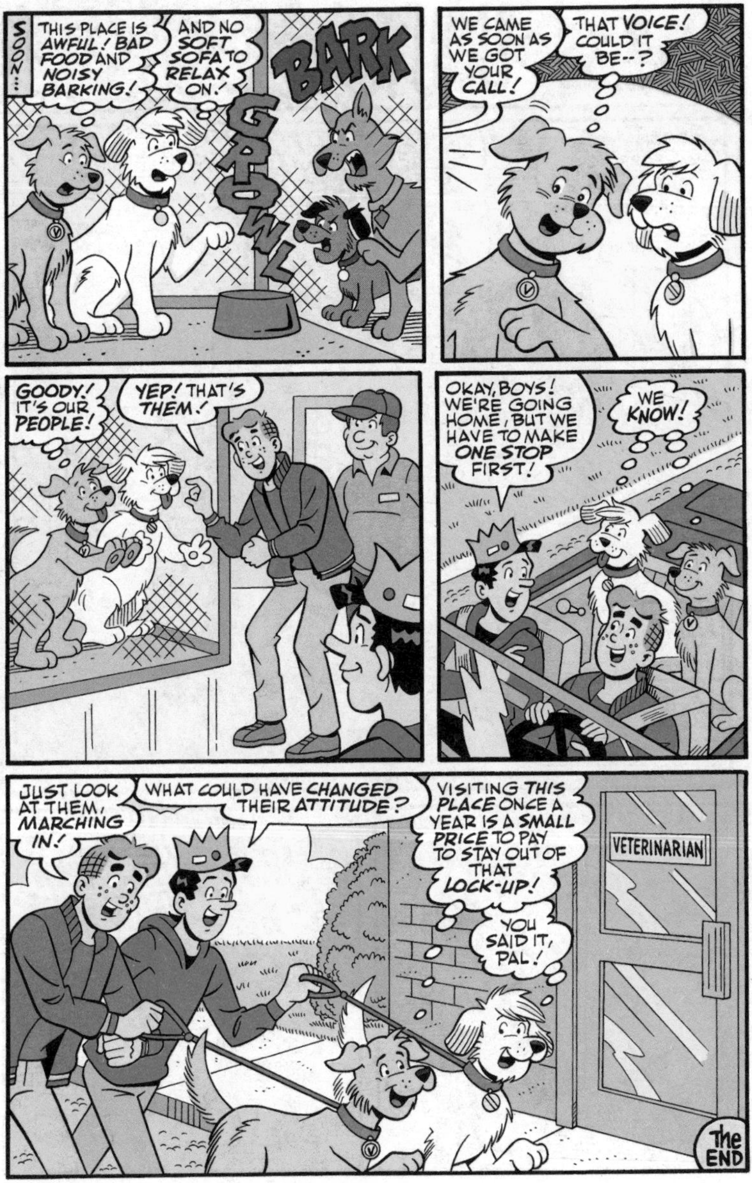
SOON...
THIS PLACE IS AWFUL! BAD FOOD AND NOISY BARKING!
AND NO SOFT SOFA TO RELAX ON!
BARK
GROWL
WE CAME AS SOON AS WE GOT YOUR CALL!
THAT VOICE! COULD IT BE--?
GOODY! IT'S OUR PEOPLE!
YEP! THAT'S THEM!
OKAY, BOYS! WE'RE GOING HOME, BUT WE HAVE TO MAKE ONE STOP FIRST!
WE KNOW!
JUST LOOK AT THEM, MARCHING IN!
WHAT COULD HAVE CHANGED THEIR ATTITUDE?
VISITING THIS PLACE ONCE A YEAR IS A SMALL PRICE TO PAY TO STAY OUT OF THAT LOCK-UP!
YOU SAID IT, PAL!
VETERINARIAN
The END

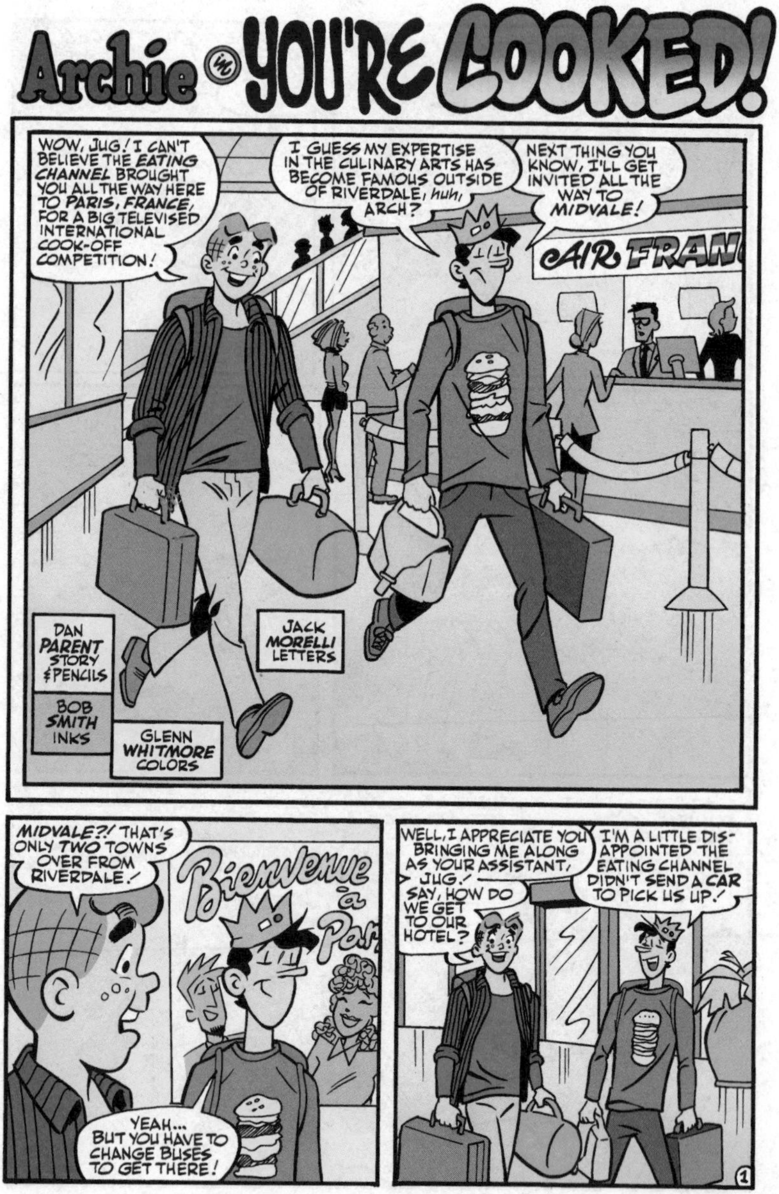
Archie in YOU'RE COOKED!
WOW, JUG! I CAN'T BELIEVE THE EATING CHANNEL BROUGHT YOU ALL THE WAY HERE TO PARIS, FRANCE, FOR A BIG TELEVISED INTERNATIONAL COOK-OFF COMPETITION!
I GUESS MY EXPERTISE IN THE CULINARY ARTS HAS BECOME FAMOUS OUTSIDE OF RIVERDALE, huh, ARCH?
NEXT THING YOU KNOW, I'LL GET INVITED ALL THE WAY TO MIDVALE!
AIR FRAN
DAN PARENT STORY & PENCILS
BOB SMITH INKS
GLENN WHITMORE COLORS
JACK MORELLI LETTERS
MIDVALE?! THAT'S ONLY TWO TOWNS OVER FROM RIVERDALE!
Bienvenue a Par
YEAH... BUT YOU HAVE TO CHANGE BUSES TO GET THERE!
WELL, I APPRECIATE YOU BRINGING ME ALONG AS YOUR ASSISTANT, JUG!
SAY, HOW DO WE GET TO OUR HOTEL?
I'M A LITTLE DISAPPOINTED THE EATING CHANNEL DIDN'T SEND A CAR TO PICK US UP!
1

I GUESS YOU'RE NOT THAT BIG OF A SHOT, OL' MAN! WHAT WERE YOU EXPECTING? A BRASS BAND?!
YOU MEAN LIKE THAT?
VIVA monsieur JUGHEAD
WELCOME TO FRANCE
BONJOUR, MONSIEUR JUGHEAD! I AM ANDRE, YOUR DRIVER.
I AM 'ERE TO DRIVE YOU TO ZEE 'OTEL!
MONSIEUR JUGHEAD
UM...GEE THANKS!
WOW! WHATTA SWEET RIDE, JUGHEAD!
I'D LOVE TO PULL UP TO THE DRIVE-THRU WINDOW AT BURGER THING IN THIS--!
2

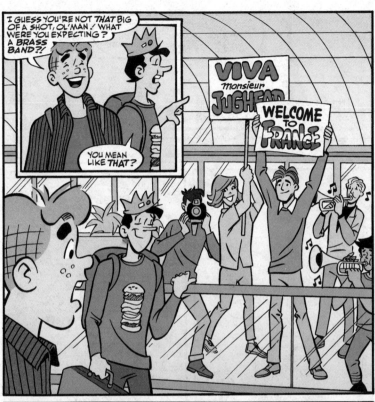

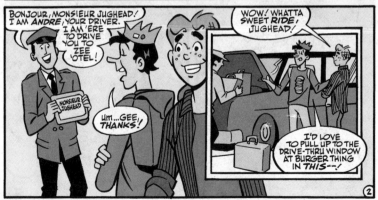

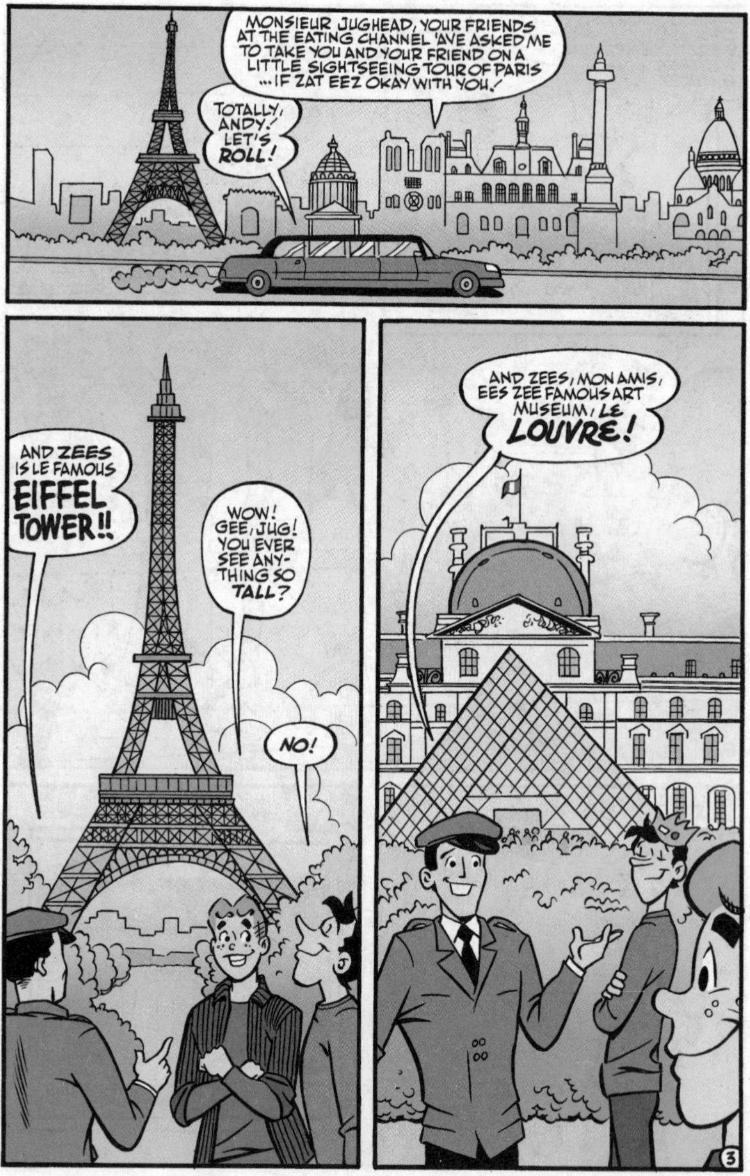
MONSIEUR JUGHEAD, YOUR FRIENDS AT THE EATING CHANNEL 'AVE ASKED ME TO TAKE YOU AND YOUR FRIEND ON A LITTLE SIGHTSEEING TOUR OF PARIS ...IF ZAT EEZ OKAY WITH YOU!
TOTALLY, ANDY! LET'S ROLL!
AND ZEES IS LE FAMOUS EIFFEL TOWER!!
WOW! GEE, JUG! YOU EVER SEE ANYTHING SO TALL?
NO!
AND ZEES, MON AMIS, EES ZEE FAMOUS ART MUSEUM, LE LOUVRE!
3

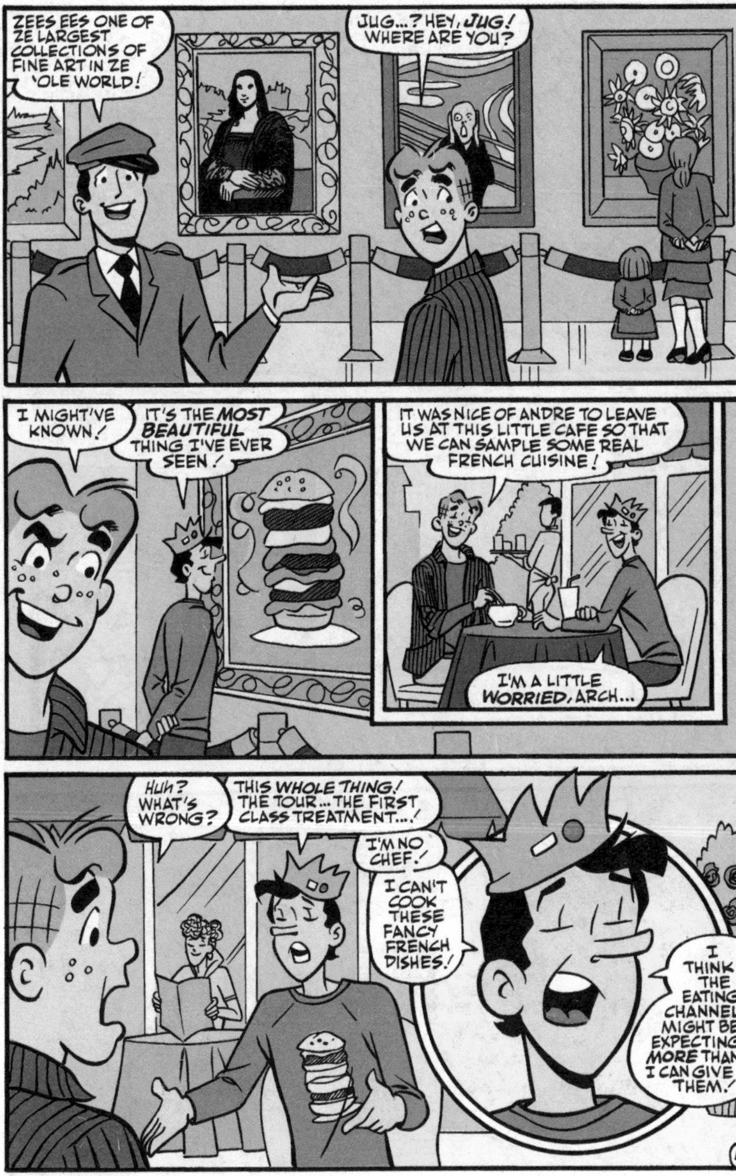
ZEES EES ONE OF ZE LARGEST COLLECTIONS OF FINE ART IN ZE 'OLE WORLD!
JUG...? HEY, JUG! WHERE ARE YOU?
I MIGHT'VE KNOWN!
IT'S THE MOST BEAUTIFUL THING I'VE EVER SEEN!
IT WAS NICE OF ANDRE TO LEAVE US AT THIS LITTLE CAFE SO THAT WE CAN SAMPLE SOME REAL FRENCH CUISINE!
I'M A LITTLE WORRIED, ARCH...
Huh? WHAT'S WRONG?
THIS WHOLE THING! THE TOUR... THE FIRST CLASS TREATMENT...!
I'M NO CHEF!
I CAN'T COOK THESE FANCY FRENCH DISHES!
I THINK THE EATING CHANNEL MIGHT BE EXPECTING MORE THAN I CAN GIVE THEM!
4

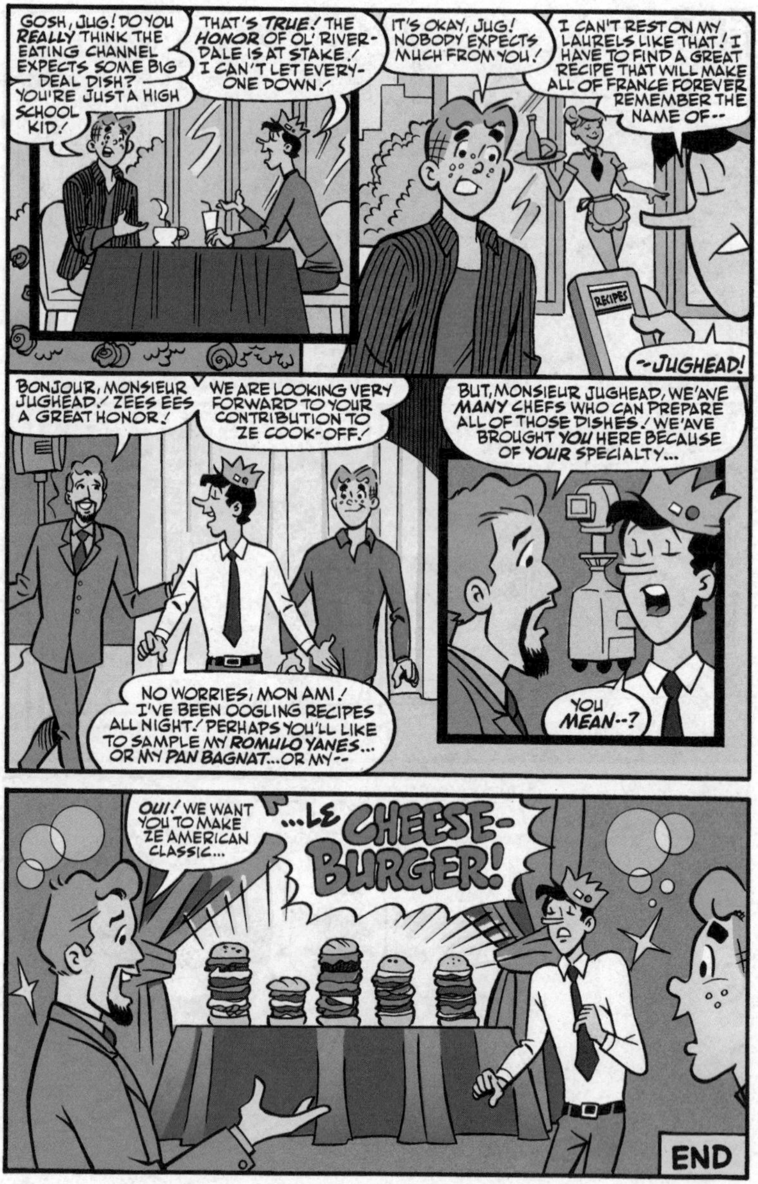
GOSH, JUG! DO YOU REALLY THINK THE EATING CHANNEL EXPECTS SOME BIG DEAL DISH? YOU'RE JUST A HIGH SCHOOL KID!
THAT'S TRUE! THE HONOR OF OL' RIVERDALE IS AT STAKE! I CAN'T LET EVERYONE DOWN!
IT'S OKAY, JUG! NOBODY EXPECTS MUCH FROM YOU!
I CAN'T REST ON MY LAURELS LIKE THAT! I HAVE TO FIND A GREAT RECIPE THAT WILL MAKE ALL OF FRANCE FOREVER REMEMBER THE NAME OF--
RECIPES
--JUGHEAD!
BONJOUR, MONSIEUR JUGHEAD! ZEES EES A GREAT HONOR!
WE ARE LOOKING VERY FORWARD TO YOUR CONTRIBUTION TO ZE COOK-OFF!
NO WORRIES, MON AMI! I'VE BEEN OOGLING RECIPES ALL NIGHT! PERHAPS YOU'LL LIKE TO SAMPLE MY ROMULO YANES... OR MY PAN BAGNAT...OR MY--
BUT, MONSIEUR JUGHEAD, WE'AVE MANY CHEFS WHO CAN PREPARE ALL OF THOSE DISHES! WE'AVE BROUGHT YOU HERE BECAUSE OF YOUR SPECIALTY...
YOU MEAN--?
OUI! WE WANT YOU TO MAKE ZE AMERICAN CLASSIC...
...LE CHEESE-BURGER!
END

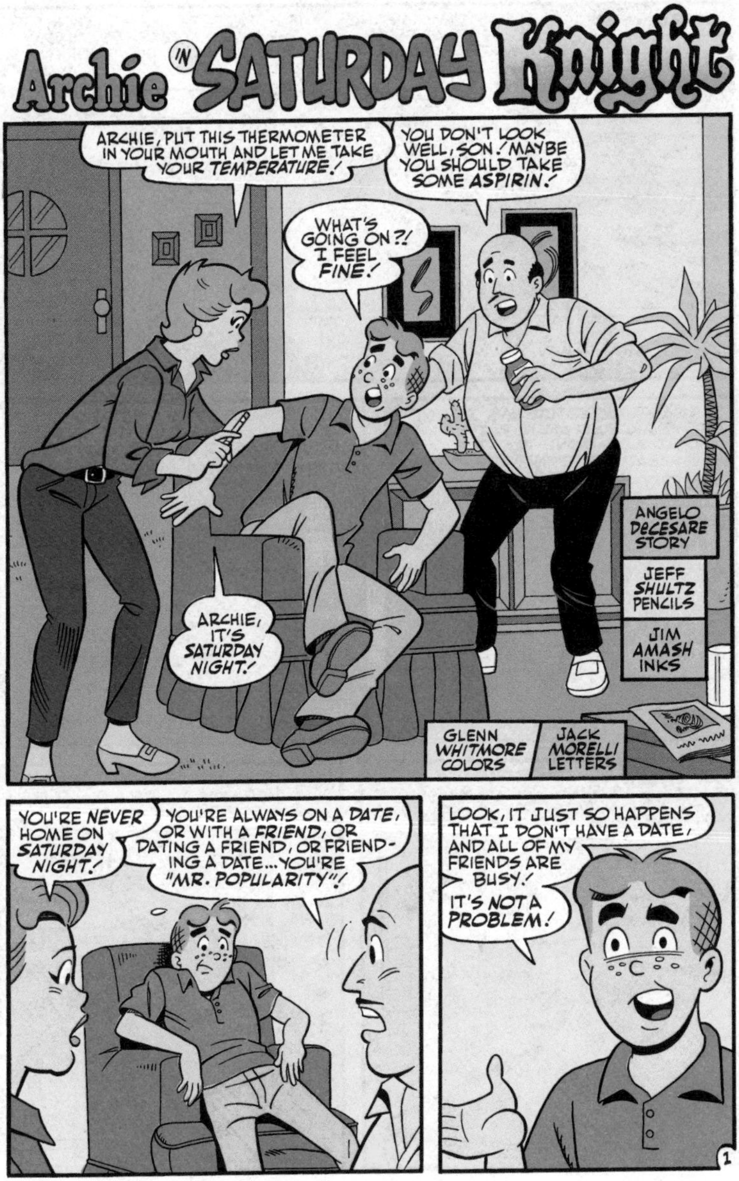
Archie in SATURDAY Knight
ARCHIE, PUT THIS THERMOMETER IN YOUR MOUTH AND LET ME TAKE YOUR TEMPERATURE!
YOU DON'T LOOK WELL, SON! MAYBE YOU SHOULD TAKE SOME ASPIRIN!
WHAT'S GOING ON?! I FEEL FINE!
ARCHIE, IT'S SATURDAY NIGHT!
ANGELO DeCESARE STORY
JEFF SHULTZ PENCILS
JIM AMASH INKS
GLENN WHITMORE COLORS
JACK MORELLI LETTERS
YOU'RE NEVER HOME ON SATURDAY NIGHT!
YOU'RE ALWAYS ON A DATE, OR WITH A FRIEND, OR DATING A FRIEND, OR FRIEND-ING A DATE... YOU'RE "MR. POPULARITY"!
LOOK, IT JUST SO HAPPENS THAT I DON'T HAVE A DATE, AND ALL OF MY FRIENDS ARE BUSY!
IT'S NOT A PROBLEM!
1

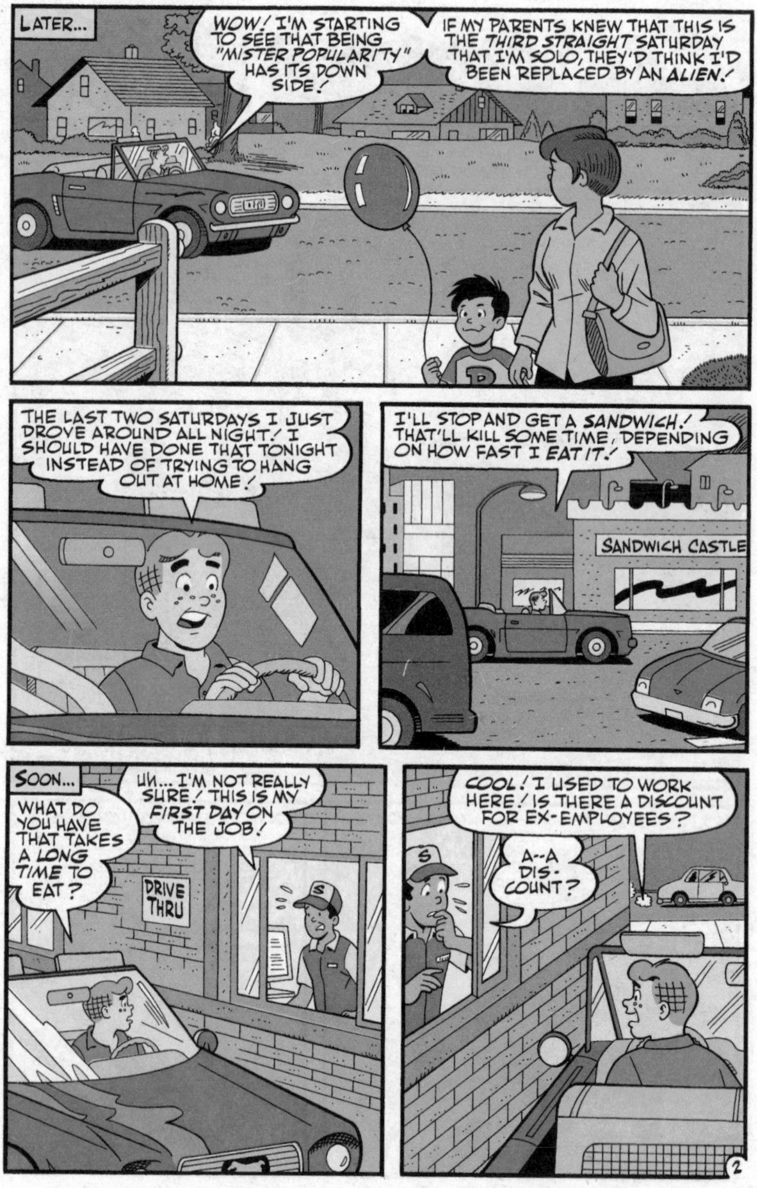
LATER...
WOW! I'M STARTING TO SEE THAT BEING "MISTER POPULARITY" HAS ITS DOWN SIDE!
IF MY PARENTS KNEW THAT THIS IS THE THIRD STRAIGHT SATURDAY THAT I'M SOLO, THEY'D THINK I'D BEEN REPLACED BY AN ALIEN!
THE LAST TWO SATURDAYS I JUST DROVE AROUND ALL NIGHT! I SHOULD HAVE DONE THAT TONIGHT INSTEAD OF TRYING TO HANG OUT AT HOME!
I'LL STOP AND GET A SANDWICH! THAT'LL KILL SOME TIME, DEPENDING ON HOW FAST I EAT IT!
SANDWICH CASTLE
SOON...
WHAT DO YOU HAVE THAT TAKES A LONG TIME TO EAT?
UH... I'M NOT REALLY SURE! THIS IS MY FIRST DAY ON THE JOB!
DRIVE THRU
COOL! I USED TO WORK HERE! IS THERE A DISCOUNT FOR EX-EMPLOYEES?
A--A DIS-COUNT?
2

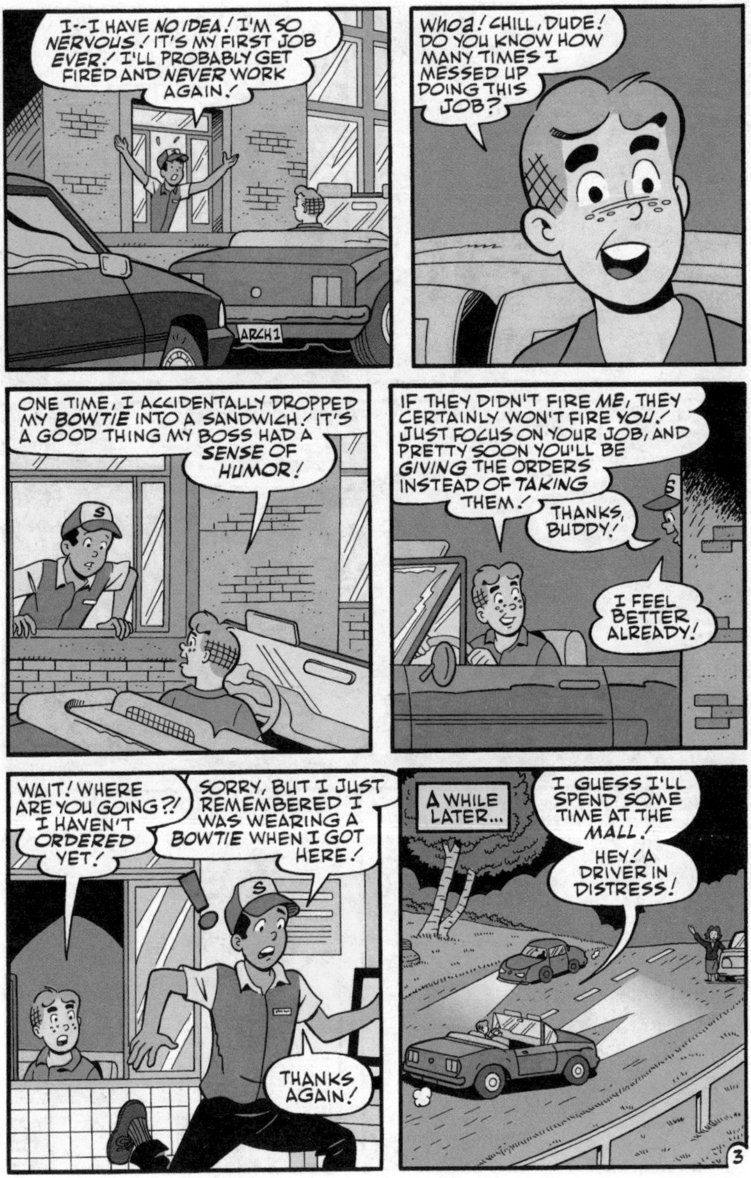
I--I HAVE NO IDEA! I'M SO NERVOUS! IT'S MY FIRST JOB EVER! I'LL PROBABLY GET FIRED AND NEVER WORK AGAIN!
ARCH 1
WHOA! CHILL, DUDE! DO YOU KNOW HOW MANY TIMES I MESSED UP DOING THIS JOB?
ONE TIME, I ACCIDENTALLY DROPPED MY BOWTIE INTO A SANDWICH! IT'S A GOOD THING MY BOSS HAD A SENSE OF HUMOR!
IF THEY DIDN'T FIRE ME, THEY CERTAINLY WON'T FIRE YOU! JUST FOCUS ON YOUR JOB, AND PRETTY SOON YOU'LL BE GIVING THE ORDERS INSTEAD OF TAKING THEM!
THANKS, BUDDY!
I FEEL BETTER ALREADY!
WAIT! WHERE ARE YOU GOING?! I HAVEN'T ORDERED YET!
SORRY, BUT I JUST REMEMBERED I WAS WEARING A BOWTIE WHEN I GOT HERE!
THANKS AGAIN!
A WHILE LATER...
I GUESS I'LL SPEND SOME TIME AT THE MALL!
HEY! A DRIVER IN DISTRESS!
3

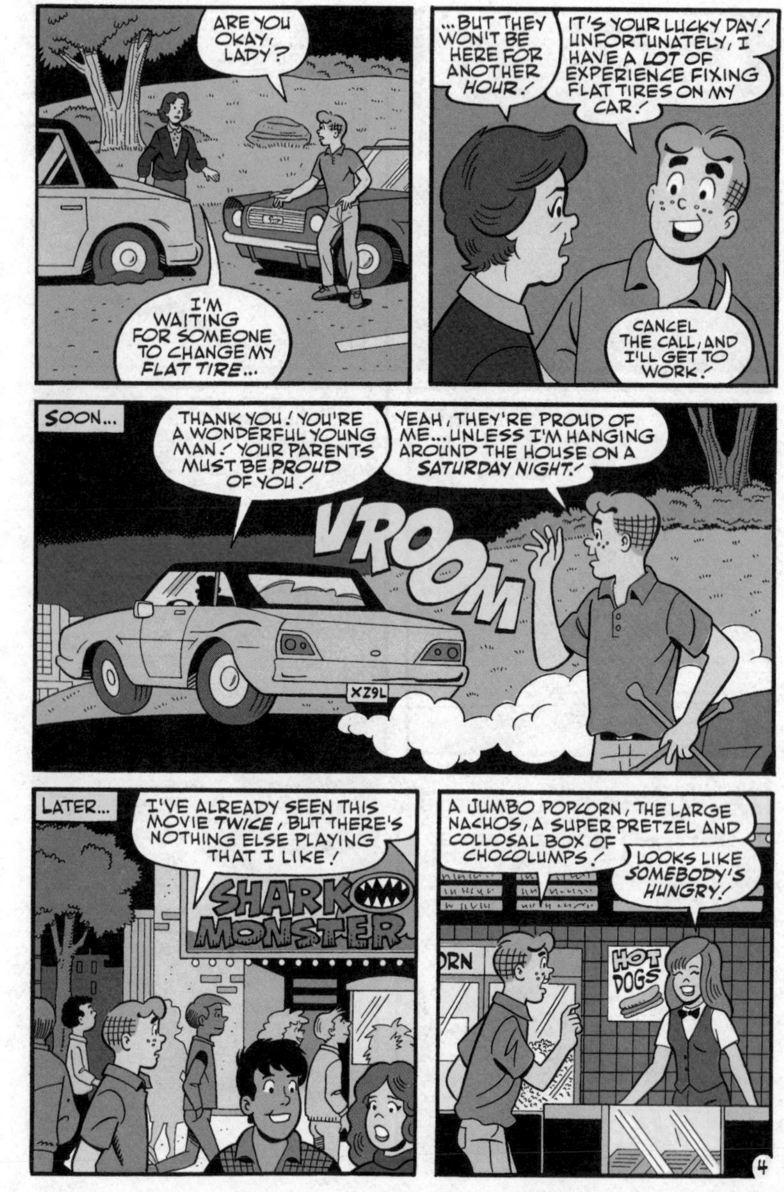
ARE YOU OKAY, LADY?
I'M WAITING FOR SOMEONE TO CHANGE MY FLAT TIRE...
...BUT THEY WON'T BE HERE FOR ANOTHER HOUR!
IT'S YOUR LUCKY DAY! UNFORTUNATELY, I HAVE A LOT OF EXPERIENCE FIXING FLAT TIRES ON MY CAR!
CANCEL THE CALL, AND I'LL GET TO WORK!
SOON...
THANK YOU! YOU'RE A WONDERFUL YOUNG MAN! YOUR PARENTS MUST BE PROUD OF YOU!
YEAH, THEY'RE PROUD OF ME... UNLESS I'M HANGING AROUND THE HOUSE ON A SATURDAY NIGHT!
VROOM
XZ9L
LATER...
I'VE ALREADY SEEN THIS MOVIE TWICE, BUT THERE'S NOTHING ELSE PLAYING THAT I LIKE!
SHARK MONSTER
A JUMBO POPCORN, THE LARGE NACHOS, A SUPER PRETZEL AND COLLOSAL BOX OF CHOCOLUMPS!
LOOKS LIKE SOMEBODY'S HUNGRY!
HOT DOGS
4

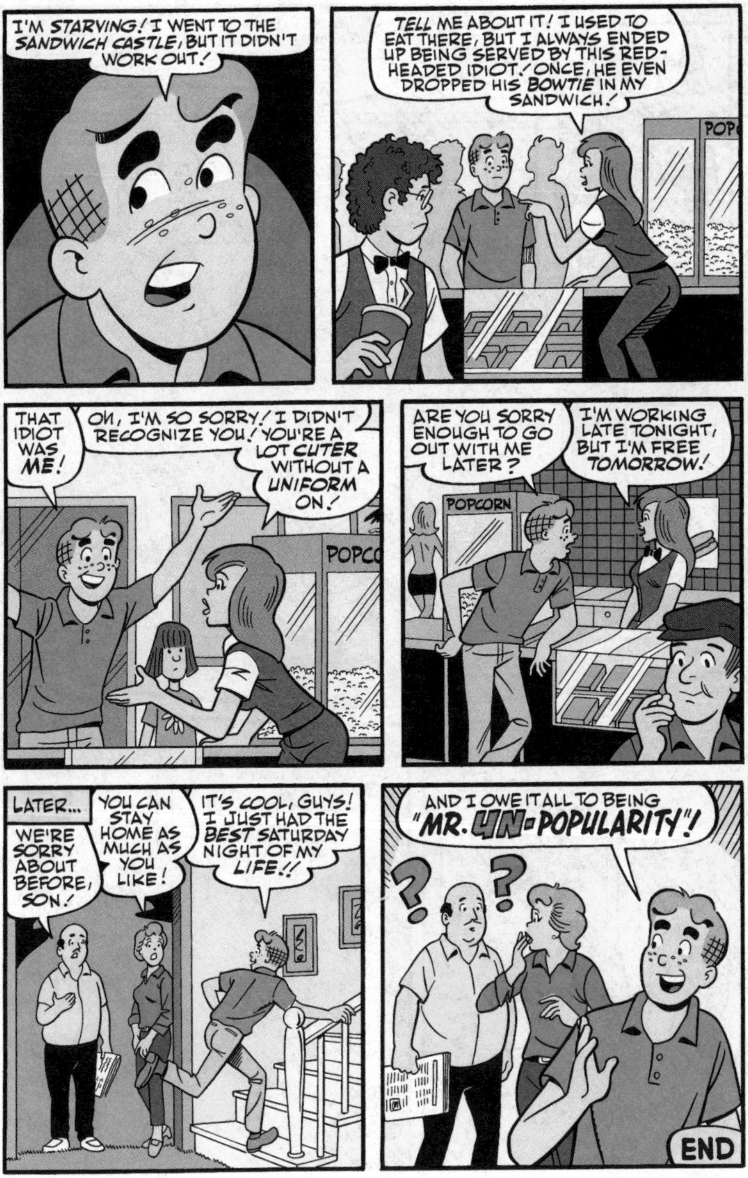
I'M STARVING! I WENT TO THE SANDWICH CASTLE, BUT IT DIDN'T WORK OUT!
TELL ME ABOUT IT! I USED TO EAT THERE, BUT I ALWAYS ENDED UP BEING SERVED BY THIS RED-HEADED IDIOT! ONCE, HE EVEN DROPPED HIS BOWTIE IN MY SANDWICH!
POPC
THAT IDIOT WAS ME!
OH, I'M SO SORRY! I DIDN'T RECOGNIZE YOU! YOU'RE A LOT CUTER WITHOUT A UNIFORM ON!
POPCO
ARE YOU SORRY ENOUGH TO GO OUT WITH ME LATER?
I'M WORKING LATE TONIGHT, BUT I'M FREE TOMORROW!
POPCORN
LATER...
WE'RE SORRY ABOUT BEFORE, SON!
YOU CAN STAY HOME AS MUCH AS YOU LIKE!
IT'S COOL, GUYS! I JUST HAD THE BEST SATURDAY NIGHT OF MY LIFE!!
AND I OWE IT ALL TO BEING "MR. UN-POPULARITY"!
END

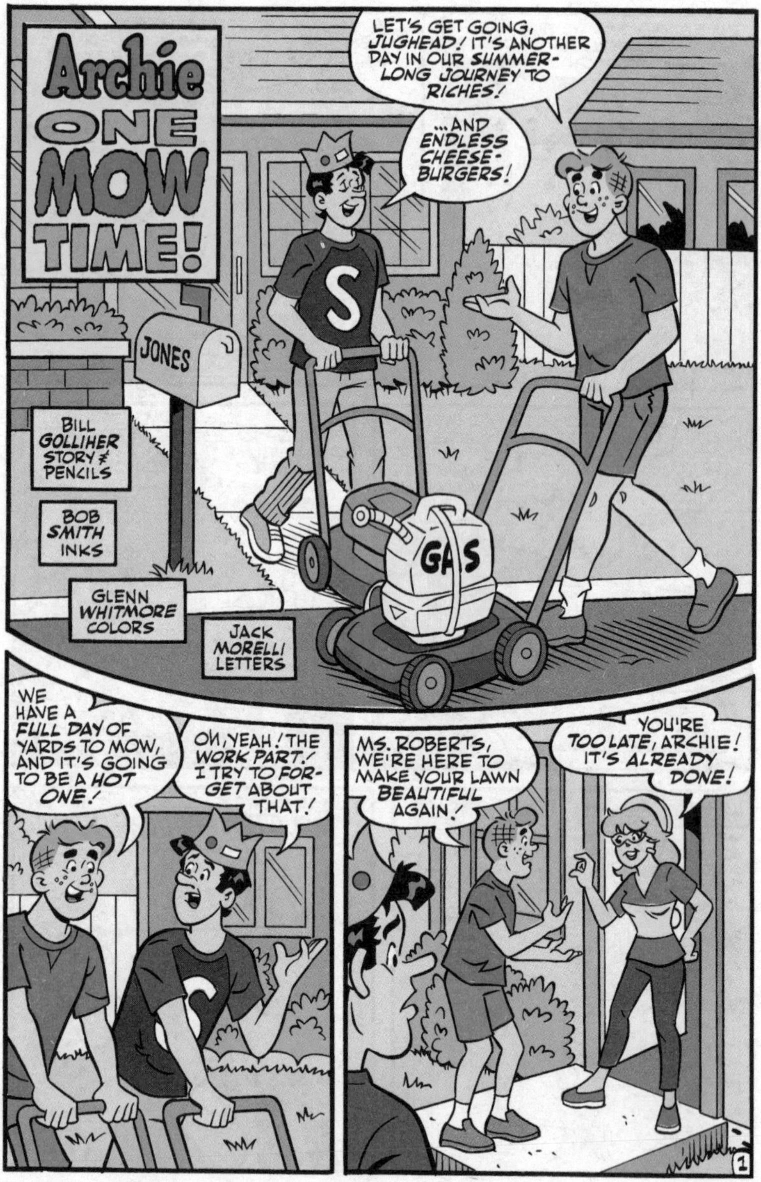
Archie
ONE MOW TIME!
LET'S GET GOING, JUGHEAD! IT'S ANOTHER DAY IN OUR SUMMER-LONG JOURNEY TO RICHES!
...AND ENDLESS CHEESE-BURGERS!
JONES
BILL GOLLIHER STORY & PENCILS
BOB SMITH INKS
GLENN WHITMORE COLORS
JACK MORELLI LETTERS
GAS
WE HAVE A FULL DAY OF YARDS TO MOW, AND IT'S GOING TO BE A HOT ONE!
OH, YEAH! THE WORK PART! I TRY TO FOR-GET ABOUT THAT!
MS. ROBERTS, WE'RE HERE TO MAKE YOUR LAWN BEAUTIFUL AGAIN!
YOU'RE TOO LATE, ARCHIE! IT'S ALREADY DONE!
1

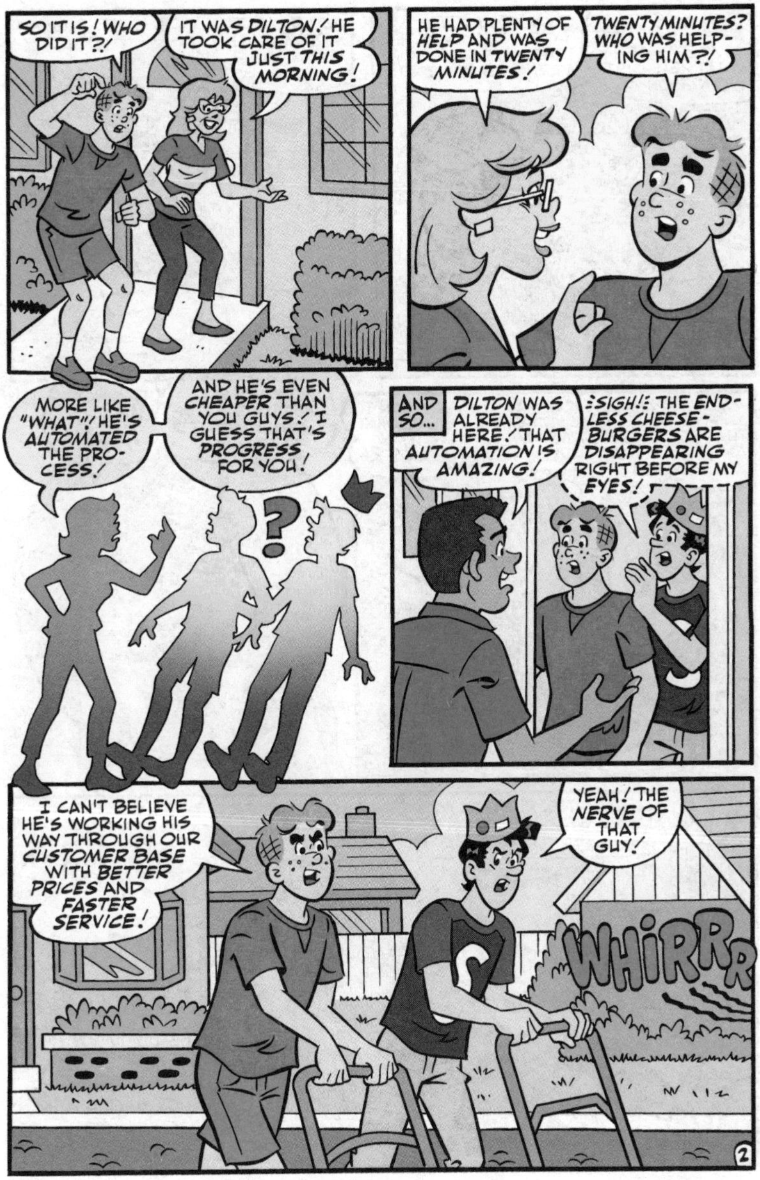
SO IT IS! WHO DID IT?!
IT WAS DILTON! HE TOOK CARE OF IT JUST THIS MORNING!
HE HAD PLENTY OF HELP AND WAS DONE IN TWENTY MINUTES!
TWENTY MINUTES? WHO WAS HELPING HIM?!
MORE LIKE "WHAT"! HE'S AUTOMATED THE PROCESS!
AND HE'S EVEN CHEAPER THAN YOU GUYS! I GUESS THAT'S PROGRESS FOR YOU!
AND SO...
DILTON WAS ALREADY HERE! THAT AUTOMATION IS AMAZING!
:SIGH!: THE ENDLESS CHEESEBURGERS ARE DISAPPEARING RIGHT BEFORE MY EYES!
I CAN'T BELIEVE HE'S WORKING HIS WAY THROUGH OUR CUSTOMER BASE WITH BETTER PRICES AND FASTER SERVICE!
YEAH! THE NERVE OF THAT GUY!
WHIRRR
2

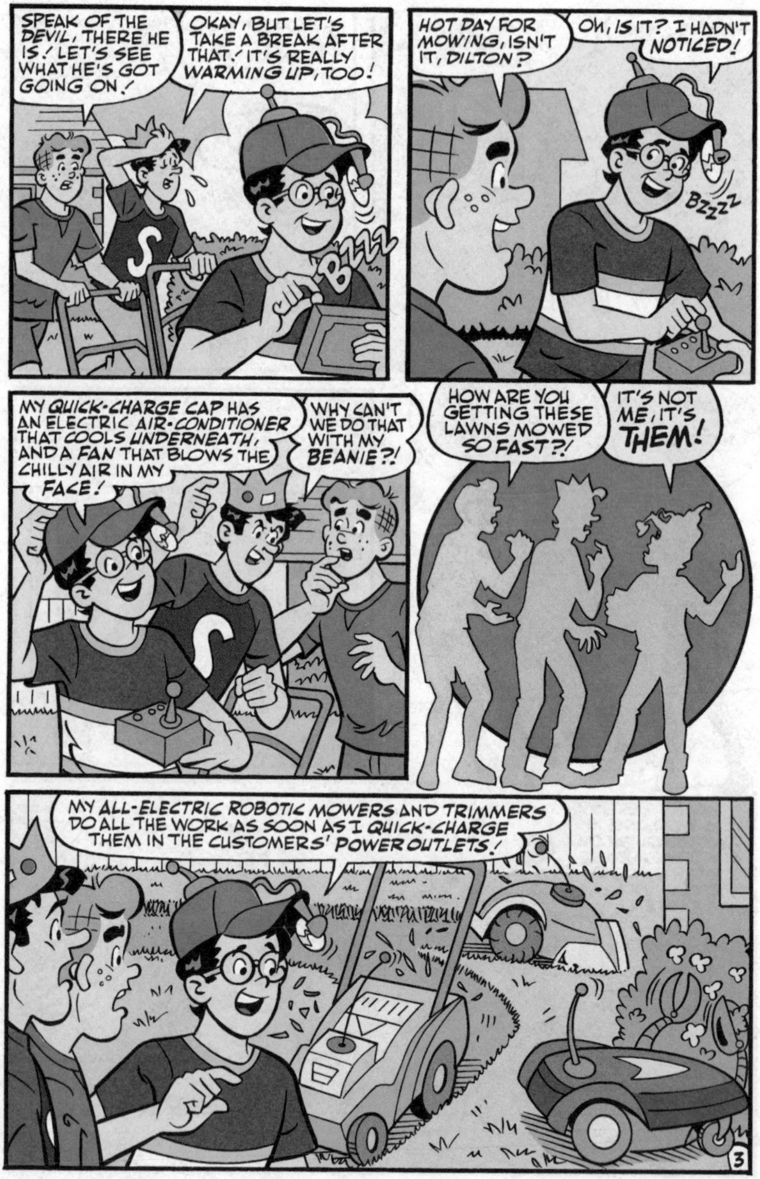
SPEAK OF THE DEVIL, THERE HE IS! LET'S SEE WHAT HE'S GOT GOING ON!
OKAY, BUT LET'S TAKE A BREAK AFTER THAT! IT'S REALLY WARMING UP, TOO!
BZZZ
HOT DAY FOR MOWING, ISN'T IT, DILTON?
OH, IS IT? I HADN'T NOTICED!
BZZZZ
MY QUICK-CHARGE CAP HAS AN ELECTRIC AIR-CONDITIONER THAT COOLS UNDERNEATH, AND A FAN THAT BLOWS THE CHILLY AIR IN MY FACE!
WHY CAN'T WE DO THAT WITH MY BEANIE?!
HOW ARE YOU GETTING THESE LAWNS MOWED SO FAST?!
IT'S NOT ME, IT'S THEM!
MY ALL-ELECTRIC ROBOTIC MOWERS AND TRIMMERS DO ALL THE WORK AS SOON AS I QUICK-CHARGE THEM IN THE CUSTOMERS' POWER OUTLETS!
3

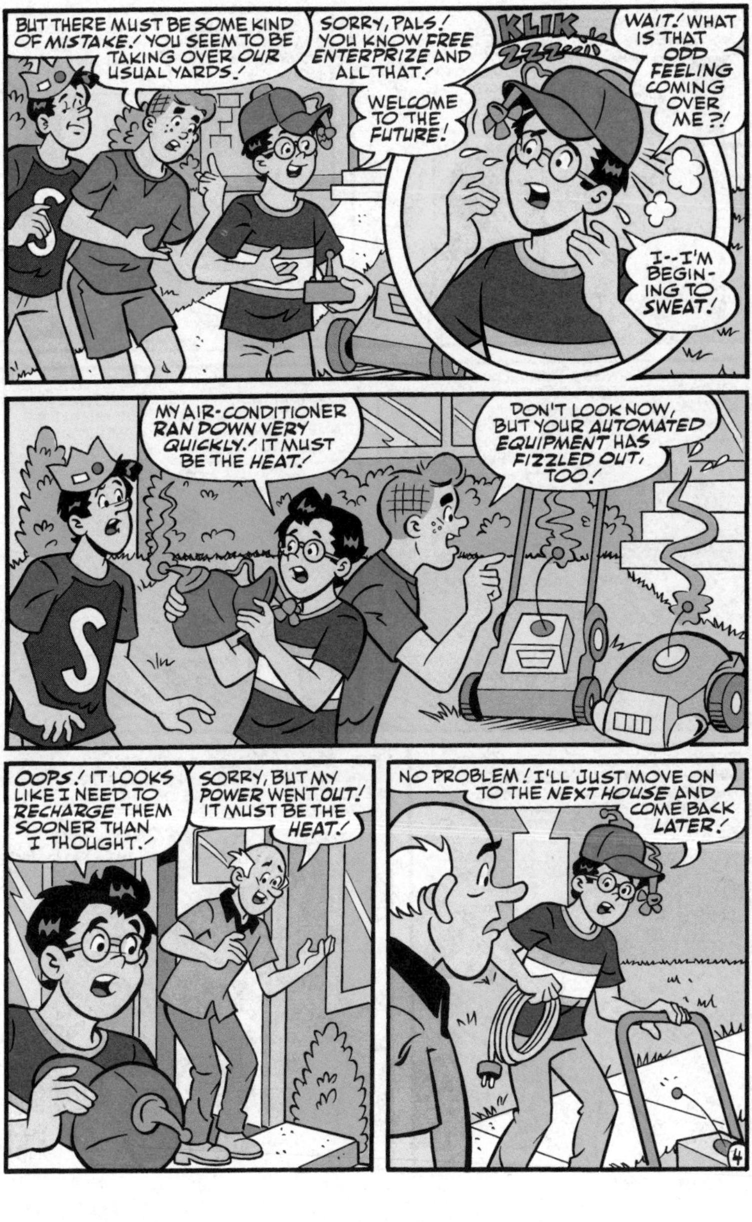
BUT THERE MUST BE SOME KIND OF MISTAKE! YOU SEEM TO BE TAKING OVER OUR USUAL YARDS!
SORRY, PALS! YOU KNOW FREE ENTERPRIZE AND ALL THAT!
WELCOME TO THE FUTURE!
KLIK
WAIT! WHAT IS THAT ODD FEELING COMING OVER ME?!
I--I'M BEGIN-ING TO SWEAT!
MY AIR-CONDITIONER RAN DOWN VERY QUICKLY! IT MUST BE THE HEAT!
DON'T LOOK NOW, BUT YOUR AUTOMATED EQUIPMENT HAS FIZZLED OUT, TOO!
OOPS! IT LOOKS LIKE I NEED TO RECHARGE THEM SOONER THAN I THOUGHT!
SORRY, BUT MY POWER WENT OUT! IT MUST BE THE HEAT!
NO PROBLEM! I'LL JUST MOVE ON TO THE NEXT HOUSE AND COME BACK LATER!
4

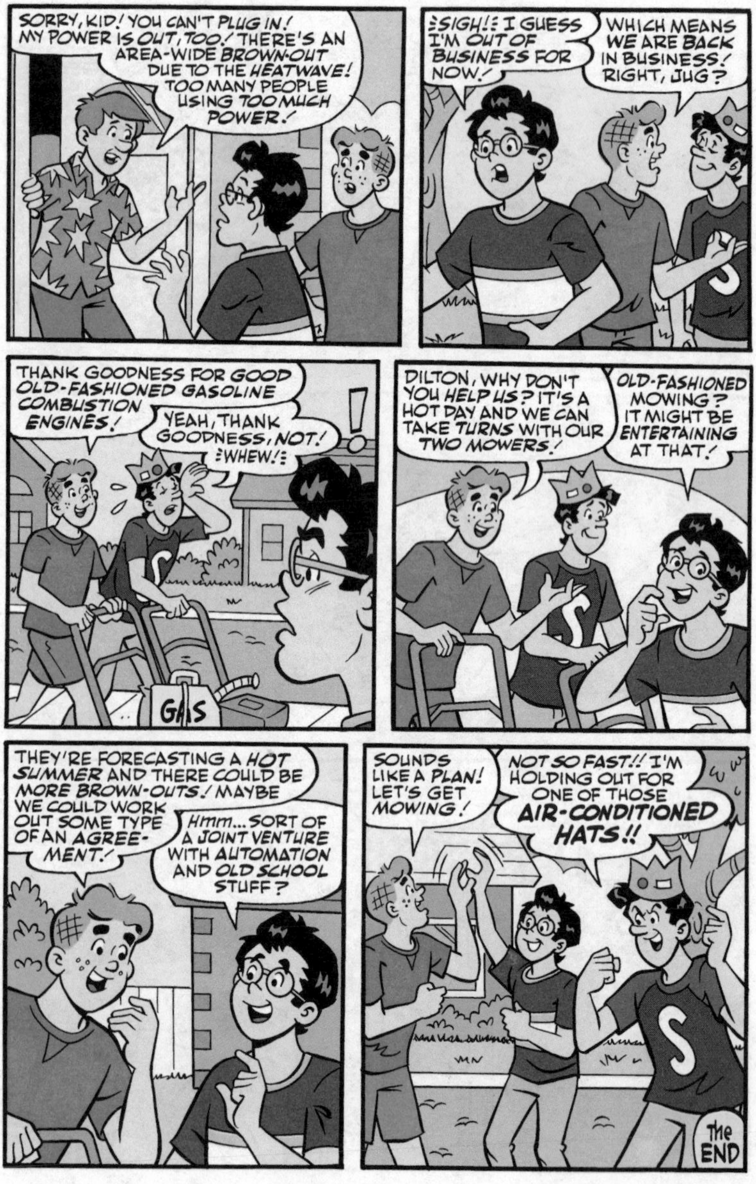
SORRY, KID! YOU CAN'T PLUG IN! MY POWER IS OUT, TOO! THERE'S AN AREA-WIDE BROWN-OUT DUE TO THE HEATWAVE! TOO MANY PEOPLE USING TOO MUCH POWER!
SIGH!! I GUESS I'M OUT OF BUSINESS FOR NOW!
WHICH MEANS WE ARE BACK IN BUSINESS! RIGHT, JUG?
THANK GOODNESS FOR GOOD OLD-FASHIONED GASOLINE COMBUSTION ENGINES!
YEAH, THANK GOODNESS, NOT! WHEW!
!
GAS
DILTON, WHY DON'T YOU HELP US? IT'S A HOT DAY AND WE CAN TAKE TURNS WITH OUR TWO MOWERS!
OLD-FASHIONED MOWING? IT MIGHT BE ENTERTAINING AT THAT!
THEY'RE FORECASTING A HOT SUMMER AND THERE COULD BE MORE BROWN-OUTS! MAYBE WE COULD WORK OUT SOME TYPE OF AN AGREE-MENT!
Hmm... SORT OF A JOINT VENTURE WITH AUTOMATION AND OLD SCHOOL STUFF?
SOUNDS LIKE A PLAN! LET'S GET MOWING!
NOT SO FAST!! I'M HOLDING OUT FOR ONE OF THOSE AIR-CONDITIONED HATS!!
THE END

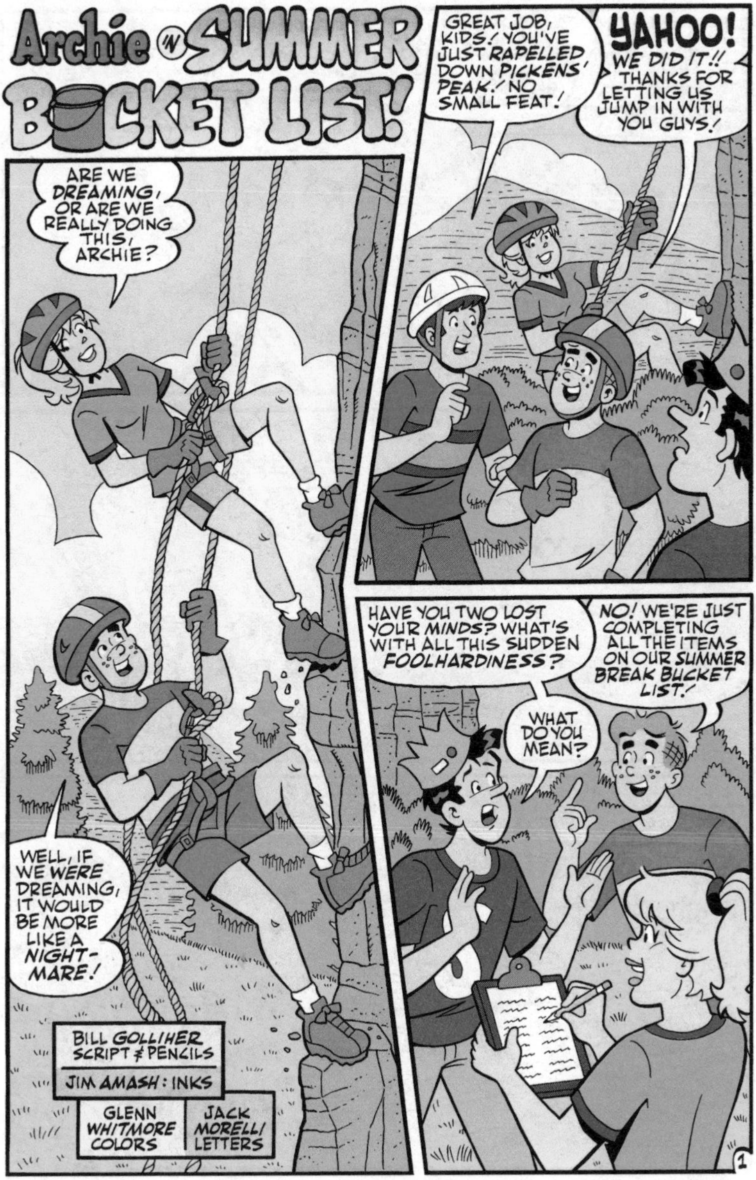
Archie in SUMMER BUCKET LIST!
GREAT JOB, KIDS! YOU'VE JUST RAPELLED DOWN PICKENS' PEAK! NO SMALL FEAT!
YAHOO! WE DID IT!! THANKS FOR LETTING US JUMP IN WITH YOU GUYS!
ARE WE DREAMING, OR ARE WE REALLY DOING THIS, ARCHIE?
WELL, IF WE WERE DREAMING, IT WOULD BE MORE LIKE A NIGHT-MARE!
BILL GOLLIHER SCRIPT & PENCILS
JIM AMASH: INKS
GLENN WHITMORE COLORS
JACK MORELLI LETTERS
HAVE YOU TWO LOST YOUR MINDS? WHAT'S WITH ALL THIS SUDDEN FOOLHARDINESS?
NO! WE'RE JUST COMPLETING ALL THE ITEMS ON OUR SUMMER BREAK BUCKET LIST!
WHAT DO YOU MEAN?
1

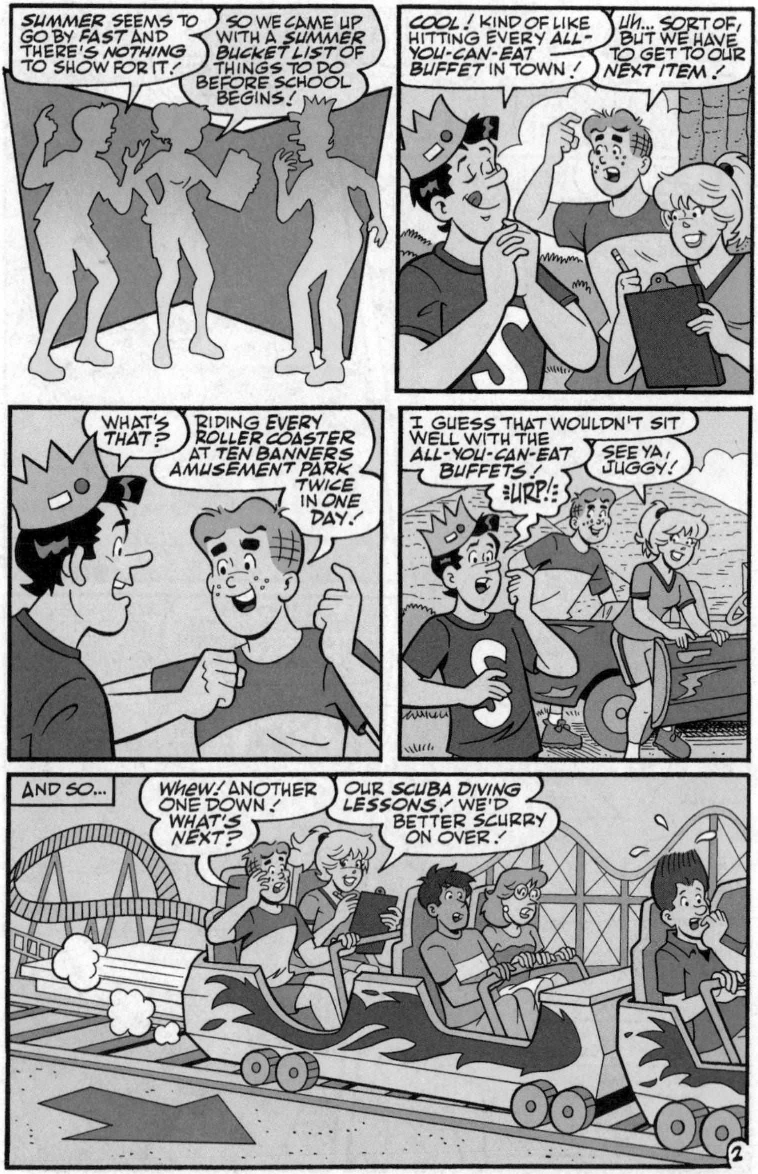
SUMMER SEEMS TO GO BY FAST AND THERE'S NOTHING TO SHOW FOR IT!
SO WE CAME UP WITH A SUMMER BUCKET LIST OF THINGS TO DO BEFORE SCHOOL BEGINS!
COOL! KIND OF LIKE HITTING EVERY ALL-YOU-CAN-EAT BUFFET IN TOWN!
UH... SORT OF, BUT WE HAVE TO GET TO OUR NEXT ITEM!
WHAT'S THAT?
RIDING EVERY ROLLER COASTER AT TEN BANNERS AMUSEMENT PARK TWICE IN ONE DAY!
I GUESS THAT WOULDN'T SIT WELL WITH THE ALL-YOU-CAN-EAT BUFFETS!
SEE YA, JUGGY!
URP!
AND SO...
Whew! ANOTHER ONE DOWN! WHAT'S NEXT?
OUR SCUBA DIVING LESSONS! WE'D BETTER SCURRY ON OVER!
2

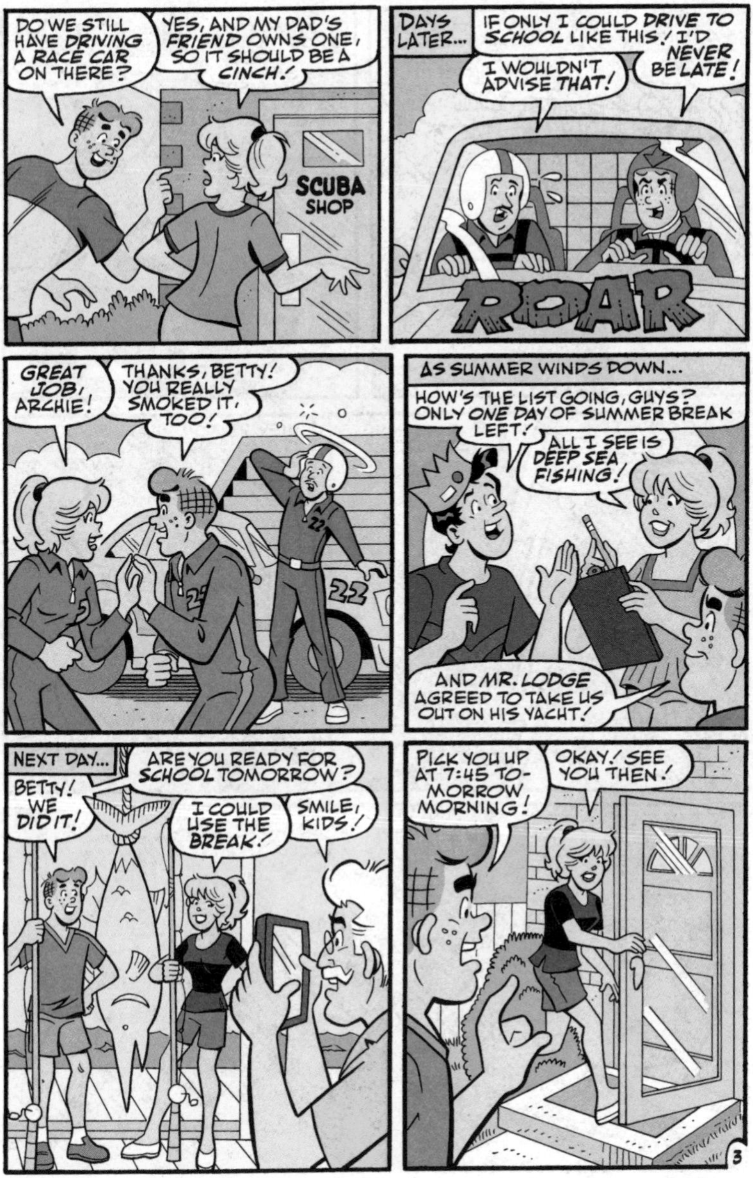
DO WE STILL HAVE DRIVING A RACE CAR ON THERE?
YES, AND MY DAD'S FRIEND OWNS ONE, SO IT SHOULD BE A CINCH!
SCUBA SHOP
DAYS LATER...
IF ONLY I COULD DRIVE TO SCHOOL LIKE THIS! I'D NEVER BE LATE!
I WOULDN'T ADVISE THAT!
ROAR
GREAT JOB, ARCHIE!
THANKS, BETTY! YOU REALLY SMOKED IT, TOO!
AS SUMMER WINDS DOWN...
HOW'S THE LIST GOING, GUYS? ONLY ONE DAY OF SUMMER BREAK LEFT!
ALL I SEE IS DEEP SEA FISHING!
AND MR. LODGE AGREED TO TAKE US OUT ON HIS YACHT!
NEXT DAY...
ARE YOU READY FOR SCHOOL TOMORROW?
BETTY! WE DID IT!
I COULD USE THE BREAK!
SMILE, KIDS!
PICK YOU UP AT 7:45 TO-MORROW MORNING!
OKAY! SEE YOU THEN!
3

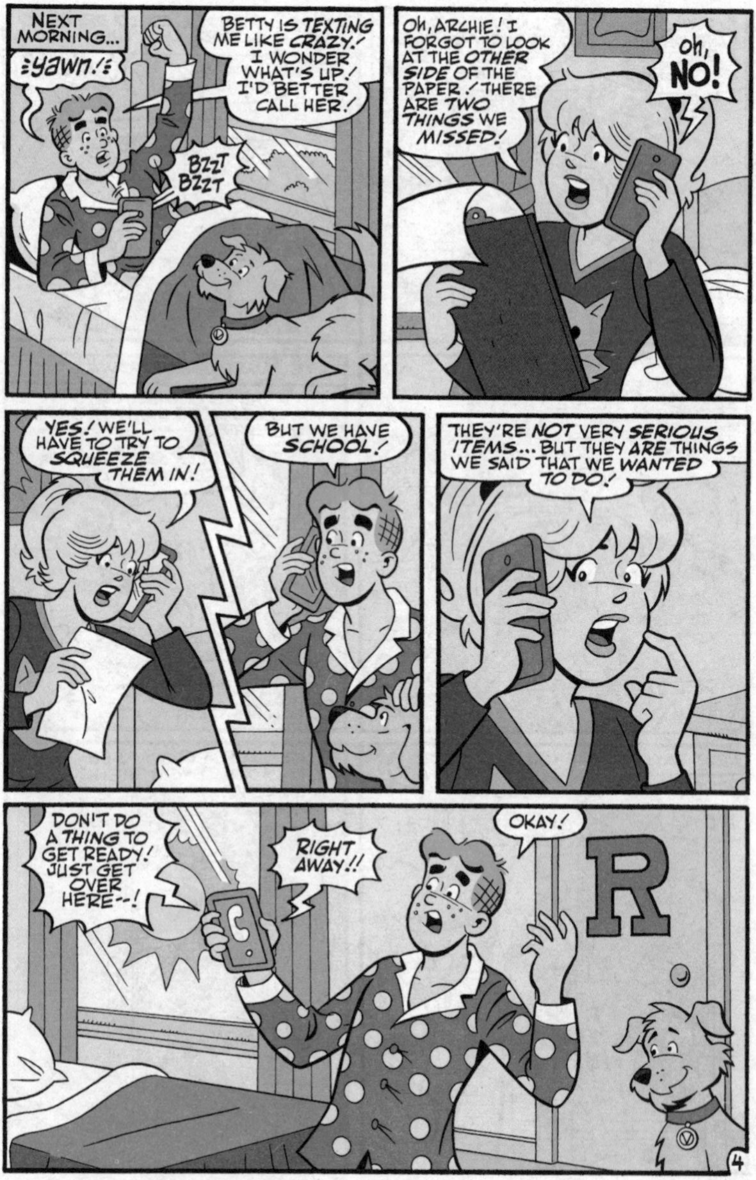
NEXT MORNING...
yawn!
BETTY IS TEXTING ME LIKE CRAZY! I WONDER WHAT'S UP! I'D BETTER CALL HER!
BZZT BZZT
Oh, ARCHIE! I FORGOT TO LOOK AT THE OTHER SIDE OF THE PAPER! THERE ARE TWO THINGS WE MISSED!
Oh, NO!
YES! WE'LL HAVE TO TRY TO SQUEEZE THEM IN!
BUT WE HAVE SCHOOL!
THEY'RE NOT VERY SERIOUS ITEMS... BUT THEY ARE THINGS WE SAID THAT WE WANTED TO DO!
DON'T DO A THING TO GET READY! JUST GET OVER HERE--!
RIGHT AWAY!!
OKAY!
R
4

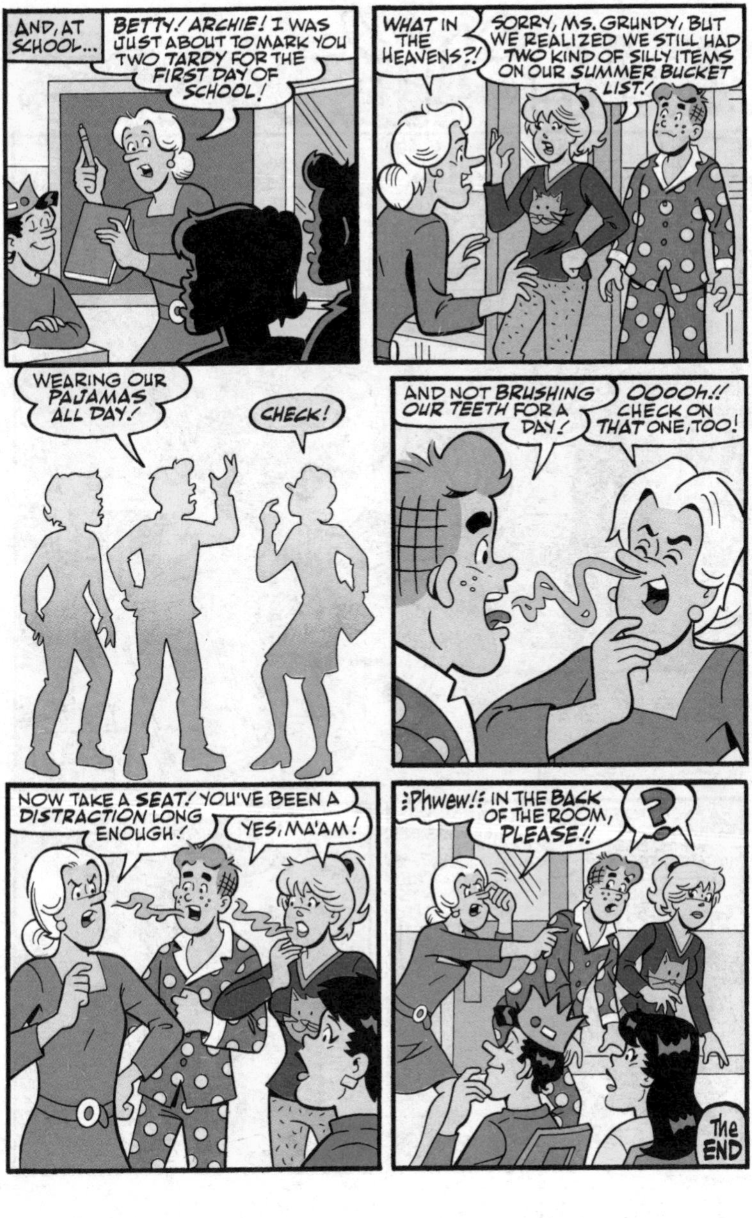
AND, AT SCHOOL...
BETTY! ARCHIE! I WAS JUST ABOUT TO MARK YOU TWO TARDY FOR THE FIRST DAY OF SCHOOL!
WHAT IN THE HEAVENS?!
SORRY, MS. GRUNDY, BUT WE REALIZED WE STILL HAD TWO KIND OF SILLY ITEMS ON OUR SUMMER BUCKET LIST!
WEARING OUR PAJAMAS ALL DAY!
CHECK!
AND NOT BRUSHING OUR TEETH FOR A DAY!
OOOOh!! CHECK ON THAT ONE, TOO!
NOW TAKE A SEAT! YOU'VE BEEN A DISTRACTION LONG ENOUGH!
YES, MA'AM!
:Phwew!: IN THE BACK OF THE ROOM, PLEASE!!
?
The END

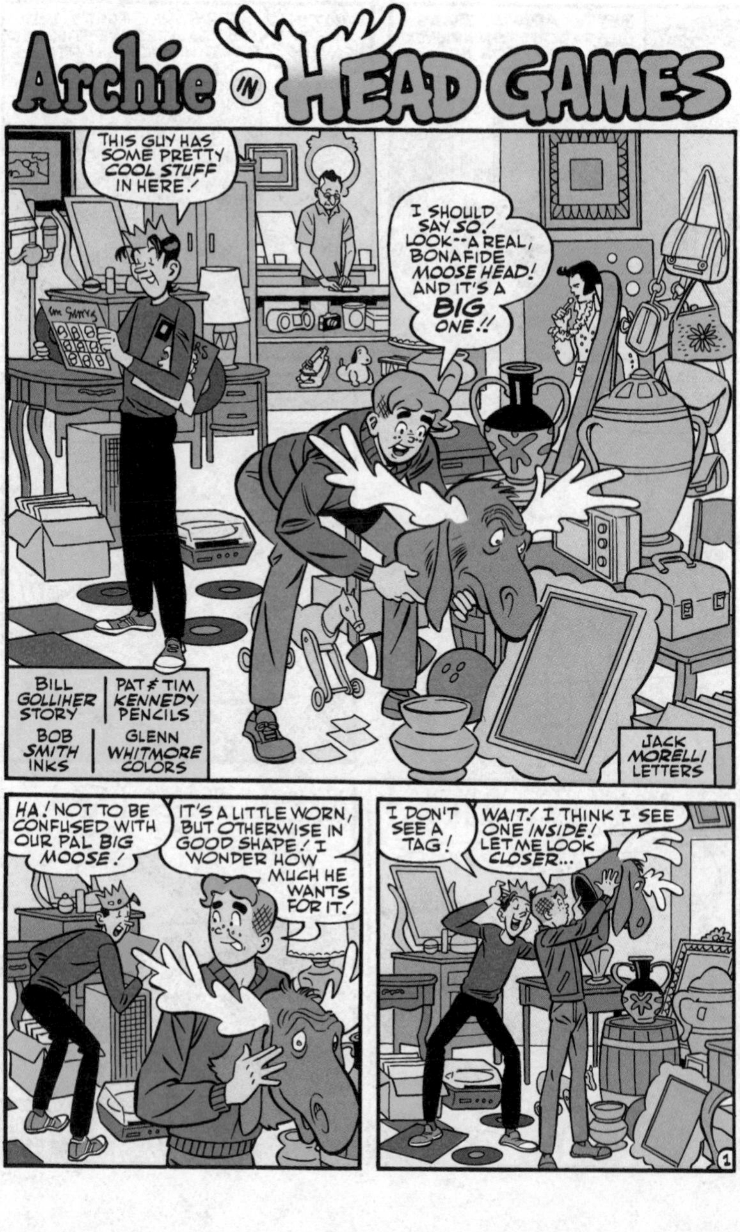
Archie in HEAD GAMES
THIS GUY HAS SOME PRETTY COOL STUFF IN HERE!
I SHOULD SAY SO! LOOK--A REAL, BONAFIDE MOOSE HEAD! AND IT'S A BIG ONE!!
BILL GOLLIHER STORY
PAT & TIM KENNEDY PENCILS
BOB SMITH INKS
GLENN WHITMORE COLORS
JACK MORELLI LETTERS
HA! NOT TO BE CONFUSED WITH OUR PAL BIG MOOSE!
IT'S A LITTLE WORN, BUT OTHERWISE IN GOOD SHAPE! I WONDER HOW MUCH HE WANTS FOR IT!
I DON'T SEE A TAG!
WAIT! I THINK I SEE ONE INSIDE! LET ME LOOK CLOSER...
1

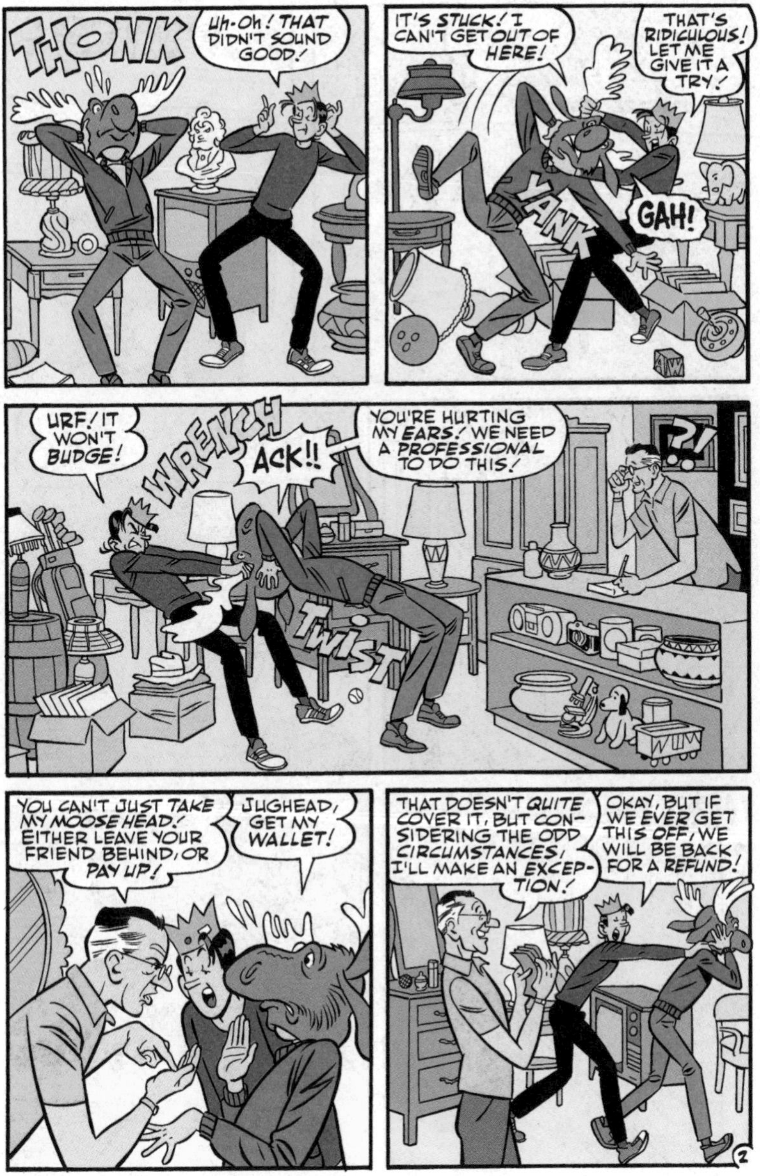
THONK
UH-OH! THAT DIDN'T SOUND GOOD!
IT'S STUCK! I CAN'T GET OUT OF HERE!
THAT'S RIDICULOUS! LET ME GIVE IT A TRY!
YANK
GAH!
URF! IT WON'T BUDGE!
WRENCH
ACK!!
YOU'RE HURTING MY EARS! WE NEED A PROFESSIONAL TO DO THIS!
?!
TWIST
YOU CAN'T JUST TAKE MY MOOSE HEAD! EITHER LEAVE YOUR FRIEND BEHIND, OR PAY UP!
JUGHEAD, GET MY WALLET!
THAT DOESN'T QUITE COVER IT, BUT CONSIDERING THE ODD CIRCUMSTANCES, I'LL MAKE AN EXCEPTION!
OKAY, BUT IF WE EVER GET THIS OFF, WE WILL BE BACK FOR A REFUND!
2

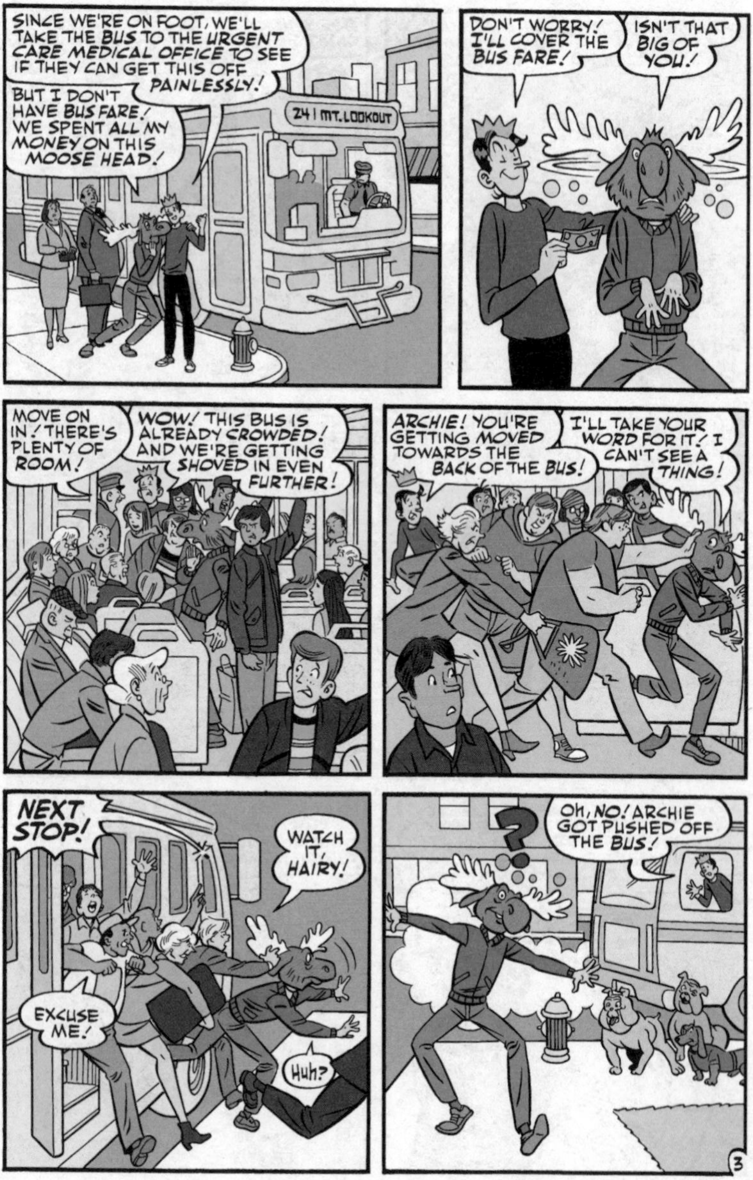
SINCE WE'RE ON FOOT, WE'LL TAKE THE BUS TO THE URGENT CARE MEDICAL OFFICE TO SEE IF THEY CAN GET THIS OFF PAINLESSLY!
BUT I DON'T HAVE BUS FARE! WE SPENT ALL MY MONEY ON THIS MOOSE HEAD!
24 | MT. LOOKOUT
DON'T WORRY! I'LL COVER THE BUS FARE!
ISN'T THAT BIG OF YOU!
MOVE ON IN! THERE'S PLENTY OF ROOM!
WOW! THIS BUS IS ALREADY CROWDED! AND WE'RE GETTING SHOVED IN EVEN FURTHER!
ARCHIE! YOU'RE GETTING MOVED TOWARDS THE BACK OF THE BUS!
I'LL TAKE YOUR WORD FOR IT! I CAN'T SEE A THING!
NEXT STOP!
WATCH IT, HAIRY!
EXCUSE ME!
Huh?
OH, NO! ARCHIE GOT PUSHED OFF THE BUS!
3

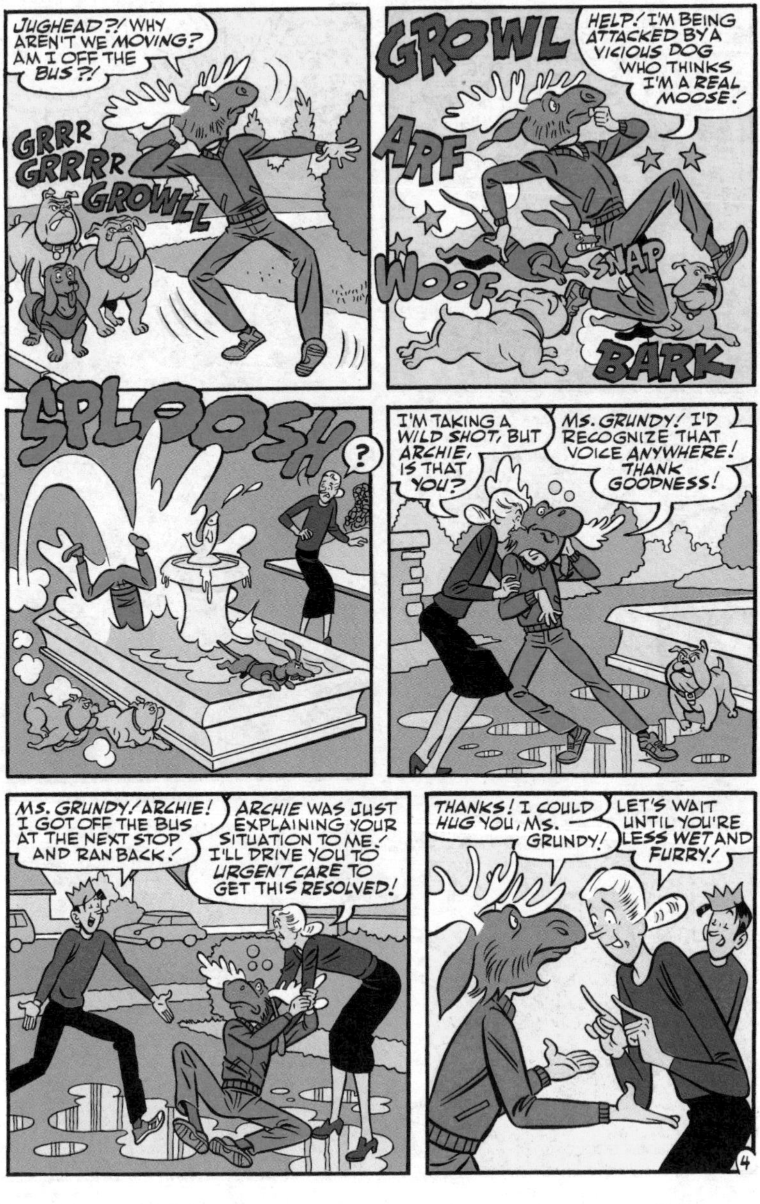
JUGHEAD?! WHY AREN'T WE MOVING? AM I OFF THE BUS?!
GRRR
GRRRR
GROWLL
GROWL
HELP! I'M BEING ATTACKED BY A VICIOUS DOG WHO THINKS I'M A REAL MOOSE!
ARF
WOOF
SNAP
BARK
SPLOOSH
?
I'M TAKING A WILD SHOT, BUT ARCHIE, IS THAT YOU?
MS. GRUNDY! I'D RECOGNIZE THAT VOICE ANYWHERE! THANK GOODNESS!
MS. GRUNDY! ARCHIE! I GOT OFF THE BUS AT THE NEXT STOP AND RAN BACK!
ARCHIE WAS JUST EXPLAINING YOUR SITUATION TO ME! I'LL DRIVE YOU TO URGENT CARE TO GET THIS RESOLVED!
THANKS! I COULD HUG YOU, MS. GRUNDY!
LET'S WAIT UNTIL YOU'RE LESS WET AND FURRY!
4

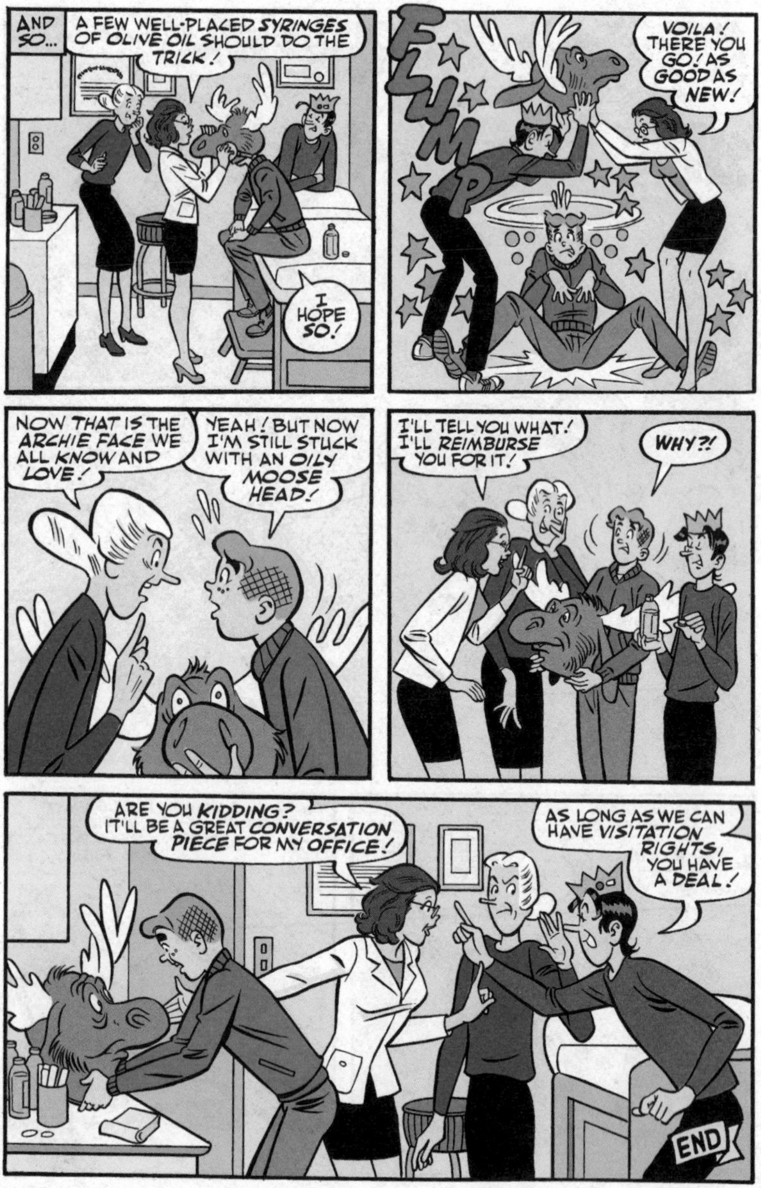
AND SO...
A FEW WELL-PLACED SYRINGES OF OLIVE OIL SHOULD DO THE TRICK!
I HOPE SO!
FLUMP
VOILA! THERE YOU GO! AS GOOD AS NEW!
NOW THAT IS THE ARCHIE FACE WE ALL KNOW AND LOVE!
YEAH! BUT NOW I'M STILL STUCK WITH AN OILY MOOSE HEAD!
I'LL TELL YOU WHAT! I'LL REIMBURSE YOU FOR IT!
WHY?!
ARE YOU KIDDING? IT'LL BE A GREAT CONVERSATION PIECE FOR MY OFFICE!
AS LONG AS WE CAN HAVE VISITATION RIGHTS, YOU HAVE A DEAL!
END

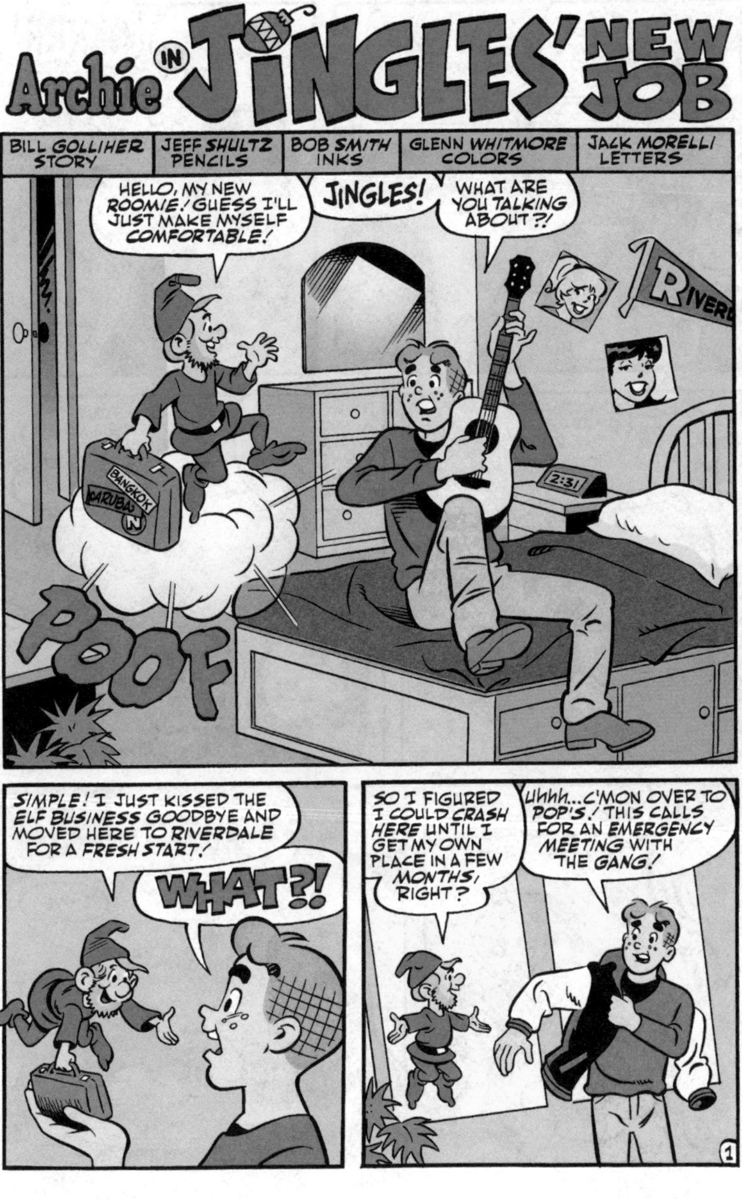
Archie IN JINGLES' NEW JOB
BILL GOLLIHER STORY
JEFF SHULTZ PENCILS
BOB SMITH INKS
GLENN WHITMORE COLORS
JACK MORELLI LETTERS
HELLO, MY NEW ROOMIE! GUESS I'LL JUST MAKE MYSELF COMFORTABLE!
JINGLES!
WHAT ARE YOU TALKING ABOUT?!
BANGKOK
ARUBA
2:31
POOF
SIMPLE! I JUST KISSED THE ELF BUSINESS GOODBYE AND MOVED HERE TO RIVERDALE FOR A FRESH START!
WHAT?!
SO I FIGURED I COULD CRASH HERE UNTIL I GET MY OWN PLACE IN A FEW MONTHS, RIGHT?
UHHH...C'MON OVER TO POP'S! THIS CALLS FOR AN EMERGENCY MEETING WITH THE GANG!
1

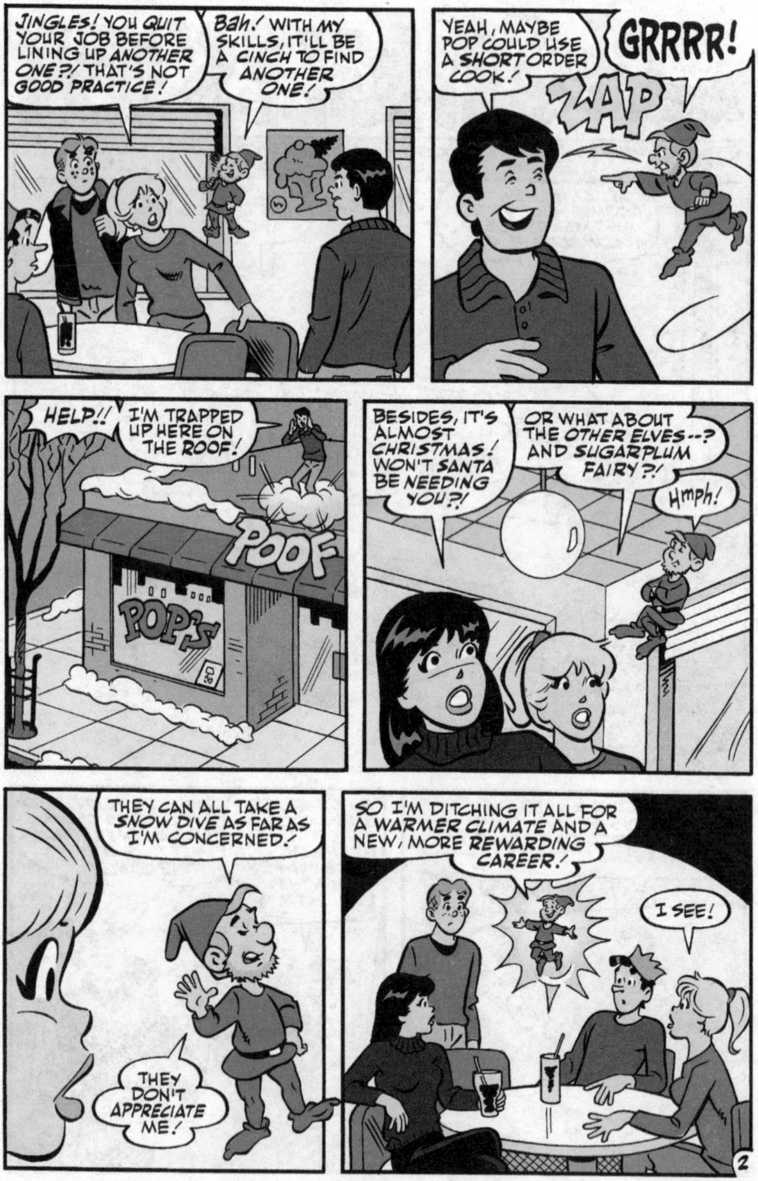
JINGLES! YOU QUIT YOUR JOB BEFORE LINING UP ANOTHER ONE?! THAT'S NOT GOOD PRACTICE!
Bah! WITH MY SKILLS, IT'LL BE A CINCH TO FIND ANOTHER ONE!
YEAH, MAYBE POP COULD USE A SHORT ORDER COOK!
GRRRR!
ZAP
HELP!!
I'M TRAPPED UP HERE ON THE ROOF!
POOF
POP'S
BESIDES, IT'S ALMOST CHRISTMAS! WON'T SANTA BE NEEDING YOU?!
OR WHAT ABOUT THE OTHER ELVES--? AND SUGARPLUM FAIRY?!
Hmph!
THEY CAN ALL TAKE A SNOW DIVE AS FAR AS I'M CONCERNED!
THEY DON'T APPRECIATE ME!
SO I'M DITCHING IT ALL FOR A WARMER CLIMATE AND A NEW, MORE REWARDING CAREER!
I SEE!
2

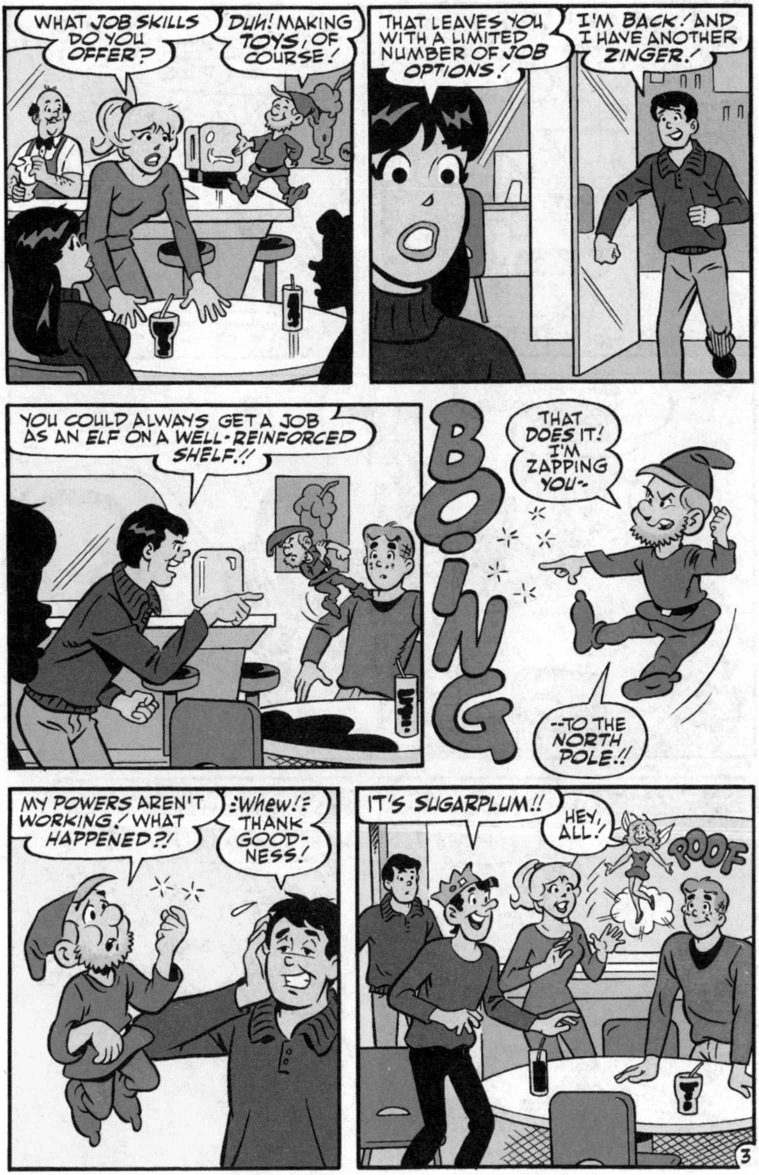
WHAT JOB SKILLS DO YOU OFFER?
DUH! MAKING TOYS, OF COURSE!
THAT LEAVES YOU WITH A LIMITED NUMBER OF JOB OPTIONS!
I'M BACK! AND I HAVE ANOTHER ZINGER!
YOU COULD ALWAYS GET A JOB AS AN ELF ON A WELL-REINFORCED SHELF!!
BOING
THAT DOES IT! I'M ZAPPING YOU--
--TO THE NORTH POLE!!
MY POWERS AREN'T WORKING! WHAT HAPPENED?!
Whew! THANK GOODNESS!
IT'S SUGARPLUM!!
HEY, ALL!
POOF
3

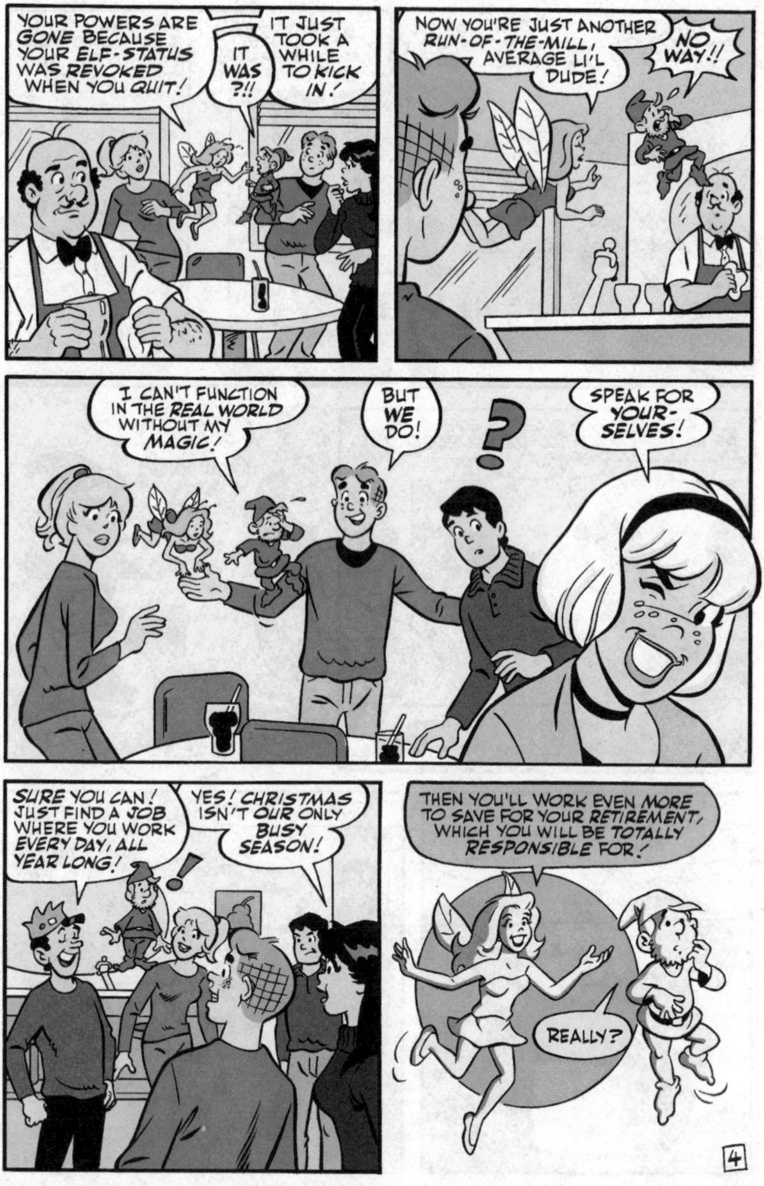
YOUR POWERS ARE GONE BECAUSE YOUR ELF-STATUS WAS REVOKED WHEN YOU QUIT!
IT WAS ?!!
IT JUST TOOK A WHILE TO KICK IN!
NOW YOU'RE JUST ANOTHER RUN-OF-THE-MILL, AVERAGE LI'L DUDE!
NO WAY!!
I CAN'T FUNCTION IN THE REAL WORLD WITHOUT MY MAGIC!
BUT WE DO!
?
SPEAK FOR YOUR-SELVES!
SURE YOU CAN! JUST FIND A JOB WHERE YOU WORK EVERY DAY, ALL YEAR LONG!
YES! CHRISTMAS ISN'T OUR ONLY BUSY SEASON!
!
THEN YOU'LL WORK EVEN MORE TO SAVE FOR YOUR RETIREMENT, WHICH YOU WILL BE TOTALLY RESPONSIBLE FOR!
REALLY?
4

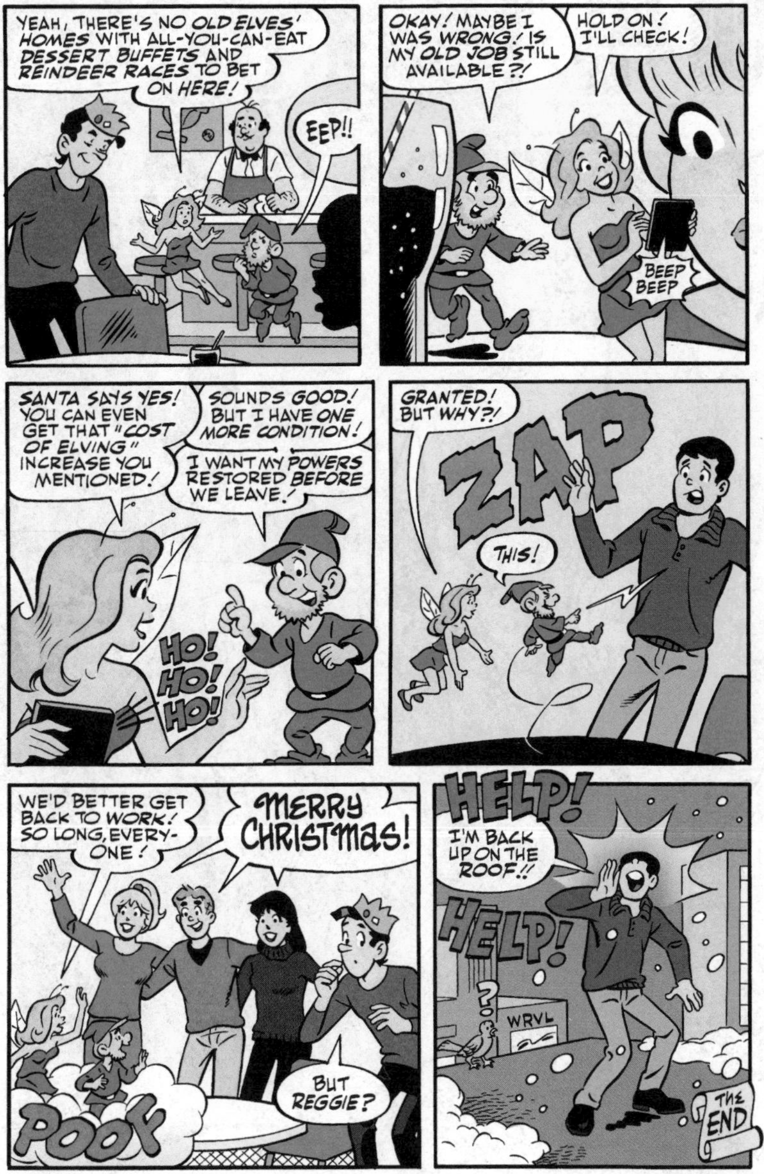
YEAH, THERE'S NO OLD ELVES' HOMES WITH ALL-YOU-CAN-EAT DESSERT BUFFETS AND REINDEER RACES TO BET ON HERE!
EEP!!
OKAY! MAYBE I WAS WRONG! IS MY OLD JOB STILL AVAILABLE?!
HOLD ON! I'LL CHECK!
BEEP BEEP
SANTA SAYS YES! YOU CAN EVEN GET THAT "COST OF ELVING" INCREASE YOU MENTIONED!
SOUNDS GOOD! BUT I HAVE ONE MORE CONDITION!
I WANT MY POWERS RESTORED BEFORE WE LEAVE!
HO! HO! HO!
GRANTED! BUT WHY?!
ZAP
THIS!
WE'D BETTER GET BACK TO WORK! SO LONG, EVERY-ONE!
MERRY CHRISTMAS!
BUT REGGIE?
POOF
HELP!
I'M BACK UP ON THE ROOF!!
HELP!
?
WRVL
THE END

04 B&V FRIENDS

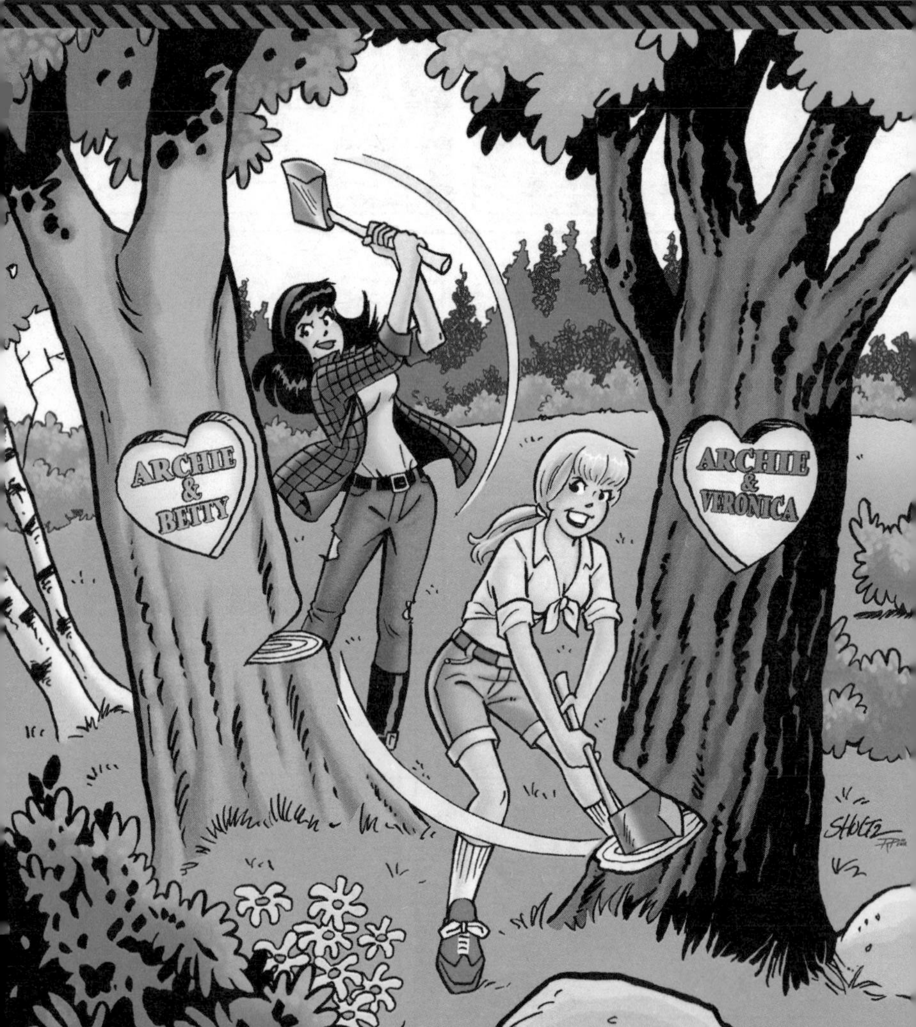
ARCHIE & BETTY
ARCHIE & VERONICA
SHOLTZ

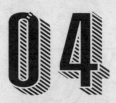

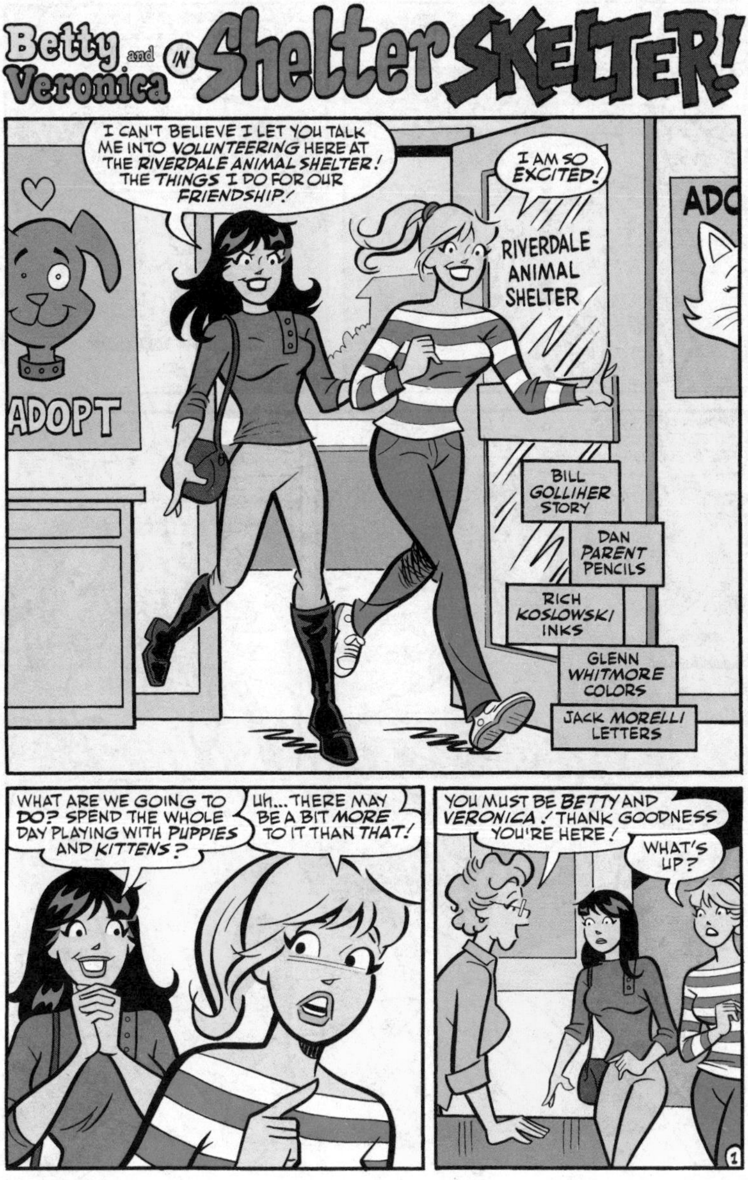
Betty and Veronica IN Shelter SKELTER!
I CAN'T BELIEVE I LET YOU TALK ME INTO VOLUNTEERING HERE AT THE RIVERDALE ANIMAL SHELTER! THE THINGS I DO FOR OUR FRIENDSHIP!
I AM SO EXCITED!
ADOPT
RIVERDALE ANIMAL SHELTER
ADO
BILL GOLLIHER STORY
DAN PARENT PENCILS
RICH KOSLOWSKI INKS
GLENN WHITMORE COLORS
JACK MORELLI LETTERS
WHAT ARE WE GOING TO DO? SPEND THE WHOLE DAY PLAYING WITH PUPPIES AND KITTENS?
UH... THERE MAY BE A BIT MORE TO IT THAN THAT!
YOU MUST BE BETTY AND VERONICA! THANK GOODNESS YOU'RE HERE!
WHAT'S UP?
1

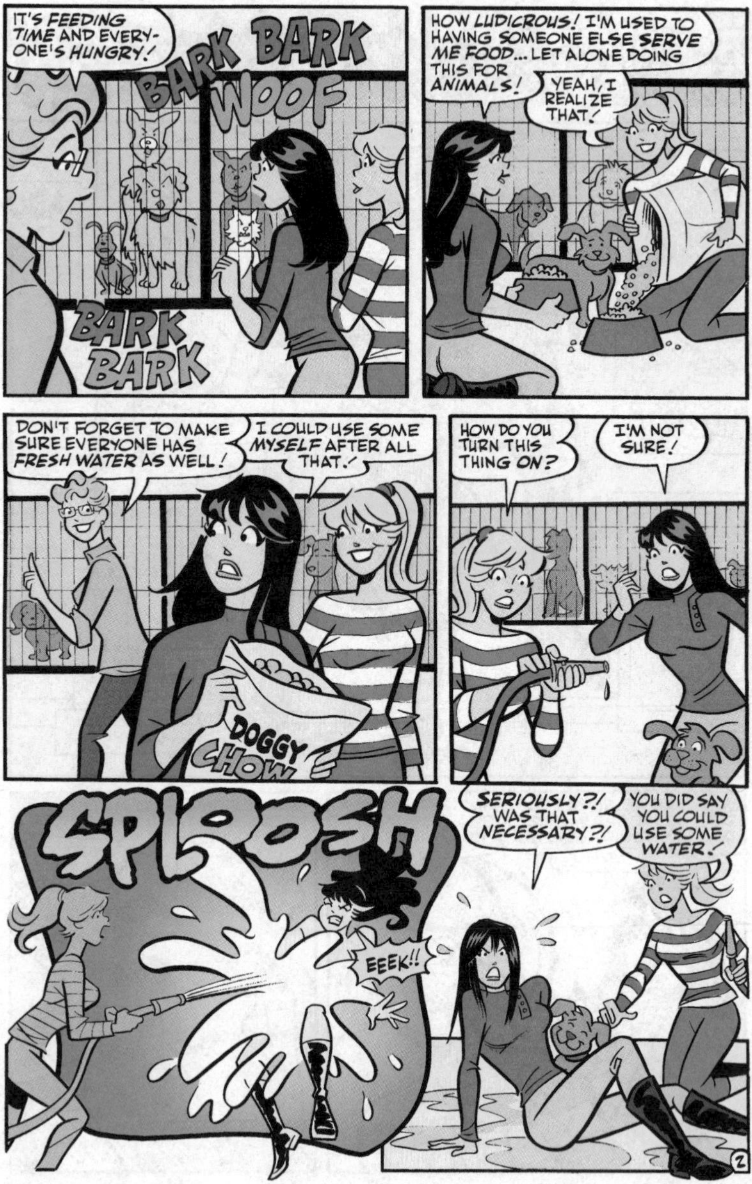
IT'S FEEDING TIME AND EVERY-ONE'S HUNGRY!
BARK BARK
WOOF
BARK BARK
HOW LUDICROUS! I'M USED TO HAVING SOMEONE ELSE SERVE ME FOOD... LET ALONE DOING THIS FOR ANIMALS!
YEAH, I REALIZE THAT!
DON'T FORGET TO MAKE SURE EVERYONE HAS FRESH WATER AS WELL!
I COULD USE SOME MYSELF AFTER ALL THAT!
DOGGY CHOW
HOW DO YOU TURN THIS THING ON?
I'M NOT SURE!
SPLOOSH
EEEK!!
SERIOUSLY?! WAS THAT NECESSARY?!
YOU DID SAY YOU COULD USE SOME WATER!
2

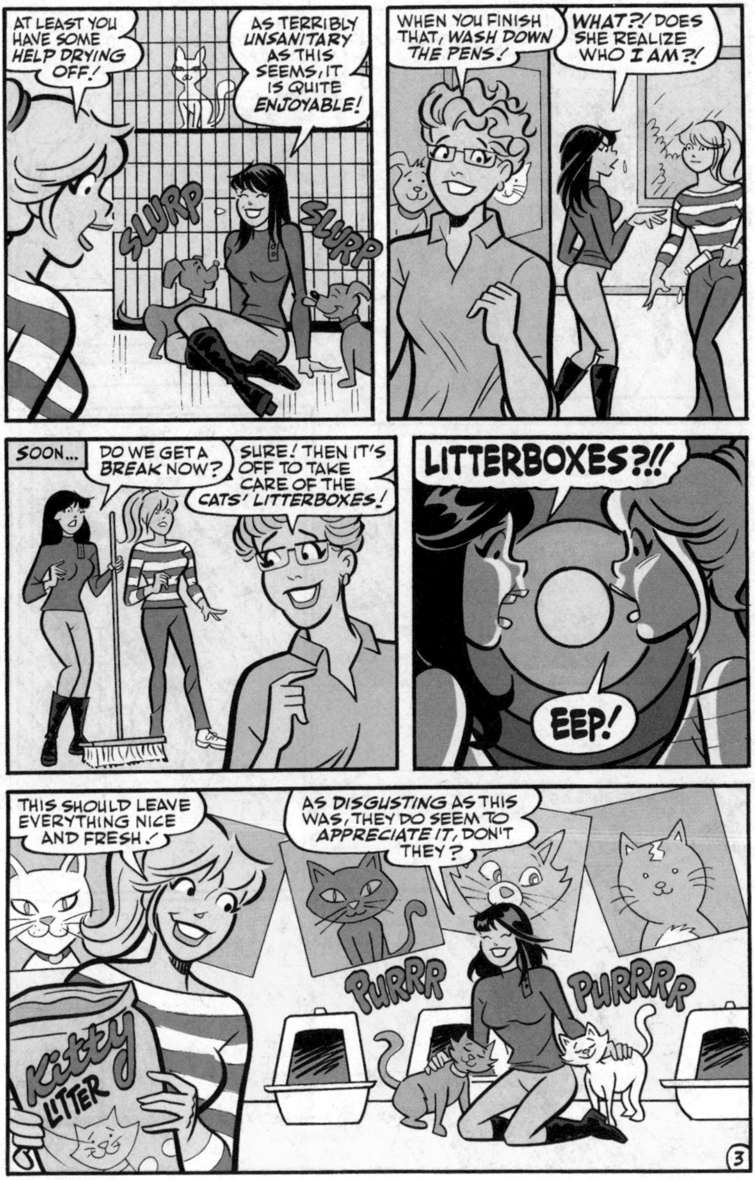
AT LEAST YOU HAVE SOME HELP DRYING OFF!
AS TERRIBLY UNSANITARY AS THIS SEEMS, IT IS QUITE ENJOYABLE!
SLURP
SLURP
WHEN YOU FINISH THAT, WASH DOWN THE PENS!
WHAT?! DOES SHE REALIZE WHO I AM?!
SOON...
DO WE GET A BREAK NOW?
SURE! THEN IT'S OFF TO TAKE CARE OF THE CATS' LITTERBOXES!
LITTERBOXES?!!
EEP!
THIS SHOULD LEAVE EVERYTHING NICE AND FRESH!
AS DISGUSTING AS THIS WAS, THEY DO SEEM TO APPRECIATE IT, DON'T THEY?
PURRR
PURRRR
Kitty LITTER
3

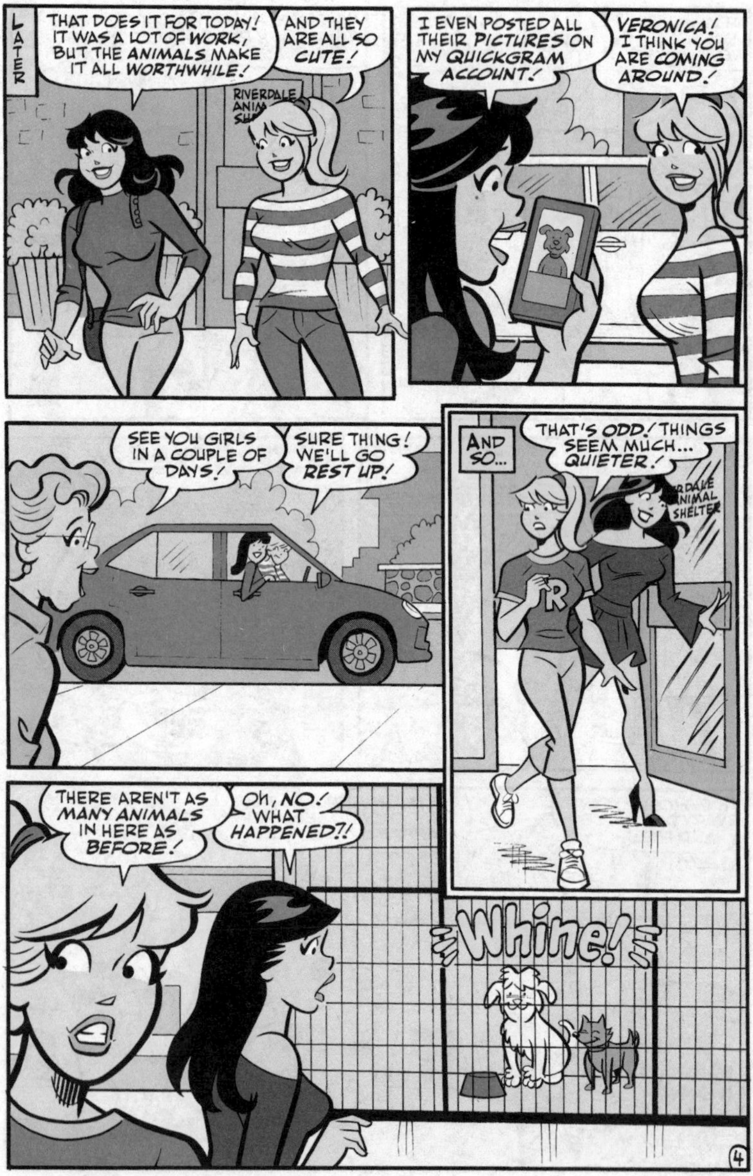
LATER
THAT DOES IT FOR TODAY! IT WAS A LOT OF WORK, BUT THE ANIMALS MAKE IT ALL WORTHWHILE!
AND THEY ARE ALL SO CUTE!
RIVERDALE ANIM
I EVEN POSTED ALL THEIR PICTURES ON MY QUICKGRAM ACCOUNT!
VERONICA! I THINK YOU ARE COMING AROUND!
SEE YOU GIRLS IN A COUPLE OF DAYS!
SURE THING! WE'LL GO REST UP!
AND SO...
THAT'S ODD! THINGS SEEM MUCH... QUIETER!
RDALE NIMAL SHELTER
THERE AREN'T AS MANY ANIMALS IN HERE AS BEFORE!
OH, NO! WHAT HAPPENED?!
WHINE!
4

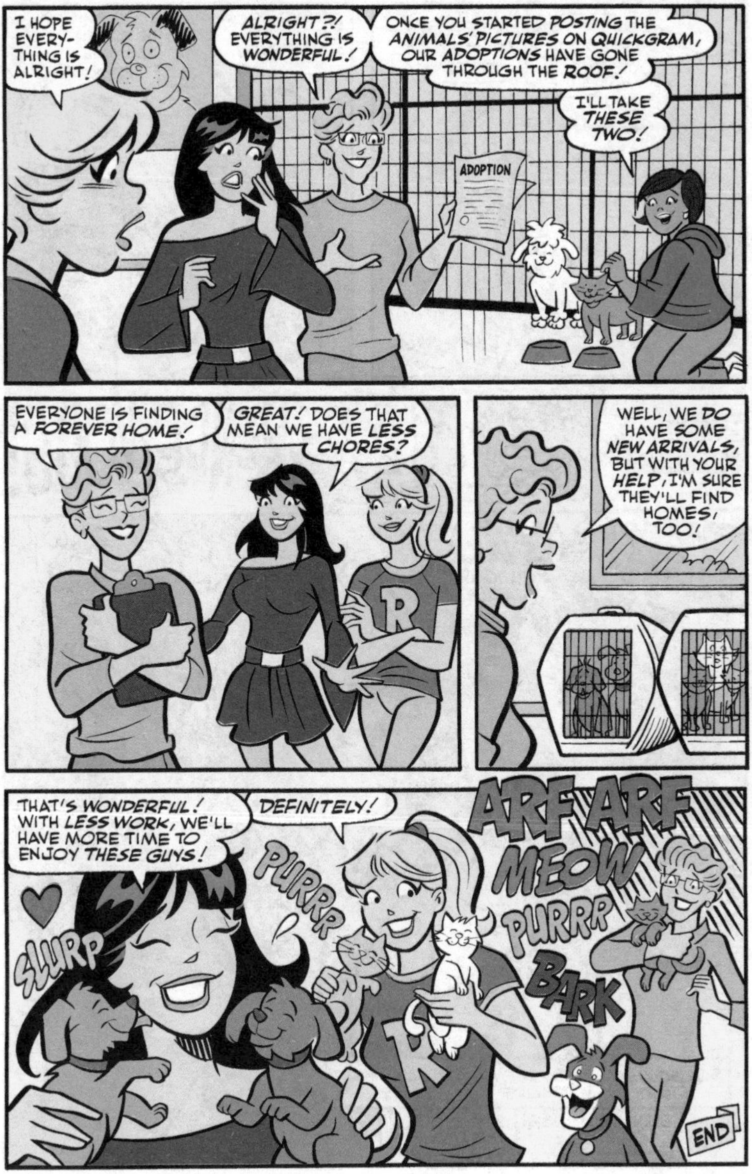
I HOPE EVERY-THING IS ALRIGHT!
ALRIGHT?! EVERYTHING IS WONDERFUL!
ONCE YOU STARTED POSTING THE ANIMALS' PICTURES ON QUICKGRAM, OUR ADOPTIONS HAVE GONE THROUGH THE ROOF!
ADOPTION
I'LL TAKE THESE TWO!
EVERYONE IS FINDING A FOREVER HOME!
GREAT! DOES THAT MEAN WE HAVE LESS CHORES?
WELL, WE DO HAVE SOME NEW ARRIVALS, BUT WITH YOUR HELP, I'M SURE THEY'LL FIND HOMES, TOO!
THAT'S WONDERFUL! WITH LESS WORK, WE'LL HAVE MORE TIME TO ENJOY THESE GUYS!
DEFINITELY!
ARF ARF
MEOW
PURRR
PURRR
SLURP
BARK
END

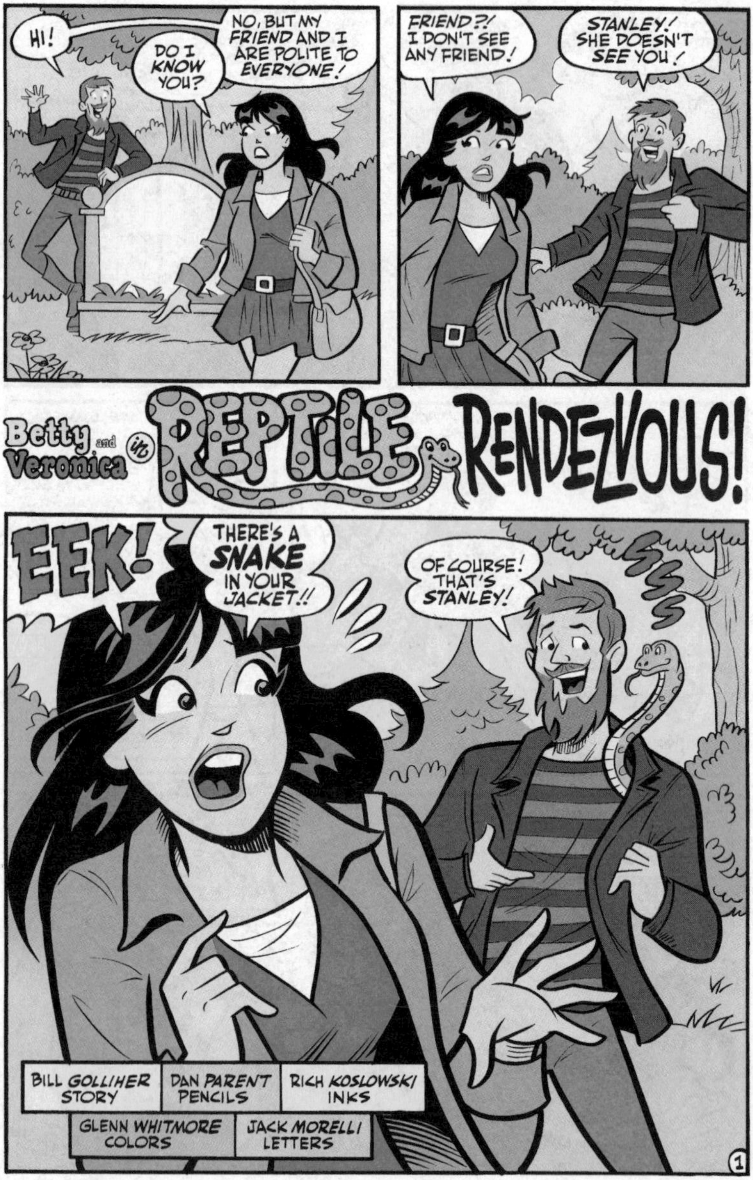
HI!
DO I KNOW YOU?
NO, BUT MY FRIEND AND I ARE POLITE TO EVERYONE!
FRIEND?! I DON'T SEE ANY FRIEND!
STANLEY! SHE DOESN'T SEE YOU!
Betty and Veronica in REPTILE RENDEZVOUS!
EEK!
THERE'S A SNAKE IN YOUR JACKET!!
OF COURSE! THAT'S STANLEY!
SSS
BILL GOLLIHER STORY
DAN PARENT PENCILS
RICH KOSLOWSKI INKS
GLENN WHITMORE COLORS
JACK MORELLI LETTERS
1

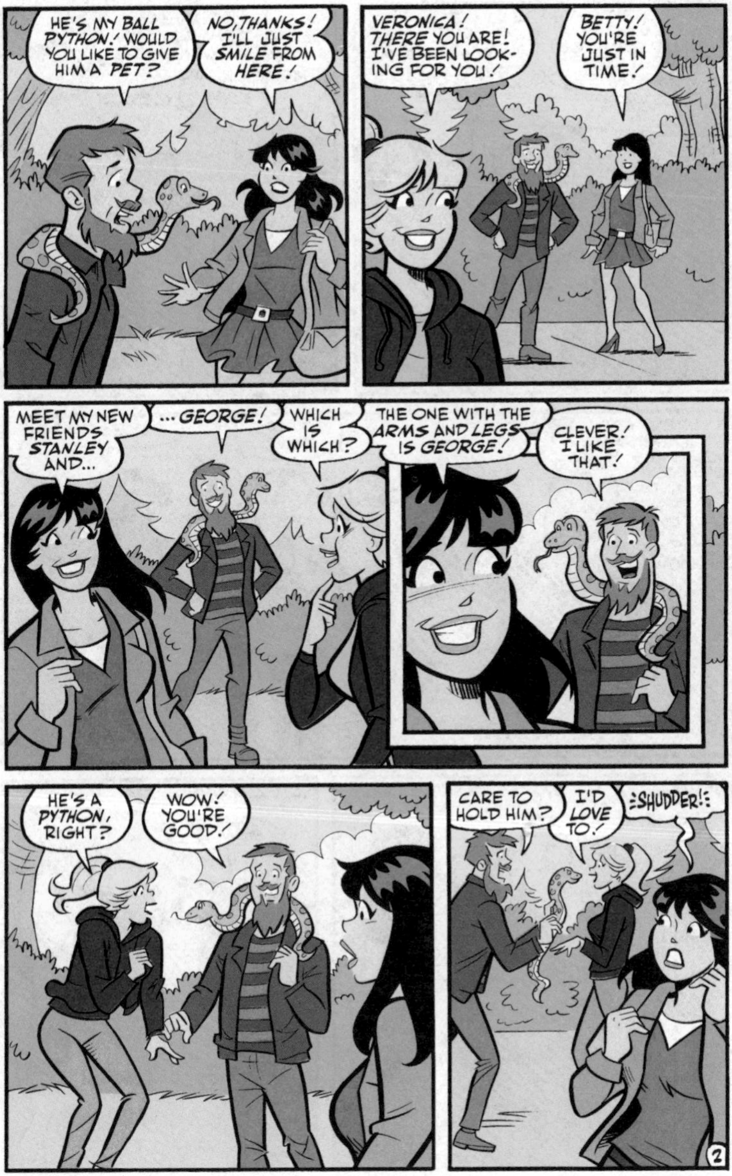
HE'S MY BALL PYTHON! WOULD YOU LIKE TO GIVE HIM A PET?
NO, THANKS! I'LL JUST SMILE FROM HERE!
VERONICA! THERE YOU ARE! I'VE BEEN LOOKING FOR YOU!
BETTY! YOU'RE JUST IN TIME!
MEET MY NEW FRIENDS STANLEY AND...
...GEORGE!
WHICH IS WHICH?
THE ONE WITH THE ARMS AND LEGS IS GEORGE!
CLEVER! I LIKE THAT!
HE'S A PYTHON, RIGHT?
WOW! YOU'RE GOOD!
CARE TO HOLD HIM?
I'D LOVE TO!
SHUDDER!
2

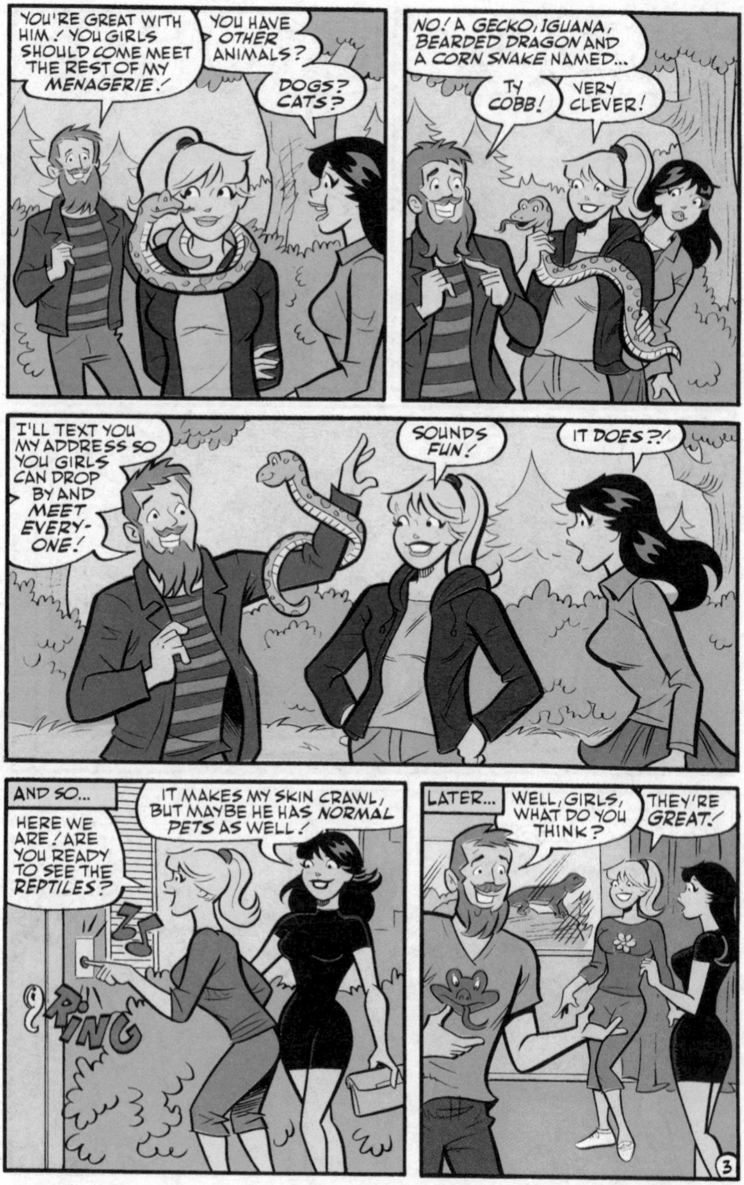
YOU'RE GREAT WITH HIM! YOU GIRLS SHOULD COME MEET THE REST OF MY MENAGERIE!
YOU HAVE OTHER ANIMALS?
DOGS? CATS?
NO! A GECKO, IGUANA, BEARDED DRAGON AND A CORN SNAKE NAMED...
TY COBB!
VERY CLEVER!
I'LL TEXT YOU MY ADDRESS SO YOU GIRLS CAN DROP BY AND MEET EVERY-ONE!
SOUNDS FUN!
IT DOES?!
AND SO...
HERE WE ARE! ARE YOU READY TO SEE THE REPTILES?
IT MAKES MY SKIN CRAWL, BUT MAYBE HE HAS NORMAL PETS AS WELL!
RING
LATER...
WELL, GIRLS, WHAT DO YOU THINK?
THEY'RE GREAT!
3

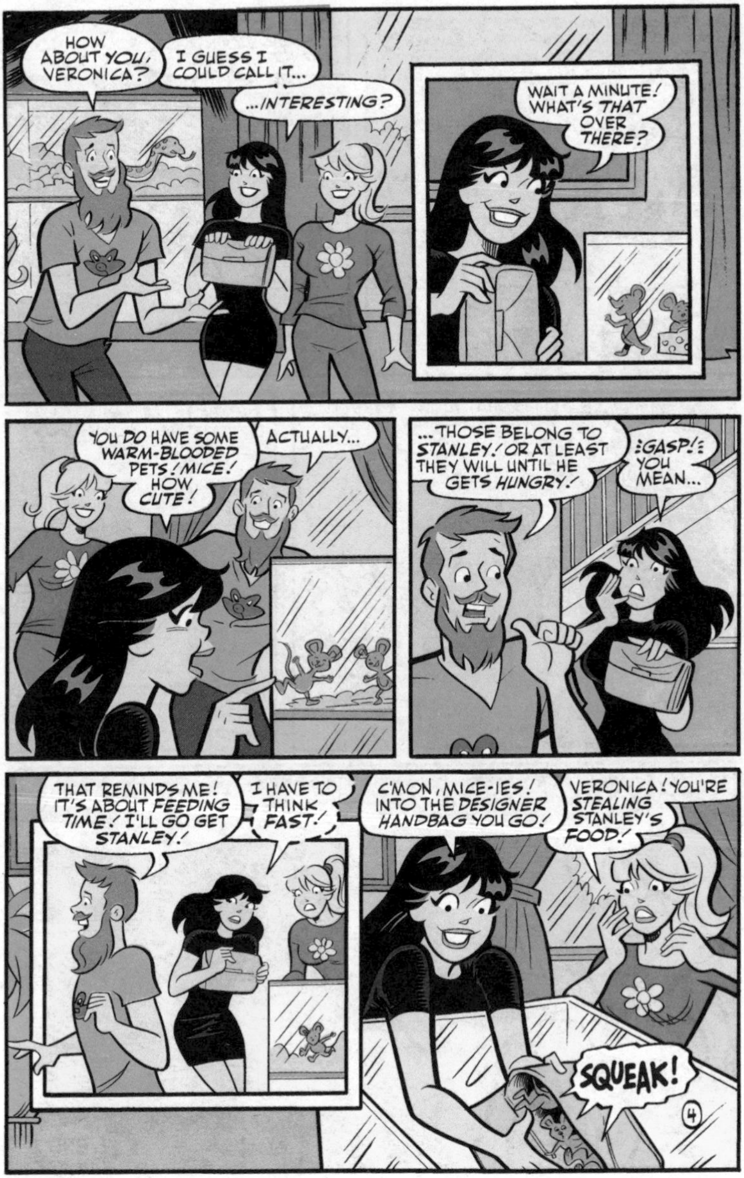
HOW ABOUT YOU, VERONICA?
I GUESS I COULD CALL IT...
...INTERESTING?
WAIT A MINUTE! WHAT'S THAT OVER THERE?
YOU DO HAVE SOME WARM-BLOODED PETS! MICE! HOW CUTE!
ACTUALLY...
...THOSE BELONG TO STANLEY! OR AT LEAST THEY WILL UNTIL HE GETS HUNGRY!
GASP! YOU MEAN...
THAT REMINDS ME! IT'S ABOUT FEEDING TIME! I'LL GO GET STANLEY!
I HAVE TO THINK FAST!
C'MON, MICE-IES! INTO THE DESIGNER HANDBAG YOU GO!
VERONICA! YOU'RE STEALING STANLEY'S FOOD!
SQUEAK!
4

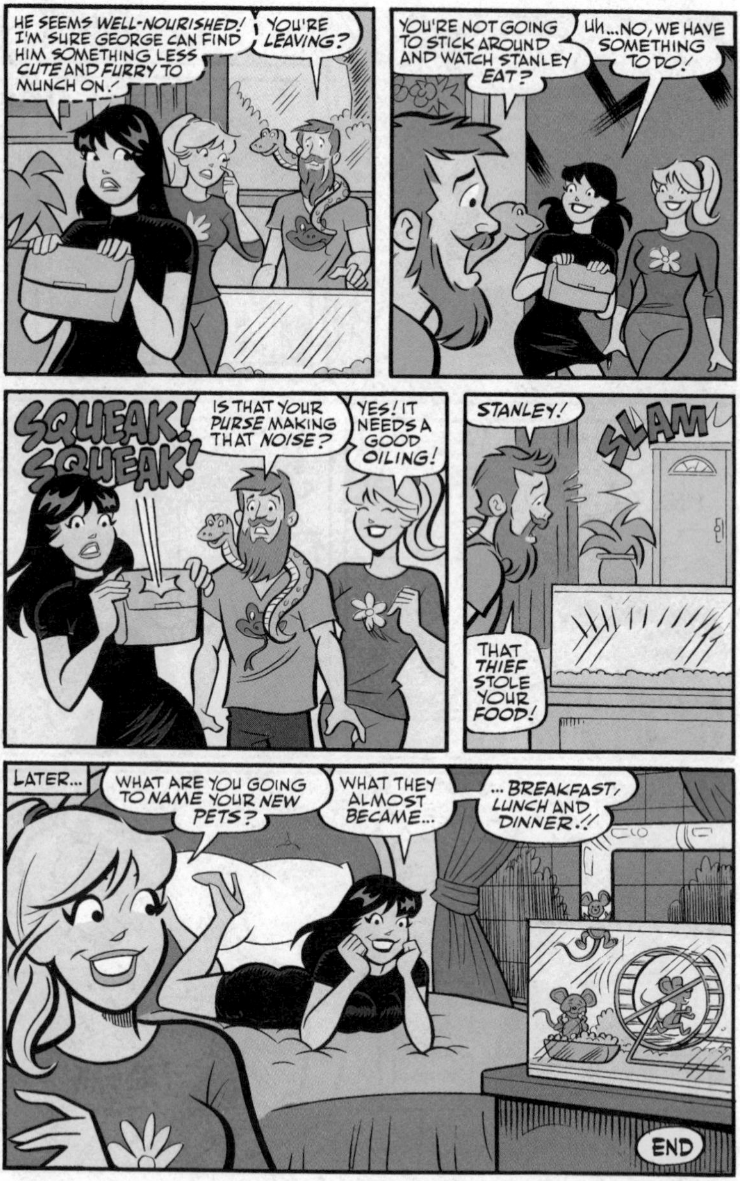
HE SEEMS WELL-NOURISHED! I'M SURE GEORGE CAN FIND HIM SOMETHING LESS CUTE AND FURRY TO MUNCH ON!
YOU'RE LEAVING?
YOU'RE NOT GOING TO STICK AROUND AND WATCH STANLEY EAT?
UH...NO, WE HAVE SOMETHING TO DO!
SQUEAK! SQUEAK!
IS THAT YOUR PURSE MAKING THAT NOISE?
YES! IT NEEDS A GOOD OILING!
STANLEY!
SLAM
THAT THIEF STOLE YOUR FOOD!
LATER...
WHAT ARE YOU GOING TO NAME YOUR NEW PETS?
WHAT THEY ALMOST BECAME...
...BREAKFAST, LUNCH AND DINNER!!
END

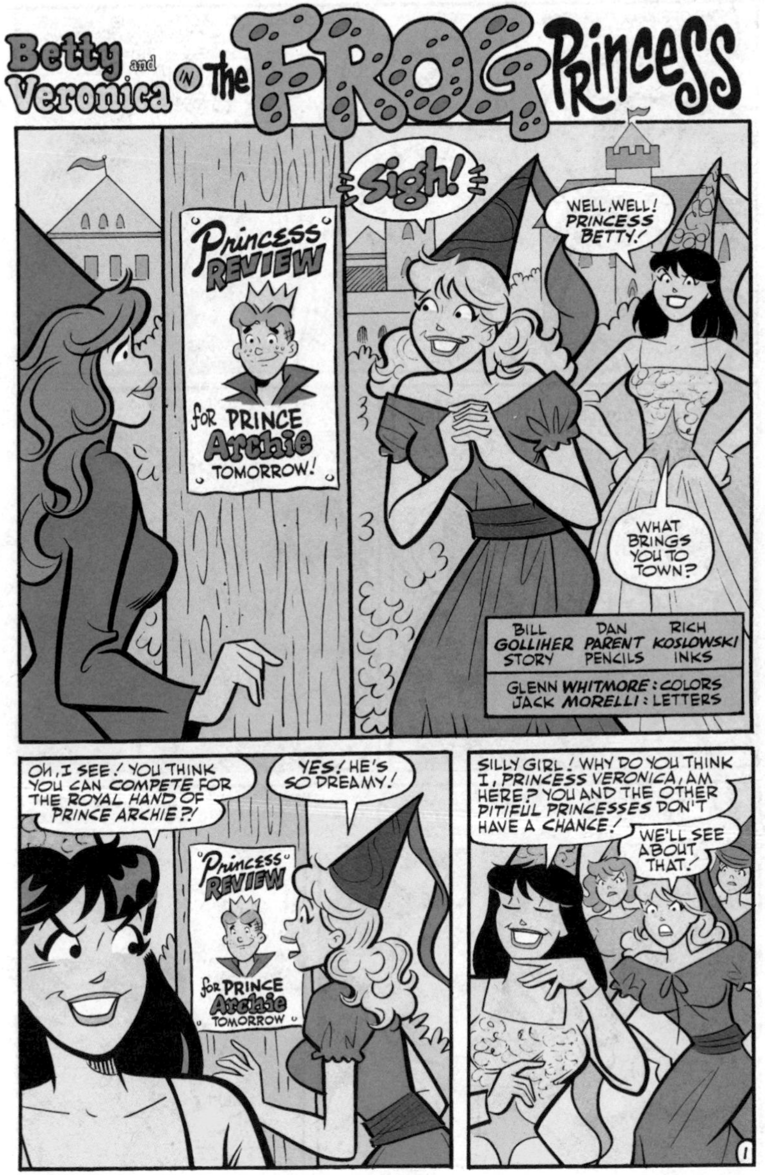
Betty and Veronica in The FROG Princess
Princess REVIEW for PRINCE Archie TOMORROW!
SIGH!
WELL, WELL! PRINCESS BETTY!
WHAT BRINGS YOU TO TOWN?
BILL GOLLIHER STORY
DAN PARENT PENCILS
RICH KOSLOWSKI INKS
GLENN WHITMORE: COLORS
JACK MORELLI: LETTERS
OH, I SEE! YOU THINK YOU CAN COMPETE FOR THE ROYAL HAND OF PRINCE ARCHIE?!
YES! HE'S SO DREAMY!
Princess REVIEW for PRINCE Archie TOMORROW
SILLY GIRL! WHY DO YOU THINK I, PRINCESS VERONICA, AM HERE? YOU AND THE OTHER PITIFUL PRINCESSES DON'T HAVE A CHANCE!
WE'LL SEE ABOUT THAT!
1

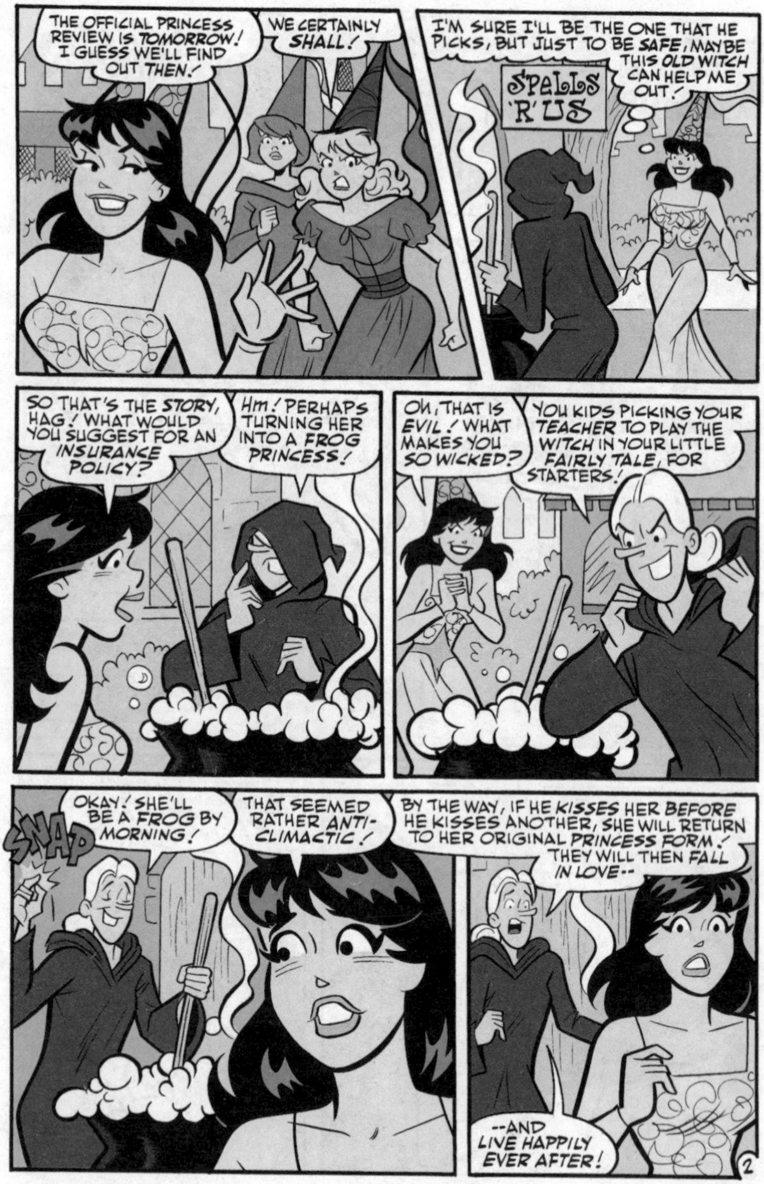
THE OFFICIAL PRINCESS REVIEW IS TOMORROW! I GUESS WE'LL FIND OUT THEN!
WE CERTAINLY SHALL!
I'M SURE I'LL BE THE ONE THAT HE PICKS, BUT JUST TO BE SAFE, MAYBE THIS OLD WITCH CAN HELP ME OUT!
SPELLS 'R' US
SO THAT'S THE STORY, HAG! WHAT WOULD YOU SUGGEST FOR AN INSURANCE POLICY?
Hm! PERHAPS TURNING HER INTO A FROG PRINCESS!
Oh, THAT IS EVIL! WHAT MAKES YOU SO WICKED?
YOU KIDS PICKING YOUR TEACHER TO PLAY THE WITCH IN YOUR LITTLE FAIRLY TALE, FOR STARTERS!
SNAP
OKAY! SHE'LL BE A FROG BY MORNING!
THAT SEEMED RATHER ANTI-CLIMACTIC!
BY THE WAY, IF HE KISSES HER BEFORE HE KISSES ANOTHER, SHE WILL RETURN TO HER ORIGINAL PRINCESS FORM! THEY WILL THEN FALL IN LOVE--
--AND LIVE HAPPILY EVER AFTER!
2

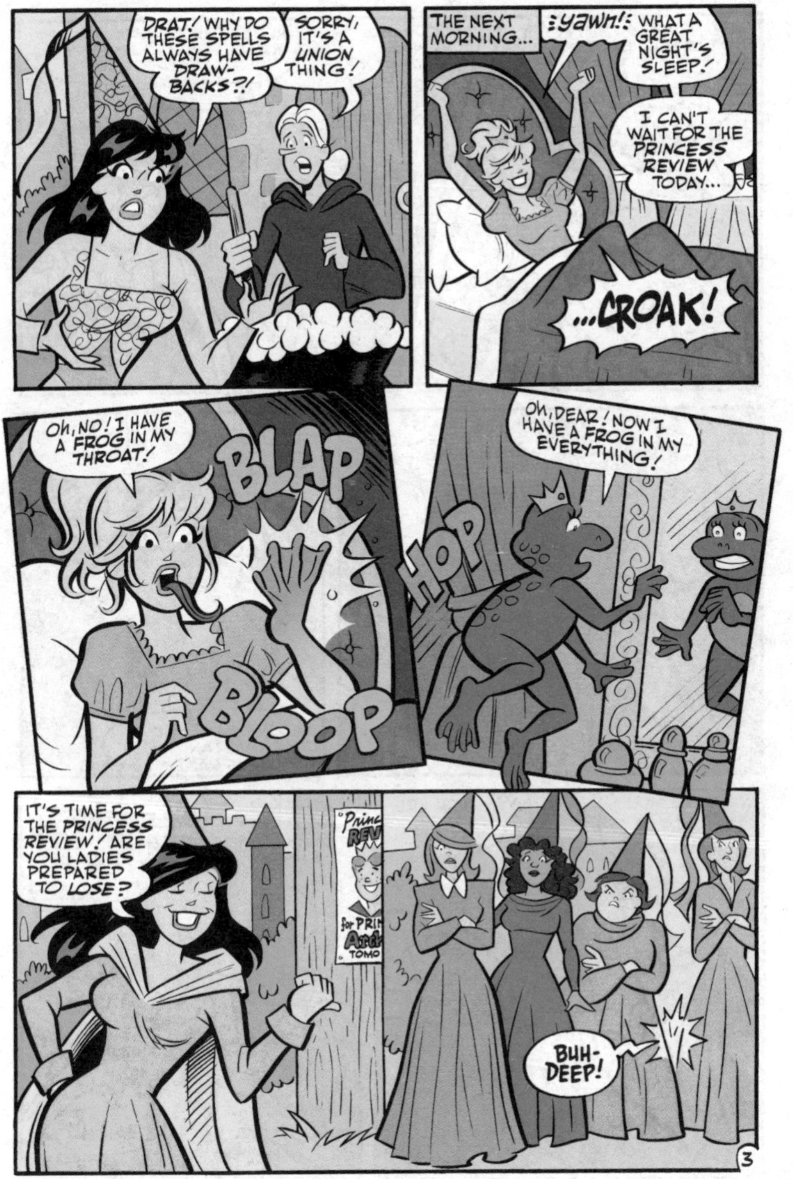
DRAT! WHY DO THESE SPELLS ALWAYS HAVE DRAW-BACKS?!
SORRY, IT'S A UNION THING!
THE NEXT MORNING...
:YAWN!: WHAT A GREAT NIGHT'S SLEEP!
I CAN'T WAIT FOR THE PRINCESS REVIEW TODAY...
...CROAK!
OH, NO! I HAVE A FROG IN MY THROAT!
BLAP
BLOOP
OH, DEAR! NOW I HAVE A FROG IN MY EVERYTHING!
HOP
IT'S TIME FOR THE PRINCESS REVIEW! ARE YOU LADIES PREPARED TO LOSE?
BUH-DEEP!
3

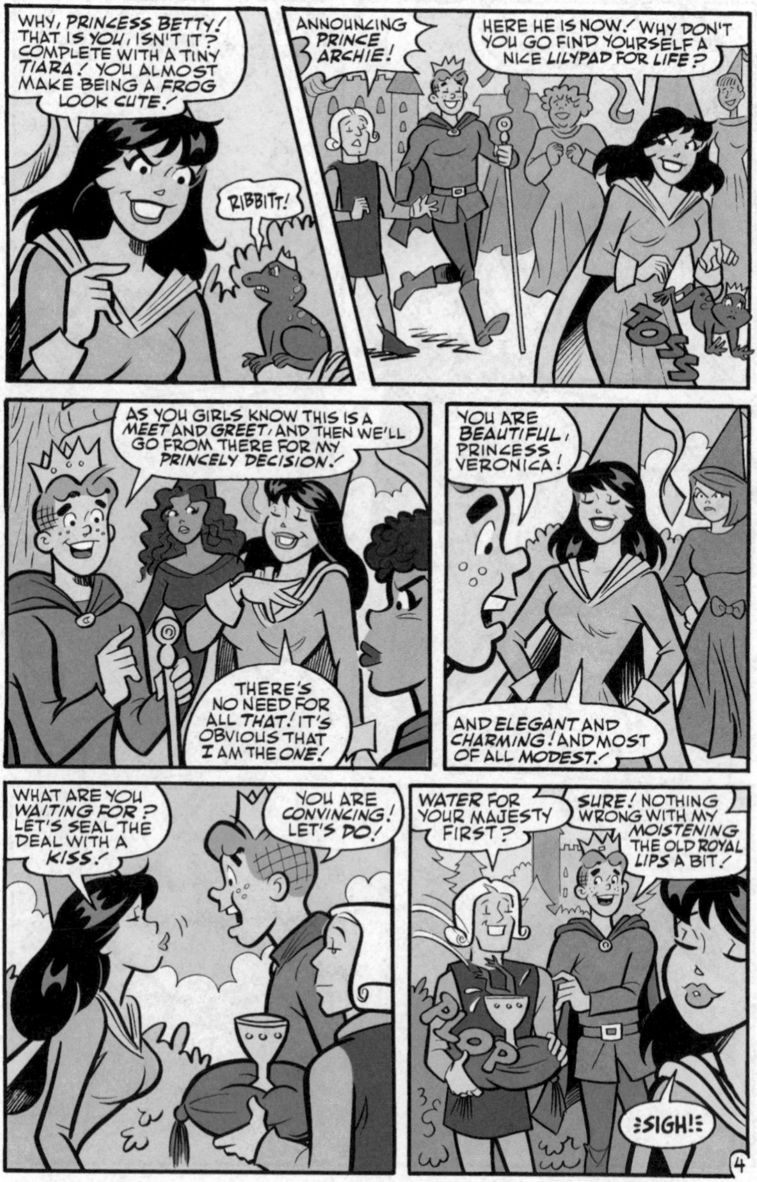
WHY, PRINCESS BETTY! THAT IS YOU, ISN'T IT? COMPLETE WITH A TINY TIARA! YOU ALMOST MAKE BEING A FROG LOOK CUTE!
RIBBITT!
ANNOUNCING PRINCE ARCHIE!
HERE HE IS NOW! WHY DON'T YOU GO FIND YOURSELF A NICE LILYPAD FOR LIFE?
TOSS
AS YOU GIRLS KNOW THIS IS A MEET AND GREET, AND THEN WE'LL GO FROM THERE FOR MY PRINCELY DECISION!
THERE'S NO NEED FOR ALL THAT! IT'S OBVIOUS THAT I AM THE ONE!
YOU ARE BEAUTIFUL, PRINCESS VERONICA!
AND ELEGANT AND CHARMING! AND MOST OF ALL MODEST!
WHAT ARE YOU WAITING FOR? LET'S SEAL THE DEAL WITH A KISS!
YOU ARE CONVINCING! LET'S DO!
WATER FOR YOUR MAJESTY FIRST?
SURE! NOTHING WRONG WITH MY MOISTENING THE OLD ROYAL LIPS A BIT!
PLOP
SIGH!
4

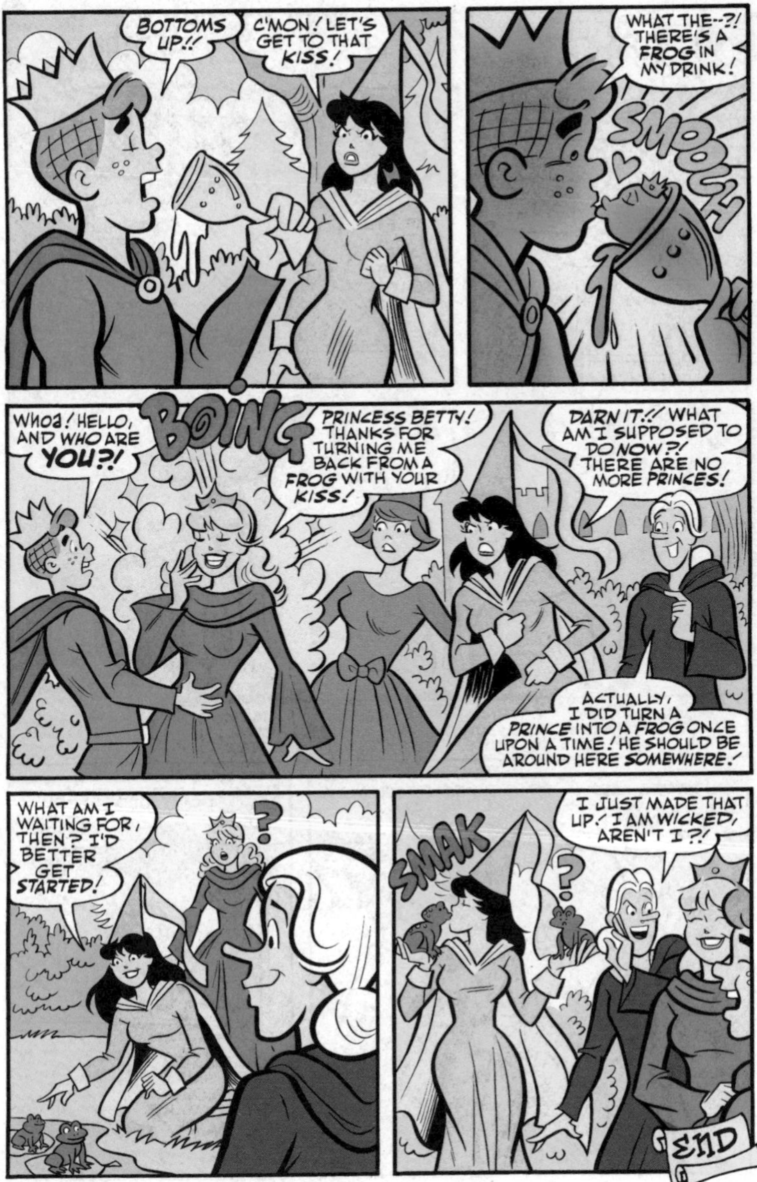
BOTTOMS UP!!
C'MON! LET'S GET TO THAT KISS!
WHAT THE--?! THERE'S A FROG IN MY DRINK!
SMOOCH
WHOA! HELLO, AND WHO ARE YOU?!
BOING
PRINCESS BETTY! THANKS FOR TURNING ME BACK FROM A FROG WITH YOUR KISS!
DARN IT!! WHAT AM I SUPPOSED TO DO NOW?! THERE ARE NO MORE PRINCES!
ACTUALLY, I DID TURN A PRINCE INTO A FROG ONCE UPON A TIME! HE SHOULD BE AROUND HERE SOMEWHERE!
WHAT AM I WAITING FOR, THEN? I'D BETTER GET STARTED!
?
SMAK
?
I JUST MADE THAT UP! I AM WICKED, AREN'T I?!
END

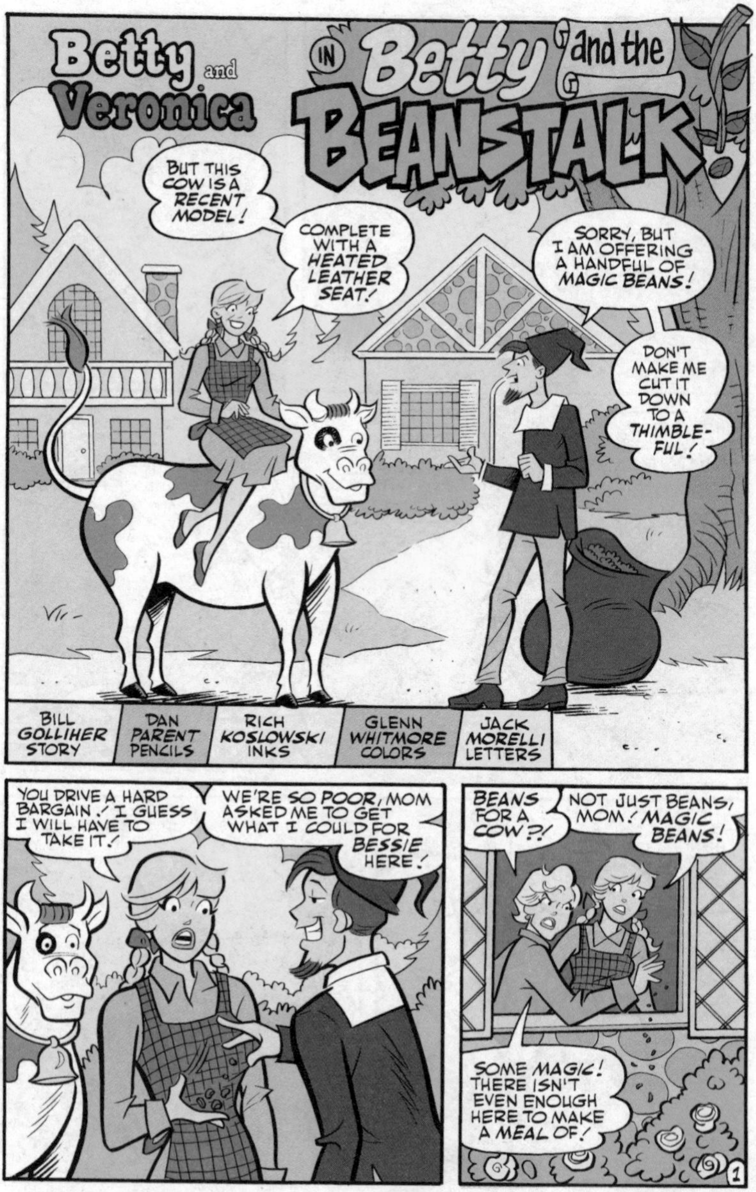
Betty and Veronica
IN Betty and the BEANSTALK!
BUT THIS COW IS A RECENT MODEL!
COMPLETE WITH A HEATED LEATHER SEAT!
SORRY, BUT I AM OFFERING A HANDFUL OF MAGIC BEANS!
DON'T MAKE ME CUT IT DOWN TO A THIMBLE-FUL!
BILL GOLLIHER STORY
DAN PARENT PENCILS
RICH KOSLOWSKI INKS
GLENN WHITMORE COLORS
JACK MORELLI LETTERS
YOU DRIVE A HARD BARGAIN! I GUESS I WILL HAVE TO TAKE IT!
WE'RE SO POOR, MOM ASKED ME TO GET WHAT I COULD FOR BESSIE HERE!
BEANS FOR A COW?!
NOT JUST BEANS, MOM! MAGIC BEANS!
SOME MAGIC! THERE ISN'T EVEN ENOUGH HERE TO MAKE A MEAL OF!
1

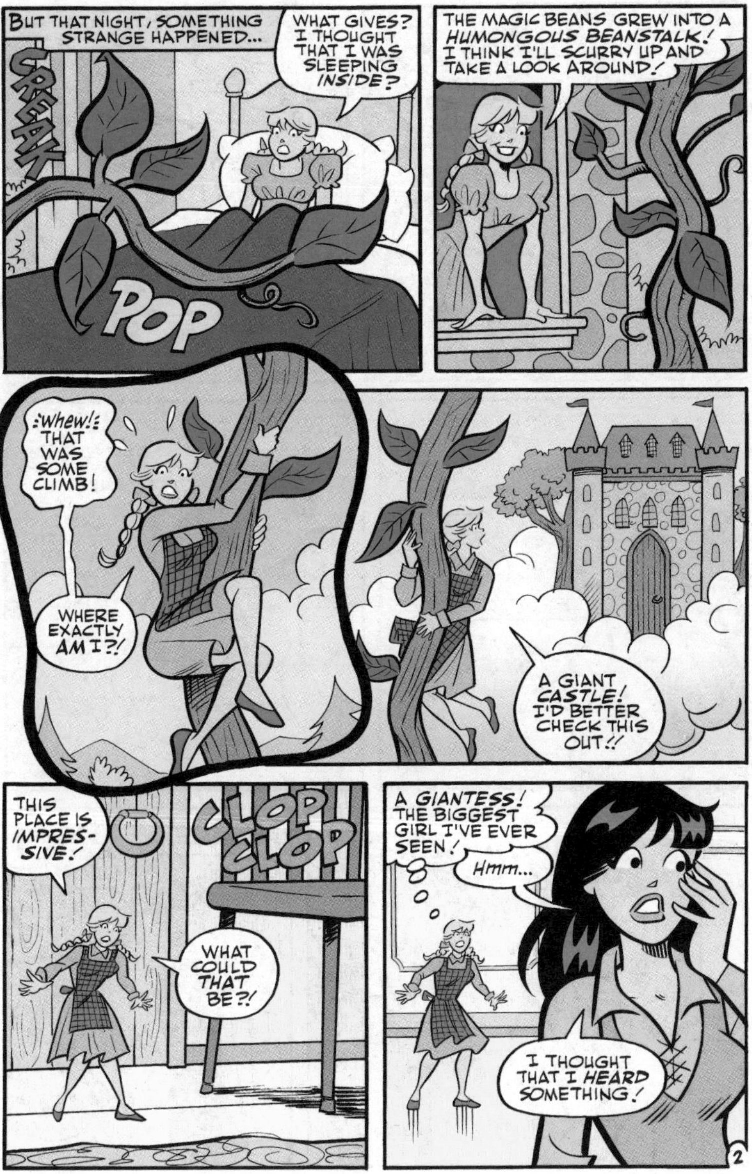
BUT THAT NIGHT, SOMETHING STRANGE HAPPENED...
CREAK
WHAT GIVES? I THOUGHT THAT I WAS SLEEPING INSIDE?
POP
THE MAGIC BEANS GREW INTO A HUMONGOUS BEANSTALK! I THINK I'LL SCURRY UP AND TAKE A LOOK AROUND!
WHEW! THAT WAS SOME CLIMB!
WHERE EXACTLY AM I?!
A GIANT CASTLE! I'D BETTER CHECK THIS OUT!!
THIS PLACE IS IMPRES-SIVE!
CLOP CLOP
WHAT COULD THAT BE?!
A GIANTESS! THE BIGGEST GIRL I'VE EVER SEEN!
Hmm...
I THOUGHT THAT I HEARD SOMETHING!
2

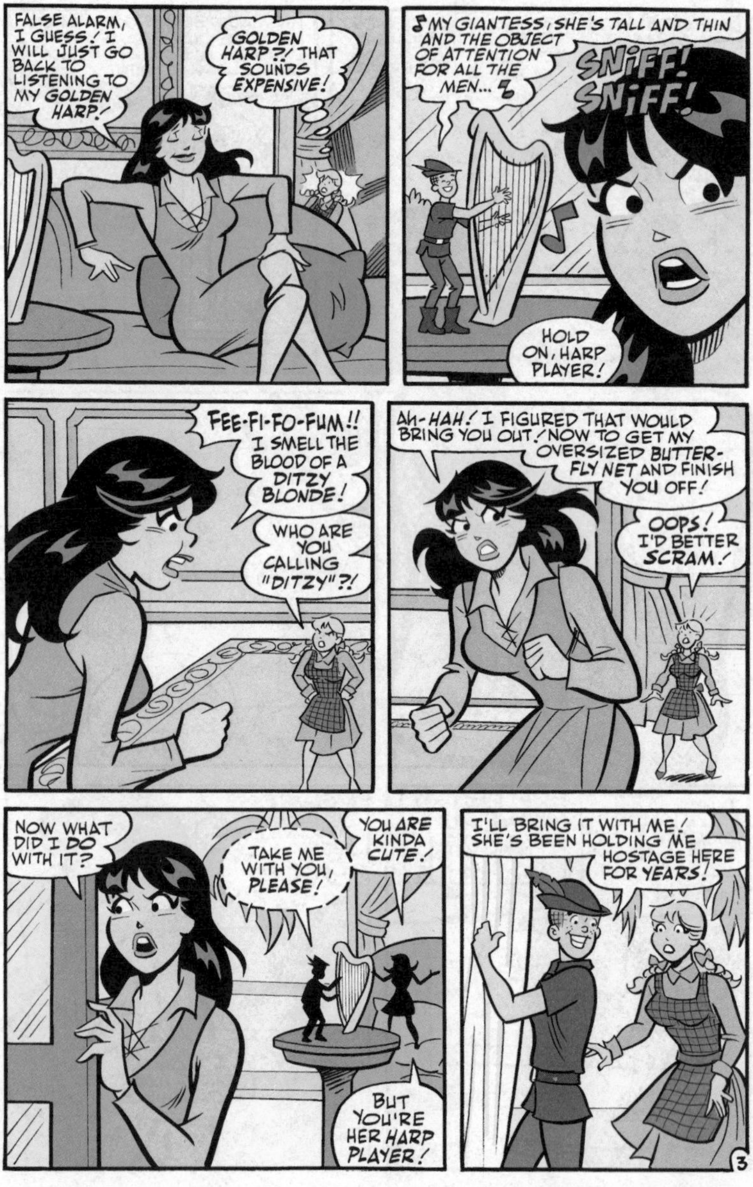
FALSE ALARM, I GUESS! I WILL JUST GO BACK TO LISTENING TO MY GOLDEN HARP!
GOLDEN HARP?! THAT SOUNDS EXPENSIVE!
MY GIANTESS, SHE'S TALL AND THIN AND THE OBJECT OF ATTENTION FOR ALL THE MEN...
SNIFF! SNIFF!
HOLD ON, HARP PLAYER!
FEE-FI-FO-FUM!! I SMELL THE BLOOD OF A DITZY BLONDE!
WHO ARE YOU CALLING "DITZY"?!
AH-HAH! I FIGURED THAT WOULD BRING YOU OUT! NOW TO GET MY OVERSIZED BUTTER-FLY NET AND FINISH YOU OFF!
OOPS! I'D BETTER SCRAM!
NOW WHAT DID I DO WITH IT?
TAKE ME WITH YOU, PLEASE!
YOU ARE KINDA CUTE!
BUT YOU'RE HER HARP PLAYER!
I'LL BRING IT WITH ME! SHE'S BEEN HOLDING ME HOSTAGE HERE FOR YEARS!
3

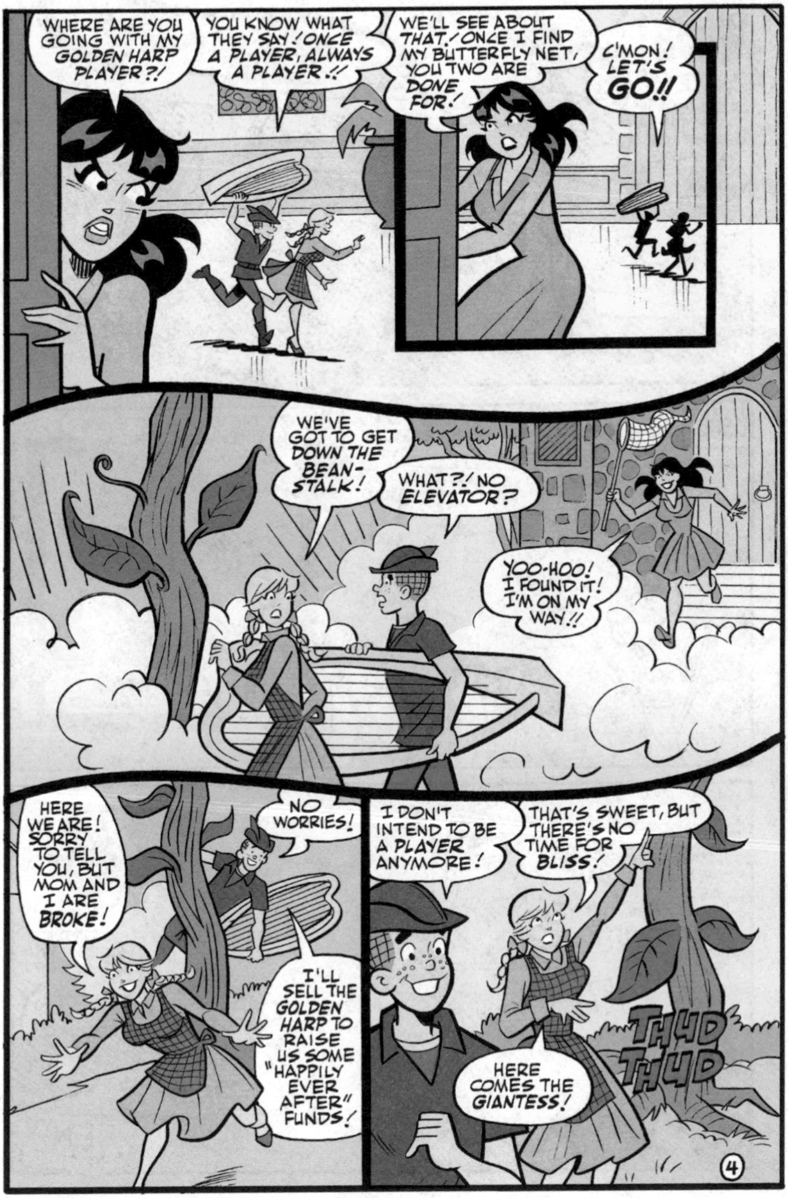
WHERE ARE YOU GOING WITH MY GOLDEN HARP PLAYER?!
YOU KNOW WHAT THEY SAY! ONCE A PLAYER, ALWAYS A PLAYER!!
WE'LL SEE ABOUT THAT! ONCE I FIND MY BUTTERFLY NET, YOU TWO ARE DONE FOR!
C'MON! LET'S GO!!
WE'VE GOT TO GET DOWN THE BEAN-STALK!
WHAT?! NO ELEVATOR?
YOO-HOO! I FOUND IT! I'M ON MY WAY!!
HERE WE ARE! SORRY TO TELL YOU, BUT MOM AND I ARE BROKE!
NO WORRIES!
I'LL SELL THE GOLDEN HARP TO RAISE US SOME "HAPPILY EVER AFTER" FUNDS!
I DON'T INTEND TO BE A PLAYER ANYMORE!
THAT'S SWEET, BUT THERE'S NO TIME FOR BLISS!
HERE COMES THE GIANTESS!
THUD THUD
4

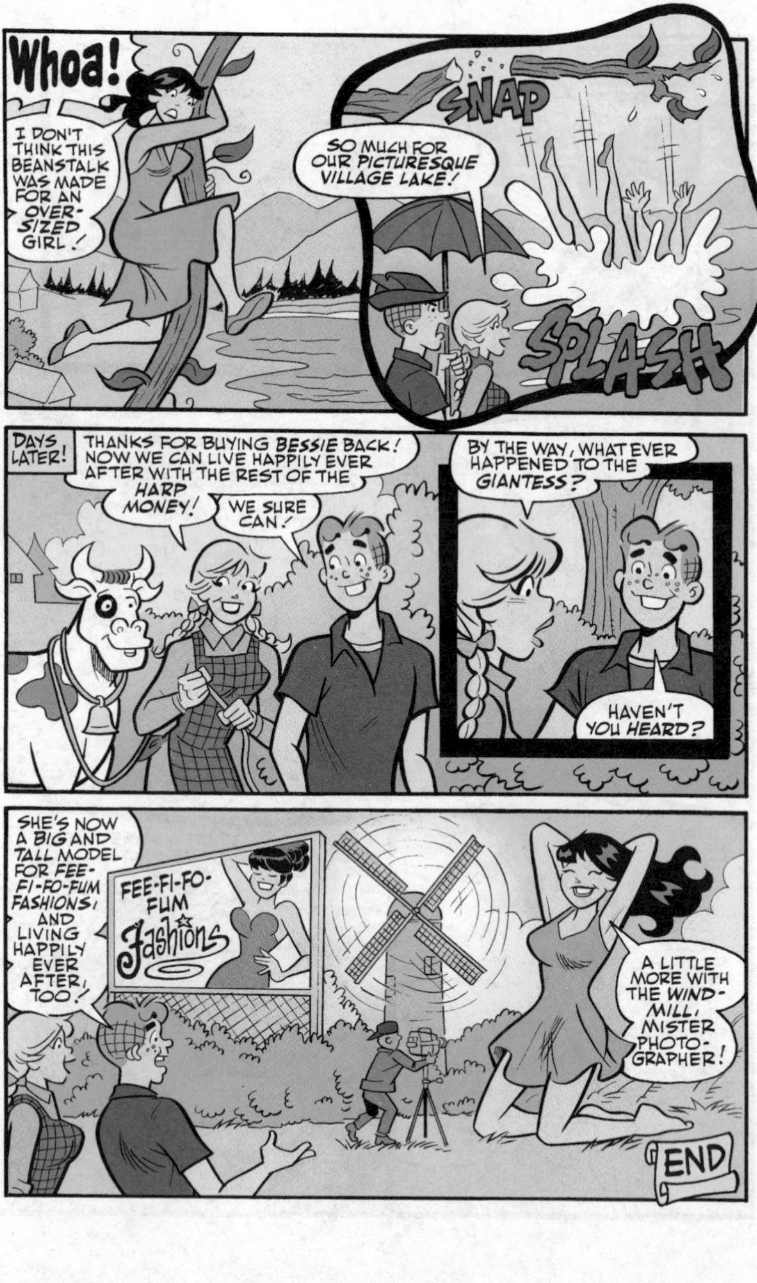
Whoa!
I DON'T THINK THIS BEANSTALK WAS MADE FOR AN OVER-SIZED GIRL!
SNAP
SO MUCH FOR OUR PICTURESQUE VILLAGE LAKE!
SPLASH
DAYS LATER!
THANKS FOR BUYING BESSIE BACK! NOW WE CAN LIVE HAPPILY EVER AFTER WITH THE REST OF THE HARP MONEY!
WE SURE CAN!
BY THE WAY, WHAT EVER HAPPENED TO THE GIANTESS?
HAVEN'T YOU HEARD?
SHE'S NOW A BIG AND TALL MODEL FOR FEE-FI-FO-FUM FASHIONS, AND LIVING HAPPILY EVER AFTER, TOO!
FEE-FI-FO-FUM Fashions
A LITTLE MORE WITH THE WIND-MILL, MISTER PHOTO-GRAPHER!
END

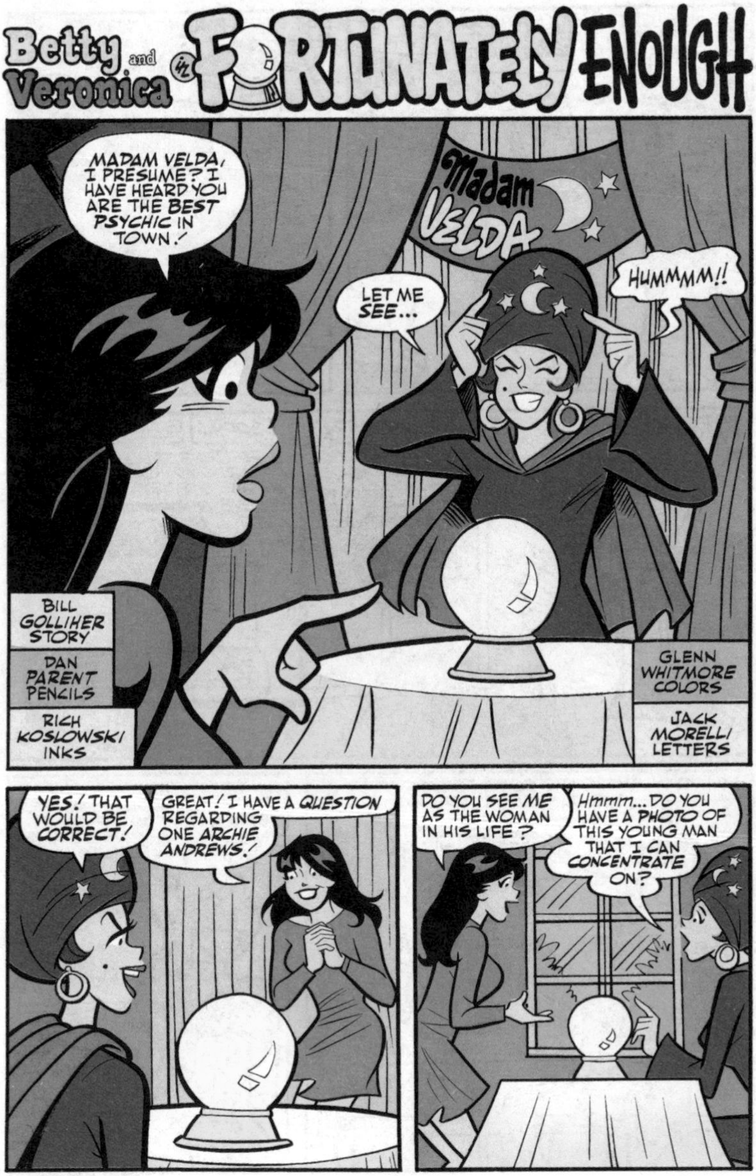
Betty and Veronica in FORTUNATELY ENOUGH
MADAM VELDA, I PRESUME? I HAVE HEARD YOU ARE THE BEST PSYCHIC IN TOWN.!
Madam VELDA
LET ME SEE...
HUMMMM!!
BILL GOLLIHER STORY
DAN PARENT PENCILS
RICH KOSLOWSKI INKS
GLENN WHITMORE COLORS
JACK MORELLI LETTERS
YES! THAT WOULD BE CORRECT!
GREAT! I HAVE A QUESTION REGARDING ONE ARCHIE ANDREWS.!
DO YOU SEE ME AS THE WOMAN IN HIS LIFE?
Hmmm... DO YOU HAVE A PHOTO OF THIS YOUNG MAN THAT I CAN CONCENTRATE ON?

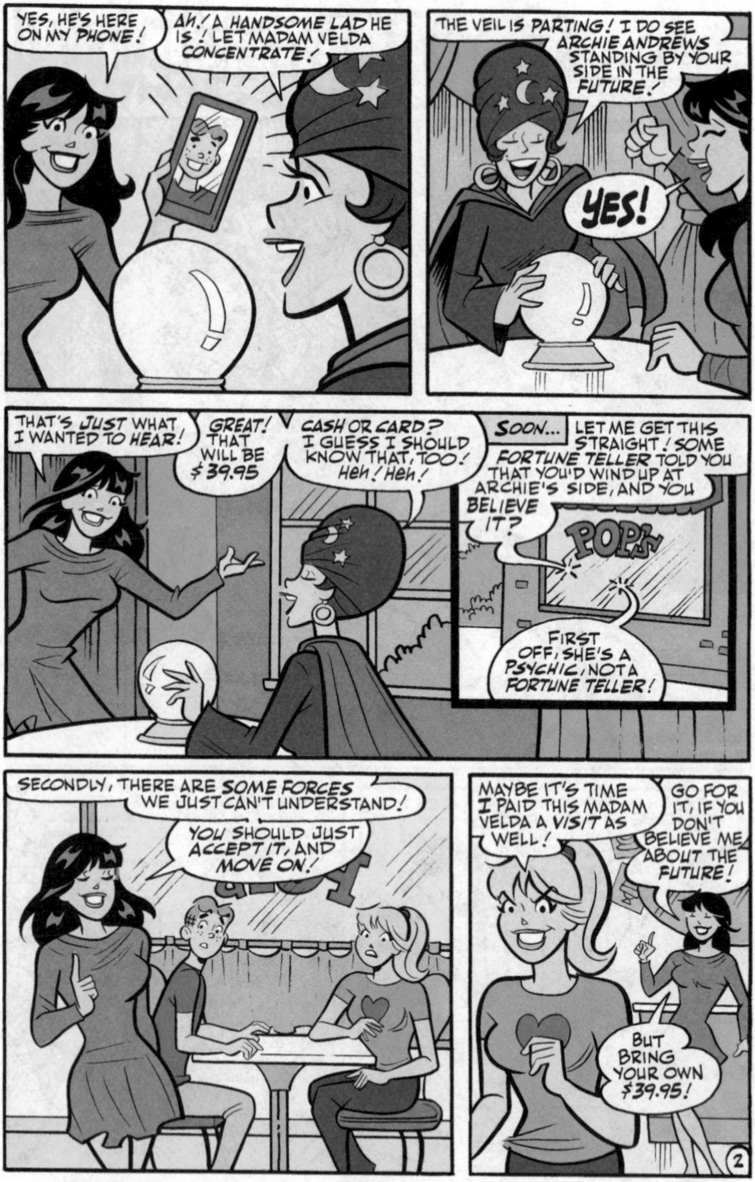
YES, HE'S HERE ON MY PHONE!
AH! A HANDSOME LAD HE IS! LET MADAM VELDA CONCENTRATE!
THE VEIL IS PARTING! I DO SEE ARCHIE ANDREWS STANDING BY YOUR SIDE IN THE FUTURE!
YES!
THAT'S JUST WHAT I WANTED TO HEAR!
GREAT! THAT WILL BE $39.95
CASH OR CARD? I GUESS I SHOULD KNOW THAT, TOO! HEH! HEH!
SOON...
LET ME GET THIS STRAIGHT! SOME FORTUNE TELLER TOLD YOU THAT YOU'D WIND UP AT ARCHIE'S SIDE, AND YOU BELIEVE IT?
POP'S
FIRST OFF, SHE'S A PSYCHIC, NOT A FORTUNE TELLER!
SECONDLY, THERE ARE SOME FORCES WE JUST CAN'T UNDERSTAND!
YOU SHOULD JUST ACCEPT IT, AND MOVE ON!
MAYBE IT'S TIME I PAID THIS MADAM VELDA A VISIT AS WELL!
GO FOR IT, IF YOU DON'T BELIEVE ME ABOUT THE FUTURE!
BUT BRING YOUR OWN $39.95!
2

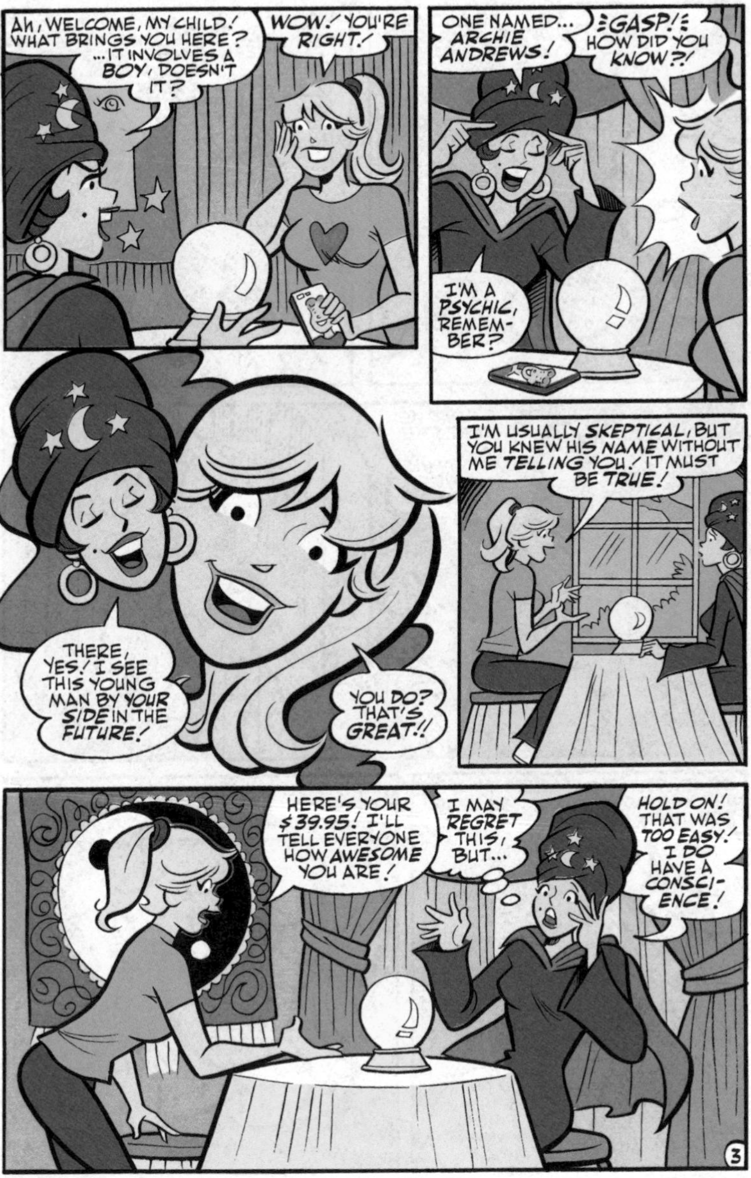

AH, WELCOME, MY CHILD! WHAT BRINGS YOU HERE? ...IT INVOLVES A BOY, DOESN'T IT?
WOW! YOU'RE RIGHT!
ONE NAMED... ARCHIE ANDREWS!
GASP! HOW DID YOU KNOW?!
I'M A PSYCHIC, REMEMBER?
THERE, YES! I SEE THIS YOUNG MAN BY YOUR SIDE IN THE FUTURE!
YOU DO? THAT'S GREAT!!
I'M USUALLY SKEPTICAL, BUT YOU KNEW HIS NAME WITHOUT ME TELLING YOU! IT MUST BE TRUE!
HERE'S YOUR $39.95! I'LL TELL EVERYONE HOW AWESOME YOU ARE!
I MAY REGRET THIS, BUT...
HOLD ON! THAT WAS TOO EASY! I DO HAVE A CONSCIENCE!
3

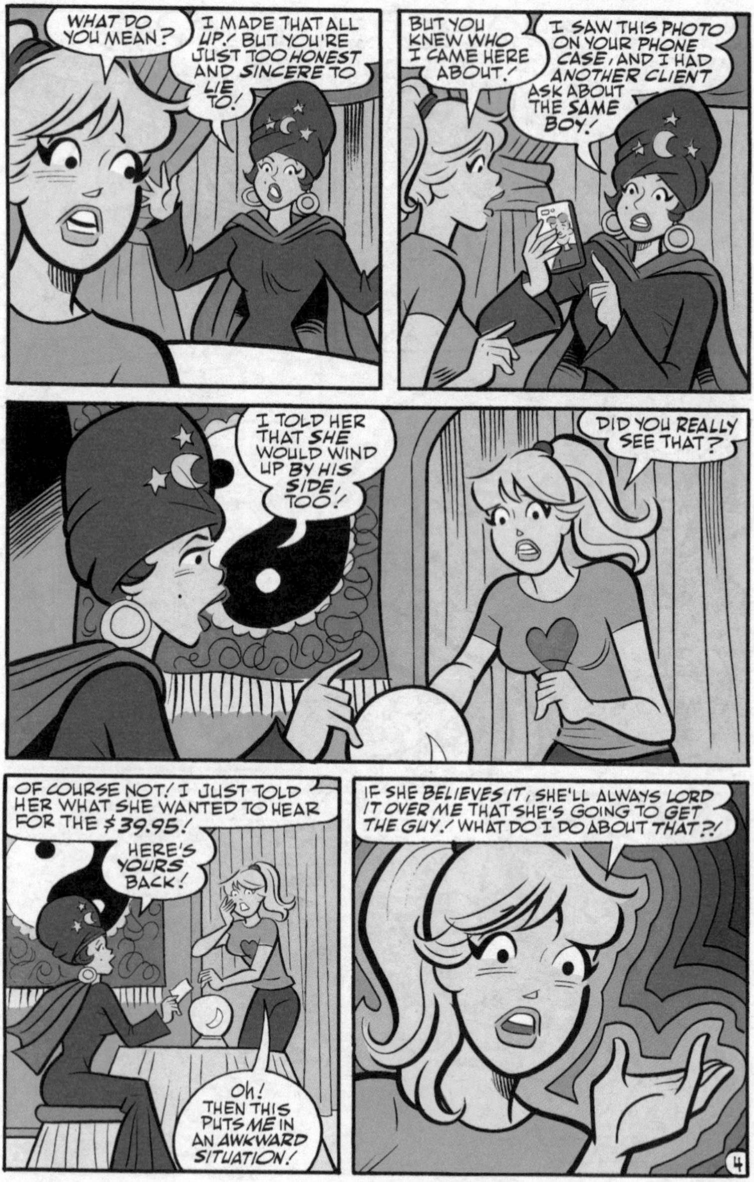
WHAT DO YOU MEAN?
I MADE THAT ALL UP! BUT YOU'RE JUST TOO HONEST AND SINCERE TO LIE TO!
BUT YOU KNEW WHO I CAME HERE ABOUT!
I SAW THIS PHOTO ON YOUR PHONE CASE, AND I HAD ANOTHER CLIENT ASK ABOUT THE SAME BOY!
I TOLD HER THAT SHE WOULD WIND UP BY HIS SIDE, TOO!
DID YOU REALLY SEE THAT?
OF COURSE NOT! I JUST TOLD HER WHAT SHE WANTED TO HEAR FOR THE $39.95!
HERE'S YOURS BACK!
Oh! THEN THIS PUTS ME IN AN AWKWARD SITUATION!
IF SHE BELIEVES IT, SHE'LL ALWAYS LORD IT OVER ME THAT SHE'S GOING TO GET THE GUY! WHAT DO I DO ABOUT THAT?!
4

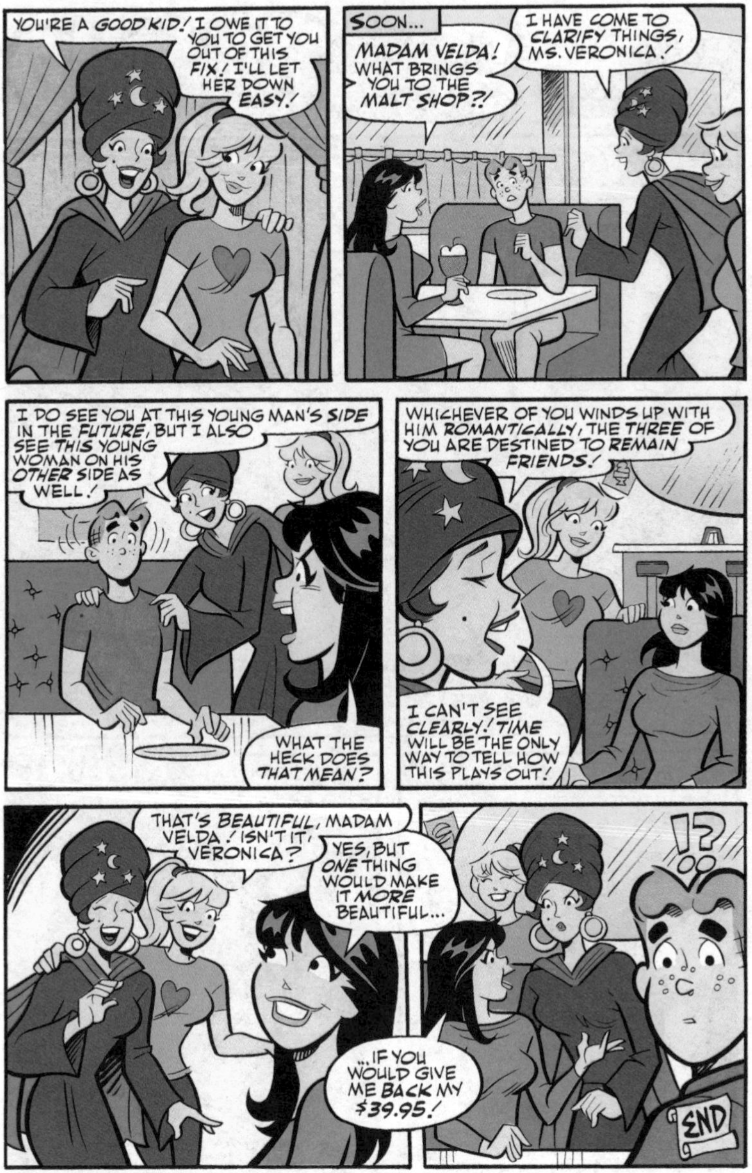
YOU'RE A GOOD KID! I OWE IT TO YOU TO GET YOU OUT OF THIS FIX! I'LL LET HER DOWN EASY!
SOON...
MADAM VELDA! WHAT BRINGS YOU TO THE MALT SHOP?!
I HAVE COME TO CLARIFY THINGS, MS. VERONICA!
I DO SEE YOU AT THIS YOUNG MAN'S SIDE IN THE FUTURE, BUT I ALSO SEE THIS YOUNG WOMAN ON HIS OTHER SIDE AS WELL!
WHAT THE HECK DOES THAT MEAN?
WHICHEVER OF YOU WINDS UP WITH HIM ROMANTICALLY, THE THREE OF YOU ARE DESTINED TO REMAIN FRIENDS!
I CAN'T SEE CLEARLY! TIME WILL BE THE ONLY WAY TO TELL HOW THIS PLAYS OUT!
THAT'S BEAUTIFUL, MADAM VELDA! ISN'T IT, VERONICA?
YES, BUT ONE THING WOULD MAKE IT MORE BEAUTIFUL...
...IF YOU WOULD GIVE ME BACK MY $39.95!
!?
END

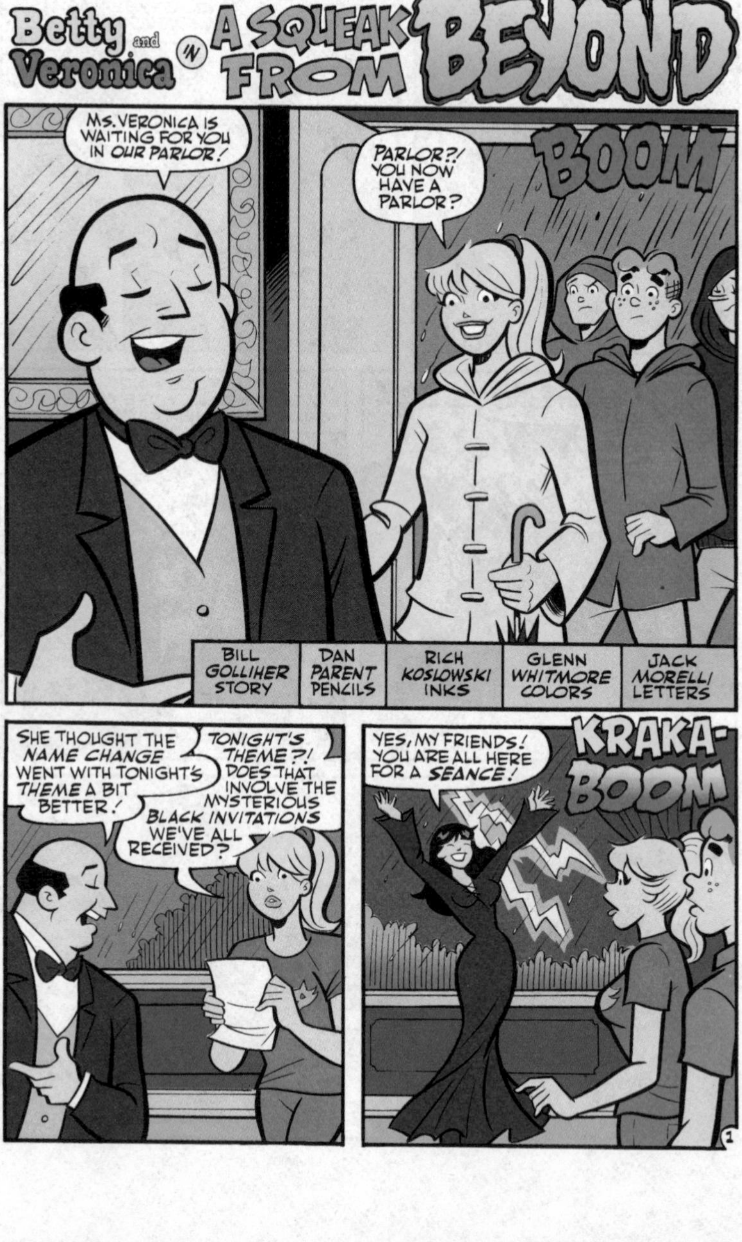
Betty and Veronica in A SQUEAK FROM BEYOND
MS. VERONICA IS WAITING FOR YOU IN OUR PARLOR!
PARLOR?! YOU NOW HAVE A PARLOR?
BOOM
BILL GOLLIHER STORY
DAN PARENT PENCILS
RICH KOSLOWSKI INKS
GLENN WHITMORE COLORS
JACK MORELLI LETTERS
SHE THOUGHT THE NAME CHANGE WENT WITH TONIGHT'S THEME A BIT BETTER!
TONIGHT'S THEME?! DOES THAT INVOLVE THE MYSTERIOUS BLACK INVITATIONS WE'VE ALL RECEIVED?
YES, MY FRIENDS! YOU ARE ALL HERE FOR A SEANCE!
KRAKA-BOOM
1

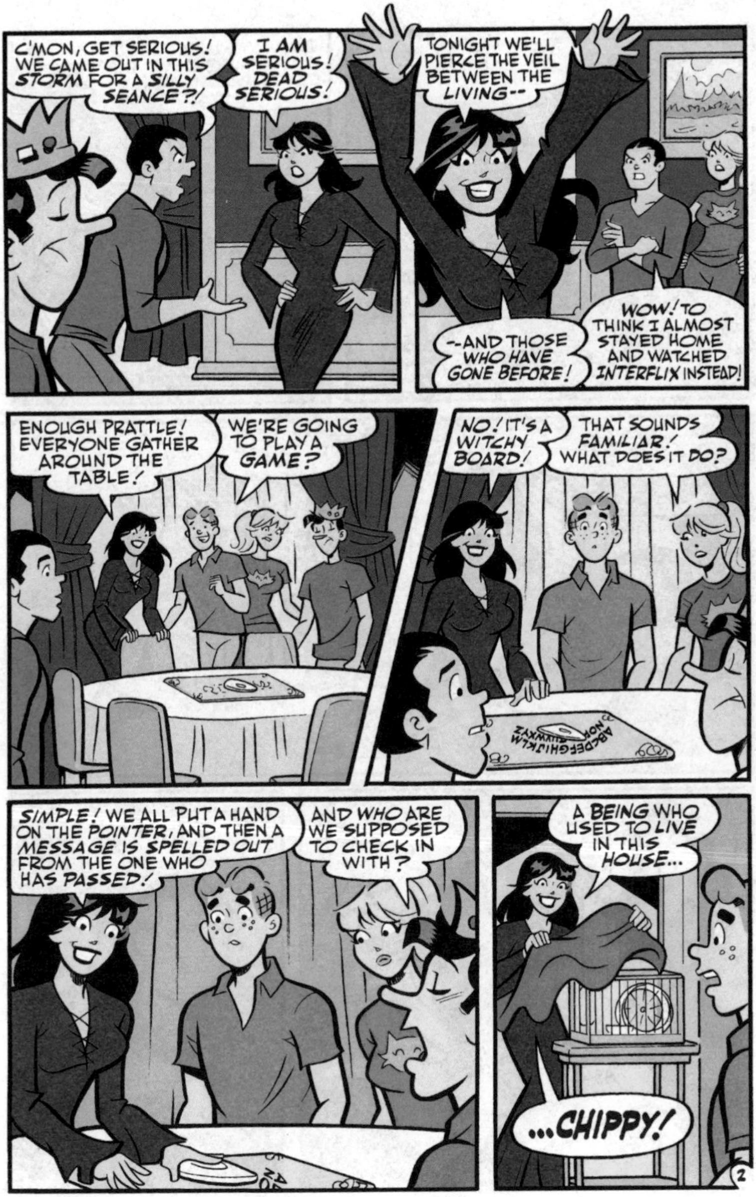
C'MON, GET SERIOUS! WE CAME OUT IN THIS STORM FOR A SILLY SEANCE?!
I AM SERIOUS! DEAD SERIOUS!
TONIGHT WE'LL PIERCE THE VEIL BETWEEN THE LIVING--
--AND THOSE WHO HAVE GONE BEFORE!
WOW! TO THINK I ALMOST STAYED HOME AND WATCHED INTERFLIX INSTEAD!
ENOUGH PRATTLE! EVERYONE GATHER AROUND THE TABLE!
WE'RE GOING TO PLAY A GAME?
NO! IT'S A WITCHY BOARD!
THAT SOUNDS FAMILIAR! WHAT DOES IT DO?
SIMPLE! WE ALL PUT A HAND ON THE POINTER, AND THEN A MESSAGE IS SPELLED OUT FROM THE ONE WHO HAS PASSED!
AND WHO ARE WE SUPPOSED TO CHECK IN WITH?
A BEING WHO USED TO LIVE IN THIS HOUSE...
...CHIPPY!
2

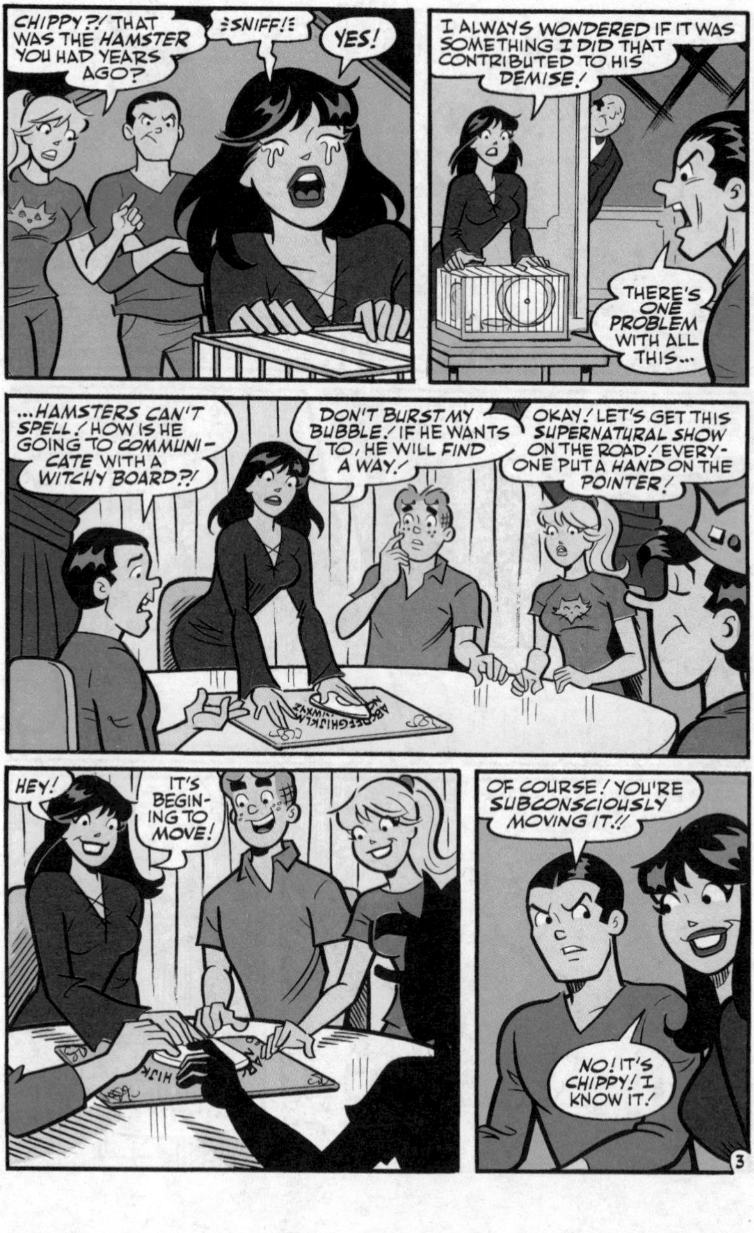
CHIPPY?! THAT WAS THE HAMSTER YOU HAD YEARS AGO?
SNIFF!
YES!
I ALWAYS WONDERED IF IT WAS SOMETHING I DID THAT CONTRIBUTED TO HIS DEMISE!
THERE'S ONE PROBLEM WITH ALL THIS...
...HAMSTERS CAN'T SPELL! HOW IS HE GOING TO COMMUNI-CATE WITH A WITCHY BOARD?!
DON'T BURST MY BUBBLE! IF HE WANTS TO, HE WILL FIND A WAY!
OKAY! LET'S GET THIS SUPERNATURAL SHOW ON THE ROAD! EVERY-ONE PUT A HAND ON THE POINTER!
HEY!
IT'S BEGIN-ING TO MOVE!
OF COURSE! YOU'RE SUBCONSCIOUSLY MOVING IT!!
NO! IT'S CHIPPY! I KNOW IT!
3

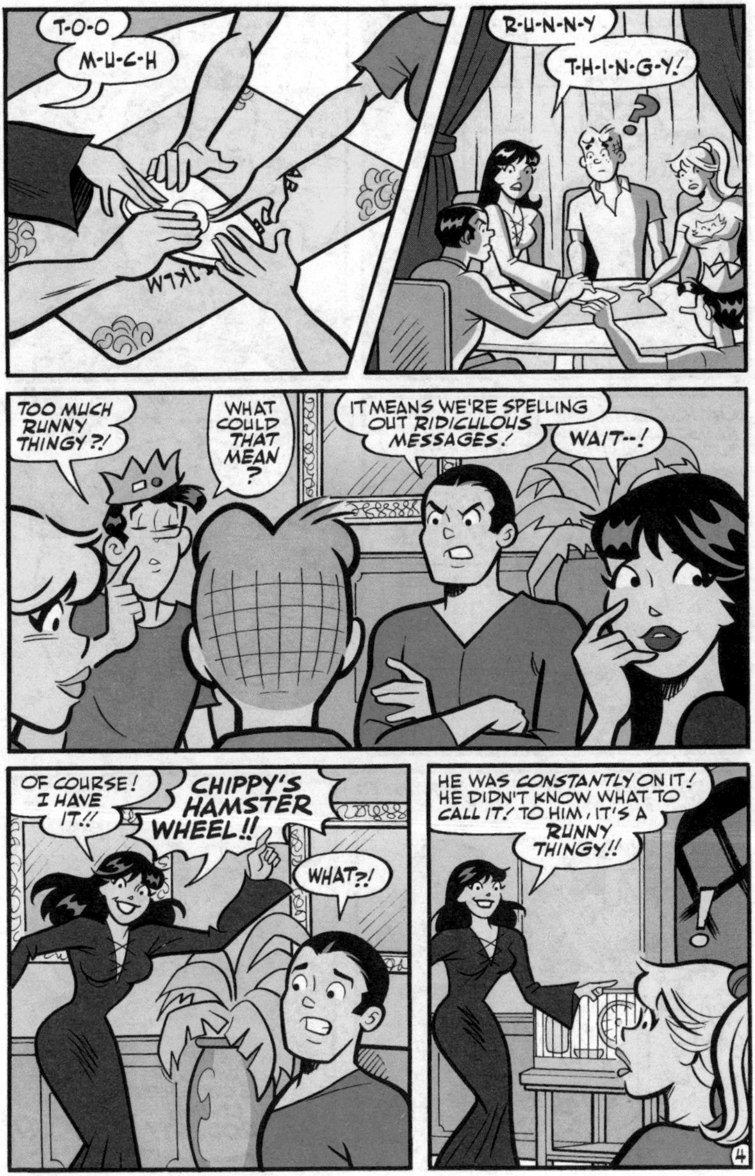
T-O-O
M-U-C-H
R-U-N-N-Y
T-H-I-N-G-Y!
?
TOO MUCH RUNNY THINGY?!
WHAT COULD THAT MEAN?
IT MEANS WE'RE SPELLING OUT RIDICULOUS MESSAGES!
WAIT--!
OF COURSE! I HAVE IT!!
CHIPPY'S HAMSTER WHEEL!!
WHAT?!
HE WAS CONSTANTLY ON IT! HE DIDN'T KNOW WHAT TO CALL IT! TO HIM, IT'S A RUNNY THINGY!!
!
4

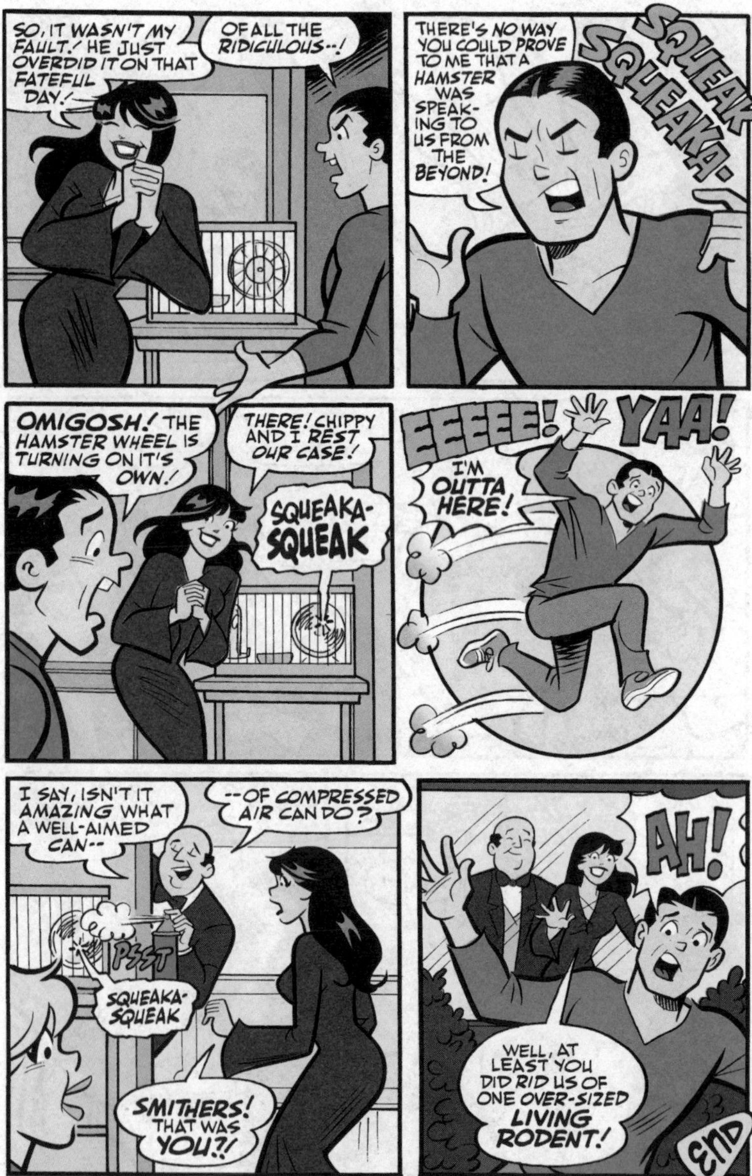
SO, IT WASN'T MY FAULT! HE JUST OVERDID IT ON THAT FATEFUL DAY!
OF ALL THE RIDICULOUS--!
THERE'S NO WAY YOU COULD PROVE TO ME THAT A HAMSTER WAS SPEAK-ING TO US FROM THE BEYOND!
SQUEAK SQUEAKA.
OMIGOSH! THE HAMSTER WHEEL IS TURNING ON IT'S OWN!
THERE! CHIPPY AND I REST OUR CASE!
SQUEAKA-SQUEAK
EEEEE! YAA!
I'M OUTTA HERE!
I SAY, ISN'T IT AMAZING WHAT A WELL-AIMED CAN--
--OF COMPRESSED AIR CAN DO?
PSST
SQUEAKA-SQUEAK
SMITHERS! THAT WAS YOU?!
AH!
WELL, AT LEAST YOU DID RID US OF ONE OVER-SIZED LIVING RODENT!
END

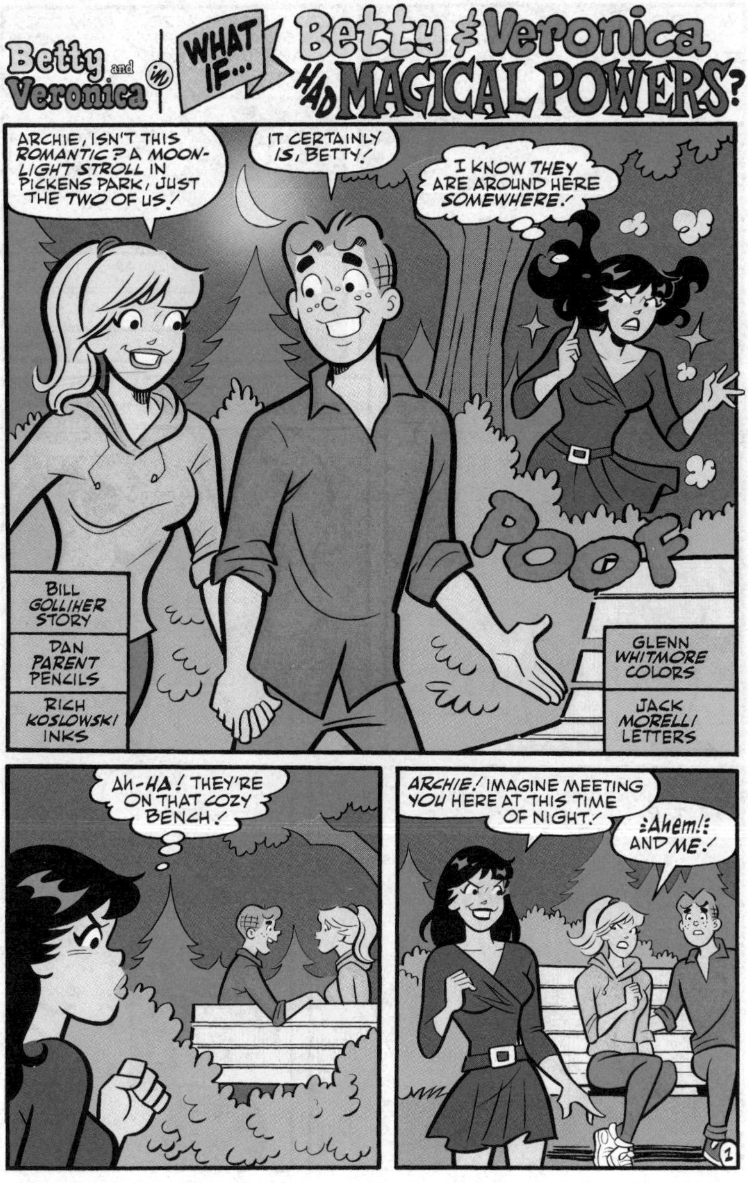
Betty and Veronica in WHAT IF... Betty & Veronica HAD MAGICAL POWERS?
ARCHIE, ISN'T THIS ROMANTIC? A MOON-LIGHT STROLL IN PICKENS PARK, JUST THE TWO OF US!
IT CERTAINLY IS, BETTY!
I KNOW THEY ARE AROUND HERE SOMEWHERE!
POOF
BILL GOLLIHER STORY
DAN PARENT PENCILS
RICH KOSLOWSKI INKS
GLENN WHITMORE COLORS
JACK MORELLI LETTERS
AH-HA! THEY'RE ON THAT COZY BENCH!
ARCHIE! IMAGINE MEETING YOU HERE AT THIS TIME OF NIGHT!
:Ahem!: AND ME!
1

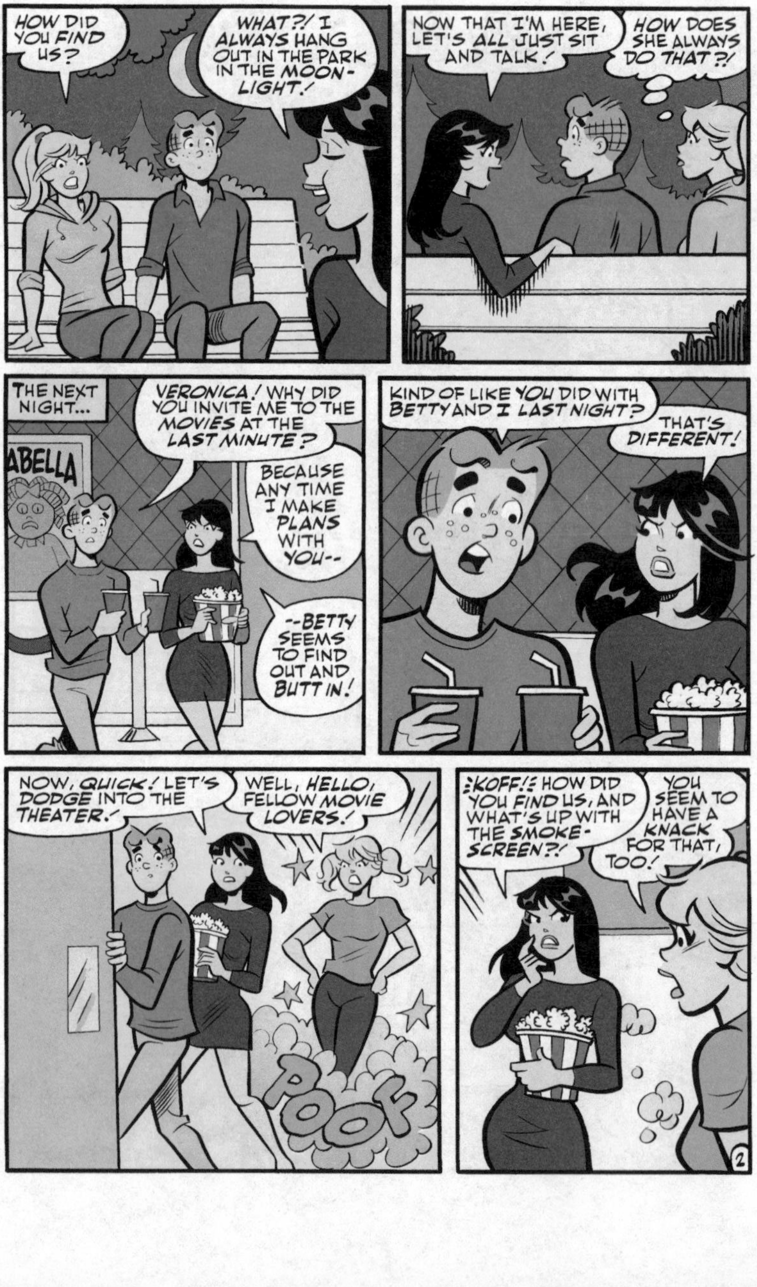
HOW DID YOU FIND US?
WHAT?! I ALWAYS HANG OUT IN THE PARK IN THE MOON-LIGHT!
NOW THAT I'M HERE, LET'S ALL JUST SIT AND TALK!
HOW DOES SHE ALWAYS DO THAT?!
THE NEXT NIGHT...
VERONICA! WHY DID YOU INVITE ME TO THE MOVIES AT THE LAST MINUTE?
ABELLA
BECAUSE ANY TIME I MAKE PLANS WITH YOU--
--BETTY SEEMS TO FIND OUT AND BUTT IN!
KIND OF LIKE YOU DID WITH BETTY AND I LAST NIGHT?
THAT'S DIFFERENT!
NOW, QUICK! LET'S DODGE INTO THE THEATER!
WELL, HELLO, FELLOW MOVIE LOVERS!
POOF
KOFF! HOW DID YOU FIND US, AND WHAT'S UP WITH THE SMOKE-SCREEN?!
YOU SEEM TO HAVE A KNACK FOR THAT, TOO!
2

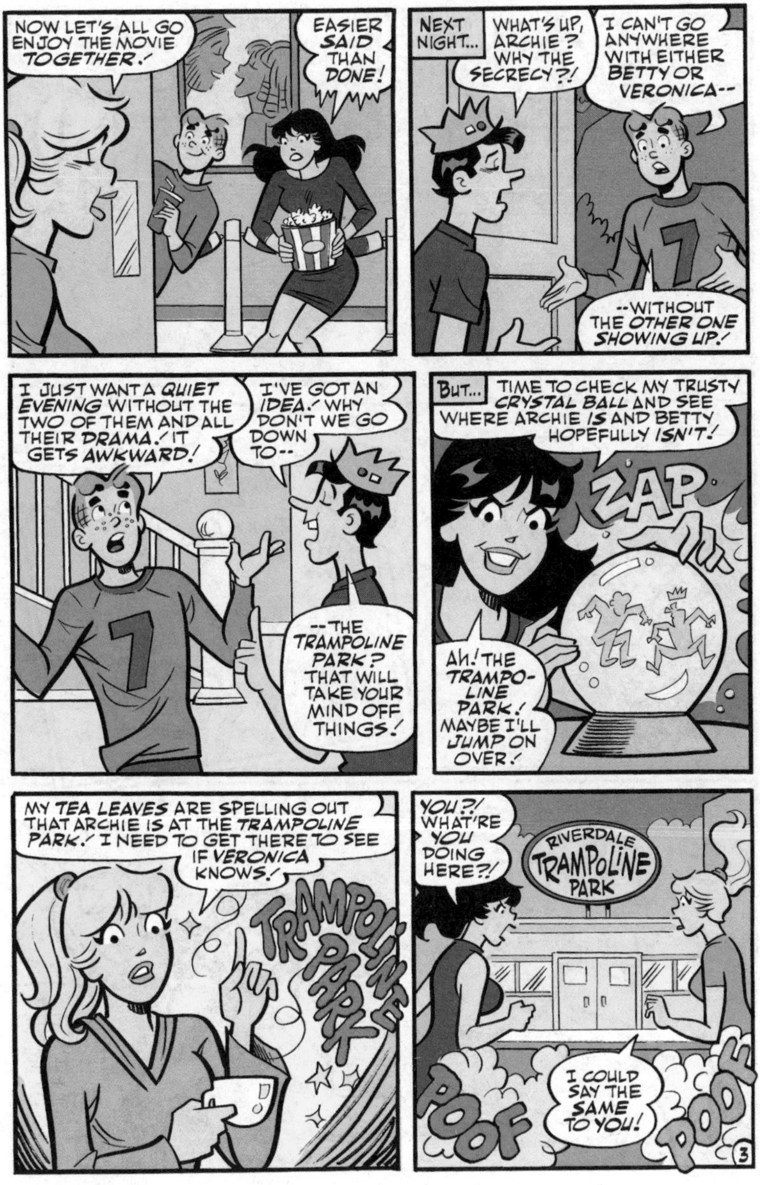
NOW LET'S ALL GO ENJOY THE MOVIE TOGETHER!
EASIER SAID THAN DONE!
NEXT NIGHT...
WHAT'S UP, ARCHIE? WHY THE SECRECY?!
I CAN'T GO ANYWHERE WITH EITHER BETTY OR VERONICA--
--WITHOUT THE OTHER ONE SHOWING UP!
I JUST WANT A QUIET EVENING WITHOUT THE TWO OF THEM AND ALL THEIR DRAMA! IT GETS AWKWARD!
I'VE GOT AN IDEA! WHY DON'T WE GO DOWN TO--
--THE TRAMPOLINE PARK? THAT WILL TAKE YOUR MIND OFF THINGS!
BUT...
TIME TO CHECK MY TRUSTY CRYSTAL BALL AND SEE WHERE ARCHIE IS AND BETTY HOPEFULLY ISN'T!
ZAP
AH! THE TRAMPOLINE PARK! MAYBE I'LL JUMP ON OVER!
MY TEA LEAVES ARE SPELLING OUT THAT ARCHIE IS AT THE TRAMPOLINE PARK! I NEED TO GET THERE TO SEE IF VERONICA KNOWS!
TRAMPOLINE PARK
YOU?! WHAT'RE YOU DOING HERE?!
RIVERDALE TRAMPOLINE PARK
I COULD SAY THE SAME TO YOU!
POOF
POOF
3

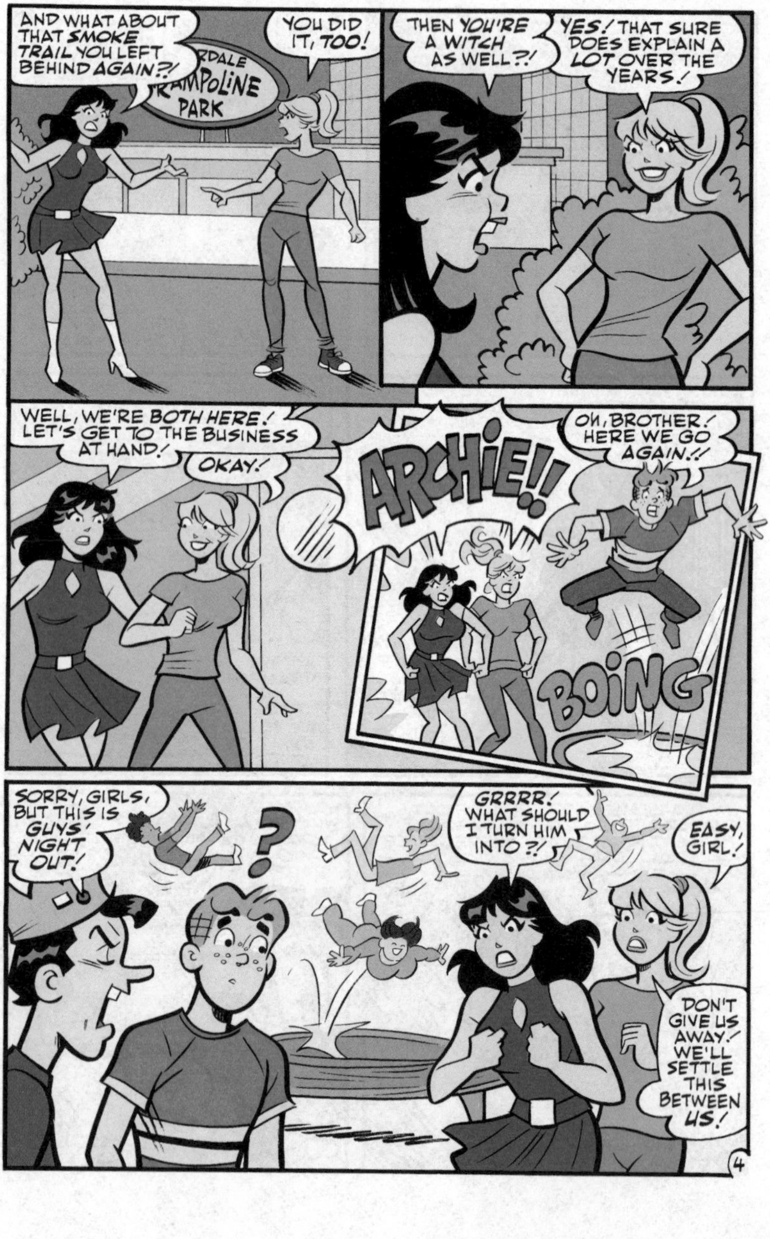
AND WHAT ABOUT THAT SMOKE TRAIL YOU LEFT BEHIND AGAIN?!
YOU DID IT, TOO!
RDALE TRAMPOLINE PARK
THEN YOU'RE A WITCH AS WELL?!
YES! THAT SURE DOES EXPLAIN A LOT OVER THE YEARS!
WELL, WE'RE BOTH HERE! LET'S GET TO THE BUSINESS AT HAND!
OKAY!
ARCHIE!!
OH, BROTHER! HERE WE GO AGAIN!!
BOING
SORRY, GIRLS, BUT THIS IS GUYS' NIGHT OUT!
?
GRRRR! WHAT SHOULD I TURN HIM INTO?!
EASY, GIRL!
DON'T GIVE US AWAY! WE'LL SETTLE THIS BETWEEN US!
4

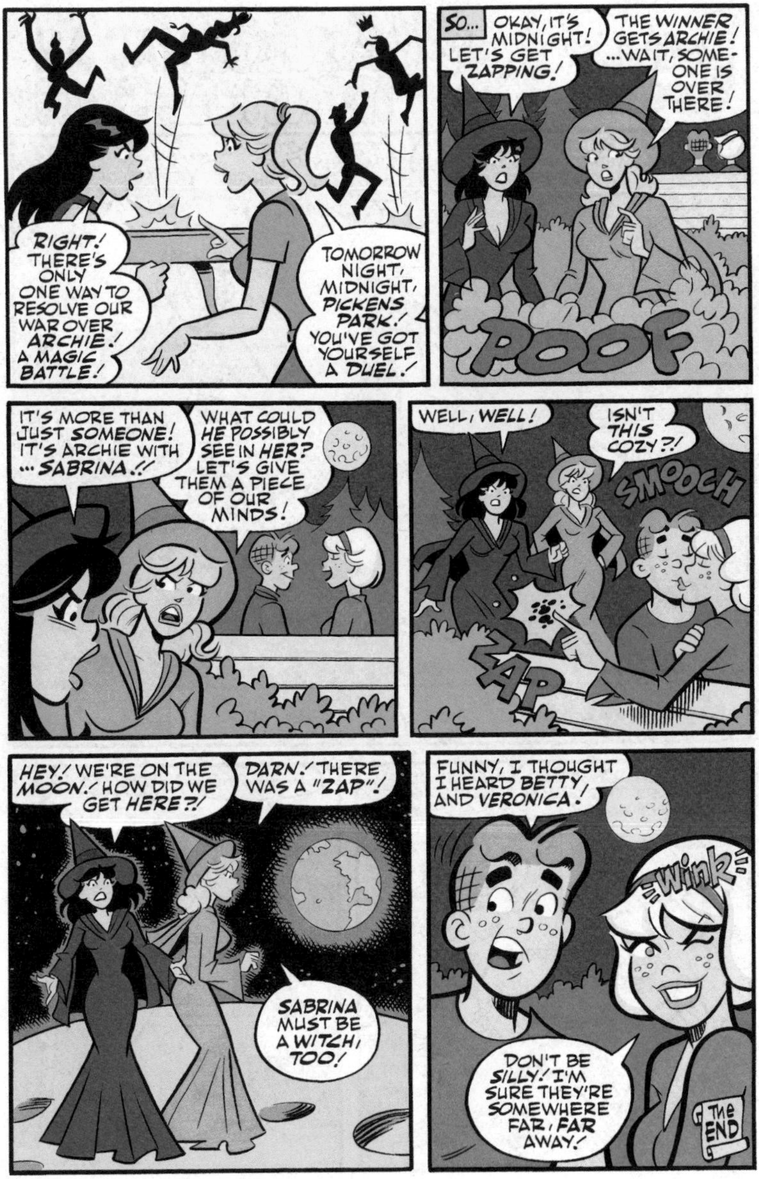
RIGHT! THERE'S ONLY ONE WAY TO RESOLVE OUR WAR OVER ARCHIE! A MAGIC BATTLE!
TOMORROW NIGHT, MIDNIGHT, PICKENS PARK! YOU'VE GOT YOURSELF A DUEL!
SO...
OKAY, IT'S MIDNIGHT! LET'S GET ZAPPING!
THE WINNER GETS ARCHIE! ...WAIT, SOMEONE IS OVER THERE!
POOF
IT'S MORE THAN JUST SOMEONE! IT'S ARCHIE WITH ... SABRINA!!
WHAT COULD HE POSSIBLY SEE IN HER? LET'S GIVE THEM A PIECE OF OUR MINDS!
WELL, WELL!
ISN'T THIS COZY?!
SMOOCH
ZAP
HEY! WE'RE ON THE MOON! HOW DID WE GET HERE?!
DARN! THERE WAS A "ZAP"!
SABRINA MUST BE A WITCH, TOO!
FUNNY, I THOUGHT I HEARD BETTY AND VERONICA!
WINK
DON'T BE SILLY! I'M SURE THEY'RE SOMEWHERE FAR, FAR AWAY!
THE END

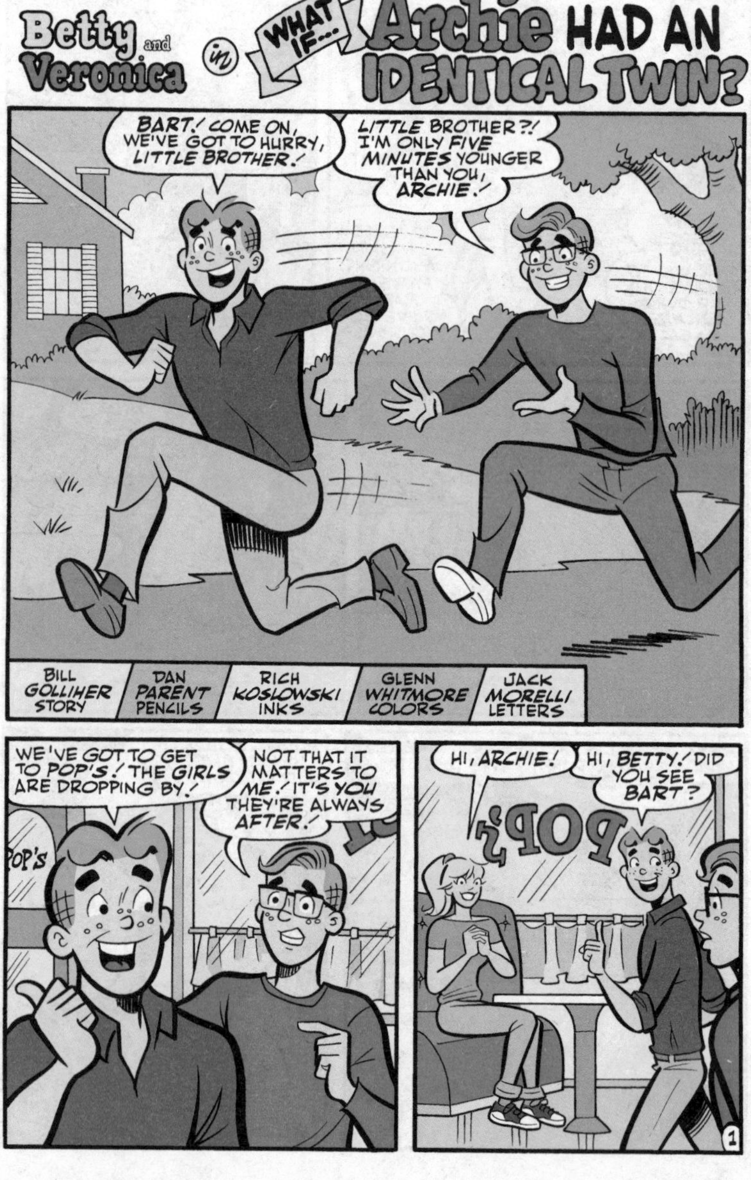
Betty and Veronica in WHAT IF... Archie HAD AN IDENTICAL TWIN?
BART! COME ON, WE'VE GOT TO HURRY, LITTLE BROTHER!
LITTLE BROTHER?! I'M ONLY FIVE MINUTES YOUNGER THAN YOU, ARCHIE!
BILL GOLLIHER STORY
DAN PARENT PENCILS
RICH KOSLOWSKI INKS
GLENN WHITMORE COLORS
JACK MORELLI LETTERS
WE'VE GOT TO GET TO POP'S! THE GIRLS ARE DROPPING BY!
NOT THAT IT MATTERS TO ME! IT'S YOU THEY'RE ALWAYS AFTER!
POP'S
HI, ARCHIE!
HI, BETTY! DID YOU SEE BART?
POP'S
1

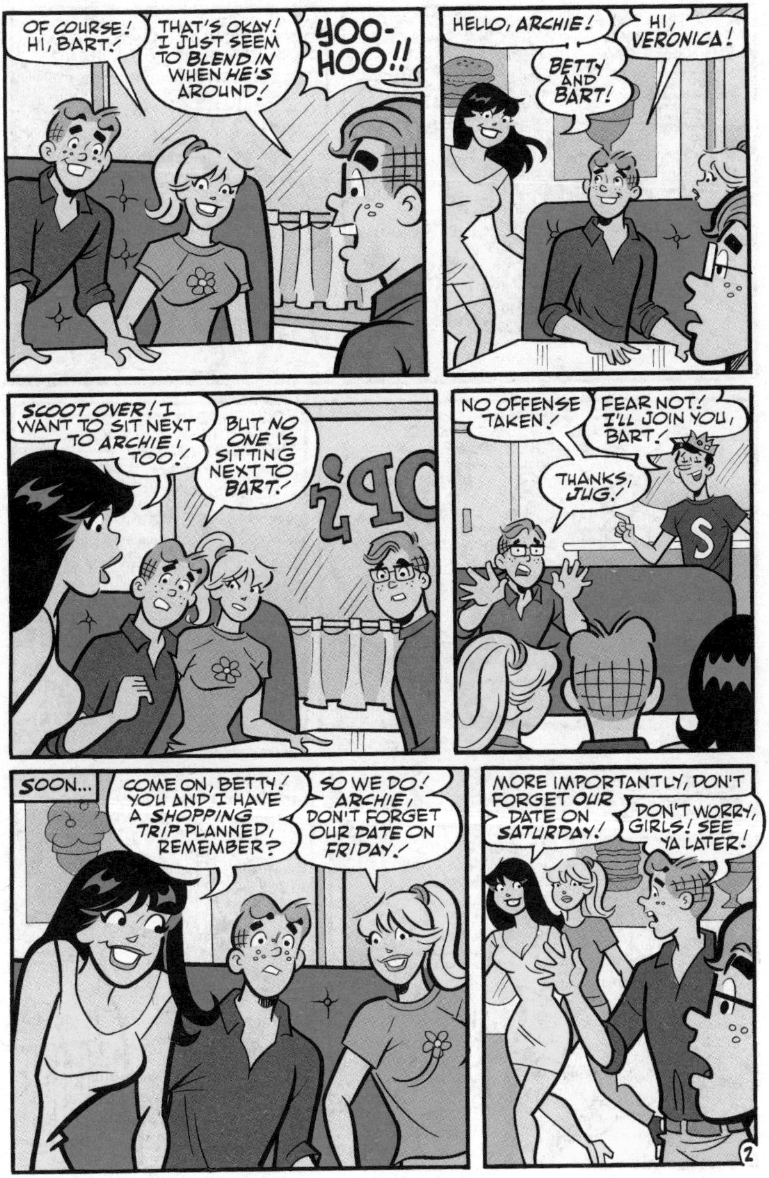
OF COURSE! HI, BART!
THAT'S OKAY! I JUST SEEM TO BLEND IN WHEN HE'S AROUND!
YOO-HOO!!
HELLO, ARCHIE!
BETTY AND BART!
HI, VERONICA!
SCOOT OVER! I WANT TO SIT NEXT TO ARCHIE, TOO!
BUT NO ONE IS SITTING NEXT TO BART!
OP'S
NO OFFENSE TAKEN!
FEAR NOT! I'LL JOIN YOU, BART!
THANKS, JUG!
SOON...
COME ON, BETTY! YOU AND I HAVE A SHOPPING TRIP PLANNED, REMEMBER?
SO WE DO! ARCHIE, DON'T FORGET OUR DATE ON FRIDAY!
MORE IMPORTANTLY, DON'T FORGET OUR DATE ON SATURDAY!
DON'T WORRY, GIRLS! SEE YA LATER!
2

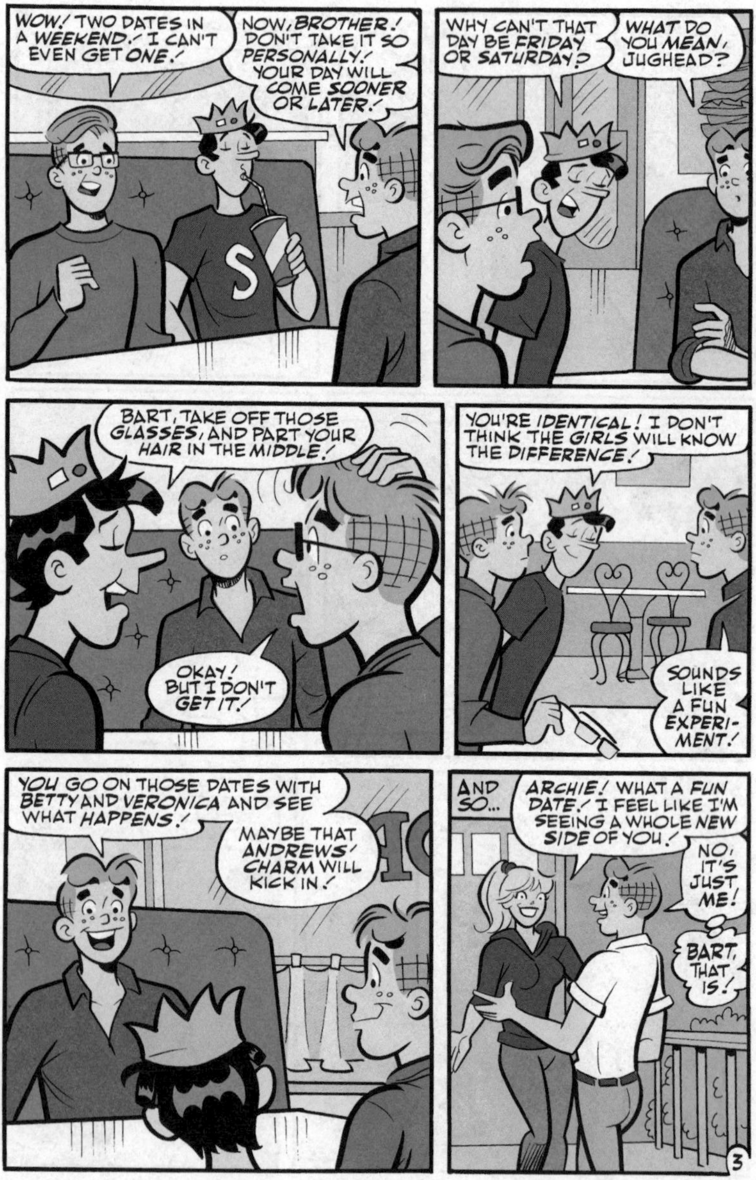
WOW! TWO DATES IN A WEEKEND! I CAN'T EVEN GET ONE!
NOW, BROTHER! DON'T TAKE IT SO PERSONALLY! YOUR DAY WILL COME SOONER OR LATER!
WHY CAN'T THAT DAY BE FRIDAY OR SATURDAY?
WHAT DO YOU MEAN, JUGHEAD?
BART, TAKE OFF THOSE GLASSES, AND PART YOUR HAIR IN THE MIDDLE!
OKAY! BUT I DON'T GET IT!
YOU'RE IDENTICAL! I DON'T THINK THE GIRLS WILL KNOW THE DIFFERENCE!
SOUNDS LIKE A FUN EXPERI-MENT!
YOU GO ON THOSE DATES WITH BETTY AND VERONICA AND SEE WHAT HAPPENS!
MAYBE THAT ANDREWS' CHARM WILL KICK IN!
AND SO...
ARCHIE! WHAT A FUN DATE! I FEEL LIKE I'M SEEING A WHOLE NEW SIDE OF YOU!
NO, IT'S JUST ME!
BART, THAT IS!
3

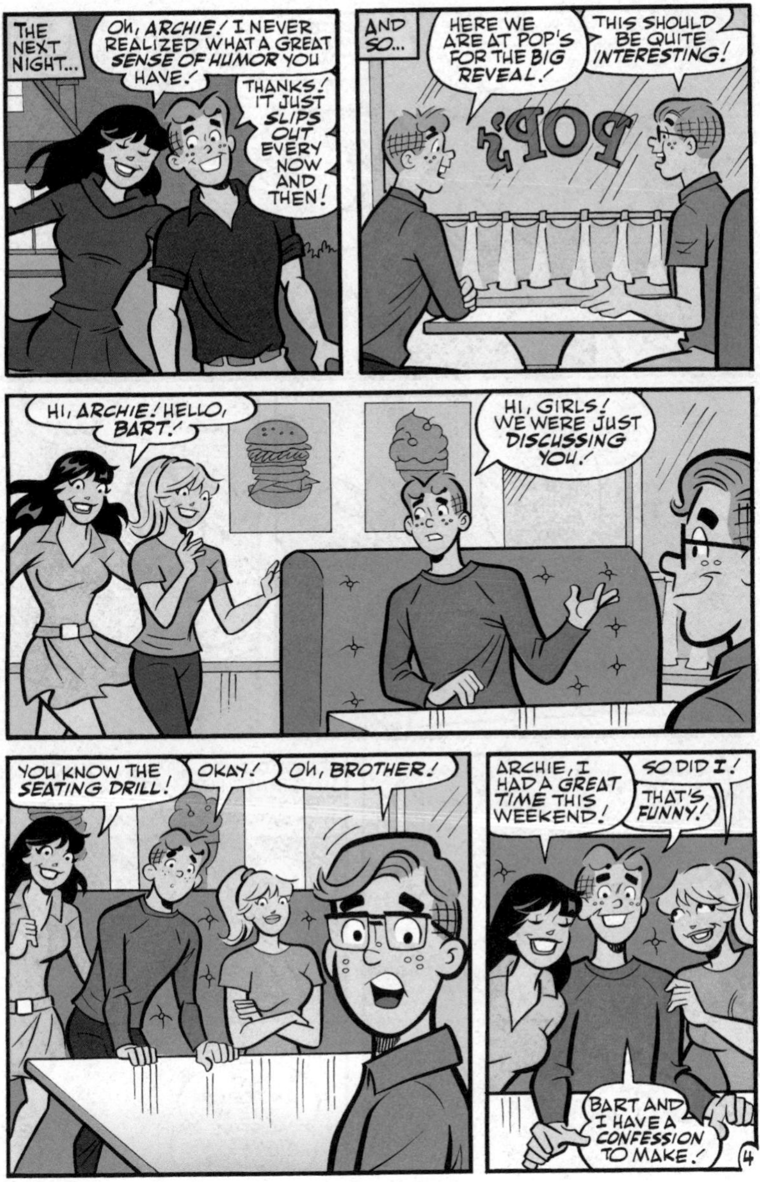
THE NEXT NIGHT...
OH, ARCHIE! I NEVER REALIZED WHAT A GREAT SENSE OF HUMOR YOU HAVE!
THANKS! IT JUST SLIPS OUT EVERY NOW AND THEN!
AND SO...
HERE WE ARE AT POP'S FOR THE BIG REVEAL!
THIS SHOULD BE QUITE INTERESTING!
POP'S
HI, ARCHIE! HELLO, BART!
HI, GIRLS! WE WERE JUST DISCUSSING YOU!
YOU KNOW THE SEATING DRILL!
OKAY!
OH, BROTHER!
ARCHIE, I HAD A GREAT TIME THIS WEEKEND!
SO DID I!
THAT'S FUNNY!
BART AND I HAVE A CONFESSION TO MAKE!
4

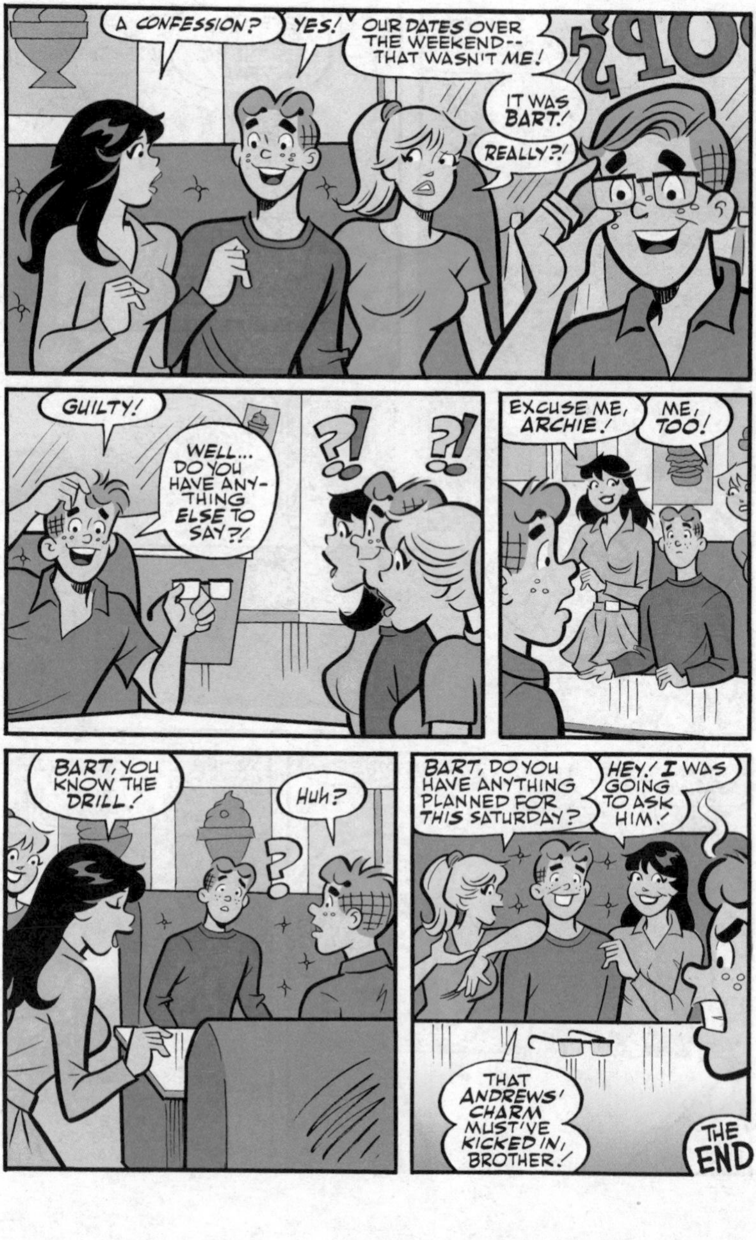
A CONFESSION?
YES!
OUR DATES OVER THE WEEKEND-- THAT WASN'T ME!
IT WAS BART!
REALLY?!
GUILTY!
WELL... DO YOU HAVE ANY-THING ELSE TO SAY?!
?!
?!
EXCUSE ME, ARCHIE!
ME, TOO!
BART, YOU KNOW THE DRILL!
Huh?
?
BART, DO YOU HAVE ANYTHING PLANNED FOR THIS SATURDAY?
HEY! I WAS GOING TO ASK HIM!
THAT ANDREWS' CHARM MUST'VE KICKED IN, BROTHER!
THE END

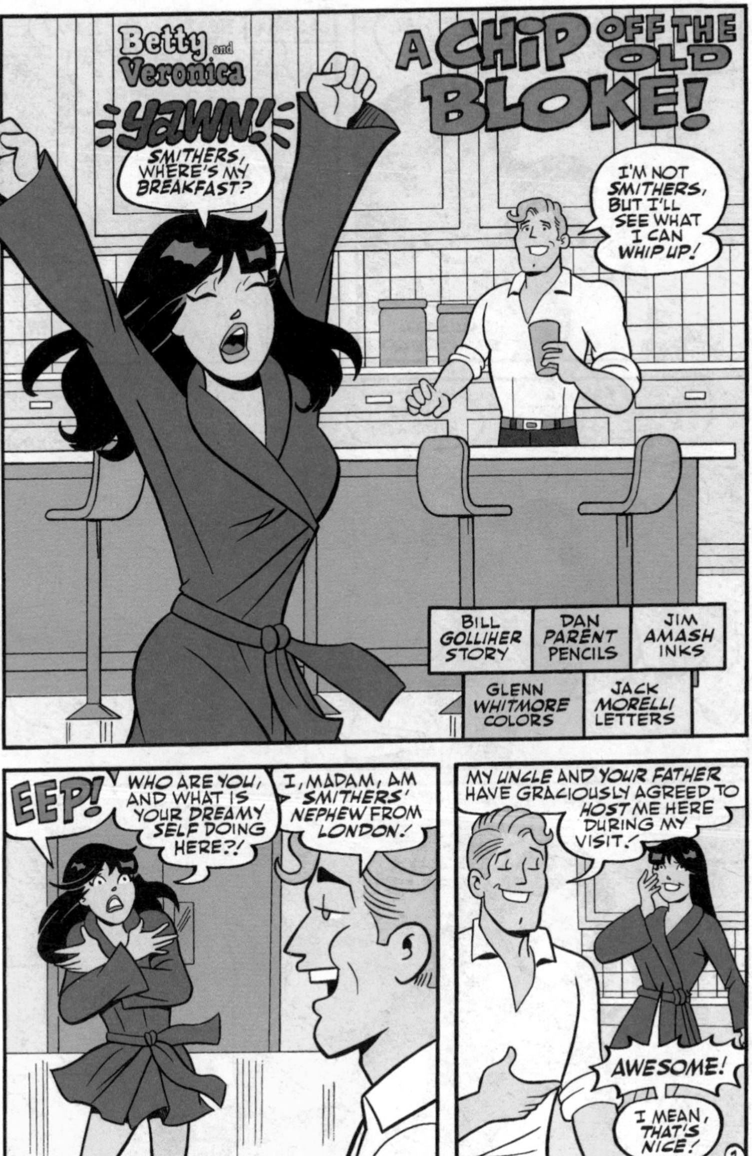
Betty and Veronica
A CHIP OFF THE OLD BLOKE!
YAWN!
SMITHERS, WHERE'S MY BREAKFAST?
I'M NOT SMITHERS, BUT I'LL SEE WHAT I CAN WHIP UP!
BILL GOLLIHER STORY
DAN PARENT PENCILS
JIM AMASH INKS
GLENN WHITMORE COLORS
JACK MORELLI LETTERS
EEP!
WHO ARE YOU, AND WHAT IS YOUR DREAMY SELF DOING HERE?!
I, MADAM, AM SMITHERS' NEPHEW FROM LONDON!
MY UNCLE AND YOUR FATHER HAVE GRACIOUSLY AGREED TO HOST ME HERE DURING MY VISIT!
AWESOME!
I MEAN, THAT'S NICE!
1

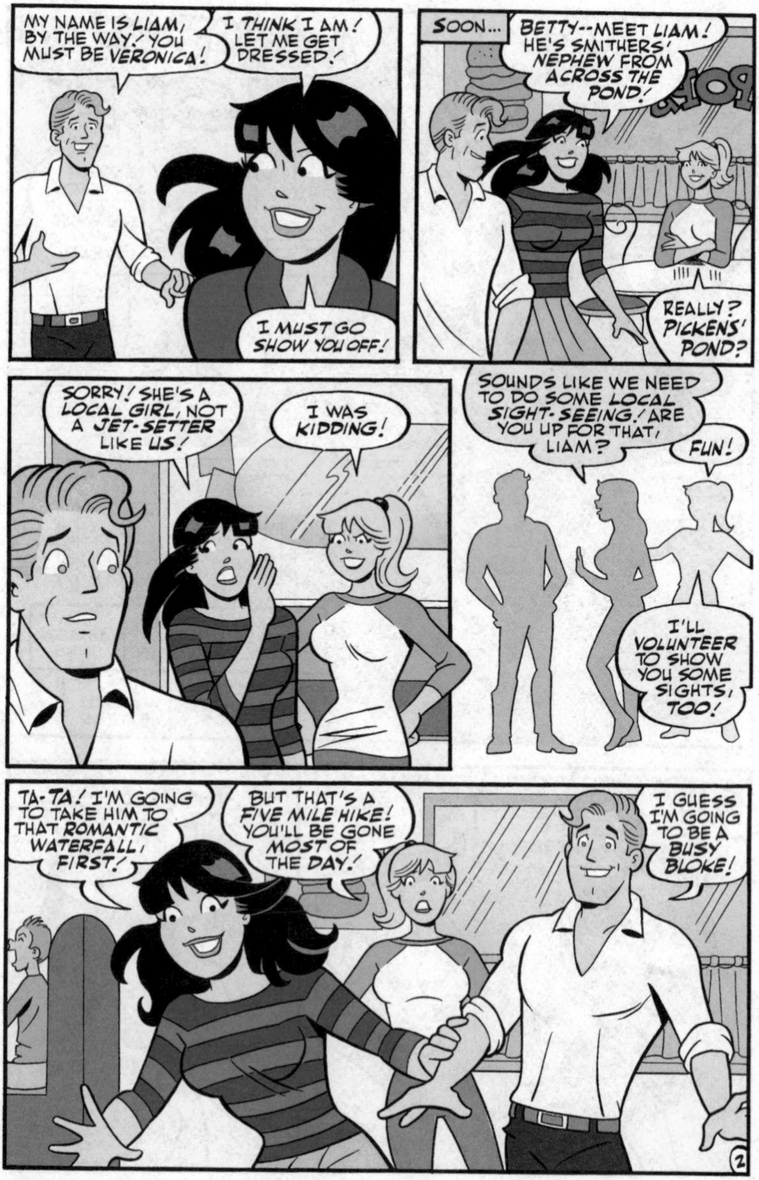
MY NAME IS LIAM, BY THE WAY! YOU MUST BE VERONICA!
I THINK I AM! LET ME GET DRESSED!
I MUST GO SHOW YOU OFF!
SOON...
BETTY--MEET LIAM! HE'S SMITHERS' NEPHEW FROM ACROSS THE POND!
REALLY? PICKENS' POND?
SORRY! SHE'S A LOCAL GIRL, NOT A JET-SETTER LIKE US!
I WAS KIDDING!
SOUNDS LIKE WE NEED TO DO SOME LOCAL SIGHT-SEEING! ARE YOU UP FOR THAT, LIAM?
FUN!
I'LL VOLUNTEER TO SHOW YOU SOME SIGHTS, TOO!
TA-TA! I'M GOING TO TAKE HIM TO THAT ROMANTIC WATERFALL, FIRST!
BUT THAT'S A FIVE MILE HIKE! YOU'LL BE GONE MOST OF THE DAY!
I GUESS I'M GOING TO BE A BUSY BLOKE!
2

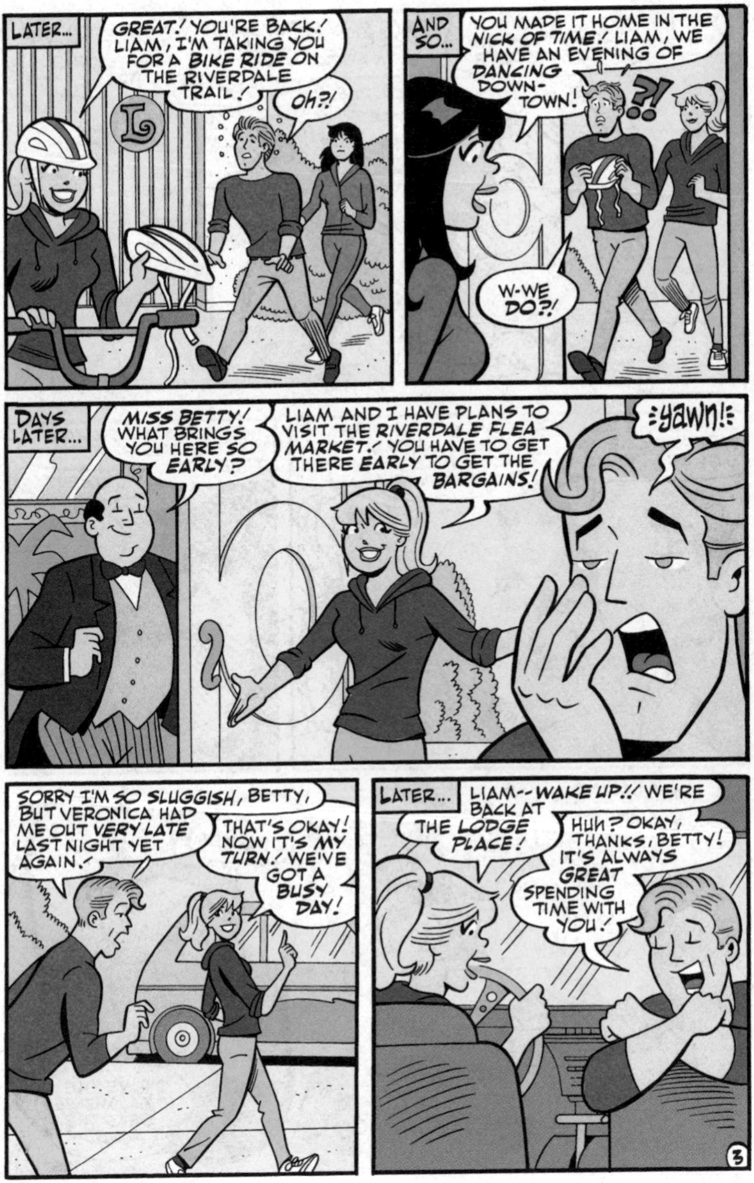
LATER...
GREAT! YOU'RE BACK! LIAM, I'M TAKING YOU FOR A BIKE RIDE ON THE RIVERDALE TRAIL!
OH?!
AND SO...
YOU MADE IT HOME IN THE NICK OF TIME! LIAM, WE HAVE AN EVENING OF DANCING DOWN-TOWN!
?!
W-WE DO?!
DAYS LATER...
MISS BETTY! WHAT BRINGS YOU HERE SO EARLY?
LIAM AND I HAVE PLANS TO VISIT THE RIVERDALE FLEA MARKET! YOU HAVE TO GET THERE EARLY TO GET THE BARGAINS!
YAWN!
SORRY I'M SO SLUGGISH, BETTY, BUT VERONICA HAD ME OUT VERY LATE LAST NIGHT YET AGAIN!
THAT'S OKAY! NOW IT'S MY TURN! WE'VE GOT A BUSY DAY!
LATER...
LIAM--WAKE UP!! WE'RE BACK AT THE LODGE PLACE!
HUH? OKAY, THANKS, BETTY! IT'S ALWAYS GREAT SPENDING TIME WITH YOU!
3

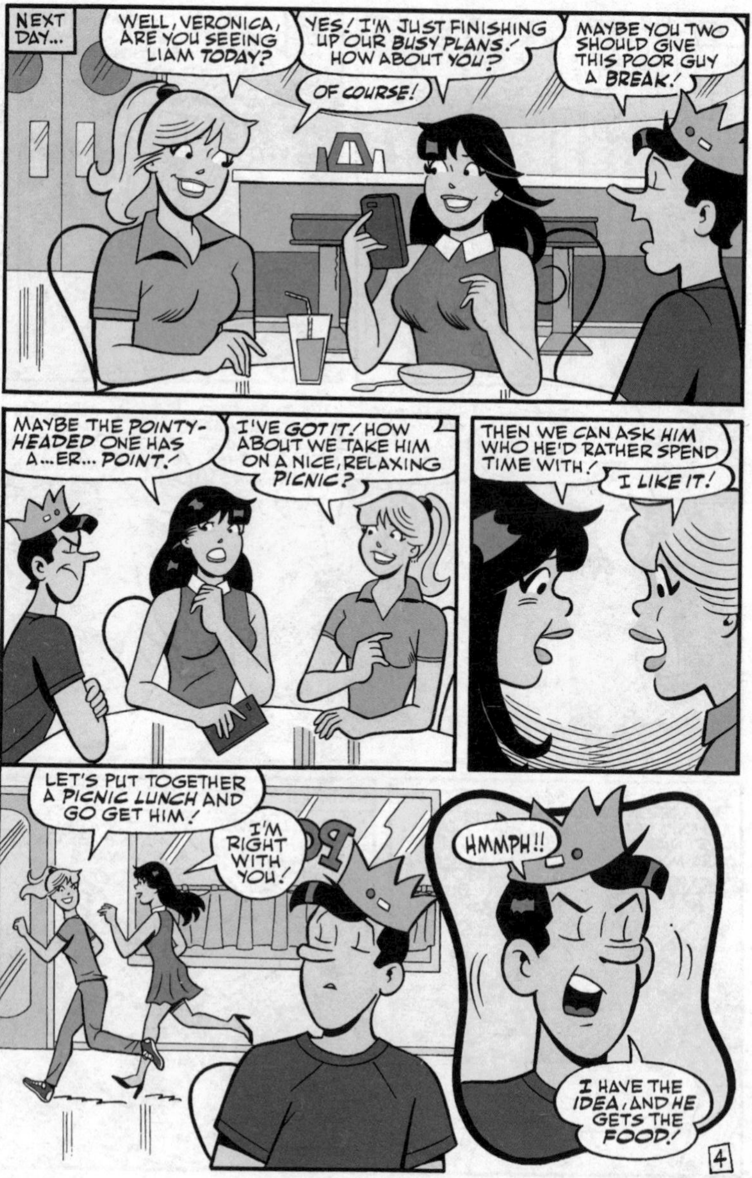
NEXT DAY...
WELL, VERONICA, ARE YOU SEEING LIAM TODAY?
YES! I'M JUST FINISHING UP OUR BUSY PLANS! HOW ABOUT YOU?
OF COURSE!
MAYBE YOU TWO SHOULD GIVE THIS POOR GUY A BREAK!
MAYBE THE POINTY-HEADED ONE HAS A...ER... POINT!
I'VE GOT IT! HOW ABOUT WE TAKE HIM ON A NICE, RELAXING PICNIC?
THEN WE CAN ASK HIM WHO HE'D RATHER SPEND TIME WITH!
I LIKE IT!
LET'S PUT TOGETHER A PICNIC LUNCH AND GO GET HIM!
I'M RIGHT WITH YOU!
HMMPH!!
I HAVE THE IDEA, AND HE GETS THE FOOD!
4

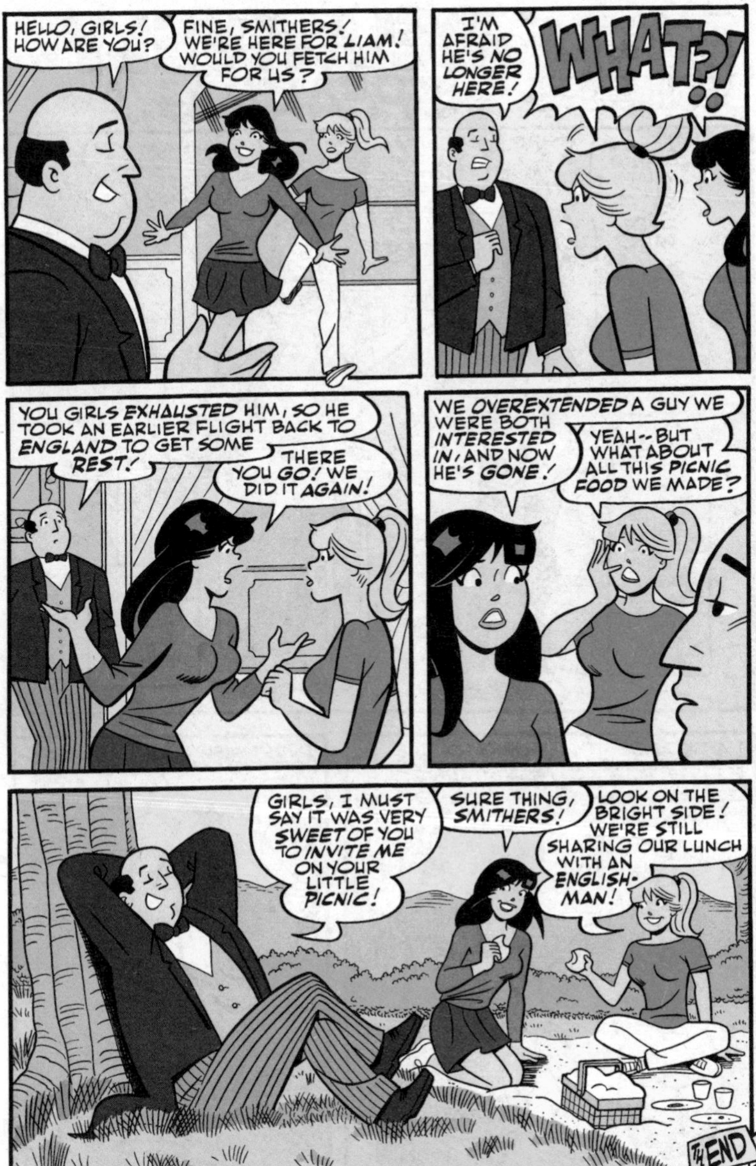
HELLO, GIRLS! HOW ARE YOU?
FINE, SMITHERS! WE'RE HERE FOR LIAM! WOULD YOU FETCH HIM FOR US?
I'M AFRAID HE'S NO LONGER HERE!
WHAT?!
YOU GIRLS EXHAUSTED HIM, SO HE TOOK AN EARLIER FLIGHT BACK TO ENGLAND TO GET SOME REST!
THERE YOU GO! WE DID IT AGAIN!
WE OVEREXTENDED A GUY WE WERE BOTH INTERESTED IN, AND NOW HE'S GONE!
YEAH -- BUT WHAT ABOUT ALL THIS PICNIC FOOD WE MADE?
GIRLS, I MUST SAY IT WAS VERY SWEET OF YOU TO INVITE ME ON YOUR LITTLE PICNIC!
SURE THING, SMITHERS!
LOOK ON THE BRIGHT SIDE! WE'RE STILL SHARING OUR LUNCH WITH AN ENGLISH-MAN!
THE END

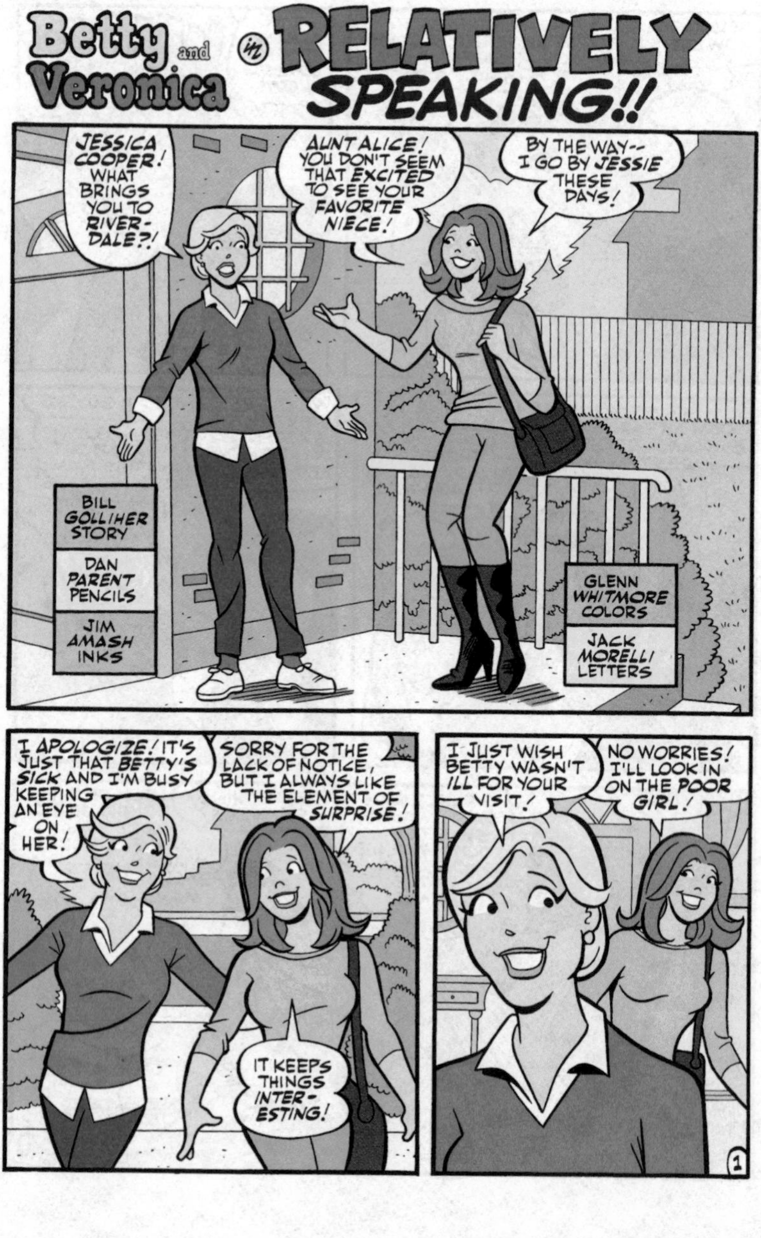
Betty and Veronica in RELATIVELY SPEAKING!!
JESSICA COOPER! WHAT BRINGS YOU TO RIVER-DALE?!
AUNT ALICE! YOU DON'T SEEM THAT EXCITED TO SEE YOUR FAVORITE NIECE!
BY THE WAY-- I GO BY JESSIE THESE DAYS!
BILL GOLLIHER STORY
DAN PARENT PENCILS
JIM AMASH INKS
GLENN WHITMORE COLORS
JACK MORELLI LETTERS
I APOLOGIZE! IT'S JUST THAT BETTY'S SICK AND I'M BUSY KEEPING AN EYE ON HER!
SORRY FOR THE LACK OF NOTICE, BUT I ALWAYS LIKE THE ELEMENT OF SURPRISE!
IT KEEPS THINGS INTER-ESTING!
I JUST WISH BETTY WASN'T ILL FOR YOUR VISIT!
NO WORRIES! I'LL LOOK IN ON THE POOR GIRL!
1

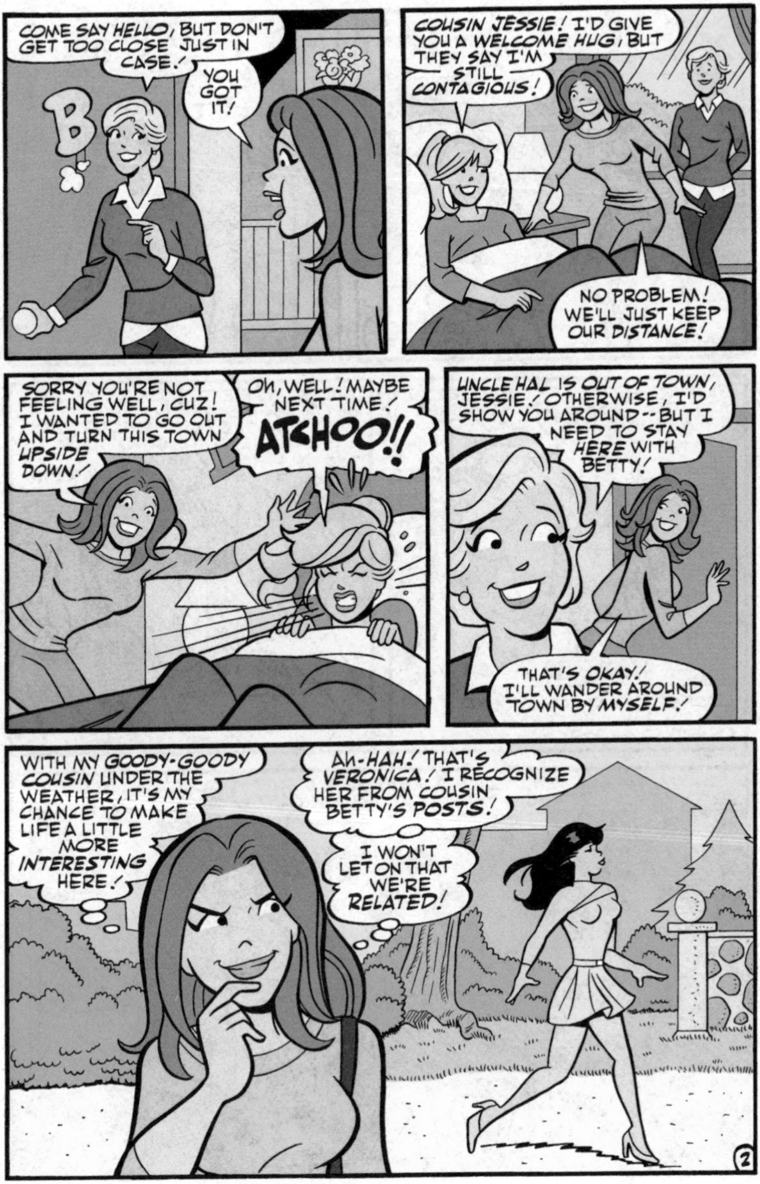
COME SAY HELLO, BUT DON'T GET TOO CLOSE JUST IN CASE!
YOU GOT IT!
B
COUSIN JESSIE! I'D GIVE YOU A WELCOME HUG, BUT THEY SAY I'M STILL CONTAGIOUS!
NO PROBLEM! WE'LL JUST KEEP OUR DISTANCE!
SORRY YOU'RE NOT FEELING WELL, CUZ! I WANTED TO GO OUT AND TURN THIS TOWN UPSIDE DOWN!
OH, WELL! MAYBE NEXT TIME!
ATCHOO!!
UNCLE HAL IS OUT OF TOWN, JESSIE! OTHERWISE, I'D SHOW YOU AROUND -- BUT I NEED TO STAY HERE WITH BETTY!
THAT'S OKAY! I'LL WANDER AROUND TOWN BY MYSELF!
WITH MY GOODY-GOODY COUSIN UNDER THE WEATHER, IT'S MY CHANCE TO MAKE LIFE A LITTLE MORE INTERESTING HERE!
AH-HAH! THAT'S VERONICA! I RECOGNIZE HER FROM COUSIN BETTY'S POSTS!
I WON'T LET ON THAT WE'RE RELATED!
2

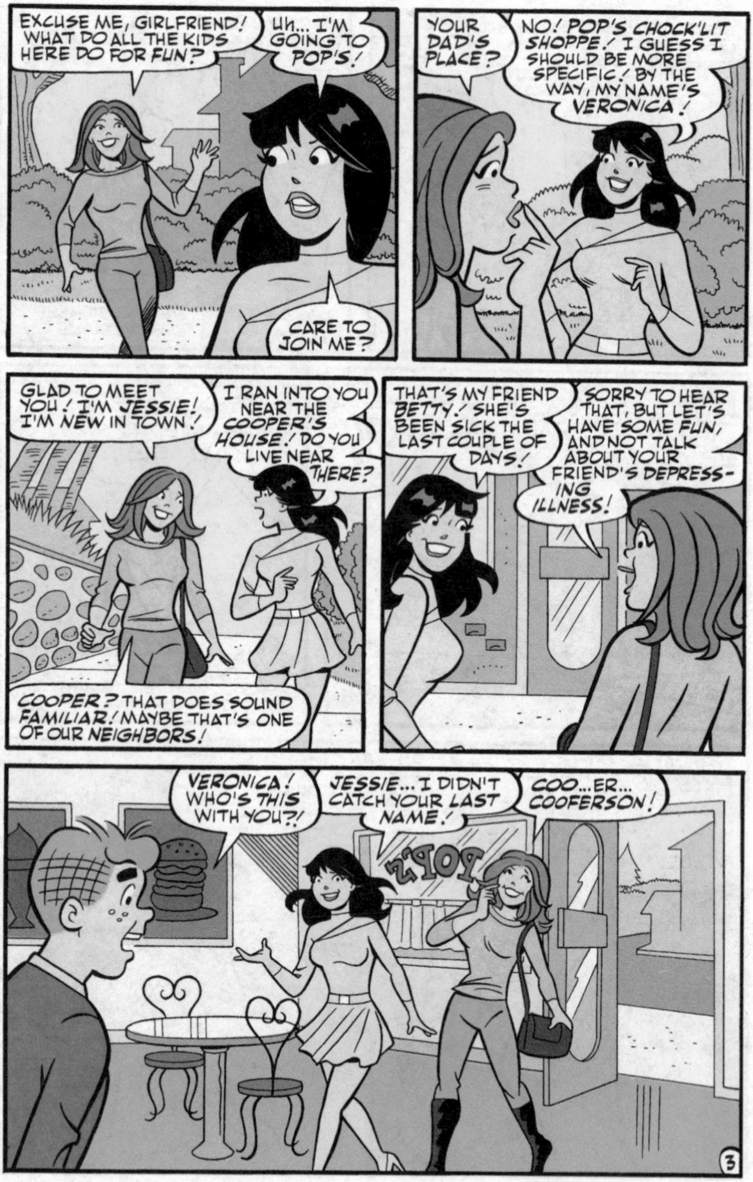
EXCUSE ME, GIRLFRIEND! WHAT DO ALL THE KIDS HERE DO FOR FUN?
UH... I'M GOING TO POP'S!
CARE TO JOIN ME?
YOUR DAD'S PLACE?
NO! POP'S CHOCK'LIT SHOPPE! I GUESS I SHOULD BE MORE SPECIFIC! BY THE WAY, MY NAME'S VERONICA!
GLAD TO MEET YOU! I'M JESSIE! I'M NEW IN TOWN!
I RAN INTO YOU NEAR THE COOPER'S HOUSE! DO YOU LIVE NEAR THERE?
COOPER? THAT DOES SOUND FAMILIAR! MAYBE THAT'S ONE OF OUR NEIGHBORS!
THAT'S MY FRIEND BETTY! SHE'S BEEN SICK THE LAST COUPLE OF DAYS!
SORRY TO HEAR THAT, BUT LET'S HAVE SOME FUN, AND NOT TALK ABOUT YOUR FRIEND'S DEPRESS-ING ILLNESS!
VERONICA! WHO'S THIS WITH YOU?!
JESSIE... I DIDN'T CATCH YOUR LAST NAME!
COO...ER... COOFERSON!
POP'S
3

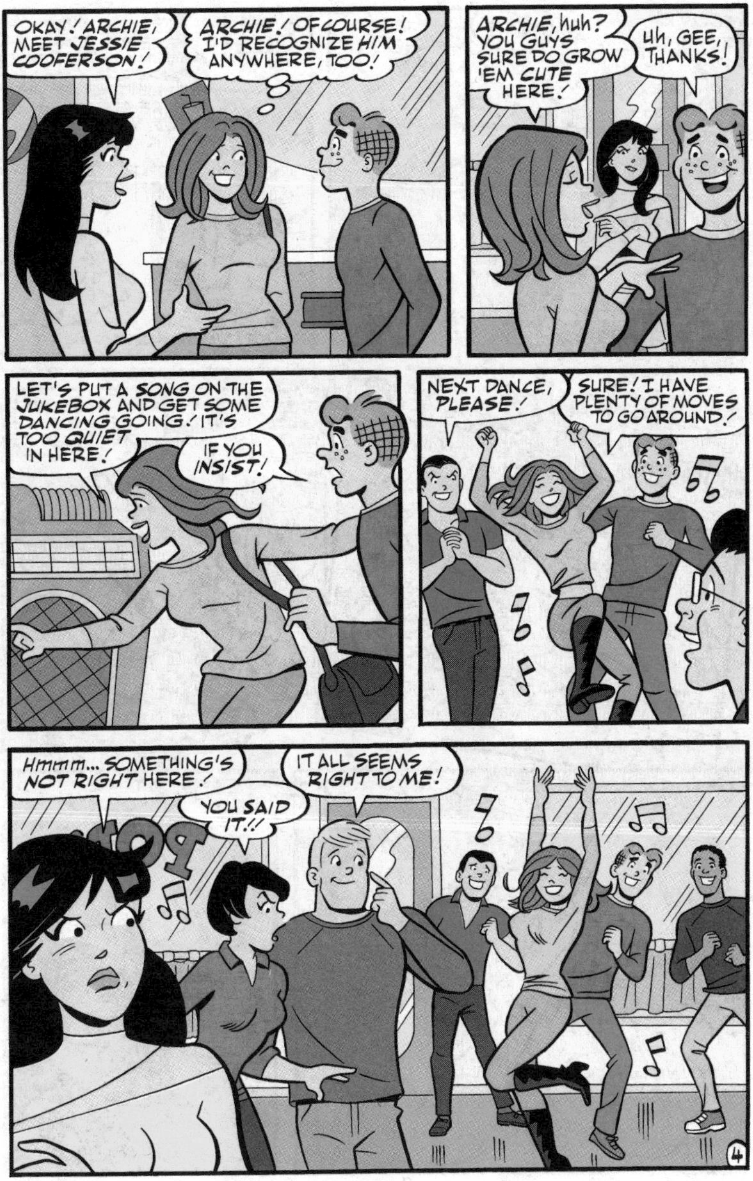
OKAY! ARCHIE, MEET JESSIE COOFERSON!
ARCHIE! OF COURSE! I'D RECOGNIZE HIM ANYWHERE, TOO!
ARCHIE, huh? YOU GUYS SURE DO GROW 'EM CUTE HERE!
uh, GEE, THANKS!
LET'S PUT A SONG ON THE JUKEBOX AND GET SOME DANCING GOING! IT'S TOO QUIET IN HERE!
IF YOU INSIST!
NEXT DANCE, PLEASE!
SURE! I HAVE PLENTY OF MOVES TO GO AROUND!
Hmmm... SOMETHING'S NOT RIGHT HERE!
YOU SAID IT!!
IT ALL SEEMS RIGHT TO ME!
4

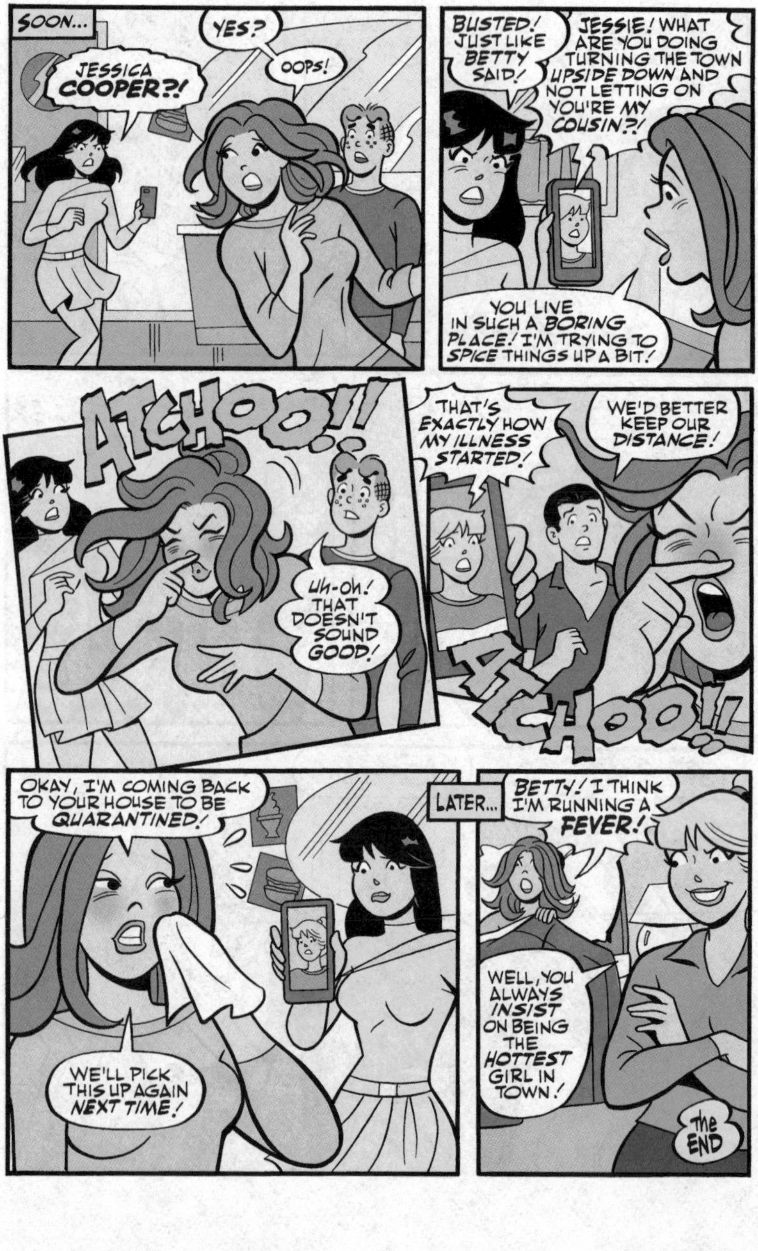
SOON...
JESSICA COOPER?!
YES?
OOPS!
BUSTED! JUST LIKE BETTY SAID!
JESSIE! WHAT ARE YOU DOING TURNING THE TOWN UPSIDE DOWN AND NOT LETTING ON YOU'RE MY COUSIN?!
YOU LIVE IN SUCH A BORING PLACE! I'M TRYING TO SPICE THINGS UP A BIT!
ATCHOO!!
UH-OH! THAT DOESN'T SOUND GOOD!
THAT'S EXACTLY HOW MY ILLNESS STARTED!
WE'D BETTER KEEP OUR DISTANCE!
ATCHOO!!
OKAY, I'M COMING BACK TO YOUR HOUSE TO BE QUARANTINED!
WE'LL PICK THIS UP AGAIN NEXT TIME!
LATER...
BETTY! I THINK I'M RUNNING A FEVER!
WELL, YOU ALWAYS INSIST ON BEING THE HOTTEST GIRL IN TOWN!
THE END

05 WORLD OF ARCHIE

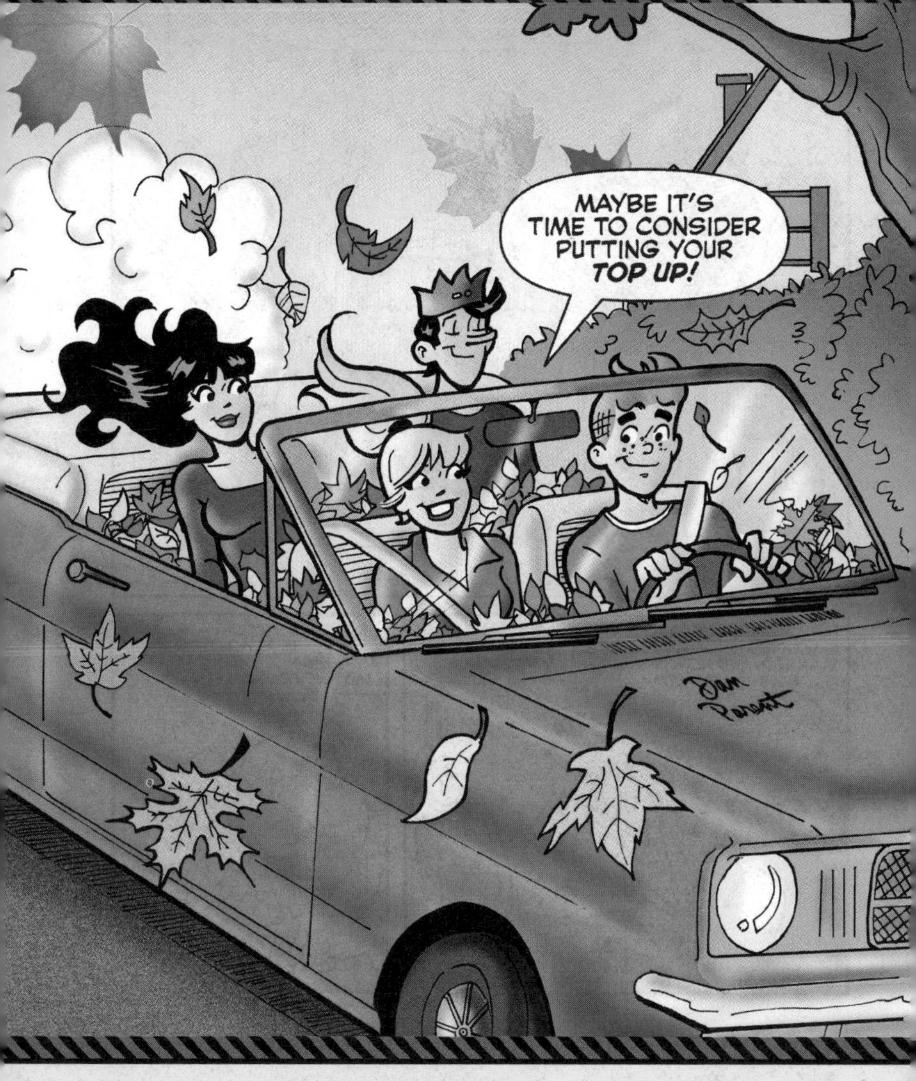
MAYBE IT'S TIME TO CONSIDER PUTTING YOUR *TOP UP!*
Dan Parent

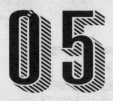

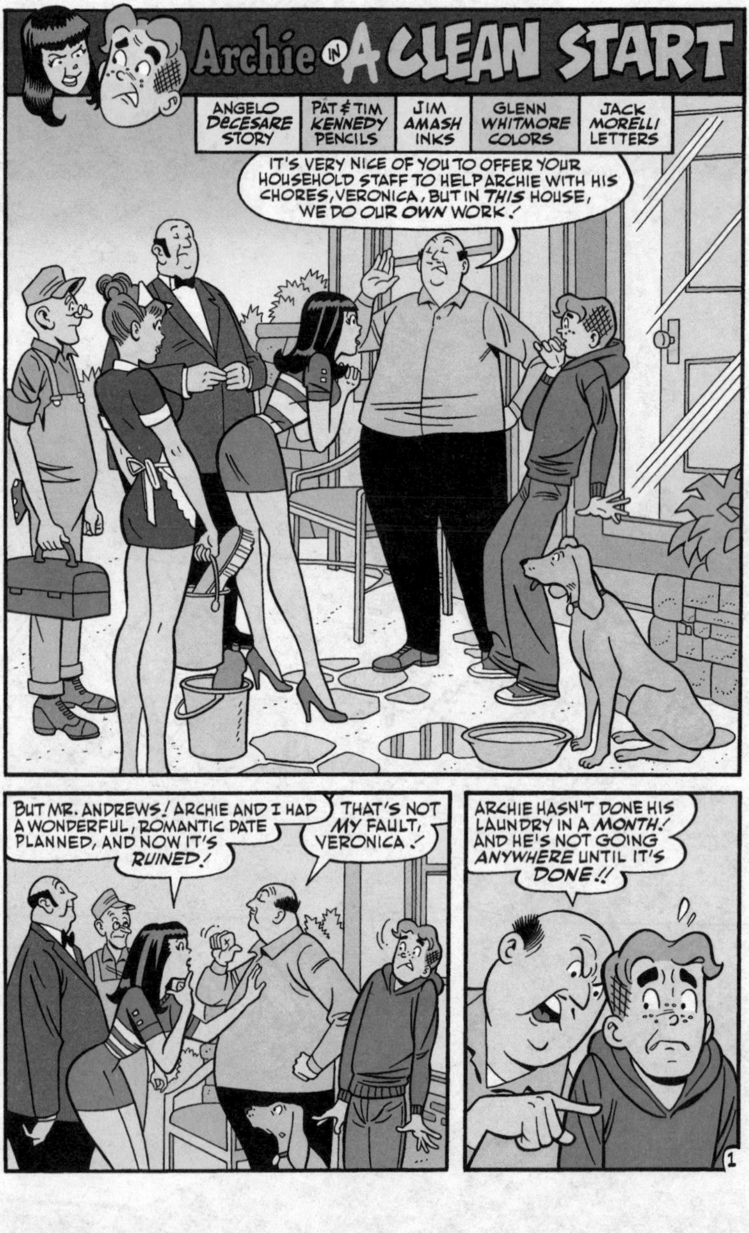
Archie IN A CLEAN START
ANGELO DeCESARE STORY
PAT & TIM KENNEDY PENCILS
JIM AMASH INKS
GLENN WHITMORE COLORS
JACK MORELLI LETTERS
IT'S VERY NICE OF YOU TO OFFER YOUR HOUSEHOLD STAFF TO HELP ARCHIE WITH HIS CHORES, VERONICA, BUT IN THIS HOUSE, WE DO OUR OWN WORK!
BUT MR. ANDREWS! ARCHIE AND I HAD A WONDERFUL, ROMANTIC DATE PLANNED, AND NOW IT'S RUINED!
THAT'S NOT MY FAULT, VERONICA!
ARCHIE HASN'T DONE HIS LAUNDRY IN A MONTH! AND HE'S NOT GOING ANYWHERE UNTIL IT'S DONE!!
1

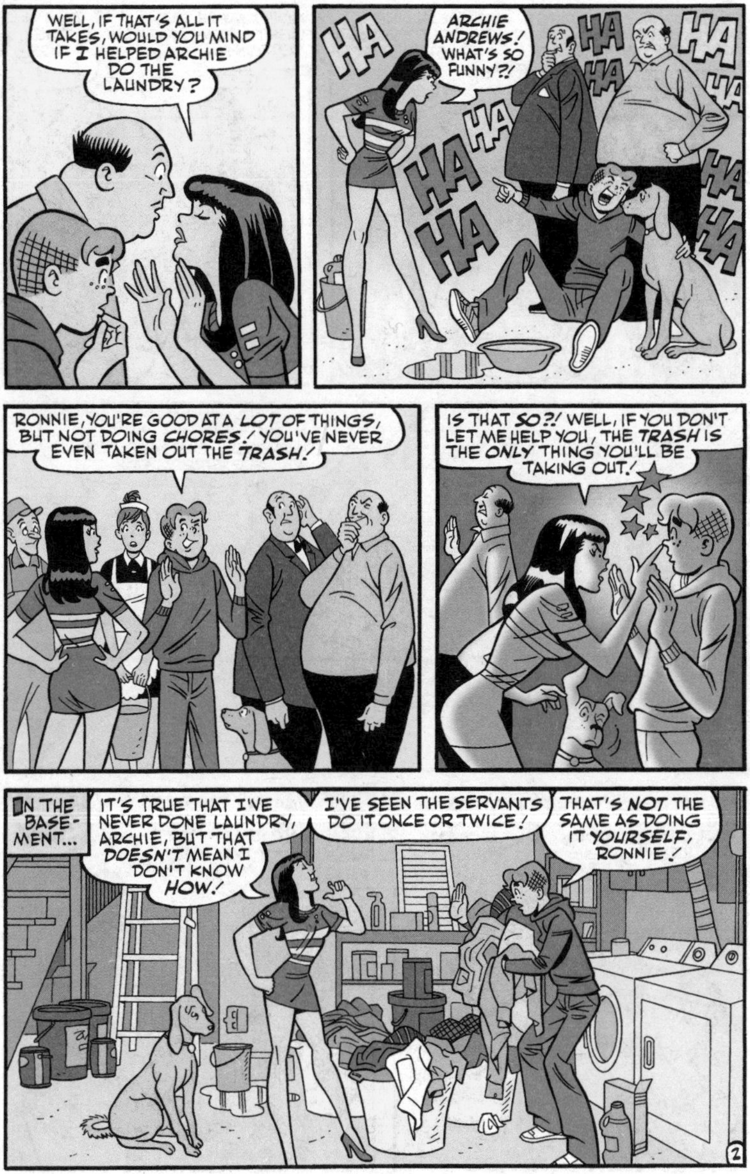
WELL, IF THAT'S ALL IT TAKES, WOULD YOU MIND IF I HELPED ARCHIE DO THE LAUNDRY?
ARCHIE ANDREWS! WHAT'S SO FUNNY?!
HA HA HA HA HA HA HA HA HA HA
RONNIE, YOU'RE GOOD AT A LOT OF THINGS, BUT NOT DOING CHORES! YOU'VE NEVER EVEN TAKEN OUT THE TRASH!
IS THAT SO?! WELL, IF YOU DON'T LET ME HELP YOU, THE TRASH IS THE ONLY THING YOU'LL BE TAKING OUT!
IN THE BASEMENT...
IT'S TRUE THAT I'VE NEVER DONE LAUNDRY, ARCHIE, BUT THAT DOESN'T MEAN I DON'T KNOW HOW!
I'VE SEEN THE SERVANTS DO IT ONCE OR TWICE!
THAT'S NOT THE SAME AS DOING IT YOURSELF, RONNIE!
2

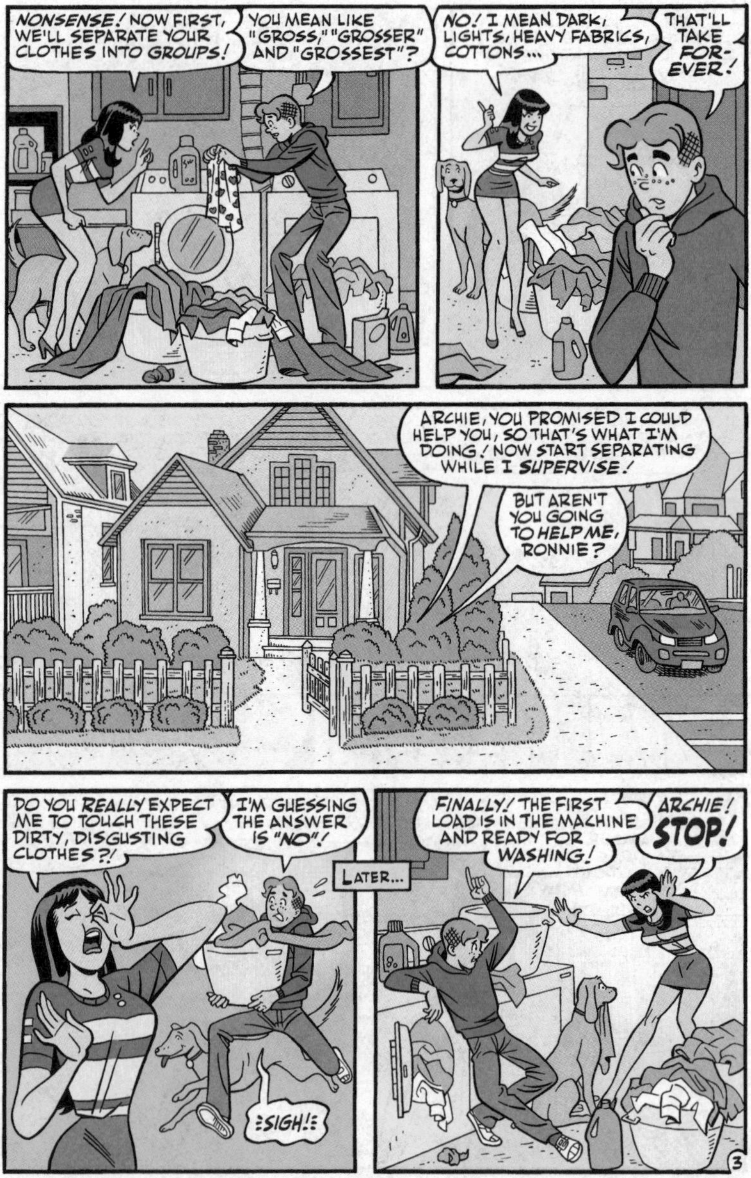
NONSENSE! NOW FIRST, WE'LL SEPARATE YOUR CLOTHES INTO GROUPS!
YOU MEAN LIKE "GROSS," "GROSSER" AND "GROSSEST"?
NO! I MEAN DARK, LIGHTS, HEAVY FABRICS, COTTONS...
THAT'LL TAKE FOR-EVER!
ARCHIE, YOU PROMISED I COULD HELP YOU, SO THAT'S WHAT I'M DOING! NOW START SEPARATING WHILE I SUPERVISE!
BUT AREN'T YOU GOING TO HELP ME, RONNIE?
DO YOU REALLY EXPECT ME TO TOUCH THESE DIRTY, DISGUSTING CLOTHES?!
I'M GUESSING THE ANSWER IS "NO"!
SIGH!
LATER...
FINALLY! THE FIRST LOAD IS IN THE MACHINE AND READY FOR WASHING!
ARCHIE! STOP!
3

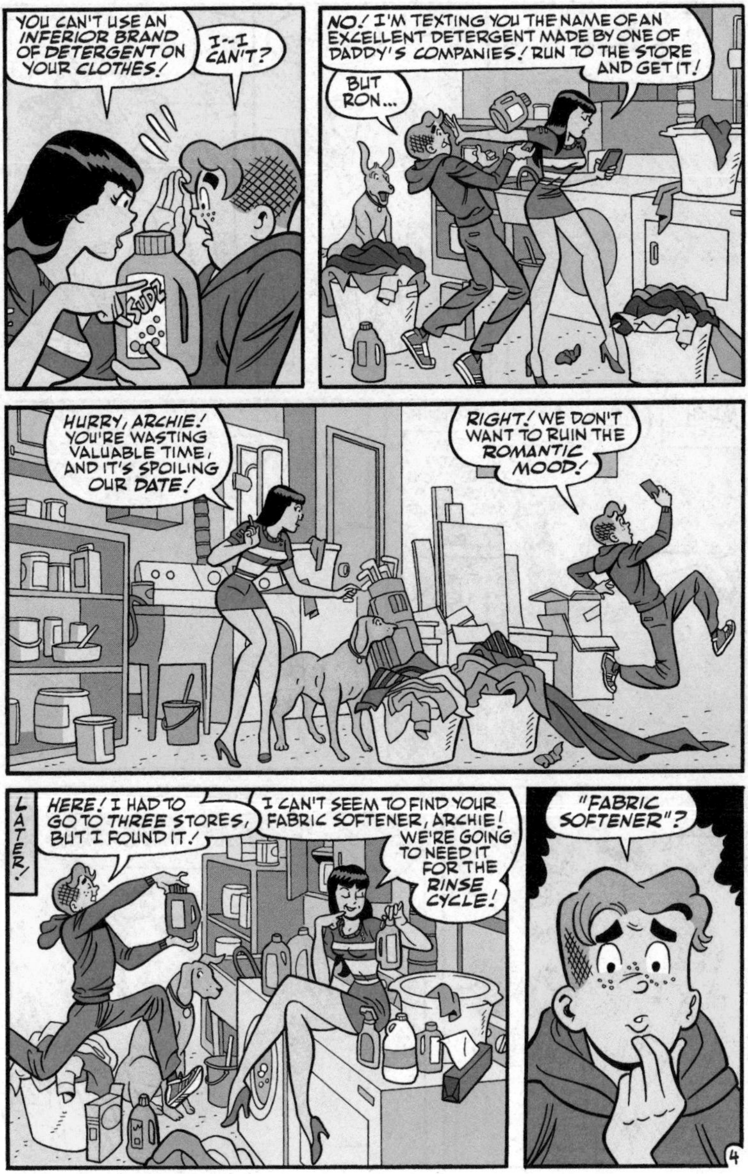
YOU CAN'T USE AN INFERIOR BRAND OF DETERGENT ON YOUR CLOTHES!
I--I CAN'T?
SUDZ
NO! I'M TEXTING YOU THE NAME OF AN EXCELLENT DETERGENT MADE BY ONE OF DADDY'S COMPANIES! RUN TO THE STORE AND GET IT!
BUT RON...
HURRY, ARCHIE! YOU'RE WASTING VALUABLE TIME, AND IT'S SPOILING OUR DATE!
RIGHT! WE DON'T WANT TO RUIN THE ROMANTIC MOOD!
LATER!
HERE! I HAD TO GO TO THREE STORES, BUT I FOUND IT!
I CAN'T SEEM TO FIND YOUR FABRIC SOFTENER, ARCHIE! WE'RE GOING TO NEED IT FOR THE RINSE CYCLE!
"FABRIC SOFTENER"?
4

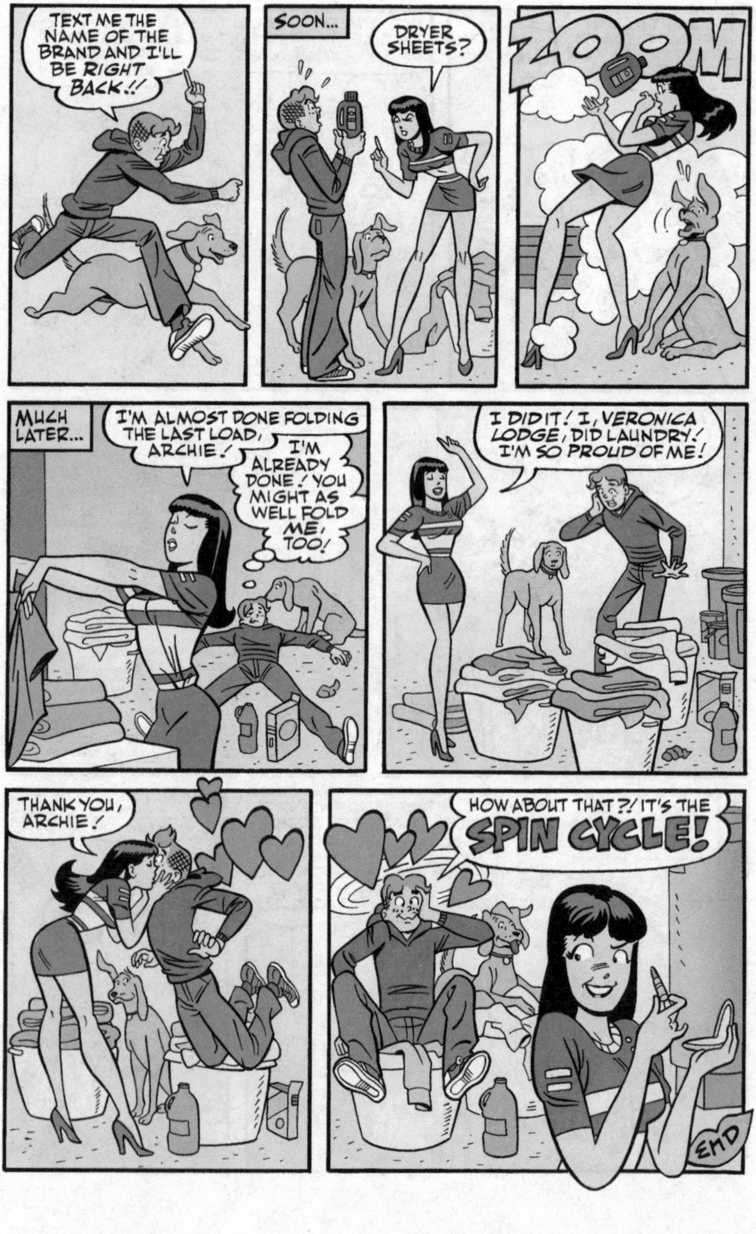
TEXT ME THE NAME OF THE BRAND AND I'LL BE RIGHT BACK.!!
SOON...
DRYER SHEETS?
ZOOM
MUCH LATER...
I'M ALMOST DONE FOLDING THE LAST LOAD, ARCHIE!
I'M ALREADY DONE! YOU MIGHT AS WELL FOLD ME, TOO!
I DID IT! I, VERONICA LODGE, DID LAUNDRY! I'M SO PROUD OF ME!
THANK YOU, ARCHIE!
HOW ABOUT THAT?! IT'S THE SPIN CYCLE!
END

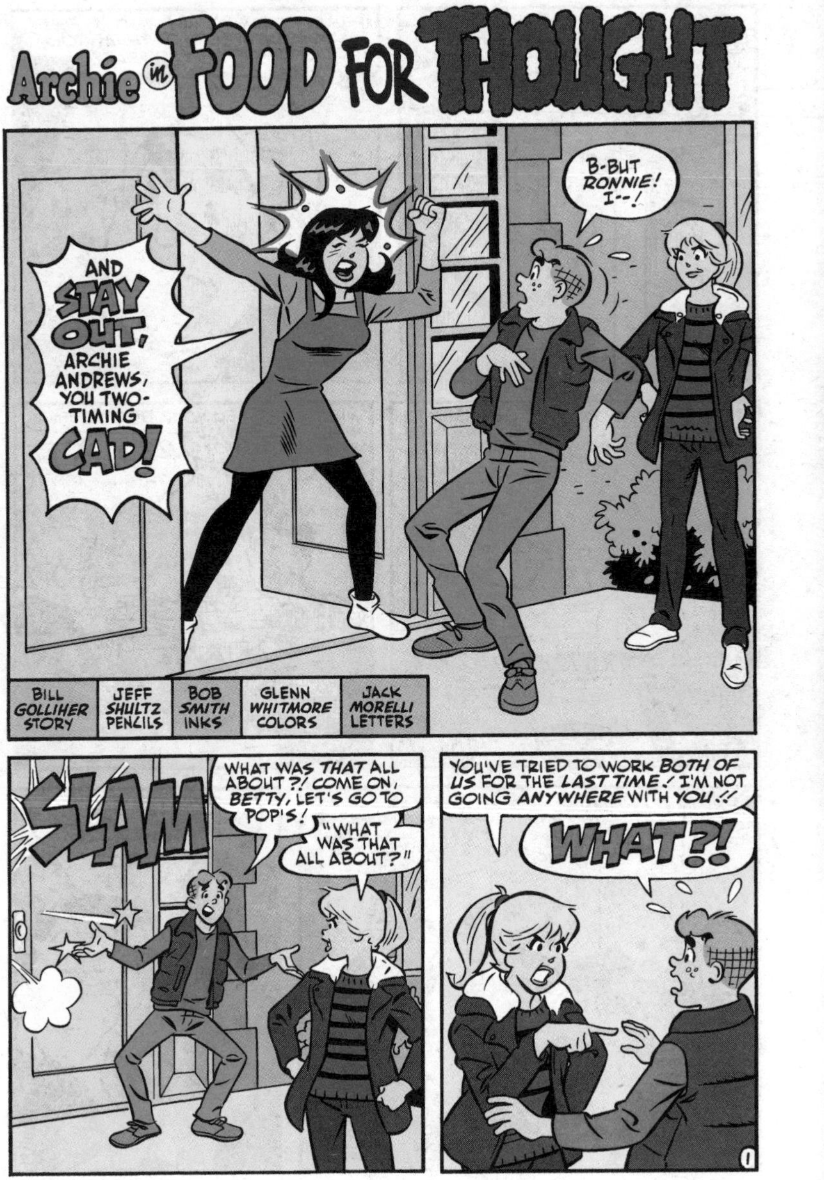
Archie in FOOD FOR THOUGHT
AND STAY OUT, ARCHIE ANDREWS, YOU TWO-TIMING CAD!
B-BUT RONNIE! I--!
BILL GOLLIHER STORY
JEFF SHULTZ PENCILS
BOB SMITH INKS
GLENN WHITMORE COLORS
JACK MORELLI LETTERS
SLAM
WHAT WAS THAT ALL ABOUT?! COME ON, BETTY, LET'S GO TO POP'S!
"WHAT WAS THAT ALL ABOUT?"
YOU'VE TRIED TO WORK BOTH OF US FOR THE LAST TIME! I'M NOT GOING ANYWHERE WITH YOU!!
WHAT?!
1

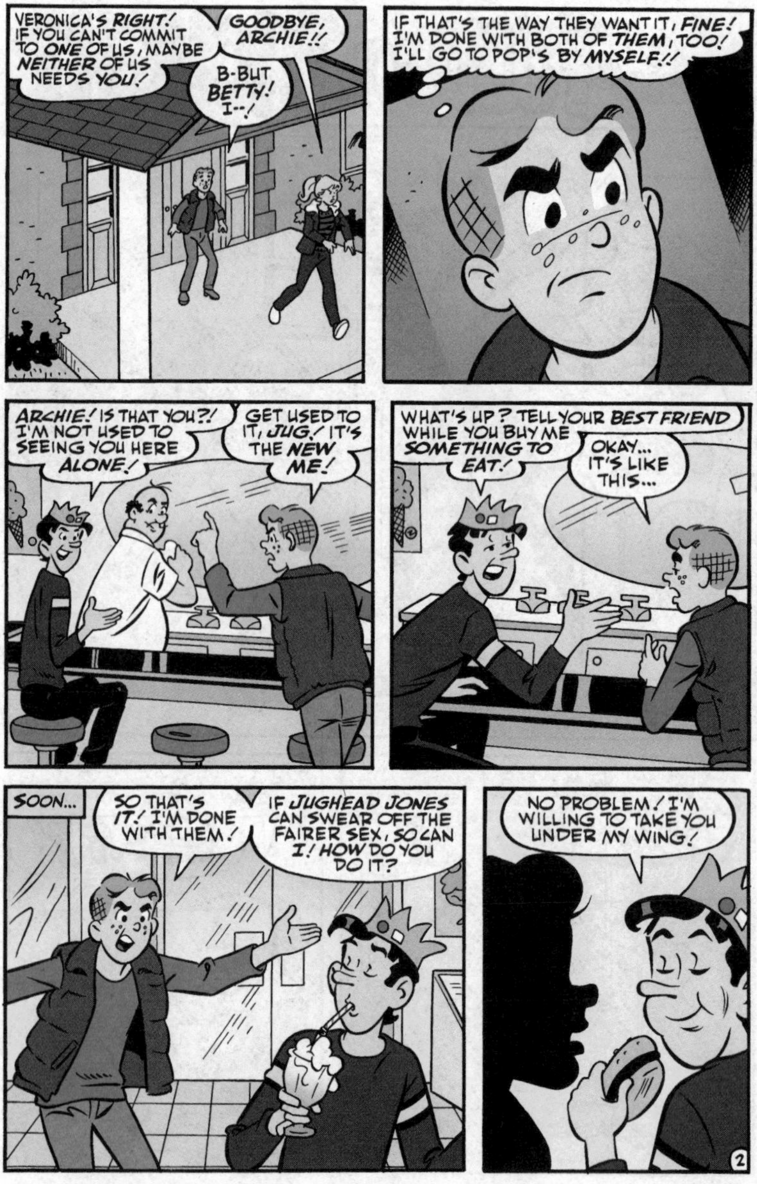
VERONICA'S RIGHT! IF YOU CAN'T COMMIT TO ONE OF US, MAYBE NEITHER OF US NEEDS YOU!
GOODBYE, ARCHIE!!
B-BUT BETTY! I--!
IF THAT'S THE WAY THEY WANT IT, FINE! I'M DONE WITH BOTH OF THEM, TOO! I'LL GO TO POP'S BY MYSELF!!
ARCHIE! IS THAT YOU?! I'M NOT USED TO SEEING YOU HERE ALONE!
GET USED TO IT, JUG! IT'S THE NEW ME!
WHAT'S UP? TELL YOUR BEST FRIEND WHILE YOU BUY ME SOMETHING TO EAT!
OKAY... IT'S LIKE THIS...
SOON...
SO THAT'S IT! I'M DONE WITH THEM!
IF JUGHEAD JONES CAN SWEAR OFF THE FAIRER SEX, SO CAN I! HOW DO YOU DO IT?
NO PROBLEM! I'M WILLING TO TAKE YOU UNDER MY WING!
2

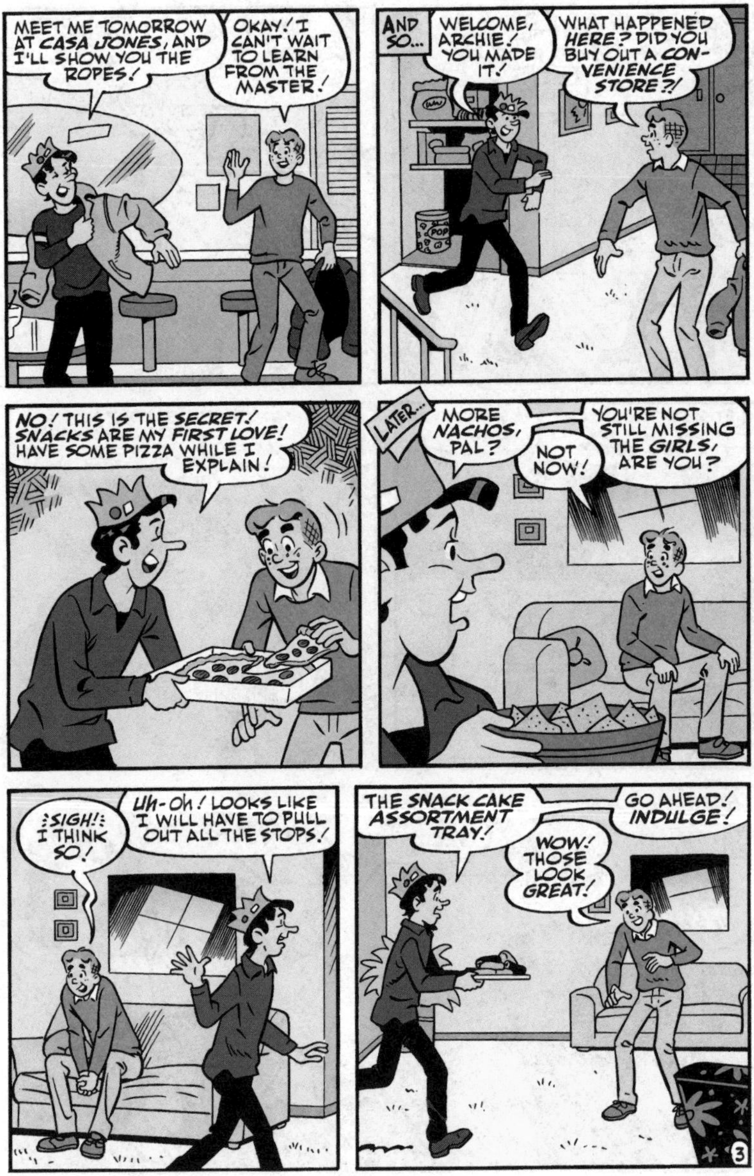
MEET ME TOMORROW AT CASA JONES, AND I'LL SHOW YOU THE ROPES!
OKAY! I CAN'T WAIT TO LEARN FROM THE MASTER!
AND SO...
WELCOME, ARCHIE! YOU MADE IT!
WHAT HAPPENED HERE? DID YOU BUY OUT A CONVENIENCE STORE?!
NO! THIS IS THE SECRET! SNACKS ARE MY FIRST LOVE! HAVE SOME PIZZA WHILE I EXPLAIN!
LATER...
MORE NACHOS, PAL?
NOT NOW!
YOU'RE NOT STILL MISSING THE GIRLS, ARE YOU?
SIGH! I THINK SO!
UH-OH! LOOKS LIKE I WILL HAVE TO PULL OUT ALL THE STOPS!
THE SNACK CAKE ASSORTMENT TRAY!
WOW! THOSE LOOK GREAT!
GO AHEAD! INDULGE!
3

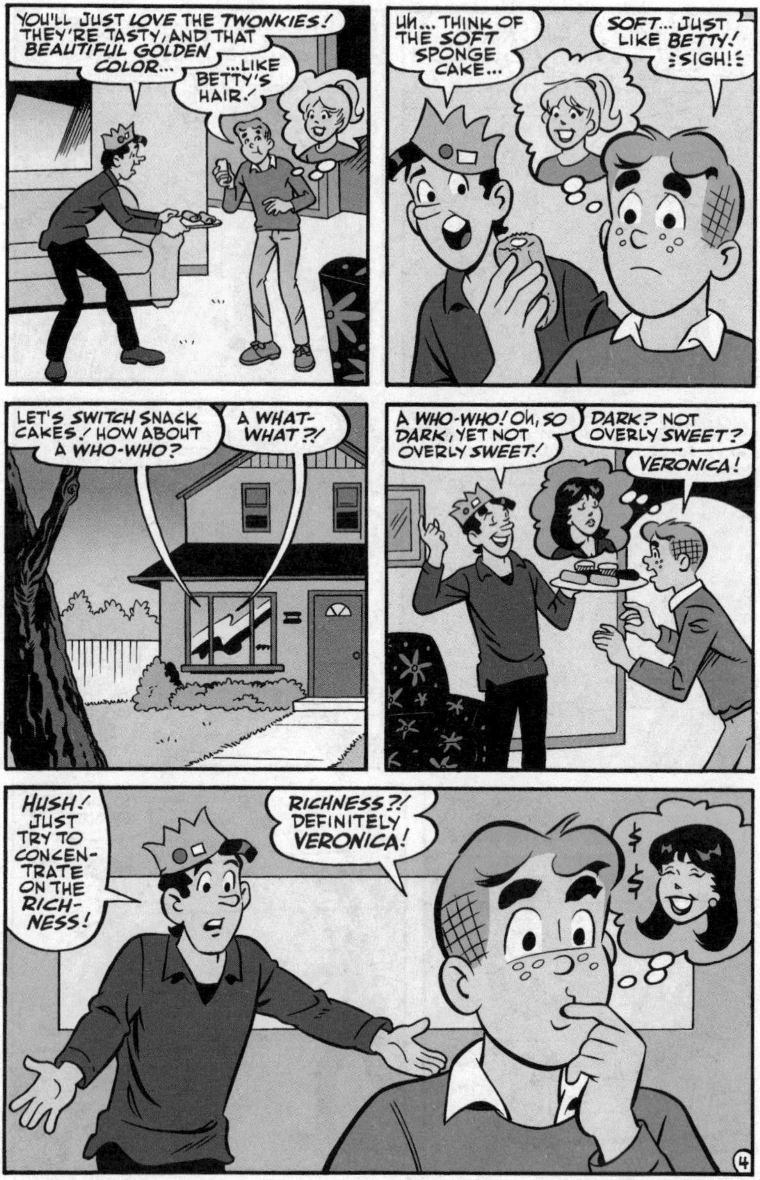
YOU'LL JUST LOVE THE TWONKIES! THEY'RE TASTY, AND THAT BEAUTIFUL GOLDEN COLOR...
...LIKE BETTY'S HAIR!
UH... THINK OF THE SOFT SPONGE CAKE...
SOFT... JUST LIKE BETTY! SIGH!
LET'S SWITCH SNACK CAKES! HOW ABOUT A WHO-WHO?
A WHAT-WHAT?!
A WHO-WHO! OH, SO DARK, YET NOT OVERLY SWEET!
DARK? NOT OVERLY SWEET?
VERONICA!
HUSH! JUST TRY TO CONCEN-TRATE ON THE RICH-NESS!
RICHNESS?! DEFINITELY VERONICA!
$
$
4

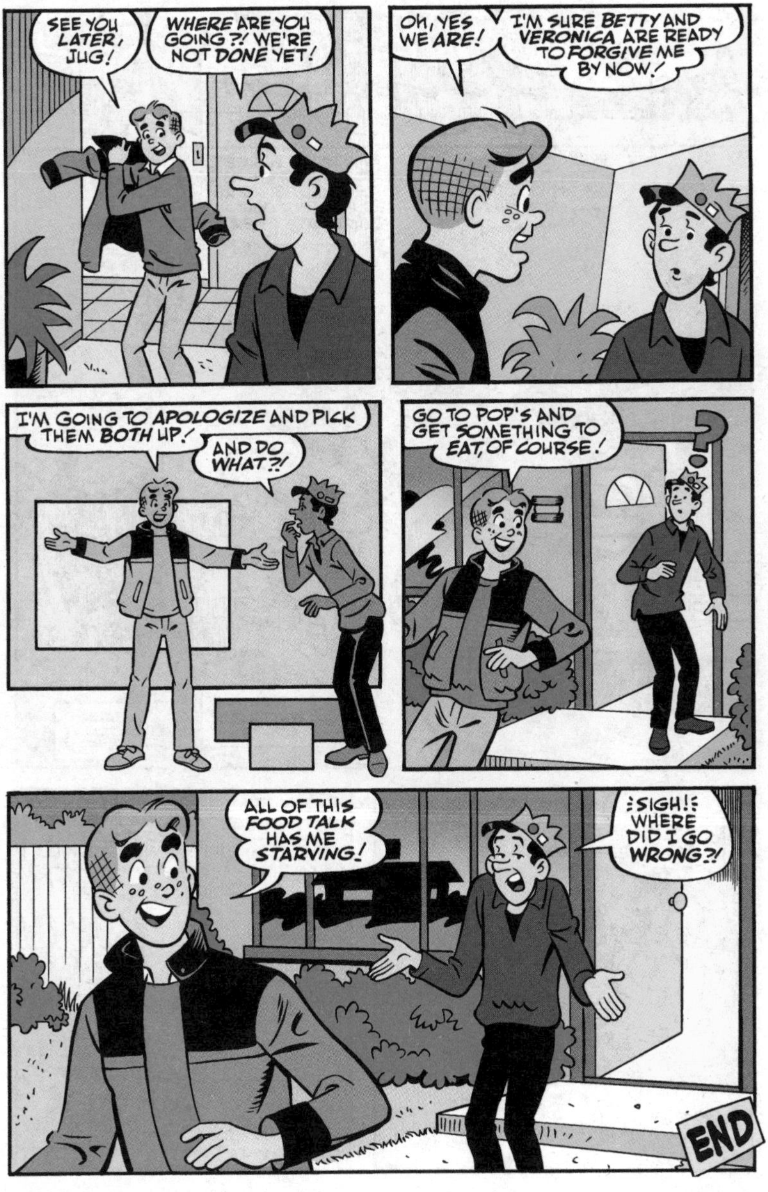
SEE YOU LATER, JUG!
WHERE ARE YOU GOING?! WE'RE NOT DONE YET!
OH, YES WE ARE!
I'M SURE BETTY AND VERONICA ARE READY TO FORGIVE ME BY NOW!
I'M GOING TO APOLOGIZE AND PICK THEM BOTH UP!
AND DO WHAT?!
GO TO POP'S AND GET SOMETHING TO EAT, OF COURSE!
ALL OF THIS FOOD TALK HAS ME STARVING!
SIGH! WHERE DID I GO WRONG?!
END

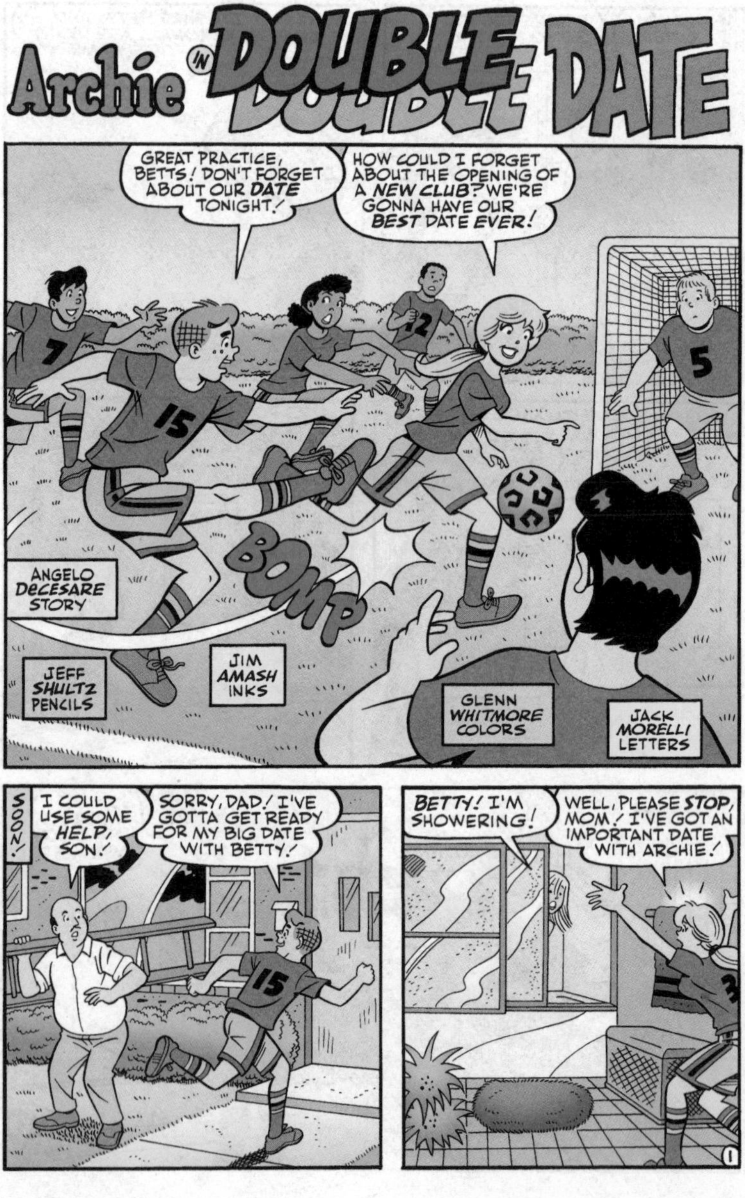
Archie in DOUBLE DOUBLE DATE
GREAT PRACTICE, BETTS! DON'T FORGET ABOUT OUR DATE TONIGHT!
HOW COULD I FORGET ABOUT THE OPENING OF A NEW CLUB? WE'RE GONNA HAVE OUR BEST DATE EVER!
BOMP
ANGELO DeCESARE STORY
JEFF SHULTZ PENCILS
JIM AMASH INKS
GLENN WHITMORE COLORS
JACK MORELLI LETTERS
SOON!
I COULD USE SOME HELP, SON!
SORRY, DAD! I'VE GOTTA GET READY FOR MY BIG DATE WITH BETTY!
BETTY! I'M SHOWERING!
WELL, PLEASE STOP, MOM! I'VE GOT AN IMPORTANT DATE WITH ARCHIE!
1

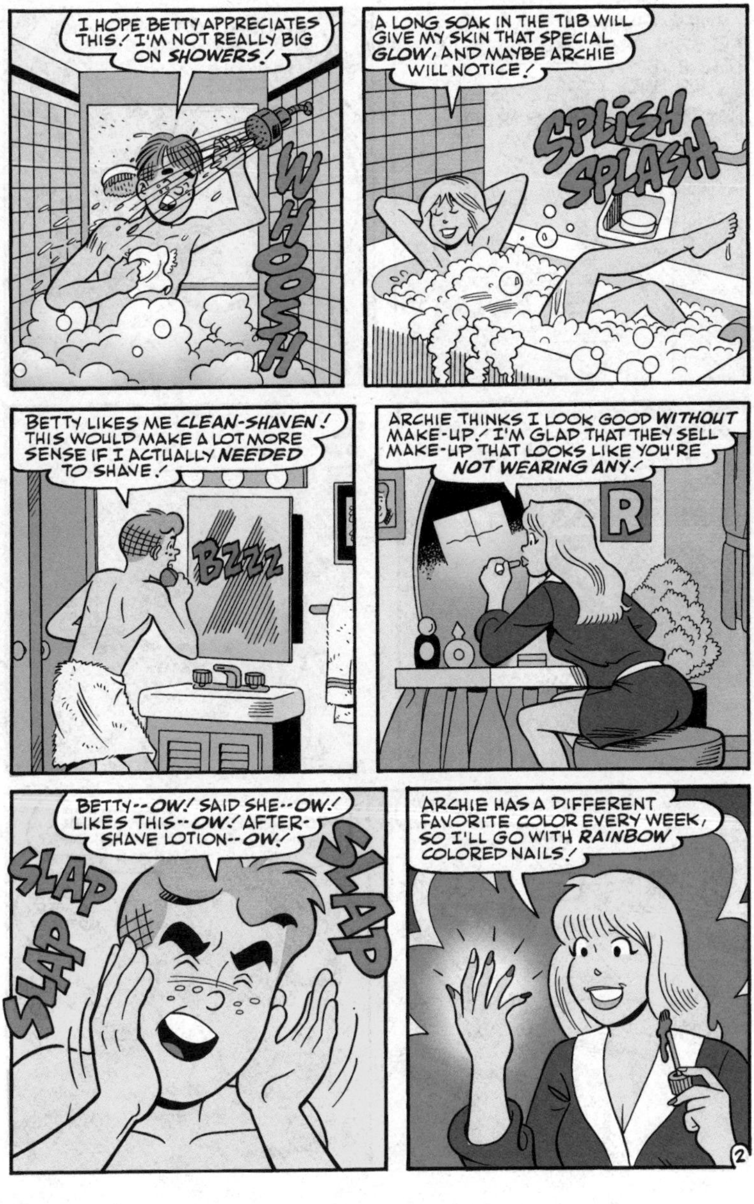
I HOPE BETTY APPRECIATES THIS! I'M NOT REALLY BIG ON SHOWERS!
WHOOSH
A LONG SOAK IN THE TUB WILL GIVE MY SKIN THAT SPECIAL GLOW, AND MAYBE ARCHIE WILL NOTICE!
SPLISH SPLASH
BETTY LIKES ME CLEAN-SHAVEN! THIS WOULD MAKE A LOT MORE SENSE IF I ACTUALLY NEEDED TO SHAVE!
BZZZ
ARCHIE THINKS I LOOK GOOD WITHOUT MAKE-UP! I'M GLAD THAT THEY SELL MAKE-UP THAT LOOKS LIKE YOU'RE NOT WEARING ANY!
R
BETTY--OW! SAID SHE--OW! LIKES THIS--OW! AFTER-SHAVE LOTION--OW!
SLAP
SLAP
SLAP
ARCHIE HAS A DIFFERENT FAVORITE COLOR EVERY WEEK, SO I'LL GO WITH RAINBOW COLORED NAILS!
2

MPHFM...FMPM...
BLMPHM...FLMB...
GLBLB...BETTY...
RGLBMP...

GLUGGLE...GLURGLE...
GLARGLE...GLUGGLE...
GLURGLE...ARCHIE...
GLUGGLE!

BETTY WILL BE HAPPY IF I WEAR THE SHIRT SHE GAVE ME FOR MY BIRTH-DAY! Hmm... MAYBE THE CLUB WILL BE DARK!

I'D LIKE TO WEAR AN OUTFIT THAT ARCHIE HASN'T ALREADY SEEN, BUT THAT'S NOT GOING TO BE EASY!

THESE SHOES WILL MAKE ME A LITTLE TALLER THAN BETTY! SHE'LL NEVER NOTICE!

ARCHIE WILL PROBABLY WEAR SHOES THAT MAKE HIM TALLER THAN ME, SO I'LL WEAR SHOES THAT WILL MAKE ME TALLER!

HE'LL NEVER NOTICE!

3

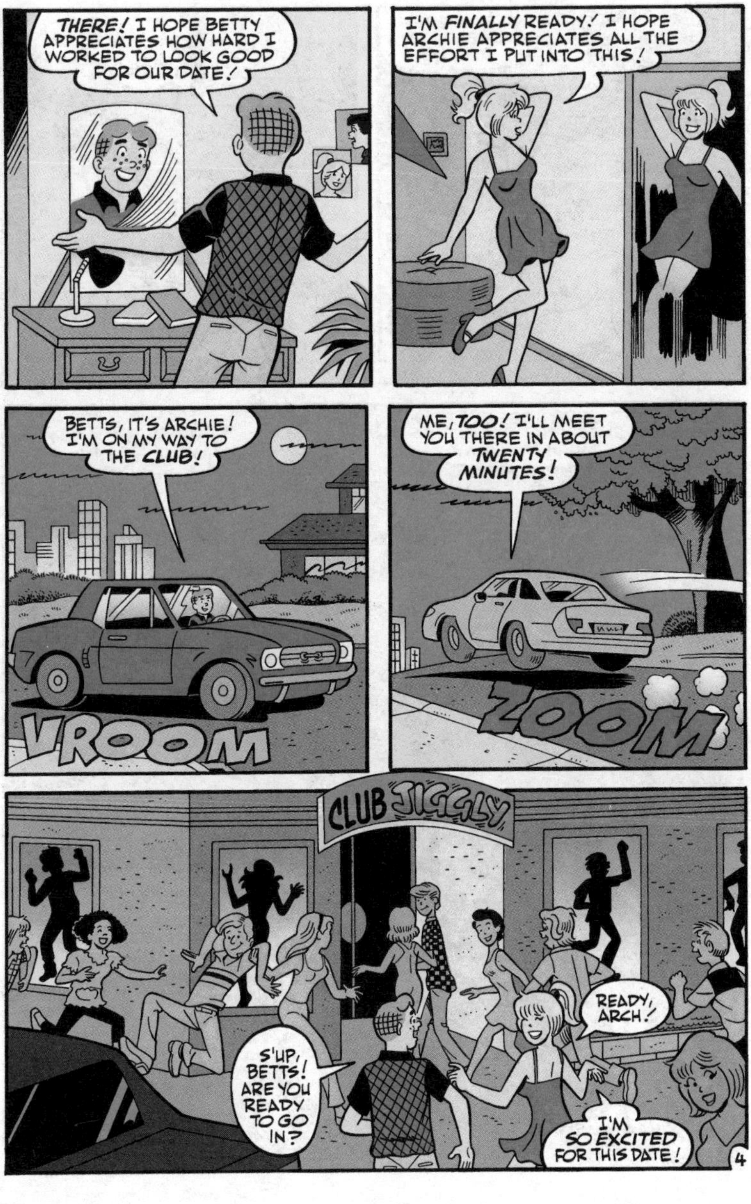
THERE! I HOPE BETTY APPRECIATES HOW HARD I WORKED TO LOOK GOOD FOR OUR DATE!
I'M FINALLY READY! I HOPE ARCHIE APPRECIATES ALL THE EFFORT I PUT INTO THIS!
BETTS, IT'S ARCHIE! I'M ON MY WAY TO THE CLUB!
VROOM
ME, TOO! I'LL MEET YOU THERE IN ABOUT TWENTY MINUTES!
ZOOM
CLUB JIGGLY
S'UP, BETTS! ARE YOU READY TO GO IN?
READY, ARCH!
I'M SO EXCITED FOR THIS DATE!
4

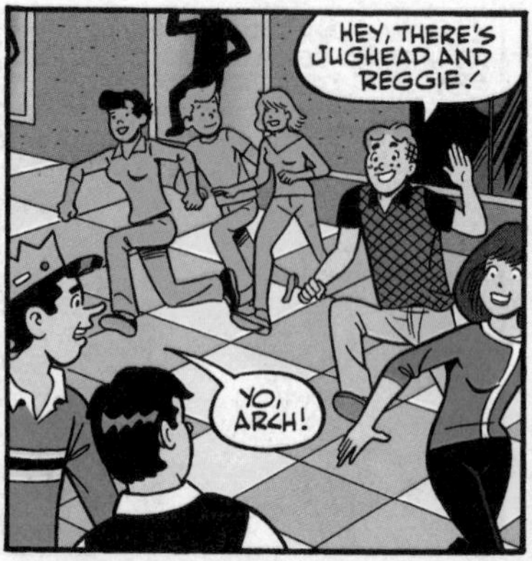
HEY, THERE'S JUGHEAD AND REGGIE!
YO, ARCH!

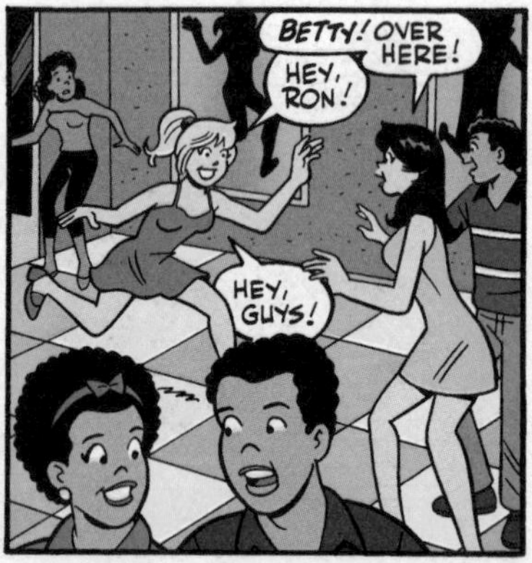
BETTY! OVER HERE!
HEY, RON!
HEY, GUYS!

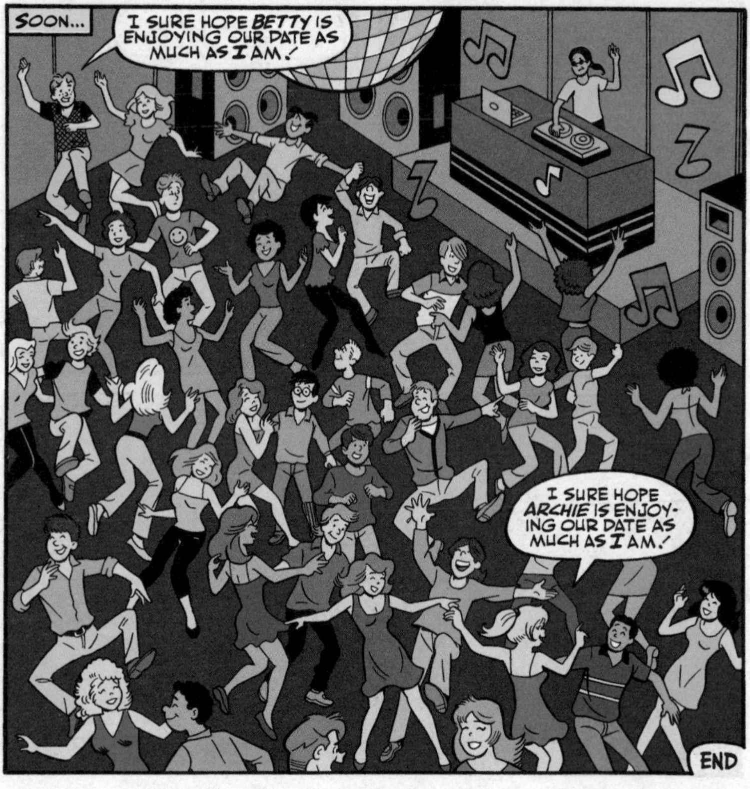
SOON...
I SURE HOPE BETTY IS ENJOYING OUR DATE AS MUCH AS I AM!
I SURE HOPE ARCHIE IS ENJOY-ING OUR DATE AS MUCH AS I AM!
END

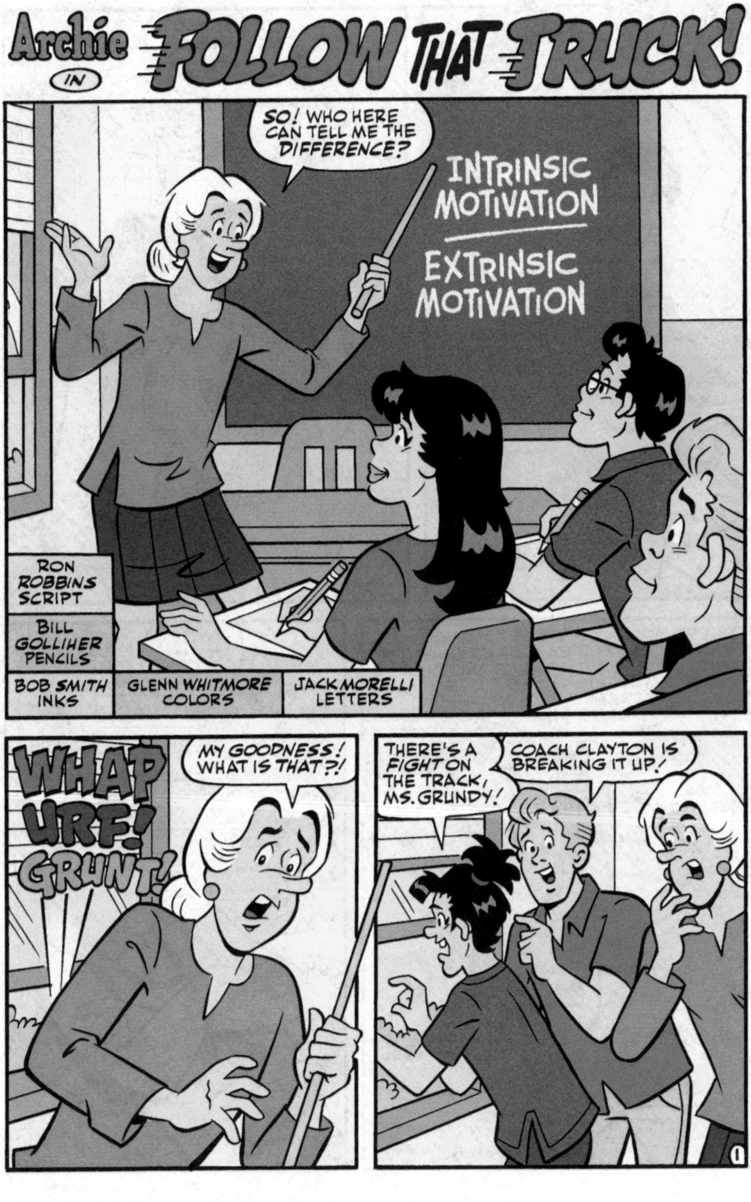
Archie
IN
FOLLOW THAT TRUCK!
SO! WHO HERE CAN TELL ME THE DIFFERENCE?
INTRINSIC MOTIVATION
EXTRINSIC MOTIVATION
RON ROBBINS SCRIPT
BILL GOLLIHER PENCILS
BOB SMITH INKS
GLENN WHITMORE COLORS
JACK MORELLI LETTERS
WHAP URF! GRUNT!
MY GOODNESS! WHAT IS THAT?!
THERE'S A FIGHT ON THE TRACK, MS. GRUNDY!
COACH CLAYTON IS BREAKING IT UP!
1

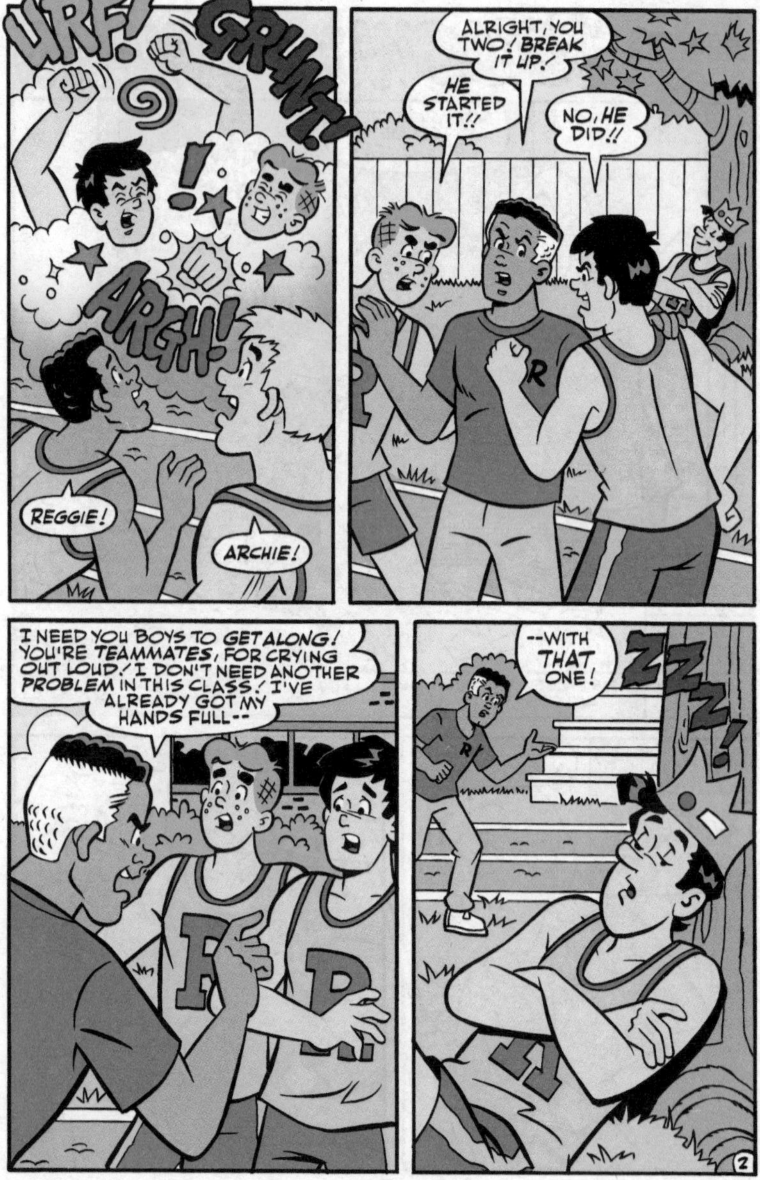
URF!
GRUNT!
ARGH!
REGGIE!
ARCHIE!
ALRIGHT, YOU TWO! BREAK IT UP!
HE STARTED IT!!
NO, HE DID!!
I NEED YOU BOYS TO GET ALONG! YOU'RE TEAMMATES, FOR CRYING OUT LOUD! I DON'T NEED ANOTHER PROBLEM IN THIS CLASS! I'VE ALREADY GOT MY HANDS FULL--
--WITH THAT ONE!
ZZZ!
2

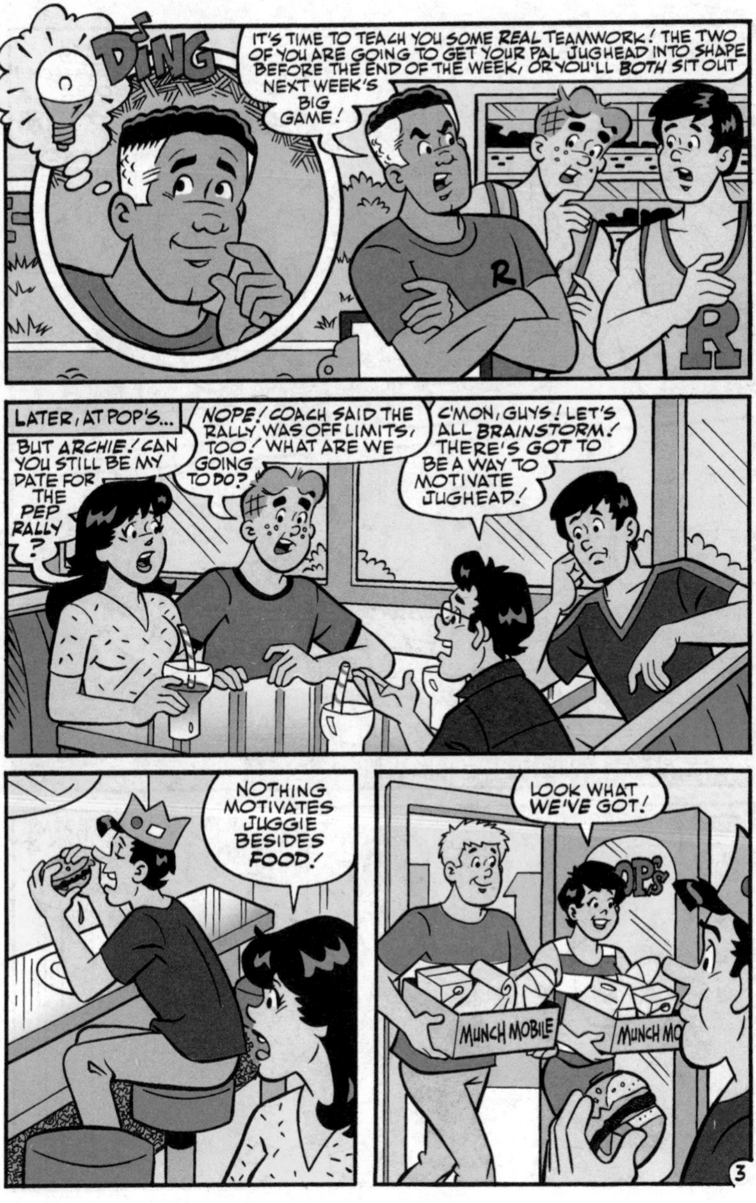
DING
IT'S TIME TO TEACH YOU SOME REAL TEAMWORK! THE TWO OF YOU ARE GOING TO GET YOUR PAL JUGHEAD INTO SHAPE BEFORE THE END OF THE WEEK, OR YOU'LL BOTH SIT OUT NEXT WEEK'S BIG GAME!
LATER, AT POP'S...
BUT ARCHIE! CAN YOU STILL BE MY DATE FOR THE PEP RALLY?
NOPE! COACH SAID THE RALLY WAS OFF LIMITS, TOO! WHAT ARE WE GOING TO DO?
C'MON, GUYS! LET'S ALL BRAINSTORM! THERE'S GOT TO BE A WAY TO MOTIVATE JUGHEAD!
NOTHING MOTIVATES JUGGIE BESIDES FOOD!
LOOK WHAT WE'VE GOT!
POP'S
MUNCH MOBILE
MUNCH MO
3

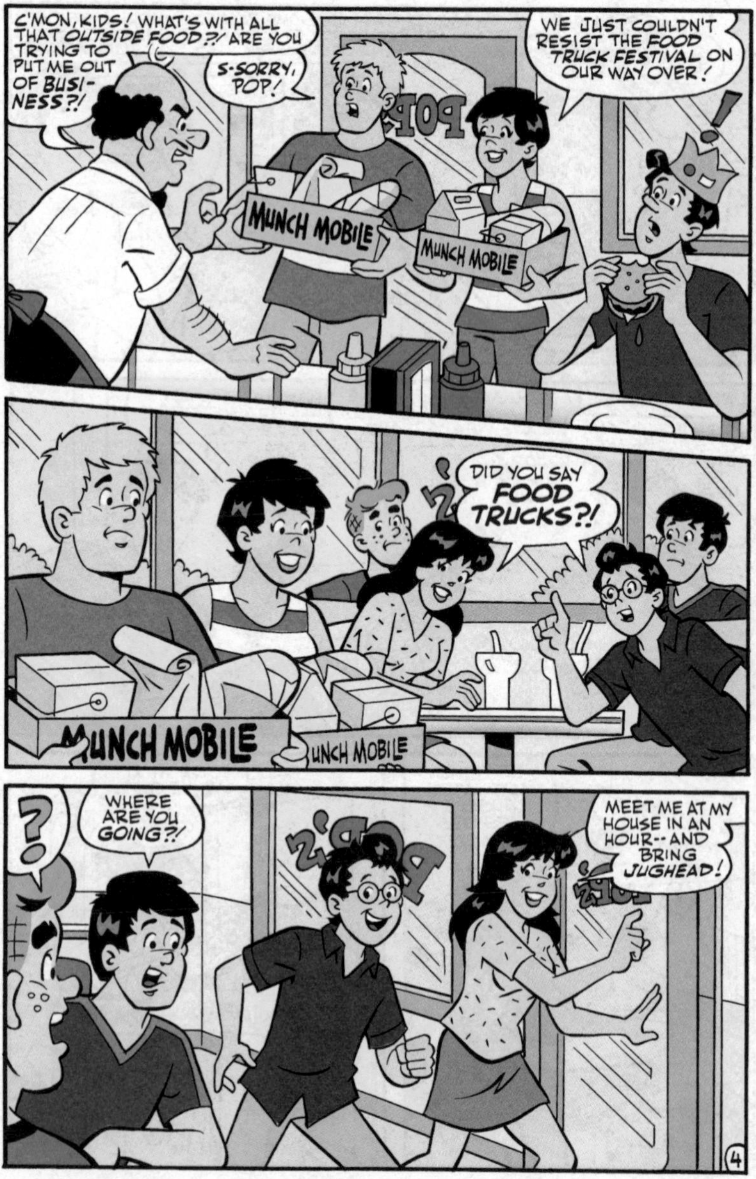
C'MON, KIDS! WHAT'S WITH ALL THAT OUTSIDE FOOD?! ARE YOU TRYING TO PUT ME OUT OF BUSI-NESS?!
S-SORRY, POP!
WE JUST COULDN'T RESIST THE FOOD TRUCK FESTIVAL ON OUR WAY OVER!
!
MUNCH MOBILE
MUNCH MOBILE
POP'S
DID YOU SAY FOOD TRUCKS?!
MUNCH MOBILE
UNCH MOBILE
?
WHERE ARE YOU GOING?!
MEET ME AT MY HOUSE IN AN HOUR-- AND BRING JUGHEAD!
POP'S
4

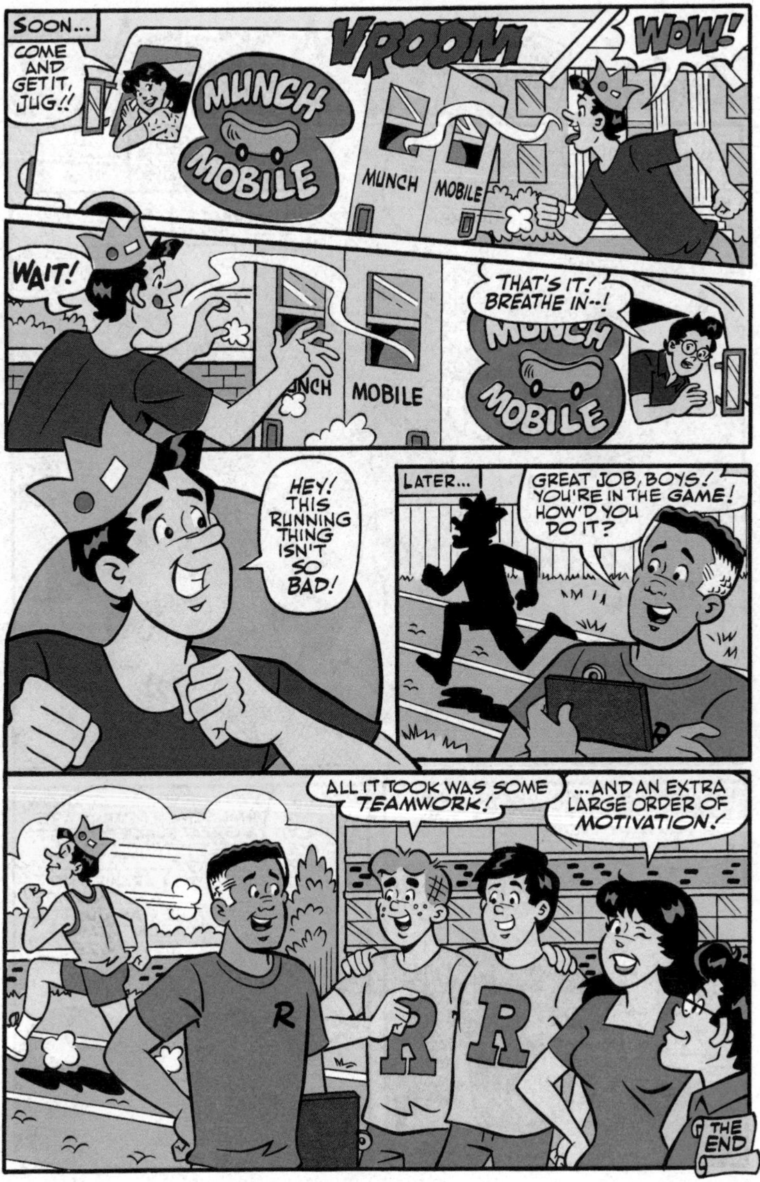
SOON...
COME AND GET IT, JUG!!
VROOM
MUNCH MOBILE
MUNCH MOBILE
WOW!
WAIT!
THAT'S IT! BREATHE IN--!
MUNCH MOBILE
MOBILE
HEY! THIS RUNNING THING ISN'T SO BAD!
LATER...
GREAT JOB, BOYS! YOU'RE IN THE GAME! HOW'D YOU DO IT?
ALL IT TOOK WAS SOME TEAMWORK!
...AND AN EXTRA LARGE ORDER OF MOTIVATION!
THE END

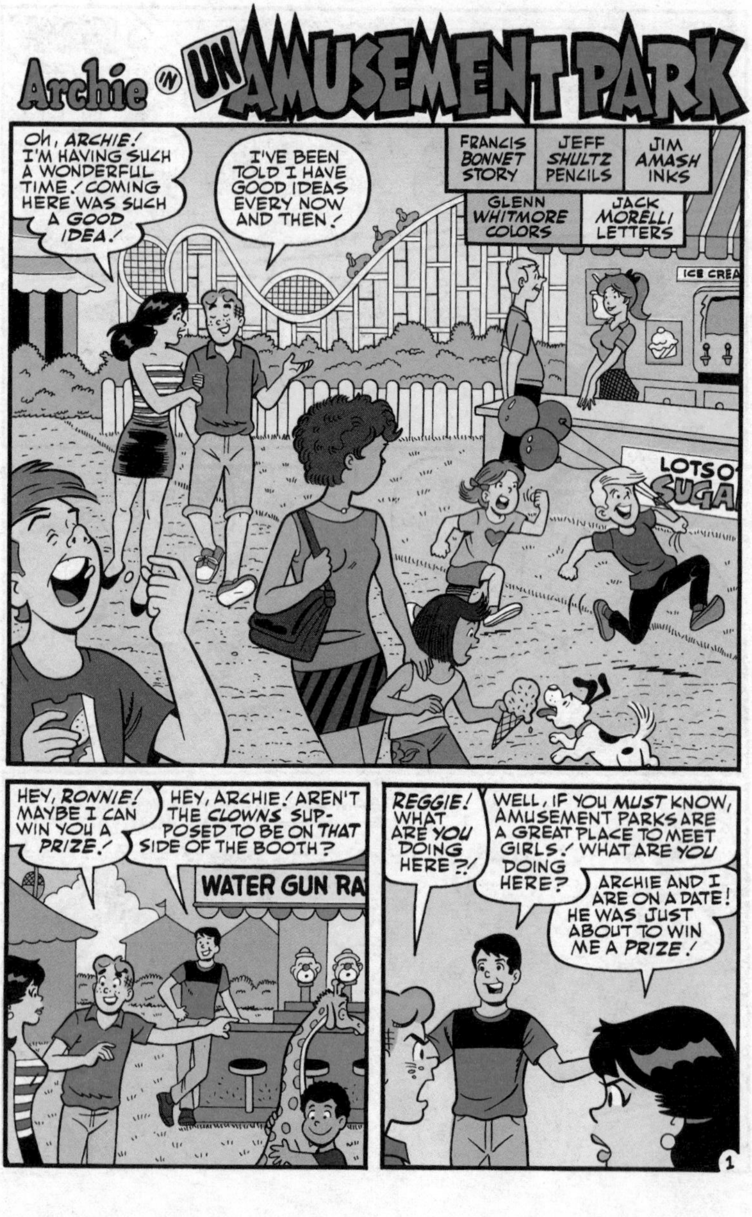
Archie in UN AMUSEMENT PARK
Oh, ARCHIE! I'M HAVING SUCH A WONDERFUL TIME! COMING HERE WAS SUCH A GOOD IDEA!
I'VE BEEN TOLD I HAVE GOOD IDEAS EVERY NOW AND THEN!
FRANCIS BONNET STORY
JEFF SHULTZ PENCILS
JIM AMASH INKS
GLENN WHITMORE COLORS
JACK MORELLI LETTERS
ICE CREA
LOTS O' SUGA
HEY, RONNIE! MAYBE I CAN WIN YOU A PRIZE!
HEY, ARCHIE! AREN'T THE CLOWNS SUPPOSED TO BE ON THAT SIDE OF THE BOOTH?
WATER GUN RA
REGGIE! WHAT ARE YOU DOING HERE?!
WELL, IF YOU MUST KNOW, AMUSEMENT PARKS ARE A GREAT PLACE TO MEET GIRLS! WHAT ARE YOU DOING HERE?
ARCHIE AND I ARE ON A DATE! HE WAS JUST ABOUT TO WIN ME A PRIZE!
1

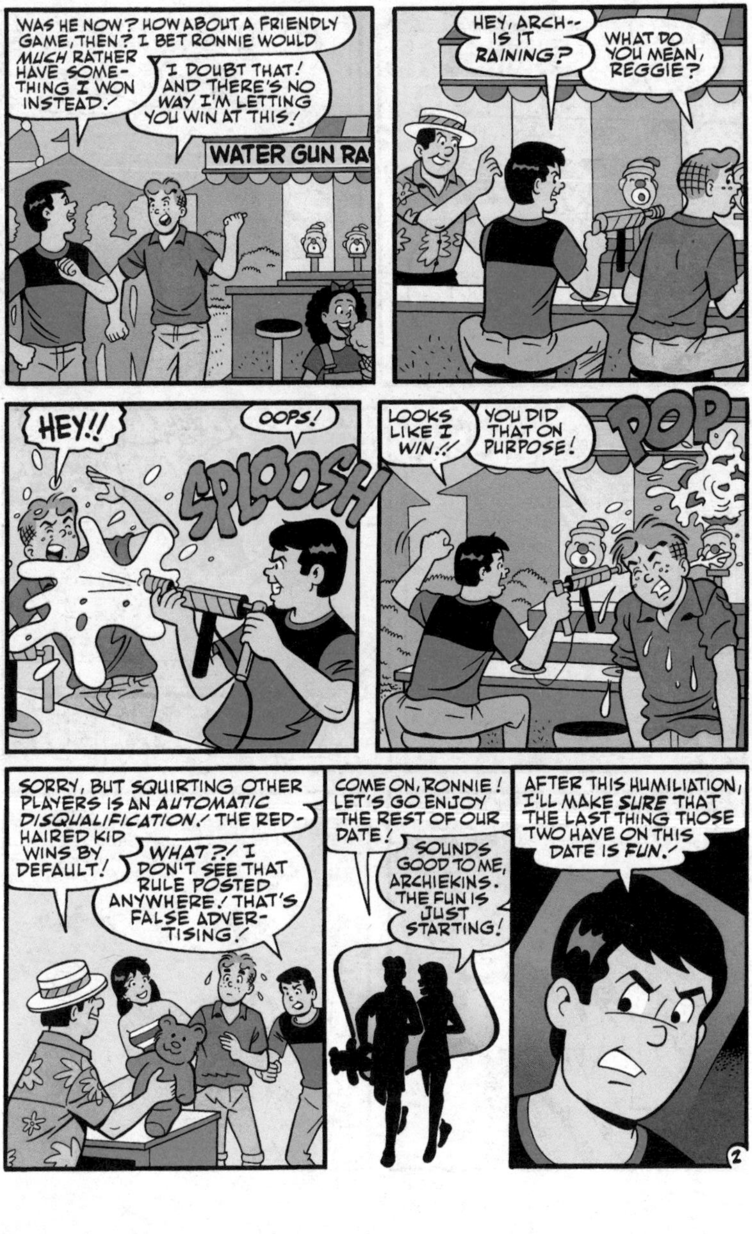
WAS HE NOW? HOW ABOUT A FRIENDLY GAME, THEN? I BET RONNIE WOULD MUCH RATHER HAVE SOMETHING I WON INSTEAD!
I DOUBT THAT! AND THERE'S NO WAY I'M LETTING YOU WIN AT THIS!
WATER GUN RA
HEY, ARCH-- IS IT RAINING?
WHAT DO YOU MEAN, REGGIE?
HEY!!
OOPS!
SPLOOSH
LOOKS LIKE I WIN!!
YOU DID THAT ON PURPOSE!
POP
SORRY, BUT SQUIRTING OTHER PLAYERS IS AN AUTOMATIC DISQUALIFICATION! THE RED-HAIRED KID WINS BY DEFAULT!
WHAT?! I DON'T SEE THAT RULE POSTED ANYWHERE! THAT'S FALSE ADVERTISING!
COME ON, RONNIE! LET'S GO ENJOY THE REST OF OUR DATE!
SOUNDS GOOD TO ME, ARCHIEKINS. THE FUN IS JUST STARTING!
AFTER THIS HUMILIATION, I'LL MAKE SURE THAT THE LAST THING THOSE TWO HAVE ON THIS DATE IS FUN!
2

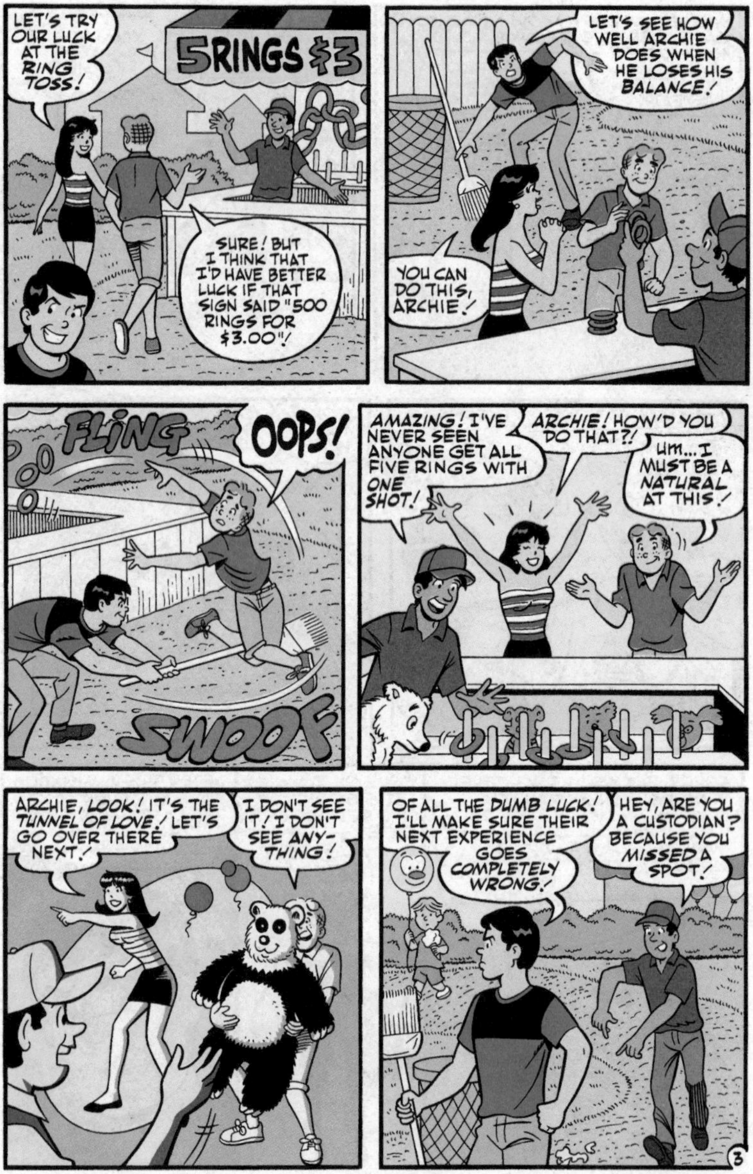
LET'S TRY OUR LUCK AT THE RING TOSS!
5 RINGS $3
SURE! BUT I THINK THAT I'D HAVE BETTER LUCK IF THAT SIGN SAID "500 RINGS FOR $3.00"!
LET'S SEE HOW WELL ARCHIE DOES WHEN HE LOSES HIS BALANCE!
YOU CAN DO THIS, ARCHIE!
FLING
OOPS!
SWOOF
AMAZING! I'VE NEVER SEEN ANYONE GET ALL FIVE RINGS WITH ONE SHOT!
ARCHIE! HOW'D YOU DO THAT?!
UM... I MUST BE A NATURAL AT THIS!
ARCHIE, LOOK! IT'S THE TUNNEL OF LOVE! LET'S GO OVER THERE NEXT!
I DON'T SEE IT! I DON'T SEE ANY-THING!
OF ALL THE DUMB LUCK! I'LL MAKE SURE THEIR NEXT EXPERIENCE GOES COMPLETELY WRONG!
HEY, ARE YOU A CUSTODIAN? BECAUSE YOU MISSED A SPOT!
3

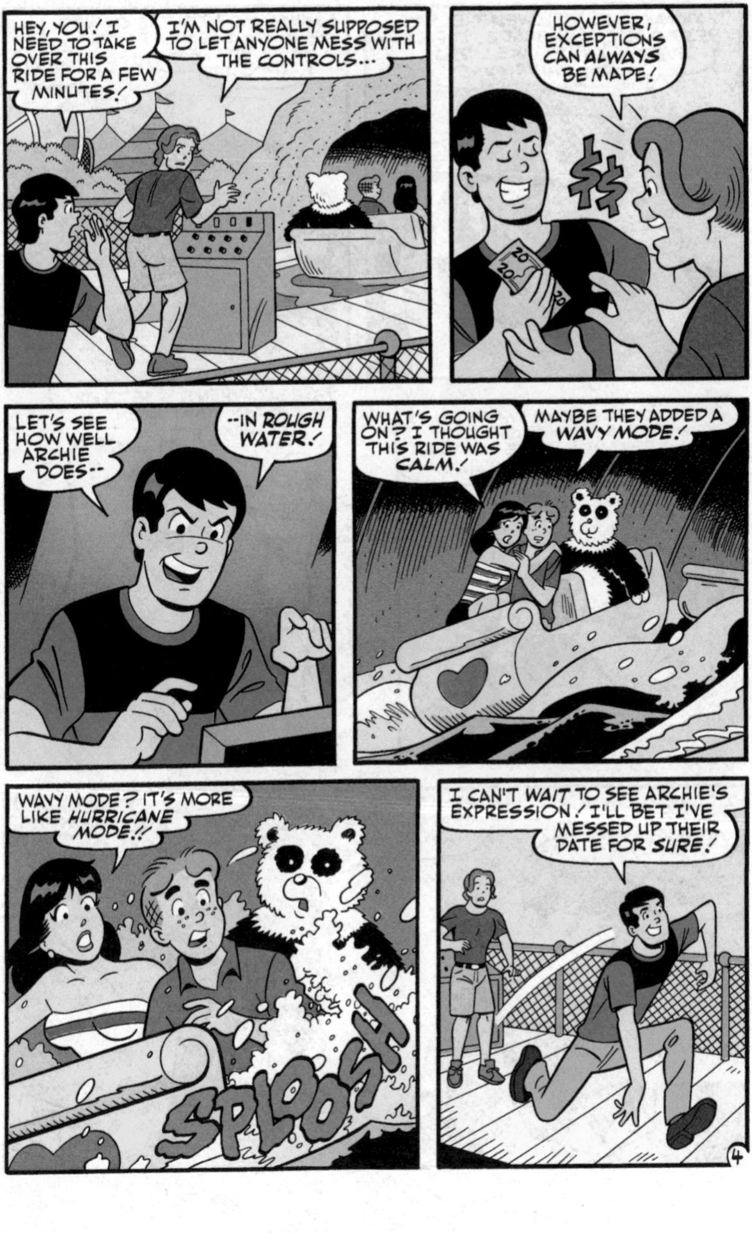
HEY, YOU! I NEED TO TAKE OVER THIS RIDE FOR A FEW MINUTES!
I'M NOT REALLY SUPPOSED TO LET ANYONE MESS WITH THE CONTROLS...
HOWEVER, EXCEPTIONS CAN ALWAYS BE MADE!
$$
LET'S SEE HOW WELL ARCHIE DOES--
--IN ROUGH WATER!
WHAT'S GOING ON? I THOUGHT THIS RIDE WAS CALM!
MAYBE THEY ADDED A WAVY MODE!
WAVY MODE? IT'S MORE LIKE HURRICANE MODE!!
SPLOOSH
I CAN'T WAIT TO SEE ARCHIE'S EXPRESSION! I'LL BET I'VE MESSED UP THEIR DATE FOR SURE!
4

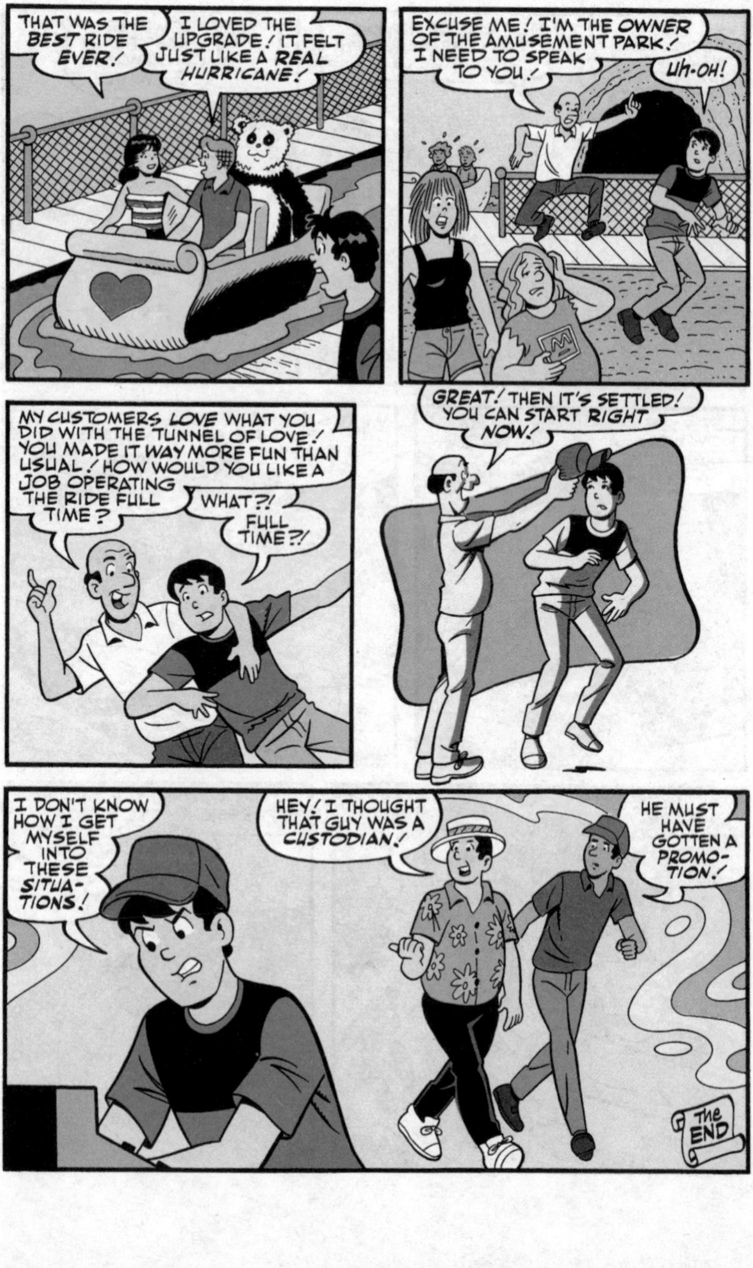
THAT WAS THE BEST RIDE EVER!
I LOVED THE UPGRADE! IT FELT JUST LIKE A REAL HURRICANE!
EXCUSE ME! I'M THE OWNER OF THE AMUSEMENT PARK! I NEED TO SPEAK TO YOU!
UH-OH!
MY CUSTOMERS LOVE WHAT YOU DID WITH THE TUNNEL OF LOVE! YOU MADE IT WAY MORE FUN THAN USUAL! HOW WOULD YOU LIKE A JOB OPERATING THE RIDE FULL TIME?
WHAT?! FULL TIME?!
GREAT! THEN IT'S SETTLED! YOU CAN START RIGHT NOW!
I DON'T KNOW HOW I GET MYSELF INTO THESE SITUATIONS!
HEY! I THOUGHT THAT GUY WAS A CUSTODIAN!
HE MUST HAVE GOTTEN A PROMOTION!
The END

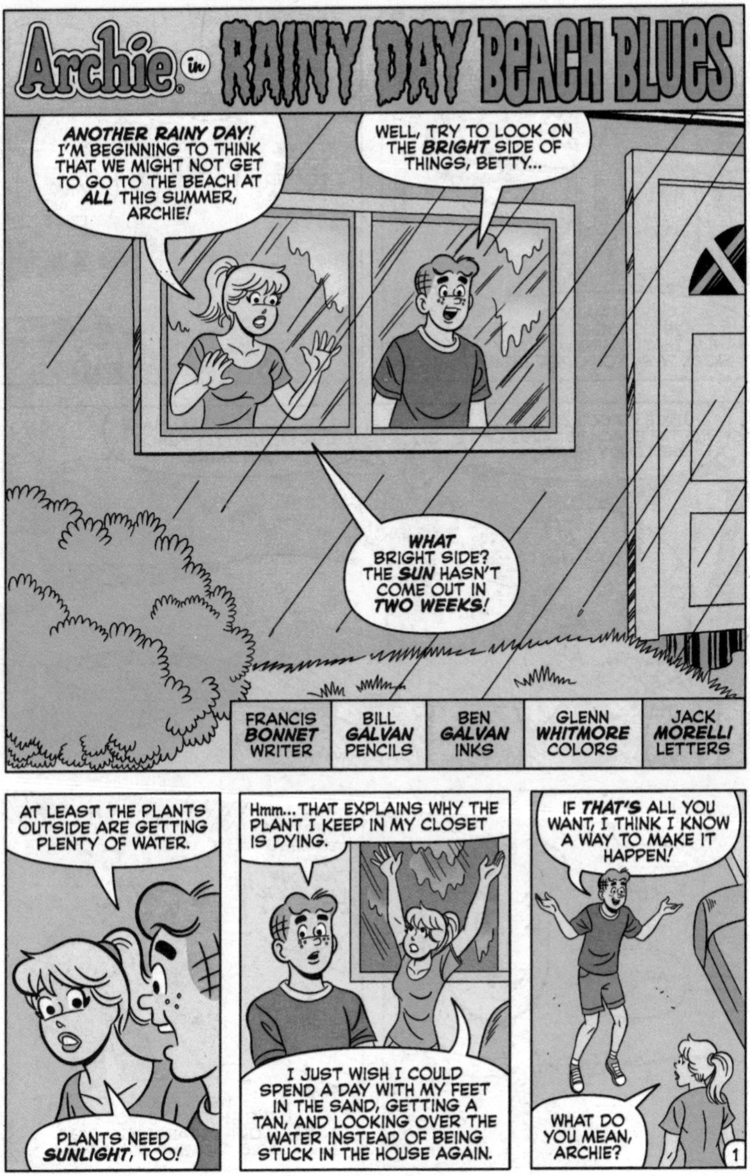
Archie in RAINY DAY BEACH BLUES
ANOTHER RAINY DAY! I'M BEGINNING TO THINK THAT WE MIGHT NOT GET TO GO TO THE BEACH AT ALL THIS SUMMER, ARCHIE!
WELL, TRY TO LOOK ON THE BRIGHT SIDE OF THINGS, BETTY...
WHAT BRIGHT SIDE? THE SUN HASN'T COME OUT IN TWO WEEKS!
FRANCIS BONNET WRITER
BILL GALVAN PENCILS
BEN GALVAN INKS
GLENN WHITMORE COLORS
JACK MORELLI LETTERS
AT LEAST THE PLANTS OUTSIDE ARE GETTING PLENTY OF WATER.
PLANTS NEED SUNLIGHT, TOO!
Hmm...THAT EXPLAINS WHY THE PLANT I KEEP IN MY CLOSET IS DYING.
I JUST WISH I COULD SPEND A DAY WITH MY FEET IN THE SAND, GETTING A TAN, AND LOOKING OVER THE WATER INSTEAD OF BEING STUCK IN THE HOUSE AGAIN.
IF THAT'S ALL YOU WANT, I THINK I KNOW A WAY TO MAKE IT HAPPEN!
WHAT DO YOU MEAN, ARCHIE?
1

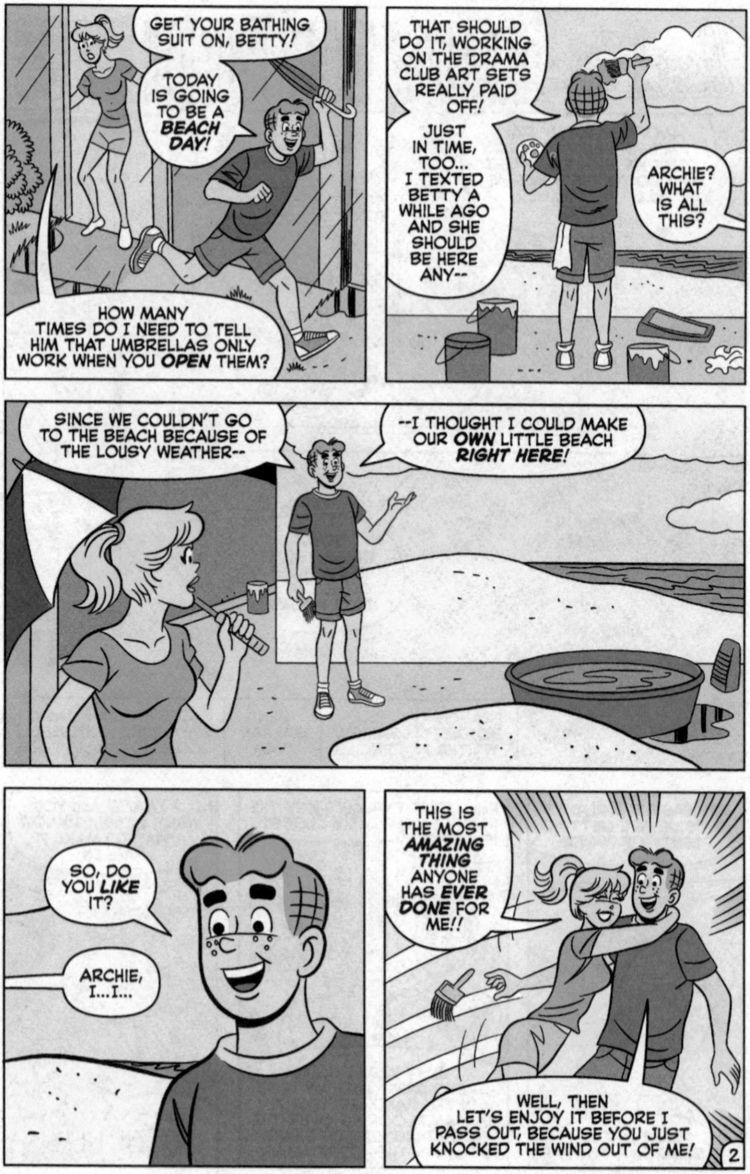
GET YOUR BATHING SUIT ON, BETTY!
TODAY IS GOING TO BE A ***BEACH DAY!***
HOW MANY TIMES DO I NEED TO TELL HIM THAT UMBRELLAS ONLY WORK WHEN YOU ***OPEN*** THEM?
THAT SHOULD DO IT, WORKING ON THE DRAMA CLUB ART SETS REALLY PAID OFF!
JUST IN TIME, TOO... I TEXTED BETTY A WHILE AGO AND SHE SHOULD BE HERE ANY--
ARCHIE? WHAT IS ALL THIS?
SINCE WE COULDN'T GO TO THE BEACH BECAUSE OF THE LOUSY WEATHER--
--I THOUGHT I COULD MAKE OUR ***OWN*** LITTLE BEACH ***RIGHT HERE!***
SO, DO YOU ***LIKE*** IT?
ARCHIE, I...I...
THIS IS THE MOST ***AMAZING THING*** ANYONE HAS ***EVER DONE*** FOR ME!!
WELL, THEN LET'S ENJOY IT BEFORE I PASS OUT, BECAUSE YOU JUST KNOCKED THE WIND OUT OF ME!
2

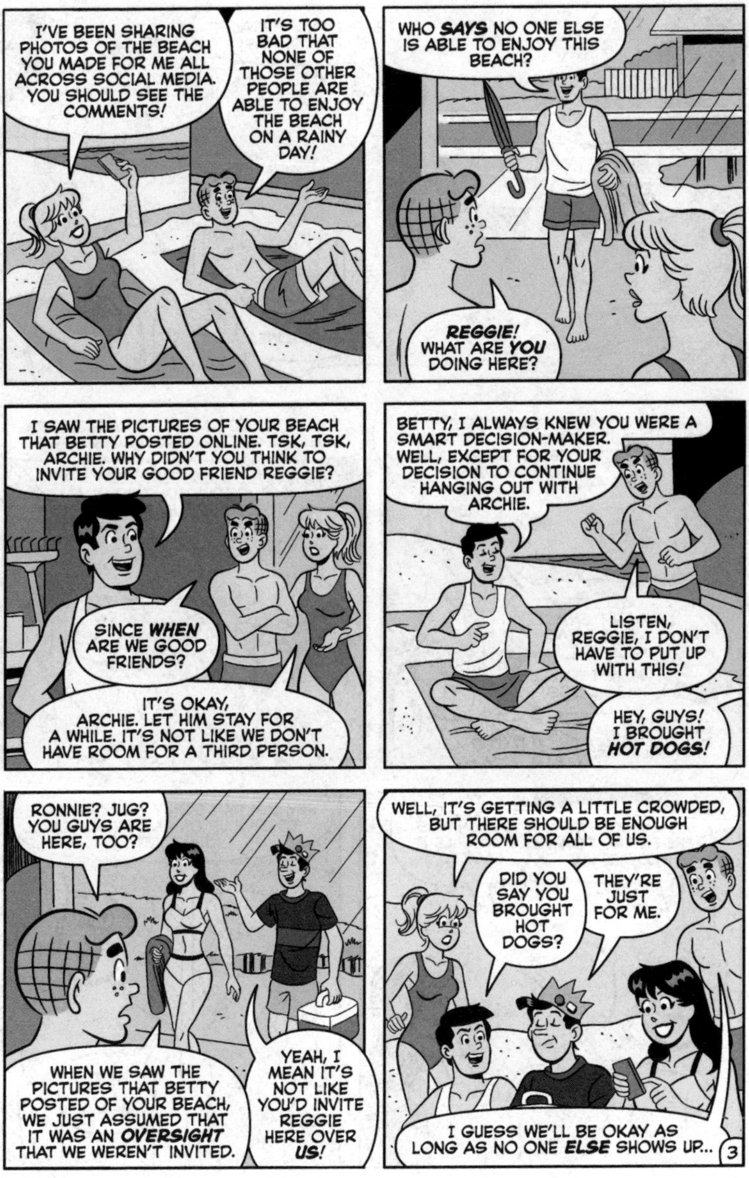
I'VE BEEN SHARING PHOTOS OF THE BEACH YOU MADE FOR ME ALL ACROSS SOCIAL MEDIA. YOU SHOULD SEE THE COMMENTS!
IT'S TOO BAD THAT NONE OF THOSE OTHER PEOPLE ARE ABLE TO ENJOY THE BEACH ON A RAINY DAY!
WHO SAYS NO ONE ELSE IS ABLE TO ENJOY THIS BEACH?
REGGIE! WHAT ARE YOU DOING HERE?
I SAW THE PICTURES OF YOUR BEACH THAT BETTY POSTED ONLINE. TSK, TSK, ARCHIE. WHY DIDN'T YOU THINK TO INVITE YOUR GOOD FRIEND REGGIE?
SINCE WHEN ARE WE GOOD FRIENDS?
IT'S OKAY, ARCHIE. LET HIM STAY FOR A WHILE. IT'S NOT LIKE WE DON'T HAVE ROOM FOR A THIRD PERSON.
BETTY, I ALWAYS KNEW YOU WERE A SMART DECISION-MAKER. WELL, EXCEPT FOR YOUR DECISION TO CONTINUE HANGING OUT WITH ARCHIE.
LISTEN, REGGIE, I DON'T HAVE TO PUT UP WITH THIS!
HEY, GUYS! I BROUGHT HOT DOGS!
RONNIE? JUG? YOU GUYS ARE HERE, TOO?
WHEN WE SAW THE PICTURES THAT BETTY POSTED OF YOUR BEACH, WE JUST ASSUMED THAT IT WAS AN OVERSIGHT THAT WE WEREN'T INVITED.
YEAH, I MEAN IT'S NOT LIKE YOU'D INVITE REGGIE HERE OVER US!
WELL, IT'S GETTING A LITTLE CROWDED, BUT THERE SHOULD BE ENOUGH ROOM FOR ALL OF US.
DID YOU SAY YOU BROUGHT HOT DOGS?
THEY'RE JUST FOR ME.
I GUESS WE'LL BE OKAY AS LONG AS NO ONE ELSE SHOWS UP...
3

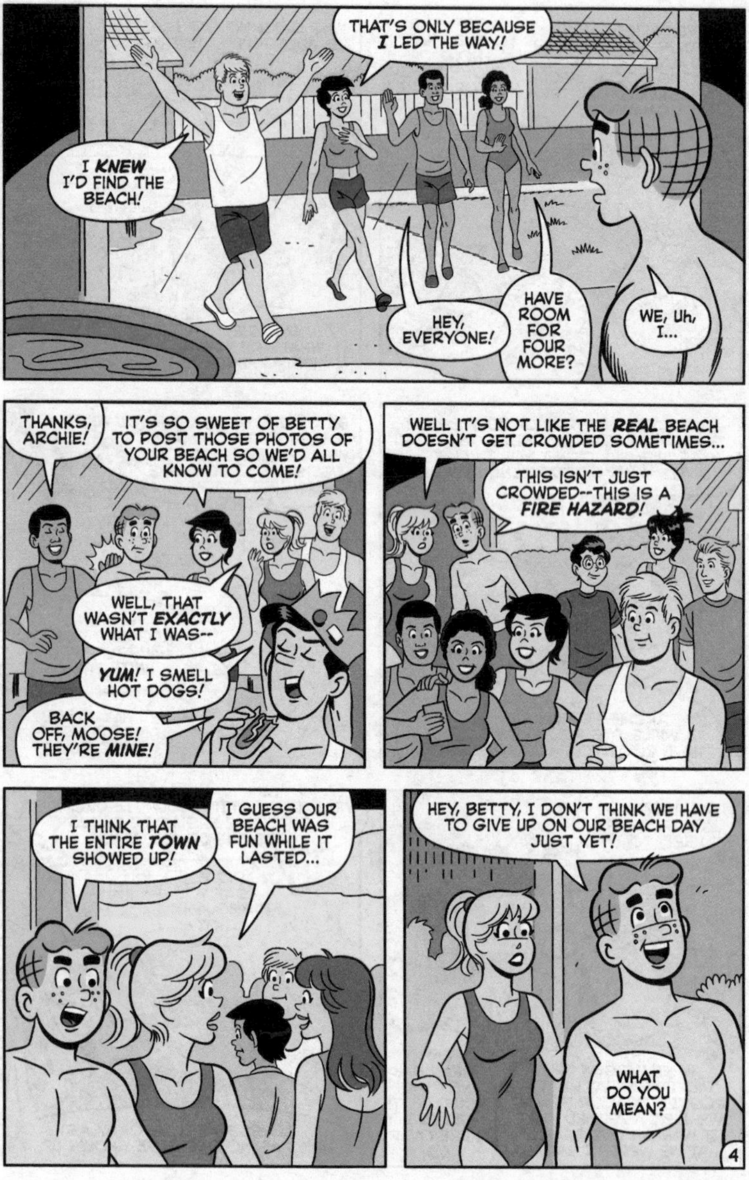
THAT'S ONLY BECAUSE I LED THE WAY!
I KNEW I'D FIND THE BEACH!
HEY, EVERYONE!
HAVE ROOM FOR FOUR MORE?
WE, UH, I...
THANKS, ARCHIE!
IT'S SO SWEET OF BETTY TO POST THOSE PHOTOS OF YOUR BEACH SO WE'D ALL KNOW TO COME!
WELL, THAT WASN'T EXACTLY WHAT I WAS--
YUM! I SMELL HOT DOGS!
BACK OFF, MOOSE! THEY'RE MINE!
WELL IT'S NOT LIKE THE REAL BEACH DOESN'T GET CROWDED SOMETIMES...
THIS ISN'T JUST CROWDED--THIS IS A FIRE HAZARD!
I THINK THAT THE ENTIRE TOWN SHOWED UP!
I GUESS OUR BEACH WAS FUN WHILE IT LASTED...
HEY, BETTY, I DON'T THINK WE HAVE TO GIVE UP ON OUR BEACH DAY JUST YET!
WHAT DO YOU MEAN?
4

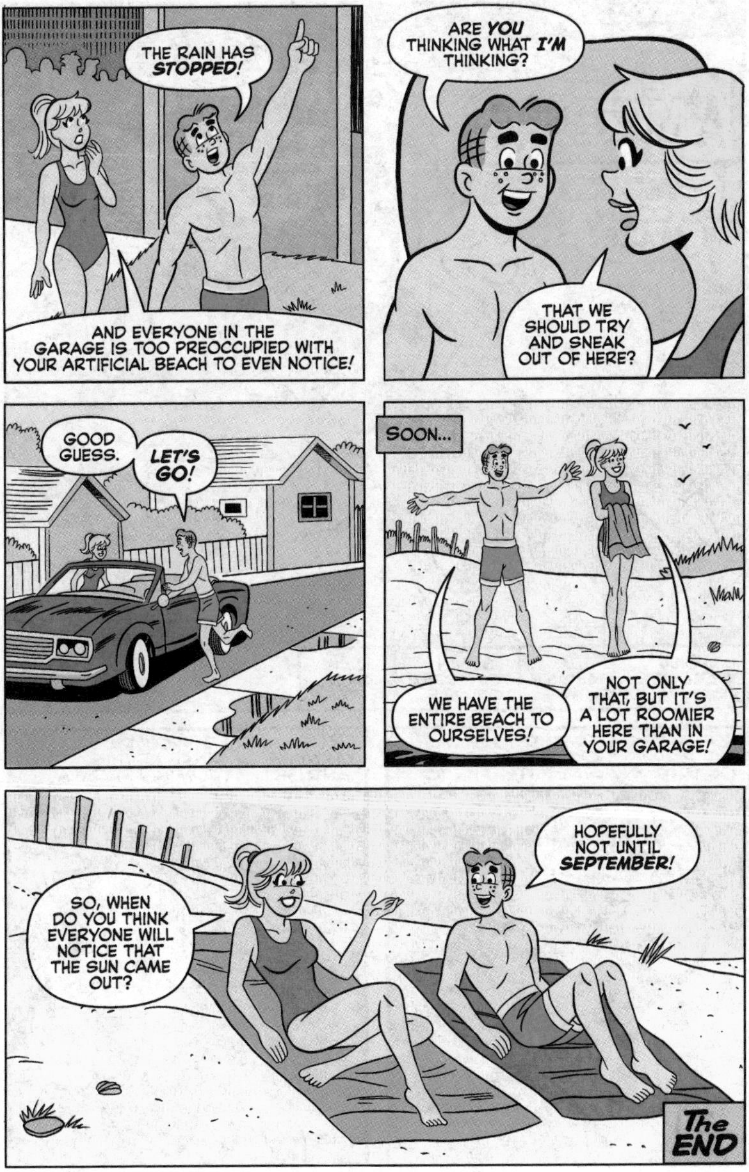
THE RAIN HAS STOPPED!
AND EVERYONE IN THE GARAGE IS TOO PREOCCUPIED WITH YOUR ARTIFICIAL BEACH TO EVEN NOTICE!
ARE YOU THINKING WHAT I'M THINKING?
THAT WE SHOULD TRY AND SNEAK OUT OF HERE?
GOOD GUESS.
LET'S GO!
SOON...
WE HAVE THE ENTIRE BEACH TO OURSELVES!
NOT ONLY THAT, BUT IT'S A LOT ROOMIER HERE THAN IN YOUR GARAGE!
SO, WHEN DO YOU THINK EVERYONE WILL NOTICE THAT THE SUN CAME OUT?
HOPEFULLY NOT UNTIL SEPTEMBER!
The END

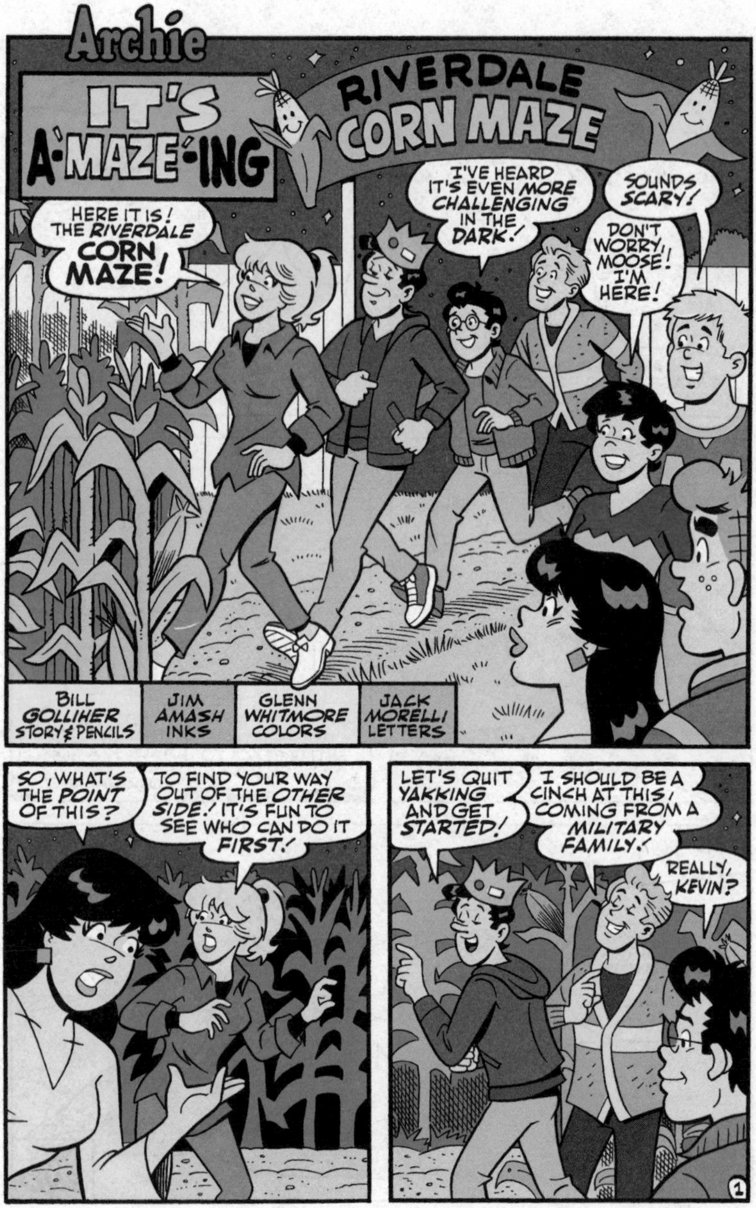
Archie
IT'S A-MAZE-ING
RIVERDALE CORN MAZE
HERE IT IS! THE RIVERDALE CORN MAZE!
I'VE HEARD IT'S EVEN MORE CHALLENGING IN THE DARK!
SOUNDS SCARY!
DON'T WORRY, MOOSE! I'M HERE!
BILL GOLLIHER STORY & PENCILS
JIM AMASH INKS
GLENN WHITMORE COLORS
JACK MORELLI LETTERS
SO, WHAT'S THE POINT OF THIS?
TO FIND YOUR WAY OUT OF THE OTHER SIDE! IT'S FUN TO SEE WHO CAN DO IT FIRST!
LET'S QUIT YAKKING AND GET STARTED!
I SHOULD BE A CINCH AT THIS, COMING FROM A MILITARY FAMILY!
REALLY, KEVIN?
1

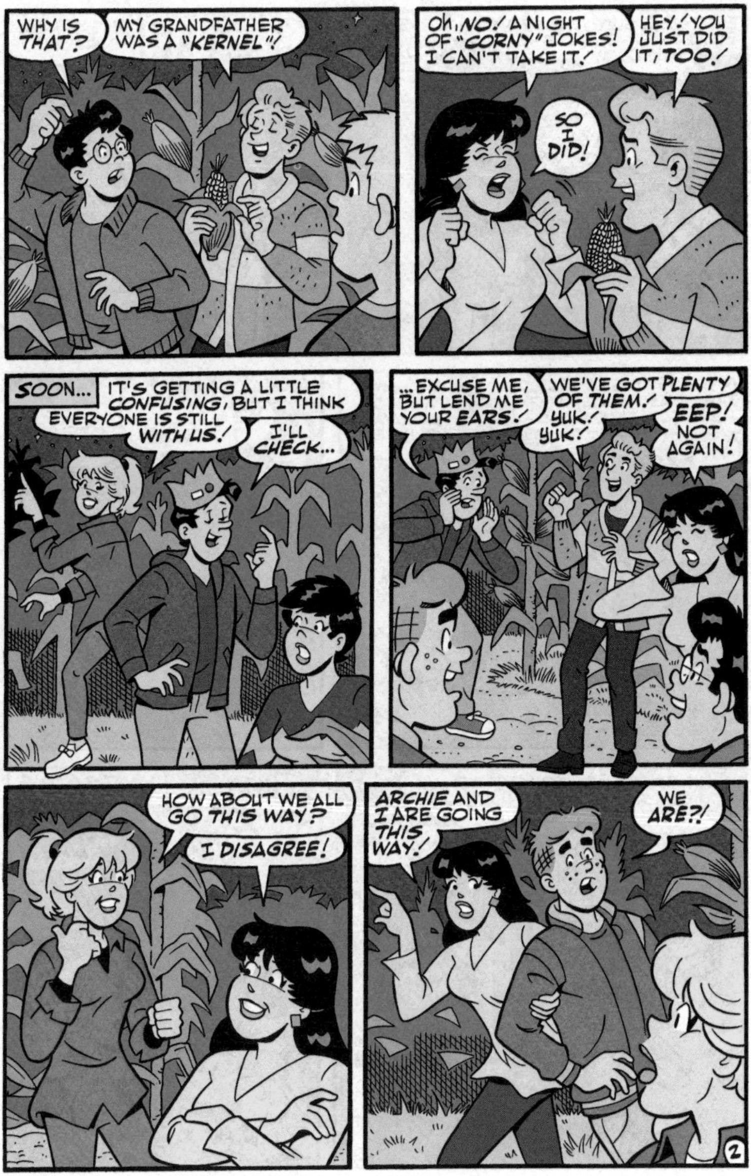
WHY IS THAT?
MY GRANDFATHER WAS A "KERNEL"!
Oh, NO! A NIGHT OF "CORNY" JOKES! I CAN'T TAKE IT!
HEY! YOU JUST DID IT, TOO!
SO I DID!
SOON...
IT'S GETTING A LITTLE CONFUSING, BUT I THINK EVERYONE IS STILL WITH US!
I'LL CHECK...
...EXCUSE ME, BUT LEND ME YOUR EARS!
WE'VE GOT PLENTY OF THEM! YUK! YUK!
EEP! NOT AGAIN!
HOW ABOUT WE ALL GO THIS WAY?
I DISAGREE!
ARCHIE AND I ARE GOING THIS WAY!
WE ARE?!
2

EVERYONE SUIT YOURSELVES, BUT I THINK *THIS* IS THE WAY OUT!

RIGHT BEHIND YOU, BETTY!

AH!

BUT WHAT'S IN *FRONT?!*

IT'S JUST A *SCARECROW!* THEY MUST HAVE PUT IT HERE FOR DRAMATIC EFFECT!

≡WHEW!≡ MISSION ACCOMPLISHED!

SOON...

WE DID IT, JUGGIE! WE MADE IT THROUGH!

THEY SHOULD HAVE LISTENED TO US!

EXIT

WHAT *TOOK* YOU GUYS SO LONG?

DILTON AND KEVIN! I MIGHT HAVE KNOWN!

EXI

KRASH

WHAT'S GOING ON?! DID THE SCARECROW COME TO LIFE?!

3

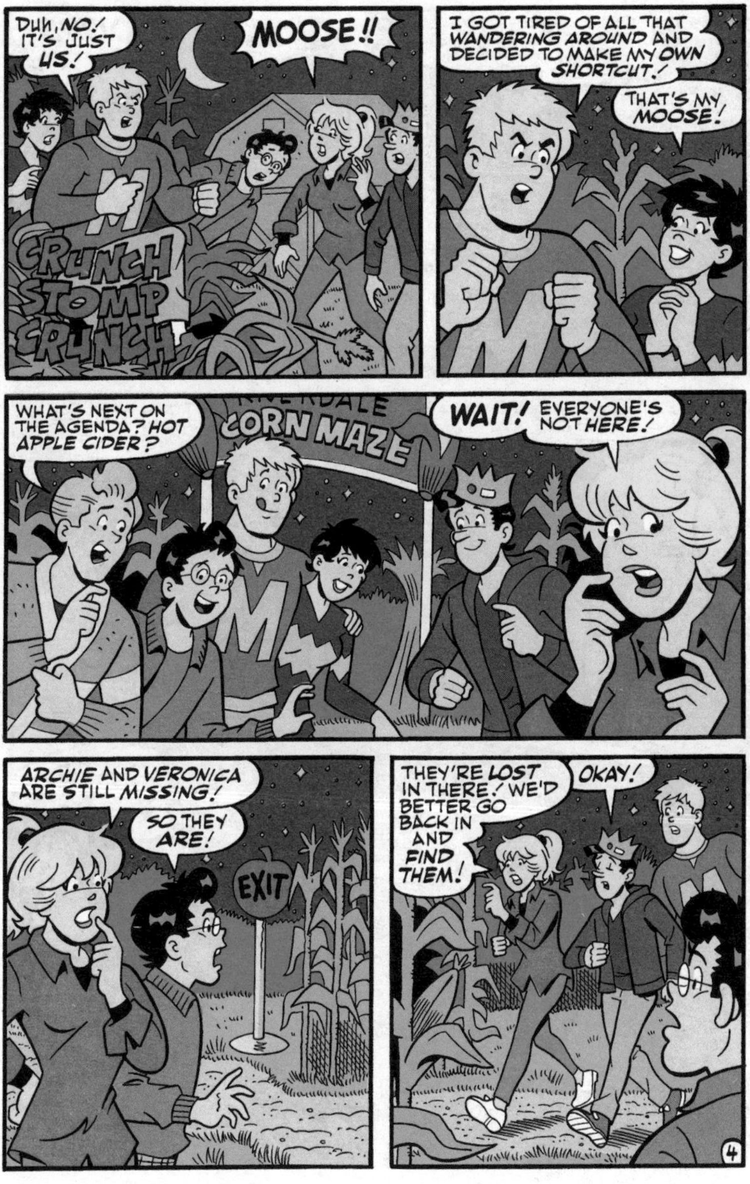
DUH, NO! IT'S JUST US!
MOOSE!!
CRUNCH STOMP CRUNCH
I GOT TIRED OF ALL THAT WANDERING AROUND AND DECIDED TO MAKE MY OWN SHORTCUT!
THAT'S MY MOOSE!
WHAT'S NEXT ON THE AGENDA? HOT APPLE CIDER?
CORN MAZE
WAIT! EVERYONE'S NOT HERE!
ARCHIE AND VERONICA ARE STILL MISSING!
SO THEY ARE!
EXIT
THEY'RE LOST IN THERE! WE'D BETTER GO BACK IN AND FIND THEM!
OKAY!
4

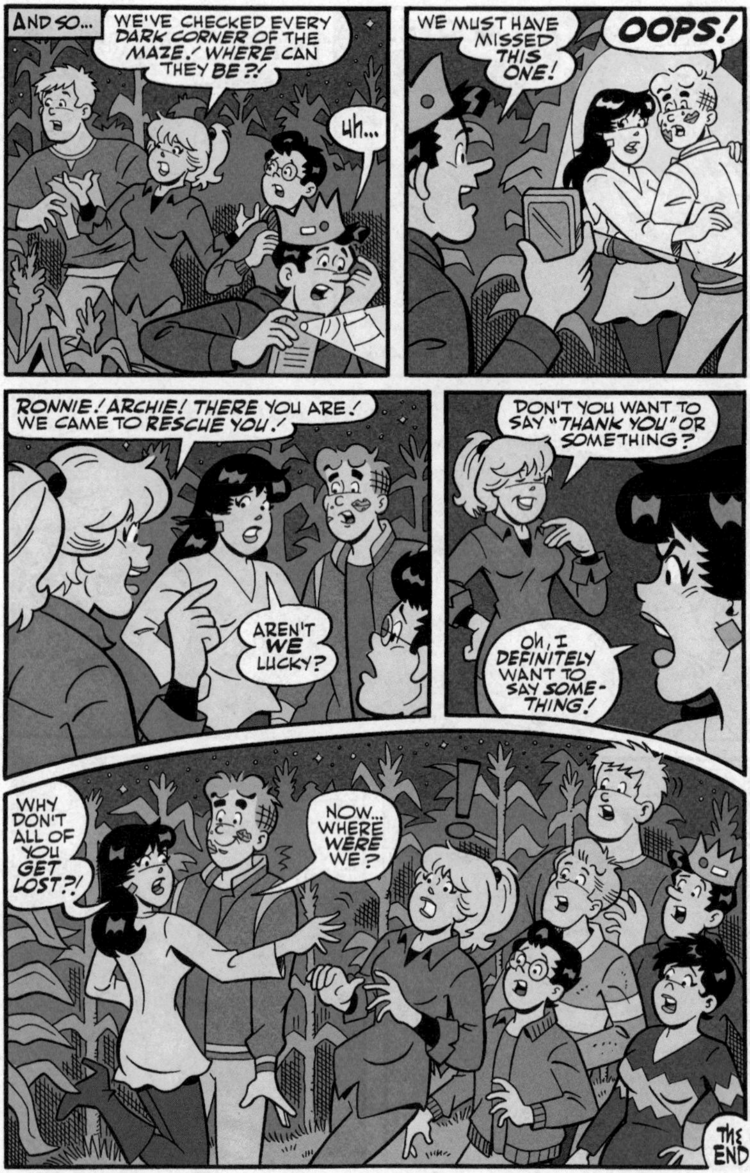
AND SO...
WE'VE CHECKED EVERY DARK CORNER OF THE MAZE! WHERE CAN THEY BE?!
Uh...
WE MUST HAVE MISSED THIS ONE!
OOPS!
RONNIE! ARCHIE! THERE YOU ARE! WE CAME TO RESCUE YOU!
AREN'T WE LUCKY?
DON'T YOU WANT TO SAY "THANK YOU" OR SOMETHING?
Oh, I DEFINITELY WANT TO SAY SOME-THING!
WHY DON'T ALL OF YOU GET LOST?!
NOW... WHERE WERE WE?
!
THE END

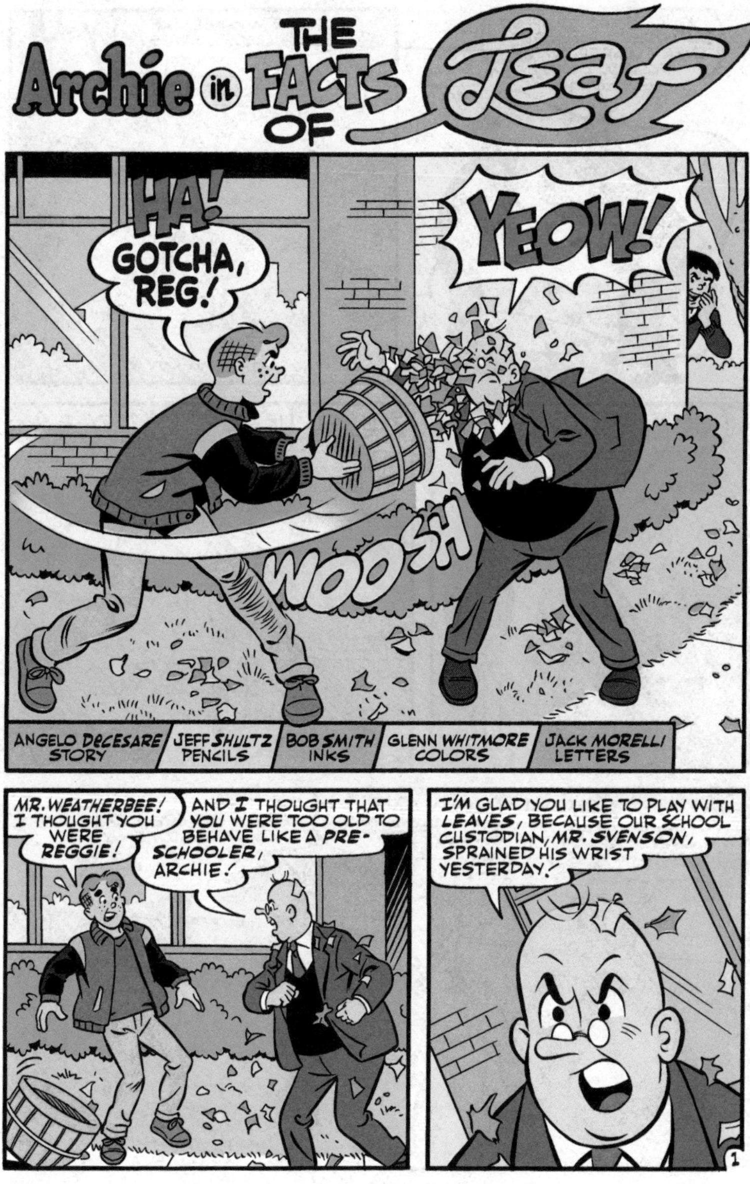
Archie in THE FACTS OF Leaf
HA! GOTCHA, REG!
YEOW!
WOOSH
ANGELO DeCESARE STORY
JEFF SHULTZ PENCILS
BOB SMITH INKS
GLENN WHITMORE COLORS
JACK MORELLI LETTERS
MR. WEATHERBEE! I THOUGHT YOU WERE REGGIE!
AND I THOUGHT THAT YOU WERE TOO OLD TO BEHAVE LIKE A PRE-SCHOOLER, ARCHIE!
I'M GLAD YOU LIKE TO PLAY WITH LEAVES, BECAUSE OUR SCHOOL CUSTODIAN, MR. SVENSON, SPRAINED HIS WRIST YESTERDAY!
1

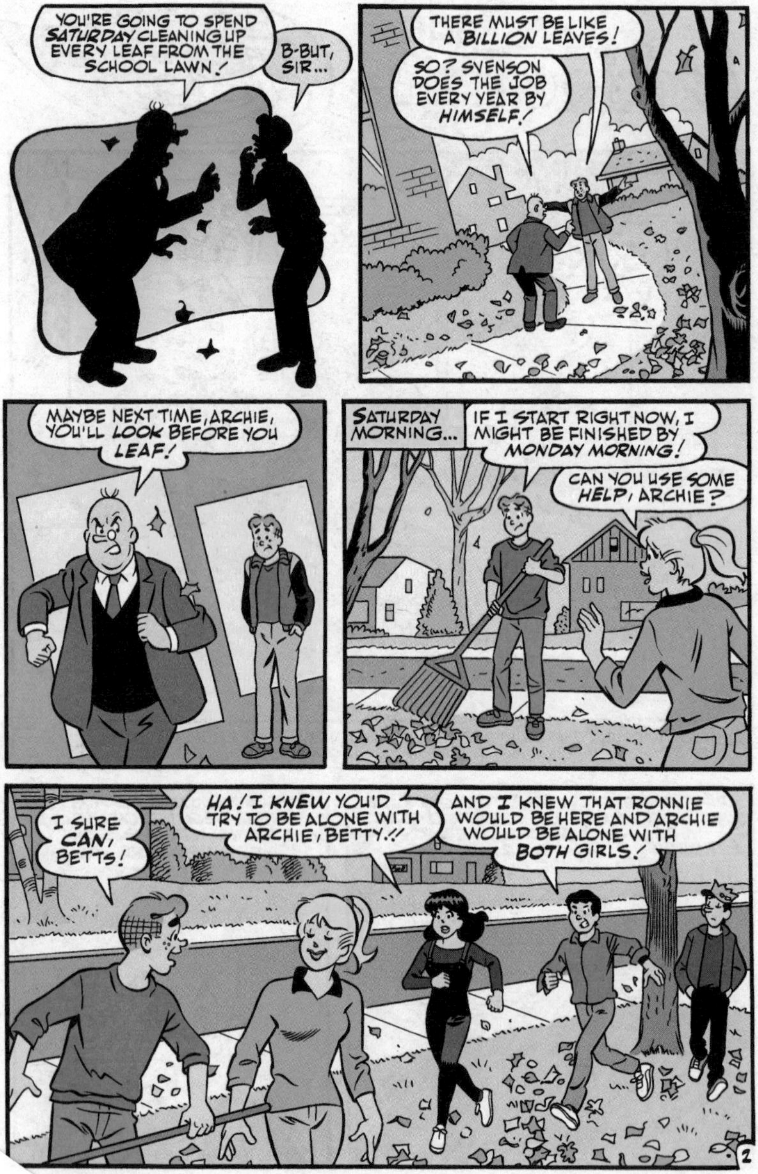
YOU'RE GOING TO SPEND SATURDAY CLEANING UP EVERY LEAF FROM THE SCHOOL LAWN!
B-BUT, SIR...
THERE MUST BE LIKE A BILLION LEAVES!
SO? SVENSON DOES THE JOB EVERY YEAR BY HIMSELF!
MAYBE NEXT TIME, ARCHIE, YOU'LL LOOK BEFORE YOU LEAF!
SATURDAY MORNING...
IF I START RIGHT NOW, I MIGHT BE FINISHED BY MONDAY MORNING!
CAN YOU USE SOME HELP, ARCHIE?
I SURE CAN, BETTS!
HA! I KNEW YOU'D TRY TO BE ALONE WITH ARCHIE, BETTY!!
AND I KNEW THAT RONNIE WOULD BE HERE AND ARCHIE WOULD BE ALONE WITH BOTH GIRLS!
2

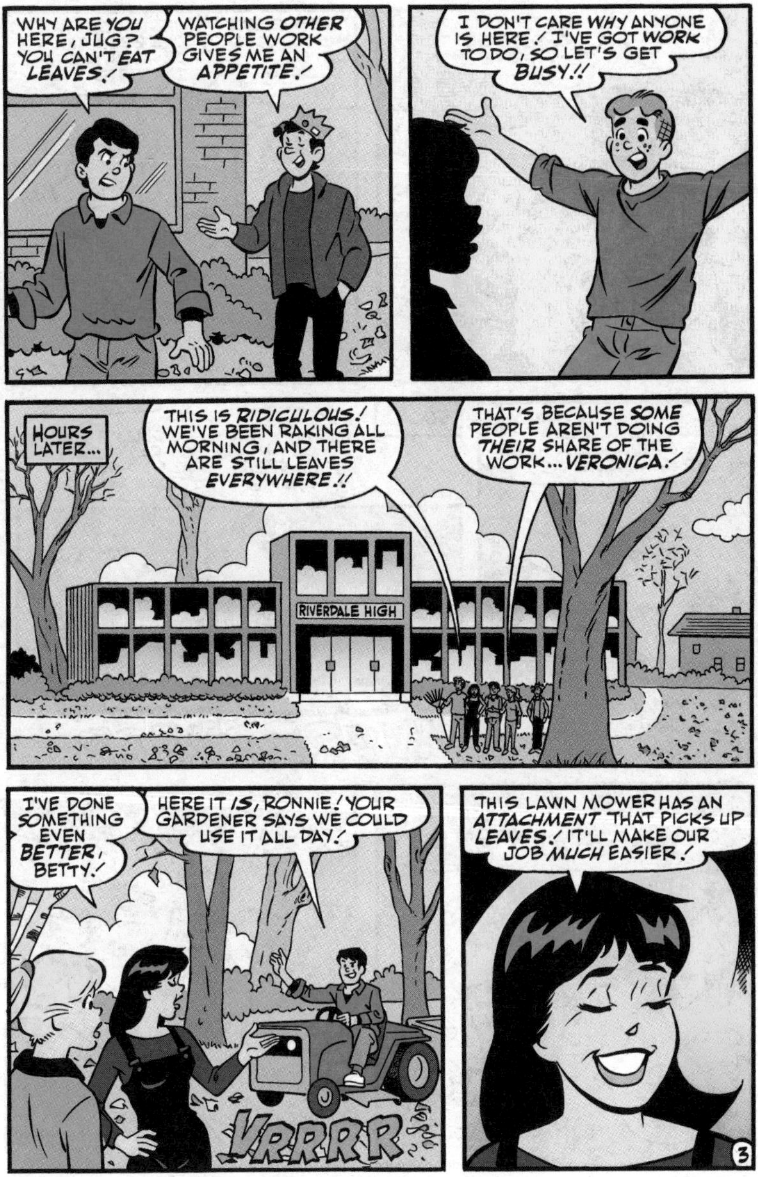
WHY ARE YOU HERE, JUG? YOU CAN'T EAT LEAVES!
WATCHING OTHER PEOPLE WORK GIVES ME AN APPETITE!
I DON'T CARE WHY ANYONE IS HERE! I'VE GOT WORK TO DO, SO LET'S GET BUSY!!
HOURS LATER...
THIS IS RIDICULOUS! WE'VE BEEN RAKING ALL MORNING, AND THERE ARE STILL LEAVES EVERYWHERE!!
THAT'S BECAUSE SOME PEOPLE AREN'T DOING THEIR SHARE OF THE WORK... VERONICA!
RIVERDALE HIGH
I'VE DONE SOMETHING EVEN BETTER, BETTY!
HERE IT IS, RONNIE! YOUR GARDENER SAYS WE COULD USE IT ALL DAY!
VRRRR
THIS LAWN MOWER HAS AN ATTACHMENT THAT PICKS UP LEAVES! IT'LL MAKE OUR JOB MUCH EASIER!
3

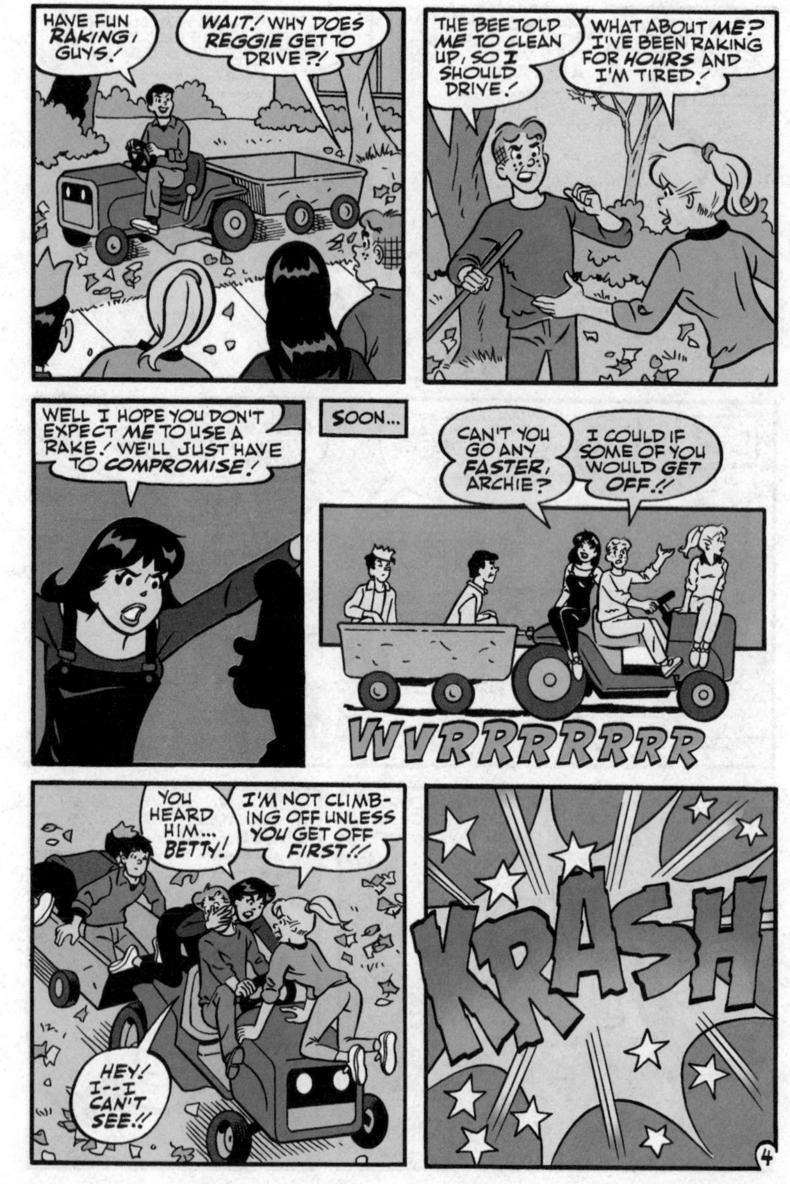
HAVE FUN RAKING, GUYS!
WAIT! WHY DOES REGGIE GET TO DRIVE?!
THE BEE TOLD ME TO CLEAN UP, SO I SHOULD DRIVE!
WHAT ABOUT ME? I'VE BEEN RAKING FOR HOURS AND I'M TIRED!
WELL I HOPE YOU DON'T EXPECT ME TO USE A RAKE! WE'LL JUST HAVE TO COMPROMISE!
SOON...
CAN'T YOU GO ANY FASTER, ARCHIE?
I COULD IF SOME OF YOU WOULD GET OFF!!
VVVRRRRRRRR
YOU HEARD HIM... BETTY!
I'M NOT CLIMBING OFF UNLESS YOU GET OFF FIRST!!
HEY! I--I CAN'T SEE!!
KRASH
4

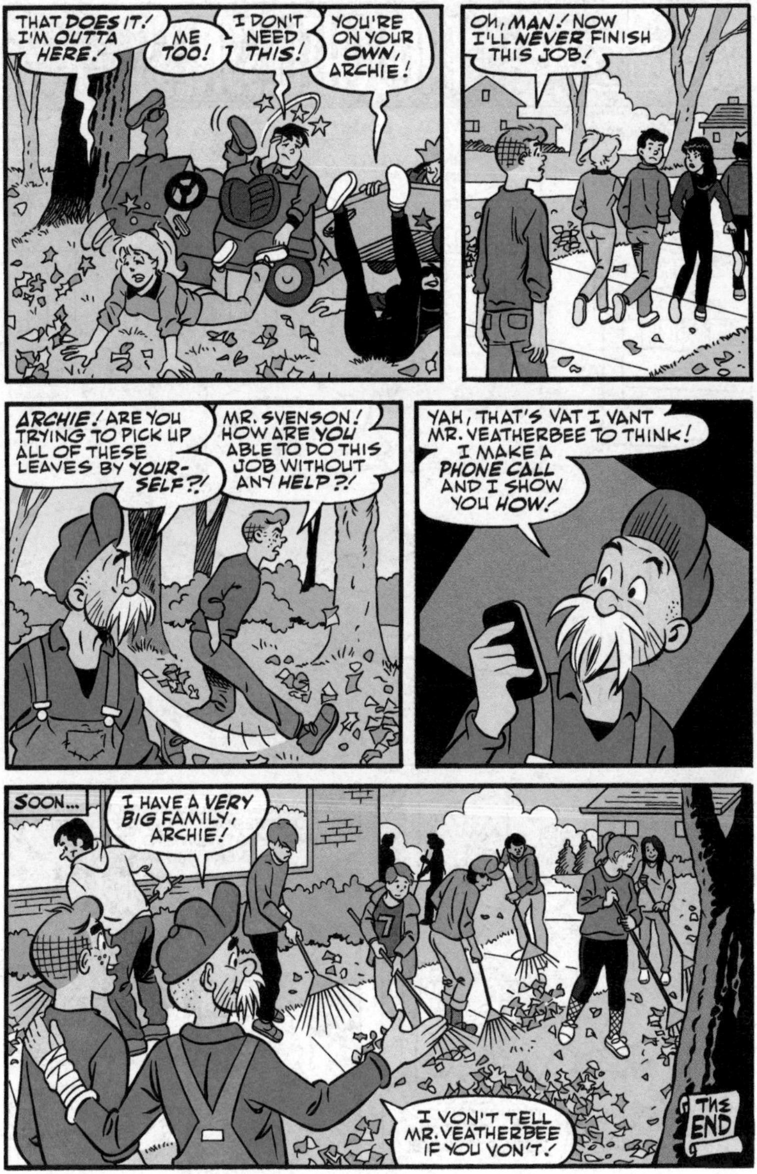
THAT DOES IT! I'M OUTTA HERE!
ME TOO!
I DON'T NEED THIS!
YOU'RE ON YOUR OWN, ARCHIE!
OH, MAN! NOW I'LL NEVER FINISH THIS JOB!
ARCHIE! ARE YOU TRYING TO PICK UP ALL OF THESE LEAVES BY YOUR-SELF?!
MR. SVENSON! HOW ARE YOU ABLE TO DO THIS JOB WITHOUT ANY HELP?!
YAH, THAT'S VAT I VANT MR. VEATHERBEE TO THINK! I MAKE A PHONE CALL AND I SHOW YOU HOW!
SOON...
I HAVE A VERY BIG FAMILY, ARCHIE!
I VON'T TELL MR. VEATHERBEE IF YOU VON'T!
THE END

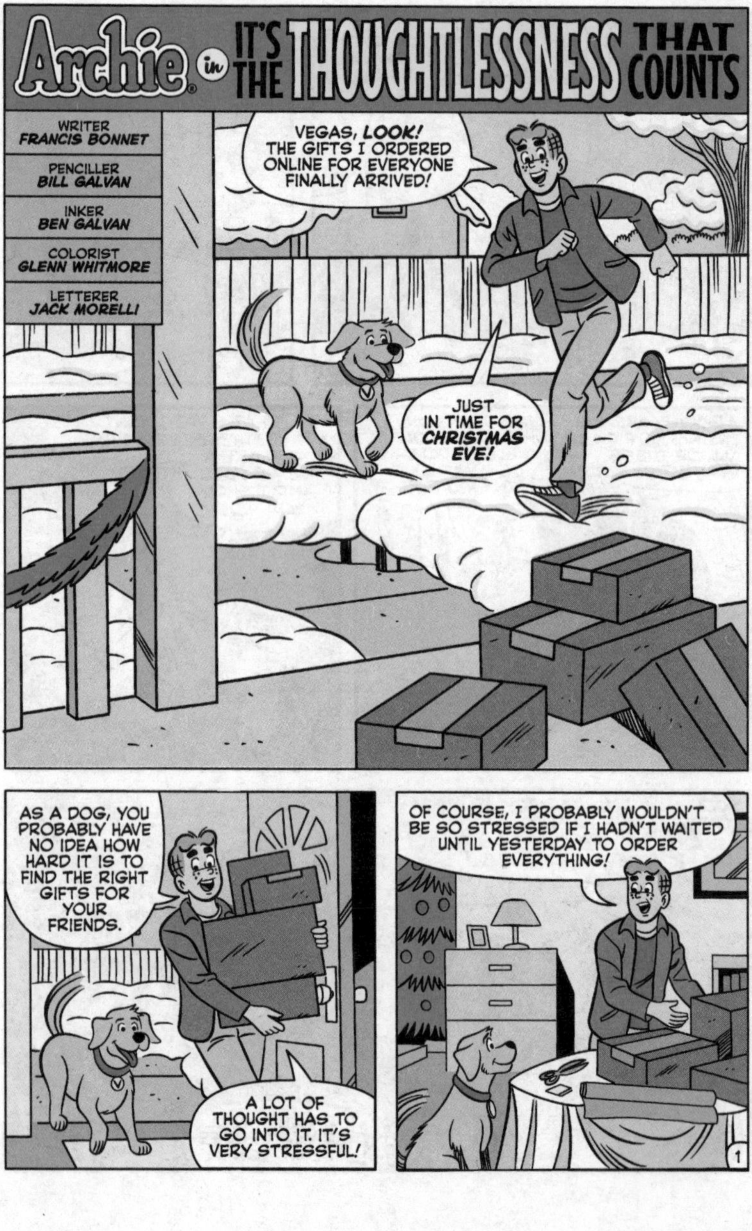
Archie in IT'S THE THOUGHTLESSNESS THAT COUNTS
WRITER FRANCIS BONNET
PENCILLER BILL GALVAN
INKER BEN GALVAN
COLORIST GLENN WHITMORE
LETTERER JACK MORELLI
VEGAS, LOOK! THE GIFTS I ORDERED ONLINE FOR EVERYONE FINALLY ARRIVED!
JUST IN TIME FOR CHRISTMAS EVE!
AS A DOG, YOU PROBABLY HAVE NO IDEA HOW HARD IT IS TO FIND THE RIGHT GIFTS FOR YOUR FRIENDS.
A LOT OF THOUGHT HAS TO GO INTO IT. IT'S VERY STRESSFUL!
OF COURSE, I PROBABLY WOULDN'T BE SO STRESSED IF I HADN'T WAITED UNTIL YESTERDAY TO ORDER EVERYTHING!
1

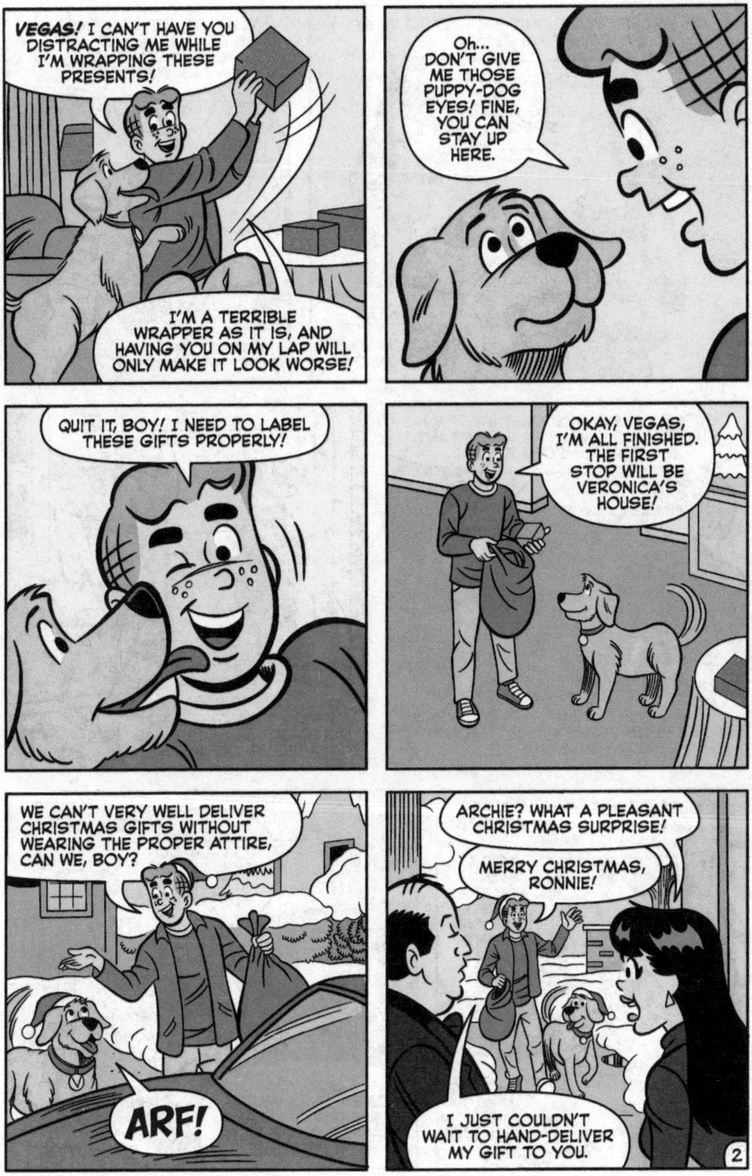
VEGAS! I CAN'T HAVE YOU DISTRACTING ME WHILE I'M WRAPPING THESE PRESENTS!
I'M A TERRIBLE WRAPPER AS IT IS, AND HAVING YOU ON MY LAP WILL ONLY MAKE IT LOOK WORSE!
Oh... DON'T GIVE ME THOSE PUPPY-DOG EYES! FINE, YOU CAN STAY UP HERE.
QUIT IT, BOY! I NEED TO LABEL THESE GIFTS PROPERLY!
OKAY, VEGAS, I'M ALL FINISHED. THE FIRST STOP WILL BE VERONICA'S HOUSE!
WE CAN'T VERY WELL DELIVER CHRISTMAS GIFTS WITHOUT WEARING THE PROPER ATTIRE, CAN WE, BOY?
ARF!
ARCHIE? WHAT A PLEASANT CHRISTMAS SURPRISE!
MERRY CHRISTMAS, RONNIE!
I JUST COULDN'T WAIT TO HAND-DELIVER MY GIFT TO YOU.
2

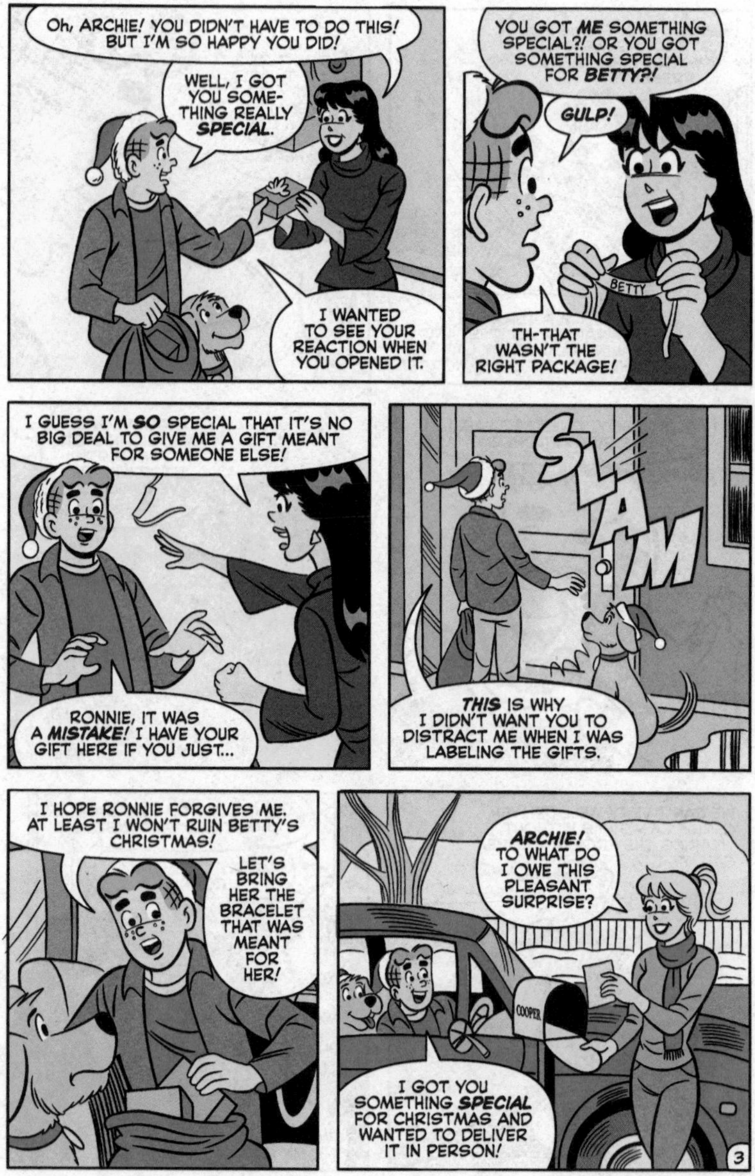
Oh, ARCHIE! YOU DIDN'T HAVE TO DO THIS! BUT I'M SO HAPPY YOU DID!
WELL, I GOT YOU SOMETHING REALLY SPECIAL.
I WANTED TO SEE YOUR REACTION WHEN YOU OPENED IT.
YOU GOT ME SOMETHING SPECIAL?! OR YOU GOT SOMETHING SPECIAL FOR BETTY?!
GULP!
BETTY
TH-THAT WASN'T THE RIGHT PACKAGE!
I GUESS I'M SO SPECIAL THAT IT'S NO BIG DEAL TO GIVE ME A GIFT MEANT FOR SOMEONE ELSE!
RONNIE, IT WAS A MISTAKE! I HAVE YOUR GIFT HERE IF YOU JUST...
SLAM
THIS IS WHY I DIDN'T WANT YOU TO DISTRACT ME WHEN I WAS LABELING THE GIFTS.
I HOPE RONNIE FORGIVES ME. AT LEAST I WON'T RUIN BETTY'S CHRISTMAS!
LET'S BRING HER THE BRACELET THAT WAS MEANT FOR HER!
ARCHIE! TO WHAT DO I OWE THIS PLEASANT SURPRISE?
COOPER
I GOT YOU SOMETHING SPECIAL FOR CHRISTMAS AND WANTED TO DELIVER IT IN PERSON!
3

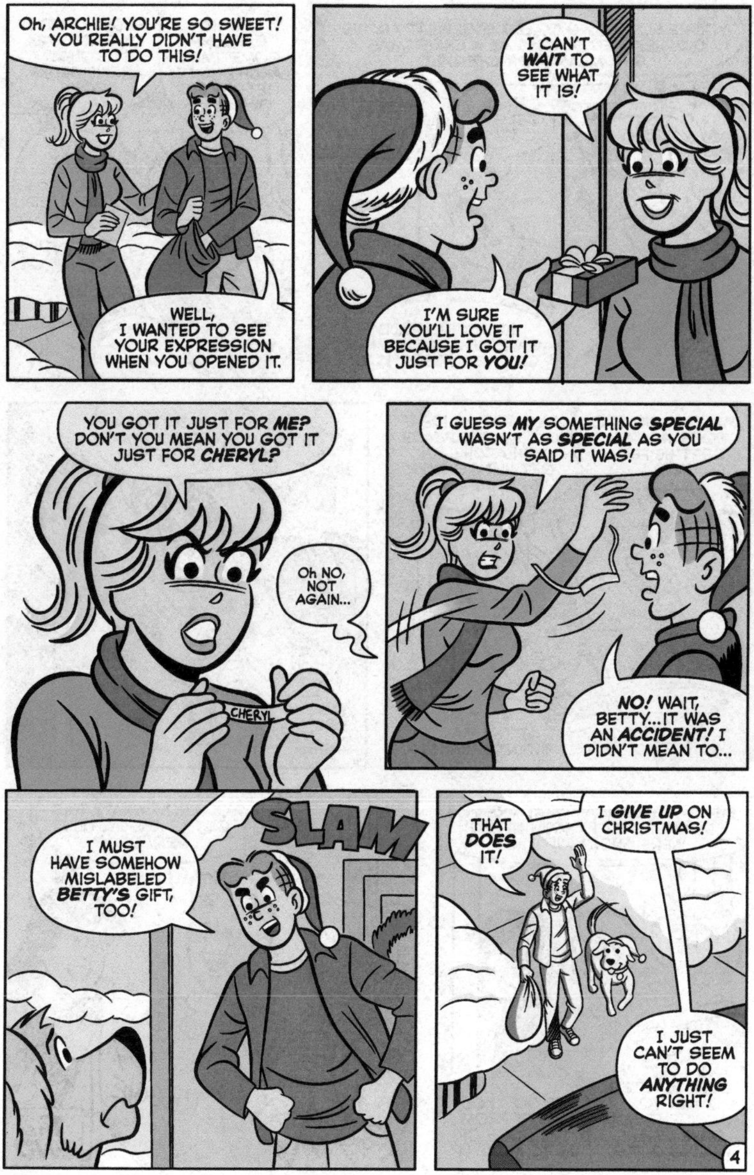
Oh, ARCHIE! YOU'RE SO SWEET! YOU REALLY DIDN'T HAVE TO DO THIS!
WELL, I WANTED TO SEE YOUR EXPRESSION WHEN YOU OPENED IT.
I CAN'T *WAIT* TO SEE WHAT IT IS!
I'M SURE YOU'LL LOVE IT BECAUSE I GOT IT JUST FOR *YOU!*
YOU GOT IT JUST FOR *ME?* DON'T YOU MEAN YOU GOT IT JUST FOR *CHERYL?*
Oh NO, NOT AGAIN...
CHERYL
I GUESS *MY* SOMETHING *SPECIAL* WASN'T AS *SPECIAL* AS YOU SAID IT WAS!
NO! WAIT, BETTY...IT WAS AN *ACCIDENT!* I DIDN'T MEAN TO...
SLAM
I MUST HAVE SOMEHOW MISLABELED *BETTY'S* GIFT, TOO!
THAT *DOES* IT!
I *GIVE UP* ON CHRISTMAS!
I JUST CAN'T SEEM TO DO *ANYTHING* RIGHT!
4

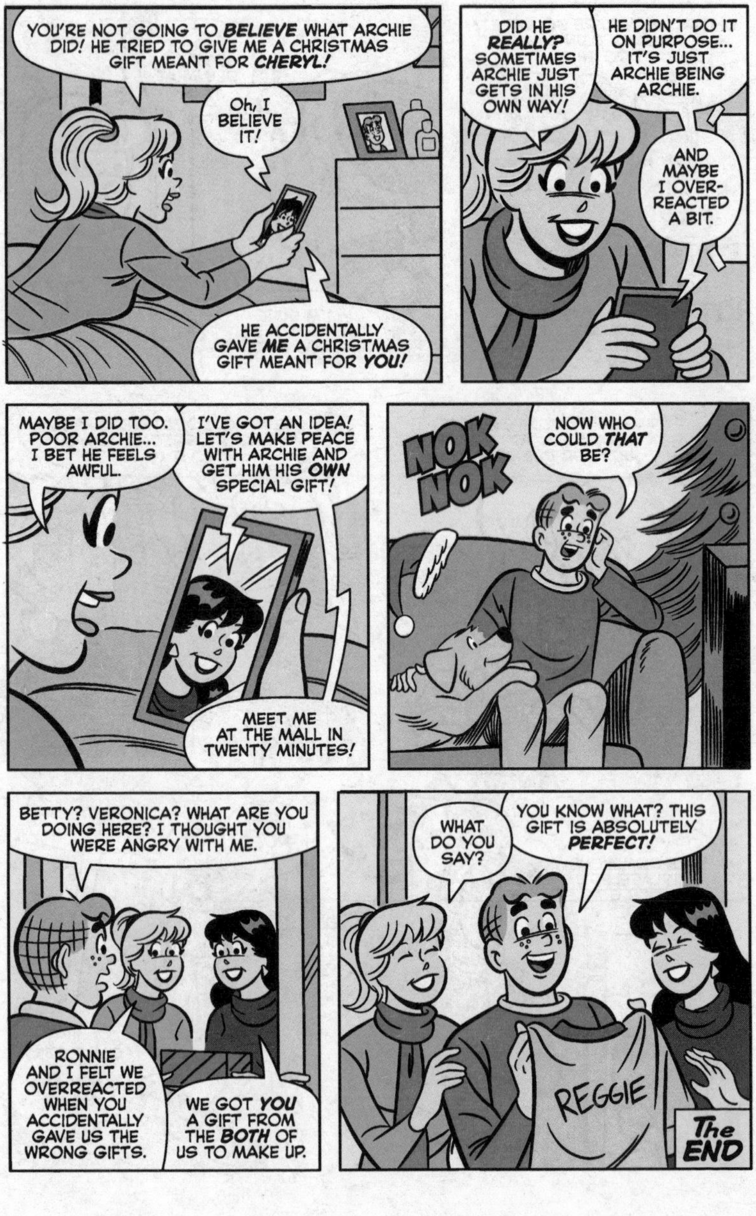
YOU'RE NOT GOING TO BELIEVE WHAT ARCHIE DID! HE TRIED TO GIVE ME A CHRISTMAS GIFT MEANT FOR CHERYL!
Oh, I BELIEVE IT!
HE ACCIDENTALLY GAVE ME A CHRISTMAS GIFT MEANT FOR YOU!
DID HE REALLY? SOMETIMES ARCHIE JUST GETS IN HIS OWN WAY!
HE DIDN'T DO IT ON PURPOSE... IT'S JUST ARCHIE BEING ARCHIE.
AND MAYBE I OVER-REACTED A BIT.
MAYBE I DID TOO. POOR ARCHIE... I BET HE FEELS AWFUL.
I'VE GOT AN IDEA! LET'S MAKE PEACE WITH ARCHIE AND GET HIM HIS OWN SPECIAL GIFT!
MEET ME AT THE MALL IN TWENTY MINUTES!
NOK NOK
NOW WHO COULD THAT BE?
BETTY? VERONICA? WHAT ARE YOU DOING HERE? I THOUGHT YOU WERE ANGRY WITH ME.
RONNIE AND I FELT WE OVERREACTED WHEN YOU ACCIDENTALLY GAVE US THE WRONG GIFTS.
WE GOT YOU A GIFT FROM THE BOTH OF US TO MAKE UP.
WHAT DO YOU SAY?
YOU KNOW WHAT? THIS GIFT IS ABSOLUTELY PERFECT!
REGGIE
The END